D0198561

Of Marriageable Age

Published by Bookouture
An imprint of StoryFire Ltd.
23 Sussex Road, Ickenham, UB10 8PN
United Kingdom
www.bookouture.com
Copyright © Sharon Maas 2000
Sharon Maas has asserted her right to be identified as the author of
this work.

ISBN: 978-1-909490-24-6
eBook ISBN: 978-1-909490-23-9

Originally published by HarperCollins, 2000.

Of Marriageable Age

SHARON MAAS

bookouture

ACKNOWLEDGEMENTS

For the original print version, published by HarperCollins in 1999:

My thanks to the following persons, each of whom helped in one way or another to bring this book to life: Pratima, who inspired it; Hilary Johnson, Sarah Molloy and Susan Watt who believed in it and brought it to birth; Katherine Prior, who helped with the history; Sridhar, my first reader and critic, whose encouragement was gold; Chris and Zarine, for putting me up, and for putting up with me; Jürgen, Miro and Saskia, my family, for the precious gift of time.

For the Bookouture, revised version you now hold in your hands:

Oliver Rhodes, who plucked this book from obscurity and brought it to life; Katie Fforde, Lesley Pearse, Audrey Howard and Barbara Erskine, my first readers and supporters; Dianne Reichart, who proof-read the revision with eyes as sharp as an eagle's; Saskia Westmaas, for her cover ideas; Amanda Richards, for your beautiful photos

Not forgetting all the wonderful people, friends and family, who have stood by me through the years, offering encouragement and support when I grew weary and discouraged:

Ann Claypole, Brenda King, Helen Zettler, Angelika Frank and Ewa Kenyeres; Mara Clark and Pratima Nath-Willard; Rory Westmaas, Peta Westmaas, Chris Westmaas, Nigel Westmaas, Yuri Westmaas, Gary Westmaas, Nancy Westmaas, Tiffany Westmaas, Susan Conliffe; Mirri and Peter Halder; Gisela Oess-Langford, Renate Boy, Elke Neukum-Kraus, Rita Coughlan, Ulrike Mack; Monique Roffey, Shahrukh Hussain;

Karin Streich and Giesla Heibel, my wonderful colleagues at GRN; Ulrike Boehm and The Ultimate Moose; Palle Jorgensen Mary Whipple, Judy Lind; Jamie Mason, Rob McCreery, Ray Wong, Jane Smith, Chris Stevenson, James Macdonald, Charles Alley and countless other AW writers; my support team in Guyana: Petamber Persaud, Salvador deCaires, Andrea deCaires, Vanda Radzig, Miro Westmaas, Jocelyn Dow, Zena Bone, Diane McTurk; Sibille and Peter Pritchard of Oveido; my Sussex-U MA Chalkmates: Sandy Tozer, Sian Thomas, Graham Hamilton, Mike Liardet, Dorothy Helme, Alison Gibb, Jacquey Piazet, Linda Baker; John G, Anda, Jo, Martina, Jeff, Mary Ann, Yamini and Richard of Toytown Germany; Guyana writers John Agard, Grace Nichols, Jan Shinebourne, Pauline Melville, Ian McDonald, Clem Seecharan; Catharina and Aliya Costanzo; my UK relatives and friends: Rod Westmaas, his amazing wife Juanita Cox-Westmaas, Gillian Westmaas Lee, Gloria Austin, Nico Kaczmarek, Chris and Zarine Pegler, Ron and Susan Sanders; Neelou Malakpour, who can't wait for the movie; Marion Kowalski, the late Uschi Mühlhause and Trudel Elsässer, Eric Arnaut and Anita Duggal, Renate Köhler, Inge and Heinz Tröndle, Monika Wittiber, Janet Kramer, Ulrike Stegmüller, Thurid Müller-Elmau, Isolde Frederix and many many more friends of India. You all did your bit, however big or small.

My husband Jürgen Münch.

Last but not least, the most important one of all: my mother, Eileen Cox. May you make your century. Thank You.

**To Caterpillars everywhere
And the Butterflies within them**

Chapter 1

Nat
Tamil Nadu, Madras State, 1947

Paul was four when the *sahib* took him away from the place with all the children. It began like every other day. He awoke to the sound of banging on a big brass plate: that was Sister Maria, waking the children, while outside the crows cawed in great excitement as if they knew the day was special, flying off in a turbulence of flapping, clapping wings. He kneeled on his mat for his dawn prayer and then, stretching and yawning, he got up and went outside for a pee.

Next to the tap by the well stood the buckets of waiting water, each with a metal cup hanging over the side. The children jostled forward chattering and laughing, and Paul was last, as usual. He ladled up a cup of water and threw it all over himself, one half down his front and the other over his shoulder, so that his skin glistened and all the pores stood out like they did on a plucked chicken. He had his very own piece of soap, now the size of a one-rupee coin, with which he rubbed himself down till he was covered in bubbles, and then he sloshed off the suds with three cups of cold water. You had to bathe with only four cups of water, Sister Bernadette said, because water was precious and the well was almost empty and no-one knew if the east monsoon would come this year, and if it didn't, well, they'd have to stop bathing and washing, and then they'd have to stop drinking, and then they'd die. Paul prayed for the monsoon every day.

A button was missing from the fly of his blue shorts. He'd shown one of the ladies in white—her name was Sister

Bernadette and she was his favourite—that a button was gone and she had made him search for it but he couldn't find it, so she told him he'd have to go without because they had no more buttons. Two buttons were missing from his white shirt, too, but that didn't matter as much as his fly button. Most of the children had buttons missing from their clothes. *Where did all the lost buttons go,* Paul wondered sometimes. How come they always disappeared, never to be found? Once he asked Sister Bernadette where all the buttons from the children's shirts and dresses and shorts ended up, and Sister Bernadette had smiled and said, maybe Baby Jesus takes them to play with. 'But if Baby Jesus takes the buttons, then that's stealing,' Paul said, but Sister Bernadette only smiled and corrected herself. 'No, no, Paul, Baby Jesus doesn't steal, it's Baby Krishna who steals the buttons and takes them up to heaven so he and Baby Jesus can play with them.'

Baby Jesus and Baby Krishna are very good friends, Sister Bernadette told Paul and all the children. Sister Bernadette knew lots of stories about Baby Krishna but she wasn't allowed to tell them, because Mother Immaculata said that Baby Krishna was naughty, he stole curd and butter, and Baby Jesus was good. That's why Sister Bernadette said it was Baby Krishna who stole the buttons, and why she wasn't allowed to tell the Baby Krishna stories. But she still did, sometimes, secretly.

It was still dark and the air was still chilly with night, but the crows were flying past overhead and in the east the sky glowed pinkish-yellow. They all gathered in the central courtyard between the home and the school and they had to be quiet now, and kneel on the sand, which hurt Paul's knees, and put their hands together. Mother Immaculata, the big fat lady in white with a large wooden cross dangling on her bulging breast, who always frowned so much and whom Paul was afraid of, strode to the front of them all. They said their prayers in unison: *'Our father, who art in heaven…'*

After prayers they had breakfast sitting on mats on the school verandah, a crumbly white *iddly* with a spoonful of *jaggary,* and sweet tea with milk, and after that a lady in white took away the banana leaf plates and another lady walked around with a big bucket and a ladle pouring water over the children's hands to wash off the *iddly* and *jaggary,* and then it was time for lessons, sitting right there on the mats.

This morning English was the first lesson and Teacher called on Paul, though all the children had stretched up their hands and waved them, all except two or three who didn't know their alphabet yet; but Paul knew his. 'A, B, C, D...' he began, and only once he hesitated, before M. He always mixed up M and N, but today he got it right and when he was finished all the children and Teacher clapped. After the first lesson came Hindi and then Tamil, and then the boys and girls went to the toilet; they had to walk in a straight line, each one holding on to the shoulders of the child in front, without running.

The toilet was the field; you had to be careful because there were thorns but the soles of Paul's feet were quite hard and thorns didn't bother him much, unless they got in deep. Paul never cried when that happened, he just told Teacher and Teacher would pull out the thorn with the rusty tweezers she kept on the ledge above the window. Teacher was nice. If you had to do a poopie she gave you a cup of water to wash your bam-bam with, and a little spade to cover it with sand. You had to be careful not to step on the poopies of the other children. But the poopies were mostly hidden behind bushes and rocks.

After the toilet there were more lessons and then there was lunch. The children sat on their mats and two ladies pushed a wagon with a huge cauldron on it between the rows, and each child got a dollop of rice on a banana leaf plate, and then a spoonful of *sambar.* Paul was always so hungry he ate up every single rice grain, wiping the plate with his forefinger so it was bright shiny green afterwards. After lunch the children lay down on their mats to sleep. The sun was high in the sky by now and the ground so hot it burned your soles, but the verandah was shaded by a palm leaf roof and though the breeze blowing through was also hot it made you nice and sleepy.

Paul was just dozing off when he heard the throbbing of

the motorbike as it turned into the courtyard with a splatter of gravel. He turned his face towards the sound and opened his eyes a slit.

He saw at once that the rider was a *sahib*, even though he wore a white *lungi* like any other man. *Sahibs* always wore trousers, Paul knew. He was a *sahib* because though his face was brown like everyone else, it was a golden-reddish kind of brown, and his hair was also golden-brown, not black. Paul had never seen a real live *sahib* or a *memsahib* before, only pictures of them in his school books, so he pretended to sleep while squinting out beneath half-closed eyes, watching the *sahib* as he flung one leg over the motorcycle seat, jacked the bike up on its stand, and walked forward, looking around as if searching for someone. Paul saw that he was limping, and, strangest of all, he wore socks with his *chappals*. Paul had seen pictures of socks in his English reader — *S is for Sock* — but had never seen anyone actually *wearing* them before. These were grey and had a blue stripe.

Mother Immaculata bustled out towards the man, the ring of fat between her sari-blouse and skirt wobbling as she ran. Paul knew that *sahibs* shook hands when they met each other, but this sahib made a *pranam* to Mother Immaculata, laying the palms of his hands together like they did when they were praying. But Mother Immaculata didn't like that. She stretched out her hand and the man shook it. Paul watched carefully, because this was very unusual and very interesting. What was the man doing here? Sometimes — not very often — the children had visitors. Men and women came; Paul knew they were aunts and uncles of the children although he himself had no aunts and uncles. But never *sahibs*. Had the man come to choose a child?

Paul's heart beat faster. It hardly ever happened, that a child was chosen, and this time it couldn't be, because then a lady would be with the *sahib*. Once, just before Christmas, a man and a lady had come in a big black car. Mother Immaculata had told the children the day before that they were coming to choose a child to be their very own, because the lady had lost a child — which Paul thought very careless of her; he could imagine losing a button, but how could someone lose a *child?* — and that the lucky child would get to live with them, and call them Mummy and Daddy. So all the children had rushed at the visitors, screaming and jumping and waving at them, swarming around them, pulling at their clothes and calling out *Namaste! Namaste!* because all wanted to be chosen.

Paul had prayed that *he* would be chosen, and in fact it had seemed he *would* be chosen, because the lady, who had sad eyes and wore a purple sari and lots of golden bangles, had stopped and looked at him and smiled. 'He has a lovely wheatish complexion,' Paul heard her say, in English. 'Is he from the north?' Paul had prayed with all his might and even began to hope, because he just knew the lady wanted him.

But Mother Immaculata shook her head firmly. She took the lady by her elbow and led her away, her head leaning in towards the lady as she told her something awful about Paul which he wasn't supposed to know, something which made the lady nod in comprehension and choose another child, a very small one, one too young to go to school.

Paul was one of the eldest children. When he was five he would go to the Good Shepherd, which was an awful place in Madras for big children who would never ever get chosen. Mother Immaculata said the children in the Good Shepherd were Jesus's own little lambs. But Paul didn't want to be a lamb, because he was a boy. *Oh dear Baby Jesus, please let the* sahib *choose me! Oh, please let him choose me, dear Baby Jesus!* prayed Paul silently, and then he fell asleep. Baby Jesus had not answered his prayers the last time, and he wouldn't this time either.

He woke up because someone was shaking his shoulders and calling, 'Paul! Paul!' Paul rubbed his eyes and looked up; it was Teacher, and she was smiling. Behind her stood the *sahib* and Mother Immaculata, and they were talking together and the man was watching him, Paul. Paul didn't dare hope; he knew Mother Immaculata would soon tell the *sahib* the awful secret about him and then the *sahib* would turn away in disgust. But no; now Mother Immaculata was stepping forward and holding out her hand to him, and when Paul didn't react right away she flapped her fingers upwards impatiently and said, 'Come, come, Paul, get up, get up!' So Paul scrambled to his feet. And stood there gazing up at the *sahib* towering over him, who had kind dark grey-blue eyes and a huge hand which he now placed on Paul's head; it felt like a nice cool hat, a cool white hat like the *sahib* in the pictures wore, but this *sahib* was hatless, as if he didn't mind the sun.

They were speaking English; Paul could understand a little of it. Mother Immaculata called the man *daktah*, which surprised Paul, because he knew he wasn't sick, so why had the *daktah* come to see him? Or had he come to poke Paul with a needle in his arm, because *daktahs* did that sometimes? And why wasn't he wearing that tube hanging from his ears, like the other *daktah* who came? Paul hoped he wasn't a *daktah,* because then he'd go away again. He hoped he'd come to choose a child, and that the child would be him, Paul.

The *sahib* was saying something Paul didn't understand, and Mother Immaculata was praising Paul because of his light skin.

'He's a clever boy,' Paul heard her say. 'A very clever boy.' And the *sahib* was nodding and looking down at him, pleased.

'Paul, count to a hundred!' Mother Immaculata said, and right away Paul reeled off his numbers, hardly pausing to breathe, and the man just kept smiling down at him with those warm grey-blue eyes that made Paul feel all cosy, like a puppy curled up to a mother dog.

Paul's heart was thumping so loud he could hear it. He rubbed the spot behind his ear and cried inside, *Please Baby Jesus, oh please, Baby Jesus, please please, Baby Jesus,* over and over again. He was terrified Mother Immaculata would tell the sahib the awful secret and then he wouldn't be chosen after all.

'. . . a tiny baby, just a few days old, wrapped in a dirty old sari . . . outside the gate,' Mother Immaculata was saying. Was she talking about him? Was that how he got here? 'A note, with his name — *Paul,* it said. And then she said something else using big English words Teacher hadn't taught him yet, and her eyes looked worried, disapproving.

Paul wanted to cry. She'd told him! Told the *sahib* the

awful thing! What did *insanity* mean? Was it worse than *awful?* Mother Immaculata was frowning so it must be much worse than *awful*. Now the *sahib* would… but the man had taken hold of his hand, was looking at it and stroking Paul's fingers while he listened to what Mother Immaculata was saying, now and then looking down at Paul and smiling, as if Mother Immaculata was only saying nice things about Paul. *She'll tell him about the day I did pee-pee in the classroom because I couldn't wait,* thought Paul. He wondered if the awful secret about him was worse than that, and thought it couldn't be much worse. Mother Immaculata had told him that time that Jesus was very, very sad about him doing that, and he had to kneel on rice grains for a whole afternoon reciting 'Hail Mary' to make Baby Jesus happy again. *Please please Baby Jesus* thumped his heart, and now the *sahib* was tugging gently at him, leading him down the verandah between the bodies of the sleeping children, to Mother Immaculata's office. Paul took hold of the *sahib's* forefinger and clutched it with all his might, so the *sahib* wouldn't leave him behind. They entered the office, and Mother Immaculata clapped her hands and when Sister Maria bustled up told her to bring two cups of tea.

The *sahib* sat at Mother Immaculata's desk, reading some papers, and Paul's heart thumped louder than ever because it seemed the *sahib* had forgotten all about him. At one point they seemed to be arguing. The *sahib* was waving a sheet of paper, and frowning, and his voice was so loud Paul grew scared and squeezed the *sahib's* finger tightly, terrified that now the *sahib* knew the terrible secret, because Mother Immaculata was arguing back and pointing at him, Paul, as if accusing him of something. But then the *sahib* looked down at Paul and smiled. 'All right,' he said, 'it's not important,' and then he sighed and everything was calm again. The *sahib* raised his right hand and chuckled, because Paul was still gripping his finger with all his might.

'I'll just have to sign with my left hand,' said the *sahib,* still smiling, and then he wrote with his other hand on the papers, and Mother Immaculata put some of them in a big cardboard folder and the *sahib* clumsily folded one other paper with his left hand and slipped it into his shirt pocket, and then he was leading Paul into the sunny courtyard, towards the motorcycle.

'Have you ever been on a motorbike before?' he asked Paul, who shook his head. 'Well, you'll have to let go of my finger so you can climb on,' said the *sahib*, peeling Paul's fingers away one by one and laughing. 'You can hold on to my wrists when we go . . . look, you sit in front; just slide forward so there's room for me behind you.'

The *sahib* pushed the motorcycle off its stand. 'Have you ever been to Madras, Paul?' he asked, in Tamil this time, while he untied a corner of his *lungi* in which he'd wrapped a key.

'*Ille,* sahib, *sah,*' said Paul.

'Well, then, off we go!' said the *sahib*, in English, and he tied the hem of his *lungi* up above his knees and swung one leg over the motorcycle, the leg which ended in a foot made of wood, although Paul only saw the wooden foot later, after they got to Madras and the *sahib* took off the grey sock.

The *sahib* leaned forward.

'Listen,' he said, 'I don't like to be called sir. From now on you can call me Daddy. And I shall call you Nataraj. Nat.'

Chapter 2

Saroj
Georgetown, British Guiana, South America, 1956

Ma pointed into the gloom at the back of Mr Gupta's market stall. 'Can you show me that?' Saroj heard her say. 'No… no, not the vase, what's that behind it? THAT… Yes.'

Saroj was too small to see over the counter so she didn't know what Mr Gupta was bringing, and even standing on tiptoe all she could see were brown bony hands wiping something long with a cloth. The thing was heavy and made a thumping noise when he laid it on the counter. Saroj strained higher and managed to peek over the countertop, but it was only when Ma lifted the object that she saw it was a sword. Ma held it up, smiling, turning it around, running her finger along the sheath. She took it out of the sheath and tested the blade carefully with her finger to see if it was sharp, before pushing it back in. She bent over holding it in both hands, and showed it to Saroj, and Saroj touched it. It was hard and cold and had curly letters engraved in the metal.

'It's from Rajasthan,' said Mr Gupta, but Ma shook her head and said, 'Probably not. But it's beautiful.' And then they talked about the price and Ma took her purse out of the basket and gave Mr Gupta some red paper money. Mr Gupta asked if he should wrap it up, and Ma said yes. Mr Gupta gave the sword to Ma wrapped all in newspaper. Then he leaned over the counter and smiled at Saroj.

'So, little girl, what's your name?'

He knew her name, of course, because she had told him many times, but Saroj told him again because he must have forgotten.

'Sarojini-Balojini-Sapodilla-Mango-ROY!' the words reeled off her tongue in a rhythmic chant, knowing themselves by heart. Mr Gupta chuckled and held out two tins, one with curly bits of *mitthai* and one with pink-and-white sugarcake. Saroj took two pieces of *mitthai* and a sugarcake and said thank-you-very-much.

People were always asking for her name and laughing when she answered: Sarojini because she was Sarojini, Saroj for short. Balojini to rhyme with Sarojini, which Ganesh always called her: SarojiniBalojini. Sapodilla because she was brown like a sapodilla (and just as sweet, Ma said), mango because that was her favourite — exquisite golden Julie mangoes, soft-yellow-squishy, sucking the seed, or green and grated with salt and pepper. And Roy because she was Roy. If your name was Roy you belonged together and you were family and family was the backbone of society. Baba said.

The sword was awkward to carry because Ma had other things as well, a full basket and a parasol. So she tucked it under her arm, hiding it in the folds of her sari, and they walked to the bus stop and took a bus home. Saroj said nothing all the way home because she was thinking about the sword. Warriors used swords to kill people. Who was Ma going to kill?

When they got home Ma didn't kill anybody. She polished the sword until it shone like gold, and then she hung it on the wall in the *puja* room.

They didn't usually take the bus, not on market day, which was Monday. On Mondays Ma walked to Stabroek, open parasol in one hand, basket in the other, Saroj trotting at her side. Because there was no hand free for Saroj, Ma always said,

hook me, my dear, and Saroj — almost five now and quite tall
for her age — reached up for the crook of Ma's elbow. Ma held
the parasol above their heads as they cut through the Promenade
Garden between Waterloo and Carmichael Streets, and crossed
over into Main Street.

Saroj liked the Stabroek Market, which was teeming with
people and noise and exciting smells, vegetables and fruit and fat
black market ladies calling out, and slippery dying fish slapping
their tails on the ground, and pink living crabs in baskets that
would snap at you if you stuck your finger at them. You could
buy swords there and everything else you needed, hairpins
and pointer brooms, Johnson's baby powder and Benadryl
Expectorant and Mercurochrome and Eno's Liver Salts. Saroj
liked the walk down Main Street, too, and the big white palaces
where you might see white people if you were lucky but Ma
said you shouldn't stare, it was rude. There were lots of palaces
in Main Street.

If you closed your eyes, it seemed to Saroj, Georgetown would
reach out and fold you into soft wide arms and let you snuggle
in. If you opened your eyes and skipped, alongside Ma, down
its wide green avenues shaded by spreading flamboyant trees,
all covered in scarlet blossoms, Georgetown watched fondly,
nodded indulgently at you and smiled, and you felt good inside,
full of light and colour. You could jump over the little ditches
on the grass verges and catch the little fishes in the gutters or
collect tadpoles. You could hide behind the flamboyants and
peek behind the hibiscus hedges at the houses, in case you saw
the white people who lived in them.

Those pristine white wooden Main Street houses seemed
to whisper to you as you passed by, bidding you come in. They
were fairy-tale palaces, with towers and turrets, pillars below and
fretwork panels above, bows and bays and Demerara windows,
stairs inside and out, porches, porticos and palisades, built by
the Dutch on vast plots because there was so much space on
this flat land by the ocean, bathed in sunshine and swept by
breezes. The houses nestled, half-hidden, among leafy mango

or tamarind trees and luxurious shrubs, and wide emerald lawns surrounded them. Their graceful elegance contrasted with the green abundance that framed them, gardens overflowing with colour and saturated with fragrance, hibiscus and oleander spilling over white picket fences, giant bougainvillea bushes climbing up the white walls and curving up against the brilliant blue sky in a riot of pink and purple clusters.

The houses in Waterloo Street were miniature versions of those Main Street palaces. Their own house, too. Ma had made a paradise of the garden: bougainvilleas in the back, so huge you could hide within them, croton and fern to offset the roses. Oleander and frangipani flourished in the front yard, their fragrances mingling. Shoulder-high poinsettia and long sleek canna lilies lined the gravel path to the front door in the tower, yellow and pink hibiscus grew along the white palings, and some long leafy nameless things where caterpillars crawled reached all the way up to the gallery windows.

The caterpillars pulled their houses around on their backs. The caterpillars' houses were mud-brown ugly things made of twigs and pieces of dried leaves and sticky threads. If you touched the caterpillar it pulled its house over its head and disappeared inside it. Some caterpillars never came back out again. They turned into nothing. The ugly twig houses hung deserted from the leaves. If you squeezed them they were full of air. But they weren't nothing. The caterpillars had turned into butterflies inside, Ma said, and pointed to the kaleidoscope butterflies fluttering through the garden. 'Ugly things can be beautiful inside,' Ma told Saroj. 'The outside doesn't count. It's the inside that's real.'

Saroj chased the butterflies all through the back garden. 'Don't chase them,' Ma said. 'Just stand still, and if you're lucky one might alight on your shoulder. See...'

And she stood as still as a statue, holding up one hand, and a big blue beautiful butterfly landed on her finger. Ma lowered her hand and leaned over to show Saroj the butterfly. Saroj held out her finger but the butterfly flew away. Saroj stood stock still so the butterfly would land on her but it didn't.

'You *want* it too much,' Ma said smiling. 'You have to be still inside as well as outside. Your thoughts are still chasing him and he's scared of you. But if you melt away he will come.'

At the centre of that house, at the centre of Saroj's life, was Ma. Ma filled the world and made it good. The house smelled good when Ma was inside it. *You* felt good. Nobody else could make you feel good like Ma. Indrani was silly because she wouldn't play with Saroj. Ganesh was loud and Baba said he was bumptious. Bumptious came from bum. Ganesh slid down the banisters on his bum. Sometimes when Baba's back was turned Ganesh pulled down his pants and pointed his bum at Baba, and made Saroj giggle. Bum was a dirty word. If you showed your bum you were bumptious. Saroj wanted to be bumptious too, but Baba would be cross. Baba was cross at most everything. When Baba came home from work you had to be quiet. Saroj didn't like Baba too much, because he was rude to Parvati. Ma said you shouldn't be rude but Baba was rude, even to nice people like Parvati.

Parvati always left before Baba came home but one day he was early and said, 'What's that woman doing here? I told you I don't want her around any more. Saroj is too old for a nanny.'

Baba didn't like Parvati because he said she spoiled Saroj. Saroj felt terrible when he said that. Spoiled things were terrible. Spoiled rice on the compost heap had blue mould on it. Spoiled eggs stank. Spoiled mangoes were slimy and disgusting. She looked at her face in the mirror and there was no blue mould and nothing slimy and disgusting. She sniffed at her armpits but they smelled of Johnson's baby powder and that smelled good. She made an ugly face at the mirror. And then she showed her bum to the mirror, pretending it was Baba. Saroj liked most everything except Baba.

Parvati had long black silky hair and took Saroj to the Sea Wall where you could gaze into For-Ever and think about things that had no end. Parvati took Saroj wading in the sea water. She showed her the crabs edging sideways out of their holes, and rushing in again. She showed Saroj how to fly a kite.

Next to Ma, Saroj loved Parvati best in the world. Indrani always teased Saroj about Parvati. 'Baby, baby,' sang Indrani. 'Baby has a nanny!' She stuck her nose in the air. 'I never had a nanny, nor Ganesh. Only babies have nannies. You always had a nanny, so you're a silly little baby!'

Balwant Uncle came to take Saroj's photo. It was her fifth birthday. Every time Indrani, Ganesh or Saroj had a birthday Balwant Uncle came to take a photo of the whole family. Saroj wanted Parvati to be in the photo too, but Ma said Parvati couldn't come to her party or be in the photo because Baba wouldn't like it. Baba was cross with Ganesh because he stuck out his tongue just when Balwant Uncle took the photo. So he didn't get any cake. The photos were all stuck in an album, and sometimes Ma sat Saroj on her lap and showed her the photos. She wasn't in any of the first photos, because Ma said she hadn't been born yet. Some of the pictures were taken at the beach. Ma said that beach was in Trinidad, because Ganesh used to have his birthday in Trinidad. Saroj was born in Trinidad, said Ma. But they never went to Trinidad any more, which wasn't fair. The beach looked nice, because the sea was blue, not like the ocean, which was brown. 'Why don't we go to the beach any more, Ma?' asked Saroj. But Ma only shook her head.

When Saroj was six Jagan became King. Several uncles had come to dinner. There was Basdeo Uncle and Rajpaul Uncle, Basdeo Uncle waving a pamphlet at Rajpaul Uncle and jabbing the air with his forefinger. Three more uncles, Vijay Uncle, Arjun Uncle and Bolanauth Uncle, sat on the shiny red sofa, laughing at some joke Balwant Uncle had just told, opposite Baba in the armchair. Baba was glowering. He didn't like the uncles to tell jokes, but Balwant Uncle was full of jokes, so Saroj liked him best of all the uncles.

Saroj was helping Ma and Indrani clear away the table. All the uncles and aunties had come for dinner, but the aunties had returned home early, leaving the uncles to an evening among themselves, because this was an important day. Saroj had felt Importance swelling in the house all day, all prickly and exciting.

The drone of the radio announcer's voice crackled. Suddenly, Baba said, 'Sssh! Now it's coming!' and all the uncles jumped to their feet if they were sitting, stopped their talk in mid-sentence, and huddled around the radio, Bolanauth Uncle fiddling with the knob and the radio voice growing louder. And then they all gave a shout of triumph, the uncles and Baba crying out, 'Jai! Jai! Jai!', waving their fists, hugging each other, slapping each other on the back.

'What happened?' Saroj asked Ma, but Ma just shrugged her shoulders and disappeared into the kitchen. Saroj pulled at Ganesh's sleeve. 'What happened?' she begged. Ganesh was two years older than Saroj and already a young man. Ganesh knew the secrets of the uncles.

'We won the election!' cried Ganesh. His eyes were burning with a fire that Saroj didn't understand. What was an election? And how come we won it? Would there be some sort of a prize, like when you did something good at school or at the May Day fair, when somebody won the raffle?

'No, no prize, Sarojinibalojini,' said Ganesh patiently. Ganesh always took time to explain things. He bent over and talked to her as if they were the same size, the same age. He stroked the hair from her face and said, 'It just means we Indians were running against the Africans, and we won.'

'Oh, you mean a race…Why didn't we go and watch it then, instead of listening on the radio? It's much more fun…'

'Yes, Saroj, a bit like a race, only the Africans weren't really running against the Indians, they just wanted to get voted, and —'

'What are you telling that child, Ganesh?' Saroj looked up into Baba's frowning face, the cross face he'd been wearing more and more these days. Ganesh jumped to his feet. Though for

Saroj he was tall he still hardly reached Baba's waist and they both stood looking up as if to a high white tower. Saroj knew they had done something wrong but she didn't know what.

'I'm telling her about the election, Baba,' Ganesh looked down at his feet as he spoke, twisting the end of his *kurta*.

'And what do you know about the elections, heh? What do you know? Do you know anything? Anything at all?'

'Baba, you said if Jagan wins the election then Indians are going to rule!'

'Yes! And you know what that means! That means this is a big day for us Indians! A big day! It's the dawn of a whole new era, what have I been telling you all along, Balwant, it's a matter of pure arithmetic... Indians outnumber Africans and as long as Hindus and Muslims stick together and vote together as one we will rule and keep those uppity Africans in their place — the country is going to the dogs I tell you, but God is on our side and I'm telling you...'

Saroj heard the words without understanding them, but she felt the rising anger behind them, and the words scared her. *Marxism. Leninism. Communism. Moscow. Imperialism. Colonialism.* Saroj fixed her eyes in fascination on Baba's face, which had taken on a coppery red colour, his eyes blazing and snapping. She could feel his passion like the swelling of a volcano, something indefinable, boiling hot and simmering just below the surface. He jabbed the air with his forefinger; his voice became a loud staccato bark. Balwant Uncle stayed cool and calm, trying to pacify him, his hands stroking the air, whereas the other uncles just stood around, listening, not interrupting. Baba's vehemence grew with every word he spoke.

She looked at Ganesh with helpless, frightened eyes. He took her by the hand and laughed to dispel her anxiety, and led her from the kitchen where Ma stood before a spitting saucepan, clapping *puris,* her back to them.

'Don't worry about Baba, Saroj,' Ganesh reassured Saroj. 'Look, here's a *puri;* you can take it in your fingers, it's not hot. You know, its just politics, it's a game grown-ups like to play, like we lil' children play with toys.'

꿍

Next door, in a lovely green-and-white wooden mansion, all louvre windows and verandahs, lived the Camerons. Mr Cameron was very black. He was an African, Ma said, and Africans were black and had very curly hair. Mr Cameron's wife was very pretty, Saroj called her Betty Auntie and she was black too, but not as black as Mr Cameron. The Camerons had an enormous garden, a tangle of trees, bushes and shrubs. Betty Auntie didn't know much about gardening, not like Ma. A man called Hussein came once a week with a load of horse-droppings in a donkey cart and dug around for an hour, but still Betty Auntie's garden was wild. To Saroj it looked exciting.

Sometimes Ma and Betty Auntie chatted over the palings, talking about gardens and cooking and children. The Camerons had three children younger than Saroj. The eldest was a boy called Wayne, who was only four. Saroj discovered Wayne through the white palings that separated their gardens. She discovered the one loose paling in the fence, pushed it aside, and squeezed through to join him.

After that Saroj often went over to play with Wayne. Neither Betty Auntie nor Ma minded when they played together. Betty Auntie was really nice. She would offer them soursop juice and pine tarts and tamarind balls, guava-jelly sandwiches and ice cold Milo. But Wayne never came over to play with her. Saroj asked Ma if Wayne could come but Ma said no. She said Saroj should only go to play with Wayne when Baba wasn't home, and she should never tell Baba that she played with Wayne, and never mention Betty Auntie either. Somehow Saroj had known that, even before Ma told her. She knew what would make Baba cross. She knew you had to keep some things secret from Baba.

Betty Auntie played hide and seek with Saroj, Wayne, and her two little girls; told them stories, sang songs with them. Betty Auntie was more fun than Ma. She was even more fun than Parvati. Even when Ma was at the Purushottama Temple, and Parvati was alone with Saroj, Saroj went through the fence to play with Wayne. Wayne was more fun than Cousin Soona, who Baba said should be her friend. Cousin Soona wasn't really a friend, because she was a cousin. Wayne was her only friend. Even at school she didn't have any friends, because the children she played with there weren't allowed to come home to visit her, and she wasn't allowed to go to anyone's homes either. Baba said so. Baba only allowed her to visit relatives. Cousin Soona was silly.

One afternoon Betty Auntie blew up the sides of a plastic pool and placed it on the grassy level land beneath the star-apple tree, stuck the end of the hose in it, turned on the garden tap, and filled the pool with water.

'You can have it to yourselves for an hour,' she said to Saroj and Wayne in her smiley voice, 'but when Caroline and Alison wake up I'm going to bring them out and then you have to share!'

They nodded and looked at each other with shining eyes. Betty Auntie helped them undress till they were both in their underpants, and next minute they were splashing and screaming in the cool water. Wayne turned on the tap and chased Saroj through the trees as far as the underbrush would let him, she screaming in delight as she ran to escape the jet of water, he calling out dire warnings. The garden was a bedlam of screams, yells and war-cries and it took an age before Saroj made out the blood-chilling call coming from beyond the fence.

'Sarojini! Come here at once!'

In a trice silence laid its death-cloak over Saroj and Wayne. They stood as if turned to stone. Saroj didn't dare look at Baba but she felt his eyes eating into her and heard him say once more in a voice that filled her with icy emptiness, 'Sarojini. Pick up your dress and come here at once.'

Betty Auntie cried, 'Mr Roy, Mr Roy...' but Baba ignored her, which was rude. Saroj did as she was told. Baba gripped her hair and forced her to walk before him, up the back steps, through the kitchen, into his study which overlooked the Cameron garden. He picked up the cane and whisked it three times through the air. Its quick sharp whistle made her blood curdle.

He whipped her to a rhythm. 'Never — play — with — the — negroes. Never — play — with — the — negroes. Never — play…' He whipped the words into her skin and into her flesh, into her blood. She screamed enough to bring down all of heaven, but nobody heard. Where were Indrani and Ganesh? Where was Ma? Where was Parvati? Why didn't they rescue her?

And through the screams she saw his face. It was so ugly. So ugly she retched and threw up the remains of Betty Auntie's tamarind balls and curdled Milo all over herself and Baba, who ignored the mess and lashed on and on and on…

When he had had enough he marched her up to the bathroom, pushed her into the shower, washed her down, dried her with a few agonising rubs of a towel and pulled a clean loose nightdress roughly over her head. He frog-marched her to her own bedroom, pulled out the chair at her desk, opened a drawer, pulled out an exercise book, rummaged in another drawer for a pencil, and then wrote on the first page of the exercise book: *I must never play with negroes.*

'You will fill this book. I want you to write on every single line. You are not to eat or rest before you are finished.'

That was how Ma found Saroj when she came home before sundown. Bent over an open page and carefully pencilling in the words Baba had given her, cheeks wet with tears. She felt Ma's hand on her head and looked up and more tears rushed out, a torrent of them. She heaved with sobs.

Ma lifted her from the chair and carried her to the bed. She took off her nightdress and turned her on her tummy so she could inspect the wounds. She disappeared into her own room and into the *puja* room. Or maybe she would bring the sword and go and kill Baba. That was what Saroj wanted most.

When Ma returned she was mixing something in a cup.

It was one of her special potions, Saroj knew. With fingers as light and soft as a feather Ma smoothed a cool paste all over the wounds, and Saroj lay there and let healing sink through her. When Ma was finished she sat the child up and wrapped a sheet loosely around her, took her on her lap and held her, not saying a word, taking care not to touch her wounds. Saroj tried to speak.

'I have to write some more!'

'No. It is over. All finished, Saroj.'

Saroj thought then it was all finished with Baba and rejoiced because they'd go away and leave Baba forever. But Ma didn't mean that. She only meant the punishment was over, and that Baba would not strike her again, which he didn't. But Saroj really hated Baba now. A few weeks later the Camerons moved out. Saroj never spoke to Wayne or any of them again. Baba sent Parvati away forever, because she had allowed Saroj to play with Wayne. Saroj never saw Parvati again, either. She hated Baba for that most of all.

Ma was making dhal puris, flinging them into the air, clapping them as they fell light as feathers like flakes of layered silk across her palms. They smelled of warm ghee and soft dough baking and aromatic spices, so tender they'd melt in the mouth.

'Ma,' Saroj began, tugging at the skirt of Ma's sari.

Ma looked down and smiled. Her hands were white with flour up to the elbows. 'Yes, sweetheart?'

'Why's negro bad?'

Ma's brow creased but her smile remained. Her hands went on working as she spoke.

'Don't believe that, dear. Don't ever believe that. Nobody's bad just because of the way they look. It's what's inside a person that counts.'

'But, Ma, what's inside a person? When people look different are they different inside, too?'

Ma didn't answer, she was looking at her hands now, kneading a ball of dough. Saroj thought she had forgotten her and so she said, 'Ma?'

Ma turned her eyes back to Saroj. 'I'll show you in a

moment, dear. I'll just finish making these.'

Saroj watched the stack of dhal puris grow into a flat round tower and then Ma said she was finished and covered them with a cloth and washed her hands. Then she opened the cupboard where she kept her spare jars and bottles and took out six jars and placed them on the kitchen counter.

'Do you see these jars, Saroj? Are they all the same?'

Saroj shook her head. 'No, Ma.' The glasses were all different. There was a short flat one and a tall thin one and a medium-sized one, and other shapes in between. Some were different colours: green or brown or clear.

'All right. Now, just imagine these jars are people. People with different shapes of bodies and colours of skin. Can you do that?' Saroj nodded. 'Right. Well, now the bodies are empty. But look…' Ma picked up a big glass jug, filled it at the tap and poured water into all the jars.

'See, Saroj? Now all the glasses are filled. All the bodies are alive! They have what we call a *spirit*. Now, is that spirit the same in all the glasses, or different?'

'It's the same, Ma. So people are —'

But Ma broke in. 'Now, can you run into the pantry and get the tin where I keep my dyes? You know it, don't you?'

Saroj was back even before Ma had finished speaking. Ma opened the tin and picked up one of the tiny bottles of powdered dye. It was cherry-coloured. Ma held the bottle over one of the jars and tipped a little of the powder into the water. Immediately, the water turned pink-red. Ma returned the cap to the bottle and picked up another one. The water turned lime-green. She did that six times and each time the water turned a different colour so that in the end Ma had six different shaped jars of six different colours.

'So, Saroj, now you answer me. Are these people here all the same inside, or are they all different?'

Saroj took her time before answering. She puckered her brow and thought hard. Finally she said, 'Well, Ma, really they're all the same but the colours make them different.'

'Yes, but what is more real, the sameness or the differences?'

Saroj thought hard again. Then she said: 'The sameness, Ma. Because the sameness holds up the differences. The differences are only the powders you put in.'

'Exactly. So think of all these people as having a spirit which is the same in each one, and yet each one is also different — that is because each person has a different personality. A personality is made up of thoughts, and everyone has different kinds of thoughts. Some have loving thoughts, some have angry thoughts, some have sad thoughts, some have mean thoughts. Most people have jumbles of thoughts — but everybody's thoughts are different, and so everybody is different. Different outside and different inside. And they see those differences in each other and they squabble and fight, because everyone thinks the way he is, is right. But if they could see through the differences to the oneness beyond, linking them all, then...'

'Then what, Ma?'

'Then we would all be so wise, Saroj, and so happy!'

Ma told Saroj it was wrong to hate. She said you should love all people, even Baba, even when he wouldn't let her play with Wayne and when he sent Parvati away. Every evening Ma ushered the three children into the *puja* room, and while they watched with folded hands she'd hold an incense stick into the tiny eternal flame till it flickered alight and a thin tendril of pungent sweet smoke rose to the ceiling. She'd gently wave the incense before the *lingam,* then gesture for them all to sit; she'd place the *sruti* box between her crossed legs and pour out her heart in song to her Lord, and they, huddled around her on the straw mat, would sing too.

Singing seemed to unseal Ma's lips. She'd tell them stories of the great heroes and heroines of Indian myths and legends, Arjuna and Karna, Rama and Hanuman, Sita and Draupadi, men and women of the warrior caste who feared neither pain nor death and never flinched in danger. She told them a great secret, the secret of immunity from pain. *Go behind the thought-body*, Ma said. *Enter the silence of spirit where there is no pain...*

Indrani listened with only one ear. She was the eldest, the

sweet, obedient one. Ganesh listened with ears all agog, drinking in every word.

At first, Saroj too had listened with both ears. But then Baba had done things for which she could not forgive him. He whipped her when she played with Wayne, and made those nice Camerons move out. He sent Parvati away. He tore her from the people she loved, and so she made up her mind to hate him. Baba was evil, a wicked demon, worse than Ravana or any of the Rakshasas, and there was no Krishna or Arjuna or Rama to conquer him.

So while Ma told her stories of love and bravery Saroj brooded on Baba, and a little seed of ire surfaced in her heart. She watched this seed, and it sprouted. She nourished it a little, and it grew. *He hurt me,* she said to herself. *One day when I'm big I will hurt him back.*

Chapter 3

Savitri
Madras, India. 1921

She was the cook's daughter, his youngest and dearest child, the apple of his eye, the spark to his funeral pyre. That long hot summer she was six years old, her hair falling over her shoulders in two thick black plaits fastened with bits of thread and twists of jasmine, and she was thin and brown and lithe and in spite of the long loose skirts that fell to her ankles, wild as a boy. She loved David, and always would.

Iyer the cook and his wife Nirmala knew of her love, and watched it with mixed feelings. It is not a good thing when servants and masters play together, and was not Savitri David's servant? If they themselves were servants, wasn't their daughter the master's son's servant? How could she be friends with the young master? It was not proper. But friends they were, and who were Iyer and Nirmala to forbid what the young master wished, and what Master and Mistress allowed?

So Savitri had the run of the house and the garden. She was not like a girl at all. She climbed trees and she played cricket, she could hit a mango with a sling-shot stone as well as David, and their laughter rivalled the birdsong in all of Oleander Gardens. When she climbed trees she tucked her skirt and petticoat between her legs and stuck the hem into the waistband, and when she played cricket she lifted her skirts and showed her knees, and she never wore the anklets she was supposed to wear. She was a most indecorous little girl. Her parents were helpless, for when they reminded her to keep her skirts down she looked at them with big innocent eyes and nodded and promised, but somehow she always forgot.

There were other children, but none like these two. Savitri's four brothers, Mani, Gopal, Natesan and Narayan, kept to their own quarters, and so did the other servants' children. The Iyers lived at the back gate that opened onto Old Market Street, which was as busy and loud as any other street in Madras. The Lindsay property, Fairwinds, ended in the row of seven servants' houses, each of which had a gate opening on to the street. From Old Market Street the row of little houses was just that, a row of houses, and no passer-by could tell that each house had a back gate opening onto paradise.

The back drive divided the servants' quarters into two areas. On one side were the Iyers — a little grander, a little apart from the others, for they were Brahmins — Muthu the gardener with family, Kannan the dhobi with family, and Pandian the driver with family. On the other side lived the sweeper Kuppusamy with family, Shakoor the night-watchman with family, and Khan, unmarried. Khan was the Admiral's wheelchair-pusher. The Admiral's male nurse, the Christian Joseph, lived in the house with the *sahibs*. And no-one entered paradise who did not work there, certainly not the children — except Savitri.

The front drive led into Atkinson Avenue, a wide, quiet street lined with jacarandas, where now and again the occasional pith-helmeted *sahib* in white drills cycled straight-backed to the Club, or two *memsahibs* strolled along the pavement, exchanging gossip and news of Home, or an a*yah* pushed a pram. In fact, *ayahs* were the only Indians to be seen on Atkinson Avenue — except of course the proud drivers of those black, hearse-like vehicles that sailed majestically down the middle of the street, and the watchmen dozing at the gates, and, every afternoon at three, Savitri.

It was a long walk from the house to Atkinson Avenue, a long sandy driveway winding through towering bougainvillea passageways, behind palms and a veritable wood of flames-of-the-forest and jacarandas. Near Vijayan's house the driveway calmed down and became more docile, lined with red, pink and yellow hibiscus bushes, a few oleanders and frangipanis,

and bordered by canna lilies. Singh and his family lived in a
pretty little whitewashed cottage next to the front gate. It had
marigolds and jasmine bushes in the front garden and papaya
trees clustered in the back around the well, and even if Singh
was not on duty his cheery wife would be washing clothes in
the back and Vijayan's dogs barked at you, but not at Savitri,
for they loved her and ran up, wagging their tails and yapping
when she came, leaping up at her, rolling in the sand so she
could rub their bellies. She wasn't supposed to touch dogs, for
they were unclean; but she did so because she loved them and
they knew it.

If you turned left into Atkinson Avenue, and walked for
five minutes past the Wyndham-Jones estate to the brilliant
red half-circle where the flame-of-the-forest reached over the
hibiscus hedge and cast its blossoms to the pavement, and
crossed the avenue right there, you'd find a little path between
the Todd and the Pennington properties. And if you walked
down this path — though Savitri never walked, she skipped,
she danced, she ran backwards alongside David and sang for
him — for another ten minutes, you came to the beach, and the
Indian Ocean, and you could bathe.

David and Savitri were learning to swim that summer.
Now, while there was still time, before the Lindsays took off for
the hill station Ootacamund; now, in the few weeks they still
had together.

It was April. The heat was unbearable and the water cool,
delicious, and it just wasn't fair. Savitri was sure she could
easily learn to swim, because she knew all the movements and
practised them at night sitting up on her mat, the frog-like
clapping of her legs and the graceful curves of her arms, and she
was envious because David had learned already from his teacher
Mr Baldwin, who took him some mornings, and she wanted
to do everything that David did, just exactly everything, and it
just wasn't fair. If she had been wearing shorts, like David, of
course she'd have been able to swim long ago; but she had to
wear this long gathered skirt, and when she swam it just would
not stay tucked into her hem. Yards of cotton clung to her legs

or swirled between them or wound themselves tightly around them like ropes, and if you couldn't move your legs freely then it was obvious — you couldn't swim. It just wasn't fair.

'Why don't you wear shorts, like me?' said David, coming up for air.

'Because I'm a girl, silly!' said Savitri. 'Girls wear skirts. And when they grow up they wear saris. I'm going to wear a sari like Amma when I grow up and get married.'

'Oh!' said David. He thought for a while. Then he said, "And I will wear long trousers, like Papa, when I'm a man!'

Savitri giggled at the thought and then she splashed him. 'But I never want to grow up and get married! I don't want to go away! I wish I could be with you forever! I don't want anything to change!'

'But if we get married, you and me, we can be together always and live here always and be happy!'

Savitri found that thought even more hilarious, and she splashed him again, and dived underwater.

'Sillybilly!' But David didn't laugh. He grabbed her two wrists when she came up for air and held them firmly so that she faced him and grew still, but still she smiled and her eyes sparkled with mirth. David didn't smile.

'I mean it!' he said. 'Promise you'll marry me!'

'Oh David!' She stopped smiling and looked past him, at the horizon, and her eyes turned hazy. She hadn't yet learnt the word *naïve* and but she could sense its meaning. How could David possibly know, living as he did with the *Ingresi?* How could he *possibly* know what real life was about? When everything you could possibly want is at your fingertips, when all you have to do is close your eyes and wish it, and it's yours, you inherit a sense of power that is completely illusory, for it is dependent on matters outside yourself. Savitri could not reason this out, yet still she understood it; and she felt sorry for David.

'Go on, promise'

'How can I promise it? It's not for me to decide. I'm just a child.'

'But when you grow up. And me too. Like in a storybook, and then we can live happily ever after.'

'I'd like that, when I grow up!'

'Then promise!' His hands loosened on her wrists and slipped down to her hands.

'But…' Savitri thought of the stories David told her, of princes and princesses marrying even though it didn't seem they would, and living happily ever after, and it seemed to her that her life too, all life, was like a story, and there could only be happiness in store, and she and David would be together for ever and ever. It seemed so real, especially with David holding her hands and the water lapping at her waist and the afternoon sun gentle on her wet shoulders. I didn't seem wrong, at that moment, to make a promise for events beyond your control. Everything just felt *right;* for now and always. How could it be otherwise? She wanted to promise. She opened her lips to speak the words.

That was how Mani found them. Standing in the water, facing each other, hand in hand, lost in their bubble of *rightness.*

Iyer had sent Mani to find Savitri, because the go-between, the boy's aunt, was waiting. Mani had searched the whole of Fairwinds for her, asking everyone he met if they'd seen her, and Singh had told Mani that they'd gone to the beach, and when Mani arrived there they were, standing in the water hand-in-hand, gazing into each others' eyes. Mani yelled and yelled for Savitri, ever more furious, but it was a long time before she heard because the wind snapped his words away. Finally, though, she heard, and spun towards him, and came out of the ocean, blouse and skirt transparent in their wetness and clinging to her body. Mani bawled at her and boxed her ears, and then not even giving her the time to turn around and wave goodbye to David he grabbed her by the scruff of her neck and marched her all the way home, dripping wet as she was.

Mani was too stupid to realise he couldn't bring her home this way. He did, and in his fury prattled out the whole story in front of the boy's aunt instead of being polite and making an excuse for Savitri and waiting till the boy's aunt had left. So the boy's aunt saw her dripping wet like a drowned rat, and opened her eyes wide. On hearing that she'd been swimming with the *sahib* boy, and holding hands with him, she excused herself and hurried off, and they never heard from that particular boy's relatives again.

Mani told Iyer that David was going to spoil Savitri and make her unfit for marriage. Iyer forbade Savitri from playing with David. Savitri told David.

That night she waited till all were asleep, wrapped in their sheets against the mosquitoes. *Thatha*, her grandfather, slept alone on the *tinnai*, the front verandah. The other men slept on the side verandah, and she and Amma, her mother, slept on the back verandah facing the garden because no-one slept inside in April, it was so hot, except the English, the *Ingresi*. As silently as a peacock's feather sweeping the sand she ran down the back drive to the manor house and round the back to David's window, which of course was wide open.

She gave the cry of the brainfever bird. Savitri could imitate all the birds and the animals so well that no-one could tell the difference. She could give a perfect peacock's cry, she could chatter like a monkey or a chipmunk, and her brainfever bird's call was so true to life it was of no use, for David did not stir. She peered into the darkness behind his window; she could not enter because of the bars but she knew that David's bed was just beyond, so she reached in as far as she could and tugged at his mosquito net. David still did not stir, not even when she whispered his name as loud as she could, so she went in search of a long stick and found the very long one used for cutting down mangoes, with a little curved knife on the end, and with some effort managed to stick this through the bars — not using the knife end — in such a way that it ran along the wall, and she poked David in the small of his back.

'Ow!' he said, and sat up with a jump.

Savitri giggled and spoke his name, a little louder now, and when he realised it was her, he came to the window and they spoke through the bars.

'They're looking for a husband for me,' she said, 'and that's why I can't play with you any more.'

'But that's so silly,' said David. 'Because I'm going to marry you myself!'

'I know. But still they're looking for a husband.'

'How could you marry anyone but me? You won't, will you? You promised '

'But, David…'

How could she make him understand, whispering here in stolen moments of the night? How could he ever grasp what it was like, not to be an *Ingresi?* What is was like when all that you want does not fall into your lap?

'You promised, so that's settled. And I won't marry anyone else but you. You know, don't you?'

Savitri's eyes were moist but David couldn't see. And he couldn't see when she nodded earnestly, just to humour him. But in her she knew, she felt, that life is not like a meal you cook adding the ingredients you want, one by one, and turning out delicious, because you have decided what goes in, and how much, and what stays out. True life is different; it is cruel and it is indifferent to your wants and even to your needs. Though she had not yet seen the full face of that cruelty, yet somehow she sensed it in every cell of her body; a sense passed down to her as was the colour of her eyes or the gentleness of her touch.

David, not knowing all this, reached through the bars and gently pulled her face so close the bars crushed her cheeks. Then he leaned forward and planted a kiss on her startled lips, and said, 'There. Now we're engaged to be married, and I'm going to give you an engagement ring as soon as I can, and they're not going to stop us playing together. Never. I promise, Savitri. I'll work things out. I'm the young master and I can do whatever I want.'

Chapter 4

Nat
A Village in Madras State, 1949

Nat dreamed of a woman with a high hysterical voice, standing outside on the verandah, calling his father's name, screaming and beating on the door till her screams pierced the layers of sleep and frayed out the dream and it was all real. He sat up on his *sharpai,* rubbing his eyes because his father had switched on the light, and in the stark glare of the single bulb hanging from the middle of the ceiling he saw that his father was hastily wrapping his *lungi* around his hips.

'I'm coming,' Doctor called out in Tamil to the woman outside. He reached up to the shelf for his medicine box, walked to the door, drew back the latch. Nat slipped down from his *sharpai,* wrapped his blanket around him and padded to the open doorway to watch through the mosquito screen. His father had switched on the verandah bulb. The woman held a bundle in her arms, under the *pallu* of her sari. It was a baby, Nat saw, because a little black foot peeped out through the folds of torn grubby cotton in which it was wrapped. His father was speaking in soothing words and trying to take the bundle from the woman, but she clasped it even closer to her body, not wanting to let go, and screaming at Doctor as if he was responsible for the child's condition which, Nat knew, was bad.

It was probably dead. When they brought their children in the middle of the night it was usually too late.

Outside the gate Nat could just make out the hulking shape of a bullock cart in the half-light, piled high with coconut-tree branches. The bullock stood with its head lowered, trying to sleep, whereas the driver had already stretched himself out on

the cart and covered himself with a sheet, indifferent to the
woman's plight. He'd sleep there till dawn, Nat knew, and then
continue his journey to whichever village he was heading for,
the bullock plodding along the dusty lanes, the driver crouching
on the cart holding its tail between his toes and twisting it
occasionally when the plodding got too slow.

Doctor persuaded the woman to lay the child on the waist-
high *sharpai* on the verandah and bent over, unwrapping the
cloth and talking to the woman, who had quietened down
considerably. He was asking her questions, speaking in that
deep warm voice which never failed to work magic with the
villagers. It was as if the healing process began with that warmth,
which seeped through the cocoon of lethargy and hopelessness
wrapped around them just like this child wrapped in rags,
waking them to life. Or, as in the case of this panic-stricken
woman, laying a balm on them like a hand on a terrified child,
easing them into a calm that allowed questions to be asked and
answered.

Since when did the child have the wound, how did it
happen? Why did she not come sooner, what had she done till
now? How far had she come, by what means of transportation,
what did her husband do for a living, how many children did
she have? The woman, though sobbing quietly, answered. She
knew, as did Nat, for his father would not have spoken so much
if he could have worked to save the child, that it was too late,
the child was already dead and not even the *sahib daktah* could
raise it.

The woman lived twenty miles to the east, Nat heard her
say. Her husband was a day labourer in the stone quarry; they
had five children of which this was the youngest and they
had all gone to help the father at work and a big stone had
fallen on the boy's foot, crushing it and leaving a glaring open
wound. She had tried to heal it herself by coating it with fresh
cow-dung but the wound got worse and yesterday a fever had
broken out. She had heard, of course, of the *daktah sahib*, but
it had not been possible to come earlier because of her work.
Then yesterday she had set off on foot and walked most of the

distance, accompanied by her second son who was six, carrying the sick boy, but when night fell and she had not yet arrived she had been afraid to walk by herself and the six-year-old boy was tired so she had given a bullock-cart driver her last *annas* to drive them and she had not eaten since breakfast the day before and the boy had still been alive when she left home but some time during the previous day he had been still. So still...

'There is nothing I can do. The child has passed away,' Nat heard his father say, and the woman broke into a loud anguished sobbing and began to cuff her forehead with her fists. Nat wanted to rush inside and hide under his blanket, but instead he stayed because his father would want him to be brave because you cannot hide from death; you can only reach down inside yourself to find the strength to help you face it. And it was their duty, his father's and his own, to stand by this woman in her hour of grief.

'Where is your boy?' his father asked the woman, and she pointed to the bullock cart.

'He is sleeping,' she answered.

'Bring him here. You can sleep on the verandah till the morning and I will send you back home on a bullock cart. Nat, bring the mats and blankets!'

Nat immediately opened the mosquito screen and hurried over to the corner of the verandah where they kept the rolled up mats for visitors. He brought two rolls and spread them on the concrete verandah and placed two folded blankets on them, and looked at his father expectantly, though he knew what would come next.

The woman had walked to the bullock cart and returned now with the sleeping boy in her arms, laying him on one of the mats. Nat's father covered him with a thin blanket. Nat saw that although the boy was the same age as him — six — he was nevertheless much smaller, frail and thin with spindly arms and legs that looked as if you could snap them like dry twigs. The woman sat down cross- legged beside him, the dead child once more pressed to her, under her sari, and sobbed quietly to herself; Nat thought she would not sleep that night. He looked

at his father, who shook his head, meaning yes, and ran inside
and opened the little fridge and removed the bowl of *iddlies*. He
took out two, placed them on an aluminium plate, sprinkled
some crukbly *jaggari* over them, and took it out to the woman,
who looked at him with eyes that bled tears and took the plate
silently, but did not eat.

'I will keep it for when the boy wakes up,' she said to
Doctor, placing the plate on the ground beside her, but Doctor
replied that the boy would get his own plate whenever he awoke,
and that this plate was for the mother. She touched the palms
of her hands together in thanks and began to eat, breaking off a
piece of *iddly* with her fingers and placing it in her mouth, and
since it was not polite to see a person eating Nat and his father
left her to herself and re-entered the house, Nat in front of his
father, whose hand lay comfortingly on his shoulder.

Nat wanted to cry but he wouldn't. He wanted to talk but
there was nothing to say. Nat had seen things like this and even
worse many times; many times they were shaken out of their
sleep by someone who had come far, usually someone dying
because if they were not dying they would wait till morning.
Sometimes Nat's father could save the person; sometimes
he took the person to hospital in Town on the back of his
motorbike; sometimes he pressed a torch into Nat's hands and
sent him running to wake up Pandu who slept in his cycle-
rickshaw in the village, and Pandu would come and take the
patient in the rickshaw to the hospital and Nat's father would
follow on his motorbike, and Nat would have to stay behind
and try to go back to sleep, but he couldn't.

Nat knew his father didn't like him getting up at night for
the emergency patients and at the beginning had made Nat stay
in his *sharpai,* but since Nat didn't sleep anyway, finally he had
allowed him to get up and help. If the treatment took too long
he'd send Nat back to bed, but he couldn't make him sleep; it
was only when Nat knew there was nothing more to be done,
because the patient had died or because his father had given a
pill or an injection to stop the pain and make the patient sleep
till morning, or the patient was able to leave and go home, that

Nat had a quiet mind that allowed him to sleep.

It had always been this way. Ever since he'd had a father Nat knew that the nights were not their own. But then, nothing at all was their own.

When Nat came to live with Doctor two years ago he had noticed at once that he was different. That was because his father was a *sahib*, and not just any *sahib*, but a *daktah sahib*. Wherever they went people would lay their hands together and bow their heads slightly in greeting. Sometimes people would bend over and touch his father's feet. Some of the men would even prostrate themselves before him on the ground, stretched out full length with their hands on Doctor's feet. Or the women crouched down before him to rest their heads before his toes. His father didn't like these prostrations at all; he had told the people hundreds of times and always bent over to raise the person up, but still they did it.

At first, when Nat saw the people bowing down to his father, he had thought his father must be God Himself.

'Why do they bow down, Daddy? Are you God?' he asked, because in the great temple in Town he had seen the people bowing down to the Lord Shiva, who lived in the innermost shrine in the temple, in the Holy of Holies, prostrating themselves before him just as they did to his father. His father chuckled, and shook his head.

'They see God in me and are thanking Him because I have cured them, and so they bow down to God in me, Nat.'

'But *you* cure them, and not God!'

'Yes, but I could not cure them without God's help and His power, Nat. It is He who cures them through me. I am only an instrument. It means I must serve God with all my life, and see Him in all who come to me, in the very lowliest, and thank Him for His gifts.'

Yet still, Nat knew that for the people his father was God, and he knew they were different. It wasn't just that their skin was not black and that they were tall and strong. Look at the house they lived in: it was bigger than all the other houses in the village, and so much better, a flat-roofed brick house in a garden at the edge of the village, painted white and with a thatched-roof verandah all around it. The house had two rooms, a small kitchen and a bathroom. The smaller room was where his father treated his patients, who would be there long before dawn, squatting in the dust on the road outside the gate and patiently awaiting their turn. Father and son slept in the bigger of the two rooms, which contained the two *sharpais,* a wooden cupboard where they kept their clothes, the fridge which was half-full of medicines, and a low wooden desk with a lid that clapped up, where Nat's father wrote his letters and did his business, sitting cross-legged on the mat-covered floor before it.

The room had several windows, arranged in threes one above the other around the room, with wooden shutters which folded inwards so you could open them to let in the breeze or close them to keep out the cold in winter. When all the windows were open it was almost like living outside, for the windows started low down in the walls and ended close to the ceiling. They had iron bars to keep out thieves and wire mesh to keep out mosquitoes and monkeys. If the monkeys came in they would wreck the room, Nat's father said. They would steal all the bananas and empty all the jars of rice or sugar or flour on the floor, and they'd open the fridge and dash the medicine bottles to the ground.

The monkeys came in big groups led by a huge monkey-king the children called Ravana, who would crouch up in the mango tree near Nat's house and glower down at the village, baring his teeth and hissing, jerking his head back and forth if anyone came too near. The other monkeys, his wives, would arrange themselves on the branches behind Ravana. Some of them had babies clinging to their tummies, and some of the babies sat beside their mothers on the branches or played together just like real children.

If there was no-one about, if the children were at school or helping their parents in the fields and the men were at work and the mothers were at the well fetching water, the monkeys would attack. They'd all of a sudden swarm down from the tree and go through the village, looking for open doors and windows or a small child alone with a banana in its hand. There was never much to eat in the houses, so in their rage they'd wreck whatever could be wrecked and that poor child would scream in terror when Ravana or one of his wives grabbed the banana out of its hand, and the mother would run out of her home shouting and throwing stones, and gather the screaming child in her arms. So it was up to the boys to keep the monkeys away.

One of the first things Nat learned when he came to the village was to use a sling-shot, and now he was six he could hit whatever he wanted, moving targets and tiny ones, and a monkey-wife up in the branches of the mango tree. He'd never aimed at Ravana yet, because if Ravana saw one of the smaller boys picking up a stone for his sling-shot he'd very likely attack that boy, jump on him and scratch and bite, so Ravana was reserved for the big boys. If all the boys attacked at once, charged through the village towards the mango tree brandishing their sling-shots, if they all stood beneath the tree yelling their battle-cries, if they all fired their stones at the monkeys while shouting and kept up that fire and showed the monkeys who was stronger, then Ravana would give the command and lead his troop away, which meant crossing a stretch of field where there were no trees at full pelt, with all the village boys tearing behind them, firing their stones and yelling. But the monkeys were faster, and would reach the grove at the other side of the field, lose themselves up in those branches, and disappear. But sooner or later they'd be back.

Nat and his father slept on *sharpais* and had mats on the floor, which was made of stone. The other people lived in huts built of mud; they used watered-down cow-dung to plaster the walls and the floors to keep them clean, and had no doors and windows, only doorways and little holes in the walls so that inside all was dark, and they slept and lived on the dried-mud floors.

Nat and his father had long wires which came on high poles from Town all the way to the house, bringing light to the bulbs and making the fridge work, and they had gas bottles under their stove so all you had to do was turn a switch and light a match and you could cook. The other villagers had to gather dried wood and dung and make dung cakes for fuel before they could cook. They dressed in rags and even though they washed their clothes often at the water tank, pounding them against a stone to beat out the dirt, somehow they never really looked clean. Whereas Doctor and Nat never had to wash their own clothes. Once a week a *dhobi* came to take away their dirty laundry and brought it back in a bundle, freshly washed, ironed and folded, smelling sweet from the Surf powder supplied by the doctor.

But the main difference between Nat and the other children was one he wished didn't exist. The other children went to the village school, if they went to school at all; which most of them didn't, especially not the girls. Nat went to school in Town. Every morning Pandu would come in his rickshaw, and Nat would take down his bag from the nail in the room and get in the rickshaw, and Pandu would drive him into Town to the Government Primary English Medium school where he learned to read and write English as well as Tamil and a bit of Hindi.

Nat was the only child from the whole village who went to this special school, which Nat thought was unfair, but which his father said was a privilege. The other children looked after goats and cows and babies or went out to gather dung or dried sticks for fuel or cut down branches of the little trees the Reforestation Agency had planted, or fetched water or planted rice or picked peanuts. And even if they did go to school Teacher came sometimes and sometimes he didn't, and the children didn't learn much. So Nat's father made him go to Town every morning with Pandu. Which was unfair.

When Nat came to live with his father he noticed the photograph of a lady hanging on the wall above his father's *sharpai*. It was a large photograph, almost life-size, showing just the lady's head and shoulders. The lady was so beautiful, Nat stared at her for a long time, looking into her soft, gentle smiling eyes, dark and shining, that seemed to say so much. The lady was his father's wife, and she was dead. She was not a *memsahib* but an Indian lady, because her skin was dark, even darker than Nat's, and she had a *tika* in the middle of her forehead, and wore a sari crossed over and covering one shoulder. If Nat could have just one more wish come true then it would be that this lady could be his mother, that she would not have died but would be living there with them, in that little house, cooking for him like the other mothers did and pressing him to her soft bosom, rubbing him down with oil till his skin glistened and telling him stories sitting in the cool of the verandah with him in her lap. But then again, if she had lived Nat would probably not have come to live with his father, for the lady would have had children of her own and Nat's father would not have had to go to that place to choose Nat. So Nat always reminded himself how lucky he was to have been chosen at all, and not think too much about the lady and what it would be like to have a mother who loved him and looked after him. He had a father; and that alone was an answer to a prayer.

The woman and the boy had breakfast with Doctor and Nat. The village was alive with sound; you couldn't see anything because of the high walls of cascading bougainvillea, pink, orange, and wild purple surrounding their house, but you could hear the clanging of the metal vessels, the swishing of coconut brooms, the splashing of water as the mothers sprinkled it outside their huts so that the girls could draw the wonderful *kolam* pictures in the damp earth before their doors, their wrists twirling and swirling to let the chalk powder flow out.

Pandu's youngest daughter Radha, who was thirteen, came over every morning to draw a *kolam* for them, and it was important to have one because it gave you good thoughts before you entered the house or left it. Doctor gave Radha one rupee every day for drawing the *kolam,* which she would accept between the palms of her hands and raise to her forehead in thanks before turning to run home and help her mother cook.

Radha did not go to school. She would be getting married in a year or two, Pandu hoped, and they were worried about the dowry, because husbands were very troublesome when it came to dowries. It had been bad enough with Pandu's elder daughter who married last year. The first boy who had offered to marry her had wanted a motorbike as dowry but of course Pandu had not been able to afford that so it hadn't worked out. The next boy had wanted a wrist-watch, but that too was too expensive. Finally they found a boy who had been content with a nylon shirt from Town, and the wedding had taken place, but now Radha's turn was coming up and Pandu never talked of anything else when he spoke with Doctor.

Ever since the trouble with Pandu's elder daughter (who, to make matters worse, was not beautiful) Doctor had presented to every family at the birth of a daughter a teak sapling, which the family could plant in Doctor's field behind the house and tend while the girl grew. When she was of marriageable age it would be a big teak tree which the family could sell for a *lakh* of rupees and so acquire a good husband for the girl. It wasn't a solution, Doctor said, but at least it got the girls good husbands and you could only hope the husbands wouldn't spend the money on drink and beat the wives.

Radha reappeared now with a tiffin carrier filled with *upma,* which was to be their breakfast today, prepared by Pandu's wife Vasantha. Doctor had sent an early morning message that they had guests, so Vasantha had cooked enough for everyone, and the woman and the boy ate with great appetite. When they were finished Pandu himself and his son Anand were already standing at the gate, waiting, Pandu with his rickshaw to take Nat to school in Town, and Anand to take the woman home on the motorbike.

Nat's father was training Anand as an assistant. Sometimes Anand worked with the patients and sometimes he ran errands on the motorbike, because Pandu worked in Town during the daytime so Anand would fetch medicines or take patients to hospital or, in certain cases like this woman, take them home if Doctor didn't think they should walk. So Anand took the woman home to her village with the dead infant in her arms and the little boy between them, which meant that Doctor would have no assistant in the clinic that morning. Which was not good, because already four people were squatting in the dust outside the gate, waiting for the clinic to open.

And that was the reason Nat had to go to school in Town instead of the village. Nat's father wanted him to get something he called a Good Education; Nat didn't know what that was, but he did know it meant he had to go to the English Medium school in Town, that one day he would have to leave his father and go far away across the seas, and one day he would be a doctor like his father, and help in the clinic. But that was a long, long way away.

He remembered this particular morning so well, the morning the woman with the dead baby had breakfast with them, because just after the woman and the dead baby and the boy left with Anand, just as he was about to get in the rickshaw behind Pandu, another rickshaw drew up, a new yellow rickshaw, and a tall man in very clean black trousers and a shiny white long-sleeved shirt stepped out, and that was his Gopal Uncle, though he didn't know it yet.

When his father saw the man he said, 'Gopal!' and the man laughed heartily and almost ran into his father's open arms, saying, 'Oh friend, my dear friend, I am very happy to see you again!'

Nat stood staring, because he had never seen his father greet or be greeted by anyone this way before. His father, as far as he knew, had no friends, no real friends the way he, Nat, had. The people in the village worshipped his father, which meant they could not be friends with him. And, whereas his father spoke Tamil with the people in the village, he spoke English with Gopal. English was their own very private world which no-one else could enter, not even Anand, although Anand understood some English words. But now this strange man in the sparkling white clothes who had come in a rickshaw, he was allowed to enter this private little English world.

The man his father called Gopal now turned to Nat with very interested, eager eyes, and said, 'And you are Nataraj!'

Which greatly surprised Nat, because how did the man know his name, just like that? And then the man stretched out his hand and pinched Nat's cheek, squeezing a slab of skin with his fingers and wiggling it. It hurt Nat so much he decided not to like this man. But he was curious so he hoped his father would keep him home from school today so he could find out more about him, but just as he thought that his father said, 'Nat, what are you waiting for? Off to school, or Teacher will be cross! Gopal Uncle will be here when you get back ... won't you? I see you've brought a valise with you?'

'Yes, yes, I was hoping I could stay ... I brought some garments with me ... and a present for Nataraj .. .' He reached into the rickshaw he'd come in and took out a shiny black suitcase, and as Nataraj settled into Pandu's rickshaw he heard his father say, 'But how on earth did you find me, old chap? I say, I heard you'd .. .'

Nat couldn't hear any more, because Pandu had mounted the cycle and was pedalling off down the dusty road. He kneeled on the seat and rested his arms on the folded-back hood of the rickshaw, and looking back he saw his father leaning down to speak to the first patient, and reaching out to help the old man to his feet. Gopal Uncle stood at the side of the road, the shiny valise in his hand, watching his father help the old man hobble into the clinic, and there was a dark look on Gopal Uncle's face that struck a cold clammy fear into Nat's heart.

Chapter 5

Saroj
Georgetown, 1964

When Saroj turned thirteen Baba threw her the gauntlet that would develop into the battle of her life, the battle *for* her life. It happened at the breakfast table.

'I have found a husband for Sarojini,' he said, as casually as if declaring he would be late in from work tonight as he had an important meeting to attend. Saroj's spoon of Weetabix-and-milk froze in mid-air, the open mouth waiting for the spoon now a jaw-dropped gaping hole of shock.

Baba's long, thin hands complacently stroked marmalade on buttered toast. He cut the toast into little orange-yellow-white squares and lifted them to his lips with an almost feminine delicacy. His fingers moved with a deft spidery lightness; Saroj imagined them spinning a web. Creepy. She shuddered and looked away, waiting for what was to come.

Everyone was waiting, but Baba took his time. Ma looked at Saroj, raising her eyebrows slightly so that the round red tika between them bobbed. Saroj turned her eyes to Ganesh, who in turn was looking at Baba, who, assured of everyone's attention, finally continued. 'After all, she will soon be of marriageable age. I have been making the necessary enquiries.'

By now all eyes were fixed on Baba except Indrani's, who was primly buttering her toast with an expression of studied nonchalance. She, of course, could afford to be blasé. She already had her prospective husband chosen and waiting, and a very good match it was too, everyone said, and only last week her wedding-sari had arrived, all the way from India, halfway round the world, sent by one of Baba's distant Bengali relatives whom none of them had ever met, including Baba.

Baba looked around, gathering his family into the tent of his authority, straightening his back for the next phase of his announcement.

'I have selected the Ghosh boy.'

Even Indrani, now, raised her eyes. Baba waited.

'The Ghosh family,' he prompted when no-one commented, no-one gasped, no-one clapped, no-one fainted. 'Ghosh of Ghosh Brothers Dry Goods on Regent Street. Mrs Ghosh is married to Narain's second cousin and they have a boy of the correct age.'

Mr Narain, a proven half-Brahmin, was Baba's law partner — Narain and Roy of Robb Street, Georgetown's second most prestigious law firm, which meant that any relative of Narain had to be suitable for Baba's children, and vice-versa. Narain himself had only daughters, a fact they all knew well because Baba lamented it so many times. Two Narain sons for the two Roy daughters would have been perfect. As it was, Narain's youngest girl was planned for Ganesh and they'd all grown up with this knowledge, but only Saroj knew that this particular marriage was possible only over somebody's dead body: Narain's daughter. Ganesh planned to murder that Narain girl and Saroj still wasn't absolutely sure he wasn't joking. She, of course, worshipped Ganesh. Every word he said was scripture, and at twelve — thirteen — all things seemed possible.

'Mr Ghosh is of pure Brahmin family. Second generation Calcutta,' Baba proclaimed triumphantly. Still the family did not break out in cheers.

'The Ghosh family? Where do they live?' Ma frowned and looked enquiringly at Baba, and while their parents exchanged words Ganesh leaned over and whispered in Saroj's ear, 'Oh, Ghosh!' and rolled his eyes.

She spluttered and almost choked on her tea. But Ma and Baba hadn't noticed so she whispered back behind a cupped hand, 'Will you help me murder him?'

'By slow strangulation.'

'Where will we hide the body?'

'Bodies. We'll make it a double murder . . . the Ghosh boy and the Narain girl.'

'We'll pickle their eyes and . . .'

'What was that, Sarojini?' Saroj jumped guiltily and met Baba's eyes, piercing and threatening — blood-curdling, she thought to herself, and shivered. *I'd rather kill* you, *Baba, and that's no joke.*

'Nothing, Baba.' She demurely turned her eyes down to her Weetabix, cut off a corner and spooned it into her mouth, trying to ignore Ganesh, who was pinching her thigh. He leaned forward for the teapot, conveniently upsetting Indrani's milk all over her frock. Indrani's yelp of annoyance and the accompanying hullaballoo covered his surreptitious whisper, delivered in a tone full of deep portent: 'I shall be making the necessary investigations.' He rolled his eyes again.

About a million people came to the birthday party that afternoon. They were all extended-family Roys and came not for the birthday girl's sake but for Ma's samosas, which were legendary, and for gossip. By that time news about the Ghosh boy was out on the grapevine. Every time some auntie grabbed Saroj to plaster her cheek with birthday kisses and press a gift into her hand squealing, 'So how's the birthday girl?' she knew by the gleam in her eyes that auntie was just bursting with the news, and dying to move on to exchange notes with the next auntie. *Do you know him? His mother? My husband's brother's second cousin twice removed is married to his father's niece . . .* and so on. They'd been through that before with Indrani. They wouldn't mention him to *her*, of course, it wouldn't be proper, but she could see the fluster in those excited knots of aunties and divine the topic from the tell-tale rustle of polyester saris as they huddled together.

She could have vomited. It wouldn't have been so bad if they'd brought decent presents, books and records or things like that, but she could tell with one touch, with one glance even, what was inside their daintily wrapped-and-tied bestowals which grew in a gaudy pile on a corner table: Twenty-five per cent panties. Twenty-five per cent handkerchief boxes. Twenty-five per cent purses. Twenty-five per cent hairbrush/manicure sets. The usual. The aunties liked to give practical, useful things. After all, what could a growing girl like Saroj want besides panties, hankies, purses or hairbrush/manicure sets?

She was still in the middle of Premavati Auntie's fat embrace, her nose nudging the prickly rose brooch holding Auntie's sari in place on her perfumed shoulder, taking in the intoxicating scent of *Evening in Paris,* when, over that shoulder, she saw Ganesh signalling and it looked urgent. She had to keep smiling and nodding at Premavati Auntie a good three minutes more while she gushed out some story about the film she'd seen with her daughter at the Hollywood and how they'd have loved to have Saroj there and how much she would have liked it. Fat chance. Everyone knew Baba didn't allow his daughters to go to the cinema, not even to Indian films.

And then Premavati Auntie pulled away and took a little flat, soft, pink-wrapped gift out of her voluminous plastic handbag and crushed it into Saroj's hand saying, 'Here you are, dearie, I do hope it fits!' She planted a wet birthday kiss on a reluctantly offered cheek, pinched the other cheek and shook it, and waddled off to chat with Rukmini Auntie.

As Saroj turned to follow Ganesh into the kitchen a little hand grabbed hers. 'Saroj Auntie, you promised to help with my kite — Shiv Sahai's is all finished and you promised!' piped a squeaky voice at her side. She smiled as she met Sahadeva's eyes. Sahadeva, her little cousin, Shiv Sahai's twin, Balwant Uncle 's little boy. Balwant Uncle and his wife were modern, teachers, he of history, she (retired) of biology, and they gave her worthwhile birthday presents. Last year a microscope, this year a chemistry set. They said she had a mathematical mind, which should be cultivated; and they were people who took her seriously. They lived in Kingston, near the sea, and she visited them once or twice a week, with the excuse of helping the boys with their schoolwork, and because Baba had selected Cousin Soona as Saroj's playmate. But she also went there to escape to the seashore, to get a glimpse of the ocean, to run for miles along the Sea Wall, to wade, barefoot and curly-toed, into the foaming sheet of warm brown water when the tide rolled gently in and licked the beach.

The ocean was freedom. Standing at its edge and gazing far out into the horizon, eastwards, she felt a deep, yearning ache that rose out of some unknown kernel within her, that reached out, far far out, to that distant horizon, to the unseen shores that lay beyond, and further, to the endlessness of the sky, to the endlessness of time.

'Yes, I know, Sahadeva. Look, I can't stop now but I'll phone you in a day or two, okay?'

'You promise, Auntie?'

'I promise.' She patted him on his tousled little black head, smiled again, and showed him her crossed fingers. 'Cross my heart and hope to die. And we'll make the best kite that ever was. Okay?'

'Okay Auntie, and we'll win next Easter, I just know it!' Sahadeva scampered off.

Ganesh had disappeared into the kitchen. She found him emptying a plate of samosas into his school bag.

'You crazy, or what?'

'I took out my books first. Come, let's go up to the tower, I'm going to lose my mind if I stay here a moment longer and I've got some news for you.'

'Okay, wait a minute.' She went to the fridge, opened it, took out two Jus-ee drinks, orange and lime crush, and stuffed the bottles down the front of her dress. Ganesh grinned.

'You think you're hiding anything? Two grapefruits would be better. More authentic.'

'Shut up.' She took the drinks out again because Ganesh was right. He held out his school bag and she laid the bottles on top of the samosas.

'The bag's going to be all greasy and full of crumbs afterwards, you know.'

'Oh, I'll give it a shake. Okay, let's go. Don't stop for anyone.' Ganesh and Saroj pushed their way across the crowded drawing room, through the milling, munching relatives, smiling into this face and that, murmuring *excuse me, excuse me please,* till they reached the square stairwell which led down to the front door and up into the tower.

The Roy mansion rested solidly on tall, heavy columns to protect the living quarters from flooding during the rainy season. But whereas most houses had an open staircase leading up to the front door, theirs had a dog-leg staircase housed in a tower shaft. The tower jutted forward at the front left corner of the house and extended above the roof into the little windowed eyrie, girded by a narrow widow's walk. House and tower were built entirely of wood; horizontally planked, pristine white, generously windowed. Rows of twelve-paned sash windows, enclosed by sloping, top-hung Demerara shutters, regulated light and shadow, heat and coolness, within the house. In the mornings and late afternoons the shutters stood open to let the cool Atlantic breeze sweep joyously through light-flooded rooms. Under the scorching midday sun Ma closed the shutters and hushed the house into sleep, to dream in a cool, moist half-light behind jalousied walls, withholding its secrets from the brash, brazen outside world.

But the tower room was all windows, without shade. Open the glass panes and the wind sailed through, a cleaning, vigorous wind that swept away care and uprooted disquiet. Up here you felt tall, free, strong. Up here, nothing could touch you. It was a refuge from the heat of the day, a sanctuary from the pain of living. An escape from the fate of being born a Roy.

Saroj and Ganesh took the stairs three steps at a time. Once in the tower they flung themselves in relief onto the bare scrubbed floorboards, gasping for breath and laughing.

'So, what's the emergency?' Saroj said.

'I spoke to Kevin Grant on the phone this afternoon and he knows him.'

'He knows who?'

'That boy, of course, that Ghosh boy, your prospective bridegroom. Now, take a deep breath, Saroj, and hold on tight, here's my hand, grip tightly and don't faint. Ready?'

'Let me guess...' Saroj paused to think. '...he's a sixty-year-old widower with dentures and a leaky bladder. Baba's importing him from Calcutta and he's bringing a brood of seven bawling snotty-nosed infants, and . . .'

'A good guess but remember, the decisive word is *boy*. Even Baba wouldn't call anyone over forty a boy.'

'Well, then. He's that lovely ten-year-old kid who sells the Argosy at Camp Street corner and Baba found out he's really the illegitimate heir to the Purushottama millions and wants to make an honest man out of him, and . . .'

'Illegitimate? Saroj, where on earth did you learn filthy language like that? I mean for heaven's sake, do you even know what it means, and does Baba know about this ?'

'Okay Gan, that's enough. Tell me before I throw myself out of the window'

'Well . . . brace yourself.'

She gripped the railing till her knuckles turned white and her arms shook, opened her eyes wide, gritted her teeth and said through them to Ganesh, 'Okay, I'm ready. Tell me the whole truth, and then I'll dictate my epitaph.'

'Well, in one word, he's a twit, a twat. He's fifteen, and he's in 5c, a puny little drip with protuberant teeth and slicked-back greasy hair and his name is Keedernat. But he likes to be called Keith. Keet for short.'

Saroj giggled, and relaxed. 'Is that all?'

'Do you need more? Oh Ghosh! Let me see, maybe he has BO, I'll get a whiff of him on Monday and let you know. Or maybe . . .'

Saroj tuned out. All of a sudden she couldn't play the game any more. She slumped against the wall, weary of Ganesh and his eternal banter, his refusal to stop joking and jesting for just one moment. Gan had taught her to see a light side to everything. To stand back from life and laugh. To see the world as a stage, the figures on it comic characters acting out their parts, they themselves the only knowing ones, the only ones with dead-pan faces but sniggering souls. The two of them side-stepped through life mocking at its vagaries and thumbing their noses at its twists.

That's the way Ganesh liked Saroj, and she played the part, for him. That is, in his company she played the part. On her own she couldn't do it. Because it wasn't real. It wasn't *her*. She was playing the part of a person playing a part, and right now she'd forgotten her lines and all Gan's prompting was in vain.

She looked at him, pleading with her eyes for him to stop, and said simply, 'What shall I do?'

She could see the word 'murder' forming on Gan's grinning lips, but then he must have caught the expression of liquid agony in her eyes because he stopped, regarded her in a moment of rare silence and said, 'I don't know, Saroj. Can't you just, well, flatly refuse?'

She gave him a look which was supposed to be withering, but it's hard to be withering when despair is nipping at your heels.

She reached into Ganesh's bag and took out the lime crush and an opener, then removed the crown with a click. But she didn't drink. The bottle still in her hand, she glanced at the window facing Waterloo Street, at the spectacular panorama of Georgetown's treetops, glittering roofs, sky, frayed clouds drifting by, and in the distance a glimpse of the Atlantic.

'As a last resort I could jump from here.'

'You never said that, Saroj, and I don't want to ever hear it again.'

'But if I don't do something, Gan, it'll all happen the way it did with Indrani. This whole Ghosh business will just keep rolling on, gathering momentum, and one fine day I'll wake up and I'll be Mrs Keedernat Ghosh.'

'Look, Saroj, just take it easy. Indrani's sixteen; you'll be sixteen too before this gets really serious. Plenty of time. What I don't understand is why Baba chose someone like that. I mean, a girl like you, good looks, respectable family, money, brains — you've got everything going for you. Why didn't he aim higher? Why didn't he nab a Luckhoo, for instance?'

The Luckhoo family was Georgetown's most prominent

Indian law clan. Now they really had everything: Oxbridge educations, judgeships, knighthoods, and a couple of boys of marriageable age.

'Well, that's quite obvious. D'you think any of those Luckhoo boys would even *dream* of having their brides chosen for them? I mean, for goodness' sake, where are we living, in some Bengali village or what? And as for you . . . you wouldn't be so flippant about the whole thing if you didn't have some trump up your sleeve about this Narain girl. What're you going to do about it? Seriously, now?'

'It's easier for me. I'm going to go to university in England and that'll solve a few problems. All I have to do is never come back. They'll get over it. One good thing about these long-term engagements is that they give you long-term time for evading them. I'll just disappear from the scene — poof!'

'Maybe this Keedernat boy will go away to study too, and never come back!'

But Ganesh shook his head. He leaned against one of the windows and stretched out his long, lean, jeans-enclosed legs.

'No such luck, Saroj. Baba'd have chosen an older fellow for you in that case, someone who's already in England and coming back in a couple of years. Like he did for Indrani. This Ghosh boy'll sit a few O-Levels next year, pass two or three, and then go straight into his daddy's business selling dry goods and saris. They'll let him work a couple of years, and then he'll marry you when he's eighteen and you're sixteen.'

He dipped his hand into his bag and took out two samosas, threw one to her, and crunched his teeth into the other one. An expression of pure delight slipped over his face. 'Mmm . . . How Ma gets them to taste this way I'll never find out. I've tried and tried but mine just aren't the same.'

Saroj felt a tweak of irritation at Ganesh. He was so *shallow!* How could he speak of Saroj marrying the Ghosh boy in one sentence, and in the next of Ma's samosas?

Ganesh adored cooking, and there was nothing Ma could cook that he couldn't, but he still hadn't figured out that certain something, the magic ingredient which made Ma's dishes exquisite works of art, and his, by its lack, just tasty food. Ma knew all the secrets of cooking. She knew which foods were *sattvic,* raising your mind to great heights, which foods were *rajasic,* exciting the mind and heating it to seething point, and which were *tamasic,* dragging it into heavy, murky depths. Cooking was a matter of control: when to add what and exactly how much, not even a grain more. Control of heat and moisture, keeping temperatures right, regulating the flame, for fire could create as well as destroy. Regulating water, which could give life as well as it could drown, and could enter the dish uninvited as drops on a callalloo leaf. But that was mere technique. Ma added mystery — touching each ingredient as if it were to be cooked for God himself. The first spoonful of each dish was an offering, not to touch human lips. Ma spoke to food and sang to it. Ganesh knew the techniques but not the mysteries of cooking.

Saroj refused to be drawn into a discussion on Ma's samosas.

'I mean, what a drip!' she exclaimed. 'The very fact of him letting himself be chosen just proves he's a drip. Any self-respecting boy would refuse.'

'Well, how d'you know he hasn't, or he won't? For all you know he's right this minute raising hell and threatening to slit your throat if they force you on him. Of course, he hasn't *seen* you yet. That'll change matters.'

'But what'll I do, Gan? I can't marry him. Apart from him being a drip, I won't ever marry anyone Baba chooses. I wouldn't even marry Paul McCartney if Baba chose him. I won't marry, ever!' It was an agonized wail, a cry of desperation.

Ganesh chuckled, his good humour rising up through the film of gloom she'd spread across its surface, like a bubble of air reaching for the sky. 'You're too much of a prize not to marry ever, Saroj, it'd be a waste. If Baba had any sense he'd let you look for a husband yourself. You'd have the choice of the pack! If Baba wasn't keeping you like a precious jewel locked away in a safe you'd have half the boys in Georgetown on their knees, licking their lips.'

'Don't be disgusting. Just tell me what to *do.*'

'Well, actually, maybe you should talk to Ma.'

'Talk to Ma? Are you crazy? Ma *approves* of arranged marriages, you know that. She helped choose Indrani's. And anyway, Ma doesn't talk. I mean, not really.'

'She does, you know. She talks to me.'

'Well, to *you,* maybe. But you and Ma are different, I mean, you're the same. The two of you live as though in a private world and you speak a private language.'

'You've never even tried to get to know her.'

'Ma's a book with seven seals. And if you looked behind them all you'd find is superstition. She's too . . . she's too *Indian.* It's as if she never left India, she just brought India here into Baba's house and continued to live there. She has no idea what the world's really about, with her Purushottama Temple and *sruti* box and stuff. She doesn't know a thing about modern life or about me and what I want to be. I don't think she's even heard of Pat Boone, not to mention the Beatles. How can I talk to someone like that?'

The Purushottama Temple was the centre of Ma's life outside the house — that, and the Stabroek Market. Mr Purushottama, the owner of the temple, was a genuine expatriate Indian who had come with a fortune to Georgetown from Kanpur to 'set the ball rolling', as he called it. He was a big, jovial man, who never wore anything but kurta pyjamas, and he opened the New Baratha Bank on High Street and encouraged, no, ordered, all Indians to deposit their savings there, which they did. As a thank-you he bought a Dutch colonial-style, wooden green-and-white mansion in Brickdam, all louvred windows and stained glass and an open balustraded gallery with ornate columns, gingerbread fretwork and arches all around the first storey. The bottom-house, the area between the pillars on which the house rested, was shielded from public view by a ground-to-ceiling lattice work, open towards the garden and yard at the back, and this is where all the ceremonies and functions took place — Diwali, and Phagwah, Krishna's birthday and whatever else the Hindus cared to celebrate. (Mr Purushottama also bought a mosque for the Muslims, but Saroj didn't know a thing about that.)

The Purushottama Temple was open to Hindus of every variety. Upstairs, in the house, was a puja room for Shiva worshippers, and one for Krishna worshippers; Rama, Kali, Hanuman, Ganesh, Parvati and Lakshmi each had a shrine where worshippers could gather at any time of day or night. Each room was a snug little refuge, complete with carpets and wall hangings from India and pictures of the various deities and decorated with brass ornaments polished and shining. The rooms were usually darkened, the louvres shut, the air thick with the heavy perfume of roses, jasmine, burned ghee and incense. Little oil lamps burned on every shrine, their flames unflickering in the half-light and surrounded with blue-and-golden haloes. At religious functions the entire temple swarmed with Indians. The lattice work was hung with garlands of marigolds; hibiscus blossoms were stuck between the wooden laths and the very air tingled with festivity.

Sometimes Ma took them all for puja to the Shiva shrine. On the weekends Baba liked the whole family — relatives near and far — to put in an appearance, all spick and span: men and boys in immaculate white and crisply ironed kurta pyjamas, women and girls in their brightest shiniest saris and skirts.

As a small child Saroj had actually liked the Purushottama Temple. It seemed a place of secrets and stories, full of deep mysteries, an exciting, exotic world aeons apart from reality. She had loved the colours and smells, the veiled idols behind thick curtains, the chanting and the singing and the atmosphere of otherworldy, ethereal ecstasy. All that changed abruptly when she reached the age of reason. Now she found the temple a reservoir of superstition. She still had to go, on Baba's command, but it was with an armoured heart and a cynical mind. Idolatry! Humbug! With turned up nose and slightly curled-up lips she sat through hours of *pujas* and *kirtans*; her hands might meet in assumed reverence, her lips might utter the prescribed responses. But inside she knew it was all a lie. It was a world of make-believe for adults.

And Ma was a part of this world that defied all reason.

At thirteen, Saroj could hardly remember the time when Ma and she had been almost one entity — a time before thought, when being alive was knowing Ma's presence as a warm, downy nest. Ma, all luminous eyes and a smile that embraced you. A time when she had worshipped Ma, as all children worship their mothers. Doesn't every mother seem like God to her child, all-knowing, all-seeing, all-forgiving? Ma, to whom the butterflies came, who spoke to the roses and brought them to bloom. All powerful. Ma could summon the sunshine and dispel clouds. The four-armed Goddess Parvati on her celestial throne.

But little girls grow up. They learn to think and reason, their horizon expands, their vision changes focus. They go to school, they read books, and newspapers. Their minds bounce free, Mother's halo fades, two of her arms drop off and she shrinks to her true, human and fallible size.

Saroj now saw Ma as what she always had been: an excellent cook, a conscientious housekeeper, a devoted mother, a dutiful wife, a fervent Hindu. A typical Indian housewife, docile, subservient. Loving, good and strong; strong in the sense that all mothers are strong for their children, but nevertheless an impotent spirit in the background, coyed and cringing under Baba's foot. Baba's rule was despotic, his rule was law, and no-one dared disobey, least of all Ma.

Ma, hanging on to the strange archaic customs she'd brought from the land of her ancestors, the silent little woman steeped in tradition, living in a world light-years away from reality, the centre of whose universe was the Purushottama Temple, a museum of dead stone idols.

'If I can talk to her, you can,' Ganesh claimed. 'It's not that difficult. Ma knows more about you than you think. She knows more about me than I thought. Who d'you think told me not to worry about the Narain girl? To go to university, get on with my life, and let the whole thing fade out of thought?'

'Ma? Ma told you that? You're kidding!'

But Ganesh nodded and there was laughter in his eyes. 'I couldn't believe it myself.'

'But I thought Ma was the driving power behind the whole

thing!'

'Naw, that was Baba. Ma played along with Baba as long as I made no objections. Then I talked to her and she swung around completely and said don't worry, it'll all work out for the best.'

'Why didn't you tell me this before?'

'Big brothers don't discuss everything with little sisters, you know. But you're a big girl now, thirteen, and you get to know grown-up secrets. There's more to Ma than meets the eye. She's on my side and she'll be on yours and help you if you trust her. Ma's pretty devious, you know. She knows how to get her own way.'

Saroj had to digest this information. The Ghosh boy vanished from her thoughts, which all turned to Ma. She bit into another samosa, closed her eyes and opened her senses, to get the feeling of Ma hidden within the subtlety of taste, and considered in silence. Ganesh's information surprised her, but, after all, Ganesh was a boy, an only beloved son. Of course Ma would take his side, support him in all his plans; that exactly proved the point! Gan's imagination was running away with him — as usual.

No. Ganesh was wrong. Ma could not, would not, help. Saroj was a girl, and that made all the difference. Childhood was over; it was growing-up time, becoming-a-lady time, and Ma was in league with Baba. And Baba had his own plans for her.

All her life Baba had been shaping Saroj to fit into the Hindu world, to make of her the tame and biddable daughter their culture demanded, a carbon copy of Ma. He had done it with Indrani, successfully. Indrani was all lined up to marry a boy of Baba's choice, and Saroj was next in line. Up to now Saroj had nurtured hostility within, cultivated acquiescence without. It was a question of survival.

But now she thought of the Ghosh boy with his protuberant teeth and from her deepest depths the cry rose up, the cry of defiance that marked the precise moment of her coming-of-age, *No! I won't!*

No more nodding on the outside and gnashing of teeth on the inside. She knew with a certainty that filled her entire being and charged her with a joyous jubilant strength that she would not, not, NOT bow to a destiny chosen for her by Baba.

Character is destiny. She said it out loud.

'What?' asked Ganesh.

'Character is destiny,' she repeated, and laughed a crazy, wild laugh that made Ganesh drop his grin and stare. Her family's destiny, till now, had been dictated more by culture than by character. Culture had moulded character to fit its own dictates so that culture, character and destiny were intermingled, intermeshed, interwoven into a preordained, predictable pattern.

Saroj was a single loose thread sticking out. It was her turn to be tucked into the pattern, according to the plan.

But she wouldn't be tucked in.

And that meant shaking off everything she had been brought up to be. She would have to peel from her soul every last trace of India, abandon the culture bequeathed to her by Baba and Ma.

Chapter 6

Savitri
Madras, 1921

The Admiral and his wife were too absorbed by their own lives to notice David's absorption with the native girl Savitri. They were happy to have him off their hands and not demanding their attention. The Admiral was wheelchair-bound, having suffered grave spinal, arm and leg injuries when his ship had been torpedoed in the very last throes of the Great War, and had found a new lease of life in writing his war memoirs. All he really needed by way of human company was Joseph, the Christian Indian male nurse, to get him up, dressed and fed in the mornings and to administer the various pills he needed during the day, and Khan, to wheel him to the library, get him adjusted into the special chair he had had made to support his back while writing, and stand to attention, to pull the *punkah* and bring him the endless cups of tea he needed for inspiration. Every Thursday evening Khan helped him into the car and the driver Pandian drove him to the Club, where he met with Colonel Hurst and spent a pleasant evening reliving the Great War and eating an excellent dinner with a non-vegetarian main course.

His wife did not allow the cooking of meat in her house. She spent her days as pleasantly as her husband. Her life was centred around the Theosophical Society at Adyar, where she went to attend lectures, talks and seminars, or simply to browse in the library, or meet her like-minded friends. She loved to walk through the shaded paths of the magnificent Adyar grounds, to spread a blanket under the banyan tree and read a book, her dear friend Lady Jane Ingram within touching distance.

Sometimes the two ladies would lay down their books and pleasantly discuss some inspiring aspect of Theosophy theory which one of their books had thrown up, or they would read to one another, which both found extremely edifying. She had once met and exchanged a few words with Annie Besant, which was the most uplifting thing that had ever happened to her, and gave food for endless conversations. Although she wasn't quite convinced about this Home Rule business. No, never. The Indians were like small children; they needed the benevolently guiding hand of the British. She herself was doing her own little part here in Fairwinds. Where would the servants be without her? Where would India be without the British?

When she was at home she read yet more, sitting in the coolness of the verandah or the rose arbour; or she wrote in her diary, or entertained her friends, who were by no means all Theosophists. She made sure the gardens and house were well maintained, for Mrs Lindsay was proud of both. The house was actually invisible from the garden, buried among the giant bougainvilleas which climbed up trellises and trees to wall in the verandah encircling the house. The house itself had a flat Madras roof, edged with a tiled roof slanting down over the verandah, and on the verandah Mrs Lindsay had arranged groups of wicker chairs and tables where she and her friends could sit in the coolness and enjoy the faint breeze blowing in from the ocean, and chat amiably about servants and children.

It was possible to get lost on the Fairwinds property. It was the most extensive of all the Oleander Gardens properties, the gardens beautifully kept up by Muthu and his ever-changing troop of Boys — each one of which, regardless of age, was automatically named Boy. Possibly only Savitri and David knew every nook and cranny, for even Muthu kept to his side of the garden, this side of the gulley. The gulley ran straight through from one side to the other, parallel to Atkinson Avenue and Old Market Street, and during the monsoon was a mighty gushing stream overflowing its banks. The rest of the year it was dry and full of stones and sediment and you could jump over it at some points, where the far bank wasn't overgrown with thorny bushes. Because over there nature ran wild. Muthu did not work it, though he lived there in the servants' quarters that lined Old Market Street. Snakes, scorpions and other dreadful wild things lived there beneath the stones and in the holes in the ground and under bushes. David was cautioned always to wear shoes, whether he was in the back or the front garden, but Savitri ran everywhere barefoot, and had never been bitten or stung.

The garden side of Fairwinds was kept constantly free of weeds, red sand spread everywhere between the flowerbeds to ensure an atmosphere of cool, clean gentility, snakes and scorpions banished. It made Mrs Lindsay feel very majestic, to stroll around Fairwinds making sure that the garden was flourishing, or to stand on the verandah and clap for a Boy, or lean over the little piles of clothes laid out by the *dhobi*, counting to make sure he had stolen nothing.

She always made an exact list of what dirty laundry had gone out and what clean laundry came in, and though in all the years she had never lost so much as a hanky, still she knew this was only because she was so vigilant, because Kannan was not only annoyingly vague but illiterate, so it was impossible to give him lists to check. He kept track of his business in his head.

'I gave you three pieces lady vests on Monday,' she now said, consulting her list. 'But you've only brought two back.'

'Three pieces you giving ma'am?' Kannan looked genuinely puzzled, scratched his forehead, did some mental calculations, and then his whole face lit up and he replied with joy, 'Yes ma'am, my washing, *naligi* bringing!'

'No, no *naligi* bringing! You going, coming, today bringing!' Mrs Lindsay said sternly, reverting to pidgin for clarity, and Kannan plucked his beard, adjusted his turban, shook his head from side to side in agreement and said, 'Serree, ma'am, my today bringing. Evening time.' Mrs Lindsay puckered her forehead in annoyance. When would her servants ever learn that shaking one's head means no, and not yes? She opened her mouth to remind Kannan. But he had disappeared.

He wasn't seen for the rest of the day. But the next day the vest, Mrs Lindsay knew from long experience, would be among that day's laundry, pristine white, ironed and folded, and Kannan, eyes shining with pride, would say, 'My one piece lady vest bringing, ma'am!'

Of all the servants Joseph was the only one who spoke English, which was annoying. But at least the Iyers' daughter was fluent. When Mrs Lindsay discussed the week's menu, or made up the shopping list with Iyer and there was some point he didn't understand, Iyer would stick two fingers between his lips and give a shrill sharp whistle, and within three seconds Savitri would appear from behind some bush, hair dishevelled, skirt awry, buttons missing from her blouse, cheeks smudged with dirt, and curtsy. Such a sweet, bright, polite child! Mrs Lindsay never failed to feel a sharp prick of pride whenever she dealt with Savitri. The girl was somehow special, if a little wild and scruffy. But she was so courteous, Mrs Lindsay's heart went out to her. She was particularly proud of her excellent English, her impeccable accent, for she knew this was all due to herself.

It was not every English wife who allowed her children to hob-nob with the servants' children. But Mrs Lindsay was a Theosophist, and theosophists knew that all humans were born equal, in spite of outer differences of colour and social standing, and Mrs Lindsay thought it was a good thing to uplift her servants — or at least a few of them. And besides, Savitri's upliftment was obviously ordained from Above. It was destiny. Right from the beginning.

Nirmala had given birth to Savitri just a few weeks after David's birth, when Mrs Lindsay's milk was drying out. That was the first Sign. Mrs Lindsay had given her David to wet-nurse, which was a great blessing for she herself found breast-feeding rather disgusting anyway — and it made your breasts sag. Of course, she could not let David grow up in the Iyer household. So she had ordered Savitri's mother to move into the nursery with the two babies, and they had grown up like twins, one white and one brown, and both bi-lingual, since Nirmala spoke hardly a word of English. As a result David called Nirmala 'Amma' and learned fluent Tamil, while Savitri, mixing freely with all the family household, learned English — the best, upper-class English. So in fact there were two child interpreters living on the Fairwinds property, although Mrs Lindsay never let David interpret — she found it somehow demeaning to hear her son speaking with servants and not be able to understand.

Nirmala was much more than an *ayah*. Mrs Lindsay had occasionally felt a twinge of jealousy, seeing how attached her son was to Savitri's mother. But her lady friends had told her time and again that Nirmala was a pearl, and so she had counted her blessings, and David had never been a problem.

Savitri kept David occupied, which was a blessing. All too well Mrs Lindsay knew what a plague children could be. The children of some of her lady friends were veritable pests, spoiled silly, and though they all had their own *ayahs* or nannies they never left their mothers alone. Fiona, Mrs Lindsay's daughter, had had an English nanny, a girl from Birmingham who had come to India to find a husband, and who in her failure to do so had grown more and more bad-tempered over the years. It had been a pleasure to replace her after David's birth.

Mrs Lindsay had been fortunate with both her children. Fiona was such a quiet, bookish girl; she had never been underfoot like some people's daughters, and now she was twelve she would be going off to Yorkshire to stay with Aunt Jemima, Mrs Lindsay's sister, where she could attend an excellent girls' boarding school. Next week they'd be going off to hill station Ooty for the summer, and immediately after that Fiona would be leaving from Bombay with the Carter family, who were going Home on Long Leave, and in September she'd start at Queen Ethelberga's. Hopefully Aunt Jemima would do her best to make the right connections, and Fiona in time would find a nicely situated husband in England and need never come back to India, except on holiday to show off her own children. Hopefully, they'd be as decorous as Fiona herself.

Of course, this child Savitri was anything but decorous; such a tomboy! Not a bit like most Indian girls, but as such she made a good playmate for David, which was a good thing. David for some reason didn't get along with any of the other English children in Oleander Gardens, and without Savitri he would have been completely alone and demanding attention.

Dear little Savitri! Whenever Mrs Lindsay thought of her she had a good warm feeling around her heart. Mrs Lindsay often had 'feelings' about people, particularly Indians, particularly servants. Most often these were negative feelings, but not in Savitri's case. Savitri, she felt, was a good spirit in Fairwinds. The way she would flit noiselessly between the bougainvilleas, just like a butterfly; you almost expected her to take off and fly, flapping her skirts and shawls, and such fantastic colours, too!

The Indians had no sense of colour. Savitri would wear a shocking pink skirt with a lime green *choli* and a tangerine shawl, all together: yes, like a butterfly. And always with flowers in her hair, placed there by her mother early in the morning at the hair-combing session. Goodness knows how these Indian mothers always found time not only to plait their daughters' hair, but also to weave little flower-garlands to decorate them with, and that apart from all their other early morning duties.

Once Mrs Lindsay had seen Savitri dancing all alone, believing herself unwatched, in the sandy open space beyond the rose arbour, and as she watched she felt the hair on the back of her neck rising. For Savitri was not of this world as she danced. It was as if she was *being* danced, as if the dance had taken possession of her and moved her limbs according to its own commands. Mrs Lindsay at once recognised the gestures: Savitri was dancing the Bharata Natyam, the classical dance of Shiva in the form of Nataraj. Her fingers formed mudras, her knees bent, her waist swayed as she took on the attitude of Shiva with his head adorned by the crescent moon, receiving the river Ganga in his hair. The bells on her ankles jingled in rhythm as she tapped the ground with her heels in the skilful play of the sacred dance, and her arms and hands moved in measured nuance to tell an ancient story. Savitri, lost in the transport of her dance, seemed enveloped in stillness, as if the whole world and all of nature beheld her in awe and only she, its centre, moved. She is *Shakti* itself, Mrs Lindsay thought, and even her breath stood still.

When Savitri brought the milk at seven each morning she would be a picture of Indian feminine beauty, grace and docility — freshly bathed and groomed, flowers in her hair, clothes clean with the obligatory shawl decorously arranged over her shoulders. On her forehead she wore the typical heathen marks in ashes and red powder (Mrs Lindsay did not forbid the servants their heathen practices; as a theosophist she was tolerant of all religions, but still these signs were, somehow, uncanny). She wore bangles on her wrists and around her ankles silver anklets, from which little charms dangled and tinkled as she walked. And during the mornings, when she came to help Iyer in the kitchen on the days she didn't go to school, she'd be hardworking and diligent. But as soon as David was released from the schoolroom off she'd run with him — shawl, anklets and bangles discarded, skirts flying, flowers slipping down her shiny black hair — to their hundred games and thousand secret places, lost to the adults.

Savitri was a blessing, and Mrs Lindsay vowed to 'do something' for the child. The Iyers had only one daughter, and as such were in a much better position than Kannan, who had three, but daughters were always a headache for the poor Hindu fathers. They had to be married off and if there were too many of them they could cause the ruin of a family. Although Mrs Lindsay frowned upon the dowry system, money was obviously always the key to a better life. Didn't she herself know that? No, definitely she would do something for Savitri.

Mrs Lindsay had been thinking along these lines for some

time, and had decided that the 'something' would be a cash gift. Mrs Lindsay's family had been connected with India from the very beginning, in the days when John Company ruled the British Empire. Things had changed since then, of course, but still there were investments. Mrs Lindsay wasn't too sure herself exactly what these investments were. She tried to keep her mind pure, free from thoughts of money and other material matters. A lawyer in London took care of business matters, and all she knew was that there was an ever-ready flow of cash, most of which she was leaving untouched so that David could one day be master of a fortune.

David would surely approve of this idea, to 'do something' for Savitri. But later; the child was only six, and there was lots of time. But when that time came, the cash would buy a first-class husband for the girl. Because you could abolish dowries as much as you wanted to — a wealthy wife still had a better choice of husband. Why, it was that way among the English too. So she herself would ensure that Savitri was not married off to the first suitor her parents could find. Give her some money, and let the girl — or her parents, or whoever decided these things — choose.

She was thinking all these pleasant, generous thoughts when David came to her with his idea, and this idea was so much in keeping with her own plans for Savitri, that she hugged him tightly — a very rare occurrence which quite took his breath away — and knew that this was a case of telepathy. Which only went to show that her idea was really ordained from Above, and that she herself was but an instrument of the Divine on Earth.

Chapter 7

Saroj
Georgetown, 1964

Like Indrani's wedding sari, Baba had imported Ma from India. That was all her children knew of her. Ma didn't count; what counted was Roy history.

Balwant Uncle had appointed himself custodian of family history. After all, he was history master at Queen's College, and well qualified to keep the family archives, drawers full of yellowing, curl-edged photos, boxes of letters falling apart at the folds, and a thick black-bound ledger recording every single birth, marriage and death of every single Roy several times removed.

The book was almost full now; yet it had all began so simply.

In 1859 three Brahmin brothers, Devadas, Ramdas and Shridas Roy, were walking through the bazaar to the Kali temple in Calcutta when they were approached by a recruiter.

'Come to Damra Tapu,' the recruiter said. 'It is a country far across the seas, a bright and sparkling country, money is growing on the trees; many Indians are already amassing a vast fortune there. When you have made your fortune in five years you can come back to India. No problem.'

The three brothers took the recruiter's words as a sign from God. Just the day before this their father, a school teacher, had been bitten by a black scorpion under the neem tree and died, and the boys were on their way to the temple to pray to God for help and guidance. Jobs were scarce, especially for young boys with no skills, and their eldest married brother Baladas could not support his own family, their mother, their two sisters and themselves. So the recruiter, they decided, was God in human form showing them their destiny. They agreed to go to Damra Tapu, wherever that might be, and accompanying the recruiter to a sub-agency. There they signed themselves to work on a sugar plantation in the colony of Damra Tapu: Demerara, British Guiana, South America, to take the place of recently liberated African slaves. Then they went to the temple to thank God for showing them the way so explicitly. Shortly thereafter they sailed from India on the ship Victor Emmanuel, leaving their mother and sisters in the care of Baladas.

The three brothers were allotted to the sugar plantation Post Mourant as indentured servants, but due to their fiery spirits and quick minds already sharpened by a basic English medium education in India they soon made swift strides forward. Ramdas, the eldest, discovered that certain Hindu ceremonies were not difficult to perform, and thus became a priest, the small fee he received being more remunerative than what he received as a cane field labourer. He went on to become *sirdar* (foreman) on the estate, saved every cent, and bought Full Cup, an abandoned sugar plantation on the East Bank of Demerara.

Shridas acquired a horse and carriage with which he ran a highly successful taxi service in the settlement of Hague, later going to Georgetown and starting a motorised hire-car business and moving into a white mansion in Kingston. Devadas became a Hindi-English interpreter, going on to teach in a private school and finally founding a school of his own, attended by Indian children; it was his nephew, Ramsaroop, who opened the first Hindi-language cinema in Georgetown, the Bombay Talkies. Thus all three brothers remained in the colony after their five-year contract ran out.

Their only problem was that they had no wives. Indian women were reluctant to leave home and family and make the long sea journey to another continent, and parents were reluctant to send their daughters far away to a country that, so rumour had it, swarmed with wild black savages, released African slaves. Which meant that women accounted for less than thirty per cent of the Indian population, which explained, Balwant claimed, the high suicide rates among Indian indentured servants.

The brothers wrote home to their mother to send three wives for them. All she could find was an old widow of twenty-seven years, a low-caste orphan girl of sixteen, and a twenty-five-year-old woman with a harelip, the latter being the only one among them who could pay a dowry. She got Baladas to bribe the same officer who recruited her other sons, and with the dowry paid by the harelipped bride got the three women on to the ship *Ganges,* which sailed for Georgetown in 1865. The bride-problem was thus solved.

The Roy family grew in size and prominence in the prospering colony. By the turn of the century the third generation of Roys was well established in Georgetown.

In 1964, the year Saroj turned thirteen, there were well over a hundred descendants of Ramdas, Shridas and Devadas — now long dead and cremated, their ashes sent back to India to be scattered in the river Ganges. The Roys continued to prosper and seek prosperity. Indians were industrious, and certain professions tended to run in families. The Luckhoo family specialised in law; the Jaikaran family in medicine; and the Roys in business. They owned four dry-goods stores, two pharmacies, a cinema, two provisions stores, an electrical appliances company, a furniture store, three hardware stores, a construction company and the Jus-ee cool drinks company. Roys were emigrating to England, Canada, the USA. Some had settled in Trinidad, some in Surinam. But nobody, as far as Saroj knew, had ever returned to India. You didn't return to India. You left India.

Back in Calcutta, Deodat Roy, Baladas's first grandson, grew up and won a scholarship to study law in England where he graduated with honours and practised as a barrister-at-law for a few years in London. But Deodat was an Indian through and through, and life in racist England, a member of the despised immigrant Indian society, did not appeal to him. England was too secular, too materialistic, too cold. Even with his education he was not treated with due respect. News of his dissatisfaction and plans to return home circulated through the family grapevine and reached Georgetown. In 1929 he received a joint letter from his three great-uncles, now old men and heads of the Georgetown Roy clan.

It was one of the most important items in the family archives, heralding as it did the New Age of Roy tradition. Balwant Uncle liked to read it aloud at family functions: *'This is a bright and shining colony, much better than India,'* the great-uncles had written, *'and there's a crying need for well-trained Indian lawyers. Do not return to Calcutta, come here and settle in British Guiana. In India, even if you are successful, you will be at best a small fish in a big pond; here you can be a big fish in a small pond.'* (This was Balwant Uncle's favourite saying.) *'You would not believe the leaps and bounds with which we Indians are progressing! We came to this colony as poor coolies owning nothing and less than nothing, yet through God's grace and our own diligence and thrift we Roys are all well-to-do and highly respected pillars of society, and we are by no means the exception! Now there are over 300,000 Indians here; we make up over forty per cent of the population! Diwali and Holi are national holidays, as well as Eid-al Mubarak for the Muslims. This is indeed Little India and opportunity is knocking on our doors! Kindly come and put your shoulder to the grindstone to help build the colony! We, your loving great-uncles, will accord you a hearty welcome. Only one thing: before you come, get married, for ladies are in short supply* here. *It would be preferable if you find a wife with several young sisters or female cousins to accompany her, for we know of many highly eligible Indian boys in dire need of a wife, and we can make excellent connections through marriage. Dowry and caste not relevant.'*

This last sentence alarmed Deodat exceedingly. He promptly married his first wife Sundari, daughter of Brahmin immigrants, in London, and brought her with two younger sisters to British Guiana. The sisters were immediately married into prominent Georgetown families so that the BG branch of the Roy clan grew further in consequence and connections.

Sundari gave birth to three boys in quick succession,

Natarajeshwar, Nathuram, and Narendra, but Narendra was
barely eleven years of age when Sundari tumbled down the
tower staircase in Deodat's Waterloo Street mansion and broke
her neck. The three boys were immediately boarded out into
various other Roy families, so all quickly recovered from the
tragedy, and Deodat set about finding a new wife. But there
were problems.

Deodat, an orthodox Brahmin, refused to take a wife born
and bred in BG. In such a woman traditions were diluted,
culture was dying, he claimed. He was appalled at the gradual
disintegration of Hindu traditions, and the spineless capitulation
of Indians to the secular spirit which ruled the colony.

In fact, Hindus were split down the middle. On the one side
were the Traditionalists, trying to uphold their culture as much
as possible but nowhere reaching Baba's strict standards. After
all, these were second, third, fourth and even fifth generation
Indians, not one of them had ever been to India, hardly any of
them spoke Hindi, and compromise had been necessary. Of this
clan Baba was the undisputed leader and authority, for he had
actually grown up in India, he spoke Hindi as well as Bengali
and a smattering of Urdu.

The Modernists were non-practising Hindus, sunk in a mire
of debauchery, growing worse from generation to generation.
Nowadays Hindu men and women even went to parties and
danced; the women wore trousers, or dresses showing their
knees; and they chose their own marriage partners. They were
all eating meat, even beef. They were converting to Christianity,
giving their children English, Christian names. A man's name
meant nothing. You could not tell a man's caste from his name,
for caste was non-existent. Brahmins no longer wore the sacred
thread, and as for the ritual purity called for in this caste, only
a few pundits knew the theories that no-one practised. In fact,
except for a few carefully-bred Roys, there were no Brahmins
left. Hindus were mongrels, a boiled-down stew where no man
knew his roots.

Balwant Uncle said this was due to historical circumstances.
The first Indians had lived cramped together in the abandoned

slave *logies* on the sugar estates, without regard for caste and clan, forced to compromise on their thousand-year rules and regulations.

But Deodat refused to compromise. He would not take a mongrel wife. His wife had to be of pure blood and orthodox upbringing. Her role was to ground a family pure in tradition, raise children as Brahmins. A devoted Hindu wife, steeped in the spirit of her religion, one to revive the dying faith. Most important, his three eldest sons should return home before they, too, succumbed to the spirit of secularism. A woman is the backbone of the family. The family is the backbone of society. Therefore, the woman was the backbone of society. But she had to be an aware woman. A woman of faith, a woman whose own backbone was held upright by God. When Woman falls, society falls, Deodat never tired of saying. There had to be a woman in the home. A good, strong woman. And he would have to import her from India.

The Bengali branch of the Roy family placed an advertisement for Deodat in the Times of India. But finding a good Brahmin wife for Deodat proved to be near impossible. Fathers stubbornly refused to send their daughters into the Antipodes, quite literally into the Underworld. Deodat considered returning to England to choose a wife: but that was defeating the purpose. He wanted a wife born and bred on India's soil. His Bengali relatives advised him to take a widow. Reluctantly, Deodat saw the necessity for compromise, and permitted the words 'widow acceptable' to be included in the ad.

Several months later Ma stepped off a ship at the Georgetown harbour. It was as easy as that.

Ma moved into Waterloo Street, and three children were born at two-year intervals: Indrani, Ganesh and Sarojini. Deodat could not have been more pleased, because Ma was exactly what he'd wanted, a still, silent, good spirit of the house, devoted to the children, a good cook, and, above all, an ardent devotee of Shiva.

The first thing Ma did when she came to Waterloo Street was install the *puja* room, and she was quite happy to hang up pictures of Krishna and Rama and Vishnu's consort Lakshmi next to those of Siva, Saraswati, and Ganesh, as well as pictures of Jesus, Mary and Buddha. So Baba was satisfied — almost. There were only two bitter drops in his life. The first was that Natarajeshwar, Nathuram and Narendra all refused to move back into Baba's household. Narendra was only thirteen at the time, so Baba forced him to come home, but he ran away nine times and was in danger of falling into extremely bad company, so Baba deemed it better for him to live on with less-than-holy Roys rather than risk complete vagabondage on his own. The three years these boys had spent in foster care had, just as Baba had feared, secularised them beyond redemption. They had enjoyed freedoms they'd never known before; never, ever would they return to orthodoxy; and they had all taken Christian names. Now they were Richard, Walter and James, and they had all settled in London. But Baba called them by their Indian names for the rest of his life.

The second bitter drop was that caste purity ended with his marriage to Ma. There was no question of importing husbands and wives from India for his children. He would have to marry them to mongrels.

Ma walked behind Baba. Ma's assimilation into the Roy clan was documented by two items in Balwant Uncle's archives: a creased, limp photo, passport size, of Ma, young, smiling, beautiful, wistful, confident, all these things at once, and more. And a clipping from the Times of India: '*England-educated Brahmin barrister-at-law, widower, well-settled in Georgetown, British Guiana, South America, excellent income and social standing, seeks remarriage with Brahmin lady of childbearing age, willing to resettle in large pleasant home in Georgetown and raise a family. Widow acceptable. Dowry not required. Condition: must be literate and speak excellent English. Please send photo.*'

Whatever steps had brought Ma to Baba were unknown to all and swept over, unmentioned, by Ma herself. She was a

woman without a past; without a name. Baba addressed her as
'Mrs Roy', referred to her as 'my wife', or simply as 'she' and
'her'. Relatives and family friends called her 'Mrs Roy' or 'Mrs
Deodat' and even 'Mrs D', or 'Ma D', depending on the degree
of familiarity with her. Balwant Uncle and his wife called her
Dee, short for Deodat's wife, her nephews and nieces called her
Dee Auntie. Her own children called her Ma. Ma, in her turn,
never spoke her husband's name in public. She called him Mr
Roy, or, capitalised, 'Him', or 'He', or 'my Husband'.

Ma spoke little. Though her English was excellent (no-one
asked, and no-one cared, why she had a perfect British accent)
it was always Baba who did the talking. Ma's stories, of course,
could go on for hours, but then only children were the listeners.

Ma did the singing. Ma performed the *pujas*. Ma
worshipped Shiva. Ma healed. Ma cooked. Ma nourished. Ma
was a cherished figure at all family festivities, especially weddings
and wakes. It was said that when Ma worked in the kitchen the
food never ran out, and even if fifty unexpected guests turned
up, which was often the case because Ma's reputation spread
and people were eager to find out if the rumour was true, there
were always leftovers.

Ma cooked not only South Indian rice and *sambar;* she
cooked Bengali, Punjabi and Gujerati. *Badaam kheer, sooji halwa*
and *kajoo barfi* melted like nectar on greedy Roy tongues. On
one occasion they discovered Ma could even bake a Yorkshire
pudding, but no-one ever asked how she learned all this, and
no-one cared. The Roy men stuffed themselves full of Ma's
creations, and with swelling tummies washed their hands and
mouths at the sink, burping and farting in deepest satisfaction.
The Roy wives watched Ma cook with envious eyes, but Ma
was too quick for them to learn her secrets. Chapattis flew out
from under her rolling pin on to a growing heap like little flying
saucers, her slender little hands flicking busily, expertly between
the little balls of dough, the heap of flour, the rolling pin. Ma
didn't give explanations; 'Cook with love,' is all she said, so
the Roy women gathered in spiteful three- and foursomes and
discussed Ma's failings.

Ma's hands were magic. Her children came to her with scratches and bruises and Ma would pass those little brown hands over the wound and all would be well. They came to her with tummyaches and earaches and growing-pains, and Ma would count out five or eight of the tiny round balls no bigger than a pinhead she kept in little tubes in the old wooden chest, or she'd sprinkle some strange powder in a cup of hot water and hold it to their lips, and their aches and pains would vanish.

Who knows what would have happened if the Roy clan had learned that Ma's hands could heal! No-one knew but her children. This was one art they kept within the family, as their own special secret; not through intention, but because they took it for granted. Ma's healing hands were a fact of life like the cool Atlantic breeze and the call of the kiskadee. No-one questioned it, and no-one talked about it, because they thought it was just what all mothers did.

Ma seemed intent on erasing herself. With every passing year there seemed less of her. She nourished herself on silence. She emitted an undercurrent of stillness as fine as the ether, and might very well have ceased to exist if it were not for her children. Almost, it seemed, she was raising them *against* her husband, yet without uttering a word against him, without so much as a raised eyebrow of rebuke.

Ma had wonderful talents, as Saroj was the first to concede, but she hadn't the resources to rescue her younger daughter from Baba and the fate he had chosen for her. Ma wasn't a fighter. Saroj would have to fight her own battles.

And Ganesh was no ally. Up there in the tower on her thirteenth birthday, at the moment of her coming of age, Saroj gazed with sober, objective eyes on her brother biting into a samosa and looking into its belly as if the secret of all creation was to be found there. This beloved brother of hers lacked seriousness and zeal. He was his mother's son: not a fighter. He might struggle to create the perfect samosa, but for a greater struggle, for the life-or-death struggle facing Saroj, he was not equipped. And she was as unequipped as Ganesh — except in determination.

A caged bird has nothing but the will to escape. In desperation it beats its wings and flings itself against the bars; for the cage's latch can only be opened from outside, and the bird's owner holds the key. And even if the bird escapes it may perish, having no knowledge of the world. Out there its innocence is its greatest enemy. But perhaps a passer-by will see that cage, and the bird within struggling to escape, and will bend the bars apart so that the bird can squeeze through. And the passer-by, now a friend, will show that bird the ways of the world so that finally it can fly alone.

Saroj had not yet reckoned with Trixie Macintosh.

Chapter 8

Savitri
Madras, 1921

When the plants cried out in pain Savitri comforted them. She knew it hurt to have their flowers picked so she always spoke to them first, silently, in her mind, and she knew they listened, and brightened up. She told them how special they were, how beautiful, that that was why she had chosen them because she only picked the fullest, most beautiful, perfect blossoms for the Lord. She thanked them, and said she was sorry.

When her basket was full she sat cross-legged on the straw mat outside the kitchen door and made her garlands — garlands of purple and white, of little orange blossoms, of jasmine; and then she went into the *puja* room and laid them at the feet of Nataraj and around the framed picture of Shiva and around the soapstone statue of Ganesh. When she was finished she placed a few perfect hibiscus blossoms at strategic points: the corners of the picture, or at Nataraj's feet, or in the crook of Ganesh's arm.

When the shrine was finished, she told Amma and went into the back room to help *Thatha* get up from his mat. She handed him his stick, and *Thatha*, one hand on her shoulder, limped into the *puja* room, where by now the incense was burning and her mother was preparing the camphor for the puja, and her brothers and Appa had gathered from their various duties. *Thatha*, old and decrepit as he was, always performed the *puja*, for he was the eldest male. He slowly waved the flame of burning camphor before Nataraj and chanted the appropriate verse, and then he passed the platter with the flame around the family members and they all touched it and placed their fingers in the ashes to make the stripes of Shiva on their foreheads, followed by the one red spot of Love in the centre. The *puja* was very short, only a few minutes. When it was over her mother clipped a bunch of fresh flowers, which had been put to one side to receive Shiva's blessing, in her hair. Savitri went outside and drew an elaborate *kolam* outside the door, after which she went to fetch water.

Amma had already fetched several vessels of water for them all to take bath, but more would be needed so Savitri picked up the big brass vessel and hooked her arm around its curved rim and set off down Old Market Street. She had to wait her turn. Several women and girls were at the well before her; some of them stood aside in the section for bathing and poured water over themselves, and others were turning the pulley to bring up the bucket from the well, filling their vessels, hoisting them onto their heads and moving off to their homes. The waiting women chattered among themselves and Savitri listened until it was her turn. She let the bucket fall into the well with a loud splash and then pulled at the rope with all her might till the bucket had reached the well's rim. She emptied the water into her vessel, twisted an old towel into a circle on her head, hoisted the vessel onto this support, and straightened up carefully. The vessel was much bigger than her head and quite heavy, but Savitri by now could balance it easily. She set off home with a wide, easy swing of her hips, her upper body, head and neck perfectly still to support the vessel. She did not use her hands. Amma said she would soon be bringing home three full vessels so she would need her hands for the other two. Even sooner she would receive the second vessel, which she would balance on her thin little hip with her arm curled around the rim.

She returned home and emptied the water into the container near the bath-house. This water was for washing clothes. For drinking water, of course, they had another well, one not used by the untouchables. Appa said the untouchables made the water impure; a thing Savitri would never understand.

Now Amma gave her the milk vessel, and she sent her off to fetch milk for the big house. She was so full of joy she could not walk. She skipped and ran and danced, and yet held the vessel perfectly still and straight so she never lost a single drop of milk. She was full of joy because of the beautiful morning, the sunshine trickling through the foliage that lined the back drive, the brilliant colours of the flowers, the sandy drive freshly swept by Muthu, the seven sisters up in the tamarind tree fluttering and twittering in a joy of their own, the sapphire blue of the sky, the peacock calling for his bride — it was all too much for a little girl's heart and the joy just rippled out of her and made her feet dance and skip, and still she never spilled a drop. She set the milk vessel carefully at the side of the path and twirled, laughing to see the way her skirt billowed out around her in a swirl of colour, and she waved her shawl as she moved so that it filled with air like a brilliant red sail, filtering the early morning sunlight. But then she heard Vali's urgent call quite nearby and a loud fluttering of wings, and Vali landed on the sandy path before her. She stopped spinning immediately, for Vali's visits were rare, and special. And when he came to her on an early morning like this it meant the day would be auspicious.

'Good morning, Vali!' she thought, and Vali, who was strutting back and forth before her, stopped and nodded courteously thrice, returning her greeting.

'I've nothing for you this morning, but later if I'm working in the kitchen I'll bring you some puffed rice. I didn't see you at all yesterday, where were you? Did you go over to see the peahens in the next-door garden?' she said aloud.

Vali jerked his head back a little crossly and Savitri laughed.

'I'm only teasing you,' she said, and then she fell silent, for Vali had begun to raise his tail and now it was unfurling into a perfect wheel and she knew Vali wanted her to behold him. She watched in respectful silence as he fluttered the long tail feathers with the thousand eyes, shivered and shuffled them so that the iridescent colours shimmered, and then Vali danced before her, swaying and sidestepping, and his beauty was so perfect she closed her eyes and her soul slipped into his and they were one. Satisfied, Vali gave a final ruffle of feathers, bowed, drew in his wheel and flew up to the topmost branches of a young coconut palm.

Savitri once believed that everyone could talk to plants and birds and animals, that everyone knew their language. When she was very small, people had been alarmed by her silences; they thought there was something wrong with her, for she had taken so long to speak; but in truth she had found speech unnecessary, for she spoke in silence. It was only when she discovered that humans didn't understand silence that she began to use words, and then they came out in perfectly formed sentences, in two languages, and people were astonished. Only the other beings, the plants, birds, and animals, understood silence.

People, she knew now, lived wrapped up in thought-bodies, which was why they could not understand silence. The thought-bodies got in the way. They were like thick black clouds through which the purity of silence could not enter, and they kept people captive and dulled. Sometimes there were gaps in the thought-bodies. Amma, for instance, had many gaps, and these gaps were the silences of perfect love. *Thatha* had hardly a thought-body at all, and babies had none. Little children had thin ones, and David's, because he loved her, was transparent. Savitri felt these thought-bodies so clearly they were almost tangible, like thick walls of brambles, and they hurt, almost, because you wanted so much to get behind them you pressed close and then they pricked. Savitri then learned that there were two ways of living: from the inside out, or from the outside in.

Living from the inside out came naturally to her. It was so easy to slip inside another being and feel the beauty of oneness, and once you felt that there was nothing more to say. What could one say to a flower, for instance, or to a butterfly resting on your shoulder, or a chipmunk eating from your hand? How sweet your perfume, how joyful your wings, how soft your fur?

You could say that, but of course they knew that already, so all you had to do was rejoice with them. Nature was constantly rejoicing, constantly singing and dancing, and all there was to do, really, was join in.

With people it was different; they lived from the outside in. They saw plants, animals, birds, and thought those beings were outside, and different from, themselves, things to grab and hold and hurt and use. They did not know that to hurt any other living creature was to hurt oneself; they did not feel the hurt of others, because they were outside others.

Especially the English, the *Ingresi*. Their thought-bodies were particularly powerful and could sweep you out of the way and crush you underfoot if you weren't careful. Savitri had grown up among the English and had learned this the hard way; if you did not address them in a certain way, if you did not show you thought they were much, much more important than you, then they would try to hurt you. This was because they lived entirely in their thought-bodies, and believed these thought-bodies to be much more real than what was beyond them. It was as if a butterfly wrapped up in a cocoon thought the cocoon to be itself. It was a form of blindness; it was a form of death.

Savitri had a thought-body too, but hers was like gossamer, like the shawl she sometimes threw over her shoulders or over her head, or waved in the sun when she danced, or simply threw over a bush to be free. It did not bind her down; sometimes it made her sad, or wistful, or bashful — especially in Mrs Lindsay's presence — but mostly her thought-body was composed of happy, translucent thought-lace, and delighted in the play of living things and their beauty.

Vali, up in the palm tree, bobbed his head a last time to her, and she curtsied and waved and hurried on her way.

She might see David.

She never knew at this time of day if she'd see him or not. He might be in the bathroom at the other end of the house, or in the nursery, getting dressed — the nursery where she, too, had lived with her mother till she was five, when it was thought appropriate that Nirmala and Savitri move back into their own house. Since then Savitri had never re-entered the big house — not because she wasn't allowed to, but because she didn't like it. It was so full of *things*. Most of the things were precious, Mrs Lindsay said. That meant you couldn't touch them. Mrs Lindsay spent a great deal of time thinking of her things, showing them to visitors, getting the maids to polish them. She was also very afraid that they might be broken or stolen. It seemed to Savitri that Mrs Lindsay's thought- body and Mrs Lindsay's things were intimately bound up with one another. Perhaps that was why Mrs Lindsay couldn't get behind her thought-body so easily, because the things anchored her down? It was a mystery to Savitri.

At any rate, the house seemed to her a huge clutter of things and she didn't like to enter it, except for the kitchen.

Today David was in the kitchen doorway, waiting for her.

Savitri's smile fled from her face, because Appa was standing behind David and in the kitchen's gloom his face was unsmiling, worried, and Mrs Lindsay was there too, looking eager and full of surprises. This morning visit to the kitchen when she brought the milk was always a crucial time, a time of decision-making, and it was Iyer who made the decision. The decision was whether she should go to school or not. If Mrs Lindsay had ordained an elaborate luncheon, with a few guests, then Savitri would have to stay and help Appa prepare the meal. If, on the other hand, Mrs Lindsay herself was invited out, and only the Admiral would be home for lunch, then Savitri could go to school and would race home again to change into her uniform. The Admiral preferred a light midday meal — a sandwich, or an omelette, nothing more. Savitri always hoped it was an Admiral day. She liked school — a million times more than the kitchen. But all was the Lord's Will, and whatever was ordained for the day through the chain of command — the Lord, then Mrs Lindsay, then Appa — she did with a happy heart and as well as she could, for Him.

But here now was David, running from the open door, lunging towards her and taking her hand to lead her forward, and Mrs Lindsay smiling and reaching out to pat her, her thought-body very thin today, and Appa, his thought-body thicker than ever, and now all of them around her, crowding her. Savitri looked from one face to the other — what was going on? Maybe it had to do with yesterday's swim; but she could not reconcile Appa's unhappy mien with the open delight on the other two faces, and so she just stood there waiting for someone to explain.

'Savitri, guess what!' chortled David. 'I asked Mummy if you could come and learn from Mr Baldwin with me, and she said yes! And Cooky said yes too, and now you're going to go to English school every day! With me! It was *my* idea!'

Savitri's heart bounced for joy, but then she looked at Appa and she knew there were problems David did not, could not, understand.

'But who will help my father?' she said dutifully, and turning to Iyer herself, for it was not respectful to speak English in his presence, she asked him, 'Appa, have you given permission for me to attend the young master's classes?'

David, who understood Tamil, did not wait for Iyer's answer.

'But of course, of course Savitri! I've already told him that Mummy's going to pay for your lessons and he's agreed, haven't you, Cooky?'

Iyer nodded, for it would be disrespectful to disagree openly with the young master, but Savitri felt the prickles on his thought-body and knew all was not well.

'But who will help you in the kitchen, Appa?' she repeated.

'Daughter, we must discuss this thoroughly at home with *Thatha* and your mother and your brothers. It is not proper for you to go to the English master when your elder brothers all attend the Tamil school. If the *memsahib* will excuse, it is not proper that a girl should have a better education than her brothers.'

Disappointment flooded David's face.

'But, Cooky, she already knows English! Proper English! Your sons only learn English in the school and Savitri is better, much better than they are! And I've been teaching her to read and write it too and she knows so much already!'

'What are you saying, David? You know I don't like you speaking Tamil in my presence. Please translate.'

So David told his mother what Iyer had said, and Savitri added, 'It's not our custom, Mrs Lindsay, for girls to be better educated than boys. I thank you very much for your kind offer, but I must obey my father.' She spoke slowly and precisely as was her habit when speaking with Mrs Lindsay. Mrs Lindsey's head jerked backwards in an affirmation of authority.

'Well then,' she said briskly. 'We'll have to educate your brothers too, won't we? We'll send them all to the English Medium school. Yes, every one of them. And Savitri, my decision is irrevocable, you must attend Mr Baldwin's classes. David has shown me your practice books and I'm most impressed with your work. I'm sure Mr Baldwin will love to have you as a pupil. Now tell your father that.'

Hope and fear struggled in Savitri's heart as she translated for Iyer. Could it be? To learn with Mr Baldwin! She had met Mr Baldwin many times, he was such a funny, jolly man, and she had struggled so hard in the tree-house with David, trying to keep up with him in his English classes. She could read his English reader almost as well as he could now, and she could write all the words she read in it by herself, without looking. Could it be, could it be? *Gracious Lord, please!*

But Appa, she could tell, would not allow it. Iyer's brow was ruffled and his eyes were shadowed and from the way he scratched his beard she knew he would not allow it. His thought-body was impenetrable.

Mrs Lindsay noticed this, too.

'What's bothering him now?' she said to Savitri, who translated.

Iyer launched into speech. A torrent of Tamil rushed from his lips, a loud, staccato, inflamed deluge of words that swept over them and stunned them into silence. Mrs Lindsay gaped numbly at her cook, whom she had known till now to be a reticent, docile little man while David, eyes wide, bit his bottom lip and fidgeted with his buttons. Savitri's eyes were misty with unshed tears, and she gazed up at Appa and nodded at his words and when it was all over and when Iyer's tirade jerked to a halt without warning she hung her head and turned half away, while Iyer turned the other way, yet still half-facing Mrs Lindsay, out of respect.

'Well? What did he say? What was all that about?' asked Mrs Lindsay.

'Appaji says it is not possible,' mumbled Savitri.

'Not possible? But why ever not? I never heard of such a thing. Savitri, I do insist you explain.'

But Savitri kept her head hanging and refused to translate, so Mrs Lindsay turned to David and said, 'David, you tell me! What did Cooky say?'

'I didn't understand everything, Mummy,' David admitted. 'He was saying something about his sons. The eldest son is going to the military. I don't know what else he said.'

'Savitri, then I'd like you to explain to me. I'm sure you understood every word!'

Savitri turned her face to the mistress then, and looked up at her with such huge pleading eyes Mrs Lindsay could hardly bear it, and then she said, 'Ma'am, my father was explaining that he has various plans for his sons. My eldest brother is to go into the army soon. My youngest brother is to be sent to my uncle to become a priest. My second youngest brother is to become a cook and will be taken into the kitchen for training. They all are not in need of English schooling.'

'But then, for heaven's sake, what's the problem?'

'The problem is my brother Gopal, ma'am, the second eldest.'

'My goodness, how many brothers do you have? Go on, go on, explain!'

'My brother is very bright. He is to go to university.'

'Well, then! He'll be the one to go to the English school.'

'Ma'am, my father says there is the problem of your daughter.'

'Fiona? Now what on earth does she have to do with all this?'

'Ma'am . . . we all know that your daughter is to be sent to England, and when your daughter leaves, then Mr Baldwin would have no girls in his class except me.'

'That is correct.'

'My father says this would not be in keeping with propriety.'

Mrs Lindsay gave a start of surprise, for Savitri spoke the word perfectly correctly and calmly, not stumbling over the unaccustomed syllables though it was almost certain she had never spoken it in her life before. Mrs Lindsay was torn between the urge to question Savitri on her unusual vocabulary, and to understand the connection between *propriety* and her second brother's education. A strange logic, zig-zagging between all sorts of seemingly unconnected factors and linking them all together in an unspoken causality, governed the lives of these Indians, and though Savitri obviously understood perfectly well what the one had to do with the other, she herself was at a loss — and David even more so. Little David: next to Savitri, he seemed so childish .. .

The four of them, Savitri and her father, David and his mother, stood outside the kitchen door in a bemused circle, each captured in their little world to which the others had no access. Mrs Lindsay was determined to have her way and to uplift this family — or one or two members of it. David wanted Savitri in his classes and hated grown-up talk. Savitri was torn between love and duty. Iyer simply knew right from wrong. Mrs Lindsay broke the silence by leaning over to Savitri and placing a hand on her shoulder.

'What does your father mean by this?' she asked. She heard Savitri take a deep breath as if gathering the strength and the courage to interpret one world to the other.

'My father says that I may not take lessons with two male persons, as this would stain my character and my reputation. I may only take lessons with male persons if one of my brothers accompanies me for protection.'

'You mean, chaperone you?' Mrs Lindsay wasn't sure at first if Savitri would understand this long word but she needn't have worried, for Savitri, eyes soft and liquid as if she were on the verge of tears, nodded vigorously. Perhaps she reads the dictionary, Mrs Lindsay suddenly thought, and remembered she had been searching for the dictionary only last week to look up a word she'd found in one of her books, and it had been missing. Remember to ask David, she told herself, but afterwards, not now. Because now she needed all her concentration to hold back the laughter, and laughter, she knew, would completely spoil the atmosphere of great dignity needed to bring this conversation to a satisfying end.

And now, now that she'd arrived at the crux of the problem, she knew that the answer was, in fact, easy. Ridiculously easy.

'So your father wants your brother to chaperone you? Then he shall.' She said it with a great finality, stamping her foot for emphasis, but Savitri was just as vigorous, stepping forward and shaking her long plaits so that the flowers fell to the ground.

David bent over to pick them up and handed them back to Savitri, who said, 'No, no, ma'am. My brother must go to school and to university, so he cannot guard me.' She spoke the word 'guard' very naturally, though it must be clear to her and to her father that she would need no guarding from anyone on this property, least of all from dear Mr Baldwin. Mrs Lindsay sighed in frustration. It was all a matter a form, of rules that must be adhered to, so that there could never be any doubt as to the purity of the girl when the time came for her to marry. Marriage — that rang a bell . . . Oh yes, there was still the question of the dowry, but that could be dealt with at another time, surely it would be just as complicated to deal with as this matter of schooling, and Mrs Lindsay was now exhausted.

She wished she could reach out and take Iyer's hand to convince him of her goodwill, and to shake him out of that stubborn pride that had him standing there before her as stiff as a poker.

'No, child, no. You don't understand. I don't mean your brother should just come and stand guard over you. I mean he should come and *attend lessons*. When we come back from Ooty he shall have private tuition with Mr Baldwin, just like you, and I shall pay for it, and he shall go to university just as planned, so tell your father that and please stop worrying, and stop looking as if you're going to cry. Go on, tell your father!'

But The Admiral's male nurse, the Christian Joseph, lived in the house with the sahibs. Savitri could do nothing but stand there with her hands folded, for right now Mrs Lindsay's thought-body had dispersed entirely, it just wasn't *there*. . . and the simple gesture of folded hands was, in the absence of thought-bodies, all the thanks that were needed; for the thanks she gave were to God, who sees in silence.

'It is not right, that a girl should have an education. And much worse, with these sahibs.' Mani, though only seventeen, often felt the need to voice truths his father would not. Appa was too much under the sway of his English lords. It was therefore up to Mani to speak up, for, though a son must obey his father, when a father is under bad influences then an eldest son must warn him.

'But it is a chance for Gopal.'

'She will be polluted, mixing with the *sahibs*. Already she has broken caste.'

'As long as she does not take meals with them.'

'But she is mixing with them. It will ruin her reputation. Already people are talking.'

'But Gopal will be with her. She will come to no harm.'

'It is best she is married right away. Let us send a message to Bombay, to Uncle Madanlal; let him make arrangements for a match there. She could then be sent to Bombay to her father-in-law and we would be rid of the problem.'

'That is a good idea. But let us consult with *Thatha*. After all, Gopal's education is at stake. It is a fine opportunity for him.'

Chapter 9

Nat
A Village in Madras State, 1949

When Nat came home from school that afternoon his father was still busy in the clinic, but only one more person was waiting outside the gate, a woman with a girl whose spindly legs were bent forwards at the knee. Nat knew what was wrong with the girl: she had polio, and he knew his father could not help her. He could only advise her mother to take her to Vellore or Madras to a specialist who would give her braces or crutches or a wheelchair, but most likely the mother would do nothing; she would not have the time or the money to go to Madras or Vellore. And even if his father gave her the bus fare, she would not have the time. The girl would stay the way she was, walking by using her hands to shuffle forward on her bottom. Nat had seen lots of children with polio, who could not walk but only shuffle, crawl or hobble. He knew they broke his father's heart, and that one of Doctor's main crusades was to see that every child for miles around was vaccinated, just as he himself had been.

Nat hung up his satchel on its nail inside the house, then went to the clinic and stood in the doorway, watching. His father was speaking to another patient, a very old woman whose breasts hung against her chest in two thin wrinkled flaps, uncovered except for a torn and threadbare length of sari across one shoulder. Anand stood at the table at the back of the room, carefully pouring a measured amount of powder onto a small sheet of brown paper, which he then folded into a little sachet and placed in a paper bag, on which he wrote a few words. He didn't really have to write anything, Nat knew, because the woman surely could not read. But perhaps one of her children or grandchildren could.

His father sensed his presence in the doorway and looked up, smiling.

'So there you are, Nat. Why don't you go and look for Gopal Uncle, he went for a walk in the village. Bring him home and make some tea for all of us.'

So Nat ran out into the village, past the groups of children who, their day's work done, called out to him, inviting him to join them; but today Nat had no time.

Nat met Gopal Uncle returning from the village, and the two walked home together. Gopal Uncle had lots of questions. He wanted to know how Nat's day at school had been, what he had learned, what his favourite subjects were, and when Nat answered promptly and knew all the answers he looked down and said,

'Nat, you are a very lucky boy going to this English school in town. Do you know, I was talking to some children of your age in the school and they said Teacher did not come back to school this afternoon and all they did was play; most of them went home to work in the fields. They don't know half as much as you! I am very happy that you are having a good education, because when you grow up you can be a doctor like your father, which is a very fine profession. You must thank God for your good fortune.'

'Every day when I get up I thank God, Gopal Uncle!'

'Very good, very good, excellent!' Gopal Uncle stopped to pat Nat on his back. But then he looked around him to see if they were alone and bent down very low and whispered, 'But, Nat, how would you like to live in Madras? In a very big city, where you will wear shoes to go to school, and you will have toys to play with like the one I brought… Oh! You have not seen that yet! We have a radio in our home and you will have your very own bicycle, and you will go to school in a big black car, and you will have a mother…'

Nat could vaguely remember Madras, where his father had taken him after they left the place with all the children. He remembered hundreds and hundreds of cars weaving in and out of each other and honking their horns, all kinds of other sounds and strange smells, nice ones and nasty ones, black mounds of dirt on the pavements and everywhere people hurrying, hurrying, hurrying. And then the cool quiet garden with lots of mango trees and lovely flowers, and a big, big stone house, all dark and cool inside with round things on the ceilings, like the wheels of a bullock cart but small and of metal, with wide spokes, whirling around and making a breeze. There had been a *memsahib* in the garden. A *memsahib* in a sari walking around with a baby in her arms but it wasn't a baby, it was a doll. That's what Doctor had said. A doll. After that his father had brought him here on the motorbike, and they had never returned to Madras.

'Daddy took me to Madras once,' Nat said to Gopal Uncle now. He didn't know what else to say; it would not be polite to say he didn't like Madras, when Gopal Uncle was smiling so kindly. He rubbed the spot behind his right ear, which he always did when nervous.

'I would like to take you there too,' Gopal Uncle said. 'I would take you there to live with me in a wonderful big house. You would not have to work with all these poor sick people any more.'

'I'm going to be a doctor like Daddy!' said Nat.

'Yes, yes, that is a very fine profession, very fine. But you know, all doctors do not work so hard like your Daddy does and they do not live in such a place. They have nice patients who lie on lovely white beds in a hospital, who pay lots of money to get healthy again, and the doctors drive in big cars and their wives and children have very fine pleasant lives! You can be such a doctor, Nataraj, when you grow up!'

Nat did not understand what Gopal Uncle was talking about. He didn't know about the people who could pay lots and lots of money for a doctor. He didn't know of any other life than the one he was leading, and he didn't want to go to that horrid noisy place Madras. All of a sudden Nat felt completely stupid, and very, very frightened. He pulled his hand out of

Gopal Uncle's grasp and turned and ran, all the way home, to his father, to safety.

Nat tore through the gate but left it swinging open for Gopal Uncle. His father was still in the clinic, so he immediately busied himself so as not to have to talk to Gopal Uncle when he arrived. He made a pot of tea and opened a new packet of Milk Bikis, laying them all out on a plate. He took a tin of Amul Spray powdered milk and the tin of sugar from the shelf over the kitchen sink, and brought everything out on a tray to the verandah, where he unrolled a mat. Then he stood at the clinic door watching his father and Anand clean up after the last patient, the girl with polio, and when they were finished he took his father's hand and the two of them walked over to have tea with Gopal Uncle.

He listened to Doctor and Gopal Uncle chatting. Gopal Uncle told Doctor about a man called Henry, who was 'back in Madras'. Henry's wife had run off to Sydney with somebody and his father sounded shocked to hear that. 'Poor fellow, I'll go and see him,' Doctor said.

While his father poured out the tea Gopal Uncle turned to Nat again and gave him a little box wrapped in coloured paper and tied with ribbons.

'This is my present, Nat. Go on, open it up!'

Nat carefully untied the bow and removed the paper, which was very pretty. He thought he would take the paper to school, to show the other children. Perhaps they would hang it on the classroom wall. Inside was a box as long as a new pencil, and as high as Nat's hand. On the box was a picture of a very strange car, long and red with many wheels and things sticking out of it. Nat had never seen a car like this before; not even in Madras had he seen such a strange thing… but yes, of course! He had; last year there had been a picture of such a thing in his English reader, a picture of a very big house on fire with flames leaping out of the window, and a car like this outside, shooting water into the windows. It was a… Nat tried to think of the word but he'd forgotten.

Gopal Uncle was watching him, and now his father also. 'Go on, Nat, open it up, open it up,' said Gopal Uncle, impatiently, because Nat was turning the box around and looking at it from all sides, and shaking it. It rattled. Nat didn't know what Gopal Uncle meant with 'Open it,' so he handed the box to his father; maybe his father had already seen cars like this, but maybe he hadn't. His father took the box, smiling gently, and pulled at one side of it, and to Nat's amazement it flapped open and a real car came out, just like in the picture, small and long and red and with all kinds of things sticking out of it, a long vine-like thing, and a ladder that his father was actually moving back and forth. Nat could hardly believe his eyes, he held out his hands and his father laid the car in them and Nat saw that the wheels turned and he could roll it on the ground.

'Aren't you going to say thank you to Gopal Uncle?' said his father. 'For the nice fire-engine?'

A fire-engine. That was it. This was a fire-engine, and it was used for putting out fires in the city, because the houses were so big that when they burned you couldn't use buckets. There would be things like this in Madras. You didn't need them in the village because mud houses don't burn. And when Govinda's roof had caught fire last year the whole village had helped to put it out, passing along buckets of water from the well, but the roof was ruined anyway. His father had bought a new one for Govinda.

Nat turned his eyes to Gopal Uncle at last, then looked away again and stammered in a weak, thin voice, 'Thank you, Gopal Uncle, it's very nice.' Then he put the fire engine carefully back into the box and placed it on the ground and picked up a Milk Biki and ate it.

'Don't mention it,' said Gopal Uncle, who didn't look so happy any more. 'Aren't you going to play with it?'

'Later,' said Nat, taking another Milk Biki and not looking at Gopal Uncle. Out of the corner of his eye he saw Gopal Uncle and his father exchange a look and he had a bad feeling inside his tummy, as if something horrid was going on that he couldn't understand. He rubbed behind his ear. His father looked at his watch.

'Nat, it's time to go and get the milk,' he said, and Nat got to his feet reluctantly. He didn't want to fetch the milk today; somehow he felt he ought to stay to protect his father. But his father had to be obeyed, so he went inside and took the metal milk container from the shelf and left the house, running along the road to the other side of the village where Kanairam lived with his wife and his cow.

There was a line of ladies and children waiting for milk, and as always they all greeted him with big smiles and folded hands when he came, and tried to push him to the front of the line, because Nat brought them luck. They did this every day, but his father had told him he must never accept any special favours, so as always Nat smiled and joined the end of the line.

Usually, he liked fetching milk. He liked Kanairam and his wife and his cow. They kept the cow under a thatched roof outside their hut, and when it was milking time they tied the calf up to one of the posts holding up the roof and Kanairam squatted down beside the cow and pulled at her teats, squirting the warm foaming milk into an old battered bucket. His wife squatted near him with another bucket, out of which she ladled the milk into the containers the women held out; most of them bought just a few ounces, and Nat always liked to be last because he was the only one who bought a whole pint, which somehow shamed him. But his father said he must drink lots of milk so as to grow big and strong and learn well. Every evening his father made him a cup of steaming Horlicks, and every morning there was milk with sugar, although this morning he had had only half a cup of milk because he had given the other half to the dead baby's brother.

Today he was distracted. He hadn't wanted to get the milk, he hadn't wanted to leave his father with Gopal Uncle, and now he couldn't wait to return home. He raced through the village lane, not greeting anyone, but had to stop and pick up the lid that had fallen off the container because of the milk swirling around inside, and he couldn't put it back on because now it was covered with dirt, and he couldn't run any more because the milk would spill and he'd already spilled so much, which was very naughty. His father always said he must never, ever, waste food because it was an insult to the villagers.

His father and Gopal Uncle were still talking when he got back, and in a way that verified what Nat had felt, that something very horrid was going on. His father's eyes looked up and met his, and contained a deep hurt and a deep anguish he'd never seen in them before, and Gopal Uncle — no, he didn't want to call him Uncle any more, because how angry his eyes looked!

'Nat, go to the back verandah and do your homework, please. Gopal Uncle and I have to discuss some matters!' said his father, and more reluctantly than ever Nat fetched his satchel and half carried, half dragged it to the back verandah, which looked out on the paddy fields and scrubland that stretched out towards the sky, which was now bright and tinted with orange because the sun was preparing to go to rest. Over there, where the sun went down, Nat knew there were far-off countries, that land where his father had once lived for some time, and where he, Nat, would have to go one day to become a doctor.

Nat didn't want that day to come. He wanted to be a doctor, yes, but he never, ever wanted to leave his father. But it seemed you couldn't have one without the other. And now this uncle, this Gopal — Nat knew it was rude to call grown-ups by their first names, without Uncle or Aunt or Ma or Appa as a term of respect, but he didn't want to be polite to this uncle — had brought some new danger with him, a danger he couldn't understand, and it was simply not possible for Nat to do even a scrap of homework, even though Teacher would be cross, although he wouldn't flog him as he did the other boys because he was the *sahib daktah's* son.

Nat listened. And though he couldn't understand what the men were saying, he knew that Gopal Uncle was a threat.

'I am his father and I have the right to bring him up the way I see fit!'

'What kind of a life he is living? The life of a peasant! If I had known you would do this to him I would never have allowed...'

'Allowed! Allowed! You're talking of *allowed!* Who are you to allow anything! If what you are saying is true why didn't you speak up two years ago!'

'I am telling you, Mani would not allow it! Only because of your money! You think you can buy a child and then the child belongs to you!'

'I did not buy him! I have every right to him and you know it!'

'Mani was a rogue and you believed every word he said but I alone know the truth, I and Fiona…'

'And now Mani is dead you think you can burst in just like that and take him to Madras!'

'And you want him raised as a peasant!'

'I want him to be a doctor, just like me. Isn't that the Indian way: that a boy should follow in the footsteps of his father? Isn't that what all this caste business is about?'

'You are very right, but there are other doctors for the kind of work you are doing. You belong in another world and you could offer Nat that world instead of this.'

'This happens to be my world, and the world Nat knows and loves.'

'But this is not your rightful place. You are an Englishman. You should be among your own people.'

'I'm an Indian. You seem to have forgotten.'

'Only on paper.'

'I'm as much an Indian as you where it really counts, or even more so. You of all people should know that!'

'To us Indians you will always be an Englishman, a *sahib*, and you can't change that. You cannot change Indians and the way they think and you cannot change India. This is a big country and there is so much poverty. What you are doing is just a drop in the ocean. You cannot heal all the millions.'

'But I can do my part. I'm not trying to change anyone or anything. I'm just doing my part and teaching Nat to do the same. I'm showing him a way of life he'll one day thank me for!'

'*Thank* you for! One day he will curse you for not opening up to him every opportunity a boy should have! If I had known

I would never have let you… how much more you could have offered him! That is the only reason I did not speak up sooner, because I knew you could offer more — the West, a good education, but not *this!* If you had taken him to England, let him grow up there and be a doctor worthy of the name and with all the privileges he deserves I would not have interfered, but this…'

'Privileges! I remember a day when there was no talk of privileges but only of shame.'

'Times and circumstances change, you know that as well as I do. But the fact remains: he is born with privileges and he should take advantage of them. You, of all people! You're an Oxford man! Eton and Oxford! And Nat should have the same!'

'I want him to grow up with values and substance and not with glitter and so-called privileges. I don't care how prosperous you've become, Gopal. With me he'll have a better life, a life of quality. It is what his mother would have wanted.'

'Leave *her* out of this!'

'No, I won't! Now we've come to speak of her let's stay with her. Because this is all about her.'

Nat pressed his hands to his ears. He could not take it any more. It was too much for a boy to bear. No, not his mother!

Of course, he knew very well that every child had a mother, you couldn't be born otherwise, and he knew that some mothers died early and those children grew up without mothers, or with other ladies when their fathers remarried. But Nat also remembered clearly that place with all the children, and he knew all too well that his father was not really his father. Nat knew that his father had forgotten about that place with all the children, had forgotten that they weren't really father and son, because he always referred to Nat as 'my son'; and Nat didn't want to remind his father that it wasn't strictly speaking true. His father was his whole world.

But inside his heart Nat knew one little piece of that world was missing. He didn't often think about it, but today again, when Gopal Uncle had said, 'Your mother would be very proud of you!' it had come back, a stinging pain, a very sharp ache deep inside, as of something that ought to be, but wasn't.

Now, listening to his father and Gopal Uncle arguing, for that was what they were doing, shouting at each other and shouting about his mother, he knew that ache could only grow and all he could do was shut it all out, squeezing his palms to his ears so not even a whisper filtered through. His mother was already lost. Let her stay in that lost land! *But please, please, let me not lose my father, too!* He buried his head, with his hands still over his ears, between his knees, and stayed like that for a long, long time, so as not to hear the shouting.

When he cautiously took his hands away only silence met his ears. It was dark, and time for meals, which Pandu's wife sent over in the tiffin carrier, and which they took in a cold, hostile silence, and then it was time to sleep, and in the morning Gopal Uncle had already left, and it was as if that day had never been. Nat shut it out of his life, for Gopal Uncle never came back, and his father never mentioned that name again.

Nat gave the fire-engine to the village boys. They all shared it, each boy keeping it for one day and putting it back in its box for the night. But whenever it was Nat's turn he passed it on to the next boy. The fire engine was over ten years old before Ravana the monkey-king found it in somebody's hut and pulled it to pieces. Murugan, the village smith, tried to repair it but it was too badly damaged, and four of the wheels were lost.

Chapter 10

Saroj
Georgetown, 1964

Saroj's thirteenth birthday fell on a Saturday, mid-September. The following Monday the new school year began.

In this new school year they — they being Miss Dewer and the rest of the Bishops' High School staff — leap-frogged her over one class. Saroj found herself sitting next to Trixie Macintosh.

She had noticed Trixie before, of course, when she'd been in her former class. You couldn't help noticing Trixie, the big, brown, gawky colt of a girl who seemed to cavort and caper constantly along the decks of Bishops' High, falling up the stairs and over her own ungainly legs. Trixie was always in the middle of every knot of giggling schoolgirls. She was funny and witty, with a contagious laugh that sprinkled mirth like confetti on all those in her orbit. Her laughter began as a deep chuckle down in her belly, and bubbled out in a rippling fountain that spiralled up into a pealing crescendo, sparkling like champagne. Even if you didn't get the joke you had to laugh.

Trixie in the classroom was an experience. Sitting next to her seemed to Saroj the heights of bliss. Trixie would look at you and raise her eyebrows in a quizzical way that made you burst out laughing for no other reason than her expression. She would look up at a teacher when called to attention and wiggle her ears and say, quite seriously, 'My ears are all agog!'

And the way she walked: deliberately falling over her own flailing legs, or bumping into a lamppost or a wall or a closed door with a loud crash, and falling in a heap to the floor so that you rushed anxiously to her side to see if she was hurt, only to have her laugh up at you with that endless toothy grin that almost split her face in two.

And the stories she told, that would split your sides, and the comments on the teachers, and the caricatures she drew during lessons on the edges of her work, so accurate you could tell at a glance who she was depicting. She specialised in cartoons with witty captions, passing them on to the girl next to her who would pass it on to the next girl, till the whole class was a quivering mass of smothered giggles. Saroj would grow anxious when Trixie spent an entire maths lesson drawing such a cartoon, not listening to a single word the teacher said, all concentration, and far away from maths. Lackadaisical to a fault, she earned Saroj's admiration for precisely this fault.

It was the same survival instinct that inclined Saroj towards Ganesh's comic levity. She gravitated towards life's clowns like plants seek light; her own latent seriousness, the clay-footed realism that placed her squarely in the company of bores, terrified her. If she gazed at it too long it threatened to devour her. Ganesh brought relief. So did Trixie. They were cut of the same light wood. Up to now she had clung to Ganesh to save herself from drowning in the mire of her own distress, but Ganesh was no longer enough. Now that life had presented her with a new and seemingly insurmountable distress bearing the name of Ghosh, she needed new inspiration. To every poison, its antidote.

Trixie went one stage beyond Ganesh. Ganesh's clowning was basically passive. He made fun of life, but took good care not to get himself into trouble and never faced obstacles head-on. He wouldn't fight his marriage to the Narain girl, he'd simply swim around it. Gan would never raise tempers. Trixie specialised in doing just that. Walk along the long, silent verandah that linked the class rooms of Bishops' High School on any given day and chances were you'd find Trixie cooling her heels outside her class, carving her initials into the wooden railing, having been thrown out by the teacher in charge. There was something in her grin that caused a teacher's blood to boil. Her cheekiness raised storms of wrath, her complete lack of reverence for the subjects taught. In fact, everyone knew that Trixie, when she chose to be, could be brilliant, which was the reason she was in this selective school, and in the A form. It was the *teachers* that bored her to tears, the drone of their voices, their lack of inspiration. She was a rebel against the inherent humdrum of academia. She had no respect for learning. Dead knowledge, she called it.

Whereas Saroj was just the opposite. She was the quintessential Indian girl with her long-plaited hair and below-the-knee uniform. And in this class she was the New Girl, and the drip. Most Indian girls were drips. That's what they all thought, those African and Portuguese and Chinese and mixed-race girls. Indian girls were quiet and well behaved, chaste and studious. They were the teacher's pets and the prefects, perfect head-girl material. And Saroj fitted the mould perfectly.

But there was an outer and an inner Saroj. The outer Saroj was the Baba-trained, docile, obedient, soft-spoken, sweet-natured, aloof, dignified, paper-doll shell of an Indian girl who walked, moved, breathed, followed, spoke when she was spoken to, and did what she was told. Beneath that veneer was the real Saroj; the inner one. Beneath the smoke of what-people-thought-she-was, was the fire of the real, squirming, kicking, bull-headed, fighting-to-get-out me, the what-she-really-was. But nobody would have believed it, at least not before the thirteenth birthday that changed everything. The inner Saroj must live. The outer Saroj must die. That much was clear. But how? The inner Saroj, struggling for life, needed a hand to hold on to, and here within her grasp, less than an arm's length away, was the ideal model for the new character that would shape her destiny. Trixie. To be as free, as uninhibited, as that!

When Saroj went to see Balwant Uncle's boys, she went for a walk along the beach dreaming her dreams of freedom. Trixie was there, galloping her piebald horse along the water's edge, slightly raised in the saddle, leaning slightly forward, the picture of freedom. Saroj stared after her in envy. Trixie by now was no longer a stranger; how could a girl be a stranger who seemed nearer to your soul's true being than you yourself? But Saroj knew that this intimacy was false, because it was one-sided. Except for a vague, occasional grin, Trixie seemed unaware of Saroj's very existence. Trixie would never notice her, despite their physical proximity. She'd have to prove herself. Somehow.

Saroj's imagination had worked overtime. She had laid awake at night devising schemes, making up stories in which Trixie and the others would stand gaping, open-mouthed and goggle-eyed, while she, Saroj, the dare-devil heroine, rushed into burning houses to rescue screaming children, or joined a circus and swung on the trapeze, flying through the air with the greatest of ease…

But the morning would come, bringing Ma and her hairbrush, Baba with his squares of toast, her uniform, neatly laid across the high-backed chair next to the tower door. The spell over, the silver coach turned back into a pumpkin, the heroine a long-skirted schoolgirl nobody noticed, least of all Trixie. She was Baba's prisoner. Chained and gagged, a vestal virgin to be sacrificed on the altar of marriage. On her wedding day Baba would place the chain in the Ghosh boy's hands, and that would be her life. Forever more. She lacked the courage to rebel. She lacked the courage even to address a word to Trixie. Two weeks into the new term she was still no nearer to friendship than the foot-and-a-half between their desks.

'Auntie! Come and help me!' Sahadeva jolted Saroj out of her reverie. The two of them were a team; they had made the glorious blue-and-yellow kite that had to win the best kite prize at the kite competition next Easter.

'It's not fair!' Shiv Sahai complained. 'You get to practise with her and Pratap never comes to practise!'

'Your fault! Your fault! Your fault!' Sahadeva laughed, because they had tossed a coin to choose a teammate and Shiv Sahai had won the toss and chosen their big brother Pratap, who might be good at making kites but didn't make the time to practise. Shiv Sahai had to make do with their fat old nanny Meenakshi, who waddled back and forth at his command. Sahadeva had Saroj, who was always eager for the temporary escape that kite-flying granted.

'You stay here and hold it good, Auntie,' said Sahadeva. 'I'm just going to run off with the kite. Hold it good, okay?'

The kite soared up and Sahadeva ran back, took the spool from Saroj, and ran off, dancing sideways to watch the kite's ascent.

'Look how high! Look how high! Shiv Sahai, look! Mine's much higher than yours!'

In excitement he ran backwards along the beach, releasing more twine as he ran. The kite soared and sailed, its bright yellow crepe-paper ears flapping gaily against the cobalt blue of the sky, its long tail of scrap-cotton bows tied to a cord — which Sahadeva had made all by himself, without any help whatsoever — curling gracefully back and forth.

All of a sudden the kite took a dive downwards, like a hawk plunging for the attack, right into the path of Trixie's horse cantering back towards them.

'Look out!' Saroj yelled. But she was too far away, and it was too late.

The kite hit the sand directly before Trixie's horse's nose. The horse shied, reared, tottered, and plunged off in a wild gallop. Trixie lay on the ground. Saroj was at her side in a trice.

'Are you all right?'

'I'm fine,' Trixie said gruffly, and tried to stand up, but the moment she touched the ground with her right foot her knee gave way and she collapsed.

'Ouch!'

'You're hurt! You've sprained your ankle, or broken it.'

'Well, yes, maybe... where's Vitane?'

'The horse? He went that way, he's all right, but if you can't walk...'

'Look, I'll be all right. I have to catch Vitane. Ouch...' Trixie tried to walk again and collapsed again.

'Look, I'd better go and get help!'

'But Vitane — you've got to get Vitane first, I'm going to be fine, once he's here you can help me onto his back, then I can ride again. Look, there he is, over there, can you...'

Saroj looked down the beach and there indeed was Vitane, standing still with his head lowered, as guilty as the cat who stole the milk.

'Look, I'll go and bring your horse, you sit down here on the sand, I'll be right back.'

'He's a pony,' Trixie said, 'and he doesn't like strangers so you have to be very careful, approach him slowly from in front, and…'

Saroj didn't bother to listen to Trixie's instructions, and she didn't need them. The horse, pony, whatever, was glad to be rescued. She just walked up to him and he came to meet her. She patted him on the neck, and he nuzzled her hand. She whispered into his ear and stroked his glossy black-and-white coat, and she had to wipe a grin from her face as, leading the docile Vitane, she approached Trixie, sitting helplessly on the sand, so Trixie wouldn't think she was laughing at her.

By this time Meenakshi and the boys were with her, Meenakshi fussing over the twisted ankle, the boys fussing over the kite, which was ruined. Sahadeva was crying.

'It's all right, Sahadeva, we'll make a new one,' Saroj said in passing, and to Trixie, 'He was quite easy to catch!' trying not to brag.

'Thanks, now if you could just give me a leg-up I can ride him back to the Pony Club,' Trixie said, grouchily. She was trying to get rid of her, Saroj knew.

But Meenakshi, thank God for grown-ups, said, 'Girl, you hurt bad, you should go and see a doctor!'

'Who's this?' said Trixie, nodding towards Meenaskshi. 'It's Meenakshi, the boys' nanny, and she's right.'

'But I've got to take care of Vitane!'

'Don't worry about him,' Saroj said, and patted him again. It felt good, crouching there at Trixie's side with the reins slung over her arm, casually, as if he were her, Saroj's, horse, and not Trixie's. 'The Pony Club isn't all that far; I'll walk him over. Look, he likes me. We've got to get you to a doctor though, maybe you've broken something!'

Trixie looked sulky. She tried to stand up again but it was

no good; she yelled in pain.

'I'll telephone your mother. What's her number?'

'She's not at home.'

'Your father then. Is he at work?'

'My father's in London,' Trixie said quickly, 'so I wouldn't bother calling him, and I've no idea where my mother is right now. Just… just call a taxi and get me to the hospital, I'll be all right, really, and if you could walk Vitane to the Pony Club…'

'Shouldn't I come to hospital with you?'

'No, I'll be fine, really.'

They looked around for a telephone booth but of course there wasn't one; there never was when you needed one, and then Meenakshi pointed out that just across the road was the police headquarters, and she waddled off to seek help. And before long Meenakshi was back with two strapping policemen who lugged Trixie up as if she were a sack of potatoes and carried her off the beach to the street, where a police jeep was already waiting.

Saroj stood waiting till the jeep was out of sight. And when it was gone she sent Meenakshi off home with the little boys and the broken kite, and then she stood on the Sea Wall, which was just the right height to get her leg over Vitane's back. Then she kicked his sides like she thought you were supposed to, and clicked her tongue and said *giddy-up,* and she was off ! Riding! With her skirt all hoisted up around her knees… her very first taste of freedom. A tiny step, perhaps, one Trixie would think nothing of, nothing like plunging into a raging inferno to save somebody's life.

But for Saroj, it was a single tiny step. And she had taken it alone, with no-one's help, only Providence.

Later that evening, while Ma was still at the Purushottama Temple and Baba was still at the Maha Sabha, the telephone rang. It was Trixie.

'I just wanted to say sorry I was so bitchy and thank you for looking after Vitane.'

'Oh, no, that's fine, really, and how are you? How's your foot? Is it broken?'

'No, just sprained.'

After that it was as easy as anything. Trixie was all alone at home, lying, as she explained, on the sitting room couch with her bandaged foot up, reading Teen magazine, bored to tears and ready for a chat. Naturally gregarious, she didn't need much prodding to release the avalanche of conversation waiting inside her. It didn't even seem to matter that Saroj happened to be one of those Indian drips. It was as if they were already best friends.

Within the first five minutes she had promised to give Saroj riding lessons, to lend her Beatles records, and on hearing that she had no record-player, to make cassettes of her records which she would give her the next day at school, and on hearing that she didn't even have a cassette recorder promised to lend her her own.

'But better still, just come over here. We can listen together then. What about after school tomorrow? Oh, hell, no, I've got this gammy foot and can't ride a bicycle. Guess what, I've got crutches! Mum'll have to pick me up in the car. But as soon as it's better you'll come home with me, okay?'

'Well, er, okay, but…'

'But what?'

'Well…' Saroj didn't know how to explain it. How to tell her that she wasn't allowed to go anywhere. Not to visit, except to relatives. Not shopping, not to the swimming pool, not to the cinema. Nowhere. That she couldn't ride a bicycle. That she was her father's prisoner, his captive, his possession. The porcelain doll he kept swaddled in cotton wool.

But then the real Saroj, the Saroj she longed to be, slammed her fist right through the porcelain facecrust of that doll.

'Yes! Yes, I'll come, but listen, I haven't got a bicycle so can I come home with you tomorrow, in the car? When your mum picks you up?'

They settled that matter there and then, and Saroj replaced the receiver with a feeling of jubilant, singing joy surging up within her. She danced away from the telephone with a wide grin splitting her face, and twirled slap-bang into Ganesh just coming home from cricket, and they both lay sprawled on the floor. Saroj laughed, and Ganesh, who never needed an excuse to do so, laughed too. She scrambled to her feet and pulled at Ganesh's sleeve.

'Ganesh, come quick, up in the tower. I've got news, you won't believe it!'

Trixie opened the back door of her mother's white Vauxhall and Saroj slipped in, feeling suddenly terribly shy. Suddenly scared. But then she was sliding back into the seat behind Trixie's mum and Trixie was in the passenger seat and they were driving off to a place where Baba could not find her.

'Mum, this is Saroj; Saroj, this is Mum,' Trixie said quickly. Trixie's mum was half-turned towards Saroj. She had a perfectly round two-inch Afro and her profile showed sharp features, a full mouth and high cheekbones. Her skin was an unblemished mahogany brown, and on the crest of the cheekbone nearest Saroj was a black split-pea of a mole, which together with the rest of that profile looked strangely, vaguely familiar.

Saroj slid forward in the seat to take her proffered hand and said, 'Pleased to meet you, Mrs Macintosh.'

Trixie's mum smiled and shook her head and Trixie let out one of her cascades of laughter.

'No, no, no, don't ever call her that or she'll bite your head off. She's not a Mrs and she's not a Macintosh. She's Lucy Quentin!'

And then Lucy Quentin smiled again and nodded this time, and Saroj almost died of shame and awe. *Lucy Quentin!*

Lucy Quentin was famous, so famous her face was in the papers all the time, Lucy Quentin this and Lucy Quentin that, Minister of Health, head of this commission and that advisory board, president of this association and chairwoman of that corporation. Lucy Quentin, quote, unquote, shake hands and curtsey.

And Saroj was Lucy Quentin's greatest fan. First thing she did whenever she got hold of the *Chronicle* was scan page one for any news of her. Had she given a speech? A press conference? Had words with the Minister of Education? Lucy Quentin was always crossing swords with men of consequence. She had a hundred axes to grind — but her sharpest, heaviest axe was the one raised on Baba's talon grip on his daughter's life. Lucy Quentin wanted to raise the minimum marriageable age for girls and abolish arranged marriages. She had plans to institute a commission where girls being forced into marriage by their parents could find legal assistance, or, after such a marriage had taken place, have it annulled. She envisioned a home these girls could flee to, secure from their fist-waving fathers. She wanted laws against the unlimited power of fathers!

She outraged the entire adult Indian community with these unspeakable demands; but their daughters — and surely Saroj wasn't the only one — devoured her words in the privacy of their homes, made secret scrapbooks of *Chronicle* clippings, rooted for her in their hearts, cheered her on in their thoughts, and prayed for her success every time their parents called them to the family shrine for *puja*. And smiled demurely to themselves when their fathers ranted about Lucy Quentin's latest heresies.

It was none of her business, the Indian fathers said; first, she was an African and had no understanding of Indian ways. Second, she was Minister of Health and marriage wasn't her department. It jolly well was, Lucy Quentin replied. Forced marriage was bad for a fourteen-year-old's mental health.

And here was Saroj, now, sitting behind the great Lucy Quentin, on the way to her home to spend the afternoon with her daughter who, Saroj determined, was about to become her very best friend. In that moment she knew there really was a God.

Later on, when Lucy Quentin had dropped them off at their Bel Air Park home and driven off again to some important meeting, Trixie told Saroj her story. Trixie's mum's name was Quentin, not Macintosh, she told Saroj, because when she divorced Trixie's father she took back her maiden name and called herself

Miss.

'Did your father remarry?'

'Yeah. He married a rich white lady, and they live in a fancy house in London.'

Trixie's dad was a Trinidadian artist. Improvident, happy-go- lucky, non-political and real, real cool, said Trixie. When Lucy Quentin threw him out he went to England to recover and start a new life, without a penny. As it was just before Christmas he painted ten black Santa Clauses on thin cardboard, folded them into cards, wrote a witty Christmas message on them and stood on a street corner somewhere in London holding them out in a fan to the passers-by, wearing a red fur-lined coat himself. In five minutes the cards were all gone. So he went home and painted some more, and they were snapped up too, mostly by West Indians, but also by white Londoners who thought them original and exotic and ethnic. Because Trixie's dad was a gifted painter, and his black Santa Clauses were tiny works of art. That's how he met this rich white lady who at the time ran a small advertising agency. She took him off the streets and got those cards marketed and got him going as an 'ethnic illustrator'.

'Finally she married him and gave him two sons and they opened their own greeting card business, and since then he doesn't care a fig about me.'

'Of course he does.'

'He doesn't. He's got this white lady and two half-white sons, why should he care a fig about me?'

'Because you're his daughter.'

Saroj's experience of fathers was such that a father's indifference to a daughter was absolutely unthinkable. Impossible.

'Well, why doesn't he send for me then? This place is so utterly dead boring. I'd give anything to live in London. I keep begging him to let me come but he just says Mum won't let me, but if he really wanted to he'd fight her for me. I bet it's that white woman he's got.'

'Well, I don't know. Perhaps he thinks you're better off with your mother. And she hasn't got anyone but you. I think it's fair enough. And you must admit she's brilliant. I'd give anything for a mother like that.'

'Why? What's yours like?'

'Oh, you know... nothing special. Old-fashioned housewife type. She's very religious. Boring. But my dad's worse. Much worse. He's lethal.'

And then she told Trixie all about her family. About Ma and Baba, and about the Ghosh boy, and having to marry him. About the prison of her life.

'It's like living in a convent,' she complained. 'I've got to break out else I'll just go crazy, I tell you. And it's so unfair. All my half-brothers and my brother get to go to London to university, and me? No way. Why can't I go to London too? Just because I'm a bloody girl!'

'Well,' said Trixie, flashing her long white grin, 'we'll soon see about that. You came to just the right person. Saroj, why don't we just run away to London? I mean, not now, but later, like when we're sixteen? If we start planning for it now, then...'

Their eyes met then, and they grinned at each other, and both of them knew.

They knew; not in the sense of knowing this or that. Not that they could see into the future and sense what it held for them, or that they knew of Destiny's plan for them, or about Ganesh and Nat and London and the babies they would or wouldn't have, and all the rest of it. They simply knew. They recognised. They cognised.

As if some little spark in Trixie cognised some little spark in Saroj, and those two bright little sparks leaped in joy and bounced out at each other saying, Hi, here I am! Been missing you all my life. That's the way true friendships begin, those rare friendships as true as gold, that stand the knocks of time. Trixie yelped.

'Saroj: you and me in Carnaby Street, okay?'

They clapped and slapped their hands, hugged and laughed. A battle-cry was born.

Chapter 11

Savitri
Madras, 1921

M r Baldwin had been David's tutor for two years now. Fiona's governess, Miss Chadwick, had resigned to marry a civil-service chap, and in fact it was through this very man that the Lindsays were introduced to Mr Baldwin, who was immediately employed to replace Miss Chadwick. Mr Baldwin's father was also a civil servant, and Mr Baldwin had been born in Bombay. He had gone 'home' for schooling, of course, but as soon as he could he had come back to his real home, which was India, to seek a position as private tutor. The Lindsays were his first employers, and he was only twenty-one when he was given charge over Fiona, nine, and David, four. From the very start they loved him.

Mr Baldwin made learning a delight. No subject was so boring that Mr Baldwin could not bring to it the light of humour, and reflect it with a fascination that made them eager to learn. He was a small, wiry, energetic man, perpetually in motion. Children must learn with movement, was his devise. He had them climbing trees to count the leaves, and digging holes to bury stones. He took them for nature walks, talking first to David, on his level, and then to Fiona, on her level, explaining and discussing their discoveries. Mrs Lindsay, at first perplexed by these unorthodox methods, quickly saw the amazing results, and left well alone.

Mr Baldwin had long been aware of Savitri. He had first discovered her in January that year, hiding in the middle of a thick bougainvillea bush just behind the rose arbour, silently watching and listening while he taught Fiona long division and David the addition of single digits. He might not have noticed her at all if it had not been for the hairs on the back of his neck. They stood on end. Mr Baldwin knew he was being watched, and from behind. He let the children work for a while on their own simply to give himself the time to adjust to the situation and figure out how to react.

The feeling of being watched was insistent; he was quite certain of it. But there was nothing unpleasant about it. The watcher was not hostile. Mr Baldwin held his thoughts still for a while to see what would happen... and there! In the space between two thoughts he felt it; something soft and gentle, like the tendril of a honeysuckle vine, perhaps, reaching out, easing in, settling down comfortably right there between his thoughts, with a cosy warm stillness, like honey, seeping in through the spaces in his mind and filling him with sweet, benevolent warmth. Its source was the thick silence behind him, behind the lattice-work of the rose arbour.

Mr Baldwin moved so that he half-faced the lattice. He did not turn his face but strained to see out of the corner of his left eye, and when that told him nothing stretched out for David's exercise book. Pretending to correct the exercises David had just done, he managed to turn in the right direction and carefully peered over the edge of the book. The diamond holes between the criss-crossing slabs of green wood were black, for the bougainvillea was tall and thick. But in one of those dark diamonds something shone, something small and living, which Mr Baldwin knew to be an eye.

He looked at David then. 'What's the name of that little girl you like to play with? The girl who waits for you after lessons?'

'Savitri?' said David, looking up. Mr Baldwin's sharpened hearing noted a swift intake of breath from the depths of the bougainvillea.

'Yes, that's it. Did you know she's watching us?'

The moment he spoke the words Savitri took off. Like a frightened chipmunk she charged from the midst of the bush and would have disappeared into the foliage beyond had Mr

Baldwin, anticipating her flight, not been faster, and had her skirt not caught on one of the branches blocking her path. But there he was, waiting for her as she emerged from behind the cascading orange blossoms, torn, scratched and dishevelled, a taut, tiny thing with arms so skinny he thought they'd snap as he closed his fists around them.

She did not struggle. Her nature was not to struggle against but to face up to adversity in all calmness. So she looked into his face with innocent capitulation and said only, 'Excuse me, Mr Baldwin. Please don't tell the madam.'

But that was far from Mr Baldwin's mind. He let go of the child, only to take her little hand in his and lead her around the latticework into the rose arbour where Fiona and David stared at her, Fiona in surprise, David in joy.

'Come on, sit down, sit down,' said Mr Baldwin, patting the bench beside him, and, her shyness put to flight by his very heartiness, she slipped onto the bench and looked up at him in expectant silence, her fingers interlocked on the table before her.

'Do you go to school, Savitri?' asked Mr Baldwin.

'Sometimes. When I don't have to help my father.' She said it matter-of-factly, without complaint.

'Do you like school?'

She nodded vigorously.

'Can you show me what you've learned?'

Savitri nodded again, drew David's book towards her and picked up his pencil. She bent over the exercise book and, the tip of her tongue licking over her bottom lip in concentration, wrote for several minutes, watched by Mr Baldwin and the two children.

When she was finished she pushed the book over to Mr Baldwin and he read, written in a small, disjointed, childish but nevertheless precise script:

I wonderd lonely as a cluod...

Mr Baldwin read the poem aloud and then he looked at Savitri and said. 'Who taught you to write this?'

'I learned it from David's book, sir. From David's poetry book. He lent it to me.'

'Do you know what a daffodil is?'

She nodded. 'It's a flower, a yellow flower.'

'Do you know what daffodils looks like? Have you seen a picture?'

'No, sir, but I think they must look like marigolds. Marigolds are yellow too, and gold, like little suns. So it's like a whole field of marigolds, and they're dancing in the sunshine. I closed my eyes and I saw them.'

Mr Baldwin had looked at her intently for a long time, not saying anything, and she felt the spaces in his thought-body and knew he was not like other grown-up people. But after that she was careful not to be caught again.

Mr Baldwin first discovered that Savitri could speak with animals on the day the king cobra came. David screamed when the cobra glided across their path through the swampy area in the back drive, and Mr Baldwin cried, 'Look out! Get back!' He looked around for a weapon, but there was none. The cobra reared his hooded head and shook his tongue, hissed, stared at them as if considering where to strike, and there were waves of venomous anger all around them, and waves of fear. But Savitri silently edged forward in front of David, pushing him gently back. She closed her eyes and bowed to the cobra, asking his forgiveness, for they had disturbed him in his kingdom. She faced the cobra and drew the waves of fear and anger into herself, dissolving them, and the cobra, seeing the danger was gone, slid on his way into the undergrowth.

When the cobra was gone Mr Baldwin laid a hand on Fiona's upper arm, which was cold from fear and shaking, and David's sunbrowned face looked pale with fright. Only Savitri was unperturbed. She looked up to meet Mr Baldwin's gaze.

'Child, you were very brave!' said the teacher. But she shook her head.

'No, sir, I wasn't brave. He's my friend. I've often seen him, he lives near the anthill and he doesn't hurt anybody. He's the King, here, you know.'

'Muthu must get one of the boys to kill him. You can help

to find him.'

'No, no! You mustn't kill him!' Savitri cried. 'He won't hurt anybody, I promised him nobody would hurt him and then he won't hurt anybody and if I break my promise he'll be angry and then he will hurt somebody! Please, please Mr Baldwin, don't tell Mrs Lindsay! He's my friend and he trusts me! I'll talk to him and tell him not to come on this path again but please don't tell the mistress!'

'What do you mean, he's your *friend?* Do you go near him of your own accord?'

'But of course, Mr Baldwin. I talk to him and he talks to me.'

'How do you talk to him?'

'I bow down. Inside me I bow down and at the very bottom of myself I find the space where I can talk to him. We can be friends because we are both in that space.'

Mr Baldwin nodded. 'I see. And can you talk to other animals this way?'

'Oh yes, with all animals because all animals are in that space. And birds too.'

Mr Baldwin turned to David. 'Did you know that, David? That she can talk to animals?'

David nodded proudly. 'Oh yes, sir. I know. All the animals love her and come near. Even the little squirrels and the birds.'

Savitri wasn't sure if Mr Baldwin approved or not, and was a little anxious for the cobra, because killing the King would be very inauspicious and bring bad luck on the whole family — the Lindsay family, for killing him, and the Iyer family, for she, an Iyer, would have broken her promise to the King.

But Mr Baldwin only gave her that curious look and said nothing.

He had given her that curious look before — last week, when the Lindsays returned from Ooty and school had started again, this time without Fiona. Savitri had showed him the exercise book she had filled in the holidays. He had leafed through it, read the pages filled with writing, poems copied from David's book, and passages from the Bible. He had looked at her and said nothing. This was strange, for an Englishman. Usually they had so many words they left no spaces at all, which was why they were so difficult to know. But Mr Baldwin spoke Savitri's language. He knew about silence.

Chapter 12

Nat
Madras, 1949

A few days after the day that never was, Doctor said to Nat, 'Tomorrow we are going to Madras, Nat. I want you to meet someone.'

So that Friday afternoon the two of them mounted the Triumph and set off for Madras. It was a ride of over seven hours, but they broke it several times, stopping at wayside coffee shops where Nat had a Gold Spot and Milk Bikis and Doctor drank coffee and ate a whole bunch of apple-bananas, and they stopped for tiffin at a restaurant called Ashok Lodge where Nat ate two *puris* and Doctor ate an enormous paper *dosai* at least two feet long, crisp and folded over. Arriving in the city, Doctor wove his motorbike through an alarming medley of buses, motor-rickshaws, lorries, cars, all of which seemed to have no other goal in mind than to attack the two of them perched on their defenceless Triumph, charging into them and swerving away at the very last second with a deafening blare of the horn.

On the other hand the pedestrians, cows, goats, cyclists, pushcarts and cycle-rickshaws all seemed in mortal danger of being smashed into by them, meandering as they were with total unconcern across the streets; more than once they touched another road user and Nat clung to his father's waist as a baby monkey clings to its mother, squeezing his eyes together and praying. But Doctor was an expert motorcyclist and brought Nat safe and unharmed to a tall but narrow pink concrete house in a quiet side street. They descended from the Triumph, Nat's knees still trembling a little, and Doctor banged loudly on a big knocker on the front door, and called out 'Henry!' just for good measure.

Almost immediately the door flew open and Doctor was in the arms of another, shorter, man, another *sahib*, each patting the other on the back and exclaiming, 'Good to see you again, old fellow!' and such things. This went on for some time, and finally the two men separated and Nat saw, when the shorter man turned to look down at him, that he was also older.

'So this is your little lad!' said the man.

And Doctor said, 'Yes, this is Nat. Nat, this is Uncle Henry!'

Yet another uncle! Nat was wary of uncles now; after all, his father's greeting with Gopal Uncle had been just as joyful and warm as this one, and look how that had ended! Nat felt a tug of fear; he wasn't really sure what an uncle was, and his first experience with this species had been fraught with untold dangers; also, uncles all seemed to be connected with Madras, and Nat knew for himself what a dangerous place Madras was. But there was nothing he could do about it. And anyway, he was dead tired after the long ride on the motorcycle, and now it was dark. Uncle Henry showed him a *sharpai* in an upstairs room he was to share with his father, and after a quick wash and cleaning his teeth Nat dropped down and curled up on it. He was too excited to sleep, so he dreamily listened to his father and Uncle Henry talking.

'I'm a bit worried, Henry,' said Doctor. 'In a way Gopal's right. I've kept Nat away from the world far too long, sheltered him and kept him out of harm's way.'

'You're only doing the best you can,' said Uncle Henry.

'I've raised him like one of those tamarind saplings the Reforestation Agency planted all over the hill, with high walls of mud bricks around them to prevent the cows and the goats from eating them and the scavenging children from cutting them down to take home for firewood. One day the saplings will be little trees, strong and resilient, and it won't matter if goats nibble at their lowest branches or if a child breaks off a twig or two. And one day those trees will be so tall and strong they can give shade and take in a family of monkeys in their branches, and bear fruit

for the women to make *sambar* with. That's the future I see for
Nat. But what if I'm wrong?'

'Don't be too ambitious for him. Children have a way of
doing what they want, despite the best laid plans.'

'That's why I built those walls, Henry. And it will hurt to take
them down; will he be strong enough?'

'You can't shield him for ever,' said Uncle Henry.

'Henry, I know,' said Doctor. 'It's time to start taking down
those walls, brick by brick. It's time for Nat to meet the big wide
world outside the village. That's why I brought him here. To meet
you.'

The next morning Nat found out more about Uncle Henry,
because his father went out soon after breakfast, leaving him
alone with the man. Nat didn't want him to go. He was afraid
he'd never come back; that this uncle, too, would want to keep
him for ever. Hadn't his father said, last night, that Uncle Henry
was to show him the world? But Doctor seemed to understand
the boy's fear and said, 'I'm just going to do some boring things
at some offices, Nat, and I have to buy some more medicines, do
grown-up things, so stay with Uncle Henry, you'll have fun. I'll
be back for lunch.'

And truly, Nat had fun with Uncle Henry. The first thing
Uncle Henry did was tell him that, long ago, he had been Doctor's
teacher, right here in Madras, and that he'd known Doctor way
back when Doctor was as small as he, Nat, was now. This was a
revelation for Nat. Somehow he believed his father had always
been big and all-knowing, like God. It was strange to think of
him being a little boy, and having to learn things.

'Did Daddy go to the English Medium Matriculation
School?' Nat asked, and Uncle Henry chuckled.

'No, Nat, your daddy didn't go to school till much, much
later. I used to come to his home and teach him there, all by
himself — well, not quite. There was another little boy and two
other little girls. But it wasn't really a school, like the one you go
to. Come, Nat, I want to show you some things . . .'

What Uncle Henry had to show him were books — but not
like the ones he knew at school. Uncle Henry's books were in

boxes; they were story books that had once belonged to his own children, and they now belonged to Nat. Uncle Henry settled down on a couch, leaning on some cushions against the wall, with Nat on his lap, and read to him, and when Daddy came back they were still like that, both laughing their heads off with tears streaming out of their eyes. After that Nat no longer feared Uncle Henry would keep him.

They went places together, the three of them, in Uncle Henry's motorcar. To a wonderful big garden, with lots of flowers in all colours and an enormous tree, which Daddy said was the biggest banyan tree in the world. This place was called Adyar, and Daddy said he used to come here often when he was a boy. Nat wanted to ask him more about when he was a boy, but now he and Uncle Henry were talking about grown-up things he couldn't understand. And the next day they went to the ocean, and Nat played with the sand on the beach, and even went into the water. But it was difficult to swim because the ocean moved around a lot, rushing forward in long foaming rolls which made him shriek in delight and run away, as if it were a living thing out to get him. It was the most marvellous day in his life, except for the day his father had taken him from the place with all the children.

That afternoon Nat and his father got on the Triumph to return home, but now Nat knew he had a grown-up friend, that uncles were not necessarily bad, and that Uncle Henry would come to see them soon. In the side-bags were three storybooks. His father had promised to read them to him, and Uncle Henry would bring the rest when he came.

Uncle Henry came regularly after that visit, and after a year he built a house of his own next door to Doctor's and moved in permanently. Now Nat had his very own teacher, but so did the village children, because Uncle Henry said that any child who wanted to could come and join Nat. The problem was that the children did not speak English, so Uncle Henry had to give them extra English lessons, which he did in the evenings. And some of them almost caught up with Nat, but most of them didn't, and many had to leave again to help their parents with their work. But, Uncle Henry said, 'It's a beginning, Nat, it's a beginning. When you are big we will have a school of our own, a good school where all the children can go.'

Chapter 13

Saroj
Georgetown, 1964

Ma began her day with sweeping. Each morning Saroj awoke to the faint slash-slash of Ma's pointer-broom in the yard as she swept away the night and the cobwebs. Ma said sweeping cleared the mind. For Ma it was much more important what you thought than what you did or what you said. 'Everything begins with thought,' Ma said. So when she finished sweeping she'd spend half an hour drawing a rice-flour *kolam* at the front door's threshold, every day a different one. She'd begin by letting the rice powder drop from her fingers in a gridwork of dots, and then she'd connect the dots in swirls and lines till a wondrous, complicated symbol emerged, perfectly symmetrical, fragile, a temporary work of art that, by midday, was worn away by the uncaring feet of people leaving and entering the house.

Ganesh, who spoke to Ma about these things, once told Saroj the meaning: 'When you walk across the *kolam*,' he said, 'it draws all your bad thoughts and all your sins out through your foot-soles, so you enter the house purified.'

Saroj had only sneered. Another one of Ma's superstitions.

Yet the day she brought Trixie home she stalled for just a second before leading her over the *kolam*; an eerie sense of guilt, of doing something forbidden, shameful even, overcame her. Suppose there really was some magic, some kind of spell in that *kolam*! Some kind of curse, if you crossed it with wrong intention! It was there still: superstition. So ingrained in her was culture. A diffuse fear of unknown forces seeing all; karma coming back to grab her. Nonsense, she reasoned. Superstition. And anyway, this wasn't really *wrong*. What was wrong about showing Trixie Indrani's wedding sari?

Saroj hadn't foreseen that Trixie was a diehard romantic of the prince-on-a-white-steed and lived-happily-ever-after variety. Mention the word 'wedding' and stars gathered in Trixie's eyes and she'd dream aloud about her own future prince. And though she'd giggled at the idea of Saroj's pre-arranged wedding to a puny prince with protuberant teeth bearing the name of Keedernat Ghosh, and promised to rescue her from such a dire fate, it was only in order to 'fix Saroj up' with a suitor of her own choosing. For Trixie knew lots of boys. Highly marriageable ones.

Saroj wrestled the admission from Trixie that Lucy Quentin thoroughly disapproved of her romantic dreams, and forbade her the Love Picture Library and Mills and Boon novels she thrived on and kept hidden under her mattress.

Trixie in turn wrestled from Saroj the story of Indrani's impending wedding, and a reluctant description of that most exquisite of wedding saris hidden in Ma's sandalwood trunk in the *puja* room, and, with the bull-headed but charming persuasiveness so typical of her, the promise to show it to her, one of these days, when the house was empty.

Today was that day.

'Sshh!' Saroj pressed a finger to her lips and warned Trixie with her eyes. She showed her how to edge along the wall, like thieves, because the middle floorboards were loose and creaked, and they still had a long way to the master bedroom at the far end of the upstairs gallery. In fact, there wasn't all that much danger because Baba was at work and wouldn't be back till late, and Ma had taken Indrani to talk marriage business with the Ramcharans, Indrani's future in-laws, and Ganesh was at a cricket match and wouldn't come home till dark.

But Baba's threatening spirit, dour and disapproving, loomed everywhere, hiding in the very breath of this house, and made you scared even if there was nothing to be scared of. He'd be livid if he knew she'd taken Trixie into the private quarters, and the very idea of Trixie's impure African eyes on Indrani's consecrated wedding sari — well, that didn't bear imagining. But Trixie had pleaded and begged, and self-importance swelled up inside Saroj now as she turned the knob, opened the door, and beckoned her inside, exchanging a smile of conspiracy with her. It gave her a rush of excitement to think of defying Baba so blatantly, bringing an African into his sacred home, into the most sacred room. She felt daring, heroic. A pity that Babu would never find out!

There were two staircases to the upper storey of the Roy house: the hardly-used tower stairs and the main stairs leading from the drawing room to the upstairs inner gallery, a square surrounded by bedrooms and bathrooms. All the rooms had a door into the gallery and another into the next room, so it was possible to circle the house by walking through them.

Saroj's parents' room was the biggest of all, a corner room overlooking the magnificent back garden, huge and light and airy because of the sash windows lining two of the walls, all pushed up to let in the Atlantic breeze. Ma kept the room meticulously neat, which wasn't hard to do because it was so sparsely furnished, just the big bed in the middle with the mosquito net twisted up and slung into the hoop which held it, a polished wardrobe and matching vanity table on top of which was a doily, a hairbrush and comb side by side, the red pencil with which she carefully drew the round red tika between her eyebrows, and the little white jar of Pond's Vanishing Cream which held the entire repertoire of Ma's beauty secrets, a metaphor for Ma herself. Vanishing Ma.

The vanity table had a full-length mirror with side wings and as the two girls tiptoed across the room Saroj saw herself and Trixie in stark contrast: Trixie in a tie-dyed T-shirt and shorts, she herself in the grey-and-black chequered dress Baba made her wear because it was modest, the hemline six inches below the knee, a high neck that emphasised the flatness of her chest. She looked away quickly, cringing, disgusted. She couldn't bear to see herself in a mirror.

When Ma brushed and plaited her hair every morning and evening it was at this mirror, Saroj sitting on the little vanity stool, Ma standing behind, slashing away at the hair with a vigour that seemed to curl out of her little body and whirl all around Saroj.

Her hair would bristle and crackle with static; it seemed Ma was charging her with silent strength at these hair-brushing sessions, the way her right hand with the brush swept briskly to and fro, up and down, back and forth, and Ma's slight torso remained as still as a statue, her left hand firm on Saroj's shoulder to keep her from rocking in time to the sweeping curves of the brush, the gold bangles on her right wrist jangling in rhythm, her little heart-shaped face a centre of calm in the midst of all the crackling movement. And when she'd finished Saroj's hair would fall down her back in an unbroken black glossy sheet, reaching down, down below the vanity stool. Ma would plunge her hands into the mass and hold it up, inspect it for split ends, bend over to open the little door of the vanity and take out the bottle of coconut oil, carefully pour four or five drops onto the palm of her right hand, rub her palms together and then into Saroj's scalp, and finally with deftly flicking fingers plait the hair into one thick bulky rope which when Saroj stood up would dangle way past her bottom. By the time Saroj was of marriageable age, Ma said, it would reach her knees.

Never, Saroj swore. She'd cut it off, before then; or kill herself, depending on her mood.

The sari was in the *puja* room, a windowless little room which must once have been used as a walk-in closet just off the master bedroom. It was dark in there, but a little eternal flame burned still and smokeless from the spout of a small brass lamp on the shrine. The lamp itself was of brass so highly polished that it glimmered gold beneath the flame. In the darkness you could see the aura of blue-rimmed light surrounding it in a perfect halo.

Saroj wasn't superstitious, but even for her, and against her will — this room was holy. You could actually feel the holiness in every intaken breath, with the lingering perfume of that morning's incense mingled with the faint scent of rose and jasmine from the blossoms on the shrine, the sacred ashes from the little brass bowl and the oil from the little brass lamp. You could feel holiness in the way time stood still when the girls entered: time, and even thoughts, absorbed by the power of the dawn mantras Ma sang here daily, even before she went down to sweep under the house.

Guilt rose up in Saroj once more. She knew from years of experience what kind of thoughts you were supposed to think here, but Trixie didn't. *I shouldn't have brought her*, she said to herself, and glanced uneasily at her friend. She could see the whites of her eyes in the half-light, and the irreverent curiosity in them as she looked around, taking in the pictures of Shiva and Ganesh and Saraswati on the walls, the soapstone lingam and the black statue of Nataraj dancing, the rosary of *rudrakshra* beads on the shrine, and Ma's sword. She'd be having the wrong kind of thoughts, gross, worldly, curious, unholy thoughts, and she'd leave them here all sticky and heavy when she left, and Baba would know she'd been here, and when Baba the bloodhound came sniffing in he would...

Saroj didn't dare think further but quickly focused on the task at hand, kneeled down on the straw mat, opened the clasp of the heavy sandalwood chest next to the shrine, and beckoned Trixie to kneel beside her. But Trixie's hands reached out and picked up the statue of Nataraj and turned it around so she could inspect it, and she said, 'What's this supposed to be? One of your Hindu gods?' flippant as can be, so Saroj answered just as flippantly, 'That's Nataraj.'

'And who's that little guy under his feet?'

'Oh, I think that's supposed to be the ego or whatever. You'd have to ask Ma, I don't know all these myths and stuff.' She took the Nataraj from Trixie and replaced it firmly. She saw Trixie's hands wandering towards the Ganesh but before she could pick it up Saroj said quickly, 'Look, Trixie, the sari!'

And she raised the lid of Ma's chest.

Ma had brought this chest from India when she came to British Guiana to marry Baba. It was full of secret things. Saroj had inspected it many times when Ma was at the Purushottama Temple. Most of it was filled with wooden boxes containing little glass bottles, and those glass bottles containing all sorts of powders, little pills, herbs, dried flowers and all sorts of mysterious things. They were Ma's medicines. They rested on a wad of folded cotton, faded blue and slightly torn. It might have been an old folded sari but Saroj never unfolded it to make sure because she never wanted to waste time. Ma usually spent an age at the Purushottama Temple but you never could tell.

Beneath this folded cloth were some books which, arranged side by side, formed the chest's bottom layer. There was an ancient book of English poetry, called The Swallow Book of Verse, and another book of poems by some Indian poet called Tagore, and a book in some Indian script Saroj couldn't read, and an English autobiography of Gandhi.

There was a little gold cross on a gold chain in The Swallow Book of Verse, like a bookmark, which surprised Saroj because Ma wasn't a Christian. So why did she keep a cross? This was just another of Ma's little secrets — the secrets of a suppressed Hindu housewife who, not having much of a life, built her own from household banalities, symbols, artefacts, curiosities found in the Stabroek Market or brought from India centuries ago.

The chest itself was carved all over with the most wondrous figures, peacocks and gods and goddesses and flowers and trees, each tiny leaf in meticulous relief, three-dimensional scenes on all four sides and on the curved lid. Saroj's earliest memories were of tracing the labyrinth of branches, vines and snakes with a chubby forefinger in the semi-darkness, of delving with her toddler's mind into that wooden sand-coloured world, while Ma sat on the mat beside her, working her *sruti*-box with one hand, eyes closed in rapture as she sang for Shiva, her ardent voice sinking and rising and held by the full round single sruti note. Now Trixie, too, reached out to touch the carvings.

'It's so beautiful!' she whispered, and the awe in her voice consoled Saroj for whatever sin she might be committing.

'Yes,' she agreed, and opened the box.

The sari now lay on top of all Ma's secrets. A flat red square the size of a lady's handkerchief, protected from the medicine boxes by a folded bedspread. It was of a silk so sheer, so fine, so exquisite, that even folded it was not much thicker than a child's finger. Saroj lifted it and held it up tenderly. It felt as fragile, light and frail as a living baby bird, so slippery it felt alive, sliding across her little hands so that she had to cup her palms to stop it from slipping down to the floor.

Trixie's mesmerised gasp gave her deep satisfaction; she wanted her to see more, to wonder more.

'It's too dark in here, you can't see the colour properly,' Saroj whispered. 'Come, I'll show you in the light. The *colour's* the thing.'

'Are you sure?' There was worry in Trixie's voice, but already Saroj was on her knees, on her feet, walking to the door, across to the bed, holding the sari carefully and fixing it with her thumbs, placing it carefully on the white sheet where it shone in a pool of sunlight, in a thousand iridescent shades of red: carmine, and ruby, cerise, and blood.

'Red!' Trixie sounded shocked. 'I thought it would be white. You didn't say it was red!'

'Blood-red!' Saroj agreed.

'No, ruby-red! Look how it shines, like it has jewels in it!' Trixie slid a finger under a layer of silk and raised it slightly so that it caught a ray of sunlight and a breath of breeze, making it shimmer with liquid softness.

'It's Indrani's lifeblood,' Saroj insisted. 'She's giving her life away. That's why she has to get married wrapped in blood.'

'Don't say that!' Trixie raised her voice, horrified, but Saroj just laughed.

'But you should see the *border,'* she continued. 'That's the most incredible thing.'

Because, despite the biting sarcasm so carefully cultivated, turning everything into a joke the way Ganesh did, Saroj couldn't help it: the whole business of Indrani's wedding and the tradition out of which it arose alternately fascinated and appalled her, made her sick to her stomach, made her heart race and her own blood tingle.

The Ghosh boy came to mind. They'd send for a sari like this for her. They'd powder and perfume her and rub her with sandal-wood paste and turmeric and whatever, and draw henna pictures on the palms of her hand, and place jewels on her body, and wrap it with a sari, like this one. The sari symbolised the horror of it all — and yet it was so beautiful!

Now Saroj wanted to show it off, to get a few more *ahs* and *ohs* from Trixie, who had all the things denied Saroj, who led the life she wanted for herself, and to pay her back for being here, now, in faded frayed shorts and a tie-dyed T-shirt, looking American and casual and modern, with her black hair clipped so short it hugged her head in a tight cap like a boy's. Trixie and Saroj had exactly the same colour skin: dark chocolate. They had laid their arms together to see if one of them was lighter, but they were both the same shade. Exactly the same. And they were both tall and slim, Trixie a bit taller. They both had full lips, Trixie's a bit thicker, and huge black eyes, Saroj's a bit huger and blacker. But all similarities ended with their hair. Trixie's was African and as short as possible, Saroj's Indian and as long as possible. Trixie's crinkly, Saroj's straight.

What a glorious thing was this sari! Saroj couldn't help but feel its spell.

She clapped back one of the folds, and then a second, and a third, so that the sari now lay in two sleek square yards on the bed, the magnificent border revealed. Peacocks and roses; that was the pattern. The border was six inches wide, peacocks woven into the sari's blood with a cobweb-fine golden thread, in and out, depicting in minute detail and intricate artwork the eye of each spread tail, every tiny petal of every rose and rose-leaf, every tiniest feather, peacocks dancing among the roses, their heads held high and proud, their tails wide open to full circles, wheeling along the sari's edge.

'Wow!' said Trixie, and Saroj quickly clapped the sari together, some inner sensibility deeply offended. Trixie was so crude! Couldn't she feel that you can't say 'Wow!' to a magic like this!

'Do you know how to put on a sari?' Trixie asked.

'You mean *wrap* a sari,' Saroj corrected, putting deep dignity and authority into her voice. "Course I do!'

Indrani had been wearing saris for a couple of years

now, ever since she got her first period. Saroj had been there when Ma taught her to wrap one, and she'd always watched, fascinated in spite of herself, whenever Indrani got dressed for special occasions; she'd seen her, and she'd seen Ma, wrap a sari a thousand times. There was nothing to it. It was in Saroj's blood, you could say.

Longing shone in Trixie's eyes.

'Saroj, you think . .

Saroj knew instantly what Trixie was thinking; their eyes met and they smiled in unison. Saroj unfolded the sari again and inspected it. Actually, there wouldn't be much of a problem, folding it back the way it was. It was creased along the folds, all she'd have to do was follow the creases. Ma would never know. It wouldn't take long. She'd be in and out in an instant. Just this once, to have Trixie envy her the way she envied Trixie, for something she could never do and never be: an Indian lady in a magnificent blood-red sari.

'Sure. But I have to wear a petticoat and a sari-blouse. I'll have to borrow those from Indrani.'

'But will it fit you?'

'Saris don't come in sizes, just in lengths,' Saroj said knowledgeably, though she couldn't be quite certain. But anyway, Indrani was thin and not all that much taller than her. 'Wait a sec.'

She flitted out the door and was back in a trice, clutching a crisp white petticoat and a blue sari-blouse. 'These won't match the sari of course, but it doesn't matter, it's just to show you how it looks.'

She stripped down to her underwear, put on the midriff blouse and buttoned it up, stepped into the cotton petticoat, wiggled into it and tied the drawstring tightly at the waist; it was three inches too long so she pulled up that much overlap and bunched it into the waistband.

The secret was to feel confident. Trying to look as if she'd been doing this every day of her life, she held up the sari by its upper edge and let it fall open to its full magnificence; so smooth, so light, so slippery, a delight to the touch; she held it against the petticoat where it swung gently as she confidently tucked in a corner; then, as she'd seen Ma and Indrani do, she grasped the rest of the sari in her left hand, and, holding the end in place, wrapped it once around her hips. She reached for it behind her back and there she made her first mistake. She hadn't counted on it being so very slippery, so very long. She missed some of the slack and yards of blood-red silk flowed gracefully to the floor to form a limpid pool around her feet.

She clucked her teeth in annoyance and bent to pick it up, but in doing so the tucked-in end untucked itself and that, too, fell to the floor.

'I'd better start from the beginning,' she said, a little nervous this time.

'Can I help?' asked Trixie, sitting on the bed and watching.

'No, no, sometimes that happens,' Saroj lied. Indrani and Ma had never dropped a sari, at least not while she was watching, and picking it up she found that the next problem would be getting hold of the whole long thing along one edge while it slithered and snaked around, billowing gently in all directions.

'Close the windows, will you, that breeze isn't helping much,' she said irritably, and Trixie sprang to her feet and closed all four sash windows so that a deathly silence and stillness descended on the room, all the better for Saroj's concentration.

Saroj struggled with the sari for an age. She managed to get it all bunched up into one hand and tuck it into the petticoat again and wrap it once around her waist, and breathed a sigh of relief. Now for the fun part. She flung a long loose train nonchalantly across one shoulder and tried to weave the remaining yards of loose fabric in and out between her fingers for the pleats, the way Ma did it, so expertly, deftly, this being the most important skill in wrapping a sari, but invariably it slid away, like a live thing evading capture. In the breezeless room, gathering heat from the sun's glare through glass, she broke into a sweat and knew it was time to stop.

'I can't!' she said miserably. She looked up at Trixie in an admission of defeat. 'It's no good.'

'It's all right, Saroj,' Trixie said comfortingly, jumping up again. 'But we'd better fold that thing up so that no-one sees we've been at it.'

'Okay, can you help? Look, you hold this end and I'll take the other and then we hold it between us like a sheet, see, and then we fold it . . .'

So they began folding it, and this time it was Trixie who broke into a sweat because the sari really came alive this time, slithering out of alignment every time they got it right so they kept having to start from the beginning. Saroj had her back to the door so it was Trixie who first saw Baba.

She froze. Saroj saw the horror in her eyes and swung around, expecting the worst, and there he was.

That face. The very same face. That face distorted by ugliness, the face he had worn when he had wrenched her from Wayne, a face filled with disgust. Baba took one step towards Trixie.

'Run!' Saroj yelled, and Trixie ran, squeezing past Baba and down the stairs and out of the house.

Standing there, paralysed for the moment, Saroj felt the impending eruption. When Trixie ran, her instinct was to run too, and she tried to slip between Baba and the open doorway and fly down the stairs behind Trixie, but Baba grabbed her arm. Anger spilled out of his eyes. His arm raised to hit her. This time she would not let him.

This time she fought back.

She writhed like a mad thing, kicked his shins, hit him with her free fist. She yelled her own hatred into his face, cursed him with the dirtiest words she had ever heard. Baba, unaccustomed to reaction, could do no more than hold her at a distance as she kicked and wriggled. He pushed her forwards into the room, tried to get his arms around her to hold her still, but that was his mistake because it placed his arm before her face and she dug her teeth into his flesh and bit with all the might and with all the hatred she could muster. Baba cried out in pain and let go. Saroj almost fell down the stairs, out of the front door, into the street and into Trixie's arms.

She was hysterical with laughter.

'I bit him, Trixie! I really did! I bit him, good and hard!'

'What will he do to you?'

Trixie's eyes were opened wide, her brow creased with concern.

'What'll he do? Why, what do I care? Let him do what he likes. What can he do? He'll have those tooth marks a long time.'

It was one thing, though, to declare open warfare on Baba in an impulsive outburst of rage; quite another to re-enter the house and actually face the dragon. Saroj was a sensible girl, not normally given to eruptions of emotion. Euphoric triumph at her bravado lasted but an instant. Trixie's words sank in and she woke up to bitter reality.

Far from having won the battle with Baba, she'd put a load of fresh ammunition into his hands.

'Go home. Quick,' she whispered to Trixie, who leaped onto her bike and sailed off as if a pack of hounds was behind her. Saroj looked up at the windows. No Baba watching. She slipped between the hibiscus bush and the palings and curled up to wait for Ganesh. Her heart throbbed so loudly she could hear it. Baba's revenge, she knew, would not be of the volcano-erupting sort. It would be of the key-turning-slowly-in-the-lock variety.

She was right. Biting Baba only proved to him that she was too hot to handle.

Baba did not strike her this time. Instead, he brought forward the wedding date.

She was to be married the moment she turned fourteen, the minimum marriageable age for girls.

Indrani refused to wear the sari Trixie had touched. Baba sent a telegram to Calcutta, asking for a new one to be rushed over by express air-mail. The exquisite peacock-and-roses sari was still perfectly usable, though polluted by an African hand. Saroj's punishment was to wear that sari on her own wedding day.

'Oh Ghosh!' said Ganesh when he heard.

Chapter 14

Savitri
Madras, 1923

Gopal did not take his babysitting role very seriously, and was not with them the day the king cobra came. He was a dreamy, sensitive lad of thirteen and, not accustomed to Mr Baldwin's unorthodox methods, preferred to sit by himself in the school room or in the rose arbour, reading, for Gopal was not only clever, he was ambitious. One day he would write the Great Indian Modern Novel. In English. He already had a title for it: *Ocean of Tears.*

What good fortune, this babysitting for Savitri! For babysitting was the only way to escape the government school, where the standards were low and the teachers indifferent. This job would open doors for him. It was a matter of influence. The Lindsays had influence. Learning with their private English tutor was the best way to get ahead, and Gopal knew he was fortunate indeed.

Of his brothers he was the only one who felt fortunate. Natesan and Narayan couldn't care less about the English, and Mani still boiled with rage at the insult of David's birth, when Mrs Lindsay had stolen his mother. As simply as that, and without a by-your- leave. He had adored his mother, and that *Ingresi* woman simply said, *come,* and Amma had obeyed, leaving him, Mani, behind.

Mani, eleven at the time, was the eldest and could reason. Why should the English lady simply say: *do this*, or *come,* or *go,* and Amma obey? And why should the English lady have the power to disrupt a whole family and never even spare a thought for this disruption? A family of four boys, a girl, and a husband, left without a mother and a wife. It was atrocious, and Mani, had been appalled at such imperiousness! But the English were like that; they snapped their fingers and you had to run, and that was it.

That was when *Thatha* and Patti moved in, who till now had lived with their eldest son in the north. Patti had managed the family well, but she was exhausted after raising thirteen children of her own and burying four, and when Amma, no more needed in the big house, returned to the family, Patti had quietly and simply taken her leave, and died.

Thatha sat on the east verandah where he lived during the summer months, and gathered the girl Savitri into his mind. The time was coming, he knew. The body, this earthly frame, was growing weak and he would have to release it soon.

Thatha wore only a loincloth and a sacred thread, and an upper cloth across his shoulders. His skin was dark and spotted with age, hanging in leathery folds on his brittle frame. His head was shaved at every full moon and at these times was as shiny as a round brass pot. *Thatha,* permanently fixtured, it seemed, on his ragged mat on the east *tinnai,* the front verandah, surrounded himself with the objects of his trade: bottles containing strange milky liniments, vessels wrapped in rags containing pieces of bark and roots, seeds and dried leaves, pills and ointments and pungent herbs. None of the bottles, jars and boxes had labels. *Thatha* knew what each was for, and when someone came with a problem all he had to do was reach out and his hand would find the right remedy.

Not so many people came these days. They preferred the medicines of the English, even if they had to pay huge sums for these. Nobody had faith any more. Only the little girl Savitri, and upon her *Thatha* fixed his hopes and gathered her into his mind.

His youngest son, who was cook for the *sahibs,* had long forgotten the trade, though he too had once learned the secrets of healing. He also had once been taught that cooking and healing, food and medicine, are two sides of the same coin; that one cannot cook and nourish the body without understanding the balances of the body and how to correct them when they are out of joint. *Thatha* himself knew those secrets, handed down through the family for generations; when his father had been cook in the kitchen of the Maharaja of Mysore many had come to him with their ailments, even the Maharani herself, and he had healed them, and *Thatha* had watched and learned.

Two of his sons, his eldest and his youngest, had become cooks after him, but both had eschewed the other side, the healing; neither had inherited the Gift, and not one of his children carried the Sign. The eldest son now worked in the Hotel Ashok in Bombay, and the youngest son here in Madras. *Thatha* had worked and raised his family in Madras, then moved to Bombay to live with Madanlal till summoned back to Madras, and now he understood why Destiny had ordained this move. It was because of the girl Savitri.

She was only a girl but she had the Gift. And she had the Sign; the tiny round mole behind her right ear. He, *Thatha,* had it too, and his father and great-uncle. When it was time *Thatha* would activate the Gift with his blessing. Now she was receiving instructions, but instructions were not enough. You had to have the Gift. You had to have the Sign. You had to have the Hands. Savitri had them all.

Thatha had one day taken the hands of the girl Savitri in his own and had felt it then: the flow of power — the power to absorb through the one hand, to bestow through the other. To absorb ill, which was nothing but obstruction, coming from the mind, and bestow blessing so the illness could not return and take root again. The girl had it. The flow. The Gift. It lay dormant within her, which meant she could not yet use it consciously. For that she needed Initiation and only he, *Thatha,* could give that, passing along the Gift just as he himself had received it from his father before him. This time, one generation would be skipped, and it would pass to the female line. But that was of no account. Because the Gift came from the Great Spirit which was neither male nor female, but contained the essence of both.

The girl Savitri would receive the Gift, and pass it on to her own children or grandchildren, and so it would not die out. Never. The Gift would always find a way. It was self-perpetuating. *Thatha* smiled to himself and belched. That daughter-in-law of his, Iyer's wife, she was a good cook. But what is cooking if you did not have the Gift? *Thatha* gathered the little girl Savitri into his mind and held her there in silence.

Savitri had been learning with Mr Baldwin for six months when finally the letter came. Iyer took the letter to Mrs Lindsay and humbly begged permission to remove Savitri from schooling.

'Cooky! But no, I cannot allow that! Why, she is making such progress... Mr Baldwin says so, and besides, David would be all alone! Why on earth?'

Savitri said only, 'The mistress begs for an explanation, Appa.'

Iyer played with the paper between his fingers. He handed it to Mrs Lindsay, who only gave it an impatient glance and handed it back, saying, 'It's in Tamil. What is it about?'

'It's about my daughter's marriage, madam,' said Savitri.

'Which daughter? You only have one daughter!' Savitri translated these words for her father and he replied respectfully.

'That is correct. I am speaking of my daughter Savitri,' translated Savitri.

Savitri herself was not present at the conversation. Only her body was. She herself had withdrawn from her thought-body so as not to become entangled in the words she spoke. They had nothing to do with her. She spoke words without thinking what she was speaking. When Mrs Lindsay spoke Savitri turned her words to Tamil, and when her father spoke she turned his words to English. She was a mere vessel of translation through which language flowed back and forth.

'You don't mean Savitri's marriage!'

'She is my only daughter, madam.'

'But for heaven's sake, Cooky, she's only seven! She's a child! You can't marry her off yet! And she's so bright in school, you can't ...' Mrs Lindsay launched into a long speech and Iyer and Savitri heard her out, their faces blank, till she had no more words, Savitri faithfully converting all into Tamil. Then Iyer said, and Savitri repeated, in English:

'My brother Madanlal has found a suitable boy for her in Bombay. He is a cook in the Ashok Lodge. My brother says he is very eligible, despite his clubfoot. Savitri is to go to Bombay to live in my brother's household, until she is of marriageable age, and then she will marry the boy.'

'Yes, but if he is a cook he can't be a boy any more! How old is this fellow?'

'He is twenty-two, madam. A very suitable age, for he will be twenty-eight when they marry. When my daughter is fourteen she will become his legally married wife. But for now she will live in my brother's household.'

It was very important to establish this difference: that it was not to be a child wedding, which would be illegal, but a *betrothal*, an agreement to marry.

'It is only a betrothal. But she shall go to Bombay with my eldest son Mani.'

'If it's only a betrothal why must she go to Bombay now? Why can't she go when she's older, old enough to marry?'

'The boy does not speak English or Tamil. My daughter must go to Bombay so that she can learn his languages Marathi and Hindi,' said Savitri earnestly.

'But, Cooky, no. I cannot allow this. And why Bombay, of all places? Surely there are suitable men in Madras?'

'We have tried to find a husband in Madras but without success. The girl has been polluted by your son.' Savitri said this without once blinking, looking up into Mrs Lindsay's eyes as if begging to be excused.

'Polluted? What on earth do you mean?'

'She has been mixing with him, touching him.'

'Oh, but, for heaven's sake, Cooky, they're just children! They play children's games!'

'It is said in Madras the daughter of Iyer the cook has been polluted by the *sahib* boy. Therefore she must be married away from Madras.' Savitri spoke the words, her own sentence, without the least trace of emotion. They were Appa's words. But her heart understood and was all turmoil, and her thought-body now returned and began to heave and surge in rebellion. And yet she brought forth Appa's arguments as if they were her own, and argued with Mrs Lindsay even while she longed to throw herself at her mistress's feet and beg her for refuge, from Appa, from her brother, her uncle, the clubfoot cook, Bombay, her culture, her land, her people.

That night Savitri came to David's window again, and this time the moon was full.

'They have a husband for me, David! I am to go to Bombay next week!'

'But you promised to marry no-one else but me!'

'But Mani is taking me to Bombay! What can I do?'

'You could run away!'

'Where would I live?'

'With me, of course!'

But Savitri shook her head vigorously and tears stung her eyes, and she wiped them away with her shawl.

'Your mother would not allow it, David. I am only a servant.'

'I'll tell her I'm going to marry you!'

'David! No! Don't tell her that! Promise you won't tell her that!'

'But why not, Sav? If I tell her that then all problems are solved. She always does what I want!'

'David, she won't like that, I just know it. She'll get all red and angry like she did that day when Boy cut down her favourite rose. She'll shout and send me away and then I really will have to leave.'

'It's not true, Sav. Mummy always does what I want. If I say I'm going to marry you she'll tell Cooky and then you can come and live here in our house and when we're grown up we'll marry! Look, I haven't got a ring but keep this! This is my promise to marry you!'

And he slipped a gold chain over his head and handed it to her through the bars, and she took it. She knew what it was:

a gift from David's granny back in England, and it had a little golden cross dangling on the end, and Savitri knew that the cross was something from David's religion, it had to do with their God, and it was like Shiva, so she respected it and knew it was the holiest thing David could have given her. She slipped it over her own head.

'Thank you, David,' she said. 'I shall always keep it with me, and I promise to marry you. But still you should not tell your mother, promise me you won't!'

'But then, Sav, what shall we do?'

And the very helplessness of their position struck them into silence. Who were they, after all, but children? Children at the mercy of merciless adults who had the ultimate control to move them around the face of the earth as if they were mere counters on a gameboard, as if this love did not count, this love which was above all and more powerful than all the thought-bodies in the world. And yet it was powerless against the small group of men in Savitri's family who would carry out their plan, and tear them apart.

'It's just not fair!' said David, and stamped his foot, because for the first time he knew that he, too, was helpless, even against the insubordination of the natives who, he had learned from the very start of his life, were subject to his will. Even he, the young master, could not prevent a servant daughter's marriage.

'No matter what, Savitri, do you promise to marry me? Do you promise? No matter what, Sav, do you vow?'

'Yes, David, of course! I love you with all my heart and I vow to marry you.'

Exasperated by the stubborn logic and insubordination of her cook, Mrs Lindsay lay tossing in her bed. She could dismiss him, of course, but that wouldn't change anything for Savitri. Or she could threaten to dismiss him, if he continued with this plan. Or threaten to turn him in to the authorities for trying to circumvent the law against child marriage — for what was this, in effect, but a child marriage, even if it should be consummated at a later date?

She simply could not allow it. Here in Fairwinds she was mistress, and not Iyer! How dare he go against her will, even if Savitri was his daughter! *She,* after all, knew better. And Savitri must finish her education, or at least continue it a little longer. Cooky was being too, too ridiculous. Pollution, indeed! If anyone was being polluted it was David, from mixing with a servant's child — (but no, it was wrong to think along those lines. We are all equal.) Any other father — any *English* father — would be happy for his daughter to receive such an excellent education. And such a bright girl, too. And what about David? Who would he play with, if Savitri left? This thought struck Mrs Lindsay as no other. David would be devastated. He would have not a single friend in Oleander Gardens — it was too late to make new friends now, and he'd be all alone, isolated, and it was years until he could be sent to school in England — four at least. For David's sake, she must do something.

And that was when Mrs Lindsay remembered her vow to 'do something' for the girl, so many months ago, before they'd gone to Ooty, before she'd started lessons with Mr Baldwin. And knowledge hit her like a snap of lightning. She knew exactly what she would do.

She would write to her solicitor.

She would make arrangements to have some money set aside in some sort of trust fund for Savitri. She was vague about such things but her solicitor would surely know. Yes; money, a dowry... Mrs Lindsay's mind ticked out a plan. The money should be promised now, under contract, and handed over when Savitri was eighteen — on the condition that she was not yet married. On the condition that she continued her education at least until she was fourteen. On the condition that she lived in her father's house till then, and was not shipped to Bombay or anywhere else to wait for marriage.

Mrs Lindsay was so excited she sat up in bed. Brilliant!

She got out of bed and padded to the window, her mind hard at work. The moon was full and the garden was cast in a silvery light, as though enchanted — the fragrances of rose and jasmine, even the very subtle strain of frangipani, met her nostrils and she breathed deeply. Ah ... wonderful. Fragrances carried far in the thin Indian atmosphere. Fragrances — and sounds. The breeze, whispering among the bougainvillea and the roses — whispering, as if human. As if human ... Mrs Lindsay listened, her senses sharpened by the underlying magic of the garden, and it was then she realised that the whispering was human, that it came from the next window, David's. And peering through the moonlight Mrs Lindsay saw a small shadowy form which could only be Savitri's, and though it was too late to hear the entire conversation, she did hear the last desperate words spoken by the children, their voices raised now in the forgetfulness of their fervour, and as clear as bells:

'No matter what, Savitri, do you promise to marry me? Do you promise? No matter what? Say, do you promise?'

'Yes, David, of course! I love you with all my heart and I promise to marry you.'

Chapter 15

Nat
A Village in Madras State, 1950 — 1957

Nat, the villagers believed, always brought good luck. They noticed that when he played cricket with his friends his team always won, and so they said he had a Golden Hand, and they adopted him as their lucky mascot. When a house was to be built, they asked Nat to lay the first brick, and when it was finished, they asked him to be the first to enter it, leading in the cow with the garland around her neck and her horns painted yellow and red, and hung with bells. When the weeding season started in the fields they asked him to pull the first weed, and at weddings they asked him to touch the statue of Ganesh at the beginning of the ceremony, for Ganesh removes obstacles. But the best part of being a good luck mascot was the eating of sweets. Whenever condiments were prepared for any special occasion the mother of the house sent for Nat to eat the very first one, after the Blessing, and to pass his hand over all the rest. These things his father allowed.

'If I can take the first sweet, why can't I be the first to get milk from Kanairam's cow?' Nat asked Doctor. And Doctor had answered, 'Because sometimes Kanairam's cow does not have enough milk for everybody and they need the milk more than you. So I want you to go last, and then buy two cups, if he has so much. And if Kanairam's cow does not have enough milk then you can come home without and you can have Amul Spray powdered milk, but the villagers cannot do that. So I want you to be the last to buy milk, so that everybody gets milk, and Kanairam sells all his milk.'

Doctor did not believe that Nat brought good luck. He

said the villagers only thought Nat brought good luck because his skin was so light, and they thought if Nat touched them or their things their babies would be born light-skinned too, and this was the real reason, and Doctor told Nat that the villagers believed light skin was better than dark skin, but it was not true. Nat thought much about these things, about what the villagers believed and what Doctor told him. He knew his father always told the truth, but he also knew it was true that the team he was on would win, even though he wasn't the best bowler — that was Gopal; or the best batter — that was Gautam; or the fastest — that was Ravi, Anand's son.

And yet Nat's team always won, and the villagers put Nat first in all they did, to bring them luck.

Still his father taught him to put himself last.

One thing was certain: Nat certainly brought luck to Gauri Ma. Somehow Nat had always noticed Gauri Ma, sitting in the first court of the temple near the Parvati tank, holding out her stumps to him and his father. Gauri Ma had leprosy. She didn't have feet, just two clumps at the end of her legs, wrapped in rags, and her wrists were bent curiously forwards, so that they formed two hooks, in which Gauri Ma, though she had no fingers, could manage to hold things by pressing the stumps of her hands to close the hooks.

Although she was a grown woman Gauri Ma was as thin and slight as a girl of twelve. Her skin hung on her little bones like a loose sack of thin, soft, black leather, and the ragged piece of cloth she wrapped around herself as a sari barely covered her lower parts. Like all the poorer women of the region she wore no upper clothing, but simply draped the shawl of her cloth across her sagging breasts and over her left shoulder. Nat noticed Gauri Ma the very first day she came to the temple, because of the lovely way she smiled at him, a smile much too wide for the little wizened face and much too joyful for the ragged piece of misery that she was, and showing a haphazard array of teeth reddened by chewing *paan*. That first day Nat, walking through the temple with his father, was stopped by just this smile. He stood in front of Gauri Ma (he didn't of course know her name), clamped the bunch of little bananas he had bought for the Mother gently under his arm, and greeted her with a smile of his own, the palms of his hands together, then pulled at his father's lungi.

'I'm going to give her something!' he said to his father. Doctor usually did not give anything to the beggars; or if he did, he gave to all. He would change about thirty rupees into one-rupee coins and distribute them among the beggars. He said he had to do it this way, because the moment they saw you giving to one beggar, they would swarm around you and follow you into the temple as far as they could go, calling out behind you, so it was better to give to none, or all. So Nat's words were very extraordinary, but this did not occur to him until he had spoken them, and realised that they had no one-rupee coins to give to all the beggars.

But the words were spoken, and words once spoken could not be withdrawn, and since Nat knew his father had no one-rupee coins he knew he'd have to give something of his own, so he took the bunch of bananas from under his arm, which were gold-yellow with not a trace of green, bulging with ripeness but not yet overripe, perfectly unblemished and as fit an offering to the Goddess Parvati as anything to be found in Town, and held it out to Gauri Ma, and she took it with her hooks and her smile widened all the more.

'Thank you, oh thank you,' she said, and touched it to her forehead several times, bowing her head in gratitude, and smiling her lovely smile which made Nat want to cry.

And from that day, whenever Nat saw Gauri Ma in the temple grounds, he would stop and smile and exchange a greeting with her. Sometimes he gave her a coin, but secretly, so no other beggar could see, and sometimes a banana, till all the other beggars came to recognise that Gauri Ma belonged to Nat and she to him, and they no longer minded when she and she alone received her offering from him. He was her *tamby*, her little golden-handed brother.

For many years they were friends, and then, when Nat was fourteen, Gauri Ma got married, to a leper like herself but with a dirty beard, whose hand-stumps often oozed pus, whereas Gauri Ma's stumps were dean and dry and covered with scarred skin. Doctor told Gauri Ma's husband to come to the clinic to get his stumps bandaged, but he said it was too far to walk, so one day Doctor came with his doctor's case and told Gauri Ma's husband to follow him into the outer-outer-outermost court of the temple, to that strip of land all around the temple where trees grew and cows grazed and people attended to their excretions and dogs ate it up, and took him to a clean place under a jacaranda tree, and cleaned the wound and dressed it in a fresh white bandage. Nat did not much like Gauri Ma's husband but he supposed it was nice for her to have a companion, and Doctor told him that if she did not have a man to protect her, the other leper men would attack her at night and trouble her and steal the money she had begged that day. So it was good that Gauri Ma got married.

Soon after Gauri Ma got married Nat was on his way home from Town, riding his bicycle along the dusty road, when he saw Gauri Ma walking along the side of the road. Of course, Gauri Ma could not walk properly, it was more a limping, hobbling sort of movement. Nevertheless she had covered much ground by the time Nat saw her. He recognised her from behind, not only because of her gait but because of the dirty-purple sari she always wore, and as he drew up alongside her he pulled the bicycle brakes and swung to the ground. Nat was now a very stately young man, towering over Gauri Ma's little bent body. They greeted each other with the accustomed affection, but then Gauri Ma said something about her foot and when Nat looked down he was appalled. Both feet were now open at the front. Where till now there had been healthy — healthy for a leper — skin covering the end of the stump, there was only a purulent, bubbling ball of flesh. Gauri Ma said she was on her way to Doctor's surgery, so Nat helped her to sit on the bicycle's carrier and brought her home.

Since his father was away on the Triumph visiting a patient in the next village he cleaned the wound himself and bandaged it, the way he had seen his father do it; and where he had been disgusted at the sight of his father touching the sick flesh, even though he had been wearing thin rubber gloves, for some reason Nat felt not the least disgust.

Nat went into the room he still shared with his father and brought back a pair of his own leather *chappals*, which he buckled to Gauri Ma's feet. They were much too big, but the straps passed around her ankles and held them on, and they would offer a protection and so keep the bandage clean for a while.

While he was treating her Nat had the feeling that something was worrying Gauri Ma, so he said to her, 'Ma, you have still another problem? How is your husband?'

'Oh, no, *tamby*, I am extremely fortunate, Lord Shiva is most kind to my husband and myself, yet still . . .'

Nat probed some more and then Gauri Ma poured out her story: the other lepers, ever since the day that Doctor had treated her husband, had taken an intensive dislike to the couple and refused to allow them to share their common lodgings, which was an old ruined hut not far from the temple, where till now they had all gathered at night after the temple closed its gates. There had never been any problem, apart from the usual squabbles, but now they had all ganged up and pushed Gauri Ma and her husband away, and they had not yet found another place to stay, so they were sleeping on the corners of streets, but the people in the houses would kick them or hit them with brooms or throw water on them and make them move on, because it was inauspicious to have a leper sleeping outside your door.

That evening Nat spoke to his father. Doctor decided to buy a small plot of land between their village and Town, and to build a hut on it for Gauri Ma and her husband to live in. True, they would have to walk somewhat to get to the temple to beg each day, and back home in the evening, but nobody could ever chase them away, for the property would be Doctor's. And this is what they did. Two days later the hut was standing and Gauri Ma and her husband moved in.

Nat removed Gauri Ma's bandages and found the wound perfectly healed. People heard of this. Soon it became known that Nat had a Golden Hand for healing. Nat had recently been helping his father more and more in the surgery, but now the villagers liked Nat to touch them, or to give them their medicines, to place his hand on the heads of their babies, because they noticed that when he did so, wounds healed faster and infections disappeared sooner, and that Nat brought luck.

Chapter 16

Saroj
Georgetown, 1964

Baba had only two interests in life: Indian culture and his family. It was his sacred duty to protect them both. He was the custodian of all that was high and noble and pure, ordained, by the Higher, to contain and to preserve them from evil. Both were under siege. Modern society was evil. It could not be allowed to infiltrate the stronghold of culture, or his family

It was imperative to marry off his daughters well. It is the sacred duty of every Hindu father, and Deodat took this duty seriously. He had succeeded — more or less. He had had to compromise, it is true, for there were not enough Brahmins to go round in the colony, and hardly a pedigree was pure. He had done the best he could within this limitation, and God would forgive him the rest. But preserving a family and a culture from evil was an uphill struggle and took a toll on his soul.

By the time Saroj was thirteen Baba was like the dried-out skeleton of a tree on a dark winter's day. He had forgotten how to smile, and how to laugh. He stalked round the house like a dark shadow shrouded in white, looking for transgressions, punishing the wrongdoer, and falling back into that cold dormancy.

His children dared not giggle or play in his presence. Every afternoon a pall, a grey sadness like mist would fall over the house when he walked in the door. In all their doings they'd listen for his car, scuttle at his coming when the downstairs door opened, like young puppies running from the whip of a cruel master, tails between their legs. He would disappear into his office adjoining the living room and all would be still for the rest of the day, for they dared not utter a squeak, and they dared not leave the house. There was something almost reptilian about the way he would slink around the house, leaving his study silently to check on them, then slink back to his work. Saroj might sit in the gallery, sunk in a library book — reading was her only solace, her only refuge, and she devoured books like a hungry dog gulps down fresh meat — and feel his cold eyes resting on her. She would wait, eyes fixed on a single word, convinced of her knowledge of being watched, and then look up to meet that insidious stare. Their eyes would lock across the room; Baba would nod, satisfied, and slink away.

The Ghosh boy wasn't perfect, but he was the best Baba could do, and he was as pleased as he could be within the narrow mental space he had allotted to pleasure. Now that his family was taken care of it was time to devote himself to the greater cause, the insulation of Indian — Hindu — culture.

Here, too, as in the case of his daughter's marriage, Baba had been forced to compromise. On first arriving in British Guiana, Baba had been aghast to find that caste differentiations did not exist in the Indian diaspora. Indians had been thrown together for generations, had survived and flourished as one distinct group, holding together for strength and companionship. There were Hindu Indians and Muslim Indians, even a few Christian Indians, but Indians were Indians and none were low and none were high.

He had been loudspoken in his objections, and eager to bring about those reforms which would restore his people to their origins — in other words, reinstate a caste system. But that was impossible. Hindus had been mixing castes for generations — he might as well try to unscramble an egg. Acceptance of the odious circumstances and compromise was forced upon him; it was either that, or return to India. His great-uncles had deceived him in several matters in calling him here, but in one thing they were right: here he could be a big fish in a small pond, and his influence within that pond could be enormous. He chose to stay. And having made that decision, he saw new possibilities. He could make his own rules; his own reforms.

Caste distinguishes between the pure and the impure, the sublime and the base, and only when the low exists can the high know itself as high. Very well then. High and low would exist again, and he, Deodat Roy, would model this new society according to his own insights and dictates. In India trouble was brewing between Hindus and Muslims, but to reject Muslims would be self-destructive, for Muslims were needed for the vote which would place Indians, all Indians, at the top. It was quite clear who had to be below.

After all, there were Africans.

It was Baba who first coined the slogan *Aphan Jhat,* Vote For Your Own; it was Baba who went among the Indians preaching separate development. It was Baba who brought about those first successes at the polls: the winning of the 1957 election and the 1961 election, merely because an Indian ran against an African and Indians outnumbered Africans.

Baba was becoming a big fish. He had found a new breed of pariahs — Africans. Africans were the natural opposite of Indians — according to Baba. Indians represented spirit sublime, the summit of human evolution. Africans were at the nether end of that evolution. And they played right into his hands.

For Africans flatly refused to accept Indian leadership. Over the years their rebellion and insurrection swelled and finally erupted. For Baba it was soon clear: Africans were not only the natural opposite, they were also *the enemy*. Africans were resentful of Indian prosperity, progress and political leadership. Africans would bring down the legally elected Indian leader, and if they couldn't do it by legal means then it would be illegal, by violence. Africans were setting fire to Indian businesses; Africans were striking, rioting and looting.

And Baba's good friend and supposed ally Cheddi Jagan wasn't any help.

'Cheddi can't control those Africans!' raged Baba. 'The differences are inherent! Africans and Indians can never work together, never live together! He's selling the rights of the Indians,' said Baba to everyone who would listen, first within the family, later to close Indian acquaintances.

'Africans lack the qualities to build a nation,' he said 'They should either go back to Africa or be quiet and take the Indian lead! Where are all the great ancient cultures? In the East! India! Arabia! China! Not in Africa! That's a historical fact!'

Baba broadcast these words for the whole Indian world to hear, words others didn't even dare to think; and didn't care whom he offended. Baba wanted to introduce a sort of caste system in the colony. Caste, said Baba, was a natural fact of life.

'Some races are born with a higher spirit, born to lead, others are born low, capable of menial tasks!' shouted Baba at weddings and wakes and birthday parties. 'God has ordained that Africans should be society's feet! Just as a human body has a head and feet, so the body of society has a head and feet! The feet are just as important as the head! Without the feet the head is useless! Without the head the feet are useless! Indians are the natural head of this society, Africans the feet! But the feet should not try to be the head!'

Baba had the instinct not to say these things in public, at least not yet, but he practised his speeches on his family. Many an evening they sat around the dining table, eyes fixed on him, petrified into silence while he hammered on the table. Three children and a silent little lady were not much of an audience, but these were just trial runs: Baba knew that one day he'd have other, more worthy listeners. Occasionally, about once a month, he brought one of the uncles home from work, a few willingly, others obviously unwillingly, squirming in their seats in embarrassment.

Outside the Roy home, the world was exploding with violence. Baba's call of *Aphan Jhat* had borne fruit; Indians, being in the majority, had again won an election. Africans voted African and lost. Both sides plunged into a hell-pit of mutual hate. Trade unionists and the sugar-workers shook their fists in rage, politicians screamed at each other in Parliament, and the sabre-rattling on both sides of the racial divide led to an eighty-day general strike which crippled the country and brought it to a virtual standstill.

Indians began to fear for their lives.

In the year 1964, the year Saroj turned thirteen, the year the plans were laid for her marriage to the Ghosh boy, the year of her own private coming-of-age, the violence came to a head.

Early that year, an Indian woman called Koswilla was run over by a tractor at Leonora estate; her body was cut into two. The tractor was driven by an African, who was charged with the death of the woman, but acquitted by an African jury at the Assizes. Indians seethed. Africans laughed.

The home of an Indian in Third Alley was set on fire, turning the whole street into a flaming inferno. African gangs roamed about setting more fires, looting businesses and terrorising the Indians as they tried to escape. They beat the men on the streets, tore away the clothes of women and girls and raped them in public.

In November of that year an African gang grabbed an eighteen-year old Indian girl on her way home from a political meeting. They threw her to the ground and stripped off her clothes. Two mounted policemen, Africans, looked on in interest, doing nothing.

Indians feared to go out onto the street. They were attacked, robbed, mutilated, killed, raped by Africans, and even in their homes they were not safe. All this was just fuel on the fire of Baba's rage. He hired two watchmen to protect his house, one by day and one by night. He promised to put up a fire escape around the house.

Georgetown burned. And Africans, said Baba, had made this hell.

The British government sent in the navy.

In December 1964 new elections were held under proportional representation. Though the Indian leader, Cheddi Jagan, received the most votes he lost the election to a coalition government. Forbes Burnham, an African, took up the reins of government. It was a slap in Baba's face. He railed against the British government and the CIA, both of whom, he shouted, had plotted to bring down the Indian leader, suspecting him of Communism.

No-one was surprised when Baba left Jagan's PPP in disgust and announced the forming of the All-Indian Party for Progress, under his own leadership. Immediately all the Roys joined, for after all, which businessman, Indian or not, wants to join a Communist party, even one led by an Indian? So Baba's AIPP was a collecting bowl for those wealthier Indians disillusioned with Jagan's Marxist politics, but willing, if necessary, to form a coalition government with Jagan to keep Indians in power. Jagan could concentrate on the masses, the Indian sugar workers and rice farmers, keep them happy with his Marxist slogans. The elite — Hindus and Muslims alike of high standing — should follow Baba.

Baba rented a two-storey wooden house in Regent Street as AIPP Party headquarters, moving his own office out of his home and into the new house. From that time on home became a quieter place, a haven, even. When Baba discovered political action his interest in his children's doings receded. By now they knew the rules, and knew they were inviolable. They were well trained.

When Baba caught Trixie with her polluted black fingers on Indrani's sari, a millennium of cultural prejudice combined with his own private cauldron of smouldering white rage — personal, private rage — exploded against Saroj. For she had violated the most sacred rule of all. She had allied herself to the Enemy. She had brought the Enemy into his home.

Chapter 17

Savitri
Madras, 1923

'Nonsense, Celia, they're only children, for heaven's sake!'
The Admiral could not bear interruptions. He
drummed the desk with his fingers in impatience and willed
his wife to return to her household duties. He was one Chapter
before the greatest battle of his life and the urge to get on with
it — to write, day and night, pausing only for necessities like
eating, sleeping, urinating, and Thursday evenings — drove
him to marathon sessions fortified by endless cups of tea, hastily
swallowed in the reading pauses during which he reviewed
the last few pages belched out by his typewriter, pencilled in
corrections, arrows, exclamation and question marks. Progress
was slow. The Admiral insisted on rewriting, correcting and
retyping each and every page to perfection before he could
progress to the next; and he insisted on detail. His right hand lay
atrophied and useless on his knee. He had the use of only one
hand, his left, and had to pick out each key carefully with one
finger. In six years he had written almost four hundred single-
spaced pages in this way, stoically ploughing through battle
after battle, and now the end was in sight.

The end of a long hard war, it seemed to him, his most noble,
for with this war he was keeping history alive, and himself, for
these memoirs would be the ultimate history book of the Great
War, and every schoolchild would one day copy passages from
it, and schoolmasters would struggle with tears as the book
divulged those poignant, secret moments when the human
spirit rises far beyond itself to unknown heights, as it can, it

seemed to the Admiral, only during War. Memories crowded him, and this was the only way they accepted release. The book was modestly named The Great War — A Memory. What a clever understatement! His heart swelled with the greatness of it all, and his humble role as chronicler. And here now was Celia, intruding on his precious privacy with some preposterous tale about David and the native girl — before breakfast!

Mrs Lindsay wrung her hands in anguish.

'I know, I know... that's what I keep telling myself. And yet... I can't tell you the very seriousness of their vow... John, it gave me gooseflesh!'

She wished there was someone, anyone, she could talk to about this. Her husband was hopeless, in more ways than one, and she couldn't think of confessing to one of her friends — why, the rumour would run like wildfire through the English community, and how they would all titter! Unless she made a silly joke of it all — but it wasn't a silly joke. There was something of... Mrs Lindsay struggled for the right word. Not *solemn* — a solemn vow — no, that was banal, a cliché, not at all what she had sensed. No, something of *prophecy* in Savitri's promise of marriage.

That was it. As if the girl *knew*. And it gave her, Mrs Lindsay, the shivers. And that was why she had to talk to someone, and it couldn't be an English friend, because then she couldn't reveal her fears... that somehow she had made a mistake. She should never have thrown the children together, never. The child's words seemed to have cast a spell on her, holding her so that all logic, all reason, took flight and all that was left was fear, because the child had spoken words of truth.

'Well, what do I care, good Lord!' spluttered the Admiral, impatience bursting out of him. 'Separate them! Dismiss the cook! Send David to England. Marry off the girl. This is all your business, Celia, not mine. Now, if you don't mind . . .' he signalled to Khan standing in the corner.

'Breakfast, Khan. I'll have it here, at my desk. Thank you Celia . . . please . . .'

And Mrs Lindsay knew that her husband had already closed

his door on her. She sighed and withdrew, but as she closed the study door she smiled, because the Admiral, bless his dear soul, had broken the spell with the words spoken in innocence: 'Marry off the girl.'

'Silly me!' she thought. 'To get myself all worked up like that! All I have to do is do nothing. The girl's going to Bombay anyway, to get married to this clubfooted cook.'

The muezzin call did not wake Savitri that morning, for she was already awake. She listened, as she always did. The muezzin to the west was always a few seconds earlier than the one to the north, but slower, so he caught up and they sang in unison, far away, over the roofs of Madras, meeting and mingling and drawing all souls who would listen to meet the Lord. The hair at the back of her neck stood on end at the holiness of the call.

She was not supposed to listen. She had asked Appa, once, if that was the voice of God himself, and he said no. It was only the Muslims. They were not Muslims, so they should not listen. Khan was a Muslim and so was Ali the potter down Old Market Street, and Mr Bacchus who had been the school-teacher in the government school, which was why Appa hadn't liked her going to school, because she had a Muslim teacher. Savitri could not understand it. When the muezzin voice rang out, the call entered the space behind her thought-body and she knew it was really God calling. So why should one thought-body call itself Muslim, and respond, and the other call itself non-Muslim, and not respond?

So Savitri prayed with the Muslims every morning when it was still dark and it was the only sound in the world. She prayed with Khan and Ali and Mr Bacchus, and Appa would never know.

When the muezzin's call was over there was a space of silence, but not quite silence because there were faint noises of waking all over Madras, like little tender strains of sound rising in tendrils, tentatively at first, then gathering courage until all the city was crowned by a dome of daybreak noise. But something was different today, and Savitri listened. An early cock crowing, a flutter of wings, a brain-fever bird with his hysterical three-tiered cry ascending into madness. Water from a tap, a bucket dangling down a well, a rope fluttering behind it. The swish-swish of thresholds and bridges and streets being swept. A baby crying, a wife shouting at her drunken husband. One horn, another, a rickshaw's klaxon, the creaking of a bullock cart, horses' hooves. *'Hare-Rama-Hare-Krishna'* from a temple, and *puja* bells, the hollow blaring of a conch, rattling drums. But a single familiar strain was missing.

Thatha called.

Savitri, her ears finely tuned to the morning, was on her feet and with him in a trice, for it was she he was calling, and the call did not belong to the morning chorus. *Thatha's* chant, Savitri now realised, was that single strain that had been missing all along, the mantra of *'Shiva-Mahadeva'* he always sang for two hours before dawn, and that was what had been different today.

'Yes, *Thatha*, I am here,' she said, greeting him with folded hands and sinking to the ground before him. *Thatha* sat leaning against the wall, all swathed in a blanket, for there was a chill in the morning air, and his face was the only part of his body unswathed.

'Beloved child,' he said.

He spoke no more but his hands emerged from the folds in the blanket and he took hers in his, and she felt the space and the vast power filling that space, until she was all space and all power without even a trace of a thought-body, and neither she nor *Thatha* existed nor all the world — and then she was back, and the darkness was gone, *Thatha's* face was wrinkled, his eyes were smiling, and he let go of her hands and, without a word, raised his palm and dismissed her. She withdrew, backwards, with folded hands and head bowed to *Thatha*, humble in the power that still filled her space.

She knew she would not be leaving for Bombay. She knew it, as much as she knew that David was a part of her.

Smiling to herself, glowing from the warmth and light of the power, she cut herself a twig from the neem tree in the back yard and cleaned her teeth, and then went to the wash-house at the back of the yard to bathe, and then her mother was there, and the day and all its duties. On her way to deliver the milk Vali danced for her again. But she already knew the day was auspicious.

In fact, the morning passed in a very ordinary way. It was not until the late afternoon that the Admiral — alone at home except for the servants, for Celia had taken David to the dentist in an effort to separate him from Savitri for that day — felt a sudden inexplicable urge to leave his study. He simply could not write a further word. *Writer's block,* he thought. *It happens to the most brilliant of writers.* This morning, after breakfast, a rush of emotion had overcome him, to such an extent that his left hand had begun to tremble and he could not hit the keys. He had reread the last few Chapters, just to win time, and for inspiration, but that had not helped. All morning he had struggled with words but had not proceeded further than a few paragraphs, which, he felt, contained nothing more than hot air. It wasn't the words, he knew now, it was the *memory…*

So he signalled to Khan, and for the first time in several years he asked to be wheeled about the garden, so as to clear his mind and prepare it for the Climax.

Savitri had not seen the Admiral for several years. When she'd been a toddler, of course, and had kept nearer to the house, the figure rolling here and there in a wheelchair had been quite familiar. But over the years the Admiral had withdrawn more and more to his study, into himself and the pages of his growing memoirs. The only times he left the refuge of his home was on Thursday evenings, when Khan pushed him across the verandah and helped him into the waiting car, so Savitri had never really seen him. Not from close up. And he had never seen her.

And he had never seen his own garden; *seen* it, of course, but never really *looked* at it. The garden was Celia's world. Now, as Khan pushed him along the quiet paths of reddish sand he opened his eyes and thought himself in paradise. Such a wealth of colour, of fragrance! Thick heavy grapes of bougainvillea cascaded down from above, in brilliant, translucent shades of violet, vermilion, shocking pink, orange, and maroon. Between the bougainvilleas the hibiscus bloomed in a last triumphant flush of glory, before the dusk came and then the night, where they would close for ever, to be replaced in the morning by fresh new blossoms as young as the day. And roses of course, lilies and camellias, and a hundred other points of colour he had not names for. Glorious! The Admiral felt lifted out of a battlefield and into heaven.

The Great War had never ceased for him. Long after Victory the torpedoes of his mind had rattled on, the fire and the screaming, the blood and the gore, the horror and, yes, the *glory* twisting and turning within him and finding no escape but into the keys of his typewriter.

The glory, the final glory. The Admiral could not think of the *glory* without a shudder. That moment when all was lost, when all was fire and death and blood and screaming and he knew it was the end, he was about to die, and he had made his own personal, intimate, surrender, laid down his inner arms and given himself up to death — then had come the glory, an unutterable bliss filling all space and all mind, and all the horror and terror that had gone before had been worth even one fraction of that glory — and he had died into it, but miraculously returned to life, a mental life of agony, and a physical life of decrepitude.

Since then this physical existence on earth held no more joy for him. Life, for him, was waiting for the second death, and final Glory. He was useless to both his wife — he had married late, and she was much too young for him, and he knew it had been a mistake — and his children, to whom he was more of a grandfather than a father, for the younger had been born when he was long past fifty, conceived during a brief convalescence in the last years of the war. Another grave mistake. His life held nothing but the hollow clang of cymbals. That was why he was waiting for death: *O thou last fulfilment of life, Death, my death, come and whisper to me!*

But the butterflies! As large as your hand, almost, and he

had to smile; for once, when he was young, he had chased butterflies and loved life. He bid Khan wheel him further into this paradise his wife had created not a stone's throw from the city, this riot of peace and colour, flowers, greenery, feathery ferns, birds and butterflies — his eyes swam.

An enormous butterfly alighted on the path before him, silent as breath, wings of coloured light spread open, twirling slowly in the soft afternoon light filtering through the treetops.

It was not a butterfly.

It was a little brown girl, but her clothes were the colours of butterflies' wings and her lilac shawl, slung over her outspread arms, hung wide and open like wings of sheerest gossamer. She was dancing dreamily on the path before him and her eyes were closed, and she had not seen him.

But then, suddenly, as if she had felt his gaze on her, she opened her eyes and looked directly into his, and the Admiral was swept away, for the second time in his life, by the Glory.

It was only a split second. And then the battle-worn and battle-weary veteran smiled at this slip of a butterfly girl and it was the first time he had smiled in — oh, in years.

It all happened so quickly then that even the telling of it is too slow.

Savitri knew you didn't do *Namaste* to the English; you didn't do praying hands, you *shook* hands, so when the Admiral smiled she smiled back and, being a courteous and friendly girl, approached him the way she knew you approached the English, with your right hand stretched out to shake the other's hand, saying,

'Good afternoon, sir.'

And the Admiral stretched out his right hand and took hers.

After that there was no more talk of Savitri's marriage. The Admiral would not hear of it. If Savitri could cure his right hand then maybe she could also cure his legs; it was a miracle, and he had felt the miracle at the moment of its happening, and where miracles are concerned the human mind has no right to utter the word *impossible*.

That is what the doctors said, when he told them his hand was cured. They shook their heads and said *impossible,* but the Admiral only smiled smugly and showed them how he could move his fingers now, and raise his hand, and one day, with perseverance, he would type. And Savitri had done it.

Word of the miracle quickly spread, of course, and the English came to be healed. In the Theosophical Society Savitri was a sensation — maybe even a new Master; (in this case, a Mistress?) She was Mrs Lindsay's possession, her mascot, and Mrs Lindsay would have loved to hand her around, to give demonstrations and lectures and invite the press, but Savitri was as shy as a butterfly and at the very approach of a stranger flitted away into the bushes and could not be found, no matter how they searched the garden.

Mrs Lindsay asked her how she had done it, but all she did was look back with huge melting-chocolate eyes, shake her head, and say, 'No, madam, I didn't do it, truly I didn't, it was God that did it, God's power.'

'But you have the Power, don't you?' said Mrs Lindsay, snatching at the word. 'Your grandfather now, he gave you the Power, didn't he?'

For following the miracle word had spread of *Thatha* and his healing powers, and there had been a sudden rush of patients to him, but they were all turned away.

'Why won't you heal my friends?' said Mrs Lindsay.

'I cannot, madam,' said Savitri.

'Yes, you can, it's just that you don't want to, isn't it? Because it's all a question of willpower. Isn't it now?'

'No, madam. If you want it to happen it won't happen. It only happens if you don't want it.'

Savitri knew very well the meaning of the word 'intention', but it was beyond her to use it in this context, to explain that *intention* is the tiny stream through which the mighty river which is the Gift cannot flow; that the Gift is as much greater than willpower as the sun is greater than a lamp-flame, and must work according to its own wisdom, and that being so, turns back when puny willpower is at work. She couldn't explain it, for at seven years of age she had not yet the words.

And so Mrs Lindsay didn't believe her. Mrs Lindsay believed it was all a question of Savitri's *will*; and that her will must be coaxed and coddled and pampered, and one day, yes one day, she would harness the Power to that will and become a true Master — no, a Mistress — and she, Mrs Lindsay, would be her protectress.

Hadn't she always known there was something special about the child? Hadn't she had that feeling, right from the beginning? It was intuition. And then there was Destiny — the Destiny of Savitri's birth, right after David's, and her friendship with David. Destiny had placed this special child in her, Mrs Lindsay's, hands. All the child needed was guidance. And she, Mrs Lindsay, was there to give it. The child had Powers. They must only be developed with her help. It was pre-ordained.

Between them, through the means of bribery, flattery, authority, written contracts, threats and outright commands, the Lindsays successfully prevented Savitri's marriage to the clubfooted cook. Savitri must stay in Fairwinds, and continue her education with Mr Baldwin, and be properly guided by Mrs Lindsay. The child, the Admiral and his wife agreed, was Special. It was the first time they had agreed on any matter for many, many years, and that was another miracle worked by Savitri's presence.

Chapter 18

Nat
Bangalore, 1956 — 1960

Nat went to boarding school in Bangalore. For the most part, he hated school. He was not the most brilliant of pupils, not through lack of intelligence, but because of the way he had to learn his lessons, by rote, reeling off entire passages out of textbooks without making a single mistake. He passed through stages of rebellion, boredom, apathy, laziness, lethargy, and spells where his mind just refused to comply, wandering into far-off regions where the words he'd tried his best to memorise just filtered through his brain and, when he tried to retrieve them, were lost entirely.

As a matter of fact, Nat was distracted. Seriously distracted. Nat had discovered Girls.

Nat had grown up with village girls. When they were very young they played alongside the boys and it seemed there was not much difference, but the older they grew the more it became clear that there was a very major difference; that girls were a species apart, slowly fading out of sight and into a world of their own where boys were not admitted, into a world of women where men were not permitted.

In fact, there was a very precise moment when a girl became part of this secret female world. She simply disappeared into her home for several days, and then that same girl who till now had run and jumped and played on the streets like a half-child but helped her mother with housework and child-care like a half-woman, re-appeared. And she no longer wore her long gathered skirt and little waist-length blouse and shawl, but a sari; and she sat enthroned in womanly silence, garlanded in jasmine and rose, and men, fathers of sons, prospective sons-in-law, came to appraise her and talk to her father about weddings and dowries, and now it was said of her: she is *of marriageable age*. And from now on she lived in a secret, intimate, feminine world and only one man would ever be permitted to enter that world and to know her: her future husband.

In Bangalore, Nat met girls of quite another species. Armaclare College was for boys only, but Nat was popular. He arrived a country bumpkin, but learned quickly; his agreeable temperament, his charm and his good manners easily found him friends. His schoolmates invited him home for the weekends. He became a welcome guest at their stately homes, where he met their sisters and female cousins, not to mention their mothers and aunts. He was their pet; their darling; they pitied him for his worldly ignorance (growing up in a village! as a peasant!), admired him for his wheat-coloured skin, and spoiled him silly.

Most important of all, he met the Bannerji girls.

The Bannerjis were devout Hindus, but Western-oriented. Their eldest son Govind was in Nat's form, a day-boy, heir to a stupendous fortune in the emerging computer industry, who had several sisters all of whom Nat had the pleasure of meeting the first time he went to their magnificent bungalow in a cool green and flowery Bangalore suburb.

Five sisters, two elder, three younger — one still a child, but with a sublime promise shining in her eyes — each one prettier than the next! Each one with skin as soft and lush as a rose petal, dark long eyes containing secret upon secret, the soft silk of their saris flowing like water around their slender, supple forms.

And these girls, for all their perfection, did not keep themselves apart as did the village girls. They talked, laughed, argued with him, joined him in easy banter, played tennis with him, and wrapped him gently around their little fingers. They had all been to England several times and possessed a sophistication and worldly knowledge that dwarfed him. They also possessed a quality beyond intelligence: a gleam of wisdom lit their eyes, and they looked into his in a way the village girls never had, seeing all, exposing his soul, daring him to approach their femininity, to lay down the prickly armour that separated them from him, laughing at him for his shyness, beckoning him on even while their purity held him at bay. His instinct was to bow before them. To prostrate himself. As if only in laying down the flawed, coarse dominance of manhood he could melt into and know the immaculate bliss and greatness of the feminine, denied him as penance for that very coarseness. They were Goddesses.

Nat's mind hovered constantly before the image of perfect femininity. No wonder he could not get a grasp on logarithms.

During their last year at Armaclare College, Govind married a girl he had been betrothed to for years, and Nat was invited to the wedding, held in the plush Royal Continental Hotel. The bride was of the same unapproachable beauty as Govind's sisters. She kept her eyes lowered throughout the ceremony and when Nat was introduced to her later she graced him with the barest of glances from beneath long sweeping black lashes. Yet in that one slight glance was a spark that again made Nat ache to know Woman and her inner secrets, to pace the holy fire with such a bride, his cloth tied to her sari, rounding it seven times, uttering their sacred vows, entering the union that would lead to highest, blissful Love.

Govind would be leaving India around the same time as Nat. He was going to America, to the Massachusetts Institute of Technology. His wife would be staying here in Bangalore and attending the Musical Academy, for she was gifted in the veena, the traditional instrument of South India. After the wedding ceremony she gave a short performance on this instrument, sitting on a rich carpet before the hundreds of guests and letting a rippling river of music flow out of the tiny hands that barely seemed to touch the strings over which her fingers danced. Tears of deep emotion wet Nat's cheeks, and he envied Govind with all his heart, for this bride with the power to open such depths. When he next returned home he asked his father if he himself could not possibly be married before he left for England. He asked his father to find a bride for him.

Doctor looked at him with surprise and mirth in his eyes.

'You want to marry already, Nat?'

'Why *already?* Many of my friends are already married. I'm about the only boy in my form who isn't at least engaged.'

'Even the English boys?'

'Well, no, not them. But I'm an Indian, Dad, and we have different customs.'

'Yes. The English boys will probably wait a few years, and then marry a girl of their own choice. I thought that would be the way you'd be doing it.'

'But . . .' Nat wanted to repeat that he was an Indian, but then he remembered that his father was, strictly speaking, an Englishman, a *sahib*.

'Which way is better, Dad?'

'Which way do you think is better?'

'Well . . . the Indian way is certainly easier. I mean, I wouldn't know how to go about finding a girl and persuading her to marry me. What if she likes someone else better? What if her parents disagree? What if . . .'

'Once you get to England you'll find most of these problems dissolving and you'll probably wonder how you could ever have wanted anything else, Nat. Because you'll actually realise it's not so hard to fall in love with a nice girl. Nothing easier, in fact. It's finding the *right* girl to love that'll be hard. Your hormones will probably have a lot to say about that and they might make some bad mistakes. That's a risk we'll just have to take.'

'So why don't we do it the Indian way? Govind's wife . . .'

'You were quite taken with her, eh? You'd like a girl like that?' Nat nodded, not looking at his father.

'Anyone particular in mind?'

Nat, encouraged and all at once hopeful, let the faces of the four elder Bannerji girls pass before his mind's eye. In particular he saw their eyes, each carrying a different message. Pramela's eyes laughed, and seemed to mock him, playing with him, yet hinting at depths he could not fathom. Sundari was gentle and warm-hearted and spoke not with her lips but with her eyes, which were liquid with eloquence. Ramani could talk the hind leg off a donkey. In her eyes shone the light of intelligence. Radha kept her eyes modestly lowered but, once you got a fleeting glimpse into them, they drew you into a place too secret for words...

Each one was — he searched his mind for a comparison — an orchid, a rare, unique being radiating a mystique that foiled his fumbling senses, whom you could never possess but only adore, if you were lucky enough to win her. Each one contained in herself a wondrous, special universe he could spend a lifetime discovering. He'd be happy to marry any one of them. He was ready and poised to love any one of them, to make any one of them the focus of his life. Any one of them could help him find his wholeness. True, Sundari and Pramela were already married and Ramani would be married in a year; that was irrelevant. He *could have* married any one of them. They were all fascinating. In fact, he had never met a girl who was not, in some way, fascinating. Femininity itself fascinated.

'I don't mind,' said Nat. 'Whoever you think best . . .'

Doctor roared with laughter. 'Nat, I've managed to make an honest-to-goodness Indian out of you. I just wonder how long you'll stay that way, once you cross the great divide . . . No Nat, I'm not going to choose a wife for you. Sorry, I just can't do it, I won't. I'm still too much of an Englishman. The Indian way is fine for Indians, might even be fine for you. But I want you to have a *choice*. If, after you've had the choice and can't find a suitable girl, you still want me to choose for you, then fine. But you have to remember: a Hindu family like the Bannerjis won't take you as a son-in-law. A Muslim family will want you to convert first. A Sikh? A Parsi? They all have their prejudices, their customs, and the parents will want you to adapt. And they certainly won't send their daughter to me, to keep for you till you return! I'd advise you to look for a lovely English rose when you get to London. And wait till you've finished your studies. Marriage would distract you too much.'

'But I want to marry *now*,' Nat objected. 'I can't wait . . .'

And the years ahead of him, stuck inside his coarse maleness when there was so much to discover, when there was this great need for Woman, this great ache for her . . . it seemed a hurdle too high for him to take.

He arrived at Heathrow with the intention of finding a suitable girl and marrying her as soon as possible. A bride full of secrets waiting to be uncovered.

Chapter 19

Saroj
Georgetown, 1964

Saroj! Saroj, the bridegroom is coming, come to the gate!'
said Ma, just behind Saroj's shoulder. 'Oh, and Ganesh, I
was looking for you, you should be waiting too, to receive the
bridegroom...'

Ma led Saroj away. She was reluctant to go. *The bridegroom's
coming...*

A shudder passed through her at the words. *The bridegroom.*
This man, chosen by Baba, approved by Ma, whom Indrani had
never seen, riding toward the house now on a white horse to
claim his bride...

Saroj could hear the distant drums as the bridegroom's pro-
cession, several streets away, made its slow way forward. It was
a quaint tradition, brought by Baba from India, and practised
only by Roys, having long died out among other Indians. But
Baba had revived the custom among his own; so whenever
you saw a bridegroom on a decorated white horse with a little
nephew sitting behind him for fertility, and men playing drums
and *shehnais* dancing around him, you knew it was a Roy
wedding; that somewhere, a bride waited in trepidation, just as
Indrani waited now in an upstairs room, surrounded by aunts
and great-aunts fussing around her, adjusting her sari, painting
her hands, scenting her hair, re-arranging her jewellery as if she
were a paper doll to be decorated, and chatting all the while like
a gaggle of geese. Saroj broke into a sweat.

'He's coming! He's coming!' Like the whispering of trees
brushed by a breeze, the guests whispered to one another
in excitement. The chattering died down and there came

a discordant outburst of the *shehnais*, wild and passionate, drowning the rumble of drums. The outburst was as short as it was passionate. The drums were nearer now, two streets away at most.

The bridegroom's coming! Did Indrani, in her upstairs bedroom, hear it? Was the hair on the nape of her neck standing on end, as Saroj's was? Does she have goosebumps; is she sweating in anxiety, like me? *Oh Lord, this is what will happen to me! That Ghosh boy!*

The *shehnais* again. No longer than one minute, wild, tuneless, brassy; and then the drums. And then the *shehnais*. And the drums. Nearer and nearer came the bridegroom's party. *Shehnais* and drums. Just around the corner now. Soon they'd be in sight! The whispering grew louder, the rustling of saris and palpable excitement increasing with the jostling forward towards the gate to see the bridegroom when he came. Ganesh at Saroj's side, Ma at the other… the crowd pushing forward behind Saroj… *Do you see him? Is he coming?* The crowd surged, pushing Saroj to the forefront with Ganesh. Baba was somewhere behind, struggling through the uncles and cousins.

'There he is! There he is!'

The bridegroom's party rounded the corner and everyone gasped and clapped in joy. The bridegroom! Dressed in white, and a little boy behind him, and the white horse clopping forward patiently. Men in white dancing to the drums, flinging themselves around in ecstasy; and now the terrible *shehnais* again, that frenzied fervent explosion of strident brass, and then the drums, louder than ever. Pushing and jostling on the bridge. Guests swarming out into the street, no longer whispering but laughing, clapping, dancing themselves in their excitement, heaving forward to welcome the newcomers. Bridegroom's party and bride's joining, mixing, merging. The horse, now in the midst of the surging throng, over the bridge and into the yard, and then the little boy lifted down and the bridegroom swinging himself to the ground, to be swallowed by the crowd. Saroj felt dizzy; sick.

'Are you okay, Saroj?' Ganesh whispered behind her, as

from a great distance.

'I think she's going to faint! Ma, help her, hold her!'

Ganesh's arm firm around her as he forged back through the crowd to the front door, opened it, and half carried, half pushed her up the stairs.

'You'd better lie down,' he said. His voice was matter-of-fact. Solid. A brother. Not a bridegroom.

The living room was filled with aunties who'd been watching through the window. Some of them saw Saroj supported by Ganesh and cried out, Saroj? What's the matter, girl? You all right? Ganesh quickly nodded and signalled to them to be quiet and pushed her up the second flight of stairs to the bedrooms. Ganesh carried her to the bed. She fell back into the pillows.

Ganesh brought her a cold washcloth and a glass of water. He smiled and stroked her forehead, made sure she could be left alone, and slipped off down the stairs to the ceremony. The moment he was gone she stood up, went into the bathroom, and vomited. She returned to her bed, where she stayed throughout the wedding, trying to close her ears and her mind to the familiar chants of the priests as Indrani married a stranger. The next time she heard those sounds would be at her own wedding. In less than a year, if Baba had his way. She pressed her hands over her ears, pressed the sounds and the thoughts and the fears away into an airtight corner of her mind. It couldn't happen. *It wouldn't.*

Not knowing how to fight the fact of her marriage Saroj simply ignored it. She sealed the threat of it away in an air-tight corner of her mind. She refused even to think about it. When that bridge came she would cross it.

The joys of being thirteen were too pressing, demanding her attention, and she had Trixie at her side, only too willing to initiate her. Saroj let Trixie make her over into that most flippant, indecorous, impertinent and footloose of human beings, the Modern Teenage Girl.

Saroj had been practising freedom for two months now. Baba, once having resolved to marry her off at fourteen, washed his hands of her and her wicked ways, and anyway, he was so involved with his All-Indian Party he was hardly ever home. When he was, he didn't notice that a red Hercules bicycle, Trixie's old one now that she'd been given a white Moulton for her fourteenth birthday, stood in the bicycle shed next to Ganesh's.

'Do they fit?'

Saroj wiggled her bottom one more time and pulled Trixie's Wranglers up over her hips. She had to breathe in to close the zip; though they wore the same size Trixie was decidedly straighter than Saroj, and these jeans were too tight around the curve of her bottom, and the waistline too loose.

'Your figure!' sighed Trixie. 'What I'd give for a figure like yours, and you're only thirteen! You look more like fifteen!'

There wasn't a trace of envy in her voice. There never was. Trixie could ramble on for hours about Saroj's face, eyes, hair, hips, waistline, legs. She'd swoon with admiration, she'd wish they were hers, but without even a shadow of resentment. And now that she had her to herself, was responsible for her make-over, she positively overflowed with wonder. Saroj was like a favourite doll for her to dress up.

'Here, try this. It might be a bit tight around your breasts,' she giggled. Certain words, like *bosom* and *breasts,* made her giggle and she used them as often as possible. 'I wish I had your bosom. You're so lucky. Mine hasn't even begun to grow. Would you lend me a bra? I'd wear it and stuff it with sponges. I'm too embarrassed to buy one myself. Did your Ma buy yours for you? How do you measure for one? Let me see — turn around . . .'

Saroj had barely managed to button up the front of a skimpy midriff blouse. These things were all the rage that year, but Trixie's was too tight around her budding breasts. She felt she would burst out of it, though there wasn't all that much of her to burst. She turned around, looking at herself critically in Trixie's wardrobe mirror.

'Fantastic! Oh God, Saroj, you look great! Like Venus! Here, let me see your hair...'

She quickly parted Saroj's hair, brushed it over her shoulders, tied knots halfway down the two thick strands. She stood back to admire her work. 'Wonderful! Venus in blue jeans! If your Baba could see you now he'd fall down dead!'

'I wish he would,' Saroj said, and frowned at the three inches of bare skin between jeans and blouse. It was the same with a sari, of course, but with a sari you covered your chest with cloth and you never showed your belly-button. Saroj felt half-naked. Too provocative.

'Don't you have a shirt or something I could wear on top?'

'Pity.' But Trixie rummaged in her closet and brought forth a long, pale-blue cotton shirt scattered with tiny white flowers. Saroj slipped into it. Trixie tied it at the waist, stepped back again, and clapped.

'Saroj, we have to go out. I have to show you to the world. I can't keep you to myself a minute longer.'

The house, now that Indrani was married, was usually empty in the afternoons. Ma spent more and more time at the temple, whereas Gan, in the manner of boys, was everywhere and nowhere.

The moment school's last bell rang Saroj was out on the road with Trixie. At last she was doing the things normal girls did. Hanging around at Booker's snack bar, guzzling ice cream sodas, hanging out at Geddes Grant record store, huddling into a booth with Trixie, clicking their fingers and singing along to the latest hit booming at them through the earphones. Wandering through Fogarty's Dry Goods fingering the bales of cloth, discussing styles and dress lengths. Saroj was, for the first time in her life, having fun.

But Ma knew. Ma behaved as if it were the most normal thing in the world for Saroj to come home, tear off her school uniform, yell, 'I'm off, Ma!' and disappear on her bike, with or without Ganesh, tearing around the corner after Trixie, hair flying out behind her in long black strips, laughing in abandonment, swerving in and out between the donkey carts drifting up and down the Georgetown streets loaded with coconuts or palm leaves or wooden planks or bricks.

Saroj learned to ride a bicycle and play ping-pong. She and Trixie stacked records on Trixie's record-player and turned the volume up to deafening and opened the windows wide to share their joy with the whole street, and danced like wild things let loose. They went to Brown Betty's and ate Fudgicles, Popsickles and Chicken-in-the-Rough. They saw Cliff Richard in *Summer Holiday*, and the Beatles in *A Hard Day's Night*. Saroj rode Vitane. Betty Grant invited them to her swimming pool and Julie Sue-a-Quan and Ramona Goveia joined them there, and that's where Saroj went every Thursday for two months, and by the end of that time she could swim. She grew daring. She stayed out later and later, going to night parties and returning on the stroke of nine, since Baba now rarely came home before ten.

See, Baba, no hands! See, feet up on the handlebars! See, my skirt tucked into my panties, my legs are bare! See, that old chequered dress lying on the floor and I'm in Trixie's shorts, I'm running in the surf, I'm dancing to the Beatles! See, Baba, just see! I'm riding Vitane!

She learned to joke and banter and tease and laugh, and to listen when they talked of the most marvellous of earthly delights, the one thing that was still ahead, that one most forbidden thing: *boys*. Falling in love. All the girls were in love. It was expected of them. It was expected of *her*.

I'm at the Van Sertimas' swimming pool, Baba, and I'm wearing Trixie's other swimsuit, my skin *is showing! And there are BOYS here, living boys! Boys, boys seeing me half-naked, seeing my golden-brown glistening wet skin, watching me with a roguish gleam in their eyes, stealing touches, smiling at me, offering to teach me to swim, their hands holding my belly under water, laughing in affection at my helpless splashing… boys whispering into my ear, passing me secret notes, appearing out of nowhere from round a corner and riding their bikes alongside mine, chattering and grinning and showing off, Derek and Leo and Steve and Sandy, riding past our house, Baba, and waving secretly, blowing kisses up to me in the tower. Black boys, even!*

୬୶ঌ

Trixie fell madly, irrevocably in love with Ganesh. The first time she met him was the day that he came to pick up Saroj at her home. Trixie, up till then so garrulous, did not speak a word but just stared at him with moist puppy-dog eyes, and ever since then she was consistently struck dumb by his presence. It was a thing they giggled at when alone; but once Trixie cried: 'I love him, Saroj, I really do. But he never even sees me. I'm just a little girl to him. He'll never marry me.'

'Trixie, for goodness' sake. You're *fourteen*. There are hundreds of things to do before you marry.'

'No there aren't. All I want is to love and be loved back and marry and have children. I'll never be happy otherwise.'

Saroj could only shake her head in exasperation.

Trixie was not the only one obsessed with marriage. They all were. The girls had but one topic of conversation: catching a boy. All they did centred on the primping of their bodies to this end. They made themselves into boy-bait; they learned to bat their eyes, to walk, to talk, to dance, to smile, to live and move and have their beings all with that one central goal, the catching of a good boy. All their dreams ended with Saroj's worst nightmare: marriage. Everything they did, what they wore, how they spoke, where they went, all had that one aim: to catch a husband.

Observing these girls Saroj learned several lessons. The fishing rules in the search for prospective husbands were almost exactly the same as those among the Indians. The girls looked at family and social standing and family's income first, and then at looks: lightness of skin and straightness of hair and thickness of lips and nose.

They assessed the boy, and then they fell in love.

There was no way you'd find one of these girls falling in love with a black roadworker's son. Not even if he won the Guiana Scholarship. Not even if he wrote poetry to match Wordsworth or played a Mozart symphony backwards or discovered a new planet. Background and blood was everything.

Wasn't that the way Baba had chosen this Ghosh boy? The goal was the same: to make a good catch, to separate good from bad quality, the salmon from the minnows. There was only one difference between Saroj and her girlfriends: they had to catch their salmon themselves. Baba had caught Saroj's for her.

Saroj already had that one prize they all coveted: a husband, signed, sealed and awaiting delivery. And she lacked the guts to say, when the time came: *Return to Sender.*

If the girls were fishing for salmon the boys were out to pick orchids, and it was Saroj's hard luck to be one. Once the initial euphoria of knowing she was desirable wore off she wished it gone. They wouldn't leave her alone. She could ride her Hercules down the street minding her own business and there they'd be, sailing round the corner on their own bikes and riding up beside her, grinning inanely. They'd show off by riding their bikes without hands, zig-zaging through the traffic, turning and grinning to see if she was goggle-eyed with amazement. They boasted about the motorbike their daddy was buying them for their sixteenth birthday.

All of them were going to get the biggest, fastest, loudest motorbike available. They dreamed of motorbike racing, while others had already begun to dream of the cars awaiting them in the not too distant future. They all wanted to be pilots when they grew up. If they ever did grow up. At parties their eyes gleamed with greed and they were all hands.

When Saroj danced with them their fingers dropped from her waist to her bottom and she had to reach behind and slap their wrists to get them to behave. They put their hands into her hair and sighed in ecstasy. They maneuvered their lips near to hers and nibbled the air. When she turned her head away they followed with theirs. They reeked; they plastered themselves with hair-oil, deodorant and cologne. Old Spice was out; shirts were soaked through with Brut and perspiration.

Saroj had wrestled freedom from Baba; but for *this?* She began to question the very concept of freedom.

She had to admit it to herself: after a few months, it was growing boring. It was all very well to grab fun by the forelock, but once you had it... well, so what? Fun seemed to exhaust itself in fizzle. She looked closely at the fizzle and it was empty, nothing but hot air.

In fact, freedom and fun were leading nowhere. Marriage still loomed on the near horizon, no matter how often she pushed the thought away. Freedom and fun would not postpone the date. Her fourteenth birthday waited around the corner.

Before now, Saroj had always known what she *didn't* want: marriage. What she wanted had been vague, diffuse, unformulated, because impossible. Yet slowly, stealthily, a desire, and a goal, took form, gained profile. She grew in the knowledge of what she really, desperately wanted but could never have, trapped as she was by Baba's plans. Trixie had provided but a temporary escape. But what could she do?

Running away was out of the question: Baba would bring her back. And anyway, where would she go? Lucy Quentin, once a potential saviour, was but a distant goddess. Saroj had met her a few times at Trixie's, always rushing off to a meeting. There was as yet no law to protect Saroj. Lucy Quentin had lost interest in the cause of Indian girls and was now up to her neck in Abortion Rights and the Control of Women over their own Bodies.

And Trixie — did she really care? And the slobbering pack of boys were moving in, even ringing her up at home.

It was only a matter of time before Baba would pick up the phone and some boy would ask for Saroj and the shit would hit the fan. But it didn't happen that way at all.

Baba came home early one evening. Saroj was out.

It was a Tuesday, Car-Load Nite at the Starlight Drive-in, and Saroj and Trixie were the only girls in a car packed with fifteen- and sixteen-year-old boys. Saroj was the first to be dropped home after the show and Baba, standing back from the window in the gloom of the unlit drawing room, was presented with the spectacle of three boys piling out of the back seat to allow his daughter to descend; grinning, pimple-faced boys of a variety of races patting her on the back as she walked past them to open the gate.

He caned her till her legs bled. He attacked Trixie's old bicycle with a cutlass, slashed off the tyres and threw it outside the gate and into the gutter, where it was picked up and carried off by some passing African youths. Baba raged all night, lambasting Ma and Ganesh for allowing her to run wild. He called her a dirty whore. He removed her from school. He locked her into her room, or rather, into a tract of rooms: hers, the master bedroom, the puja room, and her parents' bathroom. All of these had to be kept locked from the outside, he ordained, so Saroj could walk all the way through to the bathroom, and visit the puja room to pray. He imprisoned her with Ma's sewing machine, embroidery, and whatever he felt would be a chaste occupation till the time came for her to be married. Only when Saroj was safely secured did he go off to his political meetings. Her only visitor was Ganesh, who came every evening bringing her books and kind words and gossip. Every day, at four after school, Trixie rode past, stopped and wave up at her at the window, and she'd wave back. One day, Trixie would tire of these useless visits. And then what? Marriage.

It was one month before her fourteenth birthday. Her freedom had lasted for not even a year.

She lay on her bed, gazing up into the vault of the roof. Thinking, as she had ceaselessly every afternoon for the last week. Baba was stupid. Escape was easy. All she had to do was climb up onto her wardrobe when nobody was home and jump over the wall into the upstairs gallery, a mere eight feet. Then down the stairs and out the door. To Lucy Quentin. But escape, as she had already concluded, would be also senseless. Baba would only have her brought back. The law allowed him to do so. She could refuse. Make a scene, kick and scream, spit into her bridegroom's face at the crucial moment. Then what? Baba would commit her to a lunatic asylum. Or something just as drastic. There was only one escape. The tower.

ஒ௸

From the widow's walk outside the tower the people on Waterloo Street looked like little toy dolls. Saroj looked once, quickly, and closed her eyes.

It had been so easy, up to now. She had looked for a long, flat, strong tool to wrench open the flimsy double doors into the tower, which had been latched from the outside. Ma's sword had been perfect. She had slid the blade into the slit between the flaps of the door, and pressed against the sword's hilt. The nails holding the latch in place had not resisted much. The door flew open with a bang, and she'd been free, free to run downstairs, to a questionable and temporary freedom, or up, to the tower. She had chosen up. *Up* was final.

And now here she was, perched on the railing of the widow's walk, clinging for dear life to the cast-iron pillar supporting the roof, bare feet hooked into the bars below her, not daring to look down, not daring to look anywhere, eyes tightly shut. A hysterical laugh of pure terror bubbled up from within her and she had to swallow hard to suppress it; at the same time unshed tears stung her eyes and she sobbed and tightened her grip on the pillar. The rail dug into the flesh of her bottom. Her hands turned cold as her grip pressed out the blood.

Pull yourself together, she told herself sternly. *Calm down and just do it.*

Just let yourself fall. Just let go. Lean forward. Close your eyes and drop. Suicide is easy. Nothing can go wrong. Look, it's all gravel down there on the drive. Nothing to soften the fall, no trees, no bushes. Death will come so quickly you won't have time to think. Just do it.

She squeezed her eyes together and imagined it all. She planned to fall when Trixie came, at around four. She saw herself falling, Trixie staring, dropping her bicycle and rushing to the gate screaming. She saw herself lying in the yard at the foot of the tower like a broken little rag doll. Passers-by would scream and all come running. They'd ring the doorbell in a frenzy and then Ma would come rushing out and her serene expression would give way to one of horror; she'd run to Saroj's prostrate body and shake her, turn her over, slap her cheeks, call *Saroj! Saroj!* Bystanders would gather, Trixie among them. *Call an ambulance!* Trixie would scream. *It's too late,* someone else would say, shaking his head, *her neck is broken.* Ma would sob and hold Saroj in her arms and talk to her through her tears, say all the things she'd never said during her lifetime, *I love you Saroj, please come back, don't die, I'm sorry, I'm sorry,* and then the crowds would part and Baba would stride through, his face as white as ash; he'd bend over and in a choking voice say, *it's not true! Not my Saroj! Saroj, come back!* And Trixie would stand up to her full imposing height and stare him in the eye and her voice would be like thunder when she said: *See, see what you did! It's all your fault! Saroj is dead and it's all your fault! You killed Saroj!* And Baba would look down at her poor limp form like a creeper in the dust and his shoulders would shake and he'd say, *Saroj, oh Saroj, I'm sorry! Please come back!*

Come back, Saroj! They'd all sob, *come back, we love you, we'll be so good to you, come back and give us another chance! You needn't marry!* And then the wake and the women in white saris of mourning, weeping and wailing, their eyes bleeding tears, arms around Ma, Baba dumb with grief!

She came to with a jerk and realised she was smiling. This won't do. It must be nearly time. Time to go. Time to die. She wished she could look at her watch, but she couldn't because if she let go of the pillar she'd fall. Well, so what. *You want to fall, don't you? Yes, but . . . not just yet . . . just a little while longer.* She needed to practise in her mind. Go through the steps of falling and of dying. Prepare herself. Think of not being any more. Ever again.

I'll lean forward and just let go and let myself drop. It'll be like flying. What thoughts will I have, those moments before I hit the ground?

Deliverance. The end. *Think of dying. Think of the moments after death. When you won't be here any more. There'll be no more me. Just nothing. How can it be! How can there be no me? How can it come to an end? Oh God, how can I end? Oh God, I don't want to end! I can't! No, No!*

In the distance the clock of the Sacred Heart church began to chime four. At the same moment Trixie rounded the corner on her bicycle and at the same moment she screamed with all the power in her lungs, *'NO! I don't want to die! Trixie!'*

In a trice Trixie's bike was clattering to the ground and she was at the front door and the bell screamed through the house. Then there was Trixie, miles below, looking up. Through the distance Saroj could almost see her eyes, like jewels in her dark face, the sheer terror in them. Her hands were cupped around her mouth and she was screaming, and, just as she'd imagined it a few moments earlier people, came running from the street, clusters of faces looking up, people's hands gesturing as if pushing her back, cars braking, people standing beside their bicycles, staring. She saw it all as in a panorama picture far away, having nothing to do with herself, detached from herself because having screamed her 'NO!' everything in her was paralysed, thoughts immobile as in a still life picture, feelings struck into a pose as in a stalled film. She was a statue of a girl with long blue-black hair floating loosely around and about her whipped by the breeze, sitting on a railing in a wide open sky, willing to drop but her will numbed to silence by a *No*.

In the tableau below Ma appeared, looking up. She walked slowly. Where others waved their hands wildly above their hands, Ma's hands were down. She patted the air gently, walked slowly, always looking upwards, up at Saroj. Dizziness overcame Saroj. Through a long naked space she heard Ma's voice, 'Saroj, be still, I'm coming.' Not a shout but a whisper. She squinted through eyelashes laced with tears and saw a space where Ma had been below, and seconds later heard her feet on the wooden steps to the tower. Ma was behind her now, her arms around her, her lips in her hair; she was whispering. Then Saroj was falling; falling backwards, though, not forwards, and there was nothing. Only Ma and blackness.

When there was light again there was only light, sunlight all around her. She was bathed in light. I'm dead, she thought, and in heaven, but then she saw the mosquito net curled into itself above her and she knew she wasn't dead.

Ma's fingers stroked her cheek.

'Saroj,' said her soft voice, and she turned her head to face her. She leaned forwards, her eyes moist with something more than love, smiling gently, her lips moving through the smile as she spoke. 'I'm here, Saroj, don't worry. Would you like some water?'

Saroj nodded, her eyes locked into Ma's. Ma helped her into a sitting position, fluffed up the pillows behind her, and held out a glass of water. As Saroj took it she let her eyes leave Ma's and look around. She was in her own room, and all but one of the windows were open. The shutters too, letting in the sunlight and the cool breeze. A softness, a gentleness, was in the air; she breathed it in and it rocked her almost physically like a lullaby within. Sleep, she thought, delicious sleep. Sleep, and never wake up. She felt Ma's finger brushing a wisp of hair from her forehead and opened her eyes.

'The water,' Ma whispered. She took the glass. Inside it the water caught a ray of sunlight. It sparkled with rainbow colours. *A glass of sunlight. A glass of rainbow. A glass of grace.*

She raised the glass to parched lips and drained it. 'Would you like some more?' Ma asked, and she shook her head and pushed herself down under the sheet and closed her eyes.

'Sleep,' Ma said. 'Sleep, darling Saroj, that's the best thing now.' So Saroj slept.

Chapter 20

Savitri
Madras, 1927

Four years later several things happened to the Lindsay family in the space of a few months. Fiona returned from England, which she hated for its cold, grey, soggy climate, determined to live the rest of her life at Home. She arrived in the dark of night. Early next morning she rose filled with an eagerness to go out and revel in the beauty and warmth of the garden, and the first person she saw was Gopal. Every morning in the grey of dawn Gopal came to study for his matriculation exams in the rose arbour which was the only place in the whole of Fairwinds — at least the only place accessible to him — where he had the peace and quiet for serious study. He was seventeen, a tall, handsome, lanky, healthy Indian youth, well educated, now speaking perfect English. She was sixteen, and the joy of coming Home lent to her otherwise plain features an inner beauty, a radiance, and nature did the rest.

In the course of the next few days they fell in love and swore to marry.

That season Savitri healed the Colonel's carbuncles. It happened, just as in the case of the Admiral's lame hand, quite spontaneously, and again Savitri denied any personal responsibility: 'It wasn't me, madam, sir, it was God!'

The Colonel and his wife had come to tea, as they did quite often now. Since the miracle of his healing the Admiral was a changed man. He had opened up socially, conversed with his wife and her guests, and had his own guests over occasionally. He went to the cricket club and the polo club — though of course he didn't play himself. Because no further miracle had taken place. Savitri had proved unable to heal his major disability, the lameness of his legs. Unable, or, according to Mrs Lindsay, *unwilling.* She had proved to be a most intractable child in this respect. Docile on the surface, yes, but she refused even to *try* to utilise the powers Mrs Lindsay was still convinced she had. It was all a matter of *will:* practice makes perfect, Mrs Lindsay knew, and if Savriti would not practise on her friends, then how would she develop her will to heal? It was all so annoying — and so ungrateful. The most the girl would do was comfort crying babies, and bring reluctant roses to bloom.

Babies, when picked up by Savitri, stopped crying immediately. Mrs Lindsay had received several offers for Savitri to work as an *ayah* — a very young one, to be sure, but a reliable one, who spoke perfect English, and had English manners, and who had a gift for calming yelling babies. But Mrs Lindsay held on to Savitri. There was her education to think about. Mrs Lindsay was her patroness, and still had plans and high hopes for her. Perhaps, when she was older, more reasonable, when she needed money...

The Colonel's carbuncles were in a very tender place, and prevented him from sitting down to tea, which he drank standing; after which he excused himself and wandered off the verandah in search of Mrs Lindsay's roses, for he grew roses himself, and loved them.

He met Savitri eating a marigold.

'Whatever are you doing, child?' he asked in astonishment.

'Eating a marigold, sir!' she said, looking up at him with her huge melting-chocolate eyes, and in all innocence, too, as if eating her mistress's marigolds was the most everyday thing in the world.

The Colonel, of course, knew about Savitri. He had thought the story of the Admiral's healing amusing, and had ever since referred to his friend's protégée as Little Lady Doctor. She was often around when he came to tea, and once he had heard her speak and been highly entertained, those fine meticulous English words emerging from that brown native mouth. It had been something of a shock — but a pleasant one.

Being basically a kind man, with grandchildren of his own whom he saw far too seldom, for they lived far away in England, he smiled at her and leaned forward to bring his large, ruddy face closer to her little brown one, and placed his hands on his spread knees for support. She smiled back, quite unperturbed. She was ten now, but had grown little in the last years so that she was still tiny, bony, fey, and dressed in her fluttering carnival colours she looked more the butterfly than ever. The Colonel's smile spread indulgingly.

'A marigold!' he exclaimed. 'My, how interesting!'

'Here,' she said, encouraged, and offered him a few petals. 'Try them!'

To humour her the Colonel placed the golden petals on his tongue, chewed them as if relishing the taste and said, 'Delicious, dear little girl! What a delicacy! Do you always do this?'

'No sir, and I don't think they taste so good, sir, but I'm eating them for health. You see, a bee stung me and my grandfather said to rub the bee-sting with marigold and to eat a few of the petals. Otherwise I don't pick the flowers. It hurts them.'

The Colonel smiled again and said, a little condescendingly, 'Well, well. Let's hope it's good for my health too, eh, Little Lady Doctor? A good day to you, and *bon appetit!*' He tipped his pith helmet, and then, changing his mind, swept it forward graciously and bowed down low to her, as to a society *grande dame*. She, having no hat or helmet to tip, held out her hand for him to shake, and curtsied politely, saying, 'Good afternoon, sir, and goodbye!'

When he shook her hand the Colonel felt as though he had touched a live wire, for want of a better description; a gentle live wire. It was a prickling, warm sensation, but altogether pleasant, and though he told no-one about the meeting with Savitri his mind wandered back again and again to the butterfly girl with the marigold, for days afterwards.

The little satellite carbuncles around the main big one

began to recede. He wasn't quite sure, at first, but by the end of the first week there was no mistaking the fact — they were almost entirely gone. By the end of the third week the large one had disappeared too. The Colonel could sit when he came to tea. And only then he talked of the miracle, and Mrs Lindsay swelled with pride.

Hadn't she known! Her disappointment with Savitri fled and she knew, she positively *knew*, the girl had Powers. She simply refused to use them.

The day after his last exam Gopal eloped with Fiona. They took a train to Bombay, she travelling first class, he third, to avoid attention and discovery. They had had just enough money for their train tickets, plus the jewels Fiona's grandmother had left her, which she intended to pawn or sell in Bombay. They got no further than Victoria Station, however, and Fiona was brought back to Madras in disgrace. Gopal stayed in Bombay, where he was to attend university. He was a disgrace to the Iyers, and to the Lindsays an ingrate — after all they had done for him! Iyer almost got the sack, but he was the best cook around, so Mrs Lindsay gave him a good reprimand and kept him. But both families were shamed. Fiona must be removed at once.

Mrs Lindsay dropped everything and booked passages for Fiona, herself and eleven-year-old David back to England, a year earlier than planned. It was time he became a real boy, and it was time he dropped his obsession with Savitri.

Mrs Lindsay had put the incident of Savitri's prophecy to the back of her mind, but now and again it nudged forward and worried her. Best to separate them. David was too soft. He needed the challenge of rugby, horseback riding, maybe hunting. He'd have all that with Aunt Jemima, who kept a stable of fine thoroughbreds, and at the prep school Aunt Jemima had selected before he went to Eton. His mother would accompany him and see him well settled before she returned. Fiona was to go to finishing school in Switzerland, and an English husband was to be found for her. She should never return to India.

༶

That year, *Thatha* died. Over the years he had taught Savitri all he knew about his remedies, but, he told her, the remedies themselves were only distractions, because people were faithless and needed physical props. Without the Gift the remedies were nothing. And Savitri had that Gift; or rather, it was in her, but it was not hers.

'Do not use it with *ahamkara*,' *Thatha* told her, and finally Savitri had a word for thought-body.

'*Ahamkara* is impure,' *Thatha* said, and left his body.

That season Vijayan killed the king cobra. Mrs Lindsay, inspecting the garden, saw the snake and ordered Muthu to kill him, but Muthu slapped his cheeks in awe and refused, and so did all the Boys. Killing him would be inauspicious. Vijayan was the only one who obeyed her. He brought his cutlass and slashed the king cobra in two.

Savitri wept. It was most inauspicious. She thought that, somehow, it was all her fault. She had promised to protect him. The killing of the king cobra was so inauspicious Savitri knew that very bad times lay ahead for everyone.

Mr Baldwin, now married, took on a new position with a new family and Savitri was sent to the English Medium School, where she quickly rose to the top of her class. But she was a strange girl, who made no friends. St Mary's was a girls' school, the pupils the daughters of upper-middle class Indians and lower class English, and all considered Savitri beneath them. She loved David, missed him, and wrote to him every week. She thought she might become a doctor — if such a thing was possible for girls. She had never heard of a lady-doctor. Not even in a book. She knew if she asked Teacher he would only laugh. And the years slipped by.

By the terms of the agreement between the Lindsays and her father she was obliged to go to school only up to the age of fourteen. On her fourteenth birthday, Iyer set her to work in the kitchen. And even if she couldn't marry till she was eighteen, it was a good thing to scout around for a husband now, because otherwise all the good ones would be taken, and what was the use of her dowry if all she could buy with it was a widower, either with a brood of children, or an old one?

So in preparation for her marriage Savitri learned to cook, and she cooked well. She had duties in the garden, too, for Mrs Lindsay knew that flowers bloomed gloriously for Savitri, that they loved her touch and her voice. The roses grew fuller and brighter when she pruned them. Her hands in the earth nourished them, on the watering can quenched their thirst, and they thanked her with their beauty. Fairwinds had never been such a paradise.

Healings took place, sporadically. The Colonel's carbuncles were only the beginning. As well as being able to stop babies crying by having Savitri pick them up, mothers found that when they changed their baby's nappies, a certain rash had disappeared and never returned, or a certain diarrhoea had mysteriously stopped.

Then, a mother herself was healed under inexplicable circumstances. This mother had been suffering from high fever for many days and she had "borrowed" Savitri to help out with the children, since she could not trust the two *ayahs*. The second morning Savitri brought a little brown glass bottle and said to the mother, 'I have brought something that might help you. May I make a little infusion for you?'

The mother knew of the rumours surrounding Savitri and gave her permission. She drank the bitter tea Savitri put into her hands, and by that evening she was up and about.

'You know, immediately I felt better. Immediately!' Her voice rose with astonishment as she told her friends, and Savitri's reputation spread. But soon it became obvious: Savitri was at no-one's disposal. She turned down every single application in the weeks following the mother's healing.

And then another healing took place, but to a patient who had not even asked for help; and besides, Savitri had not even known of the complaint, which was an intimate and unmentionable women's one which Mrs Hull would never have spoken of herself. But she too was a lover of roses and seeing Savitri in the garden went over to admire them and slipped into a conversation about roses. Their talk turned to plants in general, and Mrs Hull was amazed by Savitri's intimate knowledge of their properties. And then just by the way Savitri mentioned a certain root-powder which was 'good for women's ailments'.

Mrs Hull, who was a Theosophist, felt a rush of blood to her cheeks and a definite Knowledge. She asked sweetly and casually if she could try that root-powder, and Savitri, smiling, had run off home and returned with a sample wrapped up in a piece of brown paper and tied with string. 'A little each morning,' she told Mrs Hull, showing with thumb and forefinger just how much 'a little' was.

Mrs Hull was cured, and others. People whispered, and nodded, and wondered about her. 'She's like a butterfly,' Mrs Lindsay warned her friends. 'If you run behind her and try to catch her she'll slip through your fingers. But if you're still she might just alight on your shoulder.'

Mrs Lindsay had learned the hard way: not all the pleading in the world could make Savitri develop her alleged Powers. And not all the cajoling would induce her to accept 'a little gift of thanks' for a healing. No, not even a *word* of thanks, or of praise. Indeed, thanks and praise seemed to embarrass Savitri.

She did not receive a single letter from David. Every week she handed over her own envelope to Mrs Lindsay, on which was carefully written, *Mr David Lindsay, England.* She had asked Mrs Lindsay for David's address so she could write to him directly, but she had only replied gaily, 'Oh, no dear, don't waste your money on stamps. Just give me the letter and we'll send it on to him with our own post.'

At first she grieved for David. It was as if the very air she breathed had been cut off. And not hearing a word from him made things worse. Had he forgotten her? Had he forgotten their vow? She hadn't. She still had the cross he had given her as a pledge of their marriage, though she didn't wear it, for she knew her father would object. But why didn't he write?

Faithfully she kept up her own side of the correspondence. For years. And still he did not reply. She was sixteen when, working in the kitchen, she discovered the reason. There were two rubbish bins, one for mango and banana peels and other edible remainders which Iyer took to feed the cow, and one for papers and other combustibles which Muthu took away to burn.

She didn't have much to do with the latter but one day, throwing away a page of newspaper in which a pound of rice had been wrapped, she found in the combustible bin the scraps of a letter, with her own handwriting, thrown there by some careless maid. Her own letter to David.

On that day Savitri lost an entire heartful of innocence and trust. She learned how underhand and deceitful people could be. She learned the meaning of betrayal. And she learned that two could play at the same game, and that subterfuge was superior to openness.

At the very next opportunity, when Mrs Lindsay and the Admiral were out at a luncheon, she searched Mrs Lindsay's private desk, found David's address, copied it down, and wrote to him directly.

At the same time she continued to pass on to Mrs Lindsay other, harmless letters addressed to *Mr David Lindsay, England*, ones which Mrs Lindsay could read and tear up and throw away, suspecting nothing.

From that day on Savitri grew bold. She knew, of course, of the plans to marry her off as soon as she was eighteen, and to David she poured out her heart, reminded him of their pledge, swore eternal love, and begged him to come before then, or to write her father and ask for her hand, to come and save her. She was ready, she told him, to elope, just as Gopal and Fiona had done. She told him of his mother's deceit, told him of the years of waiting for a word from him, told him of her happiness at finally knowing it was not his fault...

'Perhaps you have written to me, also,' she wrote, 'and those letters, too, have been destroyed and burned? Never mind. All is well now. But, David, time is growing short! I am growing into a woman, and am to be married when I'm eighteen.'

This first letter grew to seven pages. She told him all the news.

'Gopal is back in Madras. He's teaching English at a boys' primary school but he's restless. He's not living with us any more, because he doesn't get on with Mani. Besides, it's getting a little cramped in our home. Mani was discharged from the army, because he was diagnosed with TB. He coughs a lot. He and Narayan are both married, their wives are living with us and Mani's little son.

'I am earning a little of my own money now, David. Friends of your mother engage me to look after their children. They say I am very good with children, that I would make a good nanny. A nanny! Oh David, is that my future, some English lady's *ayah*? But it is good to have my own cash. I give most of it to Appa, of course, but I have managed to save a little, and the rest I spent on... guess what I bought? A spinning wheel! Every evening I sit on the tinnai and spin cotton.'

That led her on to write about Mr Gandhi, her former English teacher's enthusiasm for this great man, India's hope, her own veneration of him, Mani's growing political vehemence and hatred of the English.

'Gandhiji has just returned from England,' she wrote. 'Tell me, David, what was his reception there? What did the English think of him, when he wore his loincloth to tea with King George? Why wouldn't Mr Churchill speak to him? After all, he is our chosen leader! We don't know for sure, of course, if what the newspapers say is true, so do tell me what the English really think! And, dear David, do you really think we might one day gain independence from England? Wouldn't that be exciting! But what would happen then to you? Would your family have to leave? And what about my father's job? Mani is insisting we must throw out the English lock, stock and barrel, but surely that cannot be! He hates the English. It is almost personal, but I find I cannot hate them. The English

I have personally known have been most good and kind to me, but I know it is otherwise elsewhere, and I have been fortunate. Tell me your own thoughts, David! Whose side are you on?

'No, I cannot hate the English, though my brother does, and all his friends. They have meetings in our house, imagine! On the property of an Englishman! (Please don't tell your parents!) I know Gandhiji himself does not hate the English, he just wants them to stop interfering in our own Indian affairs, and there I can only agree with him. And what he says about the Harijans, there I am also of one mind! I have always thought the same myself, you know! I always felt my father's aversion to the untouchables was in itself impure, more so than they could ever be themselves . . . it is hateful, arrogant thoughts that make us dirty and impure, the thoughts that we are better than others . . .'

She finished her letter, signed and folded it, and was just about to put it in the envelope when an afterthought struck her. Quickly she unfolded it and wrote, on the final page beneath the signature, 'PS is there such a thing as a lady-doctor? Do they have them in England? Do you think I could become one in England, after we are married?'

Even before she could expect a reply she wrote again, and again. Four letters had been sped to England when, finally, David's reply to the first one came, addressed to her personally at her father's home.

He described to her, in minute detail, the horrid English weather. He told her he missed Fairwinds, and her, in that order. He was thinking of entering the Navy, like his father. He wrote a few non-committal paragraphs on Mr Gandhi. He made no reference to coming home, or to their marriage, or elopement. It seemed he had forgotten her, except as a childhood friend. She did not write again.

It was not wounded pride. It was the acceptance that David's mind was, obviously, occupied. That, for now, love was beyond him. Savitri was not one to force; hers was the strength of waiting, waiting in knowledge, waiting in the wisdom of what is real and indestructible, waiting in the bedrock of love.

Chapter 21

Nat
London, 1963

Nat was met at Heathrow by Henry's son Adam and his wife Sheila. Though Doctor had several relatives living in London, it had not been convenient for Nat to stay with any of them and Adam, who had known Doctor since he was a boy, was happy to take Nat into the bosom of his family, and so was his wife.

They let Nat sleep out his jet-lag and then Sheila took him shopping, because his Indian wardrobe was atrocious.

'If you're not with-it the girls will tease you, Nat. You can't possibly wear those tight shiny trousers! Really, they're almost pedal-pushers! And those pointy shoes! My goodness! Not in London in this day and age!'

There was money. Nat had always known there was money, enough to support his father and himself in India, and buy medicines and teak saplings, repair roofs for the villagers, for Armaclare College, and now to support Nat in England as Adam and Sheila's paying guest, and to buy him a suitable wardrobe, books and whatever else he might need in the coming years, and, of course to pay his University fees. Nat never asked where the money came from. He only knew: there was money.

Sheila and Adam lived in a pretty, semi-detached house in Croydon. Both were secondary school teachers and from the first day they went out of their way to make Nat feel at home. They showed him all the London sights. They took him to the obligatory Museums; he saw the Changing of the Guard, fed the pigeons at Trafalgar Square, tried fish and chips (and was violently sick afterwards, having never ever eaten fish before), learned to use the Underground, and was desperately, heart-wrenchingly homesick. He felt he was living in a world out of joint, part of a jigsaw puzzle whose pieces were scattered far and wide, irretrievable, that all that was precious and whole was lost for ever. His mind was an upturned rubbish bin. He missed his father, and the villagers: the shining dark eyes in black Dravidian faces. The turbulent flapping of crows' wings, silver stars scattered over the black nights, the full yellow moon rising over the hill. But his father had thrown him in at the deep end, and he had to swim.

In early August Nina and Jule came home from their school camping holiday in the South of France. Nina and Jule were Adam and Sheila's twin daughters: fifteen, freckled, flaxen-haired, blue-eyed, long-legged, freckle-faced, gawky and identical. They made no secret of the fact that they just adored Nat; *he's ever so sweet*, they giggled to their friends over the phone, in Nat's hearing: so innocent, so shy, and s-o-o-o handsome, just fabulous, and they were absolutely *sure* he was a virgin.

'Don't take any notice of them, Nat dear,' said Sheila, 'they're just silly girls and they're trying to take the mickey out of you. Don't let them.'

This, when Nina and Jule stole all of Nat's underwear, replaced it with their own, and locked themselves in the bathroom where for the best part of an hour piercing shrieks of laughter and shrill bursts of giggles emerged. All of a sudden the bathroom door flew open and the girls raced out and down the carpeted stairs dressed in nothing but Nat's underpants, two long white streaks of almost-naked flesh pushing past Nat and Sheila in the hall. They leaped up on to the dining-room table, and, holding on to the oversized underpants at the waist, wriggled and writhed there, screaming, '*Let's twist again, Like we did last summer!*' into their fists before streaking back upstairs and collapsing on the bathroom floor in a chortling, squirming, screeching heap of adolescence.

Nat's lips twitched and he shook his head indulgently.

'It's all right, Sheila, they don't bother me. I'll get even,' he said.

And when the girls slammed the bathroom door again and hooted, 'We're going to have a bath now, Nat, just knock if you want to join us,' he was ready.

'I'm fine, thanks,' he called in return. 'But I'll take you up on that another time,' whereupon a double scream of mirth forced him to cover his ears and make a face at Sheila, who laughed and retired to watch the television.

While the girls were having their bath Nat proceeded to decorate their room with underwear. He carefully laid out their little lacy bras and panties over their chairs, their desks, their beds, their window sills; he tacked them to the walls, he hung them over their books and from the shelves, he dressed their teddy bears in them, he placed them across their pillows and pulled them over the lamps. For some reason, the girls sobered up after that. In fact, they turned almost shy. But Nat had seen the light.

One thing about girls he had known back home: whether a girl was a peasant or a Bannerji princess, the aura of chastity surrounded her like an inviolable sweet-scented armour, an integral part of her secret inner world, to be one day presented as a precious gift to her bridegroom.

But for Nina, and Jule, and the hundreds of girls Nat was about to discover, chastity was a joke, a kicked-off relic of childhood. These girls had no secrets, or if they had, they did not know it. Their gift to Nat came unconditionally, and its name was freedom. They had one thing to teach Nat: enjoyment.

Chapter 22

Saroj
Georgetown, 1964

M a brought her supper in her room, a luxury only afforded those children who were too sick to leave their beds. This time she wasn't *physically* sick, but Ma surely could see the fever burning up her soul. She picked at her food. She wasn't hungry, but wasting food in their house came second only to murder and Ma had not brought much, just a chapatti and a few spoons of potato curry. She ate slowly, thinking of how to say what had to be said. Ma moved around the room as she ate, drawing the curtains, tidying up the dresser, folding some sheets. As she mopped up the last stains of curry with the chapatti Ma came and sat on the edge of her bed, a hairbrush in her hand. She began to brush Saroj's wild hair with her accustomed vigour, occasionally stopping to attack the knots that had nudged themselves in during sleep.

'Ma, I don't want to marry yet. I don't want to marry ever!'

'You need not marry yet, Saroj. You should have trusted me, dear, and spoken to me about your fears. I'm sorry; I neglected you. I should have paid more attention to the signs... paid more attention to you. I've been a little preoccupied lately, I should have known, and then this could have been prevented.'

'But Baba said . . . !'

'Baba said, Baba said! Don't you know yet that men are full of words that mean nothing? The silence of a woman is a thousand times weightier. You must learn to trust silence. To load it with truth, and to wait. A woman cannot survive by physical violence, by biting and jumping from towers: on that level men are always mightier, and women will always lose such unequal battles. Women must be quiet, and cunning. Men possess blatant power, but the power of a woman is latent, secret, and more potent by far. It must be tapped like an underground stream, and your trust in it must be absolute. Why did you not come to me with your despair? Do you think I would have let you marry in such a state? If I had known I would have helped you, and he could not have done a thing. If the mother does not consent, how can a wedding take place? You will marry, when the right time comes, the husband who is your destiny. Not this one.'

Her eyes twinkled and her lips twitched in a girlish smile of complicity. She had never spoken so much in all Saroj's life, except for her stories.

'Ma: I don't want to marry at all! Not this Ghosh boy nor any boy Baba chooses and not anybody, never.'

Ma was silent. Saroj's hair was now brushed clean, knot-free and silky; with the side of the brush Ma parted it right down the middle, laid down the brush on the bedside table, and picked up half of the hair, the hair on her side of the bed, in her two hands, dividing it expertly into three equal strands with strong, calm fingers.

'And if you should love someone?'

Her fingers and the strands of hair flicked back and forth, the plait growing out of her hands, and as it grew she moved backwards on the bed.

'Love! What is love! There's no such thing!'

'In a way you're right. What most people call love is only passion and it ebbs. But true love never ebbs.'

Saroj felt the tide of irritation rising within her, and pushed it back before it turned to exasperation. Ma was full of clichés, pat statements, reeled off as if learned from a book. What did she know about life? What *could* she know! But Saroj had to talk to her, desperate as she was, knowing that neither Ganesh nor Trixie could help her now. Ma was all she had, and she'd have to do.

'Look at Baba. How could any wife love him?'

Ma tied a piece of ribbon round the end of the finished

plait, stood up and walked around to the other side of the bed to begin the second plait. Her hands in Saroj's hair, the rhythmic working of her fingers, the soft lashing back and forth of the silken strands brought a kind of comfort, a degree of calmness, into the girl's mind.

Ma said quietly, 'I do.'

'You don't! You can't! He's so awful! Ma, he's so cruel, he's such a monster!'

Something like naughtiness flashed into Ma's eyes.

'But it's the monsters who most need love! They need the strongest, rarest kind of love!' She paused. And then she continued.

'And anyway, he's not really a monster. Don't ever think that. Some things are only ugly on the outside. If you look below the surface you can see the truth. And in truth, Baba loves you very much; he loves us all. We are his whole world and without us he is nothing. But his mind has distorted the truth and that is why he appears such a monster. In truth he is not hateful. Only desperately unhappy. How can you hate anyone so unhappy?'

'Well, I hate him! I hate him with all my heart. I hate him with all my heart and soul and all my life and one day I want to hurt him the way he hurt me! I swear it, Ma, I do! I wish Baba were dead, dead, dead!' Saroj sobbed and flung herself against Ma's bosom. Ma's eyes grew moist and she took Saroj in her arms. Silently she rocked back and forth.

She said, 'Your hatred will destroy you, Saroj. Learn to rise above it. You are so like him: stubbornly courting feelings that eat you up inside. You've been resenting him since you were a tiny child and that's not healthy — you hurt yourself even more than you hurt him. You have made an image of your father and you go through life battling this image, and you will never see him as he really, truly is. You make an effigy of him inside your soul, and burn him up — but in fact you burn yourself as well. It hurts, Saroj, don't you see how hate hurts!'

'You always told us not to fear pain! That pain is good!'

'There are good pains, and bad pains. Do you know why I keep a sword in the puja room? It's to remind myself of the meaning of pain; to remind myself that there is something in me stronger than all pain. That's what I mean by good pain. Good pain is pain that forces you to rise beyond it — then you are stronger than suffering.

But your kind of pain, Saroj, self-afflicted pain, is the opposite. Hate is like a tiny weed growing in the mind: pluck it out at the roots, as you would the weed! But what you did is nourish it with attention — and now it's grown into such a tangle you're caught within it — it's strangling you. You're a prisoner of your own hatred. Can't you see?'

'No, Ma, it's Baba who's imprisoned me! It's he who locked me up in my room and locks me up in the house and wants to lock me up in marriage! It's Baba who's trying to plan my life for me and make me do things I can't, I just can't do! Why won't he let me do what I want!'

And what is it that you want? That you *really* want?'

Saroj lowered her eyes. Ma laid an arm around her shoulder, drawing her closer, and said, 'Child: you must talk to me. Tell me what is in your heart. Don't worry about the Ghosh boy and don't worry about your father. I will take care of that. But you must trust me, and talk to me.'

Saroj swallowed. She took a deep breath. And then it all came rushing out.

'Ma, Ganesh is going to England to study and I would like to do that myself. I want to finish school. Get my A Levels and then go to university. I want to go to England like Ganesh. I want to study law and then come back and change all the laws, so girls like me aren't forced into marriage. I know it's impossible but that's what I *really* want.'

So. It was out. She'd put the impossible into words. Ma would be shocked and brush it away and tell her to forget it because girls did not need an education, only boys, and it was just her hard luck being born a girl. She'd tell Saroj to accept her destiny, for the *karma* of a girl was to marry and have children. These were the facts Saroj had grown up with and even to think of an alternative was ludicrous. She couldn't think of a single Roy girl who hadn't married after leaving school. Not one. Not even the clever ones who shone at school. Not even the ones with Christian names and the ones who wore trousers. Not even the ones who went to work in a bank or an insurance agency for a few months before their weddings. Not even Balwant's wife. Sooner or later they dropped their jobs to marry.

Every one of them had a husband before she was twenty. Every one of them had a baby before she was twenty-one. Marriage was their ordained lot in life and they all knew it and there was no exception. And why should Saroj, Deodat Roy's daughter, the strictest and most conservative Roy of the lot, be any different? But she had spoken the words. It was heresy, but she had spoken them.

Ma was so silent she pulled away to look into her face, which was as inscrutable as ever. You could never read Ma's thoughts. She stood up now and walked to one of the windows and pushed out the jalousie on its stick to let the moonlight into the room. She opened the second jalousie. Then she walked to the dresser and lit a candle and came back to sit on the side of the bed and took Saroj's hand. The flickering flame cast grotesque shadows on the wall; they looked like witches, Ma and Saroj, leaning in towards each other. Ma's hand was cool, her touch like silk. Saroj's hand lay limp in hers, and she stroked the back of it with light, feathery fingers.

And then Ma laughed. Not a loud laugh, for Ma was never loud. A round, happy, bell-like chuckle, and she turned to Saroj, and in the flickering candlelight her eyes were bright and expressive, the inscrutability gone, and Ma was like an open book, inviting Saroj to read its pages.

'That's what I wanted too,' Ma said.

Saroj hadn't heard right. 'What, Ma? What did you want?'

'I wanted to finish school and go to university. I wanted to be a doctor.'

'You wanted to be a doctor, Ma? *You?*'

It was like hearing the moon say it wanted to be the sun. Saroj couldn't believe her ears. But Ma nodded. She had opened wide the book of her past, and shown Saroj a single page. Before she could close that page Saroj said hurriedly, 'What happened, Ma? Did you go to university?'

'No. My parents wouldn't let me. It wasn't the done thing. They forced me into marriage. I was seventeen. Old, for an Indian girl. Time to marry.' Reluctantly she spoke, eager to close the book, but one tiny crack was still open.

'And what happened then, Ma? Tell me!'

'My first husband died. And then I came here and married your father.'

Bang. It was over. The book banged shut and locked with a key. Ma seemed suddenly in a hurry.

'You should try to get some sleep now, dear!' she said, and stroked Saroj's hair away from her face, leaned over and kissed her.

'Ma . . .'

Ma spoke hurriedly now, and in a whisper, conspiringly. This was just for the two of them and the words were the most beautiful in all the world.

'Listen, dear. I spoke to Miss Dewer. She says you have been very lazy this past year but you have a brilliant mind and if you work hard you can win the British Guiana Scholarship. If that's what you want I will help you. But you must trust me implicitly. You must stop worrying about the future, and simply trust. Come, sleep.'

Saroj slipped down into the bed as Ma pulled up the sheet to cover her. Ma kissed her again. She walked over to the dresser and blew out the candles and in the ghostly moonlight that filtered in through the open windows Saroj saw her glide over to the gallery door, an evanescent spirit forever out of reach. In the doorway she paused.

'I'm not going to lock you in, dear. That's all over now.' Then she was gone. But her words rang on in Saroj's mind.

The British Guiana Scholarship! Awarded each year to the boy and the girl with the best A Level results in the whole country! The very thought of winning it made her dizzy But then, why not? Indeed, why not? If even the strict and hard-to-please Miss Dewer believed in her, why shouldn't she believe in herself?

Saroj smiled herself to sleep. Ma was on her side. Anything, anything in the world could happen. Because Ma's words were well chosen and carried all the weight of truth, and truth, Ma said, was more weighty than the universe. As children they had believed that anything Ma said would automatically come to pass, simply because she had said it. And because they believed it, that was the way it had always been. Ma had been their private prophetess. By the mere fact of speaking she brought forth events. Saroj felt herself transported back into the safe predictable world of childhood.

Ma was still sweeping the yard next morning when Ganesh poked his head around the door. Saroj had never been so happy to see his boyish grin and tousled head in all her life. He bounded to her side with the exuberance of a half-grown puppy, and by the time she could sit up in bed he was all over her. Ganesh was such a very physical boy; he liked to hug and kiss and squeeze and stroke, and that's what he did now. They laughed together and he brushed the hair out of Saroj's eyes.

'Well, at least you haven't forgotten how to laugh! And look what I brought for you!'

From behind his back he brought out a packet wrapped in birthday paper and tied with a bow, big and oblong, and when she took it in her hands, it rattled — the kind of present that was exciting because you couldn't guess what was inside.

'Oh Gan! But what is it?'

'Go on, open it! Your birthday isn't till next week but I grant you permission.'

She tore at the paper like a little girl. Inside it was a box, and inside the box was a radio-cassette recorder. She flung her arms around Ganesh.

'Oh, Gan! I can't believe it! I never dared own one of these before!'

'Well, if you dare to jump from the tower this is just small potatoes!'

'Gan, don't let's talk about that, okay?'

'But that's exactly what I'm here to talk about. I couldn't believe my ears when I came home and heard. I looked in on you but you were sleeping else I'd have come and given you a good telling off. Saroj! It's not that bad, is it?'

'If they marry me off to that boy it is.'

'Look, they're not going to. They postponed the wedding. Ma and Baba were up late last night and I joined them, and Ma and I pleaded and wheedled with Baba not to do it. Ma said a wife needs an education these days. I confirmed it. We persuaded him to postpone the wedding at least till you get your O Levels.'

'Okay, they can postpone it but it's still hanging over me and what use is it getting O Levels if I jump from the tower on my wedding day?'

'You won't. We won't let you.'

'All right, I won't kill myself, but I swear I'll run away.'

'That's a much more sensible idea. I'll even help you. But don't forget, you can't hide for ever. Baba can have you brought back. And where'll you be then?'

'I'm not going to marry any boy Baba chooses for me, Gan. It can't be right, I bet it isn't even legal. Trixie said I should get a lawyer; her mother will help. I'm going to fight, Gan, and I've been thinking. Listen, Gan, when you go to England I want you to send for me. Get me a plane ticket and let me come! Please!'

'Saroj, I'd love to and I will, but don't forget, you're not even fourteen yet! You'll need all sorts of papers and things and parental consent and don't think Baba's going to sign anything!'

'No, but maybe Ma will!'

In the silence that followed those words they heard the faint swish-swish of Ma's broom downstairs, a rhythm and pace that was comforting and inspiring at once, like the steady beat of the earth's inner heart as Ma set her little world in order.

Chapter 23

Savitri
Madras, 1934

After Eton David came home. It was his final holiday before Oxford.

He had not forgotten the little butterfly girl fluttering through the Fairwinds garden. That was the way he held her in his memory: as a skinny ten-year-old tucking a long skirt into her waistband to scramble up a mango tree, her clothes dishevelled and her plaits unravelling, and he was as fond of her as ever. He had not forgotten her as he had not forgotten the peacock dancing and the hibiscus blooming. She was a part of the natural beauty, the unchanging tableau of his perfect childhood, a background he had left and outgrown, still a part of him, yet left behind.

He himself had grown into a tall, limber young man, whose hair, the colour of wheat-straw, refused to stay parted but fell unruly over his forehead, whose blue-grey eyes were flecked with russet gold, and whose generous smile had charmed and captivated many a flippant debutante.

He had woken late that first morning and the house was empty, except, of course, for the servants, the little maids scuttling out of his way as he entered the dining room. His mother had left a note — sorry to have missed him, gone to Adyar — and she'd be back for luncheon. His father was in his study.

David had one overwhelming desire: to bite once again into a juice-dripping mango or a slice of ripe golden papaya. So he entered the kitchen to see what Cooky could offer. He was eager for the old world to fall back into place, to ensure that nothing had changed. And of course it was all the same, the kitchen with its red-tiled floor and the baskets of fruit and vegetables hanging from the rafters, the little brass vessels containing spices on the shelves along the walls, the black-bottomed pots, the clay pitcher containing sweet ice-cold water, all the familiar smells and sounds. It was all the same, but in the corner sitting cross-legged on the floor on a straw mat, her hands rolling chapatti dough into soft little balls — he had requested chapattis for lunch today — her arms white with flour up to the elbows, there was Savitri.

He didn't recognise her at first glance, for her head was bent forward, over her work. And yet some sound must have escaped his lips, or else she sensed him standing there, speechless, for she looked up and gave a cry of delight and sprang to her feet, and ran to him.

The name *Savitri* was forever connected in his mind with wild, bare-footed skylarking; how could he simply detach it, and reconnect it with this… this… *woman!* In the seconds it took her to run to him he took in every change: gone, the flapping shawl and the fluttering skirts, the skittish leaps and bounds. She wore a sari, originally cobalt blue but faded to pastel. She wore it with the end crossed over her hips and tucked into her waistband for freedom of movement in the way of peasant women. It had one long rip across her thigh, torn where she'd caught it on a rose-bush, and rudimentarily repaired with white thread, not to hide the rip but to prevent it ripping further. It was of the cheapest cotton but she wore it as if it were of the finest, costliest silk; it covered her form only to reveal all the more its grace and sleekness, for soft and fluid it flowed into her curves and followed her every movement.

As she crossed the floor he saw her as if in slow motion, growing into herself before his eyes, into that name *Savitri,* and the love he had known for the little girl grew to fit the woman. The shock of knowing that it was, indeed, *her,* overwhelmed him, and his knees almost gave way. He clutched the door-jamb so as not to fall. She did not notice. Ignoring the horrified reprimand of her father she flung herself at him and her floury arms around him, and then his arms were around her too and he was lifting her up, and spinning her around; she was almost crying with joy.

'David, oh David!' she said. And he replied, 'Savitri! It's you!'

But his voice was muffled because of the lump in his throat.

She leaned into his hands on the small of her back and looked up at him in silence, and he down at her, and saw her face so eloquent with unveiled delight and so radiant with beauty and grace, his eyes misted over. Her own eyes were the same melting-chocolate brown but larger now than ever, wiser, calmer, the eyes of a woman: without guile, and without greed, simple and clear. Her lips smiled, but her eyes spoke and told him there had never been a time without loving, because loving was her very being. Her face was framed by thick, full hair pulled loosely back so that it waved gently around her face, and tied at the nape of her neck, where it was clasped by a bunch of purple and white flowers, and fell down her back to cover his hands in springy curls of black silk. He drew her to himself.

They clung to each other wordlessly till a furious Iyer pulled them apart. Men and women may not touch in public but both had forgotten and neither cared, for they were together again and all that remained was to breathe in and absorb the other, to make up for the years they had been apart.

Savitri drew away, looked at him again, and her silence too was full. And he, unbelieving in the light of her beauty and the sweetness of her love, could do nothing but gaze back and smile until his cheeks hurt, for his heart was too full for words and all words which had ever been spoken and ever been invented were inadequate, and could never match what he felt. She was exquisite.

David had seen many beautiful women in England. In fact, his silence towards Savitri during the previous years was the result of a distracted, adolescent mind growing into an awareness of female charms.

Savitri, though, was more than a beautiful body, more than mere symmetry of features. Her body seemed to him to be a vessel containing the very *essence* of beauty itself. That beauty poured from her every cell, from her eyes and her smile and her every gesture, it radiated from her in a warmth as enrapturing as the fragrance of an exquisite rose, folding him into itself.

Her beauty was more even than that inner warmth. He had seen it in the fleeting moment when she had sprung to her feet and run to him. It was the smoothness of her movements, her grace and suppleness acquired through years of carrying heavy water-vessels on her head, balancing them even without hands; it was the sum all of these things that had made of the fluttering butterfly of then the sleek gazelle of now; whose fluid buoyancy of being radiated from inside to transfix him into stillness.

Iyer, horrified at their indiscretion, pushed David out of the kitchen door and slammed it — a serious transgression of a servant towards the young master, but Iyer, as a wronged father, could be forgiven. Besides, David did not even notice. He leaned against the kitchen door in a daze, eyes shut, smiling like an idiot. He saw stars — literally, he saw stars. It had all been too sudden. He was in shock. But even in shock, he knew.

He had never stopped loving her.

Iyer lambasted Savitri for her indecorum and sent her home. And when the *memsahib* came back and the family had been served lunch and his duties for the morning were over he went home and lambasted Savitri again, and complained to her mother that she had raised her daughter badly, that she was completely spoiled and without morals.

Savitri sweetly apologised. 'He is my milk-brother,' she explained. 'I have not seen him for so long, Appa. You must forgive me but I was so full of joy.

And because he too was under the spell of his daughter and because he could not resist her contrite smile he only grunted and turned away.

'You must not see him again,' he said in final reprimand.

Savitri replied, 'Appa, but how can I avoid seeing him? I must help you in the kitchen, must I not, and don't you want me to serve the family when they sit to eat? I have always done so and it would not be fitting for you to serve them yourself.

And I have always discussed the meals with the mistress, have I not, and the young master will surely want to eat this and that, he has been away for so long without eating proper food. I am sure he will want to discuss meals with me, and you cannot do so because you speak no English! So please, Appa, do not forbid me to speak to him for it would be most inconvenient!'

Iyer saw the sense of her argument so only grunted again. He then turned back to her and said: 'Very well, then, but remember you are an unmarried young woman and you may not speak to a young man alone and you must never touch him again. Remember you are betrothed, and what would your bridegroom say, if he heard you are associating with another young man, even if the young man is your master? Your reputation has been ruined once by your lack of discretion when you were a child and now that you are grown up you may not behave as you did then. You must attend to the proprieties. You and the young master are no longer children and you do not know of the dangers of young men and women mixing. You must discuss nothing but meals with the young master. Think of your bridegroom.'

Savitri's face clouded over.

'Very well, Appa.' This last was a command she could easily promise to keep, because her betrothal to Ramsurat Shankar was constantly in her thoughts, though not in the way her father meant. Ramsurat Shankar was perfect for her. He was a teacher in the technical college with an excellent salary, and his previous wife had died in childbirth, and the child too, and his two elder children were already living with his younger brother's family and he did not expect to take them back into his household when he remarried. It was only thanks to the generosity of the Lindsays that such a good suitor could have been found for Savitri—who was so far above marriageable age—and they were all delighted, except for Savitri.

It was not that she did not *like* Ramsurat Shankar. She had seen a photograph of him, for he was a modern man and had insisted on an exchange of photographs before the wedding. He was quite a handsome man of thirty-one and she knew he was an excellent match. If there had been no David it would have been a happy marriage. But there *was* David.

'You must honour and respect your bridegroom,' Iyer added, and Savitri nodded sadly. That was nothing new. But to do so would be effort. Whereas to honour and respect David was joy, and to love him yet more so.

She disobeyed her father twice before the day was over. She met David in their old tree-house that afternoon. He was waiting for her when she came, and leaned over to give her a hand up as he had never needed to do when she was a child. She didn't need the hand now but took it nevertheless, laughing up at him. She had met him alone, and they touched, and in these two things she disobeyed her father.

She had never disobeyed her father before, except when she knew obedience was in conflict with obedience to that within her which was Truth, and wiser than her father. Thus she had touched the dogs and prayed with the Muslims and loved the Harijans. Always. Because these were important things and it was more important to obey the Truth within her than to obey her father's words, which were not words of Truth, but words of ignorance. For if he could have known that the muezzins' call was truly the call of God, and that God lived in the dogs and the Harijans, he would not have given her those orders. And if he could have known that God lived in her love for David, he would not have given her that order either. These things were Truth. But it was the tragedy of her life that not Truth, but ignorance should be given authority over her, in the form of her father.

This tragedy was in her eyes now, as she turned them to David. She laughed, because not even such tragedy could completely stain the joy she felt at being with him. But she could not hide the sadness, and David, who felt her soul as intimately as if it were his own, and could read every flicker of feeling in her eyes, touched her cheek softly and said, 'What's the matter, Say? You're sad.'

She told him then of her betrothal. She told him of Ramsurat

Shankar, whom she would have to marry when she was eighteen.

'You can't, Sav. You're going to marry me . . . you promised! Do you still have the cross I gave you?'

She smiled then.

'Of course! But I don't wear it. I've got it hidden in a safe place. And I've got your Swallow Book of Verse and your Bible.'

'You'll have to break the engagement. I'll speak to your father if you like.'

'Oh David, you don't understand! I'll never be able to marry you!'

'Why not? Maybe not yet; I'll be at Oxford for a few years, but when I come down, when I'm finished. Why can't you just go on working with your father, or better yet, go back to school…

Savitri chuckled ruefully. 'Go back to school! That's over, David.'

'I don't see why. You were always the cleverest of us all!'

'Oh David, David. You don't understand. That's just not our way.'

'But you're different; you've always been different. You grew up with us and that makes you different. And not just that — you *are* different. Inside, you're different. My mother always said you were special, you know. That you had gifts, secret powers. Do you still have them?'

She laughed again, and looked at the palms of her hands, spreading her fingers. 'Who knows? I certainly haven't been trying them out. Remember the Colonel's carbuncles? I suppose she was disappointed. I never thought about it. I never did anything special at all. Things just happened.'

'Maybe she was right, you know. If you'd developed them the way she wanted maybe you'd have been rich and famous by now. Instead of…"

She looked at him fiercely.

'Instead of a poor little nobody?'

'I didn't mean that. But you'd have been independent, you'd have had your own money to do what you want, and nobody could have ordered you about. You wouldn't have to mind other people's children or cook in other people's houses or prune other people's roses. Or marry someone you don't want to.'

'If I do have the gift of healing, David, then it's just that. A gift. You don't sell gifts.'

'It can't be a bad thing to have your own money!'

'Spoken like an Englishman!'

Her eyes softened. She turned to him, eager to explain. 'Not everything of value is for sale, David. Some things are more precious than money. And if you put a price tag on them they disappear.'

'Like the gift of healing?'

'Yes. If I tried to use it, to enrich myself through it, it wouldn't be what it is.'

'What's the point of having a gift, then?'

Savitri smiled and shook her head, as if marvelling at his thick-headedness.

'It came to me for free. I didn't ask for it, I didn't do anything to deserve it. I can't say it's mine; it isn't. It's just there. It doesn't come from me; it flows through me. It goes where it wants to.'

'And where does it want to go?'

She shrugged. 'To those who need it. There are so many millions who have no doctor, David! Who cannot afford one! I think I was given my gift in order to serve.'

He looked at her fondly, stroked her arm.

'You've been thinking about this, haven't you? It's not true, that you don't care!'

She lowered her eyes and smiled, a secret smile as at a pleasure only she knew of.

'Oh yes, David. I do care, I care a lot. All I said was that I never thought about what your mother calls my powers. But there are other things I care about… long for…'

She stopped, as if afraid of revealing too much, but then her eyes lit up with the fervour of purpose and she blurted out: 'Oh, David! I wish I could join Gandhiji! He's such an inspiration to me, I could just drop everything and go out with him to India's poor and serve them. Oh, that would just be heaven on earth!'

'And what about us?'

'Us?'

'Yes, us! How do I fit into your plan? Before or after Gandhiji?' There was a challenge in his words, and hardness. Her eyes clouded over.

'David, it's all just a dream, don't you see? It'll never happen. Not Gandhiji and not marrying you. None of it is going to happen!'

'Sav! Don't say that! The way you talk, it sounds as if you've given up! If you only *want* it we can do it! We can fight and win and marry and do everything we want to! Really we can! All we have to do is want it strong enough! Listen, did you know I'm going to study medicine?'

'You? Medicine! No! I thought you were going into the Navy! Since when?'

'Don't look at me like that, Sav! I'm just not a Navy man!'

'So you're going to be a doctor?'

'Yes.'

The silence fell thick and heavy between them. Her shoulders slumped. He reached out and raised her chin, and saw the pain in her eyes as sharp as an accusation.

'I know you wanted to be a doctor yourself. I know you'd be a far, far better doctor than I'll ever be. I know you have a gift and all I'll have is learning. I know it all, Sav. I know you deserve much more . . . you're like a rose that's not allowed to bloom and I'm sorry. But listen. We can do it. Together we'll do it. There's so much waiting for you, for us, Sav.'

'Ramsurat Shankar is what's waiting for me, David.'

'No. I am. But first you have to wait. A few years. Wait for me, and then I'll be a doctor, and we'll work things out together.'

Their eyes met, and she allowed herself to hope, and to believe; to believe all that he believed, and to allow him to believe for her: for faith of this kind came hard to her, faith in a destiny apart from the one laid out for her.

But David was fired with this new dream, which even as he dreamed it took on form and contours and became reality within grasp.

'Sav, don't you see? We'll have a hospital and… and… and I'll treat the rich, and earn the money, and you'll heal. Anyone you want to. You'll be the healer my mother wanted you to be, but for free… all the poor will come to you and you can be all that you're made to be…'

She had to laugh, then, for he was being carried away by a dream and she knew what was real, and the reality was painful, but she would bear it for him.

'Oh, David. I do love you so much.'

'I love you too. And it's all going to work out, you'll see. I believe in miracles. I've seen them myself. Yes, I remember the Colonel's carbuncles… does he still come?'

'Oh, yes! He's never forgotten, either! He always has a special word for me, you know, and he even flirts a bit! That old man!'

'I can't blame him. Any man . . . but Sav, what about that fellow? You've got to get your father to cancel the betrothal! Look, we'll go to my mother . . .'

'You're forgetting something, David. It's not just my father, it's your parents too. They'd never allow a marriage between us.'

'Of course they will! They do everything I want!'

'Not when it's a matter of your marrying an Indian girl, David. Believe me!'

'Nonsense. My parents were never racist. At least, well I don't know what my father thinks, but not my mother. She's a Theosophist, you know. She believes passionately in equality. Look how she treated you: you were almost a part of the family, all your life! I know some of the English are terrible, Sav — most of them. I know why you Indians want us out, and I agree, we've made a mess of things. But not my parents. And they both think so highly of you and want to see you happy. When they know we love each other they'll be happy for us. I know it. Most especially my mother.'

It was Savitri's turn to stroke his face. 'David, you're so naive. Of course your mother was good to me. I know it and I'm immensely grateful. If it weren't for her I'd have been married to some clubfooted cook in Bombay years ago. Remember?'

They smiled together at the memory and David squeezed her hand, now enclosed in both of his.

'What if I were clubfooted?'

'But David, you know that's not the point. I'd love you if you had four arms and eight legs!'

'Like one of your Hindu gods?' David let go of her hand and waved his arms in the air as if he were an octopus.

Savitri's smile faded. 'Don't make fun of our religion, David, please don't. None of the gods has eight legs and if they have four arms it's just symbolic. Just as the gods themselves are symbolic. I wish I could interest you more in my religion. It's not what you think. Not if you go deeper.'

'Oh well. When we're married you can teach me.'

'That's what I'm trying to tell you. She'll never let us get married, in spite of all her tolerance and liberal ideas. She can only be good to me because she knows, she thinks, she's better. I'm the poor little girl she raised up. I'll never be her daughter-in-law! The mother of her grandchildren!'

David took both her hands in his now and drew her close.

'I don't believe you, Sav. She's not that way. She loves you almost as a daughter and she'd love to have you as a daughter-in-law and I know, I just positively *know,* that when she finds out about us she'll be delighted and we'll get engaged and in a few years we'll marry. You wait. She always gets what she wants.'

'You're wrong, David. Maybe you have to be one of us to feel these things . . .'

'Don't argue, my darling. I can't bear arguing with you. It's such a waste of time. And time is so short. Listen, there's the gong for supper and I have to go but I'll see you tomorrow. We'll sort this all out, and you'll see: you won't marry this chap, never, ever!'

'David, promise me you won't talk to your mother!'

'But why not? That's the best, the quickest way to put an end to this betrothal thing. If my mother agrees, then your father —'

'Please, David, don't let's discuss it. Just promise you won't tell her. Not yet. Let's wait. Please. Do it for me!'

'I'll promise if you give me a kiss!'

Savitri smiled and pecked his cheek. David chuckled and pulled her close.

'No, silly. A proper one.'

And he tried to kiss her properly, but she pulled away.

'I told Amma we'd go to the Ganapati temple for evening *arathi,'* she murmured, and swung herself out of the tree-house and down the rope ladder. He followed her down; grabbed her wrist. She pulled away; he pulled her back.

'David...' she murmured, but whatever else she wanted to say she couldn't, for his lips were on hers, pressing, urgent; and his arms around her waist. She struggled for a moment, and then her body went limp against his but her lips urgent and responsive, locked to his... and then she pulled away again, gasping for breath; turned and ran.

'Savitri!' he called. She stopped, turned, waved, and turned away and ran on. David watched her go. The blue of her sari flashed in and out of sight as she fled along the winding path home, and he watched her go until she disappeared behind a bougainvillea bush, and he grinned to himself with all the faith and the exuberance and the idealism and the megalomania that is youth.

Chapter 24

Nat
London, 1960 — 1964

Nat discovered Woman. He didn't have to marry to do so, for each one was his bride. They offered themselves to him: he could take his choice, and the longing ache within him was stilled, for he found in London a garden of earthly delights. Women here were not rare out-of-reach orchids but a riotous summer-bed of flowers nodding in the sunshine, inviting, pleading to be plucked. They brought fulfilment to his starved senses. He drank their intoxicating nectar, drowned in their overwhelming fragrance. He made bouquets of them, works of art, perfumed garlands to wear around his neck. He worshipped them, no longer with his soul, but with his body.

The first time, of course, had stunned him. That an ordinary woman — that is, a woman who was not a whore — could be so quick and so willing, so eager even, to offer him her body! Before marriage! Without even a *promise* of marriage! But this was the era of Free Love, and Nat was too polite to show his shock, too charming to betray his embarrassment, too tolerant to condemn, and, of course, too gracious to refuse such a precious gift. Instead, his mind scurried into fast forward and his body, with all the impulses held so long in abeyance, followed suit. And though his body was the bait, the first offering at the shrine of womanhood, he soon discovered that it was not his body they truly wanted; they were after his soul. And Nat, raised to share his all, gave willingly.

Women adored him for the sweetness of his disposition, for his guileless, almost child-like openness, his humour and generosity and for the fact that he truly, genuinely, *loved* them, each one of them, that he was genuinely in search of what he called the Inner Goddess and fell to his knees before Her in each new English woman.

Women of all kinds loved him, and he was all things to all women.

Younger girls found in him greatness and strength, the hero of their dreams, the fairy-tale prince they could look up to, which made them feel great and wonderful and unique themselves, as if they could do anything and be anything, as if the wavering, rickety structures of their personalities, lacking foundation, at last found an inner structure, through him.

Older women, turned brittle by battling a hostile male-dominated world, laid down their arms. Their sharp corners turned round, their prickly thorns fell off, and they flourished and blossomed as never before. For Nat could see, and summon, the Goddess within each one, and raise her to life through the ashes of discontent and bitterness.

But in time Nat grew choosy, and a certain preference for younger goddesses of perfect, or near perfect, face and form established itself. Nat told himself and explained to all who would listen that outer beauty was the logical consequence of inner beauty; that the body of a beautiful woman was the outer symbol of the Inner Goddess, demanding love; that the act of love was in fact an act of worship; that there was no difference between profane and sacred love, between Eros and Agape, or, in Indian terms, between Kama and Bhakti. The body of a beautiful woman was an altar to which he brought his love-offerings. And he, in turn, possessed that mysterious, elusive charisma which made of his own body a beacon.

For, of course, Nat himself was beautiful. His skin was the creamy colour of *café au lait,* but glowing as if layered with a veil of gold, and around his oval face fell thick, heavy, bouncing black curls. He was tall, lean, sinewy, his body strong yet supple, and he moved with the languorous grace of an Afghan hound, regal almost, with an economy of energy in which perfect relaxation merged with perfect control. His eyes were huge and soulful, deep dark pools which showed great emotion and promised answers to all mysteries, heavy-lidded, veiled enigmas, and his black silky eyelashes were the envy of women, wasted on a man, they said; but no, not when that man was Nat. He dressed casually, preferring wide trousers with deep baggy pockets, over which he wore long pastel T-shirts in summer and thick woolly Norwegian sweaters in winter. He also favoured white long-sleeved Afghan shirts embroidered with shiny white flowers down the front, and over that a Kashmiri waistcoat. Sometimes he wore a turban, for the touch of mystery it added. An exotic glow radiated from him, invisible to the physical eye but sensed by women, which drew them to him as to a warm fire after a walk through snow and sleet.

In Nat, East met West in a perfect, seamless synthesis: the mysterious Orient untrammelled by convention, released into and made available for the modern world. For he personified both, embodied both. The Indian connection served him well, and to be fair it must be said that it forced itself upon him. Invariably, the girls he met would inevitably refer, giggling, to the *Kama Sutra* and ask him what he knew of it, which was, at first, virtually nothing. Then came the questions about Tantra yoga, and about the erotic temple statues of Khajarau, and Nat made it his business to educate himself in all these subjects. It was his duty as an Indian, for every Indian knows that the Western mind is gross and needs guidance in the ways of love, away from the crudeness of mere physicality to the spiritual heights it is capable of. Nat knew intuitively that what a woman really seeks is not physical enjoyment but spiritual unity with her man, to melt into his being and he into hers, and he found his women starved for love like this, wandering, lost, in a wasteland. Once they discovered him they could never go back; after loving Nat the crude pokings and pantings, the gross lurchings and thrustings of lesser men seemed ludicrous. Nat was a gardener, watering their thirsting souls with nectar.

He had his difficulties with men; or rather, men had their difficulties with Nat, since it was they who built walls around themselves. Nat had no walls. But he soon discovered that he was different from other men, which is why they built walls. Nat did not play their games. He had no need to work at building a personal image, bigger and better than everyone else's. Nat, having grown up with the lowest of the lowliest, and serving the lowliest, having been taught from the very beginning that he was no better than the meanest beggar, had a natural humility, a humility which did not debase him — on the contrary. For where English men spent their lives adding layers to their egos, in the hope of appearing strong, Nat's ego was so thin as to be transparent, allowing the great love and generosity which formed the core of his being to shine through, and that was the secret of his great charisma, and his greatness. He was Krishna with his flute; women were his *gopis,* dancing all for him.

Nevertheless, even that thinness of ego was enough for the seeds of dissatisfaction and self-indulgence to take root and grow in, and finally to flourish.

As for his studies—what a bore. The indifference he had known at Armaclare College grew to alarming proportions at University College. At Armaclare his mind had drifted off to fantasies of his own invention; here, the realities taking place in his spare time provided much more lurid detail. Learning was dull, dead; it was in his spare time that life really began, and his irritation at having to waste his time like this, being duty bound to get an education, as Doctor had drummed into him, lamed his memory, his attention span, his concentration, his motivation.

And yet. Sometimes, at night, in the spaces between waking dreams and sleep, he remembered India. Home. A place where the peace was so ineffable it seeped through body and soul and mind, holding a personality together as a cinema screen held moving pictures. A song of such sweetness, singing in the lonely stillness at the back of his being. Sometimes tears came, tears at beauty, lost, it seemed, for ever, torn apart by a hunger for life that grew the more he fed it, into a jarring, grasping monster over which he had no control. He wept like a little boy. Is this really me? Who am I? But new mornings came with new food for the monster, and Nat forgot his tears and flung himself at life.

Nat soon found that living with Sheila and Adam cramped his style, and early the following year he moved into the Notting Hill Gate flat of a fellow student, another Indian in his third year of law, a rather studious fellow from Gujarat who shut himself in his room and did not interfere with Nat's goings-on. And anyway, this fellow usually spent the weekends with relatives in Windsor, perhaps because the weekends grew increasingly busy with all the comings and goings of Nat's girls. Nat had a room to himself in the flat, quite small, but suitable to his purpose, which more and more became not so much learning but loving. Like a lost traveller emerging from the desert he felt he had to make up for lost time, for the years of his young life spent in forced deprivation of sensual enjoyment. He felt a certain resentment towards his father for having so deprived him.

On the other hand his father was, after all, providing the financial means for his stay in London, so in his letters home (which in time grew shorter, more compact and less frequent) Nat chose to keep quiet about his new-found lifestyle, feeling certain that Doctor would disapprove, maybe even whistle him home. Home! The village was no longer his home. What a narrow little world that had been, how empty of all the joys a man needs to be a man, how empty of love...

'Happy Birthday!' The door flew open and a gaggle of girls fell into the flat, giggling. They all wore mini-skirts, which to Nat's great pleasure were growing shorter by the month. They were all gorgeous, and they all loved Nat. Two of them were students, the rest of them simply girls he had met at various discos and brought home. Over time they had met each other, outgrown their initial bitchiness, and even become friends, members of the exclusive and very special society of Nat's Lovers, and Nat prided himself on the fact that now they weren't jealous of each other. Each knew that to know Nat, to love Nat and know his love, was to abandon all possessiveness, all claims of having him for herself alone, because Nat's heart was so big it could hold them all. None of them noticed, and Nat least of all, that over the glowing embers that Nat had brought from India a layer of grey ash was beginning to form, imperceptible to all but the sharpest eyes; and Nat, whose eye should have been sharp, was too young, too inexperienced, too distracted to be aware of the change.

His guests had brought drinks, records, and gifts; they celebrated Nat's twentieth birthday with great gusto, much laughter and jokes, dancing into the small hours till one by one five of the girls collapsed on the carpet. Nat covered them with blankets, of which he kept a good supply, and retired with the sixth girl, the latest to join the club and his Radha of the moment, into the bedroom, where they read poems of love to each other, poems so moving they brought tears to Nat's eyes, and to hers.

Nat was so *sensitive,* which was what distinguished him from every other man in London. Most men thought tears were weak and effeminate, but Nat was not ashamed to weep for love, to let his heart overflow when he was so deeply moved he could no longer contain his tears, and this was the essence of his manliness: that he allowed his gentleness to show, and there was not a woman alive who despised him for this, for every woman knows in her heart that true strength is always gentle. So Kathy cried with him now, and their tears mingled as he took her in his arms in gratitude, and they worshipped one another till the morning came.

Chapter 25

Saroj
Georgetown, 1964 —1966

Saroj's short flirtation with freedom was over, but between her and Ma grew a bond of silent understanding. They never again referred to their conversation; but Saroj knew. It was as if Ma had lifted her up and placed her on her wing, where she sat while Ma flew through a dark sky, not knowing where she was going, not asking, but only trusting. Knowing that Ma would never let her down. Not ever.

Saroj no longer wanted the shallow freedom Trixie had offered, the temporary, illusory freedom of riding around town chasing and being chased by boys, following each fleeting impulse regardless of its long-term consequences. The fluttery flight of a hen within a coop! The coop itself must go.

True freedom lay in education.

O Levels would be in two years. Saroj determined to work so hard, to gain such excellence, that Baba would allow her to stay in school and work even harder for her A Levels. And then she would win the scholarship. And then Baba would send her to England. He'd have to. What a scandal if she won that scholarship, the best girl in the whole country, and he refused to let her take it! All the politicians in the country would rise up against him, and all the women, including Trixie's mother and the Minister of Education who was also a woman. It was a tangible, attainable goal, easily with her grasp.

So she would go to England. She would leave this mess behind and start a new life in a new country, really free. She immersed herself in books. She aimed at excellence, and swore off fun.

'All work and no play makes Jill a dull girl,' Trixie grumbled. 'I miss you, Saroj!' But Saroj didn't care. All work and no play was her password to freedom. She'd be much more dull as the Ghosh boy's wife.

'But it's such a waste! All you have to do is snap your fingers . . . the cutest boys around . . . only the other day Brian van Sertima asked me where you were hiding, and...'

Brian van Sertima was the lead guitarist and singer of the most popular band, The Alleycats. Saroj had danced with him at Julie Chan's fete. He had pressed his groin against her. She wrinkled her nose.

'I don't like his deodorant.'

The rumour spread around town, and returned to Saroj via Trixie, that she was the biggest stuck-up snob in the country, and frigid too.

'Sour grapes!' Saroj replied. But she knew they were right. She *was* a stuck-up snob. She couldn't stand those fawning, drivelling boys. She didn't want them touching her. The thought of their lips on hers repelled her. Her reputed beauty was, to her, a handicap. The attention it attracted reduced males to a horde of panting dogs worrying a bitch in heat, except that she wasn't a bitch in heat. If refusing such base attentions meant she was frigid, then that was no insult.

'One look at your face and they're reduced to jelly,' said Trixie. Saroj snorted in disgust.

'Boys are so stupid, like slobbering puppies. Ugh! Disgusting! I don't mind being a snob if it keeps that idiot-pack away.'

But she and Trixie remained friends, for what bound them was deeper than boys and books. They sat up in the tower, played music on the cassette-recorder Ganesh had given Saroj, and talked the hours away.

Saroj's attempted suicide had shocked Trixie too, and her life, like Saroj's, took a new turn. Trixie had been the undisputed leader in the days of fun and freedom. Now Saroj was the authority. Trixie confided in her her fear of failing all her O Levels except art, her anxiety at her mother's reaction, and the mess her life would be in failure.

'I'll have to get a job, but what kind of a job can I get without O's? Or else stay at school to repeat them and that would be awful without you and with all those babies laughing at me — but I haven't a hope, Saroj, not a hope!'

So Saroj volunteered to help her with maths. Almost immediately her marks and Saroj's reputation improved. The friends she'd neglected turned back to her, asking for help, and soon Saroj found herself giving lessons in maths, physics, biology, chemistry, French and geography. Everything, in fact, except for art, music and sport.

'It all sounds so easy when you explain things,' Trixie said glumly, 'but the moment I'm back in school — wham! Miss Abrams with her droning voice explaining theorems and such, it's just all so boring! So I sit and stare out the window. Or draw things in my exercise book. Yesterday I drew Miss Abrams and she recognised herself.'

Trixie grinned her old boyish grin which never seemed far from the surface. She put on a high squeaky voice in imitation of Miss Abrams.

'Trixie Macintosh, go and stand in the corridor! You should exercise your artistic talent at the right time and in the right place!'

'Perhaps she's right!' was all Saroj said. Trixie seemed not to hear.

'And I can't stand Mummy telling me to follow your example,' she continued. 'She's always saying how much she used to be like you, and how she almost won the British Guiana Scholarship and how I'm going to be a failure. I wish Daddy was here. If he were I'd go and live with him. But he hasn't sent for me since he got married, and now he has two boys — forget it!'

'Why don't you just ask him if you can come?'

'Fat chance. I've been begging Mum for years to send me and all she says is, d'you think your father wants you? And then she said, work hard and get your A Levels and then you can go to university with my blessing. I'm not sending you to London to work in a fish and chip shop and go to the dogs and blah blah blah. But, Saroj, I don't want to work in a fish and chip shop. Why can't I go to art school? Daddy'd understand if he hadn't married that white lady. She's all rich and snooty.'

And Trixie was still madly in love with Ganesh — more so than ever before.

'The only reason for staying here I could think of would be to marry Ganesh!' she said boldly. Saroj stared.

'Marry Ganesh? But Trix, he's .. .'

'Okay, okay, don't scream, you needn't rub it in. Ganesh has never even seen me properly.'

She glared at Saroj as if she were responsible for her brother's indifference. 'I think he has a girlfriend. He does, doesn't he? I know you don't tell me everything so as not to hurt me but I know he does, I saw him hanging around at Esso Joe talking to her… he didn't even notice me. And I'm fifteen going on sixteen so it's not as if I'm too young! I bet it's because I'm black.'

'Trix!'

'No, don't protest, Saroj, I just know it. One feels these things. Your Baba hates blacks so Ganesh must too, secretly. You never see an Indian marrying a black. Never.'

'Trix, don't be silly, Gan's just like me, he just doesn't think that way! Girl, so many boys like you, why can't you —'

'I've tried, Saroj, I really have! I've tried so hard to fall in love with someone else. But even when I went out with Derek I kept hoping we'd run into Ganesh and make him jealous. Make him realise that he loves me and that he'd better make a move before it's too late. And at the end of this year Ganesh is going to England and then I'll lose him for ever. But not if I go to England myself, except Mummy won't send me and Daddy doesn't want me so what am I to do with my life? I'll never get married, I'm quite sure of it. I'm going to be an old maid like Aunt Amy.'

Saroj wanted to tell her she'd give anything for such a destiny. But Trixie looked so depressed she held her tongue. She had the feeling Trixie would rather marry the Ghosh boy than not marry at all.

On 26 May 1966 British Guiana gained independence from Britain, becoming Guyana, under the leadership of the African Forbes Burnham. Black Power hit Guyana like a tidal wave, sweeping half the population along with it, and Trixie in its wake. Trixie, non-political to the core, might have stayed outside the current if she had not fallen desperately, temporarily, in love with Stokely Carmichael when her mother dragged her along to a talk at the university.

'You must meet him, Saroj, you must! Imagine, I shook hands with him! And with Miriam Makeba! I can't believe it! I'll never wash my hands again! Mum's so pleased, she's arranged for me to go to a private party of one of her friends and he'll be there, she thinks I'm getting a political conscience! You must come, I'll get you an invitation. Just wait.'

'Trixie, no. I can't. Don't you understand? I can't!'

'But why not?'

There was no answer to that. Didn't she get it? Couldn't she see? Was she so blind? Didn't she realise that this movement threatened to tear them apart? That one day she would have to take sides?

And which side would she take? For Africans were not only anti-white; they were anti-Indian. Adamantly, ferociously so. More than ever. When push came to shove what would be Trixie's choice: her people, or her friendship?

'Your mind is so mathematical, Saroj. So cool and calculating. Loosen up a bit! What you need is a bit of romance. Mark my words: one day a prince on a white steed will ride up and sing a serenade at the bottom of this tower and you'll let down your long black hair, which by then will be down to the bottom of the tower, and he'll climb up and clasp you to his broad hairy chest and your bosom will be heaving with desire, and then you'll have this long passionate kiss, the sky will turn red and the curtains will close.'

Saroj had to laugh. 'Oh Trix, you live in a dream world.'

'Yes, and I like it there! Because there Gan loves me back!'

'And what about Stokely Carmichael?'

'Oh, him! He's married and much too old and anyway, he's

gone. Ganesh is my first and final love. If he'd been mine I wouldn't have even glanced at Stokely. But all I have of him are dreams. And where's the photo of him you promised?'

Saroj groaned. 'I'll have to steal one from the family album and Ma'll notice.'

'Just get it for me and I'll have it reproduced and she won't notice a thing. Go and get the album, Saroj. You promised! If I can't have him in the flesh at least I can swoon over his photo.'

Saroj groaned, but finally stood up to fetch the family photo album. It was the rainy season, and she and Trixie, up in the tower, sat as if enclosed in a bubble in the middle of the ocean. Rain sluiced from the drenched heavens in a solid sheet and pounded on the slate roof, like thunder. Looking out at the sky of water Saroj was transported back to her childhood, when Ganesh and she would run screaming through the wetness in the back yard, up the kitchen steps dripping wet and laughing, tear off their soggy clothes and throw them in a heap on the bathroom floor, wrap themselves in sheets and cuddle into Ma's arms . . . if Baba wasn't home.

She brought the album and a sheet and squatted down beside Trixie. They had made a home of the tower by now; bought a little Indian carpet from Mr Gupta to cover the bare floorboards, hammered in lopsided shelves for Saroj's school books and Trixie's novels, hung an extension cord down the stairs to a plug in Saroj's room, so they could play the cassette-recorder.

Saroj wrapped the sheet around them both, for it was chilly and their bare brown arms were rough with gooseflesh. She drew up her knees, leaned the album against them, and opened it. She hadn't looked at it for a long time. She hated photos of herself because she always looked so stiff and corny in Indian clothes, so usually she threw a glance at the latest family picture and that was it. And now, looking through the album with Trixie, she saw the photos through another's eyes and it seemed to Saroj they were stiffer and cornier than ever. The only one of them who looked consistently good was Ganesh, who always had this funny grin across his face and liked to strike a pose.

But in the earlier pictures it was different. There, even Baba looked good. Like Ganesh. Youthful, boyish and handsome. It seemed to Saroj that things changed after her own birth. Baba's face grew progressively sour from photo to photo, Ma's progressively serious, as if she herself had somehow brought bitterness into the family. And there were some things she knew vaguely, which were now confirmed — that before she was born they used to go to Trinidad for a holiday every July to stay at the beach house of an uncle who had settled there. Ganesh's birthday fell in July, and four of those photos were taken on the beach. She was not in any of them; and yet, she was born in Trinidad. Why hadn't they ever returned?

Saroj and Trixie sat looking at this last beach photo, when Ganesh was two and Indrani four, and they were all together, a small, happy Indian family. Just Ma, Baba, Indrani and Ganesh. No Saroj. Ganesh had made an enormous sandcastle, like a wedding cake, and was naked, and Ma wore a sari which was completely wet. Ma was smiling almost blissfully, her hand in Indrani's, and so was Baba, who kneeled beside Ganesh with a proud hand on the boy's head.

Saroj reached out for the album, held it up and squinted at this photo. There was something strange about it, something *wrong*. But she couldn't for the life of her figure out what.

The next strange thing happened the very next week. They were up in the tower, and Ma as usual was out at the Purushottama Temple.

The telephone rang. It was a nurse from Dr Lachmansingh's maternity home where most Roy women went with their medical problems and to have their babies.

Indrani had just arrived, they told Saroj, and was about to give birth prematurely, and was asking for Ma. Saroj grabbed Trixie's bike and tore down the street towards Brickdam, to pry Ma away from her prayers or her *kirtan*.

She walked past the watchmen who were always posted here nowadays, entered the temple grounds and approached the first person she recognised, who happened to be Mr Venkataraman from the Robb Street jewellery shop. She asked for Ma, for Mrs Roy, and was passed along from this person to the next till she came to a pundit in a white dhoti, who said crisply, Mrs Roy is not here.

'But she must be!' Saroj said. 'Listen, it's terribly important, her daughter is in hospital and needs her!'

The pundit called someone else who called someone else and a lady in a yellow sari came and they all discussed the matter. Then the lady in the yellow sari went to look for Ma and the pundit told Saroj to sit down in a chair in the corridor, which she did. She waited and waited and after a while yellow-sari returned and said, 'I'm very sorry, Mrs Roy is not available.'

'Not available? You mean she won't come?'

'No. Mrs Roy is not here at the present moment.'

'But she's been here since three o'clock, she always comes here!'

'Apparently she attended three-o'clock Shiva puja and then she left again. Mrs Roy never spends much time here.'

'Never spends — but she always comes on Wednesdays and Fridays!'

'She usually just drops in for puja and then leaves again.'

'Are you quite sure?'

'Most certainly. We have looked for her everywhere and the watchman saw her leaving at around three thirty.'

'Do you know where she went? It's very important.'

'How would we know where Mrs Roy has gone? It's not our business. Now, if you would please excuse.'

Yellow-sari touched the tips of her fingers together and turned her back.

Ma arrived home at around six. Saroj told her about Indrani, who by this time had given birth to a premature son.

'You weren't at the temple,' Saroj said accusingly.

'I know,' said Ma calmly. Saroj waited for Ma's explanation. None came. She packed a basket and left for Dr Lachmansingh's maternity home.

Chapter 26

Savitri
Madras, 1934

That was a glorious season. Savitri and David met each afternoon in the tree-house, and no-one knew but them. Both glowed, both grew beautiful with happiness and love, with hope for the future which could only be better and confidence that their love would conquer. David charmed Savitri into putting aside the reality which was Ramsurat Shankar for the Elysium of now, so that only the now, this love, this joy, seemed real, and the spectre of marriage to another faded like morning mist. She wanted to believe, and so she let herself be charmed, allowed herself to believe. David, accustomed to having his way, could not imagine a world where his will was not final. They dreamed on.

Iyer and his wife saw Savitri's love in the radiance of her countenance and the light in her eyes, in the lightness of her being. But they shut their eyes trusting that destiny would chart her course and sort things out; and where the young master was concerned, how dare they speak up? And was he not returning to England at the end of the season? Iyer hunched his shoulders and his wife drew her sari tighter around her shoulders and gave Savitri more tasks. They spoke more and more often of the bridegoom, and the wedding. But Savitri was not listening.

Mrs Lindsay was proud of her son, and with reason. She relished the comments of her friends on his dashing good looks, his charm, his quick intelligence. If David had once, as a child, been an outsider among his peers; now he was the opposite. Young people, the cream of the next Madras generation of

English society, up-and-coming, bold and self-assured, sought him out and wanted him among them. But David held himself apart, and they could not understand. The world lay at their feet, and always had, and though there were rumblings among the Indians, and this Mr Gandhi was stirring them up and making trouble, why, the English were here and always would be here, and all this talk of Independence was nothing but rot. It would all pass away, including this Mr Hitler in Germany. They were English, they lived in peaceful pockets of paradise amidst a turbulent world, they were confident that nothing would ever shake that world, and if only David, the most attractive young Englishman in town, would even look at one or two of the prettier girls, all would be well.

But he wouldn't. His mother, who had herself made one or two matches in her mind, laughed it off when David showed no interest. He was young, only seventeen! Let him take his time and make a good choice.

In fact, David was longing to tell his mother that he *had* made a choice, and that it was irrevocable. But Savitri in her greater calm and wisdom held him back.

'But, dear, the summer's halfway through! We've got to make it final so this betrothal of yours can be dissolved!'

'There's time, David, there's still time. Please don't tell her yet.'

'But why not? We need her support against Iyer and the sooner she's in our confidence the better.'

But Savitri felt the first fraying of dreams as realities she couldn't bear to think of rolled relentlessly forward and all she could do was put off the day when all would unravel as she knew it must. For only she knew how ruthless tradition could be. It took no heed of feelings, of likes and dislikes, desires and needs, no heed even of love itself, not even of so great a love as hers for David, and there was no avoiding it, no excuse for dreaming once you knew what had to be, for dreams must crumble once reality entered. She knew it. David did not.

'David, I'm scared!' She drew closer to him and he held her in his arms, tightly, to show her she was safe with him.

'You've never been afraid, Sav; not of snakes or scorpions or deep water or high trees or anything. Don't be afraid now.'

But Savitri shivered, and though it was hot still and the sun glared between the flames-of-the-forest she drew her sari down over her elbows and crossed her arms tightly and prayed for strength. Even David's arms around her could not renew her hope.

The bubble of happiness grew closer around them as the season wore on, hot and sultry and sometimes angry, with the monsoon clouds hanging dark, heavy and low above the trees but never bursting, never bringing relief and release, the coolness and wetness of rain. The grass grew yellow and parched and the flowers thirsted and the tightness drew them in, closer to one another. If David felt the closeness he fought it with his dreams, building them higher; but Savitri knew.

Two weeks before his ship was to leave for England David could stand it no longer. Without Savitri's permission, he told his mother.

It spoke for David's innocence that he really, truly believed that his mother loved Savitri as a daughter, that she would rejoice to welcome her into the family, she who had always been a part of the family anyway, from the day of her birth, she who had won his mother's love and admiration through her own virtues and talents. For him, it was obvious, and because it was obvious to him he believed it was obvious to all.

For Mrs Lindsay it was an abomination. No less. She had other plans for David.

It was evening and the crows were fussing terribly overhead, cawing and slapping their wings on their way to roost. A middle-aged couple strolling down Atkinson Avenue heard Mrs Lindsay's voice as they passed by and stopped to listen, for here surely was an original titbit of gossip in the making, to pass on behind an upheld hand at the next cocktail party, and Mrs Lindsay with her Theosophist leanings was anyway too big for her boots . . .

'Over my dead body! Over my dead body!' The words, screamed out into the gathering dusk, were clear, and the man and the woman looked at each other and raised their eyebrows and smiled.

'That girl! That sly, cunning girl! After all I've done for her!' The man plucked nervously at the flab on his wife's arms, bidding her to move on, but the wife stood transfixed, peering between the hibiscus shrubs beyond the iron fence as if she could hear better with her eyes, but the garden was gloomy and anyway, the house, hidden as it was behind the giant bougainvilleas, could not be seen. But no other shouts came out to please her ears and anyway, the breeze was blowing in the wrong direction. The woman allowed herself to be gently pushed forward by her husband, past the wrought-iron gate behind which the turbaned Sikh in his khaki uniform sat on the wooden chair from which a lath was missing on the back rest; a vague chill passed through her body as she glanced at him. And no wonder, the way he leaned backwards tilted on two chair-legs, holding a half-smoked *bidi* in a parrot's claw of thumb and finger. His eyes were closed; it seemed he was asleep, but he wasn't. The woman could see the glinting slit which told her he was awake, his sly eyes watching them as they strolled past, unmoving, unfathomable, not sinking in respect as they met hers.

The woman shuddered involuntarily. These Indians. You couldn't trust them any more. Trouble was brewing. She longed for Devon. But whatever was going on in the Lindsay household?

'Probably that girl, Fiona,' she said to her husband. 'Remember how she eloped with the cook's son? She's turned into quite a wild thing in London, so I heard, and they had to bring her back... she still hasn't caught a husband. There's that rumour, you know, that she's still carrying on with that servant fellow. She was seen... well, I suppose we'll know sooner or later. Those Lindsays were always a queer sort.'

They strolled on arm in arm, smug in the knowledge that

their world, at least, was quite the way it ought to be, with both sons married to heiresses.

He had to find her.

He waited till long past midnight, listening to the night sounds, the chirping of crickets and the song of the frogs and the plaintive cry of the brain-fever bird. He waited till the moon was hidden behind a long dark monsoon cloud and then he slipped out and sprinted through the garden towards the back drive. He ran barefoot with his shoes in his hand for silence and stealth, the way Savitri did, light and fleet. It was dark, pitch-dark. The servants' houses loomed before him, one of them Savitri's; but he did not know which, for he never came this far and in the blackness they all looked alike. But hadn't Savitri once said that theirs was the last house; that they lived slightly apart, because they were Brahmins, and that theirs was the house with banana trees in the backyard, and no papayas, for her father did not eat them?

Then it must be this house. David tried the garden gate and it creaked slightly. Somewhere a dog barked, and then another, but it was not here in this yard. Iyer did not keep dogs.

David tiptoed up the path towards the house but here was a new problem: all the family slept outside, on the verandah, their bodies covered with sheets from head to toe, and there was no knowing which body was hers.

Despair clawed at his heart. It could not be! It could not end this way! Not such a love! A thing so perfect must survive, it must! *Oh, dear God, let there be a way, oh let there be a way! Savitri! Savitri! Come, wake up, hurry! We have no time!* He gave the cry of a brain-fever bird but he had never mastered the art as Savitri had. It was all hopeless.

One of the sleeping bodies stirred, gently first, then rolled over and sleepily sat up. David crouched behind a bush and watched. There was still no moon and all he saw were shadows, but the dark form against the white of the wall was that of a female. Four women lived here: Savitri, her mother, and two sisters-in-law.

The woman stood up and wrapped her cloth around her. She stepped down from the raised balcony and walked out some way into the garden. In the moment that she began to hunch up her clothes and squat down, David saw it was Savitri and whispered her name, for he did not want her to know he had been there, watching her attend to nature.

She heard the whisper and stood to attention, letting her clothes drop, and he left his bush and came out to meet her.

'David!' Her voice was too loud, too surprised, and he laid a finger on her lips and drew her away.

'Something woke me up, David! I felt it in my sleep and it woke me up. Once I was awake I thought it was only nature calling but no, I know now: I heard my name in my sleep!'

'Sssh!' was all he said, and led her out of the garden gate, far from the house, and then the words gushed out quickly, urgently:

'Savitri, we have to leave! Tonight! We must run away together for I won't give you up. But tomorrow my mother is taking me to Bombay to stay with Aunt Sophie before my ship leaves. And you are to marry this man! She is releasing some money for an early marriage — so we must leave now!'

'Now! But ... David, I have nothing! The streets are deserted! Where shall we go to? What shall we do?'

'I have packed a few things and some money and some papers. You need nothing, just come. I have a plan.'

Savitri looked up at him. In the darkness of night his paleness seemed ghostly, and in his white shirt and white tennis slacks he appeared to her ephemeral, like some spirit from another world. His eyes seemed almost liquid with urgency, and his desperation was contagious. Savitri's senses were wide open and caught his insistence in all its pleading and all its wilfulness, and the tender framework of duty fell away, and she was all his.

'I'll come!' she whispered. 'But I'll have to get some clothes...'

She turned as if to return to the house, but David took hold of her arm.

'Don't go. It's too dangerous! What if you wake someone up?'

'Shall I go... like this?' Savitri swept her hand downwards to show David what she was wearing, which was an old sari, crumpled from sleep, and above that the thin blanket she used at night to cover herself, which now lay doubled around her shoulders like a shawl.

'It doesn't matter. No one will look at you.' David removed the blanket which was, in fact, no thicker than a heavy sheet, wrapped it around her slight torso and arranged it so that it covered most of her body, including her head, so that only her face showed, so sincere and trusting with the wide eyes turned silently to him that he would have taken her in his arms and held her to him, if there had been time. He took her hand and led her around the back of the servants' houses to that part of the back drive that was never used, the last few yards that led to the back gate. That was kept closed, and latched, and a heavy padlock hung from the latch, but David had made his preparations and took the key from his pocket.

He fumbled for a few precious seconds until he found the key-hole, and turned the key. The padlock snapped open. David removed it and slipped it into his pocket. He tried to open the latch but it was rusty from lack of usage and stuck fast. David swore and bent over it to work it free. Savitri watched him. She looked over her shoulder once, imagining Mani appearing out of the darkness with a crowd of his cronies, waving sticks and yelling at her, and the terror was so great she closed her eyes and prayed, and calmness filled her. Only with strong pressure steadily applied did the latch finally give way, and sprang back with such suddenness that David almost lost his balance.

In triumph he looked at her and beckoned her to follow. The gate creaked as he opened it and Savitri's heart missed a beat, for in the great silence that hung over Old Market Street at this time of night that creaking seemed as loud as a round of gunshot. But no-one seemed to have heard. A dog barked and another replied, but from a far distance, while the dogs of Old Market Street slept on as if in complicity with Savitri, and happy to be on the side of her who had always been on theirs.

The street was deserted. They walked down its middle so

as to avoid the cows sleeping on the roadside, the abandoned bullock carts, the occasional dray, its horse tied up to it and sleeping with drooping head.

Once or twice a dog woke up and barked at them, but never for long because Savitri's mind bid them be quiet, and they obeyed, circling and settling again into their snug holes in the roadside dust.

Savitri and David walked towards the bazaar. Savitri whispered, 'Where are we going, David?'

He turned to her, looking down at the small shrouded figure hurrying along beside him, and smiled to her through the darkness, pressing her fingers reassuringly.

'Let's not talk now,' he whispered back. 'I'm looking for a rickshaw, there ought to be one or two near the bazaar.'

There was a cycle-rickshaw, but it was abandoned, its driver nowhere to be found. But with the very next one they were lucky, for the rickshaw-*wallah* slept inside it, covered from head to toe with a ragged blanket. David took hold of what appeared to be a shoulder and shook it. The man stirred but did not wake, so David shook again and called out, 'Wake up, wake up!' The rickshaw-*wallah* was awake then, sitting up and folding his blanket with the placid obedience of one whose work is never done, who has no right to rest.

David and Savitri entered the rickshaw and settled into its seat, which was badly ripped with cotton stuffing hanging out of one long diagonal gash. David rattled off some directions and the rickshaw-*wallah* pushed the carriage onto the road and ran a short way with it before expertly catching hold of a bicycle pedal with a naked foot and leaping onto the bicycle and pedalling off. Their progress was swift for the street was empty and rickshaw-*wallah* was in a hurry to deliver his fare and perhaps catch a last hour of rest before the next day's toil began. David and Savitri bounced behind him on the seat, giggling in release as the potholes threw them together.

I am his, now! thought Savitri, *I can never go back!* In his eyes she saw that all worry had vanished and given way to a rush of excitement: David's head was thrown back and he was looking at her and laughing. In her eyes David still saw the absolute trust with which she had cut all ties of duty and tradition in one strong moment of decisiveness. In a split second Savitri had leaped from a fixed course and into nothingness, with nothing but her complete trust in him to lean on. This realisation came suddenly to him, stifling his laughter. Something new, bigger, more solid began to grow within him, and that was *responsibility*. He had taken Savitri out of all the security she knew, and thus he was accountable for whatever happened to her. His eyes misted over and he laid his arm around her, drawing her near. He leaned over to her and said into her ear, 'Thank you for coming, Savitri, thank you for trusting me. It's all going to be all right.'

'Will you tell me now where we're going?' She smiled up at him, snuggling against him. Having once thrown away conventions she didn't care; she felt light, and free, as if the whole world was open to her, and the whole world was good, and would embrace her.

'It's to be a surprise,' David said, and grinned as she wrinkled her nose in puzzlement. 'Try and guess!'

'I've no idea! How'm I supposed to know?'

'Well, anyway. It's too late now, we're there!'

He called out and the rickshaw-*wallah* pulled the brakes and the rickshaw jolted to a halt. David swung himself down to the ground. Savitri descended behind him. He paid the *wallah*, who nodded, turned his vehicle around, and creaked off into the night.

David stood now at the door of a tall, narrow, pink-painted house, banging a huge iron knocker against it loud enough to awaken the whole street. Slowly, A light went on in an upper storey and a figure appeared in the window, but Savitri could not see the face because it was in shadow, the light behind it.

But then whoever it was called out, 'What in heaven's name is going on out there? Have you gone mad, whoever you are?'

'Oh, my goodness!' she cried. 'It's Mr Baldwin!'

Chapter 27

Nat
London, 1964 — 1969

Nat was scheduled to return to India the summer following his first arrival in England. He didn't go. The distance to his father was too wide to breach, wider that the physical space between them.

His father lived in another world; going home would be going backwards instead of forwards. Besides: his father would want to know how his studies were going and… well, there was nothing good to say. He could always go next year; or at Christmas, when the climate would be more pleasant and the holiday shorter. He couldn't imagine the village, nor what he would do there, nor what he would say to the villagers. He had nothing in common with them, everything in common with his London friends.

Besides: there was that invitation to join Alice and some friends for a holiday on the Costa Brava. In fact, he had already agreed to go. His hotel was booked, and all that was left was to write his father (if he left it much longer he'd have to cable) to say he wasn't coming. Which he did.

He didn't go home at Christmas, either, nor the following summer. Another year passed, and still Nat did not return. In the meanwhile his lifestyle went through several changes. Women still turned their heads when he passed, but not as much as before. His beauty had lost its bloom; or rather, it had gone through a metamorphosis. He was no longer Krishna with his *gopis;* now he aimed for the Wiseman-of-the East look. Nat had grown a beard, and his hair was now way past his shoulders. By wearing a turban all the time he emanated a certain exotic-oriental mystique, and to enhance this image he started to smoke; not ordinary cigarettes, no, it had to be the tiny Indian bidis he found in an Indian shop. But these were externals. The glow, the charisma, was gone.

His mind refused to obey him, would not concentrate, his memory failed him. Nat thought it would be best just to break off his studies and do something else; get a job, be independent. He wasn't cut out to be a doctor, and anyway, he'd never go back to the village to join his father, so what was the point? The whole venture had been a waste of time. And money. Well, not quite; coming to England had been right; he'd needed these experiences, for they had shown him his true self, and now he could consider himself a man of the world, a cosmopolitan.

But the goal and the idealism which had inspired the move was long dead. It had anyway not been his own idea, but his father's. Doctor had chosen his goals for him. Doctor had decided what he should be, and where, and the more Nat thought of his father's manipulation of his life the angrier he became, and resentment gnawed at him for the wasted years which had come to nothing.

At the end of his third year he left university and found a job as a waiter in a small Indian restaurant. He made an excellent waiter, not merely polite and attentive but naturally friendly, with a charm that easily held the balance between amiability and respect, and the Indian customers loved to engage him in conversation, as Indians away from home tend to do, posing the usual questions as to where he came from, his name, his father's name, his father's profession, and so on. Since no-one had ever heard of the village Nat always said he came from 'near Madras', which sounded somehow more sophisticated.

Nat had a Golden Hand as a waiter and it was not long before he found himself solicited to move on to bigger and better things. People noted his name and address; wealthy people rang him up and asked him to come and help with their weddings and religious ceremonies, and paid him handsomely.

Finally he was permanently lured away by a fat Bengali, a Mr Chatterji who actually spoke not a word of Bengali, and in fact had never been to India and was a converted Christian bearing the name of William, who ran an Indian catering service.

Five years later, eight years after his first arrival from India, Nat was assistant manager of this catering service, an attractive and successful young man: a true-blue Londoner. He drove a green van with a caricature of an Indian waiter on the side, turbaned and in a dhoti, holding up a plate piled high with chapattis, smiling and winking at the world, and next to that the inscription: *Bharat Catering Services — Veg and Non-Veg Meals — Weddings, Religious Functions — Bengali and Tandoori Specialities — Best Quality for Price.*

It wasn't, strictly speaking, quite the thing to take the girls out in, but for some reason they adored it, thinking it quaint, and would rather go out with Nat in his Bharat van than with the Barclay's Bank manager in his Jag. Nat had never cared much for mere *things*, and he was never for one moment lured by possessions — *perishables,* he called these — or tempted to enhance his image by expensive cars, stereos, watches, and so on. Nor did he give expensive presents, nor did he feel the need to move to a bigger flat. He still lived in his Notting Hill Gate room, which he now shared with another Gujarati student, a cousin of the first one, now an up-and-coming solicitor in a Chancery Lane firm.

He hardly ever wrote to his father. He had found his way in London. He never lost his touch with women.

One evening Nat poured himself a whisky, reached for the telephone receiver with his free hand, clamped it under his chin, leafed through his dog-eared telephone book — S for Sarah — and dialled a number.

'Hallo, Sarah, how's my favourite lady?'

She giggled. 'Oh, come on, you, I bet you say that to every single girl!'

'No I don't, you really are! Any plans for tonight? Can you fit me in?'

'Any time... where to?'

'*Les Enfants Terribles?* I'll pick you up about eight, all right?'

'Wonderful!'

A few hours later Nat and Sarah tumbled up the stairs, wrapped in each other's arms, laughing, eager, all arms and legs and swinging hair, his as long as hers. Nat fumbled for his key, turned it in the lock, they tumbled into the flat, into his room, leaving a trail of shoes and Nat's shirt across the hall, Nat tearing at her blouse, she shrieking at the fun of it all, as they tumbled into his room...

The light was on.

In the corner between the bed and the couch a man rose to his feet, from the floor. A small man with a friendly face and great flapping ears, coming forward with his hand stretched out, saying, 'Hello Nat . ..'

'*Henry!*'

'Yes, it's me. Sorry for barging in like this — would have rang you up first, but Adam didn't have your telephone number; all we had was your address, so I just came in the hope that you'd be here.'

Sarah stood with her back turned, buttoning up her blouse. Nat grabbed a shirt from the back of a chair and slipped his arms into it, glowering.

'Who let you in?'

'Well, who do you think? That nice Gujarati chap in the next room. He even gave me a cup of tea and some crisps. We had a nice talk, but then he had to retire to do some studying. Said you'd be in later and I thought I'd wait. Seems it wasn't such a good idea after all...' his eyes shifted to the doorway where Sarah could be seen in the hall, shoving her stockinged feet into her shoes.

'Bye, Nat. See you next weekend!' she called, and the front door slammed. Nat collapsed on the bed.

'But... why... I didn't know you were coming... what...'

'I didn't know I was coming myself. Just flew in the day

before yesterday. Got some business in London: got to see a heart specialist, catch up with the family, a few matters to look into for Doctor... May I take a seat? Thank you.'

Henry sat down again, on the floor, as in India.

'Did Dad send you?'

'No, Nat, he didn't *send* me. But he did ask me to drop by and find out how you're doing. And he's hoping you'll come home in three weeks. I've taken the liberty of booking you onto the same flight I'm returning on.'

'Well, that certainly *is* a liberty! Who said I'm coming to India this summer? How d'you know what my plans are? How *dare* you...'

Nat's voice rose. He got up and paced from wall to wall, coming to a stop above Henry, tailor-seated on the carpet. Nat glowered down, almost threatening in his anger. Henry remained calm.

'Nat, it's been eight years! Eight years! Don't you think your dad wants to see you after all this time? I just thought, hoped, I might persuade you to come, that's all. Come on, sit down. Let's talk this through.'

But Nat began to pace again.

'And don't *I* count? What *I* want to do with my life? Henry, I'm just not into India any more. I don't know if I'll ever be. I've settled down here, I'm doing well...'

'Why did you break off your studies?'

'Well, I just decided I don't want to be a doctor.'

'And what *are* you doing? Why don't you ever write? Why don't you say a word about what's going on? Every Christmas a card: Dear Dad, I've got a new job, I'm doing fine, love Nat. What kind of...'

'Look, what is this? The Spanish Inquisition? Did anyone ever ask me if I *wanted* to be a doctor? All my life I've been maneuvered into a profession that has nothing whatsoever to do with me... I...'

'Don't talk rubbish. You know as well as I do that back home it was what you wanted. You're a born doctor and you know it.'

Nat rubbed behind his ear. 'Anyway, what's the point? It's over, I'm doing well. I've got myself a life. I'm not going to be a doctor. Finished.'

'It would have been nice if you'd at least dropped by to discuss things with your father, before making a decision.'

'Look, Henry: I was a grown man when I made the decision. Can you give me one good reason to discuss things with my father?'

'Merely as a matter of courtesy, which I shouldn't have to explain to you, for goodness' sake, Nat. Since he was the one financing you…after all he's done…'

'Look, d'you mind getting off my back? If there's one thing I can't stand it's parents laying a guilt trip on their children… "After all I've done for you…" '

Nat's voice was mocking, sneering.

'It's not your dad saying that, it's me. Because he has done more for you than you can ever imagine and it would have just been nice, Nat, if you could have come and explained things to him yourself. I shouldn't have to spell this out for you. Your father's the last one to reproach you but he does love you and thinks about you and wonders what's going on. And it breaks my heart to see him working himself almost to death, longing for a word from you, and then to see how callous you've become. And that's the reason, the *only* reason, I've booked this flight. Nat, do I have to beg you? Come home! Just for a while! Just talk to him! He'd have come himself but he can't, he's up to his ears in work and he can't leave his patients. He needs you, Nat!'

'Yes, exactly, that's it! He needs me! All his life he's been raising me just for himself, to help *him* with *his* work, what *he* wants for me. You know what I call that? That's selfishness; it's just plain egoism! What about *me*? What about what *I* want?'

But even as he said the words he felt a pain like the twisting of a knife inside him, and a picture of his father's eyes rose in his mind's eye, eyes that carried no reproach but only understanding. Nat shook his head to rid himself of that vision, and his hand rose to the back of his neck where he rubbed the spot that calmed him.

'Would you talk that way if he were a Harley Street doctor with a brass plate on his door, giving you the opportunity to be his partner?'

'Well, that's different!'

'What's so different about it?'

'Well, I'd have had the *choice!*'

'And, Nat, given your natural talent, you would have done it. That's not the problem, Nat. The problem is inside you. That's why you look such a mess. Why you *are* a mess.'

'If you came here to moralise . . .'

'I'm not moralising at all. I'm just stating a fact that's open for all to see. Look at yourself in the mirror. That's not the same chap I said goodbye to eight years ago, not even allowing for age. What's become of you?'

'Come off it, Henry. Get off my back. I've got to live my own life and I'll live it the way I want to. I'm not your little lad any more and I don't need your approval for what I do, thank you very much.'

'Nat, you're sulking. How old are you now? Twenty-seven? You act more like a sixteen-year-old in the throes of an adolescent rebellion. Well, I suppose it had to come sooner or later. Throwing you into deep water probably wasn't the best way, and if your dad had known how much times have changed since he was a student in England he wouldn't have done it. But somehow I never thought of you as a young rebel.'

'If there's one thing I can't stand it's moralizing and preaching.'

'Yes, you told me already. And if there's one thing I can't stand it's bratty know-it-alls, so I'll just bow out gently. By the way: Sheila, Adam and the twins send their love and say you should drop by again. Seems you made a lasting impression on the twins, since you were there last — what, three years ago? — they've jumped on this India bandwagon and it's been Harekrishna and Yoga and God knows what all; doesn't help that their father grew up in India himself, kind of a status symbol. Right now they're into Buddhism. Anyway, they asked me to give you this, and hope you haven't read it yet.'

Henry picked up a cloth bag from the floor and just seeing it gave Nat a little stab in his heart, for he recognised it, it was one of those cloth bags they gave you when you made a purchase at the dry-goods stores in Town, to put your cloth in, covered all over with a Tamil inscription. *Poompookar,* said the bag, in the curlicues of the Tamil alphabet which Nat found he could, miraculously, still read. *Special sari show room, artificial-silk saris, best quality. Polyester shirts and suitings.*

A memory rose involuntarily in his mind: he and his father standing at the counter chatting with Mr Poompookar while an attendant measured out a length of cotton, ripping it expertly, folding it and scribbling the price in biro on the wad of cloth, a habit the dry-goods salesmen religiously indulged in no matter what you told them. Doctor collecting the bill at the cashier's booth and counting out the limp little rupee bills and paying; having another attendant putting the cloth into a bag like this and stepping down into the pandemonium of the street, into the swirling traffic, the medley of rickshaws and cyclists and pedestrians zig-zagging through each other as in a mad dance to the music of honking rickshaw horns and bicycle bells and screeching brakes .. .

Henry threw a slender, blue-wrapped slab on to the bed. 'A present. With love from Nina and Jule.' He stood up, slinging the straps of the cloth bag across his arm, so that the bag, almost empty now, swung limp from the crook of his elbow as he placed the palms of his hands together. *Poompookar. Best quality goods.* At the door he stopped, turned, and did *namaste.*

'Namaste, Nat. Give me a call if you change your mind.'

Without thinking Nat found the palms of his own hands joining, returning Henry's greeting. Then Henry was gone, and Nat was alone with the stab of pain in his chest and the ghost of Mr Poompookar's smile still hovering in his mind and the unmistakable sweet fragrance of India permeating the room, left behind by Henry and his bag.

Tears gathered in Nat's eyes. He covered his face. A wave of shame and guilt and regret shuddered through him, and silent tears gushed forth. He picked up the book Nina and Jule had given him; read the title. He'd read it already, of course.

That's me, he said to himself. Siddhartha is me. Siddhartha, who lost the bird of happiness in the arms of the prostitute Kamala, who lost himself and all that was most precious...

'Henry ?'

'Oh, hello, Nat, how are you?'

'I'm all right . . .' He paused; Henry waited.

'Henry, did you keep that plane reservation?'

'Of course. Have you had second thoughts?'

'Yes. Henry, I — I've decided to go home.'

Chapter 28

Saroj
Georgetown, 1968

A gang of African hooligans threw a bomb into the Purushottama-Temple. Indians ran screaming from the premises and into the street, their clothes on fire. They flung themselves into the grass verges beside the street and rolled out the flames. Before the fire engine could arrive the building was an inferno, the two neighbouring wooden houses were also alight. The inhabitants of those houses fled in time, but six Indians were killed in the temple, which was completely razed.

Workers came to measure the Roy house for a fire escape. Baba received anonymous threats. 'You see?' he said. 'Animals!'

Saroj looked at her watch for the third time. Trixie was late. She had had to stay at school in detention for an extra period, so Saroj had gone to the library in the meantime and now was waiting for her at Booker's Snack Bar. She had finished her milkshake and the girl behind the counter had thrown her the second vicious glance — they liked you to go when you'd finished, but Saroj suspected that it was more because the girl was black and these days living in an Indian skin drew those kinds of glances from blacks. She squirmed on her seat, uncrossed her legs, swivelled half around to watch for Trixie.

She loosened her school tie and considered ordering a second milkshake, but there wasn't much time. This was to have been just a quick meeting, a cold drink and then a visit to Bata to help Trixie choose her latest shoes, after which they'd return to school for hockey. The man next to her paid for his sandwich and vacated his stool. Three black girls in Central High School uniforms edged themselves into the space next to Saroj. One of them slid herself on to the empty stool, and the other two glared at her.

'You finish? You not going?' said a tall lanky girl with an angry face, glowering at her.

Saroj looked at her watch once more. Trixie was twenty minutes late; she couldn't possibly wait any longer. She swivelled her stool around and was about to slip off when the second of the two standing girls gave her a shove from behind and she landed on all fours on the ground. The three girls cackled with laughter, and Saroj stood up, furious, brushing the dust from her uniform.

'Why'd you do that? I was leaving anyway!'

The girl wiggled her hips, pursed her lips, and said, imitating Saroj's accent, 'Why'd you do that? Oh my dear, listen to Miss Prim and Proper Cooly talking white!'

'I was leaving anyway!' said another girl, in an exaggerated BBC accent.

'Well, what about a nice cup of *tea?*' said the other in a stylised falsetto, carrying on the charade.

Tears stung Saroj's eyes. The way she spoke was a fact of life — after all, Ma spoke that way too, and she had never made the effort to speak Creolese. Now and then she had been teased about her English accent, but always the teasing had been friendly. This was downright mean.

The girls encircled her now — worse, they were joined by a group of boys, also in Central uniforms.

'That cooly-gal givin' ya'll trouble?' A boy with a six-inch Afro, the tallest, probably eldest of the group, pushed himself to the front of the group and stood directly before Saroj, staring down at her, almost touching her. She tried to step backwards but a girl behind her pushed her forwards so that she actually found herself in the boy's embrace — for he closed his arms around her and gripped her tightly.

'Hey, Errol, leave she alone, I jealous!' cried one of the girls.

'Give she it good, boy!' called someone else.

The boy holding her was pushing his face into her cheek, trying to nibble her ear. His hand was in her hair, kneading her back. She squirmed, grunting and protesting, to free herself, but he only held her tighter and laughed: 'Look how she winin' up! I like dem movements, girl!'

'Hey boy, you tekin' all de sweetness! Is me turn now! I never had a cooly-gal yet!' A second boy tried to push the first away and grab Saroj, but the other swung her around, clasping her to his chest.

'Oh, she sweet, man, too sweet!' He ground his hips against her. She tried to cry out but his mouth was on hers, and all the others were cheering, clapping him on.

'Go on boy, tek she! Tek she right now!'

Out of the corner of her eye Saroj saw an Indian woman, probably a housewife out shopping, peer into the group to see what was going on. Fright passed across the woman's face and she turned away and was gone. Behind the counter the girl stood smiling superciliously. Several of the customers had left; at least seven of the stools were now empty. No-one, it seemed, whether African or Indian, wanted to get involved.

What happened next happened so quickly that before she knew it, it was all over, and all she remembered was the loud thump as a thick French dictionary landed on the boy's head. Then a kicking, flailing-fisted, flashing-eyed Trixie pushed herself between Saroj and the stunned boy and in the next moment Saroj's molesters, boys and girls alike, had flown. Trixie dusted off her hands and gave Saroj her most wicked grin. She bent to pick up the schoolbooks lying scattered on the ground. She grabbed Saroj's hand, held it with intertwined fingers.

'Come, girl, we got to go. No time for a drink. Sorry I'm late; Miss Dewer came by and gave me an impromptu lecture about politeness to teachers. What a bloody bore!'

It was too much to hope that Baba would completely forget the Ghosh boy. He didn't. As was his wont, he made the announcement at the breakfast table only two weeks after the razing of the Purushottama Temple.

'The Ghosh family is coming to tea on Saturday afternoon. I am expecting you to be on your best behaviour, Sarojini.'

Ma, Ganesh and Saroj exchanged glances. No one said a word. Baba, basking in his regained authority, continued.

'That I am permitting you to meet the boy before the wedding is a concession to modern times. I am expecting you to be most polite and hospitable.'

'But Baba . . .' Saroj finally found her courage and her voice, but numbed with shock she could get no further then this mild protest.

'No buts, Sarojini. We made this contract several years ago if you remember correctly, and the Ghosh family has been very patient. The boy is ready to enter the family business and support a wife and a family of his own. Luckily the family does not know of your caprices. We have managed to keep your worst transgressions within the family otherwise I am sure they would have backed out by now.'

'But Saroj has her O Levels in two months! She can't get married now!' Ganesh snapped at Baba in a way that would surely bring down all hell's wrath. But Baba's stubbornness had lost its edge over the last few years. His was the cold clever determination of a serpent, and Saroj seethed inside.

'I know that very well, Ganesh. She will complete her O Levels and get her certificate, and then she will marry. We — myself and the Ghosh parents — have consulted with an astrologer and fixed a date for after her sixteenth birthday in September.'

Saroj looked helplessly, pleadingly, at Ma, whom Baba obviously had not consulted in any of these plans, a serious variation from the planning of Indrani's wedding. Then, Ma and Baba had worked together. Ma had met the parents of the boy, had been in on all the intricate consultations leading up to the setting of the final date. This time, it had all taken place in secret, without Ma's assent or knowledge. That meant Baba no longer trusted Ma. That meant Baba worked alone. That made him infinitely more dangerous.

'Ma, I'll run away before I marry this boy. Tell Baba that! He'll have to bring me home in chains!' Saroj lay in bed at the end of that day, Ma at her side, and finally gave voice to the rage that had been burning her up all day.

Ma only smiled and stroked her arm. 'Child, don't be so impulsive. Have patience — all will be well.'

'And what about this visit on Saturday? What if I'm just not home on that day?'

'Do what your father asks this one time and trust. All will be well. It would be impolite to revoke that invitation, and extremely rude for you not to be present. Please receive the boy and his family graciously, and let's see what our next move shall be. Who knows, maybe you will even like him!' She dared to chuckle.

'Ma, how could you say that? I'll never marry him, or anyone else! You know what I've been working for. Is it all in vain?'

'Dear, listen: if it is not in your destiny to marry this boy, then nothing in the world can force you to marry him. Not even if it were what you yourself wanted with all your heart. And if it is in your destiny to marry him, then that marriage will take place, no matter how you plan and scheme for another life than marriage.'

'Destiny! Poof ! It's all so *passive,* Ma! You would just sit back and let destiny take care of everything… but then nothing would ever happen! Nobody would ever make an effort!'

Ma only laughed. 'Effort and destiny are two sides of the same coin, dear!'

'Oh, *Ma!*'

Exasperated with her philosophising, Saroj turned her face away. Ma silently stood up, switched off the light, and left the room.

The boy's family arrived at three-thirty on the dot. He came with his mother and five older sisters, all married. Saroj supposed that these sisters owed their existence to their parents' determination to produce a boy, and here he was now, of marriageable age and all set to meet his bride-to-be — her. The boy, his mother and his sisters left the car and his father drove off without entering the house or meeting Saroj.

Baba wasn't home, neither was Ganesh. Indrani, not one to miss out on this highly interesting family occasion, was present, and she and Saroj waited at the top of the stairs for the visitors while Ma went down to let them in and lead them up.

The mother came first. She wore a sapphire blue sari; she was tall and bony with a long, thin, almost hooked nose and sharp quick eyes which took in all the details of her prospective daughter-in- law's appearance in one glance. Ma had plaited Saroj's hair on one side so that it fell over her right shoulder, over her right breast and down almost to her right knee. Saroj now realised Ma had done this so as to present her best feature without forcing her prospective mother-in-law to walk around her to see it. That hair was famous in Georgetown: if Saroj could cut it all off at the scalp she could sell thin strands of it for five dollars each and grow rich.

Whose side is she on anyway? Saroj felt a tide of distrust and annoyance at Ma's subterfuge rise up within her.

After the mother came the sisters, one by one; they all looked alike except for the colours of their saris. Their mother rolled off their names as they filed by, staring unabashedly at the famous hair, not even bothering to meet Saroj's eyes.

Then the boy himself was there, in front of her, staring like all the rest, the boy she was contracted to marry. She looked up and met his eyes. This proved difficult, for they weren't where they were supposed to be. They were half-hidden under prominent eyelids, which made him look as though he was about to fall asleep; yet obviously he saw her, for he smiled lazily, revealing a set of pearly teeth, the front two of which protruded slightly, which was about all she had expected of him. He said, 'Hello!' in a voice that broke in the middle, ascending into a squeak, which he tried to hide by coughing.

Apart from those half-closed eyes and protruding teeth he was quite a nice looking boy, with a clear complexion and symmetrical features, and even his mother's sharp nose on him seemed only masculine, not mean. He wore his hair in an exaggerated Elvis style, brushed forward and up above his forehead and slicked back over a puff. He wore a thin white dhoti tied in the orthodox way, pulled up between his legs, a plaid shirt, and black pointed patent-leather shoes. His hands were long and narrow, folded together in a *namaste* at his chest.

'This is Keedernat, Saroj,' said Ma pleasantly.

'Keet,' said the boy. Saroj's heart sank. Ganesh was right. A proper twat.

They were talking about the boy. They were sitting around the dining table, the two mothers, the boy and Saroj, the sisters, Indrani. Nine ladies and one boy. It didn't seem to bother the boy too much. Saroj supposed he was used to it.

'Keet the best boy in he class,' his mother was saying. 'He teacher say he got every chance of winning the Guyana Scholarship. Is a very talented boy. He brilliant in mathematics, science. But we don't want send him away for studies. His daddy need he for take over the business. We only got the one boy, so the one boy got to follow in the father's footsteps. Right, Keet?'

Saroj knew that to be a blatant lie. Ganesh had told her the boy had failed O Level maths and was in the Lower Sixth only in order to repeat the exam, and then, according to Gan's spies, would leave school to go into the business.

Keith meanwhile was sinking his teeth into one of Ma's samosas, having already devoured a few potato balls while his mother was making his many marvels known to the family. Even though Saroj kept her eyes lowered she could see his face. Beneath the hooded eyelids black eyes kept sliding sideways to look at her before sliding back towards his plate. She shuddered.

His mother took a long sip of sorrel drink which gurgled down her throat. Her bangles, at least six inches of them, jangled as she reached out for a samosa.

'Huh?' said the boy.

'What you say, boy? You proud to tek over de business, nah?'

'I don't mind,' he said, and looked at Saroj openly and grinned. For the second time, Saroj looked straight into his eyes and he, encouraged, winked.

'All me daughters married off good,' said Mrs Ghosh.

'Basmatti, she marry one Ramrataj boy from the East Coast. She marry six years already, got three chirren. Bhanumattie, she marry the youngest Magalee boy. He a engineer at Sprostons Dock. One chile. Satwantie, she marry one Boodhoo. They livin' in a big concrete house in Bel Air Park…'

While she went into the details of her younger daughters' marriages Keith kept trying to catch Saroj's eye but she, offended by that first wink, kept hers lowered and concentrated on the pineapple tart in her hand.

'You want to go out in the back yard?' said Keet suddenly, interrupting his mother's list of Satwantie's furniture, all new from Fogarty's. Startled, she looked up, from his face to Ma's, to Mrs Ghosh's. Keith was eating a pineapple tart now in all innocence as if he hadn't spoken a word. Ma's face was the usual picture of serenity, but Mrs Ghosh looked appalled.

'Who you talkin' to, boy? You in't got no manners? What you mean?'

'I just ask Sarojini if she want to go in the back yard with me.'

'What a t'ing! How you mean? What you want to go in de back yard for? How de girl gon' go with you alone?'

'If I suppose to marry de girl I got to talk with she, not true?'

'But what you think we come here for! You could talk with de girl right here at this table! Boy, you too rude! What dese people gon' think of you? You don't know is a respectable girl?'

Keet's sisters and Indrani all pressed their hands to their mouths or turned away trying not to giggle. Saroj kept her head bowed but still could see Keet calmly chewing his pineapple tart, eyes almost fully closed now, and Ma, next to him, looking at him with a kindly smile playing on her lips.

'If he wants to speak to her alone he may go,' Ma said then. 'Saroj can show him the garden. Saroj, take the secateurs and cut some roses for Mrs Ghosh. Don't worry,' turning to Keet's mother, 'it's all quite respectable. He's a good boy. Saroj? Have you finished eating?'

'Yes, Ma.'

'Show Keet where he can wash his hands and then show him the garden. The rest of us will sit in the gallery and chat.'

Obediently Saroj scraped back her chair and stood up. Keet, grinning now all over his face, did the same. They washed their hands in the kitchen and went out through the back door and down the steps, not speaking. Saroj could think of nothing to say to this boy, and he, it turned out, was waiting to be far out of range of the house.

'I have to cut some roses,' Saroj said to him then, and he nodded in apparent delight. She snipped at some of the best roses and laid them in the basket which hung over her arm. Since Keet was still not speaking she decided just to ignore him and start pruning one of the rose bushes. She felt him standing beside her, burning holes into her back.

Suddenly, as suddenly as he'd spoken at the table, he said, 'We going to have the honeymoon in Pegasus Hotel.'

Saroj whipped around. 'Who says there's going to be a wedding?'

'Of course there going to be a wedding. Is all fix up. Everybody want the wedding.'

'Everybody except me.'

He laughed, unperturbed. The eyes were wide open now, almost mocking, suggestive. 'Well, when you get to know me a little better you're going to beg me to marry you.'

And without warning he pulled his dhoti up over his knees, spread these, sank into a half-crouching position, positioned arms and hands to hold a guitar, and in a screeching falsetto belted out the Elvis Presley's *'Girls Girls Girls'*, gyrating his hips in slow forward thrusts in time to the music and moving the neck of his imaginary guitar up and down, his face screwed up all the better to sing.

As suddenly as he'd begun, he stopped. 'Good, eh? Elvis the Pelvis. I got all he records. How many of he films you seen?'

Saroj could only stare. But Keet, unperturbed continued: 'I got posters, I got them stuck all over the wall. Me mother won't allow any in the living room but when we married we can hang them over the whole house. My parents building a small house in the back yard for us. You can have as many records as you like. I's a modern fellow, you know, I gon' allow you to dance and wear short skirts and so. I like to dance. I like women in short skirts. You know there's a discotheque at the Pegasus? Yes, man. I been there but they don't play no Elvis. We can make our own discotheque in the house, yeah? Dance all night . . . *"Are you lonesome tonight... do you miss me tonight..."* great. Next week, *Viva Las Vegas* coming to the Empire, I'll take you. Don't worry about your parents not letting you go. We can take me sister Satwantie, she like Elvis too, and she gon' let we together. She modern too. Hey look . . .'

He glanced behind him, making sure that no-one had followed them. 'That hair of yours, man . . . lemme just touch it once . . . mmm . . . hey, why you pulling away? You don't know I's your bridegroom? I'm going to be your husband soon and then we can do what we like, oh boy, I can't wait, man, hey Sarojini, come back, where you going?'

Saroj turned on her heel and ran back to the house, Keet in her wake. As she drew nearer, and thus out of danger, she slowed to a walk and by the time they climbed the steps to the kitchen they had both caught their breath and looked what they were supposed to be, two healthy teenagers, flushed with the exuberance of life, returning from a short chaste walk in the garden. Only Keet 's Elvis haircut had lost its hold, and a few strands of hair hung over his forehead and refused to obey when he pushed them back into form. His eyelids had fallen back into hoods.

'Back already?' said Ma, putting away the leftovers in the fridge. 'Oh yes, give me the roses, I'll put them in water till Mrs Ghosh leaves. They're in the gallery, Saroj, please take this sorrel drink to them...'

Saroj grabbed the tray with the jug of sorrel and the glasses and turned away from Keet — standing sheepishly in a corner of the kitchen, watching Ma — and walked out to the visitors. She heard Keith's steps behind her: she wanted to run, no, to turn and empty the jug of sorrel over his head, no, to scream, 'Get away, you moron! I'll never marry you in a hundred years!'

They sat in a circle in the gallery, Mrs Ghosh and the girls. Saroj stood there with the tray, uncertain what to do because the little tea-table was outside their circle and no-one was making a move to bring it, not even Indrani, who should know better, because she was avidly listening to Mrs Ghosh's account of Rampatti's wedding a year ago.

As Saroj stood there she felt a deliciously warm wave move slowly downwards through her, and as it flowed it drew her strength with it. Before her, the scene turned vague, fuzzy, as through a mist. Her arms fell, with the tray and the jug of sorrel and the glasses. The warm wave... no, by now it was a river, swept on through her lower body, down her legs, to a never-ending sea, all wet and warm, like syrup, down, down her legs. Her head drooped and she saw the sea around her feet, it was red, it was blood!

A thought flitted through her mind, and she had to smile, the thought of herself standing in the sea of blood that was Indrani's wedding sari, so long ago, so many ages ago, but this was no sari, this was real, and she felt herself falling into that sea, knees crumbling, legs giving way. And she heard Mrs Ghosh's shout, distinctly, in the moments before she passed out.

'The girl getting a baby! Oh Lord! Is a miscarriage! Look at all de blood! Mrs Roy, Mrs Roy, come quick!'

But Ma was already at her side. Saroj could smell her. She felt her arms reaching out around her, breaking her fall, because she was slipping in the blood, and she heard Ma say, 'Mind the glass. Indrani, help me carry her away from the glass. Call Dr Lachmansingh.'

Chapter 29

Savitri
Madras, 1934

'No, David. Absolutely not. I'm not going to aid and abet an elopement.'

Though the night was warm Savitri shivered as she heard these words. She drew her blanket up over her shoulders, and pulled it tighter. She stroked Adam's head to calm herself. They had awakened the children with all their din, but Mrs Baldwin had quickly quieted the two elder boys, Mark and Eric, and had taken them back to bed, while Savitri held Adam, the youngest, an infant of eighteen months. Now, they sat around the kitchen table while Mr Baldwin made tea.

Adam began to whimper and Savitri got up to walk back and forth and rock him, but he would not sleep.

'But Mr Baldwin . . .'

'Absolutely not, David. What you've done is absolutely irresponsible. You'll have to go home. Immediately. Both of you.'

'Mr Baldwin! They're sending me back to England!'

'And that's where you'll have to go. Maybe one day you'll learn some sense there!'

Savitri moved near to David and he put an arm around her. Both stared at Mr Baldwin, wordlessly. Adam wiggled to get down and Savitri let him slither out of her arms. He ran to his father and flung both arms around his legs. Mr Baldwin's voice dropped, losing some of its sternness. He stood with the teapot in one hand, the other reaching down to pat Adam's curly blond head.

'Look, David, Savitri. Don't you see, you can't. You're both underage, for one. Savitri's Indian, for another.'

'That's the whole problem, don't you see! They want her to marry some man she hasn't even met and if we don't rescue her I'll lose her! Mr Baldwin, help us, please! I know we're minors but still: we do know our feelings, and we belong to each other, we always have. You know that!'

Mr Baldwin nodded imperceptibly, and David, encouraged, carried on.

'I don't mind going to England, I don't mind going to Oxford, I don't mind waiting for her, but I want her to wait for me! And she wants to wait for me, don't you, Sav?'

Their eyes met and locked and Savitri nodded, then turned calmly to Mr Baldwin. 'I can't go back, Mr Baldwin. I've left my home and my family and I can't go back. Even if you refuse to help me I cannot go back.'

Mr Baldwin clicked his tongue and placed the teapot on the table. He picked up Adam and slid him into his high chair, and signalled to David and Savitri to sit down. He poured them each a cup of tea and then said to Savitri, slowly, as if speaking to a little girl,

'You *can* go back, Savitri. It's only three in the morning. If you go back now no-one will have noticed. You can slip home and it'll be as if nothing ever happened.'

He turned to David now. 'She's an Indian, David. They have their customs which we can't understand. If you had never turned up she'd have married this man her parents have chosen and very likely she'd have had a good marriage. Indians do have good marriages, you know. Indian women are not like our women. They make up their minds to love, and they love unconditionally. Savitri has that in her. Let her go. It's unfair of you to put her in this situation. It's irresponsible. She's doing it for you because she loves you, but you have no idea what the consequences will be to her... what scandal, what shame...'

'No!'

All eyes turned to Savitri. The word was spoken sharply, authoritatively, and it was as if not Savitri herself spoke, but another being, strong and knowing.

'It's not David's decision, it's mine. Don't blame him. He didn't force me. He asked me to come and I said yes, and I'm here, and I'll stay, if you'll have me, and if you'll hide me, for a while at least, until I can find some sort of work. There's no going back. Even if they come and take my body forcefully back to my home, marry me forcefully to this man, I have chosen David and I belong to him in my soul. I will wait for him, if you will help. I've left my home, I've abandoned my duty. For an Indian there is nothing worse but I have done it and there's no going back. Before tonight it was different. I was prepared to renounce David and marry the man my parents have chosen, like a dutiful daughter, and you are right, I would have had a good marriage because I would have given my heart into it, and I would have been a good and strong wife for my husband. But the moment I walked out of our gate with David, Mr Baldwin, that moment I became another. No longer Indian, and not yet English: there is no name for what I am, but I am myself, and I will wait for David. If you will help. And —'

A burst of clapping interrupted her speech and Mrs Baldwin walked in, smiling at Savitri. June Baldwin was a big, physically strong woman, a head taller than her husband. She had changed out of the nightie she had been wearing and was dressed now in a long flowing house-dress with a faded floral pattern. She had wild curly hair, a sharp nose, a wide, generous mouth, and freckles, and crossed the room now in great strides. She joined the little group and moved over to stand behind Savitri, as if in support. She dominated the room.

'Well spoken, well spoken!' she said, still clapping. She patted Savitri's shoulders then continued, 'I for one am fully on your side, Savitri! It's about time you women stood up against the ridiculous custom of arranged marriages! Show your mettle, girl, I'll be glad to help!'

David's eyes lit up. 'You will? You'll help us?' He turned eagerly to his ex-tutor, seeking confirmation, but Mr Baldwin was looking at his wife, and she at him; a contest of wills was taking place, which Mrs Baldwin won hands down.

'You'll stay,' she said to Savitri. 'We'll employ you. We need someone to help with the children; we've had a string of ayahs and they're all no good. I know you're good with children. I know a lot about you, Savitri, Henry has told me so much. He was so taken with you, you know, when he was your tutor. I said back then, he should have done more for you.' She glared accusingly at her husband, turned back to Savitri.

'You'll have a room upstairs. It's not very big but you have the run of the house and the courtyard out in the back. You're welcome!'

'June! Do you know what you're saying? The girl's a minor. If we're found out we could get charged with ... with kidnapping, or God knows what. Her family'll be furious…"

'Oh, fiddledeedee. What do I care? We're English, aren't we? Who rules this country? We do. The law is on our side. They won't dare take us to court, and even if they do, what English judge would ever side against us? All we have to say is that the girl was being forced into a marriage she didn't want and came to us for refuge. And they needn't ever find out. We'll hide her.'

'We shouldn't interfere.'

'Oh yes we should. It's our duty to interfere! What do you expect the poor child to do? Run home with her tail between her legs and beg for forgiveness? They'll probably throw her out anyway… you know these Indians!'

Savitri nodded in eager agreement. 'That's right, Mr Baldwin. What I have done is a terrible thing. I have brought great shame to my family. They will never accept me back, once they know I've run away. In their eyes I'm a fallen woman!'

Mrs Baldwin smiled down at her and reached for her hand. It was now three against one, and Mrs Baldwin, standing behind the two young people like a mother hen with her wings spread over her chicks, glared at her husband, challenging him to disagree.

He threw up his hands in capitulation.

'Very well, then, Savitri. You can stay. But you, David!'

His voice was like a whiplash and David, exulting in those first words, jumped to attention, the triumphant grin wiped off his face.

'You're not welcome. You'd better get on home. Now. Immediately, before they miss you. I don't want your name mixed up in all this. Believe me, it's better if no-one knows you helped her escape. Go home and pretend you don't know a thing.'

'But . ..'

'I know what you want. You'd like to hide here yourself a few days, wouldn't you? Be with your lady love? Over my dead body. No, you go. Look, it's nearly four already, and you've got to find a way of sneaking back in without being seen. It's high time ...'

There was no arguing with Mr Baldwin. David knew that from his boyhood; he knew that it was only thanks to Mrs Baldwin that he'd gained any leeway at all, and there was nothing more to be gained by arguing. He stood up reluctantly, and Savitri too stood up. He took both her hands in his, and they faced each other, loath to pull apart.

'You'll hear from me!' he said. 'My ship leaves in two weeks, and I'll get in touch, I'll send you a message.'

'No!' Mr Baldwin stepped between them and pulled them apart. 'What utter nonsense! Do you want to help her, or put her in acute danger? You're to stay away from her, lad, not even a note, d'you hear? I've promised to help her but I'm not going to get myself mixed up in your intrigues! If you want to marry in a few years it's your business, but for now you must keep away! I've taken her on as my responsibility and for you, that means hands off! This is a risky enough business to begin with, and we English have made enough enemies here in India, and we don't need our boys putting their hands on their girls! So go! I'm throwing you out!'

And David let himself be thrown out, with nothing but a last wave for Savitri over Mr Baldwin's shoulder.

David had wisely not told Mr Baldwin that he was due to leave for Bombay that very day, and that his train was scheduled to leave at five a.m. and that he would very definitely be missed, and his absence very definitely connected with Savitri's escape. When he returned home, Fairwinds was in uproar.

News spreads quickly in Madras. Savitri's escape was the talk of Old Market Street by ten that morning, the gossip spreading from the Fairwinds servants' quarters and passed along in both directions till, at around ten, it reached the bazaar. When Murugan the rickshaw-*wallah* found his way back to the bazaar for his midday meal he heard about the missing bride who had run away with a young *sahib*. There was a reward of one hundred rupees for news of the girl's whereabouts. Murugan did his duty and collected the money.

Mani's thugs came before dawn, six of them but it sounded more like sixteen, masked and brandishing hammers and axes. Their cries woke the whole street, but when they started to batter down the Baldwins' door with their hammers and axes the neighbours withdrew their heads from their windows and closed their shutters. The thugs stormed up the stairs, breaking down all the doors. June stood akimbo in the doorway to the children's room, prepared to let herself be slaughtered before they could enter: three of them pushed her aside, inspected the room and its occupants, stormed out again. They weren't after the children.

They found Savitri in the little room at the top of the stairs. They dragged her, yelling and struggling, from her bed by her hair, half-carried, half-dragged her down the stairs to the road and into the waiting rickshaw.

At the very same time that Mani's thugs broke in, David and his mother were boarding a first-class carriage on the Bombay Express. As planned, David sailed back to London two weeks later.

One month later Savitri was married to the station-master of Tiruchirappalli, a middle-sized township several hours by bus from Madras. R. S. Ayyar had been found by Savitri's elder brother, who worked in the same town. Ayyar was a widower with five children, the youngest a girl of thirteen years. His first wife had died only a month previously and he was in a hurry to remarry, and not too particular about his future wife's background, for, after all, she was only a second wife. And so he did not know that Savitri was a fallen woman, sullied by the hands of an Englishman, one without caste. Which was, after all, the reason why Ramsurat Shankar had cancelled his own wedding to her. And since she married before the age of eighteen, Savitri was not eligible for the generous dowry granted her by the goodness of Mrs Lindsay.

But R. S. Ayyar was not particular about a dowry, and such a man was hard to find. All in all, Savitri could be considered lucky, since she was able to keep the gold jewellery passed down to her by her mother.

Not so lucky were Mrs Lindsay and her daughter Fiona. The Lindsay family had brought shame and scandal to the Iyer family, and, Mani proclaimed loudly, someone had to pay.

The night after Mrs Lindsay returned from Bombay a group of masked thugs, very likely the same ones who had rescued Savitri from the Baldwins, entered Fairwinds through the servants' quarters. They stormed the house, battering down the kitchen door. They lifted the Admiral bodily from the bed and into his wheelchair where he watched helplessly, or rather, tried not to watch while they tied Mrs Lindsay and Fiona to the bedstead and each of the six men raped them. The women writhed and screamed, but their writhing only made it worse and their screaming excited the men all the more. They found glass bottles in the kitchen which they broke and used the gashed edges to cut the women's thighs and genitals, and left them bleeding on the floor. The little Christian live-in housemaid locked herself in the bathroom where she whimpered and quivered in fear, but she need not have feared, for she was not English, not the enemy.

The police came but the investigation proved difficult. Mani was a prime suspect but he had spent that night at a political meeting where he had been seen by several friends who could all swear to his presence, providing a cast-iron alibi. All the servants were questioned but no-one had seen or heard a thing. The thugs were never identified.

Aunt Sophie came to Fairwinds to take matters in hand. A week after her arrival Fiona disappeared. All efforts to find her failed.

Mrs Lindsay announced she could not bear India a day longer, could not face her friends and acquaintances, could never live down the shame. And then there was David. He was the heir to a fortune, and too foolish, too emotional, to be left on his own. He must be taken in hand; a suitable alliance must be found, and in his guilt he would comply. She took a ship back to England, planning to buy a London house and settle there and then send for her husband. The Admiral, accompanied by Aunt Sophie, Joseph and Khan, followed after six months. Fairwinds was boarded up, deserted, the garden given back to nature.

Chapter 30

Nat
London, 1969

Having made the commitment to return home, Nat had second thoughts. He wasn't so sure he could actually keep the commitment. He envisaged himself walking through the village street, climbing into a rickshaw, buying oranges at a market stall, leaning over a patient to dress a wound in his father's surgery, and it all seemed impossible, the stuff of dreams; it had never happened, could never happen, not to him, not to Nat. He closed his eyes and tried to bring back that moment of truth soon after Henry's first visit when he had known, simply *known*, that he had to go back, that this, his London life, was the dream. That his life here was the surrogate and India the real. But that moment had flown, and Nat could no longer bring it to mind, and furthermore, he did not want to. Going back to India was to cross an abyss too deep, too dangerous for words; not even in his mind could he make that leap. The more he thought of India the more the fear grew.

He thought of his father, and his father's hopes for him. Doctor had given his life to the service of the poor and there was no trace left in him of that grasping, hungry little worm called selfhood. Doctor's life began in service and ended in service, and should the lowliest ragged beggar drag himself dying to Doctor's door at midnight, then Doctor would be there for him, and either fight to ward off death or be with him till death arrived, whichever was more appropriate.

In his youth, Nat would have jumped to his feet to stand by his father through the hours to fight or to wait for death, and those hours had not seemed difficult, nor wasted, nor diminishing. But thinking of it now filled Nat with something near panic; he could not! This was the life his father had chosen for himself but it was grossly unfair to expect his son to do the same. Such sacrifice of selfhood must come voluntarily, or not at all. Doctor apparently had no personal needs whatsoever. But Nat knew all too well his own needs, needs that demanded satisfaction without cease.

But his commitment to return was binding and he could not back out. Keeping his given word was one of the sacred duties Doctor had upheld so well that Nat could no more go back on a promise than he could cut off his own hand.

He needed a valid excuse not to go, but there was none. There had been no problem getting leave from work. Summer was a quiet time for catering with hardly any Indian weddings or other celebrations, so Bill Chatterji was closing his business anyway for two months and going to his maternal relations in Maharashtra, and Nat could not lie and tell Henry he couldn't get leave when he could.

What he could do was work out some kind of a compromise that would satisfy everyone's wishes and not break any promises, and Nat spent the last weeks before his departure thinking out just such a compromise. He wrote a long letter to his old friend Govind Bannerji, explaining the situation. Sealed the envelope, addressed it, stamped and posted it. There! That done, Nat felt much, much better.

By their last night in London, which he spent with the Baldwins, he was feeling quite satisfied with himself, and even looked forward to India. Seek and you will find, he thought. He could kill two birds with one stone: visit his father, and make the most of what India had to offer.

The following morning Sheila drove them to Heathrow. They were flying via Colombo instead of via Bombay because, Henry said, changing planes at Bombay was always such chaos since you didn't only change planes, you changed airports and they'd have to take a bus from Bombay International to Bombay National, whereas Colombo airport was international, thus much easier for passengers in transit.

They were well on their way to Colombo, cruising somewhere over the Middle East, about an hour after the Abu Dhabi stop, before Nat told Henry that he would not, after all, go to the village right away, but first spend a few weeks in Ceylon.

'I need some time to myself, Henry. I feel utterly exhausted in body and mind. I've been going on full power for years and now I'm absolutely burned out. All I can do right now is just lie on the beach and, well, recover. Find myself again.'

'That's your freedom for you, lad. Saps a man's strength.'

'Look, Henry, if you're going to be judgmental then we can stop this conversation right here and you just go on alone and don't bother explaining to Dad. But...'

'Don't say a word more, Nat. I understand. When can I tell Doctor to expect you?'

'Well . . .' Nat hesitated, for Henry did little to conceal his disapproval. Damn Henry. Why did he always have to lay a guilt trip on him, Nat?

'Well?'

'Henry, to be honest, I can't give you a fixed date. I thought after Ceylon I'd travel around a bit. See a bit of India, you know. When people ask me about the Taj Mahal it's a bit embarrassing to admit I've never seen the damn thing! I'd like to see Delhi, Kashmir, the Himalayas. Maybe Nepal. The usual. There's plenty of time. And then I plan to visit the Bannerjis in Bangalore. After that I'll come to the village.'

'I see. The usual tourist trail. I suppose you'll also take in a few gurus standing on their heads in caves and some fakirs sleeping on nail beds. Hope you've got your camera. Well, Nat, go ahead, you won't find me standing in your way. I'll tell your dad and pass your love on to him. Nat sends his love but he's up looking at the Taj Mahal; he'll drop in before he flies back to London.'

Henry reached up and pressed the button for service and a pretty, chocolate-skinned stewardess at once appeared, bending over Nat to smile at Henry, showing teeth as white and flawless as pearls, which unaccountably gave Nat a twinge of jealousy.

'May I help you?' she asked Henry sweetly, and Nat, who hadn't been asked, smiled up at her and asked for a beer to accompany Henry's orange juice. Nat had an aisle seat which he found very pleasant, since it offered him a much better view of the stewardesses moving up and down with such elegant ease, despite the wraps of their saris, which emphasised the roundness of their hips and showed silky brown inches of bare skin between skirt and blouse. They brought back memories which alarmed him as much for the lump they brought to his throat as for their very vagueness. Bangalore girls; the loveliest in the world. Well, it wouldn't be long before he'd see them again, in person. He hoped Govind would be there; but yes, by now he'd be back and a CEO in the family business. Govind would help him find those girls.

Bangalore seemed as far away as the village — Bangalore, and the laughing, teasing yet discreet Bannerji sisters and the intangible fragrance that to Nat contained the essence of their womanhood, wafting around them as an invisible shield, protecting, upholding, the aura of their dignity, like the sheen on an untouched peach.

Nat squirmed uncomfortably in his seat. He thought of Woman, as he'd once adored her, from afar, never knowing her. But thoughts of women, as he'd known them, kept interfering, lewd pictures: of lascivious, lustful, wanton, carnal, dissolute, lecherous, horny, beckoning… women. He nipped at his beer, closed his eyes, smiled, and gave himself up to the pictures. Sometimes he opened his eyes just a slit and watched the splendid smiling Ceylonese stewardesses swaying up and down the aisle and in his mind he stripped them and had them join the orgy. He wondered if he might get to know one or two of them when they landed at Colombo; if he got a chance he'd have a go. Surely after such a long flight they'd have a few days' break . . . a few days on the beach with a stewardess . . . he'd never had an Indian girl yet, nor, of course, a Ceylonese. It would be nice to penetrate that aura of purity. As long as Henry hovered in the wings he'd have to lie low, but once he'd gone on to Madras Nat would circle in for the kill . . . sunny beaches, sea and surf sang their siren song, and Nat knew he would have company, delicious company.

With a sidewards glance he checked that Henry was asleep. Then he smiled at a passing stewardess and crooked his finger. She bent low to hear what he had to say.

Chapter 31

Saroj
Georgetown, 1968

Through the mist Saroj saw a familiar face: Dr Lachmansingh, smiling down at her. She was floating somewhere in space. Light as air, like a feather, bodiless.

'What… where am I? Where's Ma?'

'It's all right, you're here in the Mercy Hospital.' Dr Lachmansingh's voice was low and soothing.

Saroj remembered the blood.

'What happened? All that blood . . .'

'It's nothing serious. The lining to your womb just got a little too thick so all the blood rushed out. It's all right. Now listen: we're going to give you a D and C, clean out your insides a little. You lost quite a bit of blood so we're going to have to replace it. Your parents are here right now downstairs, having their blood group determined. One of them will have blood matching yours, and will donate blood for you. It's a routine procedure.'

Questions, anxieties crowded her mind. What had caused it? Why her? Why exactly then, at that particular moment? But she was too tired to ask her questions, too tired to think, even. Saroj floated off, into a far off space, a far off time, and dwelt there for an eternity.

When she awoke the room was full of shadows.

Voices. Through the space, through eternity, floating voices, both familiar. Ma, Dr Lachmansingh, talking. Somewhere in the room, behind the bed.

'A slight problem, Mrs Roy . .

A nurse came in through the mist, bustled around the bed. Silence. The nurse left. Again, the voices .. .

'...a rare blood group, Mrs Roy and — er — this is, ahem, rather unusual, but neither your blood nor that of your husband... matches...'

'I understand,' said Ma, so calmly she could be talking of the weather.

'That means we need another donor — maybe your two elder children?'

The silence that followed was too long. When Ma broke it her voice trembled slightly, yet was clear, calm and defiant, as if Ma was telling Dr Lachmansingh: this is all the explanation you'll get. Putting him in his place.

'But their blood may not match either... they will want to know why... ask questions...'

'Well... we'll have to go to the blood bank then but you understand: it's a rare group, so...'

Ma's voice now was brisk, decisive, as if she'd figured everything out and made up her mind. 'No, doctor, I have another plan that will save a lot of time and trouble. I will bring somebody with the matching blood.'

Her voice sank. Conspiratorially she continued, 'But please, let this be very discreet... my husband must not know — do you understand? And Saroj; she would be devastated. She must not find out. Never. Just a minute...'

So calm, so serene. As always. Ma, wearing her mask of absolute dispassion. Unmoved. Cold. So far away. Through the distance, each word came to Saroj and etched itself into her mind with the piercing sharpness of a scalpel on untouched skin. No more fuzziness. No more mist.

She heard the slapping of Ma's tiny leather sandals against the soles of her feet as she walked around to the window side of the bed. She could feel Ma's eyes on her face, as if she'd sensed wakefulness. She tried to pull Saroj's hair free but she was lying on it so she stroked her cheek once and rose from the bedside. Saroj kept her eyes closed, pretending sleep.

Once more Ma spoke to Dr Lachmansingh: 'Doctor, can we perhaps talk somewhere else?'

They left the room.

Saroj fought to stay awake, stay conscious, to think, to reflect, hold on to her mother's admission of deep, shameful, unforgivable, scandalous betrayal, but it was her own mind that betrayed her, waving white, feather-like tendrils over her, enclosing her once again and carrying her off into the swirling mists of unknowing.

Grey mists parted; somewhere in a corner a naked bulb burned and she blinked, then turned her head to avoid the glare. Soft hands pushed the hair out of her face.

'Ma . . .' she murmured, and a soft voice said, 'Yes, dear, it's me.' And Saroj saw Ma before her, leaning forward over her in the half-light, but something was wrong... The fragrance? Something... She rubbed her eyes with the back of her hand. Yes, it was Ma, bent over her... No, it was... It was herself! Her own face, her own long hair drawn forward in a single plait heavy on the bedsheet. Her own face... But no, an older, a weary, worried Saroj... The face was near, and it was her own... *Ma is me... we are one...*

'Ma . . .' she groaned, and closed her eyes and drifted off to some far heaven.

Other hallucinations came and went. She saw the four-armed Shiva with the cobra around his neck and the moon in his piled-up hair. Shiva disappeared and Nataraj came, Nataraj dancing on the ugly little ego-monster, a majestic, divine, cosmic dance. Gods and goddesses in a heavenly sphere, translucent and shining and lit from within by a cool blue light. Kali with her necklace of skulls, drooling blood. She was outside her body, swirling somewhere far from earth. She heard a holy song from a region beyond time and space and her mind was as wide and endless as the universe itself.

I'm dead! Yet I'm alive! How can that be?

The mists parted again. She was all there, back on earth, trapped in her body on the hospital bed, back from her journey beyond the cloud of unknowing, bringing with her a wealth of confusion, memories mixed with hallucinations.

She remembered all she'd heard, all she'd seen, but some dreams were dreams and some were true and it was impossible to sift the truth from the dreams. She looked around. A double room, the wooden walls painted in a fresh light lime, apricot-and-lime patterned curtains fluttering at the open window. Outside, a kiskadee called. There was that fresh scintillating feeling of early morning.

The bed next to hers was empty. A smell of antiseptic and sterility, of roses and fresh sheets and sea-breeze, of lightness and air and returning health. Her body contained pains in deep places but warm strength flowed through her, and her mind was alert as never before. Truth and dreams clicked together or fell apart. It was so vivid all she needed was her own sharp logic to piece together truth and discard dreams, and the truth was sharp and clear and full of pain.

She remembered.

Looking around she saw a button on the end of a cord. She pressed it. A white-clad woman came bustling in, an Indian nurse with her hair tucked neatly into her cap, smiling with the sisterly affection of having known Saroj longer than *she* knew *her.*

'So, Miss Roy, you're back with us! How are you feeling?'

'Good, thanks. Have I had the operation?'

'Of course!' Her voice rose cheerfully on the second word. 'It all went fine, darling.'

'And the blood transfusion?'

'Yes, of course, of course! Everything's over! Now you can start to get better! Do you want to go to the toilet? Do you need help?'

'No, thanks, I'm fine... where...?'

'Just outside, the next door on the right!'

When Saroj returned the nurse was changing her sheets. She sat on the wooden chair in the corner and watched silently. On the night table was a vase with fresh ferns and roses, roses from Ma's garden. The nurse spoke:

'You can get washed in the basin over there, or you can

have a shower if you like. Do you need help? I must say, you slept like a baby; it's already ten o'clock! Your mother was here early this morning, she brought you some flowers and some fruit. She'll be back later.'

'When can I go home?'

'Well, actually, you'll have to talk to the doctor about that, but it won't be long now; he'll be along in a while to have a look at you, there, now you have a nice fresh bed ... Shall I bring you some magazines?'

'No thanks, I'm fine.'

The nurse looked at her watch. 'So, I have to go now, see you later!'

'Sister .. .' Saroj stood up, raised her voice to call her back, but she was gone and the door clicked discreetly into place behind her. Saroj walked over to her bed, picked up the vase, inspected it from all angles, gathering the determination to do what she'd just sworn. Empty out the water, then into the wastebasket with the roses. *Come on, don't be a coward, just do it.*

Ma'll be back soon. It won't be long. What do I say to her? Shall I confront her? Pretend? Bide my time? Play-act? If she can play-act, why can't I? If she can tell a lie, live a lie, sustain a lie for a daughter's lifetime, why can't I live that lie for a while, just a little while longer, just as long as it takes to throw all her lies back in her face, and grab my freedom, what's left of it?

Lies! All lies! A lifetime of lies! Dirty, filthy lies! Trixie was right! I must have suspected the truth... Yes, she always suspected that Ma had a secret. A secret lover! And everything else was a lie!

Please let this be very discreet... she should never find out... my husband must not know...

Oh yes, she understood now. She understood everything. Ma's stealth, her slipping from the house, her serenity in the midst of a disastrous marriage. Ma had been playing a part. Playing the sweet, chaste, butter-wouldn't-melt-in-her-mouth innocent angel, the saint, holier-than-thou. All Saroj's life. Play-acting. The docile, silent wife. The temple-going chaste saint.

The Hindu Madonna.

Purity is the highest virtue, Ma had told her children. Purity of thought. Your body is a temple; care for it. She had drummed it into them when they were too small even to know the meaning of the words. Take care of your mind, and where you let it dwell; for where your thoughts go, that is what you become.

And all the while... this! This *lie!* Ma has a lover! *Adultery!* The hypocrisy of it!

Ma, of all people! *Ma!* But, well, yes, Ma. Of course.

All at once Ma's silent way of sliding around corners, up staircases, entering rooms, took on a dark, threatening, sinister connotation. Sneaking about, slinking out of the house when Baba was absent, to meet her lover in some dark room somewhere. Saroj remembered other words of Ma's, words that now took on a dire significance.

Women must be quiet, and secretive, and cunning.

Ma, slinking off to the Purushottama Temple. But not actually being there.

She never stays here for very long.

And it's not over. It's still going on!

Ma *still* has a lover. She meets him almost every day. She's had a lover for at least sixteen years, *and I am that man's daughter!* Ma has a secret life. Who is this man, who sired me? Where is he? Obviously, he knows of me...

I can bring somebody with the matching blood...

And, worse than all that, worse than her hypocrisy, letting Baba ruin her life! Baba, a stranger to Saroj, no relation whatsoever, no blood, nothing... The most distant stranger, yet he had been allowed the intimacy and the rights, the privileges of a father.

Baba is not my father. He never was! And Ma had let him do this to her! Oh, cruel, cruel, Ma! Too lazy to fight, too passive to act, too cowardly to admit that I am not his daughter. Too fainthearted to leave Baba and live another life with the man she loved, with the daughter of that union!

Saroj's initial amazement and disbelief gave way to a fury so wild she almost wrecked the room.

Fury at Ma. At Baba.

Her fury lent her strength. All physical discomfort fled. She paced the room in wrath. She picked up the vase and the roses and could not bear their stench, the stench of Ma's betrayal. She poured away the water and threw the roses into the wastebasket, got the better of herself and grabbed them again, pricked her finger on a thorn, shoved them back into the vase, plonked the vase, without water, on to the bedside table of the other bed, pulled viciously at the sheets and got into bed before she caused more damage.

There she sat, sucking her bleeding finger and brooding, every cell of her being a boiling cauldron of wrath, counting off every last one of Baba's crimes against her since the day she could see them as crimes, her wrath gathering momentum, ready to unload on the first human being who dared to cross her path, who dared to open that door and walk in. She prayed it could be Ma. Pray! No! She'd never pray again. It was nothing but a tremendous lie — her whole life, a lie! Ma, who should be her protector, had in fact delivered her into Baba's hands! She had given Saroj to Baba, without need!

She gave me to him like a lamb to be slaughtered! This thought was the last straw. The world so lovingly built by Ma — *lovingly! Ha!* — crashed down around her, as irreparably shattered as a fragile eggshell under a ruthless foot. Everything she had ever believed, and everything she had *not* believed but accepted anyway because of her trust in Ma, was, in the opening of the eye of knowledge, destroyed, in shambles.

She couldn't just lie there doing nothing. She got up again, walked to the window, looked out across the emerald green of the parade ground. The mounted police were doing some sort of an exercise on the green, eight horses circling a mounted sergeant shouting out his commands. The policemen on the horses' backs looked so smart in their navy blue uniforms. Straight-backed in the saddle, they calmly trotted their circles, now turning, now stopping and saluting, now forking off to meet in pairs, riding away in diagonals, returning, stopping again, backing three paces. Now they were all walking towards the sergeant in two rows of four, these again forking away and meeting in one row of eight, walking towards the sergeant, stopping, saluting. Without Saroj realising it the horses and their riders effectively drew her attention and held it fixed. Watching them brought a calmness to her mind, and the violent emotions that had waged their war within her somehow settled into a new mode.

Thoughts began to tick through her mind in methodical, cold alignment, like marching soldiers, like horses in training, obedient, under her command.

Somewhere from the middle of police headquarters on the far side of the parade ground the sound of a bugler practicing the *reveille* drifted across, sometimes just two faltering notes, then three, repeated over and over again. A little bird flapped its wings, learning to fly.

I must leave home. I will never, ever, return to Ma and Baba. Saroj swore this with a vengeance so cold in its conviction that the pores rose on her arms despite the warmth of the mid-morning sunshine, golden on her skin and filling the room with light. But not her heart. That was dark. *I will go.* Go now, before the doctor comes, before Ma comes, before anything happens to stop this slow methodical march of thoughts, this steady, unflinching resolve. *I will never live with them under the same roof again.*

She glanced around the room to see what she would take: nothing, just slip out of her nightdress and into her own clothes and shoes. This she did, and then she walked down the stairs — nobody seemed to notice — and out into the sunshine.

Chapter 32

Savitri
Somewhere in rural Madras State, 1938

Let me keep this child. Let it live, and let it be a boy! Savitri stooped on the steps down to the Parvati Tank and paused to send this prayer up to the Lord. Oh, let this child live! The cry from Savitri's heart was so anguished that surely every living thing in the universe must hear, and nod and smile to acknowledge it!

But no answer came. The farmer ploughing the peanut field next to the Parvati Tank walked stolidly on, step by step behind the pair of oxen, holding the wooden plough that drove deep furrows into the red earth. Up and down, up and down the field. Indifferent. What a little thing was Savitri's prayer. Who would ever listen?

She lifted Ayyar's lungi from the water and wrung it into a thick rope to beat against the stone, and spoke to the baby inside her. She begged it to stay, she begged the Lord to bless it, to keep it safe within her body, but most of all, *to keep it safe once it was out,* to hold His hand above it. If she could only have a child there would be something to live for! *And ... let it be a boy, dear Lord, oh let it be a boy!*

For if it were a girl something might happen again, like with the first two. Accidents both, but nevertheless...

The first two years Savitri's body had refused to conceive, as if privately mourning for David, as if refusing to bear any other fruit but his. Ayyar's beatings had started then. They stopped when at last, as if to ward off the beatings, she finally was with child; and started again when the first little girl was born.

She was named Amrita, and had lived one day. Savitri had left the baby sleeping safely in the depths of a hammock made of a sari hanging across the room. She had gone out to fetch water from the well before dawn, as always, leaving her husband still asleep in the little room which was their sleeping quarters in the station-master's house. When she got back she found that one end of the sari had mysteriously loosened from the rafter it had been tied to, and slipped to the ground. The baby had fallen on its head and it was dead.

Ayyar was still asleep, and had noticed nothing. He had wept and pulled at his hair when she woke him, but Amrita, whose name meant *nectar of immortality*, could not be brought back to life.

The second little girl, named Shanthi, lived six months. Then she took ill and died. The doctor said it was from rat poison. Rat poison! Savitri had no rat poison in the house. But her mother-in-law did, and she often went to see her mother-in-law, who lived with two younger sons and their wives two blocks away, and maybe the rat-poison had been on the floor when she had let the baby down to crawl? No-one knew, and Shanthi, whose name meant *peace*, was dead.

'This time it will be a son,' Ayyar said when she was with child a third time. 'Certainly it will be a son. The chances are high that this will be a boy. Take heart, wife. He will bring great joy to your heart.'

The chances were indeed high. Ayyar had five children already, four of them girls, three of them married. His two brothers had four daughters between them, and no son. So the chances were high that this time, it would be a boy. After so many girls in one family, it had to be a boy!

'My mother's heart is yearning to hold a grandson in her arms!' said Ayyar. 'Twenty years since my first child was born, that is too long for a grandmother to wait! I have had to give so much dowry for those daughters. This last girl must be married soon but we have no more funds for dowry. Let us thank the Lord for his kindness in removing your two first daughters. This time he will be kind enough to grant a son. You will see.'

And so Savitri hoped this would be a son. Then it would live. She could not bear to lose a third daughter.

But even if she had a daughter who lived, she would have little joy. What can I give a daughter? she said to herself. Nothing. I would like to give her so much but I cannot. Education, and books, and the love of a man like David. The power of healing. She stopped lashing her husband's wet lungi against the flat stone near the tank where she did her washing, and looked up at the sky and a great silent cry escaped her heart: *Why, oh why!* She held the palms of her hands up before her, and looked at them. Useless, now, except for cooking and washing and fetching water. She often found herself grumbling in this way and quickly pulled herself together. *Do not complain,* she told herself. *It is a waste of time for nothing will change. Go to the place behind the thought-body, and bear it all in silence, for in silence the strength will gather and one day you will be free.*

She slapped the lungi one last time, with all her power, and then flung it out into the tank and watched it spread out beneath the water's surface and almost float away. She waded out to retrieve it, stepping cautiously down the mossy stairs of the tank into the water green from algae, wetting her sari up to the knees. *Oh Lord, oh Lord. Give me the strength to bear it. And if it is a daughter, oh Lord, then save her! Save her from him!* She stroked her tummy. *If you are a girl,* she said in her mind, *then I will protect you. I will never leave your side, not even for an instant. I will watch over you, and nothing shall ever harm you. I shall bind you to my side when I fetch water at dawn, and I will hold you in my arms when we visit his mother. This is my solemn promise. But it will be easier for you if you are a boy, easier for us both. If you are a boy you will be safe.*

Near the Parvati Tank was a shrine to Ganesa, the elephant-headed god, Shiva's son, the remover of obstacles. Behind this shrine stood an old pipal tree on whose branches hung tiny hammocks of rags containing clay figurines and stones, tied there by women when they prayed for children. Savitri too had tied her cloth to the tree, and prayed fervently for a son. She vowed to Shiva that, should he grant her prayer, she would shave her head and make the sacred pilgrimage to Tiruvannamalai for the Kartikai Deepam festival.

Savitri did not pray for herself, but she might very well have done so. The beatings were bad enough, but much worse were those nights when he came home late with stinking breath and slobbering mouth and threw his heavy heaving weight on her, and took his pleasure. Each time it was a small death. She prayed for the strength to bear it, but she never prayed for release. She had abandoned duty and had to pay a price, and these small nightly deaths — that was that price. When the price was paid she would be free. She pressed her soul into a pinpoint of strength, and bore it.

She finished her washing. She had brought a clay vessel with her which she scooped full of water and placed on a rock at waist level, to take home for washing cooking vessels and other utensils. Then she spread a dry sari on the parched grass next to the tank and piled the wet clothes onto it, then bundled them up in the sari, tied it all together with two knots on the top, tied the remains of her soap into a corner of the sari, and heaved the bundle on to her head. She hooked her elbow around the lip of the clay vessel and heaved that into the curve of her hip, and made off towards home.

She walked easily and quickly, the bundle of clothing balanced deftly on her head held high, her hip carrying the weight of the water vessel, the crook of her arm preventing it from tipping over. The other hip was free — how she longed to balance her baby there! In a year she would be doing just that. Her heart soared, and sank. *Oh, let it be a boy! Let this family not be cursed by yet another daughter! Let it be a child I can afford to love, a child that everyone will love! Or if it is a girl, let her live!*

That evening Ayyar came home drunk again, and in a particularly filthy temper. Afterwards Savitri could not remember what had so infuriated him, what had initiated his tantrum. All that she remembered were the slaps on her face, and her body, and the shouting, and the kick in her stomach, and the rape, mercifully short.

And she remembered the blood. The warm wetness on her legs as she tried to sleep later that night, the blood that would not stop bleeding. The coming of the rickshaw, Ayyar in a panic bundling her into the rickshaw wrapped in many saris to stop the blood that would not stop.

The little boy was too tiny, too weak even to take a breath. He died. She named him Anand, meaning *bliss*.

Chapter 33

Nat
Colombo, 1969

When they left the plane at Colombo it was pouring. The passengers were loaded into buses and driven the short distance to the airport building and hustled into the transit hall where they joined an interminable queue until, shortly before midnight, they were ushered into another bus bound for the Hotel Blue Lagoon.

Nat was seriously disturbed by the rain. It dampened his enthusiasm considerably, which was why he had stayed with Henry instead of going on to Immigration. The word *monsoon* was buzzing in everyone's ear and if this was the monsoon there was no point in planning a week or two on the beach. And the airline was putting them up in the luxurious Blue Lagoon till they could board the plane for Madras the next day — which meant a good night's sleep between clean sheets and a good hearty breakfast before making new plans. Nat decided to wait. It was certainly annoying, to have to change his plans like this. He'd been looking forward to a week or two on the beach and had in his mind made a tentative itinerary for his Indian holiday: up to the north, down to Goa for another beach holiday, to the village for a few days to do his duty by his father, then over to Bangalore and the Bannerjis, and finally returning Colombo for the return flight. All of that he'd have to drop now, because if there's any hell on earth, it's India during the monsoon. He thought for a while.

He would have to begin with his duty-visit to the village, which was particularly annoying. Nat had expressly planned this visit near the end, so as to rule out any designs his father and Henry had to keep him longer, and any twinges of his own conscience, once he was in their clutches, urging him to stay longer and help out. He knew his father was overworked and it would take a great effort of will to stick to his guns and go on with his tour, but Nat was determined. It seemed a matter of life and death, a matter of preserving his individuality, his self-determination, not to succumb to the call of so-called duty, which was a particularly Indian thing and since childhood deeply ingrained in him, drummed into him by his elders.

Living in the West had changed all that. He now knew freedom to be as essential as duty, no, not as essential, but a hundred times more essential. He needed his freedom, needed to be his own man, to make his own decisions, spread his wings and fly. Perhaps it was just as well that he would now be called upon to confront his father, to *willingly* make the decision to leave, instead of relying on the tactful exigencies of a return ticket. Yes; it was better to get his duty over and then enjoy his freedom, rather than to have duty waiting for him, a deep hole at the end of the journey. It would perhaps mean a confrontation with Doctor, but through the confrontation he would make his point more clearly than through tact. Become a man, liberated from the dictates of his elders. But what could he do after that? Where could he go? And then it came to him: the life-saving brainwave.

A week in the village, to pay his respects. And then, Govind. Life in the village, in this weather, would be horrible. His father would understand. There wouldn't be much work, and few patients. That was it. He's go to Bangalore, the Bannerjis, for the rest of the rainy season. Hopefully, Govind would be there. Thank goodness he'd written that letter before leaving! With any luck, the reply would be waiting for him at his father's, with the usual invitation to "stay as long as you like". Well, he'd do just that, and stay for the rest of the rainy season. The Bannerji house wouldn't be affected much by the rains. They wouldn't be able to play tennis or golf or use the pool, but he and Govind—if Govind was there—could have a lot of nice long talks and do some nice entertaining (visions of bored unmarried

Bangalore girls wafted through his mind) and he, Nat, wouldn't be stuck in the middle of nowhere. That was it: the perfect plan. Nat felt much, much, better.

That decided, Nat finally found sleep, lulled by the monotonous roar of the rain outside his hotel window.

First course at breakfast was a choice of papaya or pineapple. Nat chose papaya and as the sweet, luscious fruit melted in his mouth he felt he had come home, at last, and smiled to himself.

'Years since I've tasted anything as good,' he said to Henry, grinning. Henry smiled back.

'Might as well enjoy it while you've got it. I fear there won't be any papayas at home for some time to come, with all this rain. At least they won't complain of drought this year. The farmers will be happy for once. You can't imagine what it's been like, the last couple of years, Nat. The well's all dried up; they had to cart water from Town or we'd all have dropped dead. Your father had two bore wells dug, but the water table's so low now that if the monsoon had failed this year it would have been a real disaster. I just hope it's not too much of a good thing. The villages aren't built for rains like this; and it's been raining non-stop for weeks now, I've heard. Doctor's house will be fine, it's got a good strong Madras roof, but I'm worried about the villagers with their flimsy thatched roofs. They don't hold back a drop. You know what we'll do? We'll buy some sheets of plastic in Madras; they're sure to come in useful. Anyway, lad, we've got *you* now; I can't tell you how happy I am that you're coming back with me after all! Your dad would have been too disappointed for words if I'd turned up on his doorstep without you.'

Henry's smile was so heartfelt that Nat looked away and as he stuck the final bit of papaya into his mouth he mumbled, 'yes, well, for a week or two, just till the rain stops, then I'll be on my way.'

Henry looked up. 'On your way? Where to?'

And Nat told Henry The Plan.

Chapter 34

Saroj
Georgetown, 1969

It was not far to the Roy house from the hospital; a mere fifteen-minute walk. As she walked, Saroj made her calculations. Ma would leave the house sooner or later, on her way to the hospital. She had to be alert, in order to see Ma before Ma saw her. She would hide, then, and let Ma pass by. If she did not see Ma that meant she was still in the house, finishing off whatever Ma did in the mornings — meet her lover? Murmur sweet nothings into the phone? — when she was alone at home.

Walking to the hospital would take Ma fifteen minutes. She would find Saroj gone, there'd be a rumpus, a panic, a search. What would she do next? Assume Saroj had gone home, and hurry back? Another fifteen minutes. Perhaps someone would give her a lift which meant ten minutes less. Or she'd take a taxi. All in all, she'd be away from home at the very least for twenty-five minutes.

But Saroj didn't need more than ten minutes. At the most.

She didn't see Ma on her way home. That was good. It meant Ma hadn't left yet, which gave her more time. On Waterloo Street she walked carefully, hiding behind each flamboyant tree and checking before running to the next one. If anyone was watching they'd think she'd gone crazy, but the avenue was empty and from the houses you couldn't see through the foliage.

She arrived at the tree beyond the house and waited, watching. It was all so clear, so calm, so strong within her. She chuckled to herself, the euphoria of liberty bubbling up within. It was finally happening, then, Independence Day! So often she'd contemplated leaving, played with the thought of running away, divorcing her family. Always it seemed a mission as impossible as cutting off her own hands. Now that she was doing it, it was so easy!

It seemed to take an eternity for Ma to leave the house. Saroj knew she was still home for the downstairs windows next to the mango tree were still open and Ma never left the house before closing those, since the mango tree was easy to climb and an open window next to it was an open invitation to thieves and arsonists. Baba had dismissed Singh — both Singhs — for sleeping on duty, and hadn't yet found replacements.

Saroj waited. One or two cars passed by on either side of the avenue. A black nanny with two white children in playsuits and sunhats, who belonged to fat Mrs Richardson at the corner of Waterloo and Lamaha Streets. Nanny stared at Saroj curiously but walked on by up the avenue, stopping every now and again to call, 'Come on, come on,' to the children, who chortled with glee and threw handfuls of red flamboyant blossoms at each other, forgetting to follow Nanny.

Vaguely their play brought back a similar scene from half an eternity ago, when Baba was still Baba and Saroj a toddler, and Indrani and Ganesh played with the blossoms while Saroj peddled furiously on her tricycle trying to keep up with Baba. A wave of nostalgia swept through her and something bitter pricked at her eyes. But quickly she banished such sentimentality and pulled herself back to the task at hand, which was simply — waiting.

A dray cart loaded with planks, the driver crunched into himself, half-asleep it seemed, calling out Hey-hey mechanically and flicking his whip each time the scrawny horse stopped to pull at the wayside grass, which was every five paces.

The closing of a sash window jolted Saroj to attention. She peeped out from behind her tree and saw Ma at the second window, jerking it up an inch before letting it fall gently into place, breaking its fall with her hands. For the split second before it closed she saw Ma framed by the window... Ma... another wave of nostalgia threatened to overtake her but she steeled herself successfully against it. Now the front door was opening.

She watched from the safety of her tree as Ma glided out in her favourite plum-coloured sari, placed a basket on the concrete path and turned to lock the door. She needed both hands because the key always stuck and you had to pull the door towards you to get it to turn. Saroj pulled her head back now, trying to ignore the sickness in her stomach, and heard the lock dicking into place, Ma's latchkey turning — strange, how sounds carry when your hearing is keenly tuned for them!

Then Ma raised the clasp on the gate, the gate opened, its chain rattling slightly, it closed again, the clasp fell into place, Ma's footsteps drew nearer as she crossed the road. Saroj was safe behind her tree, but could not help looking out to watch Ma's little back as she walked down the middle of the avenue, away from her, the *palu* of her sari floating out behind her, her basket over her arm and knocking gently against her hip as she briskly walked towards the hospital. The basket, loaded with good things for Saroj in her convalescence: favourite fruits, maybe genips because it was genip season, or guavas or a golden ripe paw-paw or pineapple slices in a box; a bottle of sorrel or tamarind drink, maybe some samosas or pineapple tarts or *barfi*...

Funny how, when you resolve to do something strong and essential, something you know you need to do, a feeling as weak as sentimentality tries to creep up behind your fixed resolve and take you unawares with memories and prods of conscience and things as frail as a mouth-watering memory of a samosa made with loving hands especially for you. Oh Ma... There was a lump in Saroj's throat. She wanted to weep, to call out. But no.

Ma turned the corner into Lamaha Street and disappeared from view. In a trice Saroj was across the road; the gate she left open but not clasped, to save time at her escape. The front door was locked, but she knew where Ganesh kept a key hidden in the yard, under a pile of unused flower-pots. It was in her hand, turning in the lock, then she took the stairs two at a time, all the way up to the second storey and through the door into her bedroom. She looked around, at what had been home for so many years, smelled for the last time the lemon-scented polish. It was dark, for Ma had closed the jalousies, but bars of sunlight infiltrated through the slats casting a ribbed pattern on the white sheet of the bed.

There were no suitcases in Saroj's room, and she didn't want to waste time searching for one. She slipped the pillow out of its case, opened the drawers of the dresser, and stuffed the pillow-case with some clothes, underwear, a few blouses, school uniform, shoes. There wasn't much she cared to take with her. The high-necked dresses Baba ordained, she would never wear again in all her life, nor the grey pleated skirts. Jeans and tie-dyed T-shirts: that was her future. Trixie would help.

The pillow-case filled and bulging, she hesitated, just for one second. Dare I? Yes! Yes! Without this, this one last defiant act, without a *statement,* her escape could not be final. She opened the door into her parents' bedroom. She knew where Ma kept her sewing things, in a corner of the wardrobe, in a round basket. She opened the wardrobe, enveloping herself in a cloud of scent so filled with Ma's presence she almost drew back. But only for a moment. Her hands found the basket, delved into them, and felt the metallic coldness of the thing she sought.

Scissors in hand, she stood before Ma's mirror and held up her plait. Before she could think a further thought crunched through it. There. It was gone. Ma's pride and joy. After that it was easy. She cut it off as near to her head as possible, not measuring but just cutting, blindly, plunging the scissor blades into the black thicket Ma had tended for hours and hours of her life, letting it all fall to the floor around her. Tears stung her eyes but she paid no heed, grabbing now at the last handfuls of hair and ruthlessly snipping them off, throwing them to the floor in disgust, watching herself in the mirror through the stinging mist of threatening tears as she worked.

It was a lot of hair. And it lay there in a deep, dead pile of worthless silk. She threw the scissors onto the pile, opened Ma's top drawer where hairpins, clips, rubber bands, ribbons, jayal sticks, and other whatnots were neatly organised in little throat-drop tins. She selected a thick black stick of kohl and wrote across the mirror: *LIAR!*

Leaving the drawer open and the kohl stick lying on the vanity, she picked up the pillow-case and ran down the stairs. The postman had come in her absence, for a thick blue airmail letter with strange bright stamps lay on the floor before the door. It wouldn't be for her; probably Baba's relatives from Bengal. Saroj opened the door, slipped out, locked it, replaced Ganesh's key, went out of the gate, and down the avenue to Lamaha Street. She looked at her watch. Ma would just be arriving at the hospital.

At the bus stop around the corner she stopped and looked at her watch again. It was lunchtime. Trixie would be joining her mother at one of the restaurants in town before afternoon school began. She'd have to wait. It might take some time before Trixie came home but it didn't matter. She'd just sit on the back steps (she should have gone to Ma's kitchen and taken some food; too late now) and enjoy her freedom. She had all the time in the world; the rest of her life, in fact.

'Christ, Saroj, where's your hair? Dammit, what've you done? Your hair! You look terrible! Oh my *Gawd!*'

Trixie was in a terrible panic and Saroj just stood there smiling as she ran up, turned her this way and that, grabbed what was left of her hair and finally, realising that it was true, it was all irrevocably gone, collapsed in a heap on the front stairs.

'Why'd you do it?' she said flatly.

'Because it's all over. I've finished with them. I've left home. I've done it, Trixie, I've left them. I want to stay here, with you. You said I could.'

'You shouldn't have done it. Not cut off your beautiful hair.'

'I had to. I'll explain once you let me in the house and fill up the hole in my belly, I'm famished, been waiting here since lunchtime.'

'Come on then.' Trixie took her school bag from the bicycle carrier and walked up the stairs, Saroj close on her heels. Before turning the key she looked at Saroj again and moaned, 'Christ, Saroj, I can't believe it, I mean I just can't believe you really did that. That hair! Your lovely, lovely hair. You look a mess, a disaster. Nobody'll ever look twice at you again.'

'And what do I care?' Saroj snarled, following her into the house. 'I'm sick and tired of being looked at. What's a lump of hair? Just hair, that's all. Hair. Fibres. My God, the way people make a fuss over a few feet of dead fibres. Look at me, Trixie, I'm here, I'm alive!'

Trixie plonked her satchel down on a dining room chair and snorted.

'That's what you say now. Anyway, no use crying over spilled milk, it's done and it's a shame but it won't come back. C'mon. What'd you like?' She led the way into the kitchen, opened the Kelvinator and poked her head in. 'Not much here. Bread and cheese. Shall I make you a Welsh rarebit? Oh, and there's some old soup. From Wednesday, I think. Callalou. Mabel made it.'

She took out a small pot, opened the lid and sniffed at it. 'Should be good still. Shall I warm it up?'

Saroj thought nostalgically of Ma's samosas, her *bhindi bharva*, stuffed okras, the exquisite scents wafting from her kitchen at all hours of the day, the fridge constantly brimming over with delicacies. Hard times for her palate lay ahead; but it was a price she was willing to pay. *Nothing comes cheap*, Ma always said. *The good things in life call for sacrifice. Give your all to get your all.*

Okay, Ma, I'm ready.

'Don't bother. Just some bread and cheese.'

The bread was pre-sliced and stored in a plastic bag. Because the outer slice was hard Trixie removed it and placed the rest of the loaf on a breadboard. She took a lump of cheddar from the fridge. She cut off a slice of mould, threw that away and gave Saroj the rest. A plastic butter-dish followed. She took two Jus-ees from the fridge, plonked two glasses on the kitchen table and sat down beside Saroj before prising the lids off the drinks.

Digging away at the cork inside the Jus-ee crowns with a knife, Trixie forgot Saroj and her hair.

'Einstein,' she said. 'That's the last of my scientists. Let's see what's here.' She dug at the second crown and threw it away in disgust. 'Lord Byron. Shit. That's the third Lord Byron. I still need Jane Austen and Wordsworth. And I haven't got a single American president! Hey, doesn't your family make these drinks? Can't you get hold of the right crowns for me?'

Jus-ee drinks was running a 'Famous People of the World' competition: in all of its crowns there was a famous person in six different categories; you stuck them into a special album and the winner would get a lady's or a gent's Suzuki. That was the kind of thing Trixie got to do and Saroj, till now, couldn't. Ma usually didn't stock Jus-ee at home, even though they were manufactured by a Roy. Ma made all their drinks, except at birthdays and weddings. They might taste better than Jus-ee but weren't half as much fun. And you couldn't win anything.

'I'm going to start collecting from now on,' Saroj declared. 'You can give me that Byron. He's my first.'

And then she told Trixie her story.

Trixie shook her head in disbelief. 'You're the weirdest person I ever knew,' she said. 'You mean, you're leaving home just because your Ma had an affair and you discovered your Baba isn't your Baba? And all the time they were marrying you off you didn't run away? Now *that's* a good reason to leave — what happened about that Ghosh boy, by the way? — But your Ma having an affair? I think it's exciting! Romantic! So that's where she was when she was supposed to be at the temple! You know, I had a feeling back then, but I didn't say anything. Shows your Ma's got guts. If I were you I'd be *dying* to find out who's my real father. I wouldn't run away, I'd gang up with my Ma and get her talking. Who d'you think it is ?'

'I don't know and I couldn't care less. You just don't get the point. Ma 's always going on about purity and truth and she can't...'

'But she *did,* silly! You've got the proof, I just don't get why you're so uptight. This just goes to prove that she's not all different like you say, not the saint you were always making out she is, she's just, well, she's *normal,* she's like everyone else! Lots of married people have affairs. How many married men do you think raise kids from other men in all innocence? Hundreds — thousands, I bet!'

'And I think you read too much True Confessions behind your mother's back. I don't know how someone with your brains could read such absolute drivel and then believe it, and anyway, what counts for the rest of the world doesn't count for Indians, they're different, Ma is different, I tell you. Her doing a thing like that is like if... like if the sun began rising in the west and setting in the east! It's just unimaginable, and if she did do it, which is obvious, then everything she ever said and did is just one huge *lie!* She's a hypocrite; *that's* what bothers me. And apart from that she let me believe that monster is my father, that Deodat Roy!'

'You should at least give her a chance to explain everything! I mean, what if she's desperately in love with someone else? I once read a novel about a married lady — I was sobbing for days afterwards, so I think you should at least talk to your mother and find out what really happened, and keep her secret, because if your Baba ever finds out she had an affair he'll... Christ, I can't even imagine what he'll do! Think he'll throw her out, or what? Divorce her?'

In fact Saroj hadn't given even the slightest thought to Baba's reaction. For obvious reasons he didn't know Ma had been unfaithful and if he did find out, if he began to ask questions because of what Saroj had written on the mirror, there was no telling what he'd do to Ma. What if he killed her in his rage?

But no. Ma would be home long before Baba and she'd certainly remove the evidence, that message on the mirror. All Ma would have to tell him was that Saroj had cut off her hair and run away. Baba would believe it was because of the Ghosh boy. If Ma had any sense — and she must have sense if she'd managed to keep this love affair a secret for so long — she'd manage it. She was underhand enough. A sly, conniving bitch.

What if Dr Lachmansingh talked? He might consider it his duty, men among men, and so on. Well, that was Ma's own doing; she'd trusted Dr Lachmansingh with her secret so if he spilled the beans to Baba, then it wasn't Saroj's fault. And she, Saroj, certainly wouldn't be talking to Baba, and neither Trixie nor her mother would ever snitch. So Ma could keep her dirty little secret.

Chapter 35

Savitri
Somewhere in Rural Madras State, 1938 — 1939

Savitri's son Ganesan was born on the day Great Britain and France declared war on Germany. An inauspicious sign? Many other things had happened in the year leading up to that birth.

R. S. Ayyar seemed, after Anand's death, stricken with genuine compunction, perhaps even remorse, perhaps only fear of bad karma. That was the last time he beat her. The rape stopped too, for the most part, but that was more or less involuntary. For his drinking increased, and when he came home drunk at night he could do little more than collapse on a heap on the mat.

A month after the 'incident' — as he chose to call it — Ayyar suggested that Savitri return to Madras for a while to visit her relatives. With mixed feelings, then, she wrote to Gopal in Bombay to come and get her. She longed to relive the good things of the past, but, of course, most of those were gone forever. David was gone, and Fairwinds. Mrs Lindsay too was gone; Appa had died two years ago, and all that remained of the people who had brought her joy was her brother Gopal and Amma.

Mani was now head of the Iyer household — what was left of it, which was only Amma, and she herself was ill and dying. Mani's illness, too, had worsened — often he coughed into the night. He did not earn much money since leaving the army — he was now a salesman in a shop for electrical appliances, in downtown Madras — and the home Savitri found waiting for her was in no way the place she remembered. They still lived on Old Market Street; but on the other side, and further down, near the bazaar, in the crowded, loud, dirtier section, and instead of a garden and a huge estate behind the house there was only a paved court with a well in the middle, which they shared with two squabbling families.

Mani was gone most of the day but when he was home she knew he hated her still, and she did not know why. Gopal took a week's holiday to be with her in Madras, and between them a new depth of understanding grew. Gopal now wore Western clothes — dark long trousers, and long-sleeved shirts with a chequered or striped pattern, which he combined with leather *chappals*. He was handsome in a film-star way, with a thin moustache and slicked back hair. He was still at odds with his family and lived with a cameraman friend from a Madrasi studio, but came daily to pick up his sister and take her out. With Savitri side-saddle behind him on a borrowed motor-scooter he cut a dashing figure, and the two of them turned heads wherever they went.

Gopal had won a contract with a film production company in Bombay. His first novel, *Ocean of Tears,* had been published, and had been a great success with middle- and upper-class Indian housewives. He had been 'discovered' by the rapidly developing Indian film industry, and had developed a screenplay from the novel. In the process the studio had discovered his great talent for directing. The film was bound to be a hit. He told Savitri the story with much enthusiasm: it was a tragedy, the story of twins, violently separated from each other and from their mother at birth, and finally reunited at their mother's death-bed in a dramatic, tear-jerking climax. He had thousands of ideas for further screenplays, and stood, it seemed, on the verge of fame and prosperity.

Proudly he introduced Savitri to the fabulous fantasy world of film, to be discovered sitting in the very best seats at the Wellington Talkies on Mount Road. It was the first time Savitri had been to the cinema. She watched fascinated the story unravelling before her, the story of a beautiful heroine facing untold dangers, heart-wrenching sorrows and a ruthless villain until finally rescued by the miraculous hand of God and a brave and handsome hero, and everything ended happily.

But it is not so in real life, Savitri said to herself. In real life there is no end to the sorrows, and all we can do is learn to bear them bravely and patiently, that we may leave this world of misery worthy of bliss in the afterlife.

They went to the beach and walked along the sand together, wading on at the water's edge, in silence, each lost in memories. The water was tepid, washing forward in gentle sheets over their bare feet, and pulling back again. Savitri's sari, a fine pink one, quite new, which Gopal had bought for her, was wet up to her knees. Oh, the wideness, the greatness, the grandeur, she thought, and her heart stretched out and beyond the horizon. *If I reach out far enough, over the ocean, all around the curve of the globe, then I will meet* him. *Maybe right now, at just this minute, he is also reaching out to me. I will never forget him. I will never forget running into this very same ocean with him, and laughing with joy, our hearts full to bursting! Whatever happens, that is always there! I will never forget, for he is the air I breathe!*

Gopal interrupted her thoughts. 'Savitri, can you keep a secret?' he said.

She looked up at him. 'A secret? But of course, Gopal, you know I can! What is it?'

'I have a wife in Bombay!'

'A wife! Gopal, you are secretly married?' Savitri exclaimed, in Tamil.

Gopal replied darkly lowering his voice. 'You must keep this secret, Savitri. I have married Fiona!'

'Fiona!' cried Savitri. 'I thought Fiona was…'

'No. Fiona came to me, her only refuge, and her one true love. We were lovers over the years even after our thwarted elopement. We used to meet secretly at the home of a modern-minded actor friend in Madras, till tragedy struck in the shape of my very own brother.'

He paused. Savitri looked up at his profile and saw a pulse beating at his temple. She waited for him to continue.

'I never stopped loving Fiona,' Gopal said then. 'That is

why I never married another. I still loved her, in spite of the great shame our own brother brought on her.' Savitri looked up at him sharply, but the words were flowing fast now and he could not stop them.

'Mani raped her. My own brother.'

'Gopal! Wasn't it proven that Mani wasn't…?'

Gopal stepped away from her and clasped a hand to his heart dramatically. 'Oh, what do I care about proof! Even if his was not the male organ that sullied her, still it was his command that the deed was done. Of course it was! Who else! He was too clever for the authorities and got his cronies to do the dirty work. But he was getting even at us both, at you and me. He even so much as admitted it to me. *Your little English harlot,* he said to me smirking. *She deserved no better for whoring around.*'

'So he knew about you and her?'

'He knew everything. Mani has spies all over Madras. He knows what all the English are doing everywhere. He hates them and he hates us.'

'But why, Gopal, why? Why does he hate the English, and the two of us, his own brother and sister? He has always hated me especially, even before I ran away with David. Why, Gopal? What did I ever do to him?'

'Ha!' said Gopal. 'You don't know that? Well, little sister, I'll tell you. He hates the English because they took his mother away from him. Because his mother had to obey them and desert him, and go and live in the big house and give suckle to an English boy. He hates you because you were the cause of it all; you put the milk in Amma's breasts, you were with her in the big house and not he. That is the simple reason. He hated you the moment you were born, but you were too young to know. I knew. I saw it in his eyes. And I saw in his eyes how he hated me, when I joined Mr Baldwin's class. And now his heart is black with hate, Savitri. And I fear there will be worse, if we are not careful.'

'No. He has had his revenge. He has torn me from David and sent me into hell, and he has driven Mrs Lindsay away who was so kind to us and he has ruined Fiona's life. What can be worse than that?'

'Who knows, Savitri? Our brother has the devil in his heart. Beware.'

But Savitri only shook her head and smiled to herself. *Gopal sounds like one of those film heroes, she thought. The cinema has taken hold of him. He has seen too many Talkies. He is being melodramatic. Mani has done his worst. He has given me in marriage to Ayyar. I have lost David, and my daughters and my son. Mani has had his revenge.*

Chapter 36

Nat
Madras City; A Bus Ride into Nowhere;
A Village in Madras State, 1969

Nat and Henry had to wade through black, stinking water at Parry's Corner to get to their bus. They had bought umbrellas and raincoats and large plastic sheets; they had wrapped up their luggage in plastic, they had taken off their shoes and wore shorts and the water was far above their ankles. All of Madras was under siege. Rain fell in one solid sheet of water. Traffic was reduced to a trickle and it had seemed a miracle to even find a rickshaw willing to take them to the bus station.

They hauled themselves into the 122 bus. It was already full, but on the back seat the Indians pressed together to make room for them and they squeezed in, and very soon after that the bus rolled off.

'This is bad. Really bad,' said Henry, and his brow was wrinkled, anxiety written into every line and into the downturned corners of his lips. 'The village will be under water; those poor people!'

Nat rubbed behind his neck. He was thinking less of the poor people, more of his own poor self, because obviously, if the village was under water, there might be some difficulties in getting away, getting to Town to find a bus to Bangalore. And by the look of things he'd want to leave as soon as possible because obviously his father's house was no place of refuge in this weather. He fleetingly considered defecting here and now, while he still had a chance: excusing himself, jumping down into the black water, getting the boy to retrieve his plastic-wrapped suitcase from the bus's roof, taking a rickshaw or a taxi to the airport and the next plane to Bangalore.

However, he stayed put. Maybe it was an innate laziness, a disinclination to plunge back into the deluge after having found this temporary haven of dryness. Maybe it was lack of courage; he didn't relish Henry's barely concealed disapproval at yet another change of plans. Irresolute, Henry would call him, weak, wet and watery.

Maybe, though, it was something else. Whatever it was, he stayed put.

That *something else* in Nat began to stir, like the tiniest seedling nudging itself from its bonds, as the bus plunged through the countryside, through sheets of water falling from above and sheets of water covering the earth, water as far as the eye could see, water above and below, water, water, water. The bus lurched through an endless lake, for no road was visible, no roadside, only water. Water, collecting in some unseen pocket in the bus's ceiling, and released at intervals, gushed down on them in urgent, violent bursts, showering those passengers crouched on the back seat. Henry opened his umbrella and he and Nat took shelter beneath it. He removed a plastic sheet from his carry-all and passed it to the other back-seat passengers who thanked him and huddled, miserable, silent, beneath it. Nat saw their lips moving. They were praying.

Nat found himself praying too. It was not an act of will. It first stirred in him as they drove through a village Nat remembered, back then in another life. Driving to Madras in this same bus, and the rest-pause here in this very village, right here outside the Bombay Lodge. He recalled ragged ladies with baskets on their heads *screeching* '*Vadai-vadai-vadai-vadai,*' pushing those baskets filled with sorry little round orange *vadais* up to the bus windows in the hope of a sale, little half-naked urchins loaded with banana bunches pushing through the bus aisles selling a banana here, a banana there, half-grown girls calling out, '*Chai-chai-chai-chai,*' balancing trays of grubby thick-glassed tumblers half-filled with a brownish liquid on spindly, splayed-finger arms, strands of greasy black hair falling into their faces, looking up out of pleading great black eyes. Toddlers shitting in the dusty roadsides. Stray dogs, cows, goats, *sadhus,* cyclists, cripples, rich men, poor men, beggarmen, thieves, walking, running, screaming, calling, creeping, crawling all together in one huge mosaic of colour, sound and smell.

Now there was nothing. Just water.

The roadside stalls stood in water. The entrance to the Bombay Lodge was barred by a large metal gridwork before its wooden door, and the gridwork stood in water. The tea and coffee shops stood in water, and the coconut-frond roof of one shop lay collapsed over the counter, over the large metal vat used for boiling water. Not a living soul was to be seen.

The bus stopped for an instant somewhere in the sheet of water that replaced the main street and a few sorry sodden figures descended and melted into the grey wetness. The bus lurched off again, into the water.

Another bus lay on its side, abandoned, in what must have been a roadside ditch, in another age, before the water came and rendered it indistinguishable from the rest of the earth's surface. By some sixth sense their own driver wove his way through abandoned, waterlogged ruins of buildings, homes, shops, businesses, by some miracle keeping to the road, invisible beneath the water, by some miracle keeping his ark afloat.

Where are the people? Nat cried in his heart, and inside him he felt a constriction as if he could hardly breathe.

Where are the people? Where are they?

He closed his eyes so as not to see and not to know, but his heart knew and sent tears out from beneath his eyelids and he opened his eyes and he saw people. A small family, beneath a tree, doing nothing, waiting, a woman with a baby in her arms, a man, two small children, almost knee-deep in the water, under their tree. The man held a piece of sodden cardboard over the woman's head. The rain fell on the tree and its leaves moved in an up-and-down rhythm, bouncing almost merrily, while the family just stood there in the wetness, waiting.

Nat knew what this deluge meant for the people of his village, and of all the villages around. Not only were their huts built trustingly on ground level; they also contained no furniture. People slept not on beds, but on the earthen floor, simply spreading one thin cloth to lie on and covering themselves with another. They cooked on the ground, using dried cow-dung or twigs as fuel. They had no sanitation; they went out into the fields to relieve themselves. They could not afford raincoats or umbrellas; they usually had only one change of clothing, which when washed was laid on the ground or over a bush to dry.

What happens, then, he asked himself, when all their clothes are wet, and there's no sun to dry them? When there is no dry cow-dung or twigs to cook with; when the earth on which they sleep and cook and into which they defecate is no longer earth, but a sheet of water? When the dried mud with which their houses are built grows soggy and starts to dissolve, and their thatched roofs first leak and then cave in, and the rain won't stop? And the water keeps rising? *Oh Lord, help then!*

Six hours of water: collapsed mud huts, collapsed roofs; a world collapsed and abandoned. Nat was speechless.

When they arrived in Town they found more water, falling from above and rising from below, and no rickshaws running. Henry hired two boys to help with their luggage, Nat's, his, and the supplies they had bought in Madras, and the four of them set off through the abandoned streets of Town, out into the open countryside, through sheets of water and pouring rain, to the village.

They arrived at Doctor's long after nightfall, plodding through the water only by the light of Henry's torch, for the streetlights were not working. Henry called out but there was no answer except the whimpering of children, so he shone his torch around and they found the entire floor, inside the two rooms and around three sides of the verandah, covered with women and children; some of them lying, sleeping, covered with damp sheets, but a few mothers still up and comforting small weeping children.

'Where's Doctor ?' Henry asked one of the mothers.

She was the only woman on her feet, walking up and down between the slumbering bodies, jostling a tiny living form clasped to her bosom; covered with the shawl of her sari, it was emitting weary whimpering noises. The woman was crying, but she looked up when Henry addressed her. Although he had spoken Tamil, out of the few Tamil words Henry had mastered, she replied in English, probably for Nat's benefit, for she was looking at him, and he realised she didn't know him, nor he her, and that he was home but he knew not his home and home did not know him.

'Sahib daktah going, coming, my not knowing,' she said. 'Big wattah coming, daktah boy taking, boy sick, boy no taking meals, boy...'

She didn't know the word for *dead* so she made the gesture for dead, head lolling to one side and tongue hanging out and eyes staring, and then she began to wail, loud and penetrating, and then she said, 'No fire making, *sahib*, no cooking, no taking meals, wattah coming, coming, coming!'

Henry turned to Nat. 'Some boy's dead, Nat, I think it must be her son. Doctor must be looking into that... I'd better go and find him. Are you coming?'

Nat nodded, still speechless. Where's Dad? Where's the dead boy? Where will they burn him? What will they do with the body? And a silent horror spread through his body and he could only look at Henry out of this horror and nod, yes, he was coming.

They left their luggage there and waded through the rain to Henry's house next door, and that too was filled with wet sleeping whimpering children and comforting mothers. They plunged into the darkness, having no goal in mind except the village, but the village was deserted.

Dad, Dad, where are you? wept Nat's heart, *What are you doing with the dead boy?*

Henry's sober, calm voice cut into Nat's horror. 'Let's try the schoolhouse,' he said. 'That's the only other building that could possibly have survived this.' So they plunged through the water, following the beam of Henry's torch, and found the schoolhouse, under water, filled with Indians, and Doctor was there, spreading tree branches over the floor, and other men were helping him, one holding a kerosene lamp, another whittling at the branches with a cutlass, the others piling up the sticks to range out of the water in a sort of a platform.

Doctor had aged. He wore huge wellingtons, which he had bought in Madras once after a monsoon — but no monsoon had ever been as bad as this — large enough to cover the metal-and-leather contraption that held the wooden foot to his stump. Once, many years ago, Nat had asked Doctor what had happened to his foot, if he'd been born that way or if he'd had an accident. Doctor had only replied, 'Singapore. The war. Japanese.' And Nat knew the subject was closed, like every other subject dealing with the past. Like the portrait of the woman in their home. 'Who is she, Dad?' he'd asked, and Doctor had only said, 'a very dear old friend,' and his face had closed up and Nat had known the subject was taboo.

The past was a closed book. The orphanage, Gopal Uncle, Doctor's own family, Doctor's entire past, all was kept locked behind a wall of silence, while Doctor attended to the present. Only the present counted; the past was gone and done with, its only purpose was to produce the present, and a person's duty was to deal appropriately with that present, which in turn would give way to a future which did not, in itself, exist, because when the future arrived that, too, would be the present, to be dealt with appropriately. That was the Indian perspective, and Doctor was through and through Indian. For him only the *here and now* with its problems and challenges mattered — only the rain and the floods and the water was real, and the platform of branches and twigs they were making.

Doctor looked up when Henry and Nat entered, and far from falling into Nat's arms he only said, 'Oh, there you are, I was wondering when you'd turn up. Did you buy plastic sheets in Madras?' without stopping for an instant in his piling up of twigs and branches.

'Yes, I've got them here,' said Henry, opening the canvas bag he'd brought along and pulling out a folded wad of crackling plastic.

He unfolded it and Doctor said, 'That corner's finished, spread it over the wood,' which Henry did, forming a knobbly plastic bed of sorts.

'We've got the women and children in my house and yours, Henry; I suppose you've seen that. This here is for the men and this is where we'll be sleeping too for the next couple of days — or weeks — till the floods recede. A bit uncomfortable maybe but we'll manage. Nat, look, you can help Anand over there, try to get it a bit thicker. The biggest problem is food; we've been doing the cooking at my place, but we've used up most of the supplies in the village. We're down to nothing but rice now; we've been sending someone to Town occasionally but everything there's used up too, no vegetables, no chillis, nothing. And if this keeps up we'll have a cholera outbreak. The children are the worst off. One little boy died today; it was tragic, the mother's in a state but what can one do? I tried to save him but… well, he's gone.'

'Where's — where's the body?' Nat could hardly mouth the words but somehow the question wormed at him, as if, of all the problems in the world, the problem of how to dispose of a body when all the world is water was the very worst.

'Well, what can you do?' Doctor shrugged. 'Can't bury it, can't burn it. Sent it to the morgue in Town but they refused it, can't deal with any more bodies; they've got basically the same problems as we have, only worse. Had quite a few electrocutions there; good thing the people here have no current or we'd have had that too. So I wrapped it up in an old blanket and plastic sheets and took it out a few miles and hid it in the branches of a tree. Won't be an aesthetic sight if this goes on much longer, and I suppose it's not a very reverent thing to do with a body, but what can you do? Poor little fellow, not even three. Name was Murugan. Bright little boy, Ravi's son. Remember Ravi, Nat? Ravi married an educated woman from the next village, prides herself on her English. They've got two more children and a baby girl.'

'Yes, we met them,' said Nat, and that was all he could say. Ravi's son. Just before he'd left for England Ravi had married;

Nat had attended the wedding but the bride had kept her head lowered and so he'd not recognised her as the mother of the dead boy; and then Ravi had had children and one of them was dead, his body stuck up in a tree to rot...

'Where's Ravi?'

'Ravi's in Chetput; he's getting a proper training as a nurse at the hospital there. I sent him a year ago, promised to look after his family in the meantime. Things are growing here, Nat; we need qualified staff. Anand's not enough. When Ravi returns I'll send Kamaraj for training. Got a few girls in training, too. But we need another doctor, Nat... we need you...'

He stopped speaking,, then and looked up from his work, and Nat met his eyes just for an instant. That look and those last words hit home. The simple naked statement, telling the whole story in the choice of words: not *I* need you, but *we* need you. Not want, but need. No accusation, no moralisation, no condemnation, no verdict, not even the hint of a reproach. That was the worst. Had there been a reproach, Nat would have fought back... but this!

If it were possible to die of self-reproach, to suffocate from guilt, to drown in a deluge of shame, then Nat would have fallen over in that instant, and drowned.

Chapter 37

Saroj
Georgetown, 1969

By the time Lucy Quentin came home Trixie's maternal instincts had taken over and she had roused herself into cooking supper for the whole family, of which Saroj was now an honorary member. Rummaging in the kitchen cupboards Trixie found an open packet of Chinese noodles, a tin of peas, a tin of corn, and half a bag of chick-peas.

'Chow-mein a la Trixie!' she announced. 'Shit, I should soak the channa for a few hours… never mind, I'll do it in the pressure cooker. Now, let me see, spices . . .'

She searched at the back of the spice cupboard. 'I thought we had some soya sauce left over — damn it, the bottle's empty. You think curry powder'd do as well? Let me see, salt, pepper . . .'

Saroj's mind wasn't much on cooking so she wandered off to make herself at home, heaving up her stuffed pillow-case and lugging it into Trixie's bedroom. This was cluttered with heaps of miscellaneous stuff on the floor, under the bed, and all available surfaces: piles of papers, old magazines, records, comics, photos, you name it. Her Archie comics, which she wasn't allowed to read — Lucy Quentin had few rules, but the ones she had, like no Archie comics and no Romance Picture Library, nothing woman-hostile, she upheld to the hilt — were all stuffed under the mattress, as Saroj knew. She pulled one out, leafed through it, chucked it away, picked up a *Teen* magazine, opened it at a page with an article called *How to Know If He'll Kiss and Tell* and chucked that away too.

She wanted to unpack, just to make certain that this

was, finally and definitely, her new home, but unpacking was impossible for the wardrobes were stuffed with Trixie's things, and there wasn't a free shelf to be found. She'd have to wait till Trixie made room for her.

The telephone rang.

'Would you get that, Saroj? I'm just in the middle of stir-frying this stuff !' Trixie called, so Saroj lifted up the receiver unsuspectingly.

'Hello?'

'*Saroj!* There you are! I've been —'

She slammed down the receiver with such clumsy force that she missed the hook and the whole phone gave a twisted leap and clattered to the floor.

'What the hell was that!' cried Trixie, rushing from the kitchen waving a wooden spoon.

'Ma!' Saroj said, and plonked herself down on the tattered Morris chair next to the telephone table. Her knees had turned to jelly, her heart raced and her hands were so icy she shoved them under her armpits and clamped them there with her arms.

'Huh! What d'you think? Of course she knows you're here. Sooner or later she'll come to get you so you'd better get yourself armed and ready for battle.'

She was right. Sooner or later Saroj would have to face the consequences of her flight. Till now she'd only looked forward to liberty, to revenge, to a new life free of restraints. What Ma and Baba would do to get her back she hadn't considered. But in fact, she now realised, they must have been after her all afternoon.

She'd spent the time from lunchtime till Trixie's return in the hammock slung under Trixie's house. Though mentally and physically exhausted, her mind was still in a whirl and as she lay there unable to sleep she'd heard the telephone ringing upstairs, faintly, as through a mist. After that she'd fallen asleep, the hammock swaying in the gentle breeze seeking its way between the pillared houses of Bel Air. Now she knew for certain that the ringing had been Ma, searching for her. She'd have to think; and she'd need help. She longed for Lucy Quentin.

Saroj followed Trixie back into the kitchen and found her shoving the finished chow-mein in a Pyrex dish under the grill. She'd changed the recipe to chow-mein with grilled cheese. Trixie's idea of a gourmet meal was anything topped with grilled cheese, and though Saroj wasn't much of a cook herself, certain sensibilities had automatically rubbed off from Ma. She promised herself to take over kitchen duties as soon as tact allowed. Might as well begin now: the kitchen was a mess because in Trixie's unlimited creativity food was free to overflow and settle where it wanted, in or out of bowls and dishes, on, under or above the surfaces.

Saroj gathered up the dirty dishes and carried them to the sink and was just about to wash them but Trixie said, 'Don't bother with that, girl, Doreen comes in the morning to clean. You can deck the table if you want something to do,' so Saroj did that, and she'd just laid down the last fork when Lucy Quentin walked in.

'Oh, hello, Saroj,' she said, as if Saroj came to supper every day.

Trixie made her entrance with the Pyrex dish enclosed in a nest of kitchen towels held aloft. 'Mum, guess what!' She lowered the dish to the table and it slid from her hands and slithered right across the polished wooden surface and would have continued across the room if Lucy Quentin had not pushed her body up to the table's edge and stopped its onward flight. A yellow liquid sloshed up out of the dish, leaving a dark stain with little black spots on her immaculate, emerald-green figure-hugging dress.

'You clumsy oaf!' Lucy Quentin cried out. 'How many times do I have to tell you...' She hurried into the kitchen, returning with a wet rag, rubbing at the stain.

'This will never come out, I'll have to take it off and soak it; no, it's no good.' She disappeared again, this time to her room. Trixie looked at Saroj and shrugged, hiding her giggle behind her hand. Saroj was terrified. This was no way to begin her first evening of freedom, the evening in which so many matters had to be discussed with Lucy Quentin and which therefore promised to be long and difficult. She found a straw mat in the sideboard drawer, placed the hot chow-mein dish with the bundled kitchen towels on it, and slid it to the centre of the table, cursing Trixie for her carelessness and throwing her a look of steely reproach. Trixie responded by sticking out her long lobster-red tongue.

Lucy reappeared after a few minutes in a loose, ankle-length robe in a bright floral African print.

They all pulled out chairs around the table. Lucy Quentin turned to Saroj, smiling, shook out her napkin and said, 'So, dear, to what do we owe the honour of your visit? Oh my goodness, what happened to your *hair?*'

Before Saroj could open her mouth Trixie burst out again with, 'Mum, guess what, she's run away from home and she's come to stay with us!'

Lucy Quentin raised her eyebrows and the appraising look she gave Saroj seemed, to a mind hungry for approval, to award her two or three points of estimation.

'Well, I suppose it had to happen sooner or later,' Lucy Quentin said, and plunged a serving spoon into the browned crust of cheese topping the chow-mein. It cracked down the middle, the two halves rising on either side of the spoon like brown and yellow mottled butterfly wings and splattering yellow liquid over the table.

'Trixie, what kind of mess is this?' Lucy Quentin ladled out a soggy spoonful and sniffed at it before emptying it back into the dish. 'No thanks.' She pushed the dish towards Saroj in disdain.

'You haven't even tried it yet!' Trixie sounded so genuinely disappointed that Saroj served herself a good plateful and smiled at her, determined to praise it no matter how it tasted. *It's the love with which a dish is cooked that flavours it,* Ma always said.

'So, Saroj, now tell me this exciting news. You've really left home?' Lucy Quentin looked at Saroj expectantly. In a sudden attack of shyness Saroj glanced at Trixie for help, who launched into a garbled account of the story. Halfway through Saroj found her voice, interrupted Trixie, and finished in her own words.

'So you see, my father isn't really my father and he doesn't have the right to treat me as he does,' she finally said, and, eager to reap praise, looked expectantly at Lucy Quentin who had kept her silence all this time.

'My dear, whether he's your real father or not, he doesn't have any *right* whatsoever to treat you the way he does.' Lucy Quentin carefully laid knife and fork together on her plate and pushed it all away. Placing her elbows on the table, interlocking her long ebony fingers, she looked at Saroj intensely.

'No right whatsoever. Do you understand? That's the point you have to get straight right at the very beginning. Your father has no right to control your life, even if you are a minor. He has no right to lock you up, and no right to choose a husband for you, and no right to marry you off against your will. The trouble with you Indian girls is your absolute lack of willpower and your absolute submission to the will of your fathers. Once you've grasped how very wrong this is, then you can begin to fight for freedom. Not before. Your father is, to put it into plain English, a brute.'

Saroj was so stunned by the steel in her words her lower jaw dropped and she gaped. Here, put into clear and succinct words, was her entire rebellion, all fuzzy emotion straightened out, ironed, and laid bare for her to see in black and white, all the hate drawn out; all the speechless defiance given tongue.

'And as for your mother,' Lucy Quentin continued, 'she's as much to blame. Her fault is not brutishness, just plain . . . weakness.'

This, now, was a shock. 'Ma... weakness?' Saroj stammered, feeling a protest without the power to express it.

Lucy Quentin smiled a smile that didn't reach her eyes, shook her head and poured herself a glass of water.

'Of course, darling. Weakness. Weakness is passed from mother to daughter. You've inherited the weakness of your mother, the weakness of the Indian woman, the weakness that accepts the tyranny of the male without objection. Your mother, in bowing her head to your father's decisions, is as much guilty of wrongdoing as he is.'

'Guilty of...?'

'It's hard to accept, isn't it? That a sweet, mild-mannered, soft-spoken little woman could be guilty of anything? Nonsense!' This last word was almost a shout, she banged her glass on the table spilling half the water, and then she raised her right hand and waggled her forefinger at Saroj.

'Saroj, you're an intelligent girl. You've got to get the picture straight — especially about your mother. Your father — well that's clear enough. Your mother is the devious one. All sugar and spice on the outside — that's the way she fools the world. Even Trixie, my own daughter, adores her. Ha! Sweetness of character is certainly very appealing, especially to men, but sweetness of character will get you — yes, Saroj, *you* personally — nowhere at all. All docility and obedience, and when you do rebel, you take it all out on yourself. Suicide. Suicide! Ha! Suicide, that's weakness. Fight! Yep, that's right, fight. It's what I've been telling Trixie all this time. So you've finally done it. Congratulations, and welcome to the Quentin home!'

There followed a long stricken silence in which Lucy Quentin drank her glass of water with an expression of deepest satisfaction. Saroj played with her food, moving her fork here and there among the noodles, picking out the peas tasting of vomit, separating the corn, which she ate grain by grain. Trixie was gobbling at her own food with a gusto Saroj felt was less induced by appetite than by nervousness. Something, she felt, was wrong. She knew she had to say something, defend her mother, change the subject, anything to break this awful condemning silence. Anything to make Lucy Quentin understand.

'The... prob... my problem isn't so much... I mean, I got angry because of what... because of finding out that my mother was having... I mean, is having, well, an affair,' she stammered.

Lucy Quentin threw back her head and laughed, but her laughter sounded so mocking, so derisive, Saroj cringed for Ma's lost privacy.

'Do you know, I'd forgotten all about that bit!' she said

finally. 'Your mother's actually having an affair! Well done, no, jolly well done, as the British would say! I bet that shocked you out of your little mind, didn't it? That good, sweet, holy Mama — what do you call her? — could do something so utterly, terribly sinful! I bet that disrupted your image of chastity! How could she, eh? Give the old rascal Deodat Roy horns! My word, it's just a pity we can't make that public, wouldn't that be a laugh!'

Saroj's face was red-hot as she whispered, 'Ma couldn't... Ma wouldn't...'

'And how she could! My word, she would! She did, didn't she? You have the evidence, and your evidence is you yourself! My goodness, that's the most wonderful joke!'

'You don't understand!' the protest escaped Saroj's lips before she could stop it, and louder than she'd have dared if she'd had time to consider, and sounded like a whine.

'It's you who doesn't understand! But how can you, at your age, with your upbringing? My goodness, you Hindus are more prudish and more repressed than the Catholics. But understand one thing, Saroj: you can't stop human nature from being human nature. Your mother is a woman, just like any other, and she's entitled to get a little pleasure out of this life, and I certainly wouldn't condemn her for doing so, in fact, hats off! I wouldn't have credited her with the courage, a little mouse of a woman like that!'

'But you don't even know her!'

Lucy Quentin waved her hand dismissively. 'Oh, if you've seen one you've seen them all, these sweet little Indian women. I pity them, I really do, or I would, if I didn't know what destruction this sweetness causes to their daughters, forcing them to grow up just as sweet, and just as ineffectual.'

Lucy Quentin was an adult, the Minister of Health besides, and Saroj was raised to respect adults and not answer back. But with every critical word the woman spoke about Ma Saroj could feel her hackles rising. This wasn't the kind of support she needed. She didn't want anyone else tearing Ma to pieces, and for the wrong reasons! She wanted Lucy Quentin to commiserate with her, to tell her how awful it was for Ma to deceive them all and to give her, Saroj, the wrong father and to allow Baba to tyrannise her all these years; and here she was, saying Ma had every *right* to an affair! Saroj wanted Lucy Quentin to understand the shock of having your entire world fall to pieces around your feet, and here she was, saying it's only right and natural that this should be so! Or was she, again, blinded by some fuzzy, unacknowledged Indian moral concept?

'I… I thought…'

Again that derisive laugh. 'Oh yes, I know you're considered highly intelligent, I know you'll be a candidate for the Guyana Scholarship when the time comes, but, you know, you should use your intelligence for a little bit of reflection, self-criticism, to recognise the facts. And the fact is: your Ma is not what you thought her to be! Clear and simple!'

'Miss Quentin, you don't understand! Ma's different, she wouldn't…"

'Christ, child, I'd like to give you a good shake! *She did!* She did! She did, because human nature is stronger, far stronger, than all these cultural ideals of purity. Your mother had a romp in the hay, or several, over the years, it seems, and it's her perfect right to do so! Isn't that what men have been doing for years? Now, just get that indisputable fact into your pretty little head, which, by the way, is no longer as pretty as it used to be without all that hair, and thank goodness for that! Best thing you ever did!'

Saroj's hand closed tightly around her glass and she might have thrown it at Lucy Quentin if she'd spoken one more word, dumping all her dirty innuendos over Ma, if just then the doorbell hadn't rung. Trixie, grateful for an excuse to escape the bristling atmosphere at the table, sprang to her feet and ran to the window.

'Saroj!' she hissed. 'It's your parents!'

All resentment of Lucy Quentin vanished. Saroj looked at her, pleading with her eyes, and said, 'I don't want to see them; I can't go back, I can't! Please, don't make me go back home, Miss Quentin!'

At once the biting steel left Lucy Quentin's eyes and kindness flooded them. She reached out and patted Saroj on the shoulder, and as she rose to her feet said, 'Don't worry, child, I'm entirely on your side. Trixie, go on down and open the door, please! Saroj, I'd like you to listen to what I have to say to your parents. It's about time someone did something to help all these poor Indian girls. Now, just you go to Trixie's room and stay there, I'll take care of this. And remember, justice is on your side!'

Trixie bounded down the stairs to open the door, and Saroj scuttled off to hide.

Lucy Quentin's house had the natural air-conditioning of most Georgetown houses: rooms without ceilings, so you could see up into the eaves. And since it was a one-storey house, the bedrooms were just next door to the living room, which meant that the whole house was ventilated. If all the windows were open the breeze blew through open doors, up into the eaves and down, whirled around the house and through the rooms and out the windows again, carrying sounds, and voices.

Trixie slipped into the room, her eyes wide open in excitement.

'Your Ma's coming up — alone! Your Baba's stayed in the car! Let's listen!' Which, of course, is exactly what Saroj intended to do. Trixie grabbed her hand and pulled her down to sit on the edge of the bed.

Through the eaves Saroj heard Lucy Quentin's authoritative voice, ushering Ma into the living room. Her voice was even louder than usual; for *her* benefit, Saroj assumed. Ma's soft-spoken responses were hushed by the brassy echo that seemed to reverberate whenever Lucy Quentin spoke. It was Ma that Saroj most wanted to hear, but Lucy Quentin was what she got. Like listening to someone on the telephone, she could only guess at Ma's almost whispered explanations, conjecture at what she said through Lucy Quentin's one-sided conversation.

'Saroj is extremely upset and she would like to live with me for a while, at least until she can make an agreement with you and your husband... Yes, but you understand, this marriage business has been the last straw and I must remind you, and your husband being a lawyer should actually know this: arranged marriages against the will of the parties involved are de facto illegal. You have absolutely no right, even if she is a minor. She consented to meet the boy only as a favour towards you. What she really feels about the matter you already know — she'd rather die! You're lucky she's alive! That should have been the warning, and as a woman, Mrs Roy, you should be on her side and not on your husband's side. You yourself are living in an arranged marriage — and you yourself know the misery of such a union. But I know — Saroj now knows, and she has told me — that you have also known love; and passion, and with a man who is not your husband. Am I right?'

This time, Ma spoke. It must have been about three sentences, of which Saroj couldn't hear a word, but Lucy Quentin broke in:

'Yes, I know this is all very private, Mrs Roy, you needn't remind me of that, but Saroj has come to me for refuge; I am, you could say, her chosen guardian… No, don't interrupt, let me finish. Saroj doesn't want to speak to you. She won't return home. Of course, you do have parental rights, you could come with the police and force her to return. But just ask yourself what such an action would result in. Your only course now is for her to calm down enough to risk going home again. And since she refuses to speak to you you'll just have to use me as a go-between… but… yes, I understand, these are personal things. I understand… I'm your *friend*, Mrs Roy; I'm the friend of every woman, every woman of every race, we're all sisters and we understand each other's problems so you needn't be ashamed of anything you've done. I fully understand and I'd never, ever, condemn you, and I certainly don't believe that having an extramarital affair is the end of the world; neither is having a child out of wedlock, neither is passing such a child off as a legitimate child; morals have changed, Mrs Roy, and this isn't India, neither are we living in Victorian times! This is 1966! So really, there's no reason whatsoever for you to feel shame at all these things. It might really do you good to have a good long talk with me, I might be able to counsel you and to mediate between you and Saroj… for you both urgently need counselling. I might be able to persuade her to talk to you but, well, she's extremely upset, as I said. I've been trying to make her see the whole thing from your point of view, from the point of view of a woman trapped in a bad marriage, to help her to understand you. But you've done your work well. Saroj is very fixed in her ideas and, well, to put it into plain English: she's a prude, if you don't mind me saying so, and it's hard for her to understand that human nature will always . . .'

Ma's sandals were louder than her voice. Saroj could distinctly hear them clattering down the wooden stairs to the front door. She heard the chink of the chain at the gate, the slamming of a car door, the coughing of the car as Baba turned on the engine, the car driving off. She was bathed in sweat. Ma had walked out on Lucy Quentin!

Trixie took her hand and led her out into the living room. So numb she could hardly walk, Saroj followed her and when Trixie stood her in front of the sofa and pushed her shoulders gently she obediently plonked herself down. The imitation leather was still warm; from Ma, or from Lucy Quentin?

Lucy Quentin was still standing at the top of the stairwell, looking down it as if transfixed, a puzzled expression on her face, rubbing her chin.

When she saw Saroj she started. Her lips turned upwards in a breezy smile, and she walked over with arms stretched out towards the girl.

'Saroj dear, I did my best, you heard, I suppose? I wanted you to hear. Your mother is very soft-spoken, but that's to be expected. She's such a fearful little thing, isn't she, and so shy, she wouldn't talk about the problem with me so I'm afraid we've not come much farther. I think, dear, it would almost be better if I spoke with your father, after all, he's the villain in this piece and it might be good for him if, once in his lifetime, a woman gave him a piece of her mind, and...'

'No!'

'What? No?'

'No, Miss Quentin, I er . . . I just decided I'll talk to Ma myself. This is between the two of us, really it is, I'm sorry I tried to get you involved, I guess I was being a coward, but, well, Ma won't talk to you, I know it. She just won't. You… um, you see, Ma's different. You don't understand her. I realise that now.'

Lucy Quentin frowned. 'You're such a child, you know. You're the one who doesn't understand. You heard what I said to your mother, I hope. I called you a prude, and that's what you are. You're seeing your mother through rose-tinted spectacles and that's why you're so shocked. But it's *you* who doesn't understand, can't understand. Possibly, no, probably, your mother doesn't even understand herself. But, very well, then, have it your way. As I said, you can live on here for a while. But as long as you aren't prepared to see your mother as she is instead of how you want her to be, there's no hope for you. For either of you.'

She looked at her watch. 'Goodness, it's nine already. So late. I've given you enough of my time for today, Saroj, and if you want to solve your problems by yourself, go ahead. Trixie, it's high time you both were in bed, school tomorrow. Have you done your homework? If not you'd better…'

'Homework? At this time of night? And after a day like this?'

'Well, that's your problem. I'm off; I've got a load of typing waiting downstairs. Good night.'

She turned abruptly on her heel, obviously disgusted by Saroj's ungrateful obstinacy, and walked stiffly, elegantly down the stairs to her ground-floor office. A few minutes later they heard the clacking of her typewriter echoing up the stairwell. Trixie looked at Saroj and grinned, winking.

'Never mind her,' she said. 'Now we can have some fun. Oh boy, it's just like having a sister. Or being at boarding school. Look, I bought some new comics today, and a copy of *Seventeen*. Let's read in bed.'

Chapter 38

Savitri
Madras State, 1939 — 1941

Ayyar's behaviour improved even more after Ganesan's birth, except for the drinking. He was so proud of the boy. And he was pleased with Savitri for having, at last, done her duty, and began to be kind to her.

'What is that book you're reading?' he asked, coming home early from work to play with Ganesan, as he often did these days.

'Oh, it's a book of poetry. *The Swallow Book of Verse*. I used to read it a lot when I was a child.'

Savitri had brought back three books from her visit to Madras. It was a miracle, even, that *The Swallow Book of Verse* still existed and had not been thrown out by Mani at the time of her marriage. But with great foresight Amma had salvaged it, and kept it safely for her till the day when she could safely give it back. For her mother was a woman too, and knew of love, and knew that the book was all Savitri had left of David, and that David was now out of harm's way, and the book could do no harm.

'I want to purchase some books for you,' Gopal had said to her the day before her return, and taken her to Higginbotham's Book Store and told her to choose what she wanted. She had chosen a copy of the Bhagavad-Gita and a book of Rabindranath Tagore poems. He had encouraged her to buy more, and more costly books, but she was adamant.

'I will find all I need in these books,' she told him, and indeed, she did. She read for at least an hour every day, for somehow, since Ganesan's birth, she had less instead of more work. Ayyar thought it was beneath her dignity, as the mother of his son, to go to the Parvati Tank for the washing so she gave her laundry to a *dhobi* and all she had to do was cook and keep the house tidy, and look after Ganesan, who anyway spent a good part of every day with his grandmother. So Savitri had time to read, and life was beginning to be good. Even the nightly gropings—no longer rape!—had stopped completely since Ganesan's birth. Ayyar did not bother her at all now, and that alone was heaven. She had her son, and her books, which were a wellspring of wisdom and joy, and she had freedom in her heart. Really, she thought, to ask for more would be ingratitude.

'Read on, read on!' Ayyar said now, and smiled down kindly at her. 'I am glad you are educating your mind. I am proud I have an educated wife, for you will be able to educate our son. So I am allowing you to read as much as you please. You are a good, devout wife and I am very pleased with you.'

Savitri bowed her head and continued with her reading. *If he only knew,* she thought, smiling to herself. For, wrapped up in a piece of newspaper and glued to the inside spine of the book, was a little gold chain with a cross pendant, hidden there long ago with great prescience and presence of mind, in the days when her world was still whole and innocent. And now, when she held this book in her hands, David was with her, and all around her, and she too was whole again, and innocent, and she had Ganesan, and he was healthy, and alive.

Ganesan was the most beautiful baby ever. His golden brown skin was polished to a gloss every day when Savitri laid him, naked but for the string around his hips, on her stretched out legs and rubbed his body with coconut oil, smiling and laughing with him as he cooed and blabbered in delight, and her skilful fingers kneaded the firm flesh of his chubby legs, arms and buttocks, the softness of his back and belly and the round apple cheeks. He had a thick thatch of strong black hair, which was growing out again after having been shaved off completely two full moons ago, when Savitri shaved her own head and made the pilgrimage to the great Shiva Temple at Tiruvannamalai last Deepam, to give thanks to the Lord in keeping with her vow.

Ganesan looked up at her with his great black shining eyes as she rubbed his body, and he waved his arms and reached out to grab her fingers and pressed with the soles of his feet against her belly. It seemed to Savitri, as she lifted him up and outlined his eyes with lines of kohl and marked his forehead with a black spot, that she had always known him, that he had always been a part of her, and was a part of that great love she shared with David, for love is love and cannot be divided, it reaches out and embraces every living thing, and this little boy was the form love had chosen to approach her in, now that David was lost to her. She hugged him to her breast and laughingly kissed him all over till he struggled to get away and called out, 'Pal, Amma, pal!'

She smiled then and opened her *choli,* and replied, 'You want *pal,* little Ganesan? Come, here is Amma's *pal,* come, my darling!' And the little boy snuggled into her arms and opened his little red mouth and took her breast to drink her milk sweet with her love.

Ayyar's drinking grew worse. She knew he kept a grubby brown bottle in the back pocket of his trousers — Ayyar, like Gopal, never wore a lungi, since he, too, considered himself modern-minded — and that all through the day he took a swig or two, whenever he thought he was unwatched.

It would not have bothered her were it not for Ganesan. The boy was almost a year now, older than any child she had ever had, and at an age when fathers begin to take yet more interest in their infants. So it was with Ayyar. He loved to carry the boy around, to take him with him to work, or to see his mother, or his friends, and Savitri was certain that at the homes of certain friends yet more alcohol was passed around. Ayyar came home in a rickshaw, then, hiccupping and burping and reeking of drink, and hardly able to carry the child the short distance between rickshaw and front door. Savitri waited anxiously on the front verandah on these occasions, a book open on her lap, but looking up whenever she heard a rickshaw bell or the creaking sound as a rickshaw's wheel rounded the corner. And when she saw it was Ayyar with Ganesan she would leap to her feet and run to meet them, and gather the child into her arms, and pay the rickshaw-*wallah,* and she was so grateful that Ayyar was safely home that she was kind to him and he really believed she loved him as a good wife should, and he was pleased, even through his drunken stupor.

'What a good wife you have become!' he stammered then. 'What an excellent wife. But you would never have turned so good, wife, if I had not beaten you the first few years. You would never have borne me a son if I had not beaten you for bearing me daughters.'

And he advised his friends, 'Yes, yes, a woman needs a good beating now and then, just until she turns obedient. Once she has learned to be obedient, though, it would be a sin to beat her. Yes, yes. Look at my wife. One could not find a better wife, or a better mother. And she has borne me an excellent son. But —' and here he would waggle his forefinger at his listening friends, 'never beat your wife once she has learned her lesson, for that would be a sin. I never raise a finger to my wife any more. I adore her and worship her as the Divine Mother herself.'

And he would smile in satisfaction at his own great wisdom, assured that theirs was a perfect family life. Especially now that the youngest girl was married off, and it was just the three of them, husband, wife, and son. A perfect happy family.

Ayyar had to make some adjustments to his ledger this Saturday and so he went to work for half an hour, taking Ganesan. He had taken a swig before leaving and he set the boy down to play as he entered his office at the train station. He took the thick, heavy, yellowed ledger from its place in the overflowing cupboard, leafed through the dog-eared pages but couldn't find what he was looking for; in fact, he had forgotten what he was looking for. To give his memory a jolt he took another swig, belched, licked his thumb and leafed through the pages again. He found the right place and got up from his swivel chair to find some papers, but they seemed to be buried under a heap of other papers in the cupboard. He pulled at them and the whole lot came tumbling out of the cupboard.

Ayyar swore and went to the table to take another swig. Papers lay all over the office, now.

Ganesan thought it was delightful. He picked up a heap in both hands and threw them up into the air. Ganesan was fourteen months and had just learned to walk. His hands were everywhere, and Ayyar knew he would never get the papers back into the cupboard, and in the right order, with Ganesan in the room.

'Go and play outside!' he told the boy. 'Look, there are some goats over there. Go and play. *Po-i-va! Po-i-va!*' He shooed the boy out and closed the door. The work would take half an hour longer. He wished he had a secretary who would look after the paperwork. In Madras train station there were lots of working girls; they had typewriters and could do shorthand. He had to do everything himself. He deserved a secretary. A pretty one. He wondered if he should go and get Savitri to help him, but dismissed the thought immediately. People might say his wife was working and that would be a scandal. No, he'd have to sort out this mess by himself. He took another swig and got down to work, sitting on the floor and placing the papers in their appropriate heaps.

For half an hour he was completely lost in his work, and lost to the rest of the world. It was then that the shrill whistle of an arriving train bore into his subconscious and stirred him. He knew the times of each train by heart. He looked at his watch. Two-thirty. The through-train from Coimbatore. He frowned. He had the feeling that he had forgotten something important, but he couldn't for the life of him think what. The train's whistle stopped and the silence now was palpable. A goat bleated into that silence. The goat's bleat reminded him of something… Ganesan. He had sent Ganesan to play with the goats but that was half an hour ago. He'd better check on the child, he was so quick on his feet…

Ayyar stood up slowly. His left foot had gone to sleep and he could only limp towards the door, which he opened to cast an eye on Ganesan. The goats were still there but Ganesan was not. Ayyar frowned. Where was the little imp? Had he gone off down the road? He stepped down into the sunny, sandy courtyard in front of the station building and peered down the road in both directions. It was deserted, asleep. People were still at rest, for it was the hottest time of day. Could Ganesan have gone into one of the houses?

'Ganesan!' he called. 'Ganesan!'

The train's whistle blew again, much louder now. He heard a child call, coming from the behind the bramble hedge which flanked the track.

A dark knowledge grabbed him in the form of panic, a deep, dark premonition, a certainty of grave impending danger, like the cool breath of Yama, the god of death, at the nape of his neck. His mind cleared and he raced towards the track.

'Ganesan!' he screamed.

'Appa!'

'Ganesan, Ganesan!'

He had reached the track but there was no sign of the child at first and the train's whistle was one long drawn out piercing screech. 'Ganesan!'

He couldn't hear his own scream now, and there was Ganesan, twenty yards uptrack, with a nanny-goat who was nibbling at the hedge, Ganesan crouched beside her and pulling at her udder and smiling in contentment.

'Ganesan!'

Ayyar catapulted himself towards the child while the black, snorting, screeching engine loomed in the background. Ganesan noticed this for the first time, and pointed at it with a pudgy finger.

'Da!' he said, beaming at his father, and then with the same finger pointed at the goat.

'Pal! Pal!'

Ayyar's eyes were fixed in terror on the snorting monster storming up towards them, furious, raging, ruthless.

'Appa!' cried Ganesan anxiously, in the very moment when, simultaneously, Ayyar gathered him into his arms and the engine's cow-catcher swooped them up and flung them into the air, the two of them and the nanny-goat, and pitched them aside as if they were no more than three little rag dolls cast away by a child in a tantrum.

The moment before his head cracked open Ayyar thought:

'It is because of the daughters I killed. All things return. Shiva, Shiva, Shiva.'

The train screeched onwards, and the stillness it left behind was the satisfied silence of death.

Chapter 39

Nat
A Village in Madras State, 1969

Shortly before midnight they finished the makeshift platform of waterlogged branches. In spite of the roughness of his bed and the proximity of so many men lying foot-to-head like sardines Nat, overcome by jet lag, fell asleep almost the moment his head touched the folded *lungi* on the plastic sheet. But long before dawn he was awake again, wide awake. A word, a name, had gnawed itself into his consciousness but it took some time before it dawned on him what that name was trying to tell him.

Gauri Ma.

Where was Gauri Ma?

'Dad?' he whispered. His father slept next to him; he did not want to wake him, for Doctor needed every moment of sleep, but the question was urgent and if, by chance, Doctor was awake he'd hear the whisper and answer. No answer came. Nat fumbled in the folds of the *lungi* that had been his pillow for his torch, switched it on and looked at his watch. Twenty past three. Not an unreasonable time; in the country, people rose at four and by the time he got there it would be four. He'd have to go, there was no other way. If she was safe, then no harm done, he couldn't sleep anyway, and he'd be back by five. But he had to go.

Of course, she might not be alive at all. She might have died in the years of his absence. But maybe not.

He listened; the silence outside seemed to speak to him, to tell him something important, very important, something he'd overlooked in his worry about Gauri Ma, and suddenly he realised what — it was just *too* silent. No pouring of rain, no incessant splashing into the lake that was the world outside the school, not even a gentle patter. The rain had stopped! He said a prayer of thanks in his heart; it was a good omen.

He got up and stepped gingerly between the sleeping bodies, the beam of light from his torch cutting through the pitch darkness to guide him. Outside the school room it was just as dark, for even though the rain had ceased the night sky was still filled with clouds and Nat had only his own instinct and the narrow ray of his torch to guide him out to the road. The water reached almost to his knees, he could feel the mixture of sand and mud and grass beneath his bare feet, squishing up between his toes as he walked on through the thick blackness, through the deathly silence. It was as if the water had absorbed all sound: not a frog croaked, not an insect chirped. There was only the splashing sound Nat's feet made as he stepped onwards through the floods. Not a building, not a ruined house, not a tree or a bush or a high rock could be seen, only the shining, rippling surface of the water as it caught Nat's light and played with it, disturbed by the pair of feet moving steadily, rhythmically forwards.

It was a walk into nowhere. Since there were no stars, no landmarks, not even the hulking form of the hill in the background, Nat could not possibly know in which direction he was going. He could not even know if he was on the road, or walking through a field, or straight towards the yawning depths of the Ganesa Tank, for the whole world was one big black shining lake, opening up to him with each step he took and closing behind him again. And yet he walked on, into the nothingness.

After what seemed a small eternity, gradually, the world turned a shade less black and to Nat's amazement and deep gratitude he made out that he was right on course and almost there. He could make out the collapsed forms of isolated huts, crumbled into the water that surrounded them, the neatly woven coconut fronds that had once been their roofs cleft through the middle as if a ruthless giant hand had dealt them a quick karate stroke. He wondered where their residents had fled — but that was not his business now. A man could only do what he could, and right now Gauri Ma was his business.

Her hut, he estimated, could not be more than a hundred yards further down the road, and several steps further on he heard through the silence a quiet whimpering, as from a puppy. Probably the puppy had been left behind when the desperate family it belonged to had fled to a safer, higher place; maybe it had found refuge on an abandoned rooftop, or on a rock ranging out of the water. It was the first sound, besides the splashing of his own feet and the whisper of his own breath, that he had heard this morning.

The whimpering grew louder, and now he was almost at Gauri Ma's hut, and for the first time since setting out he felt foolish. Of course Gauri Ma was safe! His father would surely have taken care of her, evacuated her to some safe lodging; or else she and her husband would have fled to the Town and taken refuge… somewhere, or else, well, certainly they would not just have sat there and waited for the floods to capture them. He would find a soggy ruined hut with a caved-in roof, empty, abandoned, no Gauri Ma or her husband or any sign of where they had gone, and he would have to turn around and go home again, arriving back just as the others were stirring and having to explain his senseless, panic-filled rescue mission, thwarted because there had never been anyone to rescue. Idiot! Well, maybe he could at least save that puppy.

It was as he'd thought. Gauri Ma's hut was nothing but a heap of sodden rubble covered with the remains of a one-time roof, and Nat felt even more foolish. *Who do you think you are, some kind of a movie hero? No, you're not. You're a spoiled little boy back from the self-indulgent West and you'll never be even half the man your father is.* Of course Doctor had taken care of Gauri Ma and every one else he could; that was his whole mission in life and what put it into Nat's idiot mind to come out here before the crack of dawn to rescue a puppy?

But what else could he do? Better a puppy than nothing. Certainly, the last thing they'd thank him for when he

returned home was a puppy, one more useless mouth to feed —
bouche inutile; now where had he heard that before, something
from the war — but how very ridiculous, how typical of his
thoughtlessness, to plunge into such a misadventure! It would
save face, in fact, to turn back and go home empty-handed, and
just say he'd been out for an early-morning stroll through the
floods — Nat had the good humour to chuckle at his own joke.
Coward! Okay, so he'd found the puppy on his early-morning
stroll. It would be his mascot for the rest of his stay here. He
followed the sound.

It came from the mango tree, which stood a few yards
behind the hut. The puppy must have somehow managed to
scramble up into the branches, which fortuitously forked off
quite low to the ground. Goodness knows how he'd managed
that — it was still too dark to see up into the gloomy cave made
by the spreading crown of leaves, so Nat shone his torch and
let the beam of light wander along the tree's wide branches,
searching, and he made little crooning noises to quiet and
comfort the puppy.

In response the whimpering not only grew louder, it turned
into a torrent of language, human language, clearly discernible
as Tamil though the words were nothing but a disjointed,
unintelligible babble, and when Nat aimed his beam at their
source he saw her. Gauri Ma, up in the tree, not two yards away
from him, a stick-doll of a Gauri Ma wrapped in a ragged piece
of sari wound not only around her body but around an upright
branch against which she leaned, and otherwise clothed only in
an even more ragged sari-underskirt.

'Gauri Ma!' cried Nat, and he took a step nearer to the tree-
trunk but his foot hit against some hulking object in the water,
a large, slippery thing like a log. Somehow — he could tell for
his foot was bare and the thing was not rough and hard like a
log but smooth and soft — he knew it was *something else* and
he shone his torch on it and saw that it was a corpse, a bloated
black corpse, and he gave a cry of alarm and disgust and Gauri
Ma blabbered all the louder, and now he understood her.

It was her husband Biku who had tied her to the tree so she would not fall when she slept; he had tried to tie himself but couldn't, and then he had fallen out of the tree in his sleep and must have been hurt and she had called to him and called, but he had not stood up again. That had happened one, two days ago, she had been in the tree for three days, she had a pot next to her hanging from a branch and it was full of *iddlies*, which Biku had bought from a coffee stall in the market and she had been eating *iddlies, iddlies, iddlies* but now the remaining *iddlies* were all sour, and if she ate any more she would get ill and Biku was dead and she had been calling out all the time but there was no-one, no-one, no-one. And then the whimpering began again.

'It's all right, Ma, I'm here and I'm coming to get you. Do you remember me? I'm Nat, your *tamby*, I've come back from far away? I've come to get you, Ma. Do you know, I woke up this morning and I heard you calling so I came to get you; is that not a miracle, Ma? I heard you from my father's house and I walked through the big water to find you. It was very dark, Ma, but I found you. Do you see how great God's grace is, Ma? So don't worry for your *tamby* is here to help you. I will take you to my father's house and you will not die. Biku has gone home to Shiva Mahadeva, he has found rest from this world. Ma, do not think you are alone now, for your *tamby* is here to take you.'

And all the time he talked he climbed into the branches till he was sitting next to Gauri Ma on her branch. Her sari was tied very tightly to the branch, and because of the wetness the knot had hardened so that it could not be loosened, so Nat took the sari in his teeth and ripped it across and it was so ragged that it split easily. And then he gently laid Gauri Ma over his shoulder and descended back into the flood, and adjusted her weight so that he was holding her in his arms across his shoulder, and he carried her through the floods and the lightening dawn and just as the sun sent its first beams through a hole in the clouds Nat reached his father's gate, and so he brought Gauri Ma home on the day the deluge ended. And he brought not only Gauri Ma, but good luck.

Nat, they all remembered now, was the boy with the Golden Hand.

Chapter 40

Saroj
Georgetown, 1969

Saroj awoke as in a furnace. When Trixie felt her forehead she whipped back her hand and shook it as if scorched. 'Chile, you're cooking,' she said, and all Saroj could do was grunt and turn over.

Lucy Quentin came in wearing a dark green seersucker wrap, shaking a thermometer which she stuck under Saroj's armpit. She picked up some pieces of clothing, threw them across Trixie's clothes-horse, read Saroj's temperature and made some noises of her own. Saroj was too dizzy to hear what she said. She drifted into sleep. When she next awoke Ma was there, bending over her, wiping her forehead; then she was gone, and so was Saroj. She woke up again, and there was Dr Lachmansingh. Lucy Quentin. Trixie.

'We won't move her,' she heard someone say.   '…an infection,' said someone else, and, 'Too much excitement; she needs rest.'

She smelled some delicious smells, and Ma brought a tray loaded with bowls containing her favourite dishes; but she could not eat, just sleep sleep sleep. She drifted in and out of soft clouds, and every time she drifted back, Ma was there, looking down with limpid black eyes, as she'd been there in the hospital; but this time the face was her own, it was no hallucination and Saroj sighed in relief for when a hallucination seems real as it had back then, seeing her own face on Ma, sanity seems a balancing act on a razor's edge.

It was as if Saroj's body, denied the rest it had needed after the operation, now demanded it with a vengeance, keeping her nailed to Trixie's bed. Delicious healing curled through body and mind, sweet and syrupy like molasses. Rancour melted away under Ma's ministrations. She was in the hands of an angel in a space unlimited, where time could not be measured.

When her fever finally wore itself out three days had passed. Ma was still ministering to her. She finally ate; and then she sank back into her pillow with a long deep sigh and wished she could just turn back the clock, rearrange her life so it was just her and Ma in a bubble of perfection, and it would stay that way for ever.

'Ma . . .' she murmured.

'It's all right, darling, don't talk. You're much better now, I was so worried!'

'Ma . . . I want to talk to you . . .'

'I know, dear, and we will, we'll have a nice long talk, but not today. First you have to get really healthy again, and then when you feel up to it you can come home and . . .' Saroj stiffened ever so slightly, and Ma must have felt it because she went on, '. . . Or I'll come here, or we'll go for a walk together, just you and me, and I'll tell you a long, long story, everything you want to know. But not now.'

Saroj nodded, and felt the tears squeezing out of her eyes. Ma wiped her cheek with a corner of the sheet.

'Don't cry, dear, everything's going to be all right. I promise. And remember this: I love you very, very much.'

She leaned over, stroked a strand of hair from Saroj's forehead, and kissed her between the eyes. Saroj closed them; and when she opened them again Ma was gone, as silent as the moon.

The next day was Saturday. Saroj was well enough to get up and take a walk with Trixie. She felt good, better than she had done for weeks, months, even years. Strong and determined, clear and free.

Trixie rode her bike to the Sea Wall, Saroj perched on the carrier.

'It's funny,' Saroj said to Trixie as they walked up the

little stone staircase to the wall, 'I've forgiven Ma completely. Absolutely. It doesn't matter what she did. And as for Baba . . .'

'Does that mean you're going back home?'

'No, no, that's just it! I just feel clean, somehow, and yet strong and sure of myself, as if I know leaving is right, and yet without hating Ma into the bargain. I don't know. I want to have this talk with her and get things cleared up between us — it's as if I've grown up in a few short days, as if I'm willing to hear her side of the story and, well, *understand* her and what makes her tick.'

'Great! What I want to know is, who's your real father? D'you think she still loves him? It's a long time ago; nearly sixteen years. I mean, we know she has a lover now, when she goes secretly to the temple, but d'you think it's the same one? Has she had him all these years? My goodness, what a story, I can't wait to hear it.'

Saroj frowned. 'Well, she knows him well enough to ask him to donate blood; and he was willing enough to do so, so maybe..."

'Can you imagine it, your Ma getting romantic with someone? Whispering sweet nothings in his ear?' Trixie giggled and clasped her hands and mimed love-sickness, rolling her eyes and gazing at Saroj with a doting expression.

Saroj giggled too, but only for a moment. 'No, I can't imagine it. I still can't. It's just not like Ma. I can't imagine her being in love, and even less I can't imagine her doing that ..."

'Maybe she was raped?'

'No. No way. Look, if she was raped, she wouldn't have known him to ask him to give blood, would she?'

'Well, maybe someone she knows raped her.'

'Ridiculous! Who on earth! Can you imagine, if somebody raped you and you got a child from that, going to him and asking him to donate blood? It's just not logical.'

'Well, you know what I mean. Someone she really liked but she was too shy and he kind of — well you know, *persuaded* her and she gave in and..."

'Trixie, that's your imagination running away with you

again. You're crazy!'

'Well, anyway, I'm just dying to know who it is! Think she'll tell you?'

'She'll have to. I'll make her. Everything I want to know, she said.'

'When are you going to have this little talk?'

'Well, tomorrow might be a good day. Why not?'

'Anyway, d'you mind if I'm not home tonight?'

'Where're you going?'

'Out.'

'Trixie, why do you always have to be so damned *mysterious?* Why can't you just tell me straight out where you're going?'

'Okay then. To a barbecue. Up at Diamond Estate. But the main thing is...' and her eyes shone with excitement and she gripped Saroj's hand. 'The thing is, who d'you think's taking me?'

'How on earth would I know? I don't move in your exalted crowds.'

'Well then... Brace yourself... Saroj, it's Ganesh! While you were sick he called to ask after you and then we had a chat and it turned into a long conversation about four hours long and then he asked me out! Can you even believe it? I can't! To the Diamond barbecue! I've been dying to tell you all day and I thought maybe I wouldn't tell you because you might be mad, but oh Christ, I'm awful at keeping secrets and I don't want it to be a secret anyway, oh Saroj, I'm just *crazy* about him!'

Ma telephoned later that evening, when Trixie had left and Saroj was alone at home.

'I'm fine, Ma! Everybody's out and it's nice and quiet. I've started to study again.'

'Child, you're supposed to be recuperating!'

'Yes, but Ma, exams are in only a few weeks and I've lost a whole week of school. Are you coming tomorrow?'

'Yes, that's what I wanted to tell you. I got a letter this week, from a relative in India, whom I haven't heard from in years. I've been thinking about it all week and I've come to a decision.

Dear, I'm going back to India. And... would you come with me? I'd like you to meet some special people there, and...'

'Go with you to India? *Now?*'

'Well, not immediately, of course. After your exams. Why don't you take time off from school, and we could travel together? There's so much I want to tell you, and show you; we should have talked a long, long time ago and there's so much you should catch up with. And you are very young for your class, you know, so it wouldn't really matter if you repeat a year!'

'Ma! I want to go into the Lower Sixth and do A Levels and I don't want to lose a year! Maybe after A Levels!'

'In two years?'

There was such disappointment in Ma's voice Saroj wanted to reach out and comfort her. She was like a little child, and Saroj was denying her a heartfelt wish.

'Oh Ma, you've been away from India for so long it doesn't make much difference, does it, if you wait two more years? Look, I can come with you in the holidays and we'll stay for two months. Surely that's enough time?'

'Well, I suppose so. I wanted to stay longer, maybe a year, but maybe you could come back early.'

'Baba would let you go? He'd give you the money?'

'Let that be my problem. And you needn't come back here at all, you know. You could go to Richie and Ganesh in London. You could stay with them and do your A Levels there.'

'Ma! I could? Really?'

'Yes. That way you'd be a lot nearer to your goal, wouldn't you?'

'But then I can't win the Guyana Scholarship! Who'd finance my studies?'

'Let that be my problem. And maybe I would stay too. In London, with you. Or in India. Who knows? But... listen, dear, your father's home, I just heard his car. I'll come round tomorrow around ten and we'll talk some more. All right?'

'All right. Goodbye, Ma. And . . . thanks.'

'I love you, Saroj. Never forget that.'

'I — I love you too, Ma.'

There. It was said. And it wasn't half as hard saying it as she'd thought it would be. And it was true.

In the middle of the night the telephone shrilled, jolting her awake. Insistent, demanding, it screamed for attention and through the grogginess of sleep her blood curdled. She grabbed her pillow and buried her head beneath it and when the telephone stopped screaming she removed the pillow and listened into the silence broken only by Lucy Quentin's voice floating over the walls, low and stunned yet so distinct, so filled with meaning that the very first word sliced sleep and night from Saroj's mind, and she listened with a pounding, knowing heart, knowing with that knowledge that comes not from without but from some deep forgotten instinct.

'Oh Christ... No... Oh hell. Oh Christ... Are you sure? Is the fire brigade... Christ, no... What'll I tell her? Oh Christ... Yes... In the morning. Shall I come... Can I help... I see... yes, you're right, quite right. I know, she's in no condition... It's better if I tell her myself, when she wakes up. Oh Christ. This is terrible, just terrible. Oh my God. Till tomorrow then... Yes... Yes... Yes... Mr Roy, what can I say...'

Lucy Quentin stood in front of the telephone, the receiver still in her hand, frozen stiff and staring at the wall. She didn't hear Saroj approach from behind.

Saroj, still in a nightgown, cycled furiously through the silent dark streets to what had been the Roy home. Now it was nothing but fire, a mountain of fire leaping up into the black sky and licking it with furious tongues, pennants of vicious flames flying from the window holes. A roaring inferno so hot there was no approach. Six fire engines were parked in Waterloo Street, firemen and police officers pushed back the gathering crowd, while other firemen held hoses that sprayed the inferno with jets of water that sizzled into nothing.

Saroj fought through the crowd, crying aloud for Ma. She reached the front line and fell into Ganesh's arms. And then she fainted.

Chapter 41

Nat
A Village in Madras State, 1969

Though it did not rain again that season it was days before the flood receded enough to make much of a difference, and even when the soaked earth was again visible life could not return to normal. Almost all the huts in the village had been destroyed so living conditions remained the same: all the women and children in the houses of Doctor and Henry, the men in the school house which, now that the branches had been removed and they could sleep on the concrete floor, was much more comfortable.

But the sun made a difference. Even on that first day, the day Nat brought Gauri Ma home, faces that had been drawn and weary broke out in smiles, children came out to play in the water, women brought out the moist clothing that had collected over days, even weeks, and hung them over the trees and bushes to dry, and tied the ends of their wet saris to the branches of trees so that they waved like long many-coloured banners in the sunlight.

Doctor found out that those whose homes were ruined or badly damaged could apply for government aid to build new huts, but the villagers themselves had no idea of where, and how, to do this, and most of them could neither read nor write enough to fill out the appropriate forms. The men and the village elders together with Doctor, Nat and Henry held a palaver in the schoolhouse, and Nat was charged with the task of overseeing the reconstruction formalities. And so he met each villager again, his friends of old, went with them to review the damage done and salvage anything to be salvaged, heard their lamentations, filled out the forms, and took them in groups to the appropriate official in Town, where a bored civil servant collected the forms and had each applicant sign with a thumb-print.

And since whatever aid was due was slow in coming, and since living together in such cooped up quarters, eventually brought out the worst in some of the villagers so that they turned to squabbling among themselves and dividing up into groups according to caste (Gauri Ma was allotted the back verandah of Henry's house, all to herself, so that she ended up with more room than any other single person in the village), Doctor lent them the money, interest free, until such time as the emergency aid funds might — if ever — arrive. And since Doctor was fully occupied with treating the sick it was again Nat who went to town to buy the bricks and the coconut fronds for the roofs and arranged for them to be brought out in bulk to the village on bullock carts. He also organised the reconstruction teams, and settled the heated disputes as to the order in which the huts were to be built.

But Nat was one of them; their own, their *tamby*, now (as they believed) a *daktah,* and, even though he was much younger than many of those under his authority, they accepted him because of his gentle and respectful and tactful tone coupled with no-nonsense efficiency that demanded, and received, compliance. They called him the *tamby daktah*, little brother doctor, an apt merging of respect with fondness.

Nat had moreover won for himself the title of Bringer of Sunshine and Dispeller of Rain, for it was he whom they had seen that first morning, entering the gate bathed in a ray of sunshine with Gauri Ma in his arms, resplendent as a young god, and when they heard the story of how he had saved Gauri Ma from certain death (for surely she would not have been found for weeks, had Nat not appeared the way he had), how he had gone out in the night through the dark water world and found her in the impenetrable blackness, they slapped their cheeks in awe and marvelled at this miracle, and Nat was credited with being a true Son of God. And even Gauri Ma, for a few days at least, was accorded a respect she had not in her whole life received, (though this respect did not amount to letting her share their quarters, indeed, some of the women had at first objected to sleeping under the same roof as Gauri Ma, but Doctor said it was either she or them), for surely God held his hand over her, and had showered his Grace upon her, through the form of Nat.

Nat accepted their admiration, which sometimes amounted to adulation, with the appropriate humility, knowing it to be an obligation to bow his head and serve. And if he had a Golden Hand it was not his doing, he told them, but God's gift to be used in God's service.

The receding floods left a coating of filth on the earth which had to be cleared away before anything else could be done, for this filth contained night-soil, faeces, since the villagers had had no other choice but to relieve themselves into the water. The removal of night-soil could, of course, not be delegated to any but members of the night-soil-carrier caste, and so squabbling again broke out because the night-soil was all over and nobody wanted to walk on it, and the night-soil-carriers could not work fast enough to remove the filth. So Nat, fed up with the squabbling, joined the night-soil-carriers and helped them clear away the night-soil, the sight of which silenced the squabblers. And it was Nat again who helped dig a ditch deep enough to contain the night-soil polluted topsoil, and Nat who stood up to his knees in another ditch containing night-soil-polluted drainage water, and Nat who emerged from the ditch splattered with night-soil and stinking. And far from this lowering their estimation the villagers bowed before him because never, in all of history, had they seen anything like this, that the son of a *sahib* should enter a night-soil drain and pollute himself with night-soil, and surely this must be a sign of great holiness, because only a saint regards night-soil the same as gold, and is equally dispassionate to both, neither repulsed by the one nor attached to the other.

As soon as conditions permitted it the village was buzzing with activity, women carrying the pans of red mud that served as mortar in relays while the men built up the huts with baked red bricks so that the huts they now received were much more solid than the ones that had been destroyed — the difference in cost having been made up by Doctor — and when they were finished and the thatched roofs mounted they plastered the walls with cow-dung paste and whitewashed them, and the village was new and fresh and sparkling as never before.

All this work took several weeks; the day of his return to England loomed nearer. Nat would have delayed speaking up until the very end, but then the letter came; from the Bannerjis. Nat had completely forgotten about the Bannerjis, and his plan to visit them. He hadn't even noticed they hadn't replied to his letter; not till now.

The letter, the arrival of which had been delayed by the rains, welcomed him with open arms, as expected; but it also contained a proposal, a request:

Several years ago, there had been an air crash on a domestic Indian flight involving members of the Bannerji family as passengers, one of those members being Arun, the youngest son. As a result of this crash Arun (who had been only fourteen at the time, an impressionable age) had suffered an irreparable trauma and refused to enter another aeroplane. Since Arun was the next of the Bannerji sons to be sent to the West to complete his education, this trauma dictated that he should travel not by air but by sea. This in itself was no problem but, as the boy was only eighteen years old, and generally of a rather shy and sensitive temperament, the very thought of such a voyage all by himself was considerably upsetting to the entire family. And, since Nat himself would be returning to England around the same time, the Bannerji family implored him with all their combined prayers not to use his return plane ticket but to travel by sea, sharing Arun's cabin and generally acting as companion and guardian, all expenses paid. The Bannerji family did not think this alternative would be altogether unpleasant since a first class cabin had been booked for Arun on September 1st, in which there was an empty berth, and altogether they believed the trip would be quite enjoyable to both young men, who not only would have a pleasurable journey with all the amenities, delicious meals etcetera, of first class passengers, but would also have the opportunity of strengthening their acquaintance which of course could be maintained once both were settled in England. Nat's responsibility would end when the ship docked at Southampton, since Arun's elder sister and her husband would be meeting Arun and driving him to their home in Birmingham. Nat should kindly reply by telegram so that the appropriate arrangements could be made.

Nat read this letter aloud to Doctor and Henry after lunch, while they all sat on the verandah sipping their coffee and eating their Milk Bikis. He folded the letter and looked up to gauge their reactions. He himself was in two minds. The thought of a sea voyage, albeit in the company of a shy and sensitive youth who would no doubt demand much of his attention, had its temptations. Nat had always loved the sea but seen little of it, too little, in his lifetime, and there was still a residue of longing for the calming, healing effects of a seaside holiday that the monsoon had snatched from him.

On the other hand, he was at last at *home.* Ever since the village had more or less restored itself to normal Nat had been helping his father again in the surgery and knew now that he was a doctor, that life had called him to task and endowed him with the gift of healing, given him a Golden Hand, and that his place was here.

Here, in the midst of catastrophe and distress, giving all he could to ease the pain of those people who looked up to him for succour, he had found inner peace. This was his place, where he belonged. He knew it now. The thought of leaving even a day earlier than planned seemed a sacrifice he could not make. The very thought of London caused a tweak of panic that sullied that peace; he feared losing again all that he had found, all that he had learned, in the chaos of city life.

With a jolt Nat realised something extraordinary: he was happy. Not just contented but truly, deeply happy with a quiet and pure joy that had settled into his bones, into his being, and seemed so natural, so real, so really, truly him, the way he should be, his very nature, he hadn't even noticed it.

What's more: he had not been happy in London. He had had lots of *fun,* lots of *pleasure,* but fun and pleasure do not necessarily equate to happiness; they are of a different substance, a different constitution; a short buzz, a quick thrill, again and again before the dissatisfaction settled in that needed to be removed. A constant *wanting* and *needing,* a nagging sense of emptiness that had to be relentlessly served. Never satisfied, but requiring constant feeding with ever-new stimuli.

Whereas *this* — it required no stimuli. It simply *was.* It might be a cliché, but happiness really did come from within. It was a part of him. Inherent, innate, independent of anything external to his being. A scintillating, serene sense of completion and fulfilment, free of all want and need. This was *home.*

But now, the letter. The letter was an appeal, and, he had to admit it, a temptation. The Bannerjis had always been generous to him, taken him in for weekends, offered him friendship and a slice of life he could never have otherwise known, and, yes, that slice of life, though the opposite of what he knew to be his own lot in life, had been essential, for he had grown and matured and made mistakes but learned from those very mistakes. Now they were dangling another slice of that life before him, a first-class ticket on an ocean liner, luxury and pleasure and ease.

Doctor and Henry sat smiling at him, positively grinning, as if they could both witness his innermost thoughts, were privy to his private struggle. What struggle? There was, in fact, no question. He had a return air-ticket to London but in his mind he'd already cancelled the flight, so there was no reason for this letter to change anything at all. As far as Doctor and Henry knew, he would be returning in three weeks, to his job in London and his room in Notting Hill Gate.

'Well?' said Doctor. 'Will you accept?'

'I don't know, really,' hedged Nat. 'I suppose I should accept, seeing as how they've always been so kind, but, Dad, I don't want to leave you here with all the work, I mean . ..'

'Whether you go a week earlier or not won't make much difference to me,' said Doctor. 'So if that's what's bothering you . . .'

'It's not just that,' he said, hesitantly. 'But still, you see, Dad, I don't want to run away from things here, I mean, no, it won't be running away. Because how can you run away from a place you love, and a work you love? The thing is, I've decided to stay here, go on helping in the surgery. When I think of London, when I think of what's waiting for me there, my job, I'd rather say to hell with it and stay here, never leave again…'

Doctor smiled and leaned back against the whitewashed wall of the house.

'You know, Nat, sending you over to the West was a big, big risk. I could have lost you, and I almost did, and I let you go knowing the world would stretch out its tentacles to you and try its best to suck you in. But I took the risk. Because the work we do here is not for weaklings, not for escapists. You've got to be proven by fire before you can take it up, you've got to know your weaknesses before you can know your strengths, and that's why I let you go. I wanted you to be proven, I wanted you to know all there is to know, and see what the world can offer you, and then make your choice, of your own free will, and not because you never had a choice.'

'It all seems so far away, Dad, unreal. Like another person, in disguise, a clown or some ridiculous parody of myself, tripping around in circles and not even aware he's playing the fool. And now, I've grown so much. I can't go back to that. Dad, let me stay!'

'No. I told you, the first day you came back. We need you, but we need you *qualified*. When I first sent you away it was for just that: to get qualified. All right, so you had other ideas and went your own way for a time. But Nat, if you're serious there's no other way. No Indian doctor in his right mind will want to come and work here for practically nothing, much less a European one. And I can't do all the work alone. I've managed so far and if I have to I'll go on managing. Go back to university and finish what you began. Go back, Nat. Go back and become a doctor. Take the Bannerji offer.'

Chapter 42

Saroj
Georgetown, 1969

*M*a. *Dead.* The two words just didn't fit together. They nullified each other. If there was Ma there could not be death because Ma was life.

How could someone who was alive, just be *dead?* Just not *exist* any more? Just not *be?* How can anyone just stop existing?

But Ma was dead. Gone.

Saroj turned into stone. She registered the outside world. She saw Trixie, desperately trying to get the stone to react. Trixie crying, and begging Saroj to cry, but she couldn't because stones don't cry. She saw Lucy Quentin, sensible and kind and trying to make life go on as before and saying all the sensible, kind things one says at a time like this.

Baba came. Distraught and dishevelled, trying to comfort a daughter beyond comfort. Saroj heard him quarrel with Lucy Quentin.

She even knew what they were quarrelling about. She heard every word. Baba wanted her to go with him to Indrani's; Lucy Quentin wanted her to stay put. Lucy Quentin won. Baba couldn't very well carry Saroj in his arms from the house.

She was a pretty heavy stone.

So she stayed where she was. She didn't even go to the wake. She felt nothing. Stones have no feeling. Stones are impervious to grief.

And yet, the human spirit has an extraordinary power of recuperation: even a human spirit disguised as stone. At the end of the week Saroj felt the first vague stirring inside the stone of her heart, like the very light touch of a feather, like Ma stroking a healing balm into the dense clod of nothingness, and from that balm came healing, and life, and movement. And after that the awakening was swift.

Saroj cried. She cried in great heaving sobs. She wailed with grief; she pummelled her pillow in anguish, and raised her arms to the sky. *Why? Why? Oh Why?*

And then she stopped crying and started thinking again. For the first time she took in the details of what had happened. By that time the cause of the fire was clear: arson.

A witness had seen a bunch of drunk black hooligans on Waterloo Street that night, shortly before the fire, one of them carrying what looked like a bottle of kerosene, but it could just as easily have been a bottle of rum. The Persauds next door had heard rowdy singing coming from the house at around midnight; Mr Persaud had looked out the window and seen people on the bridge and shouted at them to leave, and they had gone. But the gate had not yet been locked for Ganesh and Baba were not yet home, and the hooligans must have returned, entered the property, and thrown a Molotov cocktail into the kitchen, because that's where the fire started. It spread to the living room, and fire was first seen leaping from the downstairs windows at the back of the house. By the time the fire engines arrived the house was an inferno.

Ma's charred remains were found near the door to the tower. Her sword was still in her hands. She had tried to prise open the door, even as Saroj had done the day of her suicide attempt, but the smoke had overcome her, smoke billowing up the internal staircase from the bottom to the top storey and over the walls into the bedrooms. The one blessing is that she had died of smoke poisoning, and not in the agony of being burnt alive.

Questions upon questions, and answers that in retrospect made a farce of Ma's death, a senseless, avoidable tragedy of errors. Why didn't this wooden house have a fire escape? Why, a fire escape had been ordered only recently, but unfortunately… and anyway, the tower under normal circumstances was a perfectly adequate fire escape, as long as it did not burn first. In fact, the tower was the only part of the house left standing.

Then why hadn't Mrs Roy escaped down the tower staircase? Why, because the door to the tower was bolted from *inside* the stairwell.

And why was the door bolted? Because the daughter of the family had bolted it a few days earlier in a fit of pique. And why hadn't the trapped woman circled the upstairs bedrooms to reach the tower from the other direction? Why, because the father of the house had, two years earlier, bolted the bathroom from the connecting door to the next room, that of the elder brother, in an effort to imprison the aforementioned daughter, and no-one had ever thought to unbolt that never-needed door.

And why wasn't the son of the house at home, who could have opened the door to the bathroom from his side? Why, because he was busy courting an African girl, the daughter of that black big-mouthed Minister of Health. And why was the father of the house not at home, who might have been of some use in breaking down the doors, or tying sheets together, or in some other way? Why, because he was at a political meeting ranting about African violence. The circle was complete.

The *Chronicle* tore the Roys' story apart, laid bare all the lurid details, gloated over their mistakes, dispensed guilt in all directions. The only one who escaped their wrath was Ma, the victim of all their petty bickerings and selfish shenanigans.

'Telephone, Saroj.'

'Mmmh?' Saroj looked up from the *Chronicle,* from the middle-page spread dissecting the fire. Even the editorial was about the Roy family. Deodat Roy had a big mouth, the editor said; he had been cultivating racial hatred for years and this was the predictable and tragic result.

'It's for you,' Lucy Quentin called. Saroj hadn't even heard it ringing but got up now and walked over to take the receiver.

'Hi.' It was Ganesh's voice, but a different Ganesh. A stricken Ganesh, the ruins of the brother Saroj had known. Just as she was the ruins of his sister. They were all guilty, Baba, Ganesh and Saroj. Everyone said so. It was public. All three of them, working in unconscious collaboration, had killed Ma.

They would live the rest of their lives burdened with this terrible knowledge. But this was the first time Ganesh had spoken to Saroj since the fire.

'How are you, Gan?'

'Holding up, I suppose. Look, Saroj, I can't stay in this country a day longer. I just wanted to tell you. I've booked a flight to London for next week. Maybe we could meet before then?'

'Oh, Gan!' Now this — shock, grief, guilt, and now Ganesh leaving so suddenly.

'We've got to move on, Saroj, it's what Ma would have wanted. That's what I wanted to tell you. That's why I'm leaving, just a bit sooner than planned. But Baba told me you're not talking or anything. You're better now?'

'Yes, but, Gan…'

And then it came: all the grief, all the guilt, all the darkness, poured out to Ganesh in a one a passionate, pleading, soul-wrenching gush.

'Gan, I can't stay here without you! Don't go! Don't leave me!'

Finally, Ganesh put an end to it.

'Saroj, calm down. It's over and we have to get on with our lives. You've got your O Levels in less than four weeks and you've missed two weeks of school already. I want you to go back to school on Monday and work as hard as you can and get brilliant results the way you would have if all this hadn't happened.'

'Gan! I couldn't! I can't even *think* of school at a time like this, O Levels or not!'

'You *must,* Saroj. You really must; that's what I wanted to tell you. Listen, Baba's planning again to marry you off. I heard him talking to Mr Narain. The Ghosh people won't have you any more but he's looking for a new husband. He's saying now Ma's gone you need someone to take care of you, and…'

'I don't believe it! Not after all this!'

'It's true! And once he's got you married off he's emigrating to England, having fulfilled all his duties here. So just get those exams, d'you hear?'

'That… that…' Saroj spluttered in her wrath, unable to find the words.

'Save your energy, Saroj. You'll need it for those exams.'

Chapter 43

Nat
Bangalore, 1969

A week before embarkation Nat took a bus to Bangalore, where the Bannerjis welcomed him with the warmth that only a loving family can give to a long lost son, as if somehow the years of absence had welded them all together, made Nat a part of them all. In spite of this Nat felt a stranger to them all. The luxurious house with all its comforts, the spacious, tree-shaded grounds with their English lawns carefully tended by a troop of Muslim gardeners, the tennis courts, the swimming pool (which was the latest addition to what could only be called an estate) made Nat feel as though he had strayed on to a film set somewhere and was playing a part, saying the right things, and doing what was expected of him. Meeting Govind again was more an embarrassment than a pleasure, for what on earth were they to talk about? Remembering their bawdy talk years ago, Nat made up his mind to avoid being alone with his friend, and should this be unavoidable, to only talk on serious subjects, such as the growth of the Bannerji empire.

However, the problem never arose for Govind too had changed; the dandy had become a devoted husband and a besotted father who carried his infant daughter around almost all the day, followed by a worried *ayah* anxious to reclaim the child into the folds of her sari.

Rani, Govind's wife, smiled with sphinx-like amusement at her husband's behaviour, and seeing her and the effect she had on Govind Nat wondered how many of Govind's tales of high jinks in Los Angeles, New York and London were true, and how many were wishful thinking.

'Nat, Nat, you must get married soon, you are getting to be an old man,' Govind teased him, and Nat lowered his eyes and smiled, shaking his head. They were sitting at a teak table at the swimming pool's edge, he and Govind and Arun in bathing trunks, Rani in white slacks that showed off the sleek lines of her legs and a blouse of yellow silk that seemed almost wet. She wore her hair loose; it fell straight to her shoulders in a curtain of black spun silk, held back from her face by a bundle of jasmine blossoms dipped above one ear. Govind, his skin goose-fleshed and still spotted with drops of water from his swim, jiggled his daughter on his knee.

'Plenty of time,' Nat said, and looked up at Rani, who graced him with one of her dazzling but enigmatic smiles.

'No, no, there's not plenty of time,' she disagreed. 'It is much better to marry early so you can look forward to a long life with your wife. You would make such a good husband, Nat; you must let us find a wife for you!'

She spoke as if she were several years older and wiser than he, though in fact she was one year younger. Nat had last seen her at her wedding, a remote and dignified young bride absorbed in the resonating voice of her veena, graceful as a young doe, and just as shy, about to embark on the untried ship of marriage. That ship must have weathered many storms, Nat felt, for from her eyes shone the calm strength that comes of perseverance, and when she turned them to her husband they spoke the silent language of love, not the besotted dizziness Nat had seen in the eyes of so many lovers, but a warm intimacy which seemed to close in around her husband and draw him to her.

Govind met those eyes and exchanged a knowing smile with her. 'Yes, Nat, and we've invited someone around this evening who might interest you. A lovely lady, as yet unmarried, an old school friend of Rani's.'

'You'll like her, Nat. Of course, she's quite old, twenty-three, but the only reason she's not married yet is that she's an orphan and she lives with an aunt who she's wrapped round her little finger, and she's been very picky about her husband." Rani looked at her watch. 'Govind, I'm going inside; the boys will be back from school any minute.'

She stood up, bowed her head slightly to Nat and walked towards the house, watched by Nat and Govind, Nat admiring, Govind proud.

'You see, Nat, that's a wife. A man needs a wife, believe me. Have a good look at Rhoda; I'm sure you two would suit each other.'

Rhoda was a Parsi girl with eggshell-brown skin. She was small and slight and had the first face Nat had ever seen that was truly heart-shaped. She had a pert little nose and eyes that laughed with him and a mouth which curled up at the corners; cute, Nat said to himself, and wondered seriously if he should marry her, since she made no secret of the fact that she would marry him. There were no barriers of religion or caste here, and no father to raise all manner of objections, and marriage, to Nat, seemed the very best way to regulate his life in London, if London it had to be.

Rhoda's parents had died in a car accident when she was an infant and had left her with a comfortable income from the family business, and under the charge of an elderly aunt who had little control over her. Rhoda had gone to the same music academy as Rani where she had studied piano, not an Indian instrument; for all things Western fascinated her. She also made no secret of the fact that she had made several attempts to find a Western-based husband through the *Times of India,* and all but proposed marriage herself. She wore an emerald-green silk sari which hugged her curves and rustled at the slightest movement; she was more than pretty, but not yet beautiful, and would certainly make some man a wonderful wife.

But not Nat. To everyone's disappointment, after Rhoda had left, he said no.

'Why not?' cried Govind and Rani. Rhoda was in every way suitable, they argued, and even her age was in these modern times no objection. Nat had a hard time persuading them that, yes, he was certain, and no, he couldn't explain why not, but he just couldn't marry her.

'I'll never understand you, Nat,' said Govind. 'You might have been raised by an Englishman, but your soul is Indian. Just don't let me hear you've gone and married an English girl.'

They arrived in Southampton early on a September morning. Arun was met by his sister, brother-in-law and two cousins who had driven down from Birmingham to pick him up, and who apologised to Nat that they could not possibly take him back with them as there was no more room in the car, and anyway, they were returning to Birmingham and not to London. So Nat went to the station to take the next train. By the time he reached the platform the train was already packed and he stood for a moment wondering whether to turn left, towards the engine, or right, to the tail of the train, and as his eyes strayed to the window in front of him, vaguely assessing if there were, after all, room for him in the carriage before him, they were brought up short by a pair of eyes he recognised at once — not recognised, but *cognised*, for he sort of tumbled through them, into them, or rather, into what lay beyond them. All this happened in the fraction of a second, and in the next fraction Nat became aware of the face surrounding those eyes, the face of an Indian girl which in spite of the grubby glass of the window between them shone with such innocence: guileless, so exquisite in its open-eyed wonder (he did not, in that moment, realise that he himself was the source of that wonder; how could he, absorbed as he was in his own wonder?) it made his heart ache. His hand, which he had raised to push back a lock of hair behind his ear, stopped in mid-air, startled into a greeting.

A whistle blew, jolting him to attention. He turned and hurried forward to the carriage door but the entrance there was blocked, so he hurried forward to the next door, and that too was blocked. The whistle blew once more and the train lurched forward. He hastened his stride but every single door he passed was clogged with clustering, chattering Indians and their indispensable luggage: the bundled mattresses, valises, trunks, boxes and even pieces of furniture… it was hopeless.

Doors closed. The whistle blew again. The train lurched forward, stopped, lurched again, and glided into movement, gathering force, finding its pace, moving out of reach. He stood on the platform and watched the train slide into the distance, and never in all his life had he felt so alone.

Chapter 44

Saroj
Georgetown, 1969

The first thing Saroj did when she got her O Level results was telephone Baba. She hit him with them first, and then she said, 'Baba, Ganesh told me you're planning on emigrating to England.'

'Yes, yes, that's true. And…'

'Listen. Listen carefully: I'm coming too. Either you take me with you and let me do my A Levels there, or I stay here with Miss Quentin and try for the Guyana Scholarship, and I'll win it too. I swear I'll win it. And I'll go to England anyway. But one thing is for sure, Baba, I'm not going to get married. Did you hear that? *I'm not going to get married.* Miss Quentin is on my side, and she'll fight for me against all your efforts to marry me off against my will, and she'll win. Right now you're public enemy number one in this country. So you have the choice.'

She slammed down the receiver and the gladness that washed through her was the sweetest thing she'd felt for weeks. No revenge could ever be sweeter.

'Eight A's!' Lucy Quentin could not keep the wonder and the envy out of her voice. Trixie just sat there, her head hanging. Saroj wanted to take her in her arms, shut out Lucy Quentin and her biting remarks and snapping eyes. Trixie had achieved an A in art. Everything else was abysmal. Saroj was more upset for Trixie than she was proud of herself.

'Well, Trixie, what do you say to that? Eight As! The world is open for Saroj, and what will you do now? Scrub floors?'

Trixie cringed under the withering gaze of her mother. She

picked at her food, not saying a word, and Saroj could feel the tears she was holding back in her own eyes.

'Look at me, child!'

Trixie looked up and her eyes were huge and glistening.

'I — I'm just stupid, I suppose! And you made me take six subjects, not five like I wanted, and...'

'Stupid, my eye. How could anybody fail in *geography!* You know very well what you can do if you want to! You're just lazy, spending your time buried in those comics — oh yes, I know where you hide them — dreaming up at the clouds, gathering wool all day, doodling around with a pencil. How on earth do you expect to get ahead in this world? After all I invested in you! I had such hopes for you, nothing was too expensive; you were to have every opportunity and... Anyway, now it's too late. You've had your chance and you've — oh, God, I could just...'

Lucy Quentin threw her knife at her uneaten food, scraped back her chair so that it toppled over, and strode off, the rage almost zapping out of her. She stomped down the stairs to her office.

Saroj put a hand over Trixie's.

'Never mind, everyone knows you're going to be a brilliant artist. Wait till you're famous, then see what she says.'

'I... I... Oh Saroj, I'm just so thick, just so...' She flopped forward and buried her head in Saroj's arms and sobbed with heart-wrenching abandon. Saroj held her close, trying to give comfort.

'You're not thick, Trixie. It's just that, well, you have your own special strengths.'

'To hell with my strengths!' Trixie's voice was bitter. 'Look at you, you get A's just like that . . .' She snapped her fingers. 'It means you're my mother's dream daughter, you're probably going to be a doctor or something and I'm just, just a failure and she can't stand the sight of me, and...'

'Look, Trixie, she's just angry because you can't live up to her expectations, but maybe her expectations are wrong! I mean, why can't she be proud of your artistic ability? I'd give anything to paint like you do and that's just as good as being a doctor or whatever she wants you to be!'

'Painting! Poof !' Trixie waved her hand in dismissal. 'For my mother that's just child's play. It's not *serious*. And now with these results, what can I do? Can't go into Sixth Form. Can't get a decent job. Not even in a bloody bank with that maths exam, thank goodness for small mercies.'

'You could repeat the subjects you failed.'

'Okay, and what then, some bloody job somewhere? I just wish I could… get married and have done with it. Why couldn't I have been pregnant! But now Ganesh's gone and you're going and I'll be here all alone in this dead-end country, and…'

'My goodness, Trixie, grow up! D'you really think a *baby* would have solved your problems ?'

'Yes,' said Trixie. 'I'm just a failure, can't even get pregnant properly!'

'You're not a failure. You're the best person in the world. You're so good it shines in your hair.'

That evening they were sitting around reading, Trixie her comics and Saroj a book, when Lucy Quentin called up the stairwell, 'Trixie, come down here, please. We need to talk.'

'Oh *shit,* what's she want now?'

'You'd better go and see.'

'Another tongue-lashing. Oh hell, Saroj, I can't take it again. Come with me and hold my hand!'

Together they walked down the stairs and into the office. Trixie entered first, Saroj close on her heels. Lucy Quentin sat at her desk at the far end of her office, her back to the girls. The walls were lined with bookshelves, these filled with rows of the stuffiest looking books. Piles of papers, files, ledgers, all covered the floor in some sort of order known only to Lucy Quentin herself. Saroj was positively certain that if Lucy Quentin wanted a certain paper hidden among those piles she'd know exactly where it was and would whip it out in a second. She swivelled around in her chair as they entered. To Saroj's surprise the disgruntled mask had left her face and the smile she flashed them was almost cheerful.

'Mum, I wanted to —' Trixie burst out but Lucy Quentin interrupted.

'Yes, dear, I know you're as disappointed as I am, and I've been doing some thinking. I know exactly what we're going to do. In fact, I've already more or less solved the problem; that is, if you agree…'

Trixie and Saroj exchanged a puzzled glance. Lucy Quentin beamed at them, then gestured towards the typewriter.

'How would you like to go to England? To your father?'

'To… Daddy?'

'Yes, dear. I've been contemplating your future and I've come to the conclusion that the best thing you can do is go to him. After all, he's the one you take after. He's the artist in the family, he'll know what to do… Wait, wait, what're you doing? Let me finish!'

Trixie had sprung forward and seemed about to strangle her mother, who fended her off expertly.

'Just listen, will you? Maybe, if you're good enough, he can get you into art school. I'm sending some of the paintings from your portfolio, the ones you did in school, they're not bad, really…'

Trixie was raining kisses on her mother with such violence Saroj thought she'd knock her from the chair. Lucy Quentin held up her hands and laughingly tried to push her daughter off; but Trixie was too much for her.

'Stop it, Trixie, d'you hear? Stop it, wait, I'm not finished! Wait, I said, there's more to it…'

Trixie looked up at Saroj as she drew away, her eyes bulging with disbelief, glistening with joy.

'Listen a minute before you kill me! All right, I'll let you go to art school, but under one condition: you'll have to go to a proper school for one more year and repeat your exams, those that need repeating. I want you to do your best, to work hard and be sensible and get some proper O Level certificates, including maths of course, so that if it doesn't work out at art school you can still do something else. After all, your father made a success of his art, maybe you can too. Goodness knows, he fought me like hell to get custody of you back then. Let him try his luck. I wash my hands of you. Anyway, I rang him up today and asked if you could come, it was an awful connection and I only got to speak five words but he said the most important thing — yes. So...'

She turned to Saroj. 'Saroj, you're leaving in three weeks, aren't you? D'you think there'll be a free berth, still? And what did you say the ship was called? I'll have to make a reservation tomorrow.'

Trixie and her mother left Georgetown only a week later. Lucy Quentin wanted to have a little holiday with her daughter before they were parted for who knew how long, so they went to Tobago for two weeks, where one of Trixie's uncles had a beach house. More importantly, Port of Spain was the port of embarkation for the Spanish ship Montserrat, due in Southampton three weeks following. When Lucy Quentin and Trixie left, Saroj moved in with Balwant Uncle till it was time for her own departure.

Trixie was waiting for her and Deodat at Port of Spain's airport, Piarco, jumping up and down and waving from the visitor's terrace. Baba turned to Saroj crossly.

'What's that girl doing here?'

'Well, um, she's going to England too. On the same ship.'

'What! How come? Why didn't you say anything?'

'I forgot, Baba.'

'Is she going with her mother?'

'Urn, no, actually, she's travelling alone; that is, with us!'

Baba stumbled in his shock. 'What! But nobody said anything! She can't just latch on to us! What's the meaning of this? That girl has been enough trouble already, and...'

'But, Baba, I invited her to share a cabin with me, I didn't want to be put in with a stranger, you see, so I suggested to her mother that we travel together and she thought it's a good idea. She would have told you but there wasn't time before they left the country; it was a last minute decision. I told her mother you wouldn't mind at all, that you'd be glad for me to have company. I expect Miss Quentin will talk to you about it before we leave.'

Baba threw Saroj a look of thunder but she remained gloriously unperturbed. The last two and a half weeks, the first time Baba and she had spent in any proximity since Ma's death, had shown her how much she'd grow up, how independent she was of his opinion, and how much she was ready to defy him openly. Not aggressively, not with drawn swords, but with impertinent composure, as now.

They retrieved their suitcases and entered Piarco's main hall, where a dread-locked man in a long shirt covered with brilliant red flowers played a gentle rippling melody on a steel drum, so soothing that Saroj's nervousness as to the waiting confrontation melted away.

Trixie and her mother approached them, smiling, transformed; the deep lines of stress that usually furrowed Lucy Quentin's face, her mask of permanent dissatisfaction, had vanished, and when she greeted Baba it was with a smile so serene it disarmed him completely.

'Oh, Mr Roy, I do apologise for loading Trixie onto you at the last minute, but Saroj told me it would be quite all right, you wouldn't mind in the least, and frankly, there was just no time before we left to ring you up and really we had no choice because all the flights were booked up till mid-September and there were still a few berths left on the *Montserrat,* so we were quite lucky. And I'm sure she won't be any trouble; Saroj is such a mature girl and Trixie eats out of her hand!'

Trixie and Saroj, arm in arm after their first exuberant greeting, exchanged wicked grins at these words. Trixie turned to Saroj and winked and Saroj had to smother her giggles. Baba's manners won precedence over his prejudices. He hedged and hummed and insisted everything was quite all right, that it was good for Saroj to have a friend in her cabin, and reassured Lucy Quentin completely as to Trixie's safety under his chaperonage.

Ma's death had cut Baba down several sizes. He was a ghost of his former self: for the first time, Saroj understood the cliché. Indeed, she felt that way herself; but with her, that ghost was already filling out with substance, new contours taking shape, new life stirring at the prospect of a new beginning. She had the advantage of youth. Her spirit could still sprint; and it had overtaken Baba's limping one. She almost felt sorry for him. *Almost.*

They left the terminal and plunged into the multi-coloured fray of taxi- and bus-drivers, porters, tourists, vendors, shoe-cleaners, lottery-ticket sellers and limbo dancers or whatever those loud-mouthed, grinning men in carnival colours arguing and laughing among themselves in the middle of the road were.

They took two taxis to Port of Spain. Trixie was spending the night with her grandparents, Lucy Quentin with an old school friend, Baba and Saroj in a hotel. They'd be meeting again the next morning — on board the Montserrat. But before she left for the night Trixie grabbed Saroj, pulled her aside, and whispered fiercely into her ear:

'I've got the most terrible, terrible news, Saroj! I told you Dad doesn't want me, didn't I? Well, he doesn't!' Saroj looked at her in surprise and saw that she was close to tears.

'What? What d'you mean?'

But the cars were waiting and the parents were impatient and pulled the girls apart before Trixie could speak.

Trixie and Saroj shared a tiny, outside cabin on the same deck but on the opposite side of the ship from Baba, which was a good beginning. They squabbled as to who would sleep on which berth, inspected the tiny shower and toilet and poked their noses into a few of the cupboards, flung their luggage on to the berths and hurried up to the main deck to watch the ship leave port. Lucy Quentin had been near to tears when the loudspeaker had requested visitors to leave the ship and Trixie wanted to wave goodbye. They pushed their way through the passengers with the very same idea in mind and found a place at the railing, where Trixie peered anxiously at the crowd on the pier till at last in great relief she cried out, 'There she is!' and waved frantically, screaming, 'Mum, Mum!' into a wind that tore the words from her lips. Tears slid down her cheeks and she made no effort to restrain them.

Lucy Quentin, a tiny forlorn creature in a lilac trouser suit, waved back with one hand, dabbing her own cheeks with a handkerchief with the other. She looked so small, so helpless, her power nothing but a mirage, evanescent against the desert emptiness of farewell. All she was, now, was a mother with an aching heart.

'Who knows when I'll see her again? It may be *years!*' sobbed Trixie, as the ship's horn emitted a long-drawn-out, hollow, agonised blast and the gangway and the ropes were pulled in.

At this point Trixie was crying uncontrollably. 'Now I don't have anybody except you!' she wailed. Saroj turned to her and placed her hands on her shoulders.

'Okay, Trixie, stop blubbing and tell me for goodness' sake, what's this about your dad not wanting you? You're on the ship, aren't you? What more d'you want?'

'Oh Saroj, if only you knew! Dad sent a long telegraph a few days ago and he said they're putting me into a boarding school! That they just bought a house and they don't have a bedroom for me and it's a very good school in Yorkshire! Mummy says Yorkshire's miles away from London, up in the moors somewhere! And it's some snooty school Dad's wife used to go to and she says it's the best place for me to repeat O Levels, away from London where I might get too wild, and it's time for me to get serious and more disciplined, so they're sending me away! Oh Saroj, can you believe it? It's as if they're sending me to prison! Daddy doesn't want me, otherwise he wouldn't listen to that old bitch!'

'Oh, Trixie! And I was so looking forward to us being in London together! You and me in Carnaby Street! We might even have gone to the same school!'

'Well, it's not going to be. And I tell you something, Saroj, if that school's too awful it's going to be me slitting my wrists next time! Who knows, I might jump into the ocean before we even get to England!'

Three weeks after embarkation they docked at Southampton. Saroj walked down the gangway, meekly following Baba, Trixie behind her. They no longer laughed. The passage to England had been a period of respite; they had lost themselves in the *Montserrat's* little world and now must leave its cosy familiarity. England loomed before them, not the England of their dreams but a new and unknown world, a threatening, hostile reality.

It was nearly midnight. They spent the rest of that night in a Southampton hotel, to rest before continuing to London, but neither of them slept a wink. They spent the night in speculation, winged on hopeful flights of fantasy they both knew to be vapour.

The train for London left shortly after nine. Baba met a Bengali couple just arrived on a ship from Bombay and immediately plunged into conversation with the husband. Trixie had bought a guidebook of London at a stationer's and was already lost in its pages. Saroj sat looking out of the window, watching the bustle on the platform, when her eyes caught his.

He was tall and lanky and the rich, creamy colour of coffee generously mixed with cream. His black hair was long and curled down to his neck, and one stray lock hung loose across his forehead; he had just raised a hand to brush it behind his ears. His eyes brushed hers, returned, locked. The hand raised so suddenly stiffened, remaining poised above his eyes as in a salute. Thus he stood there on the platform, immobile, just gazing, not even smiling.

He wore a *kurta* pyjama-suit like the ones Baba used to wear back home, but instead of white his was a pale ochre colour. Over the almost knee-length shirt he wore a dark brown cotton waistcoat which emphasised his slim waistline; he looked crumpled, shabby, as if he'd just rolled out of bed, or, more probably, off an intercontinental ship. The canvas straps of his rucksack pulled his shoulders back and bunched his shirt, while the strap of his woven, bulging shoulder-bag lay across his chest. The whistle blew, the train jerked, startling him back to life. He signalled, to say he was coming, and loped forward in a long leisurely stride, unhurried but nevertheless swift, moving with the loose, elegant, almost regal grace of an Afghan hound, forwards along the platform to the carriage door.

Saroj pressed her face to the glass but could not see if he'd made it. But no. There he was. As the train chugged slowly past him he shrugged and held up his hands in resignation. The train picked up speed. She opened the window and looked out, back at him. He trotted forward, grew smaller and smaller, bounded to a standstill, disappeared.

She could swear she had seen him before, somewhere.

Chapter 45

Saroj
London, 1970

Saroj ripped the letter straight through the middle and then into tiny fragments. Tears of rage pricked at her eyes, but she would not let them out. Instead, she paced her little attic room as far as the eaves would allow, picked up her pillow and smashed it into the wall — as if the pillow was to blame — and kicked at a table leg. She flung open the little window and threw the scraps of the letter out into the cold grey fog hanging over the roofs of Clapham. Then she sat down at the table that doubled as a desk to write a letter to Trixie.

In the three months since arriving in England her life had changed completely. At last, she was free. The first pleasant surprise had been that she was not, as she thought had been planned, to live under the same roof as Baba. Her three half-brothers, James, Walter and Richie Roy, were less hospitable than Deodat had expected; their wives even less so, and not one of them was inclined to augment their family by two new members — three, including Ganesh, who had arrived two months earlier. Homes in London were not as large as in Georgetown, and nobody had rooms to spare. Upon their arrival Saroj and Baba had been crisply informed by Walter's wife that the three brothers had already distributed them among themselves. Ganesh lived with Richie, the dentist, Deodat reluctantly moved in with Walter, the lawyer, and Saroj with James, the pharmacist — and so what was left of Ma's family was torn apart.

Saroj was overjoyed, more so because between her and James' English wife Colleen there was a spontaneous, wordless understanding. Perhaps Colleen was disappointed that her own daughter, Angela, had no higher ambitions than a secretarial career; at any rate, Colleen's first mission — even before taking Saroj to 'see the sights' as James suggested — was to find an appropriate school for the newcomer.

Saroj was accepted as a scholarship pupil by an excellent school, half an hour's bus ride from their home, and immediately applied herself to her studies, earning laurels from all her teachers, for a girl of such focused scholarly zeal was rare in these days of miniskirts and free love. That earnestness won her once again the accustomed reputation of prudishness among her peers, but Saroj did not mind. She had things to do, goals to achieve, and the sour-grapes griping of a few pimple-faced adolescents did not bother and could not influence her; the names they called her, Ice-Princess and Snow-Queen, fell away from her like water off a duck's back.

London had been strange, at first: the rows and rows of tall dark terraced houses, with no spaces between them, no grass between them and the streets: just forbidding stairs, doors, basement windows below your feet. The bathrooms — the two taps, cold and hot, with the cold too cold and the hot too hot. Colleen had shown her how to fill the sink with water, rub soap into a flannel, and rub her body with the cloth — what a dirty way of keeping clean! She missed her twice-daily shower. Here you had a bath two or three times a week, wallowing in your own waste, emerging from the bathwater coated with slime. And the food so bland! As bland as the sun, which shone weak, as if filtered, sapped of all strength and energy. But she had adapted. London was her Promised Land: here she would grow her wings.

And now this letter. A throwback to a bygone age when Baba had ruled supreme. Though the letter itself carried no power, as Baba had done, still the very impudence of such a suggestion, the utter *gall* of the writer to even think of making it, and, yes, the twinge of guilt it evoked in spite of Saroj's steeling over of her heart, heated her emotions to boiling point.

It had been a harmless looking blue air-letter lying on the

hall table next to the telephone, addressed to Saroj, and with Indian stamps. Saroj, hoping for news from Trixie, picked it up, checked the name, turned it over to check the sender, and carried it upstairs. It was, she noticed, from one Gopal Iyer. The name meant nothing to her, nor the fact that it was from Madras. She slipped a finger into the corner slit, ripped open the three sides of the form and folded open the flimsy paper.

Gopal began by introducing himself as her dear deceased mother's eldest living brother, and offering his heartfelt condolences. Typed with a machine which lacked the letters *e* and *m* as well as the apex of the *A* and a raised letter *d,* and somewhat garbled grammar, it was not easy reading. But Saroj understood quite well. And even before she finished she was incensed. Those references to her mother's 'last dying wish'! Which had been, according to Gopal, to see Saroj well married.

'...and now that she has passed on under such tragic circumstances it is our sacred duty, dear Sarojini, to fulfil this heartfelt desire in order that her poor soul may finally find rest having achieved this one last accomplishment. Your mother wrote to me on the very day she was to die; as if she was acting under Will of God that I may know of this her last dying wish and set about bringing it to completion after her passing over to the other side. For as she informs me you are a headstrong girl refusing the suggestions of your own father in this matter, your sister also having written me a letter informing me of your reluctance to form a suitable match. She gave me your address and suggested I write you and persuade you to change your mind.

'It was your mother's last wish that she should bring you to India to find a suitable match here and I am in agreement with her in this respect. I am the eldest living male on your mother's side of the family and I have a duty towards you. I have taken it upon myself to bring you into contact with a highly suitable young man of whom your dear mother highly approved. In fact this is the very boy she was hoping to see you married to which was the purpose of her proposed journey to India in your accompaniment. I must now humbly admit that this boy is my own son. So this boy I am thinking of is your own cousin. As your dear mother must have surely told you it is a tradition among Tamil families, and highly auspicious, when the son and daughter of brother and sister marry. And since your dear mother and I were very close, it is doubly auspicious!

'Now, dear Sarojini, I know that you are a modern-minded girl and disapprove of arranged marriages. So do I in principle. I have always done so. But I have grown in the knowledge that this is indeed the better path. I have learned this through great misery, for I disobeyed my parents and married for love, and lived to regret the day. I married a very beautiful but rather modern English woman, a friend of your mother, who was also very modern-minded, and flighty as you might know, and tended to support me in this matter.'

(Ma? Flighty?)

'The son of this union is a talented young man now living in London. He is studying to become a doctor. As he is half-English his complexion is wheatish, a most pleasing colour. Knowing that this match was your mother's last dying wish, surely you will be rushing to fulfil it as a dutiful daughter. Know that your beloved mother can never rest in peace if this burning desire is left unaccomplished! I rest assured that there will be no doubt in your own mind as to the necessity of such an action. Yet as your dear mother tells me you have been in the past highly rebellious as to your marriage, but I am sure now she has passed away you will surely change your mind as to this last dying wish. Thus I am waiting for your agreement as soon as possible so that I may proceed with the marriage arrangements.'

If only Trixie were here. She could have shared the letter, read it out loud. She'd have fumed and raged as Trixie nodded in understanding, and then Trixie would have made a farce of the letter, read it out dramatically, acted out the pathos, converted it back into the ludicrous piece of rubbish it was. With the whole matter back in perspective the two of them would have laughed till they cried. She'd have crumpled the letter into a ball and thrown it into the wastepaper basket and forgotten the whole thing. She missed Trixie more than she'd have thought possible.

꩜

The next day, another letter, this time from Trixie:

'... You won't believe this, you just won't, I love it here!

'I'm in a dorm with four girls, one of them's my best friend, her name's Alison Greer and she's from Malaya! (But she's English. White I mean. I'm the only black girl here which feels funny and some of the girls are snooty about it but Alison's on my side so what do I care?) We're in Lincoln West House, our colour is light blue and we're the best in lacrosse, there's also a Lincoln East and they're dark blue, there are eight houses but the two Lincolns are really the very best houses!! Alison and I are in a Spanish class together, just the two of us! And I'm already so good at Spanish, because of the *Montserrat* it's easy as pie! And I'm repeating O Levels in my bad subjects in December, because my French is a hundred per cent better and I'm certain to pass and even maths is okay.

'But the most wonderful thing is this art teacher, her name is Mrs Graham and she's quite old, but she says I have a real gift, a very special gift, that's why they took me into this school in the first place. She said that I should take care of it and nourish it because people with gifts have a special mission, they're on the earth to bring joy and beauty into the lives of others and if I neglect it or use my gift in the wrong way I'll either lose it or I'll lose myself, one of the two.

'She invited me into her study and we had tea and biscuits and a long long talk, when I left I was almost in tears. She says that if you have a gift and you don't nourish it to let it flower you're absolutely miserable and do stupid things and this has been my problem all my life. She says I have too little confidence, and that's because I don't see the gift I have as something miraculous, that I only see my own smallness and inadequacy and compare myself to others. She says my feeling small and inadequate doesn't matter, in fact it's good because art is something divine and great and the artist must always remain humble and grateful. Creativity is in my heart, not in my head, she says; the head must bow low and enter the heart, and not interfere. Now isn't that news?

'And how are you? Sorry to hear your cousin Angie's such a beast, you could really be having a nice time in London if she'd bother to show you around a bit! When I get back we'll paint the town red, you and me. One of my aims in life is to go to a discotheque in the West End, maybe you could do some research on this score? One thing you should not believe is that because I'm going to be a serious artist I'm not going to have any more fun! Saroj, I'm afraid your life is going to get so dead boring, I mean come on, girl, you have to fall in love one of these days and if you just stay home and study how can you meet anyone interesting? At half-term we have to do some serious liming, you and me. Oh, and my stepmother Elaine is just absolutely super … she says she always wanted a daughter and I am that daughter!

'Since Mrs Graham's talk I've been wondering about you, you know, if you have some gift too and if so, what it could be? In any case, sitting over a desk cramming all that stuff into your brain doesn't sound very joyful or beautiful.

'See you at half-term, that's in two weeks!

'Love, Trixie

'PS Tell Ganesh Hi from me, and see if you can arrange a meeting at half-term.'

Saroj could not deliver Trixie's message because by the time it arrived Ganesh had already left London for India, to sprinkle Ma's ashes in the Ganges.

He went off with a Swiss girl, Saroj wrote to Trixie, 'and right now he's working in a restaurant in Switzerland trying to earn the money for the overland trip to India, and he's broken off his studies and doesn't want to be a lawyer any more. So I think you'd better forget him after all. He's one of those hippies and he's growing his hair, can you imagine it! Very irresponsible. I hope he's not taking drugs.'

'I never see old Deodat any more thank heavens (I'll never call him Baba again!). He lives with my half-brother Walter who's a barrister and D thought he could work for him, but Walter doesn't want him and his wife hates him, so he kind of hangs around reading files and doing nothing (so I've heard). He seems to be having some heart trouble. Anyway I only wish him the worst and I hope he's getting a taste of his own medicine! My other half-brother James (the one I'm staying with) is a chemist and says I can work for him a bit in the dispensary during the summer hols, and I'm looking forward to that. So I can earn a bit of money — for what? Who knows! I'll save it.'

She opened her desk, tidied her books within it, removed those she would need, and packed them into the leather satchel she wore over her shoulder. She was alone in the classroom. The others seemed to have all vanished together, girls and boys in laughing, joshing groups, hardly throwing her a backward glance, leaving her alone to make some final notes before leaving. Whatever interest they had shown when she first joined the class had evaporated. She had felt awkward, self-conscious about her Indianness, sure that they were all staring at her behind her back, sneering at her, and had been slow to respond. What she feared she heard confirmed in the casual comments tossed out in her earshot: Saroj was an egghead, a teacher's pet, they said, and they left her alone.

She left the classroom, closed the door behind her, turned to walk down the deserted corridor, past the knots of schoolmates in the courtyard. She could feel them looking at her as she walked past, imagine their whispered comments. What do I care! She lifted her nose a degree higher, clasped her books tighter to her chest.

It had hurt, at first, this feeling of being on her own. How could she say that she was just shy and needed a friend? Someone who knew her inside and out, to open her heart to, someone who knew her past and her present and future and would not misjudge and misinterpret and stick her in a drawer with a label on it? How could she tell them that they, Londoners all, emitted a sophistication and a worldliness and a knowledge of the ways of the city which scared her and made her retreat inside herself, close her provincial wings around her, and huddle down with books as her only comfort? How could she say that she needed time, and patience, and understanding, before she could truly belong? She missed Trixie desperately, those first few weeks.

Who am I? she cried out to herself. Guyanese? Indian? English? No, certainly not English. Do I want to become English? Do I belong here? Should I have come? Should I go home? Where is home? Here, or there? Can I be reconciled to the here, give up the there completely, cast myself off and merge with these people? But they don't want me. They have shown they do not want me. They show no interest. They are happy, complete within themselves. Who wants to know a naive little me from the backwaters? Who cares?

If only Trixie were nearby, or Ganesh. Sometimes a face came to her memory, a quiet, familiar face looking at her from the bustle of a Southampton platform through a grubby train window. A face with eyes that looked into hers and recognised her, just as she had recognised him. But then the face faded, and the memory, and she was alone once more. Alone in the world. Orphaned...

But no. Not orphaned, after all. Her mother was dead, but her father? For the first time Saroj began to reflect on who he could be. The very idea of Ma *committing adultery* had seemed preposterous; that was why, at the time of discovery, it had been so hard to accept. Ma never spoke to men familiarly, never exchanged pleasantries, never engaged in small talk, never looked them in the eye. She kept her eyes lowered in their presence, or left the room. When they had male visitors Ma would serve them silently before slipping off to the kitchen. And men, in their turn, did not see Ma, never spoke to her, treating her as if she were as invisible as she pretended to be. When in the course of her duties she had to deal with men — Mr Gupta for instance, or Dr Lachmansingh — she was curt and matter-of-fact. Where would she even have met a stranger, with her retiring lifestyle and manner? But was he a stranger, even? Perhaps not. Perhaps he was someone Saroj knew... and in that moment she did know.

Now that she had guessed it was obvious, so obvious she wondered why she hadn't realised it before. Of course.

Balwant Uncle. The exception to the rule. The man who

didn't play by the rules. The only one of her male relatives who had ever shown an interest in Saroj, and more, had encouraged her and spoken to her as if she were real. Yes, and the only man to whom Ma responded, and who did not treat Ma as if she were air. Balwant Uncle teased everyone, true, but he had a special way of teasing Ma, respectful and yet somehow daring, and Ma responded to him — yes, she responded! Saroj felt excitement rising within. She recalled the way Ma reacted to Balwant Uncle's teasing: suppressing a smile, pressing her chin into her neck, looking away and yet glancing back at him coyly, in affection — and love.

How clear everything was now! Why Ma couldn't join him: he was married, happily, on the surface, and Ma was not a woman to wreck a family. Why Balwant Uncle was so fond of her, Saroj, and why she was so fond of him. Her favourite uncle. Her father. Of course. With a father like that... oh what a shame, and yet how splendid! She could not wish for a more likeable, more loveable father. She would write to him. Let him know, between the lines, that she knew, that she was anxious for a closer contact, yet willing to keep the secret from Kamla Auntie.

She wrote her letter, pages long and effusive, filled with innuendoes that Balwant Uncle could not but pick up. She addressed it, for the sake of the secret, to Balwant Uncle and Aunt Kamla. So deep was her disappointment when Aunt Kamla replied for them both, with nothing but a 'Balwant Uncle sends his love' at the end. Saroj did not write again.

Her only comfort after that was Trixie. Letters ricocheted between them, crossing and re-crossing in mid-air. At half-term they flew into each other's arms, and Saroj spent a day seeing the London sights with Trixie's family, and she and Trixie finally stepped, arm in arm, along Carnaby Street. But the three days sped by and before she knew it she and Trixie were weeping tears of farewell on a King's Cross station platform.

She missed the warm familiarity of Georgetown, the feeling of being an integral part of a whole. And yet, here she could grow, become that entity she had always missed and longed for — an individual, not bound by rules and regulations, not hemmed in by tradition and culture and a father's rule of law.

And so, huddled as she was inside herself, the new Saroj began to grow. She absorbed strength from her books; learning, she realised, lent her a power and a prestige and placed her in a world apart from her peers. She might be from a backwater colony, but here, in learning, lay her uniqueness: for here she was better than they, more focused, more determined, and here she could soar above them.

She might be without country, without nation, but inside her there was still a being that could exist and be free, that could simply say *I am* without adding a this, or a that, without saying I am Indian, Guyanese, English, or anything else in the world. She folded her wings closer about her in protection so that the inner self could grow. But while it grew those wings grew too: hard, impenetrable, shielding her from hurt.

'I'm still undecided whether to study medicine or law,' she wrote Trixie at the end of the first year. 'You know my aim was always law, so I can really do something for Indian women back home. But will I ever go back? Everything's changed since Ma's death. And I hate the idea of following in Deodat's footsteps. On the other hand medicine interests me more and more, and as Balwant Uncle never tired of telling me, I have a mathematical mind. So I think that's it. I aim to be the best. Colleen's encouraging me to go to Oxford or Cambridge, but I won't. I like it here.

'It took a bit of getting used to, though. The anonymous crowds, all those people who've never seen you and don't give a damn if you live or die. But what a relief to join them! To be really anonymous. Not to have anyone poking their nose into your affairs. Nobody saying do this or do that! It's a splendid isolation; all this personality business doesn't come between you and the rest of the world. What a difference!'

During that year Saroj received two more letters from Gopal Uncle, both of which she ignored, just as she had the first. A long silence followed the last letter, and Saroj believed herself safe from Gopal Uncle's machinations.

She was wrong.

Chapter 46

Savitri
Madras, 1941

Gopal was in Bombay when the telegram came with news of the tragedy. He rushed to Savitri's side and brought her to Madras, to Henry and June. At first glance Henry and June knew she was a widow, for she wore the white borderless sari of a widow, and June took her in her arms to express condolence. But as she did so she looked at Henry, and her eyes spoke of relief, for they both knew what sort of a marriage it had been.

But then they saw the naked searing agony shining in Savitri's eyes, and the exquisite fire of bereavement that marked her features. Savitri told them, then, in calm words free of emotion, of Ganesan's birth, and of his death, and June sobbed and again gathered Savitri into her arms, and held her there silently. Gopal plucked Henry's arm and drew him aside, and said to him, 'It would be very kind if she could live with you. It would not be good for her to live in my brother Mani's home, for Amma is now dead and she would be alone with her sister-in-law which would not be pleasant. She cannot live with me for I am going back to Bombay where a promising career in the film world is opening up to me.'

Henry, still visibly shaken, nodded and said, 'Certainly, certainly. No question,' and now that June had released Savitri he brushed away a tear and hugged her, rocking slowly, comforting the girl he had once loved almost as a daughter.

'She has brought no garments with her,' Gopal said apologetically, 'but I will supply funds to make purchases. And I will supply funds for her lodgings and victuals.'

But June and Henry were not listening. They both held

Savitri now, they held her sandwiched between them, their arms around her and each other, and they were not thinking of funds. David's presence was almost tangible. It was as if the raw youth David was still among them, crying out, 'I want to wait for her, and I want her to wait for me!'

As if that scene had been only yesterday, and there had been no deaths between then and now, no marriage, no rape, no beatings, no murder, no tragedy, no England, no war. But they all knew of these things, events that were the abyss between then and now, and the knowledge of them was like a finger on sealed lips.

After a week Savitri stepped over the abyss. 'Where is he?' she asked June, and June knew right away who 'he' was. Their eyes met; June reached out and touched Savitri's shoulder, and smiled.

'David is in Singapore, Sav. He's in the army.'

'In the army? But he was going to Oxford — he was going to be a doctor!'

'He did go to Oxford; he *is* a doctor. But then he joined the Royal Army Medical Corps, and, well, that's where he is now.'

'But why? Why the army?'

'Well, David's always known he'd work in the tropics — if not India, then somewhere else, and the Royal Army Medical College is simply one of the best places to get a training in tropical medicine. He went to Singapore as a lieutenant. I suppose he's a captain by now.'

'Singapore! Of all places! Why didn't he come home? To India?'

June shrugged. 'I think we all know, Sav. Because of you... He couldn't bear to come back, knowing you were married, and not to him. That's what he hinted. I suppose Singapore was as good a place as any. And I suppose that his knowledge of Tamil and of Indian customs would come in handy there, with all the Indian labourers.'

'But now I'm free, June! I'm free! We can marry! He can come back to India! There's nothing in our way now!'

But June shook her head. She got up to make a cup of tea, moving quietly around the little kitchen. She felt Savitri's mounting excitement, felt the need to dampen it.

'No, Sav. He can't.'

Fear shot through Savitri's features. 'He's not... married, is he?'

She looked like a little girl, sitting at the table gazing up at the elder woman with a plea in her eyes, the plea to make things right, to make things right just by saying them, a naïve little girl with no knowledge of the workings of the world, of the realities of the army. A little girl living in a perfect world where love alone counted, where love was the only reality. Affection welled up in June's heart. She walked over and placed a cup of tea on the table, then stood silently beside her, an arm around her shoulders. Savitri leaned towards her, pressed her head against June's hip, reaching out an arm to encircle her waist.

'Yes, Sav. David's married. He married just before joining the RAMC.'

Savitri's face, looking up so eagerly at June, sagged. Her body slumped. She said nothing.

'What did you expect, Sav? He's the last of the Lindsays. I expect he was pressured into it. There's a fortune at stake and they need an heir, you know! And you couldn't expect him to foresee that you'd be free, so soon!'

Savitri buried her face in her hands, still leaning against June's hip, the older woman's hand gently stroking the hair around her ear.

'I have to see him, June. I have to. I'll go to Singapore.'

At these words June kneeled down beside Savitri, took both her hands in hers, and hammered their clasped hands gently, insistently, on Savitri's lap.

'Savitri, Savitri. Listen to sense. Don't do anything rash. Don't give in to your impulses. He's married; don't barge in. Don't wreck his life. Don't make trouble. You'll only bring heartache on yourself. I beg you, Savitri — don't go chasing after him! He's *married!*'

'But we were married first!' Savitri cried. 'We were vowed

to each other! I've always been his and . . . and . . .' her voice dropped to a whisper. It was as if the rebellious English part of her bowed before the accepting Indian part, the patient, enduring core of herself.

'I won't do anything, June. I only want to see him. Really that's all I want. I have to see him.'

June shook her head, trying not to smile. 'Oh, Savitri. You're so naïve. And you think David would want to be with you on those terms? Just *seeing?*'

'I don't care! I don't know! I'll write to him! He'll come! I know he loves me, I do, I know he'll come the moment he...'

'Savitri, dear, you're overwrought. It's all the pain of recent years, I know. And now having to give up David. It's too much for you. But stop for a moment, think of it all rationally, and maybe in time you'll agree with me.'

Savitri shook her head. 'Never. I know it, June. I have to go. I just have to see him once more. Just once.'

'What will you do in Singapore?'

'I can work, June! I've got my hands, haven't I? If they need doctors they need nurses too. Volunteers, I mean, people who want to help, and especially in wartime. I can go, June, I must!'

'How will you pay for your passage? Did your husband leave you any money?'

Savitri shook her head. 'Money — no. We only had debts — he drank so much! But I've still got my jewellery. The gold ornaments Amma gave me for my wedding! I rescued them before I left my in-laws' place. I knew I'd need them. I'll sell them!'

'You'd sell your jewellery? Your heirloom?'

Savitri tossed her head in disdain. 'Gold! Pooh! What use is it to me, lying there doing nothing!'

'Sav, be sensible! You're a widow: you need to live, to build a life, without David. You're free of your family but you'll need a bit of money to start again, and...'

Savitri's eyes grew moist at the words *without David* but before the tears could spill out June looked at her watch and said, 'Oh Sav, I'm running late, Adam finishes school in half an hour and I promised to pick him up. Eric's been sleeping nearly two hours — would you be a dear and wake him for me, and entertain him a bit while I'm gone?'

Savitri nodded, quickly swallowed the last dregs of her tea, and left the room.

Chapter 47

Nat
London, 1969 — 1970

Nat was fired by a certainty, a knowledge, that somewhere, soon, very soon, this very day, he would look up and see the girl from the train again. Never mind the chances of that actually happening being one in millions. Nat knew that somewhere, among the millions of people who lived and moved in London, spilling out of the Tube and onto the pavements, in and out of buildings, restaurants, homes, offices, colleges, shops, supermarkets, cars, buses, trains, cinemas, parks, discos, milling here and there like ants and separating and marching along the pavements in the great labyrinth of streets, tunnels, mews, terraces, avenues, gardens, crossing at the traffic lights, waiting on a platform somewhere under the ground, behind that newspaper on a park bench, standing in the queue at the Wimpy Bar, somewhere just around the next corner, entering the bus at the very next stop, was that Other, the Other that was, in fact, no other but his very own, placed on the earth for the express reason of completing that which was incomplete, filling that which was empty, entering the innermost circle of one's life to make it full and whole and round, giving it a centre and a purpose and a whole new way of being.

He had seen her, so he knew she existed. On a train bound for London. There, on a Southampton station platform, separated only by a grubby pane of glass and hardly two yards of air — space, vacuum, through which, if he could only have stretched out his arms, he might have touched her. He was aware of that same power stretching out, sifting through all the millions of strangers to seek her out. He felt, he heard, he sensed, he knew that another heart was also stretching out, that from above the mass of murky mind, the composite thoughts of the million strangers thrown together in those days in that place, rose a call that could not fail to be heard, and he strained to hear that call. His eyes were restless, searching the faces of passers-by for that one face, looking over their shoulders as if by some sudden intuition — There! Now! — scanning each crowd, fine-tuning his soul to pick up signals he knew were being sent. It had to be. It could not be otherwise. He prayed, he yearned, he cried out into the silence that echoed each prayer: Where are you? Come! Oh come!

Nat, relying on his Golden Hand, woke each day with the exhilarating feeling, *Today! This is the day!* Certainty swelled within him each morning, retired each night, to be born again the next dawn, not diminished but tried through patience, stronger, matured, vibrant. Those who had known him marvelled at the change; for Nat, though kind and considerate as ever, seemed to have retreated into some inner world. His eyes still locked with others' eyes, but he looked out of them as from a distant, inviolable stronghold, and where in earlier times all were invited in, now all were shut out, confined to a periphery. And Nat, watching them from the quiet depths of his stronghold, felt a stranger to them all; their words seemed superfluous, like the babbling of apes, joined as he was in a silence of perfect communication with another soul that was no other, but his own.

Occasionally he still helped out at Bharat Catering, when there was a wedding or a large function where extra helpers were needed; for having wasted so many years of his life he found it only right to help earn his keep and not be totally dependent on Doctor's allowance, for he knew Doctor needed money for important things like medicine and roofs.

But behind these weekend jobs was also strategy and calculation. The girl he sought was an Indian. He applied logic to his search. She must have come on another ship from India, for he was sure she had not been on the Eastern Princess; and she would not have travelled alone, but with her family.

And Indian families are big, yet a minority in London; they celebrated much, and they liked to eat good food. Sooner or later, Nat reasoned, he might very well run into her at one of the functions where Bharat Catering served: a wedding, or Diwali, or Krishna's birthday. So Nat gravitated more and more into the company of Indians.

He returned to university, picking up where he'd left off, and this time he was all there, focused, his intellect lit up and enlivened by a purpose that now filled and directed him.

What a piece of work is man! Nat knew his Shakespeare. The deeper he delved into the world of medicine the more it moved and inspired him. What had once been boring and tedious became a source of marvel and awe. Anatomy! The miracle of bones, blood vessels, organs, muscles, sinews, tissues, what majesty, what utter magnificence! What held it all together, what made it work? What intelligence guided the growth of a body from the very first merging of egg and sperm till the last breath, when the life that held the miracle together left it, and all that was left was decay, disintegration, dust to dust, ashes to ashes?

Nat learned with two minds. An outer mind, which absorbed and understood and classified facts, names, results; formed logical conclusions and applied them; memorised names; wrote exams and passed them with ease. This outer mind was peripheral to the inner mind, and subordinate to it. The inner mind was a vast expanse of pure knowledge. It simply had to think — no, not even think, but feel — health and wholeness, in order to understand, and the inner mind lit the outer mind and lent it power. Just as an electric bulb is lit from deep inside, and just as the mere glass of an electric bulb is nothing without the inner source of light, so also Nat knew that it was his inner mind that made him what he was, and would be: a true doctor. For in the inner mind was the gift of healing.

Chapter 48

Savitri
Singapore, 1941

David was on duty at the Alexandra army hospital in Singapore, leaving one ward on his way to the next, when Savitri walked in. It was her eyes he first saw. An oasis, living water in the midst of the parched desert of his life. Then she was in his arms.

Savitri waited outside the hospital till David's shift was over. He took her to a cosy little Malayan restaurant, and there they sat now, in a corner niche, heads bent towards each other, eyes locked together, their *pulau ayam* untouched and growing cold.

David had aged in the intervening eight years. There were lines of care around his eyes, yet they still crinkled with humour at the corners, and savoured Savitri as if she would disappear should he once glance away. His hand shook slightly as he took a metal cigarette case and a lighter from his left shirt pocket, opened the case, lit a cigarette, and replaced case and lighter. He relaxed visibly.

'You smoke, David?'

He nodded. 'Ever since coming here . . . starting work . . . it helps . . .'

But his mind was not on his words. It was on Savitri, on the reality of her sitting there, opposite him, near enough to touch. At first glance she seemed not to have changed. She still had the clear golden complexion and the figure of a seventeen-year-old, and the radiance of youth emanated from her as from a barely opened rose. But in her eyes David saw the change. The shine of innocence had left them, replaced by a poignant depth almost painful to behold. She wore a simple cotton dress with a floral pattern, buttoned down the front, with a gathered skirt and a thin belt at the waist. It was the first time he had seen her wearing anything but a sari, and it caused him a twinge of regret. Her hair, too, was different; she wore it tied back into a knot at the nape of her neck, a style too matronly for her face, and that, too, belied the youth and vigour of her features. She seemed poised between girlhood and womanhood; the soul of a woman wore the body of a girl.

'Savitri, why did you come? Your husband, your family… Did you run away?'

She pushed a stray strand of shiny black hair behind her ear.

'I'm a widow now, David! I'm free!'

'Before we talk… I have to tell you…'

'That you're married.'

'So you know!'

She nodded. 'June told me. Is your wife here?'

David shook his head. 'Marjorie stayed in England when I came over. Mother was hoping she'd be — she'd be pregnant … Their eyes touched in pain and moved away. 'If so it would have been better…'

'And is she — was she — pregnant?'

'No.'

'Then she's coming? Here?'

'She's eager to come, she keeps writing, asking when. But I've been putting her off. I know it's wrong of me; she'd probably be safer here what with the war in Europe, Germany so near, but somehow, somehow… I've got a feeling about those Japanese, Sav, and maybe she's actually safer if she stays put. But that's just an excuse. Maybe I don't want her to come. Maybe I'm just putting her off for my own sake… you see… Marjorie and I were only married a few months before I left. We've never really had a life together, a home of our own, and, well, I've been putting it off. But now, now you're here and I want her to come still less, and I feel like an utter cad.'

'Do you still love me?'

'Oh Sav, why do you ask? I haven't stopped — ever — not for an instant. You've always been with me, constantly, you live in me, all the time! A living presence! I'd never have married if I'd known, but I'd given up hope and Mother was desperate. I'm the last of the Lindsays. She wants an heir... she pressured me, and... oh, Savitri, if I'd known!'

She nodded and their eyes locked. Her hands dropped, limp, to the side of her plate, fingers twitching slightly. His edged towards hers across the table, drew back.

David sighed audibly. 'Can't we change the subject? Talk about you? Because wonderful as it is to see you . . . I don't want you here, Sav. I told you, I have this feeling... How did you get here, anyway? Did you come on your own? What are you doing here?'

'I came because of you. I only wanted to see you once and then go back if you sent me away.'

'You crazy, idiotic, mad . . . darling! So naïve — there's a war on! The Japanese are unpredictable, they're swarming around South East Asia, looking to make trouble. I want you back home. Back in Madras. I don't want you here, it's too dangerous.' The look in his eyes was playful, tender, boyish, all at once.

So it startled him when she said sharply, 'David!' Her eyes had taken on a stern, accusatory expression and pulled him to attention. 'What's the matter?'

'David, I'm not crazy and I'm not idiotic. War isn't a joke, I know that. I'm not the same, David. My life means nothing to me, nothing at all. I have nothing else to live for, but you, and I can't have you. So there's nothing, David, truly nothing.'

She told him then, of her marriage that had been no marriage, of her two dead daughters, Amrita and Shanti, and two dead sons, the breathless one and the beloved. Anand and Ganesan.

'So you see, I'm not afraid of death,' she told him. 'Love and death are the closest of companions. Because I've loved I have touched death, and death has touched me. Once we love we open ourselves to death's touch. Love makes us vulnerable. That is the price we pay. This world holds no more pleasures for me, David. This body of mine — it is just an instrument. It has contained suffering so great it has almost burst apart — yet it survived. And if this body of mine can survive, David, what else is there left for it to do, but relieve the suffering of others? And where is the suffering greater than in war? That is why I came.

'I want to work, David. Find me some kind of work, as a nurse. I've no training, no qualification, but I've got my hands.' She smiled, a little cockily, as if to relieve the pathos or any embarrassment her words might have caused him, holding out her little brown hands to him, at last.

He took them in his, clasped them, and kissed her fingertips. 'Qualifications! Asking you for nursing qualifications, Sav, would be like asking a nightingale for its licence to sing. If that's what you have to do, I'll find you a task.'

His words showed that he took her seriously. So Savitri added, 'But mostly, I came here to Singapore to be with you. To live at your side, or die at your side.'

Beyond the visible world of forms there is a parallel universe of spirit, and that is where Savitri and David lived. Though invisible it was as real, or more real, to them than the roles they played as doctor and nurse. David advised Savitri to volunteer for the Medical Auxiliary Services of the British forces, who took volunteers of all nationalities, and civilians with little or no nursing training. She was allotted to General Hospital. She would have preferred the Alexandra, for that was where David was.

David, always closer to Indians than to the English, had befriended an Indian doctor Dr Rabindranath, who worked at Tyersall Park Hospital, which housed Indian war-wounded. His wife, a lawyer's clerk, welcomed Savitri almost as a daughter in her modest home. Thus settled, Savitri's new life could begin.

The lives she and David lived were demanding, and separate, lives that claimed every last fibre of their attention, every last ounce of strength. But beyond it all was the essence, and that was where they existed, united even when apart, linked together like Siamese twins not in body, but in spirit, for one spirit held them, a thread of life to which they could only cling, which nourished them as a sapling in a wasteland is nourished and watered by an underground spring; and even though apart, yet still they grew together, their hearts inclined towards that wellspring. And they knew joy.

Three or four times a week they were able to wrest a few private hours of togetherness from their routines, and each occasion was as a precious jewel, a coming together so exquisite, so perfect, its glow continued far into the time thereafter. They were never alone; and yet they were, for they could slip for an eternal moment into a solitude of being, a capsule of love, shielded from the gathering madness of their surroundings by a membrane so fine it was transparent, yet tough as bullet-proof glass, through which they could behold the world, and the world them, yet remain untouched, unmoved, free to love, and free to give in the totality of their being. They mastered the art of perfect communication — one that needs neither touch, nor words, and sometimes even not a glance.

Singapore swarmed with British troops, yet still many refused to believe that the war would really touch the peninsula's shores. They closed their ears to the signals.

After all, Singapore was a stronghold. Fifteen-inch guns lined the coast — a sea-borne invasion was impossible. As for an attack from the north, through Malaya, preposterous: impassable rainforest covered more than four-fifths of Malaya, and a ridge of seven-thousand-foot granite mountains formed an impenetrable backbone, a shield between the city and Malaya's silver beaches. How could the puny Japs even dare to attack the mighty naval base of Singapore? And upcountry a hundred thousand crack troops waited in defence.

'The balloon's not going to go up,' the British said. 'Let the Japanese rattle their sabres, we're British! They'll never invade Singapore. They can't!'

Yet more and more British troops arrived, as if to mock that disbelief.

Chapter 49

Nat
London, 1970

The man on Nat's doorstep almost twitched with delight. 'Nataraj!' he said. 'Dear Nataraj! I am so happy to see you!' He held his arms wide open as if he would embrace

Nat, who took a quick step back into the safety of the lobby. The man followed him inside. Nat, unused to such familiarity from men, would have tried to push him back, but he was puzzled.

The man had called him Nataraj. Nobody called him Nataraj. Nobody even knew that was his real name, for Nat never used the name and only in his passport was it recorded, and his passport was safe in the top drawer of his desk.

'You know me?'

'Yes, yes, of course I know you, Nataraj, I am coming all this long way from India to find you. I am your Gopal Uncle, do you remember me?'

Gopal Uncle... Nat racked his brain to recall the name that seemed to stir some vague memory, buried in some dark recess he preferred not to visit.

'Gopal Uncle?'

The man grinned and stroked his moustache with forefinger and thumb, looking down at his shoes. He plunged a hand into a white cotton bag he carried slung across his shoulder, took out a packet of crisps, and began to eat in embarrassment. Crumbs and salt fell on his chest and he brushed them away. He wore a suit, the jacket slightly crumpled, a white shirt and a tie slightly awry, as if he had tried his best to dress for the occasion but had fallen asleep on the Tube on his way to Nat.

'How should I know you? I don't have any relatives, none that I know of. Definitely we've never met!'

'Oh, of course we have! Have you forgotten your dear Gopal Uncle! I came to see you when you were a little boy and I brought you a nice gift, a fire engine. Surely you have not forgotten!'

'The fire engine...' Now that Nat *did* remember.

The fire engine had had a long life, treasured by the village boys but shunned by Nat for a reason he refused to acknowledge, and had quickly forgotten because of the fear it evoked. The fire engine had threatened such great loss that Nat had not so much as looked at it again. But like all things the mind rejects, and in rejecting nourishes, the fire engine had grown beyond proportion, looming in Nat's child-mind like an oversized bogeyman of fiery red steel. So when Gopal Uncle mentioned it now Nat at once knew what he meant.

'I remember the fire engine,' he said slowly, warily. 'But I don't remember you. Well, I suppose we should talk.'

He looked at his watch. He didn't want to invite the man, this Gopal Uncle, into his flat, into his life; not yet, but obviously they had to talk.

'Come along.'

Nat led Gopal Uncle to his neighbourhood café. He ordered two cups of tea and sandwiches. They took their seats at a corner table, facing each other, and Nat began.

'So, you are my uncle?'

'Yes, yes. I am your uncle and I am so very happy to meet you again at last! All these years I have been trying to find you and now finally my lifelong dream has come true!'

'But how come I never heard of you before now?'

Gopal Uncle frowned. 'That is because of your father, who is not wanting you to know anything of me and your true family, who all these years has fought to keep you in ignorance of your true ancestry and would not allow me to claim you as would have been proper. But now I am here to make you aware of the truth and tell you of my dear beloved brother and your beautiful mother, his wife, an English lady, and their tragic death by accident. Due to unforeseen circumstances their one and only child, the dear baby which was you, Nataraj, was put in an orphanage where, before I, your uncle, could claim you as my own adopted son, you were claimed by David, who would not allow me to . . .'

'Stop, stop! It's too much.'

Nat leaned forward and buried his forehead in his hands. Overwhelmed by the gush of information, he could not think, he could not follow the words. Gopal Uncle slurped his tea, bit into his sandwich and chewed vigorously, waiting for Nat to recover.

Nat's eyes were shrouded in pain; yet beyond that pain was a shrewdness, a clarity and a determination which Gopal in his romantic zeal missed.

'Oh, your dear parents! How beloved they both were to me! What a tragic story! Your mother was an Englishwoman, so beautiful, like Elizabeth Taylor. She would have become the greatest living actress had she lived, that is for certain, for she was beautiful beyond compare and so gifted! How she adored your father, my younger brother Natesan! What a passionate and doomed love was theirs, crossed by the wrath of relatives! They loved each other at first sight but neither her parents nor his would allow their union, and so they eloped to marry, and you are the first-born and only child of that love. They braved the scorn of their relatives and the disapproval of society to live their love — but they were doomed by Destiny which cruelly stepped in to claim their short lives. And as neither set of relatives would accept the half-caste child born of that union, you were given up for adoption! I would willingly have claimed you had I been in a position to do so, for I alone of my whole family stood at the side of my brother and supported him, for what does caste or class have to do with true love? But my circumstances at the time were unfortunate and so…'

Gopal, not noticing the keenness of Nat's unmoving gaze, carried on in this strain for some five minutes, pausing only for breath before plunging on with new revelations. Nat had a feeling of unreality, of being transported onto the set of an

Indian film.

'How did my parents die?' Nat's interruption came as a whiplash through the middle of Gopal's story.

'What? Pardon? Oh, they died in the most tragic of circumstances. They were killed by Muslim marauders during the Partition disturbances! What a terrible slaughter! Luckily…'

'What did you say was my father's name?'

'I told you, didn't I? Didn't I just mention that? His name was Natesan.'

'And my mother's name?'

'Your mother's name was Fiona.'

Nat was silent, then. This was it. The revelation. The story of his past, the story his father had always denied him. And it was to come from the lips of this… this garrulous clown of a man. A deep sense of anti-climax overcame Nat. A sense of not-wanting-to-know. But he had to know. It was an imperative.

'Tell me,' he said. 'Tell me the truth. And for heaven's sake, stop lying to me!'

Gopal gave a little yelp and jerked his hand forward, upsetting his tea. The cup fell to the floor and broke, the tea sloshed all over the table, onto Gopal's lap and down to the floor. Nat rose to his feet and strode over to the counter. He returned with a waiter who cast curious glances at Gopal moaning and swaying in his chair, his face in his hands. The waiter mopped up the floor, changed the tablecloth and left them again. Gopal moaned louder and swayed forward, staring at Nat with eyes widened in alarm.

'You know the truth! David told you after all!'

Before Nat's eyes Gopal's façade of garrulous self-confidence began to crumble and disintegrate. Nat pushed his chair back, and himself back into the chair, to increase the distance between them. He had to bluff it out; he'd caught Gopal in a lie and now he might just get the truth.

'Dad certainly didn't tell me that my father's name was Natesan and my mother's name was Fiona,' he said. That, at least, was the truth. Would Gopal take the bait?

Gopal stopped moaning, stopped swaying. He kept his face

lowered, bent into hands that shielded his shame from Nat. He was silent. It was a heavy, brooding silence, a silence which overturned a world. The silence of capitulation. Gopal looked up. The hands moved away from his face, reached out towards Nat, and his arms spread out wide as if to encircle him. His mouth quivered with emotion, and tears gleamed in his eyes.

'You are right! I have been lying to you. Your father was not Natesan. Natesan is my brother. Your father is… *I* am your father, Nat! And your name is not Nat; it is Paul!'

'You are my father?' asked Paul.

And Gopal closed his arms around Nat and wept as he spoke:

'Oh, my son, my son!. You are my beloved, long-lost son. I have spent years yearning for this moment when you would finally know me, when the truth would stand before us and at last I would hear you speak most precious word in all the world: father!'

Chapter 50

Saroj
London, 1970

A ngie knocked twice, opened Saroj's door and stuck in her head.

'Some fellow at the door for you, Saroj. I've let him in.'

Passing her in the narrow upstairs hall Saroj snapped, 'Why didn't you say I was out?'

'You don't expect me to lie for you, do you?' replied Angie with a suave smile.

Saroj stomped downstairs. It was probably a suitor, braver than the others, one daring to be turned away at her door. This had happened quite a few times in the six months since she'd been at university.

In the almost three years since she'd been in England she had, much to her own chagrin, blossomed into a stunning young woman. The attention her looks attracted was unwelcome to her. She hated being stared at; the undisguised male admiration she involuntarily awakened disgusted her. She tried to play down her looks. She never wore make-up, and indeed she did not need it. Her skin had the colour and the gloss of deep pure honey; long almond eyes framed by sweeping black lashes, and wide, full lips below a small, straight nose completed a face of perfect symmetry.

Her hair had never grown back to its former length, but the years of Ma's care and nourishment had given it a fullness and a sheen, a natural healthy glow that would turn the knees of shampoo advertisers to jelly. Worn loose, it swung and bounced around her shoulders in a thick curtain of satin.

While she could not hide these features, she could disguise

them by an expression of almost permanent disgruntlement. Those perfect lips never smiled, and eyes which by nature should have been soft and moistly eloquent snapped with hostility. Her hair she wore pulled back in a simple, severe pony-tail. She wore old jeans under oversized men's shirts. Thus armed, Saroj approached the world, admitting only a select few into the intimate circle of those who really knew her: Trixie and Ganesh at the core, Colleen, James and a few others forming satellites around them. At the rest of the world, more especially at the male half, she snapped and snarled, keeping it at bay.

Yet there were always a few intrepid young men prepared to brave that withering wrath by simply turning up at her door, smiling politely with a bouquet of flowers held out to her as a protective shield. This chap would be one of those. She opened the door, prepared to send him away.

She saw at once that he was different. For a start, he was old, definitely not a student. And an Indian. Thickset and scruffy, with a striped polyester shirt crudely stuffed into a too-tight waistband hanging out over his bottom. He carried a cloth-wrapped, flat packet clasped to his chest. He had greasy combed-back hair and wide bushy sideburns, and a wiry curled moustache above a far too familiar, mincing smile. Clamping the packet under his arm, he stroked his moustache once with forefinger and thumb as if to press it into place before joining his hands in a *Namaste* and bowing his head slightly, the mincing smile never leaving his lips.

When Saroj did not return his *Namaste,* but simply stood there staring three steps up the staircase, the stranger opened his arms wide and said,

'Sarojini, my dear girl! I am your Gopal Uncle!'

The words made her start. She had all but forgotten Gopal in the eighteen months since his last letter. In the past year no more letters had come. She had assumed that he had given the battle up for lost. But here he was, standing in her hall in the flesh, nervously shifting from foot to foot.

From her vantage point on the stairs Saroj looked down on him and saw that rage, now, would be futile. She had never seen such a sorry heap of humanity. Judging from his letters she had expected another version of her father, a pompous ass, an arrogant dictator of a patriarch convinced of a power he did not possess. Saroj was well matched for such an opponent.

But this overgrown chipmunk of a fellow — she couldn't fight him. She couldn't crush him underfoot. She couldn't give him a whipping with her tongue and send him packing. All she could do was what she did.

'You'd better come in. We can talk in the sitting room,' she said, clattered down the remaining stairs and held the door open for him.

'Thank you, thank you, very kind,' said the man, and the look in his eyes seemed to say he really was deeply grateful; she really was excessively kind. Saroj felt absolutely out of her depth.

'I have brought you a gift from India,' said Gopal Uncle, and handed her the packet. Unfolding the cloth, Saroj saw that it was a little bag on which was written, in English and in an unknown script, *Taj Mahal Silk Emporium, Mount Road, Madras.*

'Please, take it out,' said Gopal. 'I purchased this gift especially for you. It is an artificial silk sari, best quality, very stylish but not flashy. Indian ladies are liking this style very much these days.'

The shiny material in bubble-gum pink was neatly folded, and Saroj, unpleasant memories of unfolded saris and the trouble they brought at the back of her mind, left it that way. She thanked her uncle and laid the sari on the glass table.

She gestured to him to settle into James's armchair next to the television set, and hurried off to the kitchen for tea and buns. She needed to collect her thoughts.

She returned with a tray, which she set on the little glass table next to the armchair and, still hedging for time, poured him a cup of tea. In her absence Gopal had stood up to move around the room, and now stood with his back to her inspecting Colleen's collection of china cats on the mantelpiece.

'These ornaments are certainly very costly,' he began, holding one up and waving it at her.

'Yes, yes,' said Saroj, took the cat from him and set it firmly back in its place.

Intimidated by her gruffness, Gopal returned to the armchair and let himself sink into its protective lap. His hand reached out to fiddle with the knob on the television set but at the last moment he took control of himself and drew it back.

'I came to speak to you about your Mother's Last Letter,' he began. He emphasised the words, making them sound like Last Will and Testament. His voice was at once timid and brave. As if he himself, of his own volition, would never dare to bring up the subject again, but this Last Letter fired him with new courage.

'I know,' said Saroj, and tried to keep her voice soft and calm which, she had figured out, would be the best way to deal with a chipmunk. Soft, calm, but decisive. She sank down into the sofa opposite Gopal's chair and curled one long jeans-clad leg up under the other. Seeing this, Gopal immediately raised his two legs and crossed them into a half-lotus; the armchair offered ample room. He reached for a bun and bit into it, holding his left hand cupped beneath his chin to catch the crumbs. They nevertheless fell by the wayside and onto his shirt-front and, inevitably, the fauteuil.

'Gopal Uncle, I'm sorry to disappoint you but I have no intention of marrying whoever it is you have in mind. I came to London with definite goals: to finish school with good results, and to get a degree. And that's what I'm doing right now. I got my A Levels last year, the best results in my class, and it was hard work, and I won't throw them away for marriage. Right now I'm studying to become a doctor and I'll need all my energy and all my time for that. It will take years. I have no thought of marriage.'

'Oh, really? Very unusual for a lady. But all the same you must consider this marriage because it was your mother's wish. It is not safe for an unmarried female to live in a mixed society. And I am begging you now to hear this story before fixing your mind on an unmarried condition of life.'

'What story?'

'The story of my son, this boy your mother and I would like you to marry and why it is imperative that you fulfil her last dying request.'

'Listen, Gopal Uncle, I told you, I'm not interested. But if

I do listen, do you promise to leave, and not to pester me again with this story, and not to try marrying me off ?'

'Oh yes, I promise this in the certainty that once you hear the story you will be rushing to fulfil your mother's desire. Listen: your dear mother had a friend, a very dear friend. An English girl. The two of them were like this.' He held up two entwined fingers. 'They swore upon death to always help the other in need. This girl fell in love with an Indian boy — me! It was a very great love but had to be kept hidden because of the hostility of both our parents. Only your mother knew of the secret. Finally I was going to be forcibly married to an Indian girl of my parents' choosing, and the English girl was to be shipped to England. So in the throes of that very passionate love we eloped. But it seemed our love was crossed by Destiny because no children were born to us for several years. After many years a baby boy was born. Soon after that my beloved wife was unfortunately killed in a Partition incident. As I was struggling to make a living I could not keep my son Nataraj myself and so gave him to relatives to care for.

'Your mother at the time was married in a far-off country. She and I were always close, especially after I married her best friend. We have kept up a correspondence over the years. She has informed me of the birth of all her children and of their welfare, and she confided in me her sorrow at the fact that you refuse to be married.

'In her very last letter before her death she told me how much joy it would give her, to see our two families joined in marriage through you and Nataraj. Knowing this, Sarojini, knowing that it was her last deep desire on earth, how can you fail to comply? Are you not moved to tears?'

Saroj was silent. She had no words. She was thinking. Finally Saroj stood up, and finally she spoke.

'Very well, Gopal Uncle. You've had your say. And now please leave, like you promised.'

Chapter 51

Nat
London, 1970

'I wish with all my heart that you would address me as Father!'
'I'm sorry, I'm truly sorry, but I just can't. You see, this is
all so new to me. All my life I've called another man Father, and
to me he is my father, and always will be.'

'But I am your very flesh and blood!' Tears gathered at the
corner of Gopal's eyes and Nat turned away. All through the
last hour Gopal had plastered him with a cloying, clinging glue
he called love. If at first Nat had wished to return the favour, to
love his father even as he himself was loved, to feel some vestige
of a son's warmth for a long-absent father, now he only longed
for a moment to himself. Yet there was still so much to know.
He needed answers only Gopal could give.

They had moved on from the café to Nat's flat. Once they
were there Gopal had prowled around the walls, inspecting
Nat's radio, his record player, his records, his books, asking the
cost of everything and exclaiming over the answer.

Gopal, Nat had already found out, had been only a month
in London, and was due to return to India in two days. He had
successfully completed his business, which was to persuade a
lovely Indian actress that she would be just perfect for the leading
role in his latest film, and to lure her away from a modelling
career and living-in-sin with an English pop singer. As it turned
out, her love affair had grown stale, and the modelling career
had come to nothing.

'She is prepared to play the role for an exorbitant sum of
money,' said Gopal. 'Beautiful women are so flighty! And now I
have to speak with my bosses over there.'

He spoke the word 'bosses' with pique. His bosses were scoundrels, he declared, who refused to recognise his talent. Just because the one film he had directed was a flop he had not been given a second chance, and still they had him constantly at their beck and call, running around the place for them, promising great things but never fulfilling them. They pleaded language difficulties: Gopal's native tongue was Tamil, and though his English was excellent his Hindi and Marathi left much to be desired. There was a distinct prejudice against film directors with a Tamil native tongue.

'It is the actors who love me!' he declared. 'They respond to me as puppets to a puppeteer! They do whatever I bid them! Look at this girl in London! Only because of my influence she is returning! I know her so well!' He winked suggestively at Nat. 'She knows of my talent as a director. But what am I? Screenwriter and jack-of-all-trades. One day I will just walk out and what will they be left with? Nobody. There is no other talent in Bombay! I shall go back to novel-writing and then they will beg me to direct their films!'

'Where are you staying in London?' asked Nat, if only to change the subject.

'With the Rajkumars,' said Gopal, 'relatives of a friend. They live in Wallington which is so far away from you, my beloved son! It will make visiting you extremely difficult! And I have only the two days left, it would be most convenient if I —' he paused, as if giving Nat the chance to invite him.

'But I've only the one bed!' Nat protested weakly.

'No matter, no matter, I can sleep on floor, we Indians can sleep everywhere and in all circumstances, we are very hardy people! And look at your nice thick carpet! If you just give me one bed-sheet I can sleep most comfortably, please do not worry about me, I do not need that nice soft mattress…'

'No, in that case I'll sleep on the floor, you can take the bed.'

That little matter settled, they began a conversation that lasted well into the night. There was much Nat wanted to know, and Gopal was only too ready to talk, though, Nat suspected, information was well embellished. Gopal perched himself on a straight-backed chair, drew up his legs and crossed them. This, he proclaimed, was the best method of sitting.

'Westerners sit in such a method as to be highly disturbing to the digestive system,' Gopal explained, 'but worst of all is the system of defecation here. Do you sit on the toilet seats to defecate? You should not, you know. I myself always get up on the seat and squat like we do in India. I will show you. If you sit like this,' Gopal demonstrated a sitting position, 'the excreta cannot sufficiently pass through the digestive tract. The intestines are crushed. The result is constipation. But if you squat like this, your digestive system is in an excellent position. The knees are up, the anus is down, and excreta can pass through swiftly and emerge from the body with ease. The very power of gravity forces the faeces vertically downwards. The intestines are wonderfully loose and relaxed. And for sitting the half-lotus position is the best. I would actually prefer to sit on the floor but as you are not accustomed and as it would not be fitting for the elder to sit lower than the younger I am quite content with this chair.'

Having said that, Gopal resumed his half-lotus on the chair, and his speech.

'Your mother, even though she was born and bred in India, always maintained it was unladylike to sit in a half-lotus and refused to defecate in a squatting position. It was a subject of great dissention between the two of us. Fiona was extremely headstrong in such matters but also in matters of diet, and as a result she suffered greatly from constipation. She insisted on eating a non-veg diet which gave her stool a solid consistency and a dark pigment which could have been avoided by correct diet and correct position for defecation.'

Nat resolutely turned the subject back to his mother herself, away from her stool.

'Her name is Fiona Lindsay. So I suppose she's a relative of my father?'

'Of David, your adoptive father. I am your true father. Yes, Fiona was David's sister. I was of humble though high-born

Brahmin Indian parentage. My father was a cook at the Lindsay estate and therefore we were treated as mere lowly servants by the parents. But Fiona and I loved each other from the time we were little children. We were forced to keep our love a secret but when we were of age we eloped. Scorned by our families, nevertheless our love was strong enough to overcome all obstacles. Apart from the subject of her nourishment we were a blissfully happy couple. Our relationship was pure bliss...'

'What happened to her? Where is she now?'

'I told you, she was killed in a tragic car accident.'

'But that's not what you said. You said she was killed by Muslim marauders during the Partition disturbances.'

'Yes, yes, it is all quite true. It was a slaughter *and* a car accident. It was a burning car. It was the Muslims. I was left with the ruins of my love and with a little baby.'

'Whom you immediately placed in an orphanage.'

'What else could I do?' Gopal cried. 'I was in no position to care for you! My family would not take me in with a half-caste child and what do I know of the care of a small infant! So I placed you in an orphanage, meaning to retrieve you the moment I remarried.'

'Why didn't you?'

'Alas, my second wife refused also to take a half-caste child. She was pure Indian and wanted children of her own. However she was barren. Several years passed before she would accept the fact that she would not bear children of her own and was finally prepared to take you in. But by that time David had stepped in to gain custody of his dear sister's child and I legally handed him the reins of custody, thinking it would be in your best interest.'

Gopal beat his brow with his fists, and whined, 'Oh, what a fool I was! How I bitterly regret that move!'

Lucky for me, thought Nat.

'But why didn't you at least keep up the contact with me? I'm sure my father would have been happy to share me with you.'

'Oh, you do not know the true face of that David! He

has treated me most cruelly. He refused to let me visit you all through your childhood, for he wanted to keep the truth of your parentage from you. He is a most dastardly villain.'

'Why? Why didn't he want me to know I was his sister's child? That makes him my uncle...'

But Gopal merely shook his head and muttered something about 'dark secrets'.

'But once I was an adult you could have traced me. You could have written to me. Why do you turn up now, of all times? Why have you left it so long?'

'Oh, my son, my son! What do you know of the feelings of a father? How I have yearned for you! Yes, I should have made contact with you earlier. But how to explain my great shame of having neglected my duty as a father! Of placing you in an orphanage! But now I have found you I will never let you go again. And I have come into your life with a great purpose. This has given me the courage to make myself known to you. It is time, my dear son, that you marry and settle down. And I have found the ideal girl for you.'

'Hello, hello, hello! I have been waiting for you these past thirty minutes! I have brought somebody along!'

A grinning Gopal emerged from the anonymous crowds at Notting Hill Gate tube station, planting himself firmly in Nat's path. He gestured with palpable pride at a young man in his wake — a tall and lanky young man, Indian, with long black hair tied back in a pony-tail and a hippie bandana around his forehead, in polka-dot bell-bottom trousers and a washed-out T-shirt of indeterminate colour. The man smiled amiably and greeted Nat with a peace sign.

'Ganesh,' he said.

'Ganesh is my nephew, also long-lost. I met him first time this morning. My heart is overflowing with emotion at all these long-lost relatives I am having the pleasure of meeting in London! Today I decided to establish contact with the girl in question and also with her family and I met him. He has been abroad for several years and has just arrived day before yesterday. He is your cousin, the girl's brother!'

Ganesh rolled his eyes and Nat laughed. Their eyes locked, and Nat felt an instantaneous rapport with Ganesh. The three of them walked towards Nat's flat.

Nat turned to Ganesh. 'Don't tell me you're in on this conspiracy to marry me off!'

'But of course!' said Ganesh, laughing. 'Nothing could please me more than to see Saroj married off to a suitable boy. You look decent enough . . .' He pretended to inspect Nat, letting his eyes slide down the long, lean form walking beside him. 'But to meet Saroj's standards you'll have to have brains as well as looks. She is a studious girl. Quite brilliant.'

'Can't stand the type.'

'Oh, come on, give her a chance. If you don't marry her, who will? The poor girl'll never find a husband at this rate.'

'Thanks for the recommendation!' Nat yawned ostentatiously and kicked at an empty Marlboro pack lying on the pavement.

'No, but she's really lovely, understand? That's the thing. A brilliant girl, but lovely. Beautiful, in fact.'

'A fatal combination.'

'A most wonderful girl!' cried Gopal. 'I have never in all my life seen a girl of such spectacular facial qualities. If she came to Bombay with me I could make of her a film star. I know all about the film business. I have worked with the most beautiful actresses and never in all my life have I seen such beauty.'

Ignoring Gopal, Nat turned to Ganesh. 'Look, Ganesh, do me a favour,' he said, suddenly turning serious, 'and don't try to fix me up with her, okay? I've had enough of people trying to marry me off to their daughters, nieces, sisters, second-cousins, and friends-of-sisters. The moment I hear the words "she is of marriageable age" an alarm starts buzzing in my head. I told Gopal last night, and I meant it: I'm not in the marriage market. Definitely not. After my residency I'm going back to India, for good. There's no place in my life for a woman right now. And apart from that, this girl's my cousin, and...'

'Cross-cousin marriages are highly auspicious!' cried Gopal. 'Most auspicious. And moreover, this girl is...'

Ganesh interrupted, 'Don't worry, Nat. Apart from all your objections, Nat, Saroj herself has no intention whatsoever of marrying. I saw her myself yesterday; why don't you admit it, Gopal, she sent you packing! I could have warned you! You know what they used to call her at school? The Ice Queen. And she hasn't changed one bit since then. If anything she's worse.'

'Yes, she is rather uppity,' added Gopal, wrinkling his forehead in vague concern.

'Sounds really delightful,' chuckled Nat. 'I must say, Ganesh, as a go-between you're not much use!'

'Oh well, I tried my best,' sighed Ganesh. 'But I must say, Nat, compared to some of the prospective bridegrooms she's had, I wouldn't mind you as brother-in-law.'

'You'll have to make do with me as cousin.'

Two days later Gopal, deeply disappointed at the failure of his mission, returned to India and faded into the past. Nat was not sorry to see him go.

As for Saroj, she applied herself to her studies with doubled zeal. But Ganesh and Nat remained the best of friends.

Chapter 52

Savitri
Singapore, 1941—1942

Several months passed before, like a gift presented to them on a silver platter, David and Savitri had a free weekend — together.

Friends of David's, an English family in the rubber trade, owned a beach bungalow near Changi. The women and children of the family had been evacuated to America, and the man had no interest in going to the beach alone — especially not at a time like this. He gave David the key.

One Friday afternoon David picked up Savitri in an old Morris borrowed from a doctor friend, and drove her out to the beach. They had no need of speech. David laid a hand on her knee, which she covered with her own slim, long-fingered hand, and their fingers played together gently as David drove. Now and again they glanced at each other, their heads turning towards each other as if at a signal only heard by them, their eyes meeting and smiling for a moment of accord, and turning away again, David's to the road ahead, Savitri's to the roadside, where fleeting scenes of Singaporean life slipped past her window.

Arriving at the bungalow, David slung their two overnight bags across his shoulder, took her hand, and led her up the wooden steps on to the verandah. A slight breeze, cooling and fresh, played with the hem of Savitri's sari, and she laughed out loud in a spontaneous outburst of unalloyed joy, throwing her arms up above her head and flinging them around David.

'Oh, David, David! This is paradise! I can't believe it — alone at last, in this heaven, just the sea, and the sky, and us!'

David laughed too, clasped her around her waist, and lifted

her as if she were a feather: he swung her around, faster and faster, till he stumbled against the verandah's railing and they collapsed in a helpless heap of laughter on the floor. Then, again as if to a secret signal, they both, in unison, stopped laughing. Savitri lay still on the floor, her hair, shaken out of its chaste knot, fanned out around her face. She looked up at him, propped on his arms above her, flooding her with a silent love so profound, so brimful of joy, she could not bear it and closed her eyes. She felt him kiss her eyelids, gently, like the brush of a butterfly's wing. And then her lips, her forehead, her cheeks and chin.

'Two days, two nights. Just us, the sea, and the sky,' David murmured. 'I can't believe it.'

Eyes still closed, Savitri smiled.

'But it's true.'

The morning they left the beach hut David told Savitri: 'I've made my decision, Sav. I've written to Marjorie. I told her about you, that you're here, that I love you and always have, and want to marry you. I asked her for a divorce. When this war's over, Sav, we'll marry, and that's why I want you to leave Singapore. For me.'

Tears gathered in Savitri's eyes. She said nothing, only shook her head. 'I can't go, David. I've only just found you— how can I leave you again, just to save my own hide? Leave you in a war zone? What else have I to live for? And it's not just about you. My patients… how can I leave them? My whole life is here, now.'

They drove back to the city without speaking another word. When they got back they heard the news: Japan had bombed Pearl Harbor, and the war was upon them.

Around them the world was falling apart. Japanese air raids left devastation in their wake. Both General Hospital and the Alexandra were full to overflowing with the wounded, either from the raids or with injured soldiers brought in by the trainload from Malaya; the ambulances lined up at the railway station, waiting to rush the wounded to the various hospitals.

Savitri became an expert at changing dressings. Night after night she walked the wards, lighting her way with a torch, stopping at each wounded man, bending over him, speaking words of comfort, and with a pair of forceps carefully removed the maggots from his open wounds, laying them in a kidney basin, maggots hatched from the eggs laid by the ever-present flies. She lost count of the patients dying in her hands. Their bodies too destroyed for those hands to heal, all she could do was bring them peace in their last moments. No miracles of healing occurred. But Savitri's presence alone alleviated pain and suffering. The warmth of her voice, the compassion in her eyes, the gentleness of her touch — it was what her patients waited for day after day, and that was the true miracle.

Women and children were being evacuated from Singapore. Mrs Rabindranath, at the insistence of her husband, left. David again begged Savitri to leave. She refused.

Her eyes brimmed with tears. 'I can't, David. Don't ask me to go. How can I leave you! My patients!'

'Sav, listen: you must go. Really. It's our only chance! Look, don't worry about me. When the Japs take Singapore — not *if,* but *when* — I'll be interned. I'll be safe — but you, as a woman, a civilian, a foreigner! Foreign women will be raped and killed. Our only chance at a future is for you to leave, Sav.'

She would not answer, but only shook her head.

'Think of our future, Sav. When the war's over we'll marry and have children. Go back to Henry and June, wait for me in Madras. Please. I beg you! I'll come when this madness is over. I'll be safe as a prisoner of war — but your only chance is in leaving.'

But again, she only shook her head, wordlessly. He wept then, and so did she. They wept for they both knew that the end was near, and both knew that for all their planning and all their hoping there was nothing they could do, no trump could cancel the evil that was round about them, in the very air they breathed, and waiting around the corner.

Rooms and corridors of the General Hospital were packed to overflowing. By the end of January 1942 over ten thousand sick and wounded had been evacuated from the Malayan mainland. Savage air-raids, round the clock, played havoc with Singapore city: the menacing screech of sirens followed by a never-ending, sinister silence and then the blast of a bomb, somewhere, near, nearer. Screams and cries, the whimpering of the dying, feet running, the cry of a lost child among the ruins. Noise, fire, blood, dying, dead. Pandemonium. The noose tightened around Singapore.

Amidst it all, war's silent soldiers fought on: the nurses, military, civilian, and volunteers. Husbands sent their wives out on the last ships leaving. Many refused to leave.

'I beg you, Sav. Go!'

'No.'

On the evening of the twelfth Savitri was waiting outside the Alexandra as a weary David left the hospital. She collapsed against him; he folded his arms around her.

'Oh David, David!' she sobbed. 'They've gone! All the army nurses and sisters have gone! They've been taken away secretly, leaving us volunteers to do all the work ... but we can't! So many of us are untrained, we just can't cope! They promised they'd let them stay and that's why we stayed and now they're all gone!'

'And you go too! Tomorrow!' David knew he had won. Savitri had broken.

'Yes. Yes. You're right. I have to go. I would have stayed even now but — oh David, I'm going to have a baby!'

David's cry of relief made her look up at him, and she couldn't help smiling at his joy. 'Thank goodness! Oh, thank God! I've been hoping, praying you'd be pregnant. I knew there'd be no other reason on earth for you to leave Singapore! Why didn't you tell me before? Are you certain?'

'I'm certain, I know the signs. I didn't want to tell you

before — I knew you'd force me to go and I had to make the decision myself. I'd have stayed, David; I couldn't choose to flee, not even for the baby's sake. But when I heard how the Army deceived us, I just broke down. And I want this child. I do want this child, so much! So I'll go.'

'What a cockup!' said David. 'What a betrayal. But if that's what it takes to get you out then I can only say, in all selfishness, Sav, thank goodness.'

Chapter 53

Nat
London, 1970

G anesh became the first male friend Nat made in all his years in London, and though they were quite different in their goals and their outlook, there was an unspoken understanding between them, a bond, the comfortable feeling of being able to be oneself in the presence of the other, almost as if they were brothers. After all, they were cousins— and that explained it.

They had a similar sense of humour, a similar lightness of being. They sat for hours on the patch of grass behind Ganesh's Richmond home and philosophised about the nature of God, the universe, man, woman, the human soul, and the English, sipping rum-and-coke and nibbling the samosas Ganesh had conjured in Walter's kitchen. Nat told Ganesh about his father, the village, the work, his studies, his dream. Ganesh told Nat about his father, his mother, his sisters, his home, but did not show him any photographs, which might have explained much, and concluded more. Hearing that Ganesh was out of work, and destitute, Nat got him a job as a cook at Bharat Catering. However, they lived too far apart, Nat in Notting Hill Gate and Ganesh in Richmond, to see each other often.

Ganesh invited Nat to his birthday party. Saroj refused to attend because Deodat would also be present. Ganesh must choose between her and Deodat, she said petulantly, yet was peeved when he chose their father.

'He's changed, Saroj! Why don't you just come and see how he's changed! He's just a broken old man now. He's got heart problems, and he knows nobody wants him. If you came it would lighten up his life. He's always talking about you and why you don't come to visit.'

'Is he? Well, I'm glad to hear that. And no, I won't come. If you choose to invite him then that's fine with me. But you won't see me there. It doesn't matter all that much, Gan. Don't take it personally; I don't go to parties anyway, and I hate these gatherings of relatives.'

Nat went to Ganesh's party and with the trained eye of a waiter noticed an old man sitting on an armchair in a corner, all by himself, with nothing to eat. He approached the old man, sat down next to him, and introduced himself.

'Can I get you some food?' he offered, smiling the heartiest of smiles. The old man looked up and said:

'Thank you, thank you, very kind. The young people have no manners these days. No respect for their elders. Please. I would like to take food. But that Evelyn isn't a good cook. My departed wife was an excellent cook. What did you say your name was? Are you a relative? Are you married? Where do you come from?'

Nat brought the old man a plate of cold food and settled in for a long conversation, which he could see the old man was yearning for. The old man's eyes lit up when he heard Nat was from India.

'From Tamil Nad? What? My departed wife was from there too! Tell me, do you speak any Hindi?'

The rest of the conversation, which continued all evening, was in Hindi.

Nat grew strong and silent. He gave his full attention to medicine, cutting off almost all other activities. He no longer worked for Bharat Catering, for he had no time at this stage of his education. However, he did find time to visit the old man he had met at Ganesh's birthday party. That old man — it turned out that he was actually Ganesh's father — delighted in his company, for kindness and attention were qualities he sorely missed, and which came naturally to Nat. Nobody listened to Deodat these days; nobody cared, except that young man whose warmth and consideration could melt icebergs.

The old man spoke of the loved ones he had lost: the wife to death, the daughter to hatred. He spoke of the grave mistakes he had made in his life, and of the burning guilt that ate at his innards day after day, of the vengeful God who granted no relief.

'I am a cruel man, a wicked man,' the old man wailed. 'I pray daily to God for forgiveness but there is none. He has taken my loved ones from me in punishment. I only long for death to release me from this vale of sorrow. He granted me a saint for a wife but I sinned against her gravely. A woman pure as a lily whom I sullied with my harshness and thus God removed her from me and took her to Himself. Oh, if only He would take me to Himself ! But I have an unmarried daughter. The duty of a father is to see his daughters married. If I die before my daughter marries I will not have done my duty. But she will not marry a man of my choice. She hates me, and it is through my own doing, my own harshness. How can I tell her I was only harsh through an abundance of love?'

And Nat held the old man's hand and soothed him and told him of India, spoke to him in Hindi, and now and then made the old man laugh, and healing flowed into the old man's heart.

'You and the old man get on famously,' Ganesh commented. 'What on earth do the two of you talk about?'

'Oh, just things,' said Nat.

'You are a good boy, a very good boy,' Deodat Roy told Nat. He took Nat's young brown hand in his own old shrivelled one and squeezed it. 'Your mother must be very proud of you. She has raised you well. You are like my son Ganesh. The only son of my second wife. He is a good boy, too. A well-raised boy. He comes to see me and cares for me like a dutiful son. All my other sons are indifferent and cruel to an old man, they and their wives. My unmarried daughter too has no sense of duty. She has left me in the lurch. But I deserve it, oh I deserve it. I am a wicked, evil man and I pray that God will forgive me at the moment I leave this world. That is my only prayer.'

So Deodat Roy rambled on, and Nat came to listen to him rambling, and the old man found some measure of peace.

Chapter 54

Savitri
Singapore, 1942

On Friday the thirteenth February 1942, Savitri left Singapore on the Dutch ship *Vreed-en-Hoop*. David was working at the Alexandra, and could not accompany her to the dock.

Late that very night, after they had sailed, Savitri ran into an English nurse on the deck, a colleague of hers at the General, Molly, married to another Alexandra doctor. Molly was in a state of shock.

'Oh, Savitri, it was terrible, just terrible. You know, I wanted so much to pay a last visit to the hospital this morning, to say a last goodbye to William. I was there, Sav, and ... and the Japanese came... a group of them..'

Savitri's eyes opened wide. 'They came? To the hospital?'

'Yes! I — I was able to hide... William hid me in a closet and I stayed there until it was all over. But oh, Sav...'

Tears budded in her eyes, and her shoulders heaved. Savitri laid her hands on them, to steady her.

'Go on, Molly. Tell me the rest. What did the Japs do? Did they capture everyone? Was — was there any violence?' Yet she knew, she knew from Molly's face and her tears and the shaking shoulders that her words were wishful thinking. There was more.

'Oh, Say! They massacred everyone! Everyone!'

Molly burst into tears now. Savitri drew her close and held her.

Oh Lord. Oh Lord, don't let it be. Please don't let it be. She'll tell me he's safe, in a moment. He must be. She slid behind the cloud of thoughts into the still silent core of her being, slipping into a stronghold of spirit that held her and Molly. Coolness and detachment permeated her. Molly stopped sobbing, then began again, the words stuttered out between the sobs.

'There were curtains, no door to the closet. I was able to look between them, Sav. They were grinning! They were actually grinning; they *enjoyed* it! Oh, the screams! And blood and gore. And they were laughing, those Japs, and they killed all our people... they bayoneted them. Every last one. William's dead. I saw him being killed. Bayoneted through the heart.'

Savitri felt the coolness slipping out again, seeping away, down her body, down into the boards of the deck, leaving her alone, and unprotected, before the truth of Molly's words.

'And David? Dr Lindsay? Was he there? Did he escape?'

Molly looked at her with deep pity spilling from her eyes. 'You were lovers, weren't you? I always thought so. Savitri!' She took hold of Savitri's arms. The tables had turned; now Molly was the comforter, Savitri slowly dissolving.

'David is dead. I saw him. I saw them kill him. They herded some of the staff into a corridor, David was among them. Their hands were up, Sav! They had surrendered! And David... I saw a Jap drive a bayonet into his heart, laughing! And when he fell, another one into his arm, and into his foot. They kicked him, and he didn't move because he was dead. They killed him, Savitri. They killed every single patient, doctor, nurse, orderly. They raped some nurses before killing them. They slashed the matron's neck. They're all dead. Every single one of them. The Japanese killed them. I was lucky to get out alive.'

She wanted to say she was sorry, to comfort Savitri, to hold her. But Savitri had slipped to the deck in a dead faint.

The *Vreed-en-Hoop* was routed to pass through the Bangka Strait. The Japanese were waiting for them, with their torpedoes. Savitri's ship went down. She was rescued in a lifeboat, arrived safely on a small island where the islanders took her to Java. From there she sailed safely to Colombo, and on to Madras. She collapsed on Henry and June's doorstep.

'David is dead,' she said.

Chapter 55

Saroj
London, 1970

Trixie frowned from behind her easel, stood back and cocked her head. It was the final touch to her latest and best painting, which she wanted to have finished before the wedding, as her gift for Ganesh; and he was not allowed to see it, just as he had not seen any of those paintings lined up facing the wall, like naughty children in detention.

But five minutes later, standing back and squinting and deciding that was enough for the day, Trixie carefully placed a cloth over the easel and began to clean her brushes. Only then she looked up at Ganesh and smiled. Sometimes, she thought, I can't believe it. I can't believe he's back, he's here, and he's mine. She had Saroj to thank for that. Saroj had played an excellent cupid, working over time to bring them together again ever since Ganesh's return from India. Then Trixie's birthday: dinner for three at an Indian restaurant.

The next day, Ganesh had stood on Trixie's threshold with a bunch of seven red roses in his hand. Three years earlier disaster had torn him away from her; Ma's death had fallen like an axe into the fledgling love she had borne for him. But three years ago she had been a little girl, and he had never even noticed her as anything but his sister's madcap friend. In those three years she had grown into a woman; her zaniness had morphed into creativity, a gift that had matured and rounded her into a young woman of substance. Meeting again in London, their shared background had drawn them together with a swiftness and sureness that surprised them both. And now Trixie painted, Ganesh cooked, and both loved. The doorbell rang.

'Saroj!'

'Trixie! I haven't seen you in an age! My goodness, you've changed, let me have a look at you!'

Saroj stood back and took in the young lady standing before her, whom she hadn't seen for half a year. Saroj and Trixie had made the disappointing discovery that though they still lived in the same country, and for the last few weeks in the same city, they might just as well have lived at two opposite ends of the world, for they hardly ever saw each other. The last time had been at Christmas, when Trixie had visited her father and stepmother for a few days before shooting off for a skiing holiday in Austria. Over Easter she had visited a school friend in Scotland; in the summer she had been with her family to the South of France and then joined another group of school-friends for a camping trip in Ireland. In between times she attended art school in Paris. Trixie had matured: gone, the awkward coltishness of an unhappy schoolgirl searching for herself. She had turned into a svelte, relaxed, confident young woman, at home in her own skin and wherever she happened to be.

Like Saroj she had gone through the painful steps of shedding one culture to take on another, and yet never quite shedding the one, and never quite adopting the other. Both had learned the essential lesson: there is a *me* that exists beyond the boundaries of being English, or African, or Indian, or Guyanese; and both, in their separate ways, were struggling forward on the road to becoming that one-and-only me, more than the sum of all that had gone before, more than the sum of the parts given them by where they had lived, and among whom, and what they had done, and what they had felt till now.

Not without help, of course.

Trixie's father had spared no costs in remodelling the attic into a studio for his daughter, an open, light-flooded space. One corner was partitioned off for her work area, another for a bedroom, and yet another for a kitchen from which Ganesh now emerged, bending his head so as not to hit it against a thick black beam, a smudgy dishcloth slung around his hips and tucked into his waistband.

'Hello, little sister!' he said, folding Saroj into his arms. 'Just like old times, huh, the three of us together?'

Ganesh had also changed visibly. Having a steady girlfriend had not only brought order into his life: it had neatened him up so that his hair, though still long, looked clean and combed, and his clothes — though still no more respectable than jeans and a T-shirt with some silly slogan on it Saroj didn't even bother to read — were clean. Surprisingly so, since Ganesh himself was responsible for laundry as well as cooking, whereas Trixie looked after order, because she wouldn't allow anyone else to touch her paints and utensils, all of which took up the greater part of the room. All around the low wall at the foot of the eaves were her naughty children facing the wall. The one painting on an easel was covered with a cloth. Saroj walked over to it.

'Can I see your latest masterpiece?' she said casually and was just about to remove the cloth when Trixie sprang before her with outstretched arms which she waved violently in Saroj's face, and cried out anxiously, 'No, no, no!'

Ganesh grabbed his sister back into his arms and laid a protective, excusing arm around her. 'Nobody gets to see Trixie's masterpieces until the day of the Great Unveiling,' he said proudly. 'And when she's ready she'll have the whole world staggering, wondering what hit it!'

'She's that good, is she? Who'd have guessed it of our little clown?' Saroj laughed and looked fondly at Trixie. Trixie grinned in embarrassment at her, but then frowned critically, took her by the shoulder and turned her around.

'You're looking pale, Saroj, as if you haven't seen the sun for ages. You study too much, you know. The world won't fall apart if you don't win the Nobel Prize. Ganesh, we have to take this girl in hand, she's getting so dreary… All work and no play…' She glanced at Ganesh, who had laid his arm across Saroj's shoulder again, and gave him her unforgettably tender grin, 'We've got to see more of each other. We didn't come to England together only to drift apart. How's your love-life, girl? Any heart-broken prospects kneeling at your door? Oh, and talking about heartbroken, Ganesh's got news for you . . .'

Saroj turned questioning eyes up at Ganesh. He squeezed her and a grave shadow passed over his face.

'Yes, well, it's about Baba,' he began, and Saroj pulled away.

'Don't tell me about Baba,' she said, 'or you'll spoil my whole evening.'

'No, Saroj, really, listen to what he has to say,' said Trixie.

'What, then?' Saroj grudgingly turned back to Ganesh, but she had visibly stiffened and did her best to look bored.

'Saroj, you shouldn't hate him like that,' said Ganesh. 'He's your father, after all, and...'

'No, he's not!'

'What d'you mean, he's not? Of course he is! Even if you hate him he's still your father and you can't change that!'

'You mean, you haven't told him?' Saroj looked accusingly at Trixie.

'Told him what, for goodness' sakes? Oh... Oh, *that.*' Trixie tossed her head. 'You know, it never occurred to me to tell him; in fact I'd even forgotten! Believe me, Ganesh and I had better things to do than to talk about your mother's love affairs. That whole business is just like a storm in a teacup now. And anyway, it's *your* business to tell him, not mine. Me, I never get mixed up in family politics.'

'What business?' said Ganesh. 'What's going on?'

He looked at Saroj for an answer, whose face was at least serious, whereas Trixie, not understanding the family honour that was about to be shattered, was grinning wickedly as if the whole matter was just another snippet of market gossip.

Saroj bit her lip. Of course, Trixie had not told Ganesh, and of course, she shouldn't have told him, and of course, Ganesh shouldn't know. Ganesh had worshipped his mother; and now there was no way out of telling him the truth. Saroj herself had needed tragedy, mourning, guilt, grief, in order to deal with the fact of her mother's infidelity and of Deodat's false paternity; and though Ganesh wasn't affected by the latter certainly the former would appal him, crush him... and for no reason. There was no need for Ganesh to know; why shouldn't he retain his memory of Ma, the perfect wife and mother? It made no sense to tell him.

'So?' said Ganesh, waiting.

'It's true,' Saroj's voice was small, subdued. 'Baba isn't really my father. Ma had an affair and that's how she got me. I wasn't going to tell you but somehow it slipped out.'

She looked up at him with pleading eyes. 'But it doesn't matter at all, Ganesh, truly it doesn't! I found out years ago and at first I was dismayed and I hated Ma for doing that, most of all for lying to me about it; well, not lying exactly but for letting me believe Baba was really my father, for letting a stranger control my life. But now I know she had no choice but to hide it from us all and it doesn't matter. In fact, I'm glad if she had someone she could really truly love. I'm sure she must have loved that man with all her heart, and good for her!'

It was the first time Saroj had put it into words and she was surprised at herself; but it was true. If Ma had loved someone, if she had known true love, then good for her! If she'd had a child with that someone, then good for her! And if that someone was Balwant — Ma had made a good choice. Saroj wondered if she should let Ganesh in on that little secret but before she could come to any conclusion Ganesh's wild laugh broke it up.

'Ma, with a secret lover?' He cried out through his laughter. Ganesh threw himself onto the couch.

'Ma with a secret lover!' And then, as suddenly as it had begun, the laughter stopped, and Ganesh turned steely eyes first to Saroj, then Trixie, and said with a voice as brittle and cold as that of a Mafia boss, 'Now, would you kindly tell me how you hit upon that particular fantasy? I mean, I know you girls are hopelessly romantic but that's taking it just a step too far.'

'But it's true, Ganesh; really it's true,' cried Saroj, violently upset by Ganesh's disbelief. 'Listen, I'll tell you how I found out. It happened when I was in hospital…'

Saroj haltingly, interrupted many times by Ganesh who proved himself such a marvel at cross-examination that Saroj came to the conclusion that he really should have finished his law studies, told him the story as she knew it, omitting only the most important part — the supposed identity of her biological father.

This wildly erratic conversation had several side-effects.

Ganesh's adamant defence of his mother and his romantic veneration of the ideal of female chastity, which Ma represented for him, hurt Trixie deeply, for Trixie had certainly not been faithful to Ganesh's memory in the interval between first falling in love with him in Georgetown and finding him again in London. She had had a handful of passing lovers in this time, and the realisation that Ganesh was still Indian enough to live by the double standard of male libertinage—female chastity enraged her, and they had their first quarrel.

The second side-effect was that Saroj found herself arguing on the side of her mother, supporting the idea of her love affair, which was no longer reprehensible in her eyes but completely understandable now that she knew her father's identity; and, in fact, she was *glad* that she herself was a child of love and not of Deodat. It was only too bad that Ma had died in the interim (Saroj still felt guilt at this, for it had been her doing that the tower door had been locked at the crucial time) and that she would never have the chance to share this gladness with Ma, and, perhaps, her real father.

The third side-effect was that she concluded that between herself and Deodat there was nothing, and more than nothing. She hadn't seen him for years, and didn't wish to see him. And only on her way home did she realise that, whatever it was Ganesh had wanted to say about Deodat had been forgotten in the rush of emotions thrown up by Ma's adultery.

For a long time Saroj refused to face the fact that Deodat was ill, which was what Ganesh had tried to tell her the night of the quarrel. The following day, however, he rang to say that Deodat had suffered a heart attack, was in hospital, and would soon be discharged to live all alone in his West Norwood bedsit, where he had moved a year ago when Priya, Walter's wife, practically threw him out because, as she put it, she didn't need a crotchety old man telling her how to raise her children in this day and age, and comparing her constantly with his dead wife who, it seemed, had been absolutely perfect, a saint, and was now a goddess up in heaven.

Saroj kept her voice deliberately bland. 'What's that to do with me? He's got all of you to take care of him, hasn't he?'

'All of you' meant four sons, and their wives, if they had them; of these four, Ganesh was, in fact, the only unmarried one.

'Yes, but Priya's not going to help. And Evelyn's got her own parents living with them, and he can't move in with James because they haven't got a spare room…'

'And because I'm there. The moment he moves in, I move out.'

'Come off it, Saroj. He's changed, you know. He's just a poor old man now. I feel sorry for him, living in a crummy bedsit in West Norwood with a dragon of a landlady. And he keeps asking for you.'

'He can ask till kingdom come, as far as I'm concerned.'

'Saroj, where did you get that hard heart from? I can't believe you're Ma's daughter.'

'Leave Ma out of it, Ganesh! I mean, what can I do? I can't take Deodat in, and I'm certainly not going to go and live with him in West Norwood! And besides, he's not my father; why should I bother?'

'Don't let's start that again. For goodness' sake, he *raised* you, whether you're really his daughter or not, and he's the only father you're ever going to have!'

'So what should I do, be grateful and kiss his feet for his fatherly affection and loving care? Break my back shoving bedpans under his bottom? No thanks.'

'I can't believe it's you talking like this, Saroj! Your own father ..

'He's not…'

'Yes, he is, whether you like it or not! I mean, shucks, you could just go and visit him! Just once! Think how you'd feel if he had another heart attack, a fatal one, and died without ever seeing you again! Think how you'd feel then!'

'I wouldn't feel a thing! I told you, I hate the man!'

'And you want to become a doctor? You'll make a brilliant one, no doubt. But cold as ice. No wonder they called you Ice

Princess.'

'I'm not, Ganesh, I'm not! It's just where Deodat's concerned.'

'Why can't you forgive him? If you could see him! Last time I was there, I could have sworn he was crying because you don't come. Please, Saroj. Put aside your pride, and just go! Look, I'll come with you, if you like.'

But Saroj was adamant.

'He's not my father, and I've cut him from my life. He deserves all the suffering he gets.'

'Hi, Nat, what're you doing on Saturday?'

'Ganesh! Good Lord, I've been meaning to ring you for ages, but...'

'Yeah, yeah, don't tell me, too busy, studies, women, all the usual excuses. Anyway, I want you to make some time for my wedding. Next month.'

'Ganesh, I don't believe it, no! Not you! That was quick! The same girl? What's her name, some ridiculous thing, Trick, Trickie, or something . ..'

'Trixie. Yes, well, anyway, we're getting married, definitely and finally. And I want you as best man. That's why we're doing it now, before you take off for good to India.'

'I haven't even met the girl yet, and you want me as best man?'

'Oh, you'll meet her all right, at the very latest at the wedding; we should have all got together sometime. The two of us, you, Saroj... Well, never mind. It's this crazy city, that's what it is; keeps people apart. And now there's no time.'

'Hey, it just occurred to me, how come a best man? Don't tell me you're having a Christian wedding?'

'Well, the trouble is, she's got this thing about white weddings so we're getting married in some little chapel in Yorkshire. I don't know what the hell's going on, she arranged it with some New Age vicar who doesn't mind marrying a Hindu to a Christian, and it's all the same to me anyway. I've never been into religion, and if it's what she wants ... It's not going to be a big thing, just the two of us, family, close friends.'

'Talking about family, what about your father? Didn't he raise any objections to your marrying a Christian girl?'

'Well, that's another thing.'

'What's another thing?'

'My father. The thing is, he doesn't know yet. I've been trying to find a way to break it gently but I guess there is no way.'

'There isn't, Ganesh. I know your father. There's no way he'll approve of your marrying a Christian.'

'That's the least of my problems. It's when he sees her he's going to start pulling out his hair. She's black, remember?'

'No, I don't remember because you never mentioned it... No, you didn't... Well, okay, why should you? But that just goes to show we should all have met sooner...'

'Anyway, it's a long story but there's nothing my father hates more than Africans. And she's Saroj's best friend and they have a past... and what with the heart attack... So we're keeping the whole thing secret, at least till after the wedding, and somehow break things to him gently. Get him used to her first. We thought of smuggling her in as a nurse or something.'

'Ganesh, if you think you can keep a thing like this secret you'd better get your head examined. You, with your big Indian family! You know what Indians talk about most? Weddings. So how are you going to keep all those sisters-in-law quiet?'

'It's easier than you think. None of them can stand him and none of them visit him in that bedsit of his in West Norwood. We've got a nurse going to see him every day, and I go around at the weekends. Apart from that he's cut off from the family. And Trixie and I don't want to wait till he dies. It could take years!'

'What about that sister of yours? The brilliant unmarriageable one you tried to palm off on me? Won't she talk?'

'Saroj? No, Saroj won't talk, she doesn't even visit him. In fact she hates him.'

'Right; that's the one he's always complaining about because she won't obey him. So this poor old man's living all by himself, almost on his deathbed, and not even his own daughter's checking up on him? That's a very un-Indian thing — what kind of a family are you? I mean, he's just a harmless, slightly eccentric old man in need of a little tender loving care. Why does your sister hate him?'

'Oh, that's another long, long story and I don't think I'll tell you on the phone. Ask Saroj yourself, she'll be at the wedding; she's Trixie's bridesmaid'

Chapter 56

Savitri
Madras, 1942

'Nataraj,' Savitri said. 'His name is Nataraj. Lord of the Dance.'

'That's nice,' said Sister Carmelita, though her pursed lips belied her words. Nataraj, what a name! Ungrateful, the mother! After all, the child had been born in a Christian home, and Savitri had been cared for all this time by Christians, nuns, in fact, so mother and child were doubly blessed; it was only right that he should have a Christian name! She had even given Savitri a book of suitable Christian names weeks ago, so she had had ample time to choose. And there had been reason for hope, for Savitri's soul, it seemed, was fertile ground. She attended morning and evening services and Mass on Sundays, and read the Bible on the night-table next to her bed. It was only a matter of time before she, and the child, were baptized…

But heathen customs die hard, Sister Carmelita thought, shaking her head. Nataraj! What a name! Savitri had firmly written 'Nataraj' in the space for the baby's name, in the form for his birth certificate. Well, it could be changed, of course. Joseph was the name she, personally, had chosen for this boy, though she had not told Savitri yet. Joseph for a boy, Ruth for a girl. Beautiful names. But Nataraj ! Sister Carmelita clucked in annoyance. But then she thought of the telephone call she had made earlier in the day, while Savitri had been in labour, and knew there was still hope. The mother can do what she wants, she thought fiercely. But this shall be a Christian child!

Working in the vineyard of the Lord requires patience, endless patience. But Sister Carmelita had sown the seeds of the true faith, and prayed for this particular mother and child, and with the Lord's blessing one of those seeds would sprout in Savitri's heart — for surely that was not stony ground! Savitri was a sinner, to be sure, why else would she be here? Brought here in great shame by her brother, to hide from the world? By definition, all the women who came here were sinners. But the Lord had sent his Son just for these — the Physician visits not the healthy, but the sick, and what about Mary Magdalene? But Savitri was, basically, a sweet girl. What joy it would be to bring home this lost sheep! Sister Carmelita considered herself a Fisher of Women — fallen women. Or a Shepherdess of the Lord — what lovely metaphors one could find in the Bible!

'So, dear, try to get some rest. I'll take him with me now for he needs a rest too, he's exhausted! There! See! What did I say!'

She and Savitri both smiled fondly as the baby opened his mouth in a wide yawn and waved a little fist. Trustingly, Savitri closed the blanket around Nataraj and handed him up to the nun. She'd have liked to keep him with her, to sleep with him nestled in her arms, but she knew the rules. The babies slept in the nursery, separated from the mothers by a whole floor. At present there were six girls in the home, all in various stages of pregnancy. Savitri, until now, had been the most advanced. Now she was a mother. Again, a mother. For the fifth time, a mother, and this time motherhood would last. This was David's child.

The baby was brought to Savitri for nursing that night. She nursed him, savouring the gentle toothless motion of his gums on her nipple, relishing the closeness. Holding him, it was as if a cool, soothing balm rested on her soul. The fierce burning, the terrible piercing ache that had been with her since she had learned of David's death had at last begun its healing process. She had spent the first weeks after her return with Henry and June — as she now called them — trying, unsuccessfully, to recover from her grief. She had not thought into the future.

'When the baby is born, then I will start to order my life,' she had told June, who had been anxious to see Savitri's whole future life neatly planned and organised, and who had offered support in the difficult times ahead.

'You can stay with us for as long as you like,' June had said. 'You can work as a nurse, and we'll have an *ayah* for you, and…'

'We'll cross that bridge when we come to it,' was all Savitri had replied. However, she knew that she was an unfair burden on the Baldwins. Henry had his job to think of, which he might lose if the parents of the children he taught heard that he was supporting a pregnant, unmarried, Indian woman.

And so, early in the pregnancy, she had allowed Gopal to arrange for her to move into this home for unmarried mothers in Pondicherri. Gopal, she knew, was terribly embarrassed by the whole business. She was a disgrace to her family, she knew, for an unmarried mother was considered a whore; but what did she care? But it was too much for Gopal. Savitri, an unmarried mother, in Madras! His own sister!

'When the baby is born the problems will increase a hundredfold,' Gopal said.

'Our sons can play together, in a few years,' Savitri replied, dreamily, unburdened by such misgivings. 'Or our daughters.'

For Fiona was pregnant again, at last, and this time she had passed the six-month mark, and it seemed the baby would live. It was due a month before Savitri's, who already looked forward to the time when she and Fiona would be not only sisters but mothers together, fondly watching their children grow, children who were cousins through both sets of parents and thus doubly bound to each other.

'I am a modern-minded man,' said Gopal firmly, 'but we have to find an interim solution.'

This Catholic home had been the interim solution. As for the time thereafter — Savitri would not think of it.

'I'll cross that bridge when I come to it,' she told herself again and again as the months sped by and her girth grew greater. Gopal's son Paul was born, and then Nataraj, and now she had arrived at that bridge. Involuntarily she glanced at the bed next to hers. It was empty — the girl had had her baby last week. It had been taken from her to be adopted and the girl had left the home that very day, weeping bitterly. Savitri's arms tightened protectively around her child.

Fiona stopped dead in her tracks. A man was in the room: he was standing quite still with his back turned towards her and looking down at Paul sleeping blissfully on the straw matting of the upstairs room. The man, hearing her stifled gasp of surprise, turned, and he must have been smiling even before he turned but it was not a smile of friendship. She began to back out of the doorway but then she remembered Paul and pressed herself against the wall, hoping to edge her way around and so pick up the baby.

'Good morning, Fiona,' said Mani and his smile grew wider. Fiona didn't answer.

'Well, aren't you glad to see me? I haven't been here for some time now; haven't you been missing me?'

Still she said nothing.

'Why are you pressing against the wall like that? Don't say you're scared of me? You know I wouldn't hurt you. I wouldn't even touch a piece of scum like you. You filthy piece of dirt. How could my brother even bear to touch you, a woman who has been taken by so many men before him, low-born men at that. You are nothing but a worthless lump of dirt.'

He began to cough and once started could not stop. The coughing racked his body, bending him forward. Finally he removed a dirty rag from the waist of his *dhoti* and spat into it, inspected the spittle, replaced the rag and continued his tirade.

'You are covered in filth from head to toe. But my brother, my own brother of a highborn family, has seen fit to make you a member of my family. Well, I will tell you one thing — neither you nor my brother belong to my family. I have no brother by the name of Gopal. I have no sister at all. Filth has been brought into the family to ruin our reputation. You have given birth to scum. You English, do you know what you are? A pack of dirty rats! We Indians hate you with every fibre of our being and will fight you with the last drop of our blood. If it were not for my handicap I would join Hitler's army myself — may he destroy every last one of you, men, women and children! May he swarm with his armies over your land and may every blade of English grass be his! But now... let us go downstairs and talk. I want to do business with you. Are you scared? Very well, I will go first, you follow behind me.'

He moved towards her and like a frightened rabbit she scuttled to the doorway. But yes, she wanted him away from Paul and so when he went down the stairs she followed him and closed the curtain over the door so that Paul was safe.

He walked into the kitchen, she behind him. 'Aren't you going to make me a cup of tea? Where's your hospitality?'

She moved over to the tea and filled the kettle with water from the clay vessel and lit the fire and placed the kettle on the stove while Mani watched her silently.

'Where is she?'

Fiona swung around, staring. 'Who?'

Mani sneered. 'You know who I mean. That whore whose name I will not mention.'

'I don't know.'

'Don't lie to me. Tell me where she is. Where is she hiding? Don't waste my time. I know she is hiding somewhere. I know Gopal is hiding her. Where? I have heard a rumour about her and I must confirm it. Where is that whore? You must tell me, now. If not...'

He drew a knife from the waistband of his *lungi*. It was a small knife, but it was sharp. He held the knife in his right hand, and raised his left. With his left thumb he pointed to the room at the top of the stairs, where Paul lay sleeping.

Chapter 57

Saroj
Yorkshire, 1971

Trixie's stepmother's brother lived with his family in Four Oaks, the family mansion in a village near Harrogate, where the bride's party would stay for the weekend, and where the reception was to be held. The groom's party was to be scattered in various quarters all around the area; it consisted of Ganesh's three brothers, their wives, some of their children, and Nat.

It was a tiny chapel on the property of a local landowner, a friend of Trixie's stepmother's family, half an hour out of the village. There was no organ, but Elaine had arranged for recorded music, and when 'Here Comes the Bride' rang out from behind a back pew all faces turned and smiled, because Trixie was going to be a beautiful bride in white. Nat, standing at the altar next to Ganesh, had an excellent view of the aisle, and gazed admiringly at Trixie as she walked up in the flowing white dress she and Saroj had chosen together two days earlier.

Trixie, true to character, had managed to combine seamlessly her romantic and her bohemian tendencies. A traditional white (in this case, off-white) wedding in a church, of course; this childhood dream must be fulfilled, no matter that Ganesh was, officially, a Hindu. She'd bought her dress in some antique market, and goodness knows what century it was; the filigree lace of its high-throated top, through which the deep mahogany of her flawless skin shone, had more than a few threads snapped by age. But its full satin skirt flowed down to her ankles, the wide skirt falling in loose folds and moving freely as she slowly walked forward to meet her groom, too fast for the sedate music, as if she could not wait. She carried a bouquet of white and yellow roses and wore white and yellow roses tucked into her hair, and she held her head up and looked straight ahead, grinning very inelegantly, as she walked, her eyes like living black diamonds, shining with the great love and joy that flowed from her heart to Ganesh, who was waiting for her at the altar, flanked by Nat.

Saroj wore lilac silk, a dress of utmost simplicity which only set off all the more her own natural beauty. Her hair she wore gathered on top of her head, seemingly held in place by white roses, and tumbling down in huge, loose, shiny black ringlets. She walked behind Trixie, trying to keep up and, not seeing her friend's face but feeling the static of her emotion, kept her own face lowered, to hide the little tears that were sure to escape. She had arrived on the early train that morning and had barely met the bride's party, including Lucy Quentin who had arrived the day before and had driven up in a rented car.

Her favourite brother, and her best friend. Saroj could not, for all her effort, wear the cool mantle of reason today, because of the love she bore these two, the goodwill she wished them, the hopes she had for their great happiness together, the depth of feeling, of hope, of great yearning that perhaps, somewhere, maybe here, there was such a thing as perfect, complete love, such a thing as wholeness and an undying bond.

Marriage was a sacrament, after all, whatever the framework in which it took place, whether Hindu or Christian, whether Indian or black or white or brown; here was its blessing, and that blessing would infuse the marriage and make it strong, strong enough to weather all storms. All this she yearned for, for the bride and for the groom, who were now standing face to face before the altar and the vicar whose blond hair curled down to his shoulders.

In this complete meltdown of reason Saroj looked up, her eyes moist with unshed tears and eloquent with the depth of her tenderness. She felt like a house of glass walls, transparent in all directions, filled with a sweetness and a purity that longed to sing and soar and almost weep for joy. She struggled to hold back the tears — too sentimental!

She stepped to the left, to Trixie's side.

At this moment the vicar asked the bridal couple to step forward, which they did, and Saroj found herself face to face with Nat. Her eyes locked into his for the second time.

It might have been a moment of shock, but it was not. It was as if they had both known, long ago, had moved forward in their separate lives towards this meeting, as naturally as two rivers flow down different mountains to join in a common valley, to continue their course intermingled in one another, inseparable, for who can unjoin the drops of water so united? And as water does not leap for joy, or shout out in surprise, but continues serenely, calmly, in a much greater, fuller, wholeness, so also Saroj and Nat, at this meeting, simply knew with a deep, full calmness that they were one, and there was no other word to describe their oneness. And as the vicar spoke the words that would join Trixie to Ganesh, so also, silently, unacknowledged to the world and before God alone, Saroj and Nat met for just a moment in one perfect unity of souls.

Saroj found herself outside the chapel in a mélange of people talking and congratulating, with herself at the periphery of madness: Trixie's face always present, wreathed in smiles, Gopal grabbing her hand and pushing her into a group photo, Lucy Quentin wanting to say hello, and somewhere at the back of it all, Nat's soft eyes ever on her. Swirling emotions, and reason struggling to take command, reaching through the indefinable, precarious, vacillating waves of feeling that now, after the perfect calm of union, threatened to overcome and overthrow her.

She found herself in the back seat of a car, next to strangers. The car gliding into the driveway of a luxurious garden, at the end of which other cars were already parked before a stately, ivy-covered mansion. People emerging from the cars and milling around on an emerald lawn. Ganesh and Trixie posing for another photograph before a towering red explosion of roses growing up a pergola. Standing next to Nat for another photo, not looking, pulled away, meeting people, shaking hands, smile frozen, thoughts frozen.

Through the crowd, Nat smiling, looking her way. Those

eyes! Waiters in white jackets walking around with tall glasses of champagne precariously balanced on small round trays. Trixie's dad, deep in conversation with Lucy Quentin, his wife Elaine buzzing around introducing everyone to everyone else. Hordes of Trixie's old schoolmates with their own partners, gathering in giggling, squealing groups like on the first day of term. Those eyes again. Gan's hippie friends in headbands and bell-bottoms and flowing Indian skirts. Everyone gay and frolicsome and even the sunshine sparkling with unusual brilliance and the sky's blue richer than ever before. White people, brown, black and yellow. A day etched in vivid light and colour but Saroj, she, sloshing through a murky, rain-drenched turmoil. And then again those eyes, through the crowd.

Saroj fled unseen into the house, up the stairs and into the bathroom, locked the door. She plumped herself onto the toilet seat and buried her face in her hands. For a space of only a second, the space between two thoughts, in the first meeting of eyes, she had known perfect peace — the stillness at the centre of a cyclone. But once thrown out of that stillness she was helpless, pitched out of herself, like a leaf tossed about in a hurricane.

She tried to get a grip on herself. But who was *herself?* Who was that person she had to get a grip on? Where did she begin, where did she end? Where was her substance, her identity? Was she thoughts, feelings, that moment of stillness, this storm, this upheaval, this wild churning of emotion, this giant hand of a *no* raising up and pushing it all away, but in vain?

She hid in the bathroom for an hour. She heard voices calling her, someone knocked on the door, tried the handle, left. She waited. Calmed down. Then she stood up, splashed her face with cold water, looked at herself in the mirror as if there she could find herself; saw nothing but a frightened little girl. She ran down the stairs without meeting anyone, into the kitchen. Elaine was there.

'Saroj! Trixie's been looking for you, where on earth . . .'

'Elaine, tell her I've left, please. Tell her I feel sick, I'm going home.'

'But wait, why? You can lie down upstairs, wait, Saroj, don't . . .'

But Saroj was already out of the door, gathering her confusion like the folds of her long skirt, down the driveway at a running walk.

Half-afraid they'd come to get her, she waited fretfully for the next train south, ears pricked for the slamming of car doors on the road outside, hands fitfully opening and snapping shut her purse. Somewhere, a little lonely voice cried out to be forcibly swept up and carried off — by Nat. But it was just one tiny pleading flute of a voice.

Later, safely on her seat in the departing train, she relaxed enough to look down at herself and realise: she was still wearing her lilac maid-of-honour's dress. Her travelling clothes hung tidily in her room at Four Oaks, where only a few hours previously, untypically full of joyful expectancy, she had stepped out of them and into Trixie's once-in-a-lifetime fairy-tale wedding.

Chapter 58

Saroj
London, 1971

S aroj, you're a fool. I'm telling you for the last time: I didn't plan this. I didn't plan anything! I'd forgotten about Gopal and his plans to marry you to Nat — believe me, for once! And give the guy a chance, for goodness' sake! Nat isn't your common or garden drooling-eyed fan. If you'd just for one minute lay down your arms you'd see.'

'Gan, would you just stop interfering? Mind your own business for a change instead of sticking your nose into what doesn't concern you?'

'Well, according to your theory, this does concern me. You're looking for a scapegoat to pin your confusion on and you've chosen me. Well, let me tell you something: I happen to know Nat a whole lot better than you do, and if you prefer to act the offended little Snow Queen it's your loss, not his. And I'll tell you something else, Saroj. Snow Queen's a compliment. What you're turning into is a common, or garden, bitch.'

'You — you —'

'You're not what you used to be. Okay, you always had an acid tongue but there was always something basically — well, just basically good about you. That always shone through. And, yes, I did sort of hope for a while that you and Nat could get together because if I ever met a fellow with a heart of gold, then it's him, and that's what I wanted for you. But that wasn't the reason he was where he was on Saturday. He was there because he really is the *best man* I know; I wanted him for me, for us, Trixie and me, not for *you*. Remember, it was *our* day. We weren't thinking of you and Nat meeting. We weren't matchmaking.

The world doesn't revolve around you, you know. Why can't you just, my God, just be *normal!* The way you used to be!'

'You've changed, too. I always trusted you. I always knew no matter what, you're on my side. Now for some reason you're on his side, and not only that, you call me names, and . . .'

'I'm still on your side. But that doesn't mean I can't tell you the truth about yourself, on the contrary. It'd do you good to see yourself the way others see you. Because you know what? Remember how you used to hate Baba?'

'I still do.'

'Yes. Exactly. Then you'd better start hating yourself. Because you're turning into a carbon copy of him. People run from you the way they used to run from him. Think about that. Seems you do have his genes after all!'

Saroj slammed down the receiver.

She opened her hands; the palms were wet with sweat. She wiped them on the sleeves of her blouse, crossing her arms and hugging herself because all of a sudden she felt cold — freezing, despite the July sun outside, casting long lazy late-afternoon rays into the sitting room. She shivered, raised her knees and hugged them, pushing herself back into the arms of James's fauteuil; perhaps she had caught a bug? She felt like going up to her room and snuggling into her bed, curling up under the eiderdown in a long, blissful sleep of oblivion. Not thinking about anything. Not thinking about *him.*

He had telephoned every day, but she'd refused to speak to him. Once she'd answered the phone and it was *him,* and she'd quickly slammed down the receiver, just as she'd done with Ganesh. She couldn't talk to him. She couldn't trust her voice. She couldn't trust anything, or anyone, right now. Not Ganesh, not Trixie, not herself.

Since the wedding her mind had been in utter chaos. Gone, the orderly arrangement she had carefully given to her life: she was going to become a doctor. Making that decision had given her an invigorating sense of identity, a sense of purpose. She had a specific, concrete goal to move towards with unrelenting dedication, rigorously tailoring every other element in her life to attain it: channelled energy, no distractions. She had spent two years in the sixth form with one aim in mind: perfect A Level results. Three As. Nothing less. She had achieved that. She could, and would, achieve more. But now *this*.

Since Saturday, since looking into the dark, deep, all-knowing, all-seeing pools of his eyes, she felt the solid structure of her life crumbling away as if built of sand and gravel. Frantically she struggled to keep each tiny pebble in place. And still it tottered.

It was a battle of wills; not anybody else's will against hers, but two wills battling within herself. One she was familiar with: the clearly defined one she had trained and cultivated and coaxed into a single direction. And this other, fuzzy, ill-defined, untrained, unfathomable, like a deep unknown sea swelling within her, threatening to upset the construction to which she was clinging for dear life.

And no-one understood.

'He loves you,' Trixie had said over the phone. 'He really does, Saroj. He told us. It's the most beautiful thing I've ever heard. It's like a fairy tale. If you let this chance slip by... Look, you don't know anything about Nat. He's been in London for a long time but he's just now finished his studies and he's going back to India — for good! So you haven't got much time. He's even postponed his flight, for you. At least you could *talk* to him reasonably instead of biting his head off whenever he . . .'

'Does anybody ever think about *me*?' exclaimed Saroj. 'You're all going on about Nat, and how Nat feels, and what Nat wants. Nat, Nat, Nat. What about what *I* want? So what if he's in love with me? Why should it matter to me? And I'm certainly not even vaguely close to being in love with him.'

'You protest too much, Saroj. I smell a rat!'

'There's no room in my life for a man!' Saroj had said then, and repeated it over and over again like one of Ma's mantras. She said it now, aloud, to herself.

'Then *make* room, for goodness' sake!' Trixie had said in exasperation. She didn't know, couldn't know. Ganesh didn't know. And most of all, Nat couldn't know.

The battle of wills continued all that week. Saroj fought it the only way she knew, by forcing her mind to deal reasonably, logically, methodically with the problem. As she saw it, there were three very forceful arguments against letting Nat into her life.

The first and most weighty was her career. It was obvious to anyone with an open eye that romance did not mix well with science — and her work was science, pure and unadulterated. She wanted to keep it that way. Letting her mind grow fuzzy would put an abrupt end to that. There were people who could compartmentalise their minds, keep one area for work, another for love; but in doing so they diminished each compartment, and Saroj refused to subtract even a fraction of dedication from her work.

The second was the fact that Nat was her cousin. This little detail had revealed itself in the days following the wedding: that Nat was indeed the famous Nataraj of Gopal Uncle fame. Her cousin, Gopal's son. That explained why Gopal had so doggedly, and for years, pursued the match — pure self-interest. His motivation was not the fulfilment of Ma's dying wish — what had Ma really written? — but to get his own dear son married off.

The third argument carried the least factual but the most emotional weight. Saroj was very competent in dissecting her motivations, analysing and labelling them, and she could tell the difference. It was her own inner rebellion against what would be, once again, an arranged match. Ma had secretly plotted to bring it about, and so had Gopal. Saroj had not spent years of her life fighting Deodat's efforts to marry her off to a man of his choice, only to succumb to Ma's, and Gopal's, plot to do the same. Darned if she would. She would not be manipulated. It was a matter of her own personal integrity not to be maneuvered into such a match, and because this was a highly personal, less rational objection, all the more she had to fight to the last any personal feeling that might — *might!* — incline her towards Nat.

The only way to fight, Saroj had discovered, lay in anger.

Anger was a fuel, a force strong enough to combat her inner upheaval and bring it under control. If she could maintain anger she would not succumb. Anger, fortified by logical, rational arguments.

Thus armed, Saroj set about restoring order to her tottering life. During the day she worked at her summer job in her half-brother James's shop and dispensary. She had done so every summer since coming to England, but this year was marked by a sudden and vigorous burst of energy and an inordinate interest in the substances James produced and sold, firing questions at him, taking notes, carrying on her own private research. She worked as if she were studying for an exam. Which, in a way, she was. After work she went to the library, returned laden with books she deemed relevant to her subject, and literally threw her mind into those books, facts, details, and data. Twice a week she played tennis with Colleen, and this week she played as if tennis was not a game, but a battle, to be fought with gritted teeth and dogged ruthlessness, slamming her balls over the net like bullets.

By the end of the week she knew she'd won the battle. Her mind was once again the familiar, orderly house she felt at home in, and the surging sea of feeling had receded, vanquished. She felt strong, and strangely elated, as if she had passed the most important examination of her life. Her resolve had been challenged, and had stood the test.

Saroj felt magnanimous. She wouldn't bear a grudge; she missed Trixie and Gan, and felt that in keeping a distance from them she was adding more weight than necessary to the subject of Nat. And, after all, she had taken flight from their wedding, and it was only right that she make the first conciliatory move. On Friday evening she dialled Trixie's number.

'Hi, it's me.'

'Yes?' Trixie's voice was guarded, cold. Saroj smiled indulgently to herself. Trixie had flung herself with typical abandon into a love story that didn't exist, and now she was offended because it didn't have the happy ending she'd dreamed out. She needed soothing, and a firm hand.

'Peace?' Saroj offered.

'I don't know. What peace?'

'Between us. I just remembered I haven't even congratulated you yet. This stupid business kind of got in the way. Look, can't we just forget it, get back to life?'

'Saroj, I still think . .

'Hush, Trix. Not one more word. I want to come and visit you tomorrow but only on the condition that you don't once mention you-know-who.'

'Well...'

'Come on, Trix. I don't want this thing to come between us. You're my sister-in-law now and you're still the best friend I ever had and it's just all so silly.'

'It's not, it's...'

'Trix! Not one more word. Case closed. Tomorrow morning at ten, okay?'

'Yeah, well. Anyway. There's something here I've been dying to show you. And I miss you too. And so does Gan. Good, tomorrow at ten.'

Saroj replaced the receiver with a wide smile plastered across her face. She felt as if she'd traversed a mountain and arrived safely in the far valley; or swum an ocean, and reached the far shore.

Chapter 59

Saroj
London, 1971

Ganesh and Trixie had reckoned without the grapevine, which does not limit itself to sisters-in-law, aunts, female cousins, or relatives in general, or even Indians in general; nor is gossip and the maintenance of propriety the exclusive domain of Indians. It was a retired English colonel who set the ball of outrage rolling. In the tiny Yorkshire hamlet of R, some busybody, possibly female but not necessarily, dropped a remark on the strange wedding that had taken place in the abandoned chapel on the property of Mr and Mrs P-B. The rumour had reached the indignant ears of Colonel C, who had written a scathing reader's letter to the local Tribune, making the scandalous facts known to the unsuspecting English public. The bride had been an African immigrant. The bridegroom had been an Indian immigrant, and to make matters worse, he was said to be a Hindu; the vicar had been a hippie — was he an authentic Christian vicar? The entire wedding party, consisting of various Africans, Indians and possibly a few English men and women, was rumoured to have been high on drugs and/or alcohol, and to have ended in a tremendous orgy in an unknown country house in the neighbourhood. Various Hindu chants were rumoured to have emerged from the chapel during the ceremony, and African drums had been heard echoing across the Yorkshire moors. The whole thing had been a mockery, a masquerade, a box in the ears of the Church of England, blasphemy, an insult to God and the entire Christian world.

A copy of this letter fell into the hands of the Indian community in Bradford, was photocopied, passed along, and arrived in London, where it was whispered and conjectured about. The Indians were curious; who on earth was this Hindu bridegroom marrying an African bride in a Christian church? Investigations were made; by whom and how never quite being clear, but the results at any rate were mostly accurate, confirming the wedding and spelling out names in full. The bridegroom's name was Ganesh Roy, brother of well-known lawyer Walter Roy, son of Deodat Roy, known to be living in West Norwood. There was a small write-up in the Indian community's newsletter, to which Deodat Roy was a subscriber. There he read the bitter news, and promptly had his second, and near fatal, heart attack.

Luckily he was not alone at the time. His daily helper had brought in his post; just a bill or two, and the newsletter. Deodat had read the letter in her presence, and conveniently had his heart attack while she was cleaning the sink, on the Saturday after the wedding.

While Deodat was having his heart attack, Saroj was walking up the stairs to Trixie's studio. She tapped at the studio door.

'Come in, it's open!' Trixie called, and Saroj walked in.

It was like entering the bowels of a slowly turning kaleidoscope. A riot of colours leaped at her from all sides, intensified by the sunlight pouring in through the gable windows and the huge skylight; and a beaming Trixie, herself in a long wide robe of brilliant swirling colours, walked towards her with outstretched arms, like the empress of this psychedelic, sun-drenched realm.

Saroj rubbed her eyes and the first shock receded. She realised then what had happened: Trixie had turned around all her paintings. They circled the studio, a few on easels, most of them leaning against the sloping walls, but some of them framed and covering whichever walls were straight enough to take them. Vivid little worlds, each calling out to be approached and entered, while radiating into the space between them in a bright tangle, a brilliance so keen it hurt.

Almost in a trance, she walked up to the obvious centrepiece, an unframed painting still on its easel, in the middle of the room, the same painting she had not been allowed to view on her last visit here, now unveiled.

'Trixie. You did it!' was all she said, and stood before it transfixed, glancing up just to take in Ganesh coming towards her. She held out a hand for him and drew him to her, and they both stood there, gazing at Ma.

For it was Ma, unmistakably, though her face was turned away and only visible in profile, while her hands reached out to snip a rose from its bush, tenderly and with much love as Ma would do it, and she was going to place it gently in the basket hanging over her arm with the other roses. Ma, standing in the garden at Waterloo Street, behind her the house with its tower, not the black skeleton the house had been when Saroj had last seen it but whole and white the way it should be. Ma wore a pink sari with an intricate border, drawn up to cover her head the way she did when the sun glared down. Ma in her element. For though her face was turned away, such power and grace emanated from the painting that tears came to Saroj's eyes, and she turned to Trixie, who had crept up beside her. Saroj took Trixie's hand, letting go of Ganesh's, and placed her arms around her.

'Oh, Trix!'

'You like it?' There was pleasure and shy pride in her voice, pride in a job well done, and done with love.

'It's called The Wedding Garland,' she added. 'First I wanted to paint a portrait of her and I tried, but I haven't got a photo and I couldn't do justice to her eyes, so I've left that for when I have more experience. So this is what I painted for Ganesh, as a wedding present.'

She giggled then, as nervously as ever, and Saroj hugged her, and then she gestured to the walls. 'Take a look!' she said. Saroj walked slowly around, now and then picking up a smaller painting to inspect it closely under a skylight, now and then kneeling down to look at a larger one.

If the painting of Ma was Trixie's masterpiece, Saroj thought, it was only because it was in a class of its own. It was the simplest of all. It was the only painting with only one person in it, for instance, and it emanated something tender and subtle, which was the essence of Ma, that imperceptible radiance that didn't hit you in the eye, that you had to lean into and feel to perceive, and therein lay its brilliance.

But all Trixie's paintings were brilliant, at least all those she had chosen to grace her walls. They pulsated with life, a vibrant, exhilarating life that hit Saroj in the face, that knocked her over and left her breathless. The scenes they depicted invited you to step inside; no, they drew you into themselves. Two fat black women at the Stabroek Market squabbling over a stall piled high with pineapples, oranges and soursops, a little child cowering at the skirts of the customer, curious onlookers gathered around: you could see the beads of sweat on the market-lady's forehead and hear her shouting from the painting, and feel her anger at the customer's presumption, and you drew back for fear she would cuss you, and maybe hit you over the head with the bamboo cane in her hand with which she chased away the monkey-like urchins; and yet you laughed because, well, you were home again and could hear and smell that dear familiar market day, and fill your basket with mangoes and tangerines and a full ripe bursting pineapple, if that lady let you! You could just hear the next-door lady calling out, 'Soursop, mistress, I got a lo-ve-ly soursop today,' dwelling on the stretched out word lovely, almost singing it out as if she really did *love* that soursop.

'Come, leave those, I'll show you my favourite,' said Trixie impatiently, and led Saroj across the room to another easel in the corner.

'This is The Pork-knockers. D'you like it?'

Saroj threw her a disdainful glance for her modesty and inspected the painting.

The Pork-knockers showed a group of pork-knockers standing in a shallow riverbed, the transparent water washing white and silver over rounded mottled pebbles. One of them, a stalwart shiny black man with rippling muscles, wearing only a torn pair of khaki shorts almost falling from his hips, and belted with a frayed piece of rope, stood on a flat rock, leaning back and laughing, one hand on a hip, the other with a small flat bottle of XM Rum in his hand, holding it up to show the others. Any minute he'd place the bottle to his lips and empty it. Meanwhile two others in the riverbed, similarly half-dressed, looked up at him and shared in his laughter, one of them holding the flat round pan of pebbles in which there might or might not be a tiny gold nugget, holding it against his hip and beating the heel of his other hand against his high glistening brow. The third man, squatting, leaned forward as he laughed, about to thrust his pan into the riverbed for a load of pebbles. The fourth man was barely a youth, and he sat on a big round rock with his legs sprawled open, leaning forward and waving his forefinger. He was the one telling the joke at which they were laughing, and it was a very bawdy joke, that made you want to laugh too, while the fifth man just grinned as he rested against that same rock, his eyes covered by the rim of a wide, floppy-brimmed straw hat pulled forward against the sunshine. He grinned in his rest, as if he couldn't resist the joke, and his white teeth glistened in sharp contrast to the purple-black skin of his face.

'D'you like it?' said Trixie again, almost anxiously.

'Oh, Trix! You silly!' Saroj hugged her again. 'You must know it's brilliant! They're all brilliant! Every one of them! You really are an artist.'

'That's what I keep telling her,' called Ganesh from the kitchen. 'She refuses to believe me.'

'Miss Abrams saw it first. Remember, Trixie? "Patricia Macintosh, you should put your talent to some constructive use." '

'Yes. Well. I suppose that's what I did,' said Trixie, and turned away. 'So how about some food?' She gestured towards the dining table.

It's as if Nat never existed, thought Saroj as she walked over to the table and drew out a chair. As if he'd never entered my life and tried to upset all I've worked for. Trixie and I are friends again, and now we've got something else to talk about besides Nat. She lined up the questions she'd ask Trixie about her art and her future plans and…

The telephone shrilled. Trixie answered it, handed it to Ganesh, who listened, spoke a few words, and then turned to Saroj with an ashen face.

'That was James,' he said. 'Baba has had another heart attack.'

Chapter 60

Saroj
London, 1971

How could you hate a defenceless bundle of humanity? On a table next to Deodat the electrocardiograph ticked away his heartbeats. Ticked away his life. It was steady now, the immediate danger over, but life was a fragile thing and could snap at any given moment.

A week had passed since the second heart attack, and the doctors described his condition as stable. Though Baba had not yet spoken a word, it was only too obvious what had triggered this second heart attack. After he had been raced to the hospital, Ganesh, dropping by the deserted bedsit to pack some clothes and toilet articles, had found the newsletter folded back to the offending article, and put two and two together. So Ganesh himself was keeping his distance. Time enough for explanations when Baba was on his feet again. If ever.

This was Saroj's first visit. She had not seen him for almost two years, the last time at a cousin's wedding.

After the heart attack she had at first refused to visit him. She had been prepared to let Baba go, if go he must, to let him leave this world without the releasing benefit of reconciliation. *Who is he to me?* she had said to herself. *No relation. He is not my father, I am not his daughter.* She had enjoyed her power to hurt him, knowing as she did that Baba needed her absolution to go in peace.

She had relished her power to grant or deny absolution, had clung to it for a while, and then, over the week, let herself be persuaded, had made the decision to go, finally, to grant that absolution. 'Very well,' she had said to Gan, haughty as a grande dame, 'But I'll go alone.'

She had arrived here half an hour ago, prepared to look down on Baba in disdain and forgive him.

She had not reckoned with this.

Baba had always been thin, but now he was just skin and bones. He looked like an overstretched child, his features relaxed in an innocence so tangible it brought out in high relief Saroj's own guilt. Hers was the guilt of neglect, nourished and cultivated by a childish hatred. Baba had been wrong, from the very beginning. Wrong to hate, wrong to strike her. But that wrong itself was born of nothing more lethal than his own utter impotence. He had made himself mighty but it had been an image, a myth held in place by the willingness of others to believe in that power and cower before it, as she herself had done. She had believed; and thus was overpowered. Where was that power now? Where was hatred, where was all the past? Evaporated.

Never was Saroj so aware of her own frailty, of Baba's inherent frailty, of all human frailty. So absolute. What worth success, in the light of one's utmost inability to direct and ward off illness, and this single inevitability, death? For no man, no woman, could command death, and all power was finite and feeble except the power of death over life. What humans called power was nothing but a shadow shaking its fist at the sun. If Deodat were to slip away, now, in an hour, tonight, tomorrow, there was not a thing she could do to stop it, and this helplessness filled her with fear and with awe and with deep contrition. Between her and Baba was nothing but the moment, and that moment was filled with compassion, and her only wish, right now, was to somehow let him know, before it was too late. She willed him to open his eyes. He refused. Helplessness swallowed her once angry pride and devoured it.

His hand, now, was in both of hers. She didn't know when she had taken it; it had happened involuntarily, like the tears that now pricked her eyes and threatened to gather and roll down her cheeks.

Once more, she willed him to open his eyes. He remained

stubborn as ever, locked away from her in the drugged refuge of sleep. Gently she squeezed his hand, to reinforce her will; gingerly, for she feared to break it, so thin, so brittle was that hand in hers. Tender as a new-born bird.

Just let him live; just let him live long enough for me to say everything's all right. Oh please.

The Jamaican nurse on duty for this shift bustled in, her white clogs clattering, and with a broad smile said, 'I'm sorry, you got to leave now. Doctor coming in a minute.'

'Can I speak to the doctor?' asked Saroj, tenderly letting go of Baba's hand and placing it gently on the white-shrouded mound of his thigh.

'Well, you can wait outside and try your best,' she said in a hearty sing-song, her voice raising on the last word 'best'.

Saroj stood up to leave.

A tall lanky figure, standing in the doorway and watching, slipped backwards and melted into the corridor.

Saroj returned the next day, but this time it was she who stopped in the doorway, to watch in silence, for Baba already had a visitor. She could only see his back but she knew it was Nat. She knew, because of the racing of her heart and the sudden panic that gripped her. She wanted to turn and flee, but could not. As if transfixed, she could only stand and watch, and listen.

Baba's was the bed nearest the door. Beyond his were two other beds, the middle one empty, the last one occupied by a man of indeterminate age. Yesterday this man had had a visitor, probably his wife; now he slept. It was as if Nat and Baba were alone in the room. Nat was speaking. He was reading aloud.

Arjuna leaped forward, swarthy as a rain-cloud, shining like a rainbow lit up by lightning, his bow and quiver trembling, his armour glinting in the sunlight.

The spectators let out a roar that lifted to heaven and seemed not to stop. Musical instruments burst into sound, the hollow blare of conch mingled with the jangling clash of cymbal and the rattle of the kettle-drums. When the commotion died down Arjuna displayed his magnificence.

With the fire-god Agni's weapon he created fire, with the ocean-god Varuna's weapon water filled the arena, with the Parjanya weapon rain descended. With the Bhauma weapon he entered earth, with the Parvata he brought forth mountains; and with the next the universe vanished. In an instant Arjuna stood tall on earth or hovered above it; he was running; on his chariot; leaping to the earth; still as a rock; swift as lightning. The Terrifier shot his gleaming silver darts through moving targets and tiny ones, and his arrows swept through the arena with the stinging flash of a thousand firebolts. Drona exulted, Bhishma swelled with pride, Kunti grew faint with joy.

Saroj knew the Mahabharata story, of course; it had been told her by Ma so often as a child that the words — or rather, not the words themselves, since Ma told the story in her own words; she had not read aloud as Nat now did — and the exhilaration, the very spirit of Arjuna, seemed to come alive within her now as if she were, once again, sitting cross-legged before Ma in the half-lit puja room, Ganesh leaning against Ma as he always did, she leaning forward in thrall, dreamy-eyed Indrani resting her chin on drawn-up knees.

She started; for Nat no longer read aloud. He was speaking to Baba in his everyday voice, and with a tinge of jealousy Saroj realised, for the first time, that Baba was awake, and had been listening just as she listened.

'So, *Pitaji,* that's all for today. Tomorrow I'll come back and continue the story.'

Pitaji, Nat called him! Father, in Hindi; a term of highest respect combined with deep affection. Deodat looked as if he was melting, almost purring with contentment. No-one had ever called him that before. But his voice was as petulant as that of a child's.

'You always stop at the most exciting parts,' he complained.

Nat laughed. 'Well, isn't that how the storyteller keeps his audience coming back for more? It's an ancient trick, you see; those people who make the soap operas didn't invent it!'

'Yes, but now Karna will enter the arena and the rivalry between Arjuna and Karna will begin. It would be better if you just continue till Karna puts in his appearance. Just two more pages and then I will be satisfied.'

'Well, then, if your heart can take the excitement I'll do it, but then I really will stop, do you hear? No more ifs and buts!'

The tournament was drawing to its triumphant end when a tremendous sound like the clap of a thunderbolt echoed from the gateway. Arjuna and Drona looked at each other, deeply puzzled: for both recognised the sound of a mighty warrior slapping his upper arms, the signal of challenge.

In the perplexed silence that followed the warrior stepped forward, a warrior of long strides and upright carriage; like sun, moon and fire in brightness, he loped into the arena and stood there like a golden palm tree, regal as a lion without fear. He swept his gaze disdainfully over the gathered spectators, and brought it to rest on Drona, standing in wonder with the five Pandava brothers gathered around him, waiting.

Then the newcomer spoke, and his voice was like a clap of thunder, proud and mighty: 'Arjuna! Do not be so proud of yourself. For all that you have done, I can do too, and better!'

Nat read on for ten more minutes, and then he and Deodat debated the merits of Arjuna versus Karna: Baba favouring the classic hero Arjuna, Nat preferring the outsider Karna.

They argued pleasantly, each one putting forward his case quietly and reasonably, and to Saroj's astonishment Baba actually listened to Nat's arguments for Karna. In the old days Baba had bellowed down anyone who dared to disagree with him, even in the most trivial of disputes. Ten years ago this talk would have begun and ended with Baba's categorical statement: Arjuna is the greater, for Dharma is on his side. The voice that now responded to Nat's case for Karna was mild, amiable, and interested.

With a start Saroj realised: Ganesh was right. Baba had changed for the better, he had learned a lesson, and everyone knew it except her. Here was the proof.

She wanted to be angry. Angry at Baba, for having changed beyond the image she held of him; for having had the courage to change, to grow into a bigger, better, more generous version of himself. Angry at Nat, for being here, now, and talking to Baba in a manner that she had never found possible. Angry at them both, for the easy intimacy of their relationship, for their obvious closeness — and for excluding her. Angry, perhaps, at their betrayal of her. These two men claimed they loved her — yet seemed quite happy, now, here, cosy in the sterility of this hospital room, both relaxed enough, Baba in the face of death, Nat, in the face of his failure to win her, to discuss some utterly irrelevant ancient Hindu myth. What about me? she silently cried out.

'Excuse me, miss, are you coming or going? Make up your mind.'

The irritated question was quite rhetorical, for there was no room to go, but only to come; for a lunch trolley, and behind it a nurse, blocked her escape. She had no choice but to step into the room where all that potential hurt and a deep abyss stood waiting to gather her into itself, and where there was no way out.

Two heads turned towards her. Silence cloaked them all. Saroj waited. Let one of them be the first to speak.

It took a while for Baba to focus eyes and mind enough to recognise her. But the result was explosive, so much so that Nat laid a restraining hand on Baba's shoulder to prevent him from bolting upright in bed.

'Saroj! Saroj, it is you! You have come at last! Oh my dear, you have come! Come nearer, come here to me, let me look at you, come, dear, sit on the bed next to me!'

Baba turned to Nat and said, his voice trembling with pride and joy, 'This is the daughter I was telling you about, this is my Saroj, my youngest child, my second daughter!'

He turned back to Saroj: 'Come, dear, why do you stand there, just come, look, here there is room for you, come sit on the bed next to your old Baba, let me look at you!'

He patted the bedside and stretched out the other hand to Saroj, and she had no option but to walk towards him and tentatively let herself sit down, her eyes averted, avoiding, above all, Nat's.

She had never been so embarrassed in her life.

'Look, I'd better leave,' said Nat, and before either of them could react he was gone.

When Saroj left the hospital an hour later dusk had descended, throwing a grey pall over the already grey parking lot and the street outside where she joined the queue to wait for her bus. She found herself involuntarily looking around. It was only later, when the bus came and she entered it, and she took her place and sat looking out at the pedestrians as they passed, that she realised she was looking for Nat. She had fully expected him to be waiting for her outside the hospital. She was shocked to register her deep disappointment that he had gone. He had not waited.

Chapter 61

Savitri
Madras, 1942

On awakening before dawn the morning after giving birth, Savitri found her mind moving forward, into the days and weeks, months and years ahead. Nataraj… She smiled. He would still be asleep. She wanted to get up, go to him, watch him from behind the glass of the nursery as she had seen other mothers watching, but she was still tired and it was pleasant just to lie there and let the dreams come. Time enough, when Nataraj woke up and cried for her and Sister Carmelita or Sister Maria brought him to be nursed. They had a whole life ahead of them — and now, she suddenly realised, Nataraj had brought David back into her life.

David wasn't dead. No, he was here, right here in her heart; she could feel him as palpably as if he were actually present, sitting at her bedside, smiling down at her, holding her hand, stroking her cheek, or her hair. She closed her eyes. There he was. Tears pricked her eyes. How could he not be here? David was spirit now, and spirit never dies, cannot die — his spirit would be drawn to her, and that was what she could feel right now, enclosing her, warm and comforting. I must hold on to that, she told herself. Believe it with all my heart and all my mind and all my soul, and then it will be true.

David stayed with her for an hour, and then the sky began to grow light. She heard the noises of the home wakening up all around her. Soon Sister Anna would bring breakfast, and they would have a little chat, as always. She looked forward to showing Sister Anna her child.

She got up to go to the latrine. On her way back to bed she

passed the open window and voices in the courtyard outside drew her attention. One of those voices was familiar. Too familiar. But she realised it too late.

A car stood in the gateway just below the window, a black car with an open rear door, a driver in the front seat, and a man was just about to enter the car, exchanging words with Sister Carmelita, and she knew that man; it was her brother Mani, and Mani held in his arms a bundle, and the bundle, she knew instinctively, was Nataraj, her baby, her son, her beloved, David's son, her darling, her future, her life.

'Mani!' she screamed at the open window, and Mani looked up, saw her, jumped into the car, slammed the door, and the car was gone in a splatter of gravel, with her baby.

Savitri raced down the stairs, out of the front door, into the courtyard, the street. She raced as far as she could get before they caught her and brought her back, weeping like a madwoman, berserk.

Savitri sent for Gopal, who came to get her two days later. She would have left earlier herself, taken the bus to Madras, but she had no money and no-one would lend her any.

'You'll get over it,' Sister Carmelita comforted her. 'They all do. Think of it as the best. He'll end up in a loving Christian home, with two parents, and…'

'How could you?' was all Savitri said, and turned away.

Rude little creature, thought Sister Carmelita. *Well, what could you expect from a heathen?*

'Why did you let him?' Savitri said bitterly to Gopal, after a while. By this time she was numb with the horror of it all. 'Why did you ever tell him about the baby? Why did you tell him where to find me? No-one knew except you.'

'How could you accuse me! I did not tell him!' Gopal replied. He met her eyes and turned away again, unable to bear the accusation there.

'Well, how did he know, then?'

'I don't know! Believe me! Perhaps he followed me when I came here. What do I know?'

৵৽

Only a week later Gopal was as berserk as Savitri. The Baldwins were at supper when he burst in, hair dishevelled and eyes wide open and ringed with white, like a madman.

'Paul has gone! Mani has stolen Paul as well!'

Savitri sprang to her feet. 'No! How? When?'

Henry stood up, placed an arm around Gopal and led him to a chair. Gopal sank into it and wiped his brow on a corner of his lungi. He began to weep profusely. Nausea rose in Savitri's gorge. Not this. Oh, not this. Not Paul too! She moved over to Gopal and laid her hands on his heaving shoulders, and gradually the sobbing ceased, and Gopal began to speak.

'I — I was at work... Fiona was home alone... sitting outside on the verandah at the back. She was reading one of those books. One of those stupid love books she gets sent from England. Oh, how often I have told her not to waste her time with this kind of reading! But no, she insists and this is the result! When she went upstairs again the baby was gone! Gone! Disappeared, stolen! I must go back to her now, we are searching desperately for him, I only came to tell you.'

He tried to stand up but his knees were weak and gave way and he began to cry again.

'My son! My beloved son! He has been stolen by Mani just like yours, Savitri! How could my brother do this to me? My own brother!'

'Did Fiona see him?' Savitri asked. A wave of indignation took hold of her; and cool rationality rose up to replace utter confusion and emotional havoc that had lamed her for the past week.

'If Fiona saw him then we could have him arrested. Surely he has hidden both babies somewhere! We need to get the police on our side. We couldn't do anything about Nataraj because Mani has papers — but this is different! Surely if Paul was stolen and we give the police Mani's name they can arrest him and find out!'

For the first time since Nataraj's disappearance she felt hope. If Mani had taken one baby then obviously the police would see that he had taken the other... If they could get one baby back, then they could get the other!

'Fiona has been to the police but they are not interested. They said to wait two days. She searched the whole neighbourhood, she asked all her neighbours. She asked the vendor outside our home, and he saw the thief but it was not Mani!'

'It wasn't Mani! But I thought...'

'It wasn't Mani himself, I mean. That vendor saw a young boy about twelve years old enter our house with a basket but he didn't think anything of it. The boy came out five minutes later and the basket looked heavy so we know Paul must have been inside it — Mani must have sent that boy but how can we prove it? How?'

'We can't,' said Savitri and her heart sank. Mani, of course, was cunning enough not to incriminate himself. He had taken both babies. He would never give them back.

'But why, Gopal, why? Why does Mani hate us so?' She had asked him that before. Now she asked him again, and added, 'Why does he hate our babies who have done nothing to him?'

'Those babies are both half Lindsays. The Lindsays are English — white, foreigners. They are an abomination to Mani. It is an abomination for him to have them in his family.'

'But they are innocent! They are his blood relatives! You Indians place such value on family, on sons, why...' cried June.

Gopal looked at her in pity. 'You English, in your delusion, you believe you are superior to us Indians. But for the orthodox Hindu you are without caste, and contact with you is pollution. Unclean Lindsay blood has polluted pure Iyer blood. This is how Mani's mind works. This is why I did not want to live in Madras with Fiona. This is why I tried to keep my marriage a secret from Mani, and the birth of my son. It is my ambition that brought me to this place, my career... Oh, if I had known...'

'But what will he do with those poor babies? He won't... he won't harm them?' Savitri choked on the last words. She had used a mild word instead of the terrible one she had thought, and which she would never ever speak out loud. Gopal did not reply. Her question hung unanswered in the air.

ॐ

The back seat of the bus to Bangalore was already full but the man with the bundle headed straight for it and squeezed himself in between two other passengers who wordlessly moved aside to make room for him. The bundle was tied at the top. He placed it on the floor behind his feet, under the seat. He removed the cloth wound around his head, rolled it into an untidy ball, placed it behind his neck on the wood of the seat, and settled himself for sleep. It would be a long drive. All through the night. His employer had said it would be all right. He had administered some powder, he had said, and there would be no noise. There had been no trouble up to now, not in the first bus, though he had been anxious once when the bundle had moved and the man next to him had looked curiously at him. That was why he put it on the floor this time. So no-one would see. But in the dark who would see anyway? The powder would work for about five hours, his employer had said. That gave him quite enough time. He would arrive at the house just before dawn, when it was still dark. This house was in a city, his employer had said, not in the country like the other one. They even had a flap in the wall where one could place the bundle inside the building and leave without anyone seeing, expressly for cases such as this one. His employer knew all these things. His employer was a clever man, and cunning.

He patted the pocket on his shirt (the new shirt his employer had given him as part-payment) to make sure the letter was still there, the letter he was supposed to leave for this one. He had left the other letter with the other bundle. He wasn't quite sure if it was the right letter; though the envelopes had names written on them the man couldn't read but it didn't matter anyway. One baby was very much like another. His wife had been sad to give up the first one. She had suckled it for two weeks; she had wanted to keep it. But his employed said no. He brought another baby and told him what to do and paid him. So he had followed directions. One baby here, one baby there. One letter here, one letter there. Who cared? Satisfied, he fell asleep.

Two hours later he woke up. The bus was trundling along a deserted country lane in unbroken darkness. Not even the head-lamps were on; it was being driven, apparently, by the silvery half-light shed by the full moon. All the passengers were asleep, except himself. Something had woken him up, had penetrated the curtain of sleep and called his jangled nerves to attention. There it was again — a mewing sound, very quiet, but loud enough to strike fear into his heart. Fear, not of the bundle itself, which was, of course, harmless, but fear of discovery.

He reached behind his head, removed the balled-up cloth that served as a pillow, leaned forward and pressed it against the bundle to stifle the sound. The bundle wriggled, the man pressed harder. Harder and harder, until it was quite still. And quite silent.

Chapter 62

Saroj
London, 1971

It came to Saroj in the middle of that night, in sleep. It came as an ocean, swelling up from the deepest depths of her being and bursting the dam of reason, sweeping away the carefully constructed house of logic, engulfing her entire identity, flooding her very sense of being and transforming, so that there was only that ocean, light and warm and of a scintillating, everlasting bliss, so real, so true, so palpably present that all that had ever been before, all that she had ever known or thought, or thought she had known, or known through thought, was nothing, void and vain and insubstantial as mist; and yet it contained all that ever had been and ever was and ever would be for ever, and all life was contained in *that,* and that was *love*. Pure beauty.

She was asleep, but *that* was awake, and it woke her up, and it was still there, not a dream but a living experience. Her cheeks were bathed in tears.

Saroj went to see Baba every day and each time she thought *he* would be there, but he wasn't. Everyone else was. Walter and Richie and James and sometimes even their wives, but never him. She wanted to ask Gan, but the words stuck in her throat. She was frantic. Had he left England? She racked her memory — what had Trixie said about his return? Had she given a date, a day? Had Gopal Uncle ever mentioned where he lived? She pictured herself stalking him, waiting on the pavement outside his flat, on the street where he lived. Just a glimpse of him. Just a word with him. She'd overdone it, she knew it now. She should have said something, looked at him at least, smiled, the day she'd met him at Baba's bedside. Instead she'd ignored him.

Turned away. She couldn't expect… he wouldn't… she'd ruined everything. She couldn't work, she couldn't read, her tennis racquet swiped past balls. She could neither eat, nor sleep.

Baba was recovering. He was out of danger. He was doing well. Seeing Saroj, her daily visits, her forgiveness, had worked the miracle.

But Nat was missing. Three days passed. She'd have to ask Trixie. She couldn't ask Trixie. She'd have to. Trixie would know. Gan would know.

But finally it was Gan who called her. 'Can you come over? We have to talk.'

'About what?'

'About Baba, of course.'

'Oh.' A sinking sense of disappointment. She'd thought, about Nat. But Nat was gone. She knew it now. He'd left for India, for ever. He'd given up. And she, personally, had chased him away.

'Sooner or later Baba'll have to leave hospital,' said Ganesh, scraping back a chair and plonking himself down next to her at the round white table beneath the gable window. 'The question is: where next?'

Saroj poured herself a cup of tea, added milk and sugar, and sipped. It was too hot, so she reached out for a potato ball.

'Do you have any ideas?'

'I telephoned Indrani, and she says Baba should go back to Guyana and stay with her. I think it's the best solution. She's got the time to look after him and she's never had trouble getting on with him.'

'Baba's in no condition to travel,' said Saroj.

'I mean as soon as he's fit enough to travel. In a few weeks, or months. Whenever.'

'I suppose so, but Baba never trusted planes. He might get so scared at take-off that he'd have his third heart attack and just pop off there and then.'

'He needn't fly. He could go by ship, the way he came…'

'You're crazy, Gan! He can't travel alone, just as he can't live alone. He'd need someone to share his cabin and look after him.'

'Yes, well. Trix and I are planning on going home soon anyway,' said Ganesh. 'We could take him. We'll just bring forward the date, and take a ship.'

'You want to go home?'

'Yes,' said Ganesh. 'Trixie's homesick and wants to spend time with her mother, and have a honeymoon in Tobago; we could take him. The trouble is...'

'I'm the trouble,' said Trixie. She pouted. 'Me and my black skin and fuzzy hair. Deodat Roy hates my hide. Quite literally. And I don't see why I should...'

Ganesh scratched his temple.

'Well, you know. Time will help. If we gradually get him used to the thought of us being married. If he gets to know you better. Baba's changed a lot; he just had a shock, finding out the way he did.'

'As long as he hates me I'm not going chasing after him, thank you very much.'

'Anyway, I don't like the idea,' said Saroj. 'What about medical care over there? If he's got a bad heart he'll be better off staying here for treatment.'

'We're not going to live in the bush! Baba's best friend was Dr Jaikaran, and he's a heart specialist He'd be in good hands. And I could travel with him alone, and Trix could come later.'

'No, I bloody well won't! Either we go together, or not at all! You won't find me hiding from Deodat Roy, heart attack or no heart attack. I've a good mind to jump out on him just to...'

Gan stretched out a loving arm, wrapped it around Trixie, laid his hand on her mouth. 'Ssssh. You won't do a thing.'

'But Baba wouldn't want to live in Georgetown,' objected Saroj. 'He has too many bad memories, too many enemies there. He'd hate it.'

'Well, why don't you make a suggestion? One thing is for sure, he can't go back to Norwood. No way. Not alone. If he stays in England he'd have to stay with family,' replied Ganesh. He turned to Saroj. 'And the only ones who'd take him, that's us, Saroj. Either Trix and me, or you. And since Trixie's out of the question .. .'

'You're suggesting he lives with me? That I go and live with him in Norwood?'

They were all three silent. Gan and Trixie lowered their eyes, not looking at Saroj; A tide of refusal surged inside Saroj. It was one thing to reconcile with Baba, to pray for his recovery, to want him to live, to be up and about. It was quite another thing, she discovered now, with guilt clawing at her conscience, to take him in and care for him to the end of his days.

'I can't,' she said, and her voice was almost a squeak.

'Well, then,' Ganesh shrugged his shoulders, then stood up with an air of finality. He removed the empty teapot and disappeared into the kitchen. 'That settles it. Baba goes to India.' He raised his voice so Saroj could hear him from the kitchen.

'*India?*'

Saroj stared at Trixie, who only looked away, biting her thumb. Ganesh was back with a pot of fresh tea.

'Yes. India.'

'Gan, you've lost your senses. You can't be thinking of sending Baba back to his Bengali relatives! He doesn't know a single soul over there!'

'Yes he does. He's got a sister and two brothers, and their children,' said Ganesh. 'I met them all when I was over there. And as far back as I can remember India's been the one constant in Baba's life. The Promised Land. Baba's been in exile most of his life. He'd give anything to live out his last years there. But I wasn't thinking of Bengal.'

'Well, where then? Where?' Saroj looked first at Trixie, who still wouldn't meet her eyes, and then at Ganesh, who gazed back steadily, smiling slightly, mockingly, it seemed to her, the teapot still in his hands.

'Tamil Nadu. Nat offered to take him in.'

Saroj's heart took a running start and raced off at breakneck speed.

'Nat?'

'Don't look so shocked, Saroj. It's your own fault. You won't burden yourself with Baba, Trixie and I can't take him in, and you yourself rule out Guyana. Nat's all there is.'

'But . . . Why? How will . . .'

'Nat's a doctor, and so's his father. There's a hospital in the town near where they live, in case of emergency, and in Madras...'

'Is Nat still here, then? In London?'

'Yes, of course. But...'

Saroj jumped to her feet, almost ran to the telephone, grabbed the receiver and cried, 'What's his number?'

The doorbell rang. Trixie flew to open it. Saroj felt as shy and awkward as a veiled teenage bride at a Hindu wedding. Her heart cavorted like a hoof-flinging colt, her stomach turned somersaults and her tongue clove to the floor of her mouth. Nat walked in, a bunch of red roses in his hand. Was he glowing, or was it her imagination, or was it she herself who glowed? Or both of them?

She could not tell. She only knew that his arms had closed around her, that her face was pressed against his shoulder, that he smelled good and felt good and that in some indefinable way she had finally come home.

Chapter 63

Savitri
Madras, 1942 —1944

Savitri, with Henry's help, searched for Nataraj. She discovered she had, without knowing it, signed over the custody of her son to Mani. She had signed the paper during labour without knowing what she was signing, for it had been in Tamil, and Savitri had never learned to read or write Tamil; she had simply trusted, and not bothered to ask, for the mind of a woman in labour naturally reaches out in trust to those who would help her through that labour.

Sister Carmelita had discovered through years of experience that it spared a lot of nerves this way. Heaven knew what became of the babies so removed by fathers and mothers and elder brothers! True, the girls got hysterical when they discovered what they had done but there was no denying it: however painful for the mother, it was most definitely best for the child. This child, this Nataraj, would be taken to a good Christian orphanage, and from there he would certainly find a good Christian home, light-skinned as he was. A pity, though, about his name. She had just given the baby's uncle the baby's birth certificate and the other papers when the mother had screamed like a virago at the window, and before she could say another word the uncle had made good his escape. So the child was cursed with the name Nataraj. A pity. Well, they'd surely find a suitable name at the Good Shepherd Orphanage, which she had recommended.

A good Catholic orphanage.

Henry engaged a lawyer who tried to prove that the signing over of the child was illegal. Savitri was euphoric with hope — at the beginning. But then they found themselves up against a wall of bureaucracy. A signature was easily made but impossible to undo. Documents were signed and passed around, flying between Madras and Pondicherry and getting lost on the way, buried under heaps of other documents. Officials gave their own version of the legal situation, opened and closed ledgers, slipped bribes into pockets, sipped coffee, went out for lunch, gave their profuse apologies, let their eyes glaze over, and forgot the matter. She applied to the court; received a polite letter from the Principal Sub Judge. Another from the Under-Secretary to Government Home Department. And nobody could help. The bureaucracy dragged on. Over weeks. Over months. Over years.

Savitri went to see Mani. She begged and pleaded with him to reveal Nataraj's whereabouts. Mani smiled nastily and treated her as what she was, a woman of sin.

'Remember, Savitri, India is a country of millions, hundreds of millions. Your son could be in Bombay, Calcutta, or Delhi. He could be in Kanpur or Amritsar or Bihar. He could even be in a village quite nearby. One of a thousand villages all over India. He could be dead. How will you ever find out?' he taunted and teased. 'You won't. Never.'

He would have continued to mock but a spasm of coughs overtook him and Savitri walked out.

Her eyes devoured every male baby she saw. He could be Nataraj. Everywhere she saw him: riding on the hips of strange women on the street, looking down at her from the window of a passing bus, on the streets, the sidewalks, in rickshaws, on the carriers and crossbars of bicycles, in the bazaar, in the shops, everywhere. She found herself grabbing strange little boys, boys of the right age. Turning them around, walking around them, touching their necks. She knew she would never find peace again — not as long as she lived in a world or a country where Nataraj also lived, and where every child she met might be him, and she would not know it.

'In this country one needs to pull strings,' Henry said. 'If only we knew of someone of influence, anyone…'

'Maybe Colonel Hurst? He used to be so fond of Savitri…' June mused.

'No, no-one English! Not in today's political atmosphere! An Englishman trying to throw his weight around, to use his influence in an Indian affair would be fatal. And anyway, the Colonel isn't likely to help us find *David's* child!'

'But who would help us, then?' Savitri's voice was ragged with desperation.

But then… She gasped aloud. A sudden light of inspiration had flashed a name across her mind. She knew to whom she would turn. A man who would certainly help, for his heart was of gold. A man who would listen. A man, an Indian, whose influence in India was without limit. She would go right to the top, to a man second only to God in this country where God is all.

She took out her writing pad and wrote a letter, ten pages long, telling her story and begging for help, for the use of influence to move the wheels of officialdom. She reread it, folded it, placed it in an envelope, and addressed it to Mahatma Gandhi. She almost heard the loud thumping of her heart as she licked the stamp and pressed it into place. She walked, almost ran, to the post office. Her hand trembled as she slipped the envelope through the slot. He will help. I know it. *Oh Bapu, Bapu, please, please help.*

She no longer shed tears. Her soul was parched, scorched into tearlessness.

After six months Savitri's spirits were lower than ever. Gandhi had not replied to her letter. Inside, she was disintegrating. Do something useful, she told herself. She found volunteer work at the government general hospital in Madras, and they were glad to have her. Give yourself in the service of others, and then your own problems will shrink in magnitude. Keep on. Nataraj is somewhere, waiting. Thinking of him, worrying about him, will not bring him back. Do what you can to find him, but turn mind and body to a greater task. And so she worked on.

She held a baby who had been blinded and crippled by her own beggar father so as to earn more money; and she knew there was greater misery in the world than her own, and that sanity lay in that remembrance.

Fiona was already losing hers. When Paul could not be found she sank deeper and deeper into the slough of despond. Unable to keep herself, much less Gopal, fed, clothed, clean, alive, she had returned to Fairwinds; after all, it was hers alone, now, for her parents had been killed in a London bomb raid, and David… who knew where David was. A little Christian maid looked after her, and a Cooky cooked for her. Gopal drowned his sorrow in alcohol and a mountain of work, returned to Bombay and turned his back on the mess of his life.

Savitri alone refused to abandon hope. Henry and June regarded her with concern. Finally June said, 'Savitri, listen. Henry and I have decided to emigrate to Australia. For one thing his contract's running out at the end of this year, for another, the war's on our doorstep, and for another the English are going to be thrown out of India anyway. I've got a brother living in Perth; we're going to live there. We want you to come with us, to start a new life. There's so much strength still in you. Your life's not over, but you're wasting it here. We'd love to have you; we'll help you get whatever papers you need, get a job, everything.'

But Savitri merely shook her head.

Savitri bent down to pick it up. A letter. A personal letter, from him, from Bapu. Apologising for the delay: his wife had died earlier that year, his own health had collapsed. Malaria, dysentery and a hookworm had kept him immobile and unable to answer letters for some time. Reading her words he felt there was little he could do to intervene, but he would write a personal note to the authorities concerned. In the meantime, it was essential for Savitri to gain peace of mind. Peace of mind, Bapu said, must be found in all circumstances.

'There is a true Mahatma living not far from Madras. I will give you his address. Go to him,' he advised. 'There you will find true solace.'

Chapter 64

Saroj
London, 1971

Over the last few days Nat had gently coaxed and courted her. Like a rosebud she had opened one petal after another, hesitantly at first, for she was treading on new and unexplored ground and did not know her way; but he was gentle and he was strong, and his love was constant as a rock, and true, and the twilit areas of her soul reached out to him as to a gentle warm light, and she found words for him, and learned to transform the shadows into speech, and share all with him.

She had never really seen London, cocooned as she'd been within herself; now, Nat showed her the city. She saw, and yet she saw not, for more real than all was the love that buoyed her. Laughter spilled from her soul with Nat at her side, his eyes receiving her always, his arm across her shoulders, his hand around hers, or brushing the hair from her face, the warmth of his touch and the beauty of his laughter.

She had never known laughter like this; it transformed her mere physical beauty into brilliance, for it lit her from within, and filled her, and she flourished.

They met every day at Baba's bedside. Nat would already be there when Saroj came after work. She liked to approach silently from behind, and catch them at their conversation, and listen. Nat, she found, could beat Baba at his own game, turning up with arcane translations of Sanskrit texts, arguing him out of opinions and prejudices so ingrained in Baba's mind they seemed, to her, the very quintessence of Baba's being. In Baba's world every living creature had an established and indubitable place in the hierarchy of existence: ordained by God and eternally valid. Nat shattered that rigorously structured world with logic, tact, and humour.

'You see, *Pitaji,* I found that book I was telling you about. It's a centuries-old commentary on the Vedantic Sutras. One Sri Karapatra Swami condensed the salient points into twelve Chapters and it's been recently translated into English. It's one of the finest Advaitic texts. It says there's no essential difference between a Brahmin and a Sudra.'

'What nonsense! The difference between a Brahmin and a Sudra is like the difference between a lotus and a clod of earth! Don't play with me!'

'Yes, but what do you bet that I can refute that belief? That at the very core of the Vedas you will find the teaching that no difference at all exists?'

'The differences have been ordained since the beginning of time!'

'What do you stake on that?'

'Aha, now I know what you're up to! You're the evil Sakuni trying to defeat the good Yudhisthira with sly tricks!'

Nat chuckled, and wagged a finger at Baba. 'No no, *Pitaji,* none of that good-against-evil business! Your own Vedic scriptures say there's no distinction, I have it here in black and white. Shall I read it to you?'

By sleight of hand, it seemed to Saroj, Nat's hand, empty just a moment ago, held a little yellow book which he now waved at Baba. 'Give me that book!' said Baba, reaching for it.

'No, I'm going to read it to you. You can read it yourself afterwards. Listen.' He opened the book at a marked page. In the *Sutra Samhita* it is said that . . . Obediently, Baba listened as Nat read aloud. Turning a page, he held up his finger once more, saying: 'Now listen, *Pitaji,* here it is: . . . *there is absolutely no distinction bearing on caste, stage of life or other similar matters. Be the seeker the foremost scholar, pandit, illiterate man, child, youth, old man, bachelor, householder, tapasvi, sanyasi Brahmin, ksatriya, vaisya,*

Sudra, a chandala or a woman . . . This is the undisputed view of the Vedas and sastras.

'It can't be!' cried Baba.

Nat chuckled and continued to read, as in imitation of Baba: *Disciple: This cannot be. How can illiterate men, women and* chandalas *be qualified to the exclusion of a pandit learned in the sastras?*

Nat read on, occasionally interrupted by Baba, discussing and arguing over interpretations of the text. Almost unnoticed, Saroj slipped in, drew up a chair, and sat listening. Nat and Baba merely glanced at her.

Saroj grew bored. 'Why do you people always talk such nonsense?' she interjected at a convenient pause. 'Stop it now and let's talk about practical matters.'

Nat closed the book, turned to look at her, smiled. 'You're late today.'

Deodat stretched out his hand to her. She took it, and he pulled her gently towards him, patting the bedside so she would take her seat there.

'Nat is just explaining to me the theory of Advaita. Nonduality. He is too clever for me by far. I am terrified of these Advaitists! They would destroy the entire universe, reduce us all to one unalloyed Self without distinctions!'

Nat chuckled, and Deodat joined in.

'All this theorising is beyond me,' said Saroj. 'Me, I like to believe in what I can see and touch and prove.'

'Yes, but listen, Saroj: if this whole universe is nothing but a mental concept as the Advaitists say, what is there to prove and who will prove it?' There was excitement in Baba's voice, and he elbowed himself into a half-sitting position.

'Oh, leave her alone, *Pitaji.* Saroj says she wants to talk about practical matters so let's listen to her.'

'Even if those practical matters are completely unreal? Huh? What do you say to that? According to your theory...'

'Not *my* theory. Advaitic teaching dates back several thousand years.'

Saroj could only stare in silent wonder at Baba. It was as if a completely new person lay there before her, a relaxed, openminded, generous, affable old man, joshing with Nat, the perpetrator of this miracle. For there was no doubt in Saroj's mind that it was through Nat, and Nat alone, that Baba had found redemption. Just as she herself had. Her own reconciliation with Baba was only a part of that other, bigger miracle, its logical consequence, its result, and not its cause. It was as if something good and healing flowed from Nat's hands, turning all he touched to gold.

'So what's the practical matter you wanted to talk about, Saroj?'

'Oh, nothing in particular. Just that I wish you'd change the subject. This is all too abstract for me.'

'Well, I have a practical subject I want to discuss. Why don't Ganesh and his wife come and see me?'

They stared at him. Then Nat looked at Saroj with triumph in his eyes and a wide grin across his face, and when Saroj could only stammer in reply to Baba's question Nat said, *'Pitaji,* Ganesh and his wife will be here this time tomorrow. I guarantee it.'

'Baba, we thought, we thought...' Saroj grasped for words.

'You thought I'm a very stupid, hard-headed old man incapable of admitting his errors. Well, as Nat has just so lucidly explained, there are absolutely no distinctions between the various physical forms, so why get het up? And even a poor ignorant non-dualist like myself must remember Krishna's words on the battlefield of Kurukshetra, that the wise man remains in equanimity no matter what befalls him. So let them come and stop treating me like a senile old fool. Let them come!'

Chapter 65

Saroj
London, 1970

The papers, bundled together and tied with twine, almost fell apart in Saroj's fingers. She had found them in a suitcase under Deodat's bed, the suitcase containing his private correspondence and other personal papers. She had gone through the papers one by one, and made two piles, one to throw away, and one consisting of official papers, to keep and to deal with; Baba, having lost interest in worldly matters, had given her authority to dispose of everything. 'Everything?' she had asked, and 'Everything,' he had firmly replied. 'I am only waiting to untie the strings that bind me to this earth.'

Most of these papers would almost certainly belong on the throw-away heap, but Saroj, sighing, untied the bundle the way she had untied every other bundle.

Deodat's correspondence with India had been sparse, yet constant. But till now everything had been unreadable, all written in Bengali, except the envelopes, which were addressed in English. Of course, they could just as well throw out everything wholesale. Gan had suggested that. But Saroj had refused; her meticulous, methodical nature did not permit such slipshod disposal of material, and so it was up to her to go through it all, to sift through the chaff for, perhaps, a few grains of wheat.

What she now held in her hand was promising: four Indian red-and-blue-edged air-letter forms with return addresses in English. She turned them over, and on three of them read a return address from various Roys in Calcutta. The fourth letter was different. The spidery hand was hard to read, but, squinting in the dusky light of Deodat's abandoned flat, Saroj made out the capitalised word Madras. She started. Ma was from Madras, not Baba. But all Ma's personal correspondence had perished with her. Back in Guyana, Baba had conducted his private affairs from his office; home, he had always claimed, was too chaotic, with children running in and out all day. And it was in his office that he kept the rickety old typewriter with which he wrote his letters, both business and private, which was why these papers had survived.

Saroj unfolded the air-letter form, so thin and flimsy it threatened to fall apart in her hands. Feeling like a trespasser on forbidden territory, she read it.

It was difficult, and took some time, for the words were scrawled more than written, faded with age and almost illegible. And when she had read it she read it again, and then copied the words down into a half-empty exercise book she had found among the papers, the other half-filled with lists of numbers of some arcane meaning.

Dear Sir,

My family was very interested to read your advertisement in The Hindu *as enclosed herewith. I am hurrying to dispatch for your immediate notice a photograph of my younger sister who is a beautiful young Brahmin unfortunately widowed at a tender age, without issue, although she is proven capable of producing live healthy offspring. Unfortunately however the fine son she produced is now deceased as is her late husband. I am seeking remarriage for my sister and distance is no hindrance. Although this is not a recent photograph, having been taken before her marriage, I am sure you will deduce that my sister is a highly suitable match for your esteemed personal self. She is also beautiful and extremely homely. Her English is as you require excellent. She is also highly skilled in cooking and in all housewifely duties. Should this humble application arrest your interest, please reply to above address.*

Yours truly

The signature was illegible, but at the top of the letter was printed the name: G. P. Iyer, followed by a Madras address. Gopal Uncle.

The eternal busybody and matchmaker. This, then, was the letter that had joined Ma to Baba, the letter received in answer to the little ad pasted in Balwant Uncle's family archives, the letter that had accompanied that first photo of a young and hopeful Ma.

Saroj copied everything into the exercise book. Her thoughts were in confusion: excitement, regret, curiosity, hope, all jumbled together, but most of all the overwhelming desire to share all this with her nearest, with Ganesh and Trixie, but most of all with Nat.

She longed, as always when they were apart, for him. But now these words from the past conjured back a certain anguish, a deep abyss of unknowing. Ma was an unhealed wound within her, a wound that still throbbed with pain, behind the joy and the beauty of the present moment. She longed to share with Nat the pain of losing Ma. She wished she had a photo she could show him, but all photos of Ma except Balwant Uncle's — an ironic twist of fate, Saroj thought — had been destroyed in the fire. Nat must know this part of her life. Must know Ma. Touch the pain.

Saroj offered her wounds to Nat. He offered her the wounds of others. 'Their wounds are deeper than yours, Saroj. Come with me, to India. Come and share my work. You'll see: there's no greater satisfaction.'

'But I've only just started my studies,' objected Saroj. 'How can I?'

'There are good universities in Madras and in Bangalore. And when you're finished you'll have your hands full at Prasad Nagar. There's so much to be done. I'm thinking, Saroj, I'm thinking of the women. You'd be a godsend! Dad and I do our best but, you know, they're shy with men. We can't reach them in the way you could. We can't talk to them about things like birth control and menstruation and they don't like us attending their births. You could change all that.'

'You're talking about a vocation, Nat. I don't know if I'm made of that stuff.'

'You've always aimed for the best, for the highest. This is the highest. Believe me.'

Nat's enthusiasm was contagious. Prasad Nagar, Saroj understood, must surely be heaven on earth. Nat made it sound as if just setting foot on the soil of Prasad Nagar was the greatest good that could befall a human being; that working for the poor, for free, in primitive mud huts or under the glaring sun, with the most rudimentary of equipment, with random medicines begged from and donated by the pharmaceutical giants, was the highest honour and privilege God could ever bestow. He almost had her convinced.

'India just seems so far away, so foreign,' she now confessed.

'It's where your roots are. And it's... Saroj, look, if you love me you'll love India. Either you love India or you hate it, and all I am, all you know of me, is what it is because of India. The real India, the India behind the chaos and the dirt and the madness and the ugliness, the India of the spirit. You'll feel it. I know it. And you'll love it. You'll fall under the spell, just as I have.'

'There's a part of me, the old part from my childhood, that rejects India completely. But there's another element, it's sort of fuzzy right now but I feel it nevertheless. A fascination. A mystery, to be unfolded. And this letter, this Gopal Uncle, holds the key. I'd like to see him again, Nat. I'd like to find out more. I need to know what and who Ma really was, what her life was before she crossed the ocean and started from scratch. As if, discovering Ma, I'll discover myself.'

'You will. I guarantee it.'

And that is how Nat and Saroj found themselves on a plane to Colombo a few weeks later. Baba had been safely and temporarily settled in a small nursing home until such time as they had made arrangements for him in Prasad Nagar; then Saroj would fly back to London and accompany him over on the long sea voyage.

Flying is hovering in stillness, Saroj thought. An endless

space between past and future. All that has been has come to a standstill, doors have been closed, and new ones will open; and yet, the doors that open to my future will also open to my past, not my own personal past but centuries of ancestors, generations of men and women meeting and marrying and making children, and I am at the very peak of this process, born halfway across the globe, and now I am returning. *Home!*

The very vastness of it stunned her. Her ignorance of her roots shamed her. With all her being she strained forward, eager to absorb and to understand and to know who she was, where she came from. It seemed that a great wealth was waiting for her, just beyond her grasp; that she had ever been a chalice, but turned upside down, ignoring that wealth, and all that was required now was to reverse that chalice, hold it up, open herself, and let all that wealth flow into her.

Saroj and Nat checked into a hotel a half-hour's drive from Colombo's airport. They had a room with a balcony overlooking the beach, the sea at their doorstep, and two weeks for themselves. They arrived at night, exhausted from the journey, too tired to do more than collapse into the double bed in the middle of the room, she wrapped in his arms, their first night spent together.

Dawn called them with the sweet lapping of water on sand and the tentative chirp of a bird on the balcony railing. They woke into the sweetness of a love that was as wide and encompassing as the ocean, a love so secure and so deep they knew it had been there long before them, only waiting for their recognition, a love that welcomed them as the ocean closes around an early morning worshipper. They melted into each other as a salt doll melts in the ocean. They found each other in stillness which was movement, and movement which was stillness. Love was oneness; to lose one's identity in love was not to lose oneself, but to find oneself in the other, for the unity of two was greater and vaster than the sum of two separate parts. Two flames melted into one.

Later they swam. The water was soft and warm, their skin

golden and glistening, their eyes clear and laughing. Days melted into nights and nights into days, and there was neither day nor night but only undulating time, measured only by that love which grew and bloomed and drew them constantly closer into itself, ticked away by the ring of their laughter and their footsteps on the sand.

'Wouldn't it be wonderful if we could preserve time — hide it away in a capsule where no-one ever goes, except us? And whenever we feel like it, we could enter that capsule, return to this time, and everything is just the way it is now, and nothing has changed?'

Saroj spoke almost in a whisper. She and Nat sat at the water's edge, barely out of reach of the frothing sheets of water that slid up towards them, trying in vain to nip at their toes. It was dusk; just a minute ago the last sliver of glowing sun had slipped behind the horizon. They were alone. The beach was empty of life, and except for the blinking lights of an aeroplane circling to land at Colombo the sky was vast, cloudless, and devoid of all movement.

Nat squeezed her closer to him.

'You're cold,' he said, and then, 'are you thinking of tomorrow? Are you afraid?'

'Yes, Nat. I wish tomorrow would never come. I wish this would never end. I don't want to go to Madras or see anyone else ever again, but only be here now, with you.'

'You'll always be here now, with me,' said Nat. 'Because wherever you are, I'll be there too. Every moment of every day and every night. Even if you can't see me, hear me, feel me, I'm there. I am you, Saroj. Don't you feel it, don't you know? Always and everywhere.'

'Nat, oh yes, Nat, of course. But still. This is just so... so perfect. I wish it would never end. And it will end. Tomorrow. The minute we step off that plane in Madras the outside world will catch up with us, will grab us and claim us.'

'And that's what you're afraid of.'

'Not afraid, really. I just don't want it to happen. It's all so far away. All that matters is this. And this time tomorrow it'll be all over. Past tense.'

'No, it won't be over. Because wherever we are it's still here. Here, Saroj, here, inside us! That's what's real, and not all the things that are waiting over there.'

He waved out over the ocean, westwards, towards India. India, which had seemed like a magnet drawing Saroj, now threatened her. It was like a hulking beast that would devour her, suck her in, absorb her into itself and destroy this deep perfection she now shared with Nat. She shuddered and huddled into him. She had no name for her fear. Perhaps it was simply the awareness that such happiness, such perfection, could never be for ever, that something so precious was also so very fragile…

I don't deserve this, she found herself thinking, almost against her will. *It is so precious, so priceless. So very perishable.* She reached out to grasp it to herself, but in grasping it all she found was fear. *It cannot last,* said that fear. *Something terrible will happen. It will be shattered. It is not for me. I am too imperfect; how can I hold such perfection?*

Chapter 66

Savitri
An Ashram in Madras State; Madras, 1944

Savitri arrived at the Asramam in the searing heat of midday. There was no sign of life, except for a peacock perched on the roof of the nearest hut. Under a peepal tree a dog stretched out in sleep, its tail twitching away the flies. Savitri walked between the few whitewashed, thatched-roofed huts scattered around the open grounds, stepping gingerly on red sand so hot it tore at the soles of her bare feet.

A man in the orange cloth of a *sannyasin* sat fanning himself with a fan of peacock's feathers on the porch of one of the huts. He gestured for her to approach, and when she came near, said, 'Have you just come? Have you taken meals yet?'

'No,' said Savitri.

'Would you prefer to take meals, or shall I take you to the Maharshi?'

'Take me to him,' whispered Savitri.

The *sannyasin* rose, retied his lungi, placed his upper cloth over his head and left the shade of the porch to show her the way.

'In here,' the *sannyasin* said in a voice hushed with awe. 'He is always alone at this time but he likes visitors to come at all times. Come in, come in.'

At first, Savitri thought the room was empty. It was dark, after the glare of outdoors. The hut had a low thatched roof, the shutters to the windows were closed, and the black flagstones were cool as she stepped inside and her eyes adjusted to the darkness.

Somewhere a clock ticked; the only sound in a silence so

palpable she felt she could reach out and touch it, which seemed to fill every atom of her being.

In the left-hand corner of the room was a couch, the only piece of furniture in the room. On it a man reclined. Before the couch another man, probably an attendant, sat cross-legged on the floor, leaning against the wall, dozing. On a small wooden stool burned a tiny oil-lamp, next to which three sticks of incense burned, white, curling tendrils of scent rising up, intermingling, dissolving into thin air. Rose petals lay drying in a brass dish, along with an untidy heap of *vibhuti* and kum-kum. The mingled aroma of those fragrances, of rose and burning ghee, incense and *vibhuti,* seemed to seep all through her tortured thoughts, calming and cooling.

The man on the couch wore nothing but a loincloth. His hair was white; he was aging, perhaps in his seventies, perhaps older, perhaps younger. It was hard to tell. He was smiling slightly, and his eyes rested on her. She felt it. They were cool as the full moon. They saw through her. She felt transparent under that gaze, as if her whole life and all her agony lay spread out as a crumpled sheet between them, open for him to see. She herself could see little, for tears were brimming up in her eyes, clouding her vision. She slowly walked up to the man, raised her hands in Namaste. He returned the Namaste. Her legs trembled as she bowed; she had lost control of her body. She fell to the floor and the sobs came; they heaved through her body from an inner depth so secret, so hidden, from a remote recess within her protected from view by layers and stratums and crusts of sorrow, all of which collapsed and dissolved and melted into her tears. Her body heaved, bent double in pain as she sobbed alone on the cool black flagstones. She made great gulping, spluttering noises yet felt no shame and no inclination to shame. The tears would never dry, they flowed and flowed and would flow for all eternity, she would cry an ocean of tears, for ever and ever and still her misery would not end, it was everlasting; it was too great, too endless ever to be measured or ever to cease.

It seemed she had been sobbing for an eternity when, of

their own accord, the tears stopped. Their stopping took her by surprise.

After a while she sat up, dried her eyes on a corner of her sari, opened them. Her eyes met his. He was smiling, and his gaze still rested on her like a great warm glow. She could not remove her eyes. No words came. There was no need of words. She simply looked, and let him look, and her soul was naked and he saw every corner of it and it was good.

Savitri, she who had healed so many, felt now the healing hand on herself. But not a hand; something more subtle than a hand. A healing light. So powerful, it drew the ghostly darkness of pain into itself and left her light as ether, unburdened, and free. She felt, rather than heard, the door to the hut opening and someone enter. Gradually, the room filled with people, who entered in silence and sat in silence. The midday break was over.

Savitri spent six weeks at the Asramam. She never spoke a word with the Maharshi; in fact, he hardly ever spoke to anyone. Speech in this place seemed superfluous, like fitful ripples on a lake as smooth as glass, like the shattering of whole and immaculate crystal.

She stayed six weeks and would have stayed forever. The world outside held no more lure for her, no appeal. She had sloughed it off as a butterfly leaves its cocoon. It was pain. There could be no return.

And yet, at the end of those six weeks, the knowledge came to her, unbidden and wordless, that return she must. That new life waited for her. That she, as a new woman, must enter that life.

It was Gopal who found the personal ad in the Hindu, which he sent to Savitri in great excitement.

English-educated Brahmin barrister-at-law, widower, well-settled in Georgetown, British Guiana, excellent income and social standing, seeks remarriage with Brahmin woman of childbearing age, willing to resettle in large pleasant home in Georgetown and raise a family. Widow acceptable. Dowry not required. Condition:

must be literate and speak excellent English. Please send photo.

Savitri took her kohl pencil from her dresser and drew a large black circle around the ad. She pushed it across the breakfast table to June.

'That's it,' she said with finality.

Henry frowned. 'British Guiana? Where's that?'

'Africa!' said June.

'I don't care,' said Savitri. 'As long as it's not India.'

'I don't think it's Africa,' said Henry. 'You're thinking of Ghana.'

'Well, get out the Atlas, then.'

They got the Atlas and looked for British Guiana, and found it, but not in Africa.

'South America! That's the other side of the world!' exclaimed June.

'The other side of the world is exactly where I want to be,' replied Savitri.

'But you've never even *seen* the man!' protested June.

Savitri smiled one of her rare, wistful smiles and pushed a stray lock of hair behind her ear.

'You forget — I'm an Indian!' she answered.

'Savitri, you're an Indian, but your mind is English. You've lived among us for so long now, in fact all your life. You've loved one of us, and you were ready to marry for love. You know the difference. You know *better*. You can't just reverse all you've learned from us and bow to tradition. That's so passive — so weak!'

Savitri's head was bent. She smiled. 'I'm still an Indian, June. That means I will kindle love for this man, whoever he is, whatever he is like. True, I cannot love him the way I loved David: that was once in a lifetime, that was special, and that will never cease for David is always with me, every second of every day. So what does it matter, June, where I go or what I do, or whom I marry? What can that change?'

'But — marriage to a man you've never seen?'

'It can't be worse than marriage to Ayyar — and I survived that, didn't I?' Savitri paused. 'June, I have a feeling, a knowledge, almost, that I have some task, some duty to fulfil. Perhaps I must be a mother again. Perhaps that is the only way to exorcise the ghosts of my lost children. Who knows? Perhaps that is why I am drawn to this man. For who will marry a widow in India?'

'But how fatalistic! Savitri — I can't believe it is you speaking! After so much pain, so much tragedy, you deserve a little happiness in life, a little success, and with our help and support — oh, the world is open to you now, now that you are free of your family! You could have a career! Look, we'll help you. Go back to school. Get qualified. You can be a doctor, even. It's what you always wanted! Why risk yet more pain!'

Savitri looked fondly at her and patted her hands. June's were hot and sweaty and wringing with agitation. Savitri's were cool and calm.

'I've had my career,' she said. 'Those months in Singapore; my last few weeks there. That's enough career for five lifetimes. Any other career would be an anti-climax.' She stopped, started again. 'One of my only comforts during my marriage were the poems of Tagore. My favourite is the one — do you know it? — of the maiden who has spent a night with her beloved. She waits in anguish for his departure, not daring to ask for the rose garland around his neck. In the dawn, after he has left her, she searches the bed for a few stray petals. But:

"Ah me, what is this I find? It is no flower, no spices, no vase of perfumed water. It is thy mighty sword, flashing as a flame, heavy as a bolt of thunder..."'

She paused, as if drinking in the words, and her voice trembled slightly. June's eyes were stricken, fixed on Savitri with almost awesome fascination. Savitri seemed to have forgotten her, her eyes luminous and far away.

When she looked up at June they were free of tears. 'June! This pain has made me strong. There is no more fear. No more tears.'

The words of the poem continued in Savitri's mind: *From now there shall be no fear left for me in this world, and thou shalt be victorious in all my strife. Thou hast left death for my companion and I shall crown him with my life. Thy sword is with me to cut asunder my bonds, and there shall be no fear left for me in the world.*

Before Savitri left India she returned to Mani. Mani lived with his wife and children in a crumbling brick building not far from Old Market Street. Savitri would not enter his house. She stood on the *tinnai* outside the entrance and said:

'You have won, Mani. I am leaving India. I will bring no more shame to the name of Iyer. You are rid of me, for ever.'

She straightened her shoulders. 'I have not forgotten Nataraj. But I know your cruelty and I know you will never return him to me, and on my own I can never find him. I pray to God to look after him, to keep him safe, and that is my guarantee that he will be safe. But I will leave my address with you. If ever you change your mind and your heart and your conscience speak to you, you may write to me and tell me of his whereabouts. I will come and get him. I pray for you, too, Mani, that your soul may find forgiveness with God. That is all I have to say.'

Mani, who had been grinning his mocking grin as she entered his home, turned his eyes away and it seemed to Savitri that she, and not he, was the winner, for Mani's eyes clouded and she knew that the fear of God had entered his heart. She looked at him, and pitied him, for death was written all over his face. She smelled death. Mani would die, and burn, and the secret of Nataraj's whereabouts would burn with him. She saw it in his eyes. And yet…

He seemed to be considering, weakening. He was silent for some time. Then he mumbled for her to wait, went inside the house and returned with a folded slip of paper.

'Nataraj is dead,' he told her. 'He grew sick and died, several years ago. You need never return to Madras. Here is the proof.'

He handed her the paper. She unfolded it. It read: *Certificate of Death. One male infant. Name: Nataraj Iyer. Cause of death: Unknown.'*

Nataraj would have been ten days old, according to the

barely decipherable date scrawled at the bottom. Savitri only nodded, and returned the paper to him. She did not cry.

'Mani killed him,' she said, later, to Henry and June. 'I'm sure of it.'

'You must report it to the police,' Said June. 'The bastard!'

But Savitri shook her head. 'Would that bring my baby back? No. Mani could have just thrown the body away if the death was suspicious. Or bribed the police. And anyway, do you think they will go after him after all this time? I have no proof. He had custody. Do you think the police will listen to me, a single mother? There is no justice on earth. Mani's sins will catch up with him, in this life or the next.'

Savitri left Bombay on the Portuguese ship *Benjamin Constant*, taking the route via South Africa to Brazil and British Guiana.

She married Deodat Roy. Seven years later she was the mother of three living, healthy children: Indrani, Ganesh, Sarojini.

Chapter 67

The beast that would shatter love's perfection had a name, and that name was Madras. Not that the love itself was shattered. But love seeks to mirror itself, to see itself reflected in the world outside, in peace and loveliness and unsullied perfection. The mantle of soft magic that a Ceylon beach had spread around them had been just such a perfect world.

Madras was chaos multiplied by pandemonium, a cacophony of sounds and smells, a tangle of careening vehicles breathing stench, noise, filth. But Nat was with her, a rock in the madness, calm and knowing. Nat held his peace in bedlam, and Saroj clung to him as to a lifeline. What use are all my books, now, at this moment, she thought grimly; if it weren't for Nat...

They took a bus from the airport to Mount Road and there Nat stopped a cycle-rickshaw and helped Saroj onto its ripped and grime-encrusted seat. The rickshaw-wallah was a tall thin Dravidian, in a blue-chequered *lungi* doubled up on itself to show legs of skin, bones and sinewy muscle. With a blaring honk of his klaxon the rickshaw-wallah leaped on to his cycle and plunged into the fray, winding his way around cars, lorries, buses, bicycles, dray-carts, bullock carts, pedestrians, cows and all the other denizens of Mount Road, honking his ragged way through the medley. Saroj glanced from the chaos of the street to Nat's face. It was perfectly relaxed.

Nat seemed to be enjoying the madness, smiling contentedly to himself. A nostalgic, affectionate, indulgent smile, as a mother will smile at a toddler who has covered himself with mud, granting absolution. *He loves this crazy place,* Saroj thought. *Can I ever?*

Nat directed the rickshaw-wallah to a side street; *Vallaba Agraharam,* he kept saying, lest the wallah forget, and the wallah kept turning his head to comment, taking his eye off the traffic to Saroj's consternation. Nat seemed unbothered. He spoke Tamil, a language which to Saroj, hearing it for the first time, sounded as rough and aggressive as the city itself. But Nat spoke it with grace and melody, whereas when the rickshaw-wallah shouted back it sounded as if he were angry at Nat. But then, as he braked in front of the Broadlands Lodge and handed them their bags, he smiled as affably as ever, and when Nat gave him the fare he raised his folded hands to his forehead in thanks, the coins held together between the palms, then rolled the money in a corner of his lungi, tied it and tucked it into his waist, and lunged off down the road.

'Come on!' said Nat, and slung both of their bags across his shoulders. They had not brought a lot. Nat said they didn't need much. He himself kept his Indian clothes in India, and apart from one change of clothing for the plane and one for the city, his bag was full of medicines and other supplies his father had asked him to bring.

Saroj had given much thought to what she would wear in India. Instinct told her she should wear a sari; but she had not done so in years, and had always felt awkward in one. The sari represented the culture she had wilfully sworn off and kept at bay; but that had been before Ma's death. She had never worn a sari in England. To India she had brought cotton slacks and two long flowing skirts, which, thanks to the hippie culture, were in good supply in London. Nat had advised her not to wear any skirt shorter than ankle length, an advice she had first resented, but now that she was here she realised that he had been right. The slacks she wore made her feel awkward and out of place. Being Indian herself added to her discomfiture, plus the fact that she was, right now, confused, helpless, and completely frazzled. She followed Nat into the hotel lobby.

Broadlands Lodge was a third-class hotel. But, Nat had told

her, he had always stayed here when he was in the city, and he had reserved the best room for them.

'The honeymoon suite,' he added, with a suggestive twinkle in his eye.

The hotel rooms were arranged in three tiers opening onto the verandahs overlooking a central courtyard with a broken-down fountain in the middle. The hotel had been claimed by travelling Westerners as their Madras stopover and hang-out, and as Nat and Saroj walked along the verandahs and up the stairs to their room they were greeted now and then by long-haired men or long-skirted women passing by, leaning over the railing and chatting, or sitting in their doorways drinking *chai*.

'Do you know *everyone* here?' Saroj asked.

'No. But somehow they all look familiar. They just say hi to everyone from the West.'

'How do they know we're from the West? We're both Indians!'

'We have that Western aura,' Nat grinned.

'So, here we are. Ladies first!'

He let Saroj pass by him into the room. It was the highest room in the hotel, all alone in splendid isolation, and reached by its own staircase. Like an eagle's eyrie, Saroj thought: windowed along three of its walls, the fourth wall opening onto bathroom and toilet. Like our tower on Waterloo Street, she thought again, but cut off that thought at the moment of its birth. It was a large, clean, cool, pleasant room, and Saroj was glad it was theirs, and not one of the cubbyholes along the tiers below them. She let herself fall onto the double bed that stood in the middle, beneath a rusting overhead fan, which now, for Nat had turned the switch, slowly, creakingly, began to revolve.

'D'you like it?' Nat placed the two bags on a table against the wall and came towards the bed.

'It's perfect,' said Saroj, and held out her hands to him. 'A perfect refuge from the outside world. A time capsule.'

Later Saroj and Nat emerged from their hotel. It was evening, and a strange lustre, a bristling excitement, lay over the city. They walked, this time. Nat wanted her to feel Madras with all her senses.

'I could have taken you to a posh hotel in a shady secluded part of the city, and we could have cut ourselves off from all this —' he gestured towards a half-naked beggar crouched in a shop doorway '— and hidden ourselves away in our time capsule. But, Saroj, I want you to see, to feel, to know what poverty is, and misery, and the misery of an Indian city is like no other misery in the world. Don't turn away from it: look it in the face, and love it. Because all this is part of you, and part of us.'

He stopped outside an Indian restaurant. They stood in the doorway, looking in. Inside was darkness, but as her eyes grew accustomed to the darkness Saroj made out tables in rows, with Indians sitting around them, and round silver plates before them. They were all eating, pushing food into their mouths with their fingers. Above the doorway was a sign: Arjuna Bhavan — Delicious Vegetarian Meals. Little boys with rusty buckets scuttled between the tables collecting used glasses, and other boys sloshed water on the tables and rubbed them down with dirty cloths. The floor was wet with spilled water, and strewn with pieces of food.

'This is India,' said Nat, and his eyes were serious. 'The real India, the India of the streets. I've often eaten here. Shall we go in?'

Saroj couldn't help it; disgust shuddered across her features, though she tried to hold it back. Nat chuckled and placed a protective arm around her.

'But I see it's too much to begin with. Come on, before you throw up.'

They walked for ten minutes down Mount Road, in silence. The pavement was packed with people jostling, pushing, scrambling, edging and even crawling past each other, humanity in rags and in riches, in grimy shirts and silk ones, bare-backed and half-naked, swathed in saris, in pristine white flowing kurtas or in ill-fitting buttonless pants and shirts, torn and patched or richly ornamented — humanity, swarming from the Wellington Talkies and from Ashoka Hot Meals and from Parvati Men's Suitings and from Ramlal's Electrical Supplies; buying combs and bras and soap-dishes and lottery tickets from roadside vendors; waiting at bus stops, descending from and mounting rickshaws…

Above the chaos of the streets enormous hoardings loomed over them, etched against the night sky and illuminated by floodlights, displaying, as if in another, serene, divine world far above the real one, pink-faced chubby-cheeked heroes, gazing languorously at voluptuous doe-eyed creamy-skinned belles in bosom-clinging, seam- splitting saris.

They passed beggars and cripples and a little boy with a fortune-telling bird, piles of refuse and a mother holding out a crippled baby, and Saroj felt India, Madras, a microcosm of all of India, reaching out to enfold her, and struggled against it, lost the struggle, struggled again. This is India… Nat had said. It is a part of you… do not reject it…'

But that's enough, she thought, *I can't take any more*… just as they reached a hidden staircase between two shops, and Nat drew her in and up into the sanctuary of Buhari's restaurant, and quietude closed once more around them.

'How're you getting on?' He smiled at her across the white-clothed table, from behind his menu, and she thought he was laughing at her and her fickleness of mind. But he wasn't.

'I know, it's a shock, and I've thrown you right in at the deep end. But I know you'll swim, because I know you're strong enough to take it. I can't protect you, Saroj, not from anything, you have to see it all and know the worst, for this is India. There is no time capsule.'

She was silent. He continued.

'I highly recommend their Tandoori chicken. And they have the best sweet lassi in town.'

Chapter 68

David
Singapore; Madras, 1942 — 1945

Friday, thirteenth February began inauspiciously, with the water supply to the Alexandra hospital cut off. David and the rest of the staff carried on as best they could, trying to ignore the pandemonium outside, the screech of air raids, the bursting of shells, the boom of mortar bombs.

The attack came out of the blue. All of a sudden the Alexandra swarmed with Japanese, waving their bayonets, running through the corridors and into the wards. Lt. Weston rushed to the rear entrance of the hospital waving the white flag of surrender and was rewarded with a bayonet plunged into his heart by the first Japanese to enter.

David was preparing for an operation in the theatre block when they kicked open the door and surrounded the group gathered round the operation table, shouting unintelligible orders. David, with all the others, immediately raised his hands. The Japanese continued to shout, waving their bayonets towards the door, shooing them out. The patient, unable to move, was disposed of with a bayonet through the heart.

The staff was herded into the corridor, pushed backwards, all with their hands up. Captain Smiley edged himself to the front and pointed to the Red Cross brassards on their arms and shouting the words 'Hospital, doctor,' but he might as well have shouted 'walkies' at a mad dog tearing a rabbit to pieces.

To David's horror Lieutenant Rogers, a friend of his, was bayoneted through the throat. Before his eyes his friends and colleagues fell bleeding to the ground as the Japanese, drunk with bloodlust, attacked again and again, indiscriminately plunging their bayonets into hearts, throats, heads.

Then it was David's turn. He saw the raised bayonet and the teeth of the grinning Japanese behind it, he saw the blood-stained blade descend as in slow motion, aimed straight at his heart. He saw his end coming and spoke a prayer; he felt the blade enter and fell on to the heap of bleeding bodies.

I am alive, he thought, and wondered how this could be so. And then he realised the pain was in his arm.

How can that be, thought David, and then he remembered the metal cigarette case in his left shirt-pocket. It had saved his life, deflecting the bayonet at the very last moment. By now his attacker had gone on to the next victim; through half-closed eyes David watched the massacre, listened to the bloodthirsty shouts of the Japanese and the cries of the dying. One soldier was checking to see that all were dead, kicking the bodies to see if they moved and finishing them off with a quick thrust of a bayonet. So David kept still. He felt a searing agony as the bayonet entered his foot and bit his teeth together so as not to scream.

He thought of Savitri. *There is a way of going beyond pain,* Savitri had said, and he tried to recall her method, but before he could do so he passed mercifully into unconsciousness.

The next party of Japanese was less bloodthirsty. Finding David alive, they took him prisoner. He was a doctor, and of value, so they amputated his foot and carted him off to Changi, where he became prison doctor. He survived that hell. At the end of the war David, more dead than alive, returned to Madras to pick up the pieces of his life.

The first piece of information he picked up was devastating: in London a bomb had destroyed the house where his parents lived with Marjorie. All three were dead. David wept for the people whose lives he had ruined — for had he not run away with Savitri his parents would have spent the war in Madras, and been safe. He would never have met Marjorie, that innocent, sweet girl with dreams of romance with a man who could never love her as she deserved.

Savitri had disappeared off the face of the earth. David's enquiries revealed that almost all the women and children in her convoy had been killed, that her ship had been torpedoed, and had sunk. Desperately, he searched for news that she had been one of the lucky few to be rescued — but nobody had seen her. Surely she would have come back to Madras, to wait for him, if she were alive? And what about the child?

Through his British contacts he found out that Henry and June had emigrated to Australia just a few months previously.

Gopal. Where was Gopal? Gopal and Fiona? Nowhere to be found. It was as if everyone David had ever known in Madras had been wiped out. He went back to Fairwinds, just to remember.

'Fiona!'

The woman in the rocking chair glanced up and looked at him vaguely. 'Fiona, it's me!' he repeated, and ran up the steps to the verandah, expecting her to leap up and embrace him. But she remained seated, rocking back and forth in the ancient rattan rocking chair that had once been his mother's.

'Fiona! Speak to me! What's the matter?' He stood before her now and saw that she clasped something to her breast, something wrapped in rags.

'What's the matter, Fiona? Why won't you speak? It's me, David! I'm back!'

Something seemed to click then and she looked up and their eyes met and David saw that hers were vacant.

'David?' her voice was small and piping, almost like a child's.

'David.' She tried to stand up but slipped. David stretched out a hand for her and she took it and he helped her to her feet. The dirty bundle she kept hugged tightly to her chest, never loosening her grip.

'David,' she said for the third time. 'David. David. Have you met Paul? This is Paul. My baby.'

She held out the bundle then and David tried to take it but she pulled it back, but David had seen enough. It was a doll, a grubby-faced doll.

'Fiona,' he said gently. 'What has happened to you? Where's Gopal? Where's Savitri?'

'Gopal? Savitri?' She paused, as if thinking. And then she shook her head, slowly, sadly. 'All gone,' she said. 'All gone. Gopal. Savitri. Nataraj. All gone. Mani has won. I am scum. Dirty scum. He has left me with Paul. Paul is all I have.'

David took hold of her shoulders, shook her gently. 'Fiona, please, please talk to me, try to remember. Where is Gopal? Where is Savitri! Tell me! Who is here with you? Are you alone? Does Gopal live here too? Who looks after you?'

Fiona shook her head again. 'No Gopal. No Savitri. No Nataraj. Only Paul is left. My dear Paul.' She looked down at the doll and smiled lovingly and crooned, and David knew he would get no sensible answers from her.

He looked around. Fairwinds was overgrown, true, but this side of the verandah appeared clean and well-kept, the area before it had been freshly swept. Fiona's clothes were old, but clean, her hair was neat, she appeared to be well-fed. Somebody must live here with her, to take care of her. He went in search of that somebody. In the kitchen he found a woman, lying on a mat in the corner, sleeping. He woke her and she stood up, rubbing her eyes. A short exchange in Tamil, and he knew that Gopal had arranged for Fiona to live here and be cared for, but that he himself was, most probably, in Bombay. And that Mani was responsible for everything. For stealing Paul, and another baby, Fiona's nephew. Nataraj.

David found Mani. Mani sneered for a while, coughed, and told David that Savitri was safely married on the other side of the world.

'And what of her baby? She was pregnant when she left me. What became of her child?'

He kept his voice low, calm, respectful. He needed information that only Mani could give. And though he trembled with rage inside, he maintained a façade of composed pleasantness. He needed Mani to talk.

Mani, enjoying his power over David, sneered again and mocked while David begged. And when it became clear that David would do anything to find Nataraj a certain gleam entered Mani's eye and he said: 'What will you give me for Nataraj's address?'

'I will give you money! A *lakh* of rupees!'

'A *lakh!*' Mani laughed but his laughter turned into a violent cough that racked his body. When he came to himself he said, 'A *lakh* is a joke. Is your bastard son worth no more than a *lakh* to you?'

'Five *lakhs!*'

Mani shook his head. 'I need more than that. I need a fortune. I am sick and I need a doctor. I need money to pay for the best doctor money can buy. I will go to England, to America, in search of a doctor and for that I need money. Ten *lakhs* of rupees, in British pounds. I know that is nothing to you.'

Mani wrote down an address for David. David fetched the little boy to Fairwinds.

A week later Gopal turned up, out of the blue. He saw the child Nat and cried, 'But Nataraj is dead! Mani showed Savitri the cremation papers, before she left India! This is Paul, my son!'

David shook his head. 'He was only making sure she'd never return to Madras. This is Nataraj, my son. It is your son who is dead. Paul.' But he said it with guilt. There was the note; the scribbled one Mother Immaculata had given him. *Paul,* it had said; and *"Mother insane."* He had tried to argue with Mother Immaculate, but it wasn't her fault of course. It was Mani's. A mix-up. The child was his, and Savitri's. He knew it.

But Gopal looked at the creamy-coloured little boy and saw another truth. 'I know that this is my son. What a trick of fate! For I cannot keep him; at the moment I am without job, without wife, I have no-one to take care of him. But, David, you are rich. You can provide a good education for my boy. You keep him. I will let you have him. I will even let you call him Nataraj. But in my heart I know he is Paul. My heart tells me the truth.'

Chapter 69

Saroj
Madras State, 1971

In South India you order coffee by the yard, not the cup!' Nat pointed to the man at the next table, who expertly whipped his coffee back and forth between two stainless steel mugs. The coffee was merely a long brown streak plunging from vessel to vessel, a steaming ribbon of liquid, trapping the cooler air into crests of froth before being flung out again and into free fall, caught and flung and caught again.

A grinning youth in torn khaki shorts and a grubby singlet walked over with their own coffee, ready milked and sugared. Both stainless-steel mugs stood upside down in wider, shorter stainless steel vessels. Saroj looked into hers. There was no coffee in it. She looked up at Nat questioningly.

Nat raised his upside-down mug and coffee plopped out into the lower, wider vessel. He poured coffee into the mug, lifted it half a yard above his tilted head, opened his mouth and poured. Saroj tried to do the same but missed and coffee rolled down the sides of her chin. She spluttered and wiped her mouth with the back of her hand.

'Why can't they just do things the normal way here?'

'This is normal, dear! Didn't your mother raise you properly? One of the rules for drinking in public is never touch a vessel with your lips. You *pour*. That way the cups stay germ-free. Ingenious, isn't it?'

'Yes, well. Considering that they're all washed in the same dirty water afterwards.' She glanced with distaste at the plastic basin where the boy was now busy washing the mugs, dipping them in and standing them on the counter to be reused.

'Queasy?'

Saroj nodded glumly. She glanced around at the other tables in the coffee-house; at the men sitting around them, dressed in lungis or long trousers, with slicked-back oily black hair, leaning over the tables on their elbows and digging into the mountains of rice with their fingers. They ate in a hurry. Their fingers twirled the rice into the *sambar*, rolled it into little brown balls and popped them into their mouths. Some of them seemed to be squabbling with each other. She and Nat ate nothing. They had filled up on bananas on the bus-ride to this stop.

'Why are they all shouting so?'

'They're not. They're just talking.'

'Oh. I see.' Saroj tried again to pour coffee into her mouth and this time she got it right. She swallowed the luke-warm brew with an audible gulp and said, 'I'm learning, Nat. I'm trying hard, and I will learn. Be patient.'

'I know.' She felt his knee pressing against hers under the table, a substitute for holding hands, which, Nat said, they should not do in public. 'I told you: you either love India or you hate it. You can even do both together. I've shown you the part it's easy to hate. The other part comes later.'

Nat and Saroj arrived at the town and descended into yet another swirling mass of madness, a strident dissonance of yelling rickshaw-wallahs and blaring klaxons. All she could do was cling to Nat's side, to close eyes and ears to the bedlam and focus on his calm presence, let him lead her through the fray. She found herself next to him in a rickshaw, careening through the thronged streets converging on the bus station. Nat held her hand. She squeezed it, and gathered strength, and looked at him. His eyes anchored her. She leaned into him. *I can! I will! For his sake, and for the sake of love! This is a test, and I will stand it!*

The rickshaw-wallah drove them as if they were royalty. As they entered the village he pressed the klaxon and its steady honking drew the mothers from their huts and they stood on the roadside waving, and the children jumped up from their games, and the men turned their heads to look.

They arrived at David's home accompanied by a gaggle of half-naked boys and girls running beside the rickshaw and screaming, *'Daktah tamby, daktah tamby, daktah tamby!'*

Nat was in high spirits, laughing with the children, leaning out of the rickshaw to clasp this hand or that, calling them by name. A little boy leaped onto the running board and Nat pulled him backwards and into his lap, pinched his cheek, and the boy threw his arms around Nat and spoke to him in that strange language Nat shared with all these people, and Nat answered in that same language, shutting her out.

A white man in a white lungi stood in an open gateway, under a wide wooden arch on which was written in English and in Tamil, Prasad Nagar. The man approached the rickshaw and lifted out the little boy and Nat fell into his arms. It must be his father, Saroj thought, but in the next moment Nat was on the ground beside him and helping her out and saying, 'Saroj, this is Henry. Henry, this is the big surprise I wrote you about. Where's Dad?' He offered Saroj a hand and ushered her towards another gate, opposite Henry's.

'David's in Town, Nat. He's with a patient in the hospital. He'll probably want to stay for the operation — I don't expect him back before tonight.'

Nat's face fell. He smiled at Saroj, touched her elbow, and signalled for her to walk down a sandy path between high trellis walls. Giant bougainvilleas grew up the lattice-work. Their branches snaked up through the trellis, forming a shady tunnel of luxurious foliage.

The children tried to follow, but Henry shooed them away resolutely and closed the gate on them, rather rudely, Saroj thought. But the children didn't seem to mind. They swarmed up the gate and sat on its upper bar, still grinning and calling, while the smallest pressed their little faces against the bars and peered inside the yard, watching as Henry, Nat and Saroj stopped at the edge of the verandah and Nat and Saroj removed their sandals. Nat turned on a tap and gestured for Saroj to wash her feet. The water was cool and soothing on her tired dusty feet, and she let it wash over them for longer than was necessary.

She was overwhelmed by Nat's welcome. He is at home, she thought — absorbed again into this community which is the soil that nourished him and made him what he is. I am outside it, a stranger. She heard Nat and Henry's easy banter as they waited for her to finish washing her feet: Nat telling Henry about their holiday in Ceylon, Henry's questions, Nat's answers. She heard without listening. She was listening to herself.

He is home, and I am a stranger. Look how they love him! He knows them, they know him, they are all a part of him. I will never fit in. True, it was quiet here, at this house. It was just like home, like Ma's garden, that arch of towering bougainvilleas; pretty, and clean, not like Madras. This was yet another India. Nat's India. But still she was a stranger. *They won't want me here! He's only got eyes for this Henry. He's ignoring me. What shall I do? What am I doing here?*

Then she moved aside and let Nat wash his feet, and there was Henry summoning her up the two steps to the verandah, unrolling a mat and bidding her sit down, asking her if she preferred tea or coffee, turning a key in the door and entering, Nat joining her, plonking himself down beside her on the mat; Nat, the same as ever, smiling across at her the way he had done in London, or in Ceylon, or in the plane, and, at least for the time being, all was well.

They drank tea and ate Milk Bikis on the verandah and Saroj listened to the two men chatting. Occasionally Nat or Henry looked at her and smiled and tried to draw her into the conversation, but Saroj was distracted. She looked around and liked what she saw. David's little house was shielded from the road and from curious eyes by the same towering bougainvilleas that lined the garden path between gate and house. Cascading clusters of brilliantly orange, vermilion and purple blossoms created a flowery refuge, luxuriously overflowing walls which contained smaller, more modest shrubs and gentler colours — the creamy yellow-fringed frangipani, pink oleander, the tender mauve of hibiscus. Saroj, sitting with her back to the house, imagined herself at home — home being the Waterloo Street garden halfway across the world, where the very same flowers had been coaxed into effulgence by Ma. The agitation that had taken possession of all her senses almost since the moment of entering the airport at Madras began to recede, as well as her doubts concerning Nat. She felt her body relax spontaneously, as if a load had dropped from her shoulders, as if it too registered a homecoming, recognised this refuge as a place of safety, understood the silent welcome of nature.

She sighed audibly and leaned back against the pristine, whitewashed wall. *I can make it, she thought. I can, and I will. Here I shall let down my roots. Here I shall flourish, and grow. Nat is at my side.* She reached for his hand, and felt his fingers close around hers. Her eyes grow heavy. She barely heard Nat's chuckle as her body slumped against his, she barely felt his hands as he touched her limbs and stretched them out on the mat. *I am home,* she thought, and it was her last thought before the sleep that had evaded her all night long in Madras finally caught up with and claimed her.

When she woke up it was dark. She heard voices: Nat's, Henry's, and a third, which she knew must be David's. David was back. Her future father-in-law. Hastily she sat up, instinctively ran her fingers through her hair, straightened her clothes. She felt musty, clogged from the dust of the long bus journey, and longed for a shower and a change of clothes, things she had been too tired to consider on their arrival hours ago. How many hours? She looked at her watch, holding it up to the dim light that shone through the window above her head. Eight o'clock. The men were inside. She wanted to join them, but a sudden, violent shyness lamed her. How would David welcome her? The beloved son had brought home his bride…

She remembered the tap where she had washed her feet. She got up and walked over to the steps leading down from the verandah, crouched down and reached in the darkness for the tap. She found it, turned it on, cupped her hands, felt the cool water filling them and splashed her face with it. Delicious. She rubbed her neck, her arms, might have taken off her blouse and washed her whole body but then the screen door to the house swung open with a creak and Nat emerged and crouched beside her.

'Hello! Had a good sleep?'

Saroj splashed her face again and replied, 'Mmm! Your dad's here, isn't he?'

'Yes. I've told him all about you, he's taken a look at you sleeping, and is dying to meet you.'

'But I'm not at all presentable! I wish I could have a shower, wash my hair, change into something else! He'll think I'm a real tramp if he sees me this way!'

'No he won't. But you can have your shower if you want. Come on in.'

Saroj followed Nat into the house, into a small central room with no furniture whatsoever, doors on each of the four walls. Nat opened one of the doors and Saroj found herself in a bathroom. Beneath a tap in the wall were two buckets full of water, metal dippers hung over their edges.

'Here's soap, and a towel,' said Nat, pressing a block of Chandrika Ayurvedic soap into her hand before returning to the others.

Saroj looked in despair at the buckets with their dippers. What I need, she thought, is a long soak in a tub of deep warm foamy fragrant water. But this is India, my new home. Cold water dipped from buckets will have to do. For now and evermore.

Saroj emerged from the bathroom, her skin scrubbed clean and cool, and fragrant with the warm spiciness of Chandrika soap, her hair wet and coiled up into a knot on top of her head. She wore the *shalwar kameez* she had bought in Madras, slightly crumpled from the journey, but clean and fresh with a paisley pattern in shades of blue. Not quite the elegant young bride, she thought ruefully, crossing the floor of the central room to the open doorway where the men were still sitting and talking.

She stopped in the doorway and three faces turned to look. Nat's dear familiar one, Henry's jovial bat-eared one... and David's.

She had never seen a face quite like David's, never seen an

older man she could even remotely describe as beautiful. But David was beautiful. Not so much his features, which were even and of an almost classic handsomeness. His skin was of a weathered texture, browned and leathered from years of harsh tropical sun. His face was framed with greying hair combed back, two stray locks falling forward in boyish defiance over the high forehead. His eyes were of a marbled grey, large and wide apart like Nat's, and they too were beautiful. But it was the expression in them and in that entire face that caught Saroj's attention and held it. She could not look away, not even to Nat, though she felt her lover's expectant gaze upon her.

He is good, she thought. There is no other word to describe this man as simple, pure, goodness. Benevolence, integrity, kindness, beneficence, love — they were all encompassed in that goodness, gathered together into a radiance that literally seemed to glow from him, to stream from his eyes, to light up his smile. It was the goodness she felt in Nat's presence — but more, much more, the fulfilment and summit of that goodness, a goodness that was strength and compassion and that reached out to embrace her even before David had risen to his feet and come forward with outstretched hands to greet her.

'Saroj! Welcome!'

Shyly she took those hands; but David came closer, and his arms closed around her, and Saroj felt herself surrounded by that goodness and filled with it. She felt like crying, and closed her eyes.

Saroj opened her eyes. In doing so her gaze fell automatically on a framed photograph on the wall behind David. She started, and stiffened. David, feeling her bewilderment, let go of her. She stepped aside and walked around him towards the photo, which was the portrait of a young Indian woman, gently smiling, her hair parted in the middle, a perfectly round *tika* in the middle of her forehead. There was no mistaking this portrait, for it was the very same one, albeit much larger, that was pasted into Balwant Uncle's family archives. There was no mistaking Ma.

Saroj turned to face the room, her face lit up in radiant joy.

'That's Ma!' she said to David, and glanced at the portrait

again, turning eagerly to Ma. 'That's Ma, Nat! That's my mother, when she was younger.'

She looked away from Nat, passing quickly over Henry's face and up to David's, eagerly awaiting his reaction to the miracle, that here, in his house, should be a photo of Ma.

'This woman is your mother?' asked David.

'Yes, of course... and how... oh, but of course! Your sister! Your sister was married to her brother, my Gopal Uncle. You all grew up together, didn't you... you and Fiona and Gopal Uncle. I didn't realise that, I...'

'What do you know about Fiona and Gopal?' David's voice was sharp, and brought her to a stop.

Nat said, 'I was going to wait to tell you the whole story, Dad, but now it's out. I know all about Gopal and Fiona, that they're my parents. And can you believe it, Saroj is Gopal's sister's daughter. It's a long story, and...'

But David's voice slashed through his words. 'How is she? Where is she?'

'Well, she's dead. She died a few years ago, in a fire.'

'Dead? Savitri, dead?' The pain written across David's face, the yawning hole that seemed to open in his eyes, stunned Saroj into silence. She knew then, and so did Nat: David loved Ma. Saroj's mother. *Savitri,* he had called her.

David turned then to Nat and the look in his eyes was no longer pain but pity. 'Nat. My Nat. I should have told you. And now it's too late. I should have told you about Savitri. Your mother.'

At the word Saroj froze. And so did Nat. His hand dropped hers. Henry looked away. The candle flame flickered. Even the shrill chorus of insects outside seemed silenced by the moment. They all stood poised on the rim of that silence.

Then David spoke again. 'She was the cook's daughter...'

Chapter 70

Nat and Saroj
A Village in Madras State, 1971

David spoke for two hours nonstop. Almost at once the horror of his revelation seemed to retreat from the room, and Savitri entered in its place: Savitri as she had been, the little girl he had loved becoming the woman he had worshipped. His voice smiled. It was warm and alive with the memories that seemed to flood his being, that poured out now in words. As a river held back by a dam of twigs, a dam held in place by a single vital twig, bearing the name of Savitri, and that vital twig now pulled, and the river bursting forward sweeping all in its wake.

David's story transported his listeners back into the past and into another world, and his words were windows on the past, and the spirit of Savitri came alive and wrapped itself around them like the warm glow from a gentle flame.

But Saroj was cold, and numb with something worse than dread.

'But who am I really?' Nat cried as David ended his story. 'Am I Nataraj, or am I Paul?'

He leaped to his feet and paced the room. 'Who am I? Which of the children was killed? Nataraj or Paul? Which one lived? Which one am I?' He stopped at Savitri's photo, buried his face in his hands in anguish, leaning against the wall.

'You're . . .' Henry began, but David interrupted.

'Paul died, Nat!' David cried. 'You're Nataraj. Of course you are!'

'But how do you know? You can't! Only Mani knew, for sure!' Nat's voice was loud and agitated.

'Nat, don't ask me how I know. I just know, that's all. I

know you're my son!'

'But that's what Gopal believes too! He's convinced of it, just like you, but one of you is wrong! What if you're wrong, Dad, and Gopal's right?'

Nat's question hung unanswered in Saroj's heart. She found herself praying. A thin ray of hope was prying its way through the coldness inside her. Let him be Gopal's son after all. Oh, let him not be Savitri's! Let us not be brother and sister!

Let Gopal be Nat's father. Let Gopal be Nat's father. The words were a mantra in Saroj's mind.

Above her anguished prayer David and Nat fired words at each other, each fighting a battle for his life, not allowing Henry a word between the salvos.

'Gopal talked himself into the idea that you're his son! After all, Savitri had seen the cremation papers with Nat's name on them. One of the babies was dead, one was living, that much was certain. He convinced himself that the living one, the one I had claimed, was his son. He wanted to believe that, Nat. He had to believe that! He didn't want his son to be dead! And now one of the boys had turned up — you! He wanted you! He wanted you desperately!'

'But maybe I was his son. There's no way you can tell. Maybe it's you who wanted to believe.'

'May I just . . .' interrupted Henry, raising a hand like a child in the class-room, but Nat barked him down.

'Gopal's my father! He must be! I'm sorry, Dad, I love you more but I want Gopal to be my father! Can't you understand? Don't you see! Let him be my father! And Fiona: my mother! Where is she now?'

'She's still at Fairwinds. I engaged a psychiatric nurse to live with her there and take care of her. I did consider sending her back to England, to a hospital, but I believe she's happier in Fairwinds, with her doll. Better off than in some English loony bin. I visit her now and again. She doesn't recognise me.'

'She's my mother! I must go to her — maybe I can heal her! Maybe when she knows I'm alive...'

His voice rose in desperation, echoing the panic in Saroj's

heart. She looked up and met his eyes. Their hands reached for each other, calming each other. Perhaps, together, they could will it to be true. *Make Nat Fiona's son, and not Savitri's.* Make them cousins, not brother and sister.

'Listen, the two of you, I can —' Henry began again, but again David interrupted.

'It's possible, of course,' said David, and desperate doubt flooded his eyes. 'But no, you can't be, Nat. I've always…'

'You're just like Gopal, Dad. You want it to be true and so you believe it's true. But don't you see, I can't be Savitri's son!'

'But you *are* her son! I know it, I feel it! More than I feel you're my son, I feel you're hers! She speaks to me through you, you are her very image! You have her spirit! She has passed on all her gifts to you. The healing hands. The power! It is from her!'

'You said it runs in our family. Well, it could have been passed on by Gopal, couldn't it? He's her brother; these things need not pass in a direct line. *Thatha* had the gift; why couldn't it lie dormant in Gopal, his grandson?'

David shook his head. 'I feel it, I know it. She lives in you! Do you really believe you could be the son of Gopal and Fiona? Both spineless, colourless people? Don't you in the depths of your heart know that you are mine and hers?'

David's voice was gentle as he continued. 'When Mani told me that Savitri had left India, that she was married, on the other side of the world, I knew I had lost. I didn't even ask where she was. He wouldn't have told me, anyway. Fiona may have known but she had lost most of her mind. I didn't even ask Gopal. I knew I had lost; there was no going back. Savitri thought I was dead. That is why she married… she is an Indian woman, with the strength and resilience of an Indian woman, and I knew she would make good of her life, whichever turn it took. I knew she had no choice but to remarry — as a widow, with all the scandal, she'd have had no chance here in India, for which Indian man would marry her? She had been lucky, to emigrate, to marry again. I couldn't interfere, much as I longed to. So I let her go. But when I found you, Nat, it was as if she had returned to me. It was as if she'd reached out to me, entered my life in your form. I *know* you're hers.'

They were all silent then, and a bitterness, like gall, rose up in Saroj, because she, too, felt it. Savitri — Ma — lived in Nat. She had seen Ma in him from the very beginning. Their attraction, it seemed, was nothing more than the call of blood.

'Are you two willing to listen to me now?' said Henry into the silence. 'I could have told you from the beginning if you'd listened. Nat is Nataraj. Without a doubt.'

At last he had caught their attention. Saroj and Nat exchanged a last, agonised glance, then turned their eyes to him, waiting for what was to come, knowing it was their death-knell.

Henry's voice was calm, patient. 'Savitri lived with us for two years after Nat's birth,' he said. 'She searched for him from our house. She fought the bureaucrats for him, but she also searched for him physically. She couldn't help it. She said there was one way she'd always recognise Nataraj, and that's the reason she always inspected little boys, took them in her arms, rolled back their collars, touched their necks. The mole behind your right ear, Nat. Savitri had it, and so do you. She told us. You are Nataraj, the boy she gave birth to. You have the mole.'

Involuntarily Nat's hand flew to the spot behind his right ear. His eyes met Saroj's, and they both knew. And then Nat's eyes shifted away.

Another long, eloquent silence. In that silence Saroj felt a shifting of worlds. Nat's world moving out of her grasp, and sinking into Ma's. *Savitri's.* Silently he slipped from her. He had found something big, a miracle, a marvel, greater than herself. She had lost him — to Savitri. To Ma.

Chapter 71

Nat and Saroj
A Village in Madras State, 1971

'But, Dad, why did Gopal ignore me for all those years, and suddenly turn up in London with that stupid story of us marrying? And how did he find me in London?'

Henry coughed ostentatiously. 'Seems it's my turn to take over the story,' he said. 'I have to make a confession. I ran into Gopal by accident in Madras, a few years ago. It was when you were in England, Nat. Let me see — it must have been a few months before you came home for the first time, the year of the great flood. I asked how Savitri was; June had kept in touch with her for the first few years, but you know how these things are — it all trickled out, and when June ran off with her pilot she took Savitri's address and that was the end of that. Gopal told me she was very ill. She had cancer.'

'Cancer!' Saroj stared at Henry.

'Yes,' Henry continued. 'She had breast cancer and had decided not to have it operated. She felt her task in life was over. She hadn't told her family yet. She was quite reconciled to dying, Gopal said, and he was thinking of going over to visit her. They were always very close.'

'She never told us,' Saroj murmured. Once again, Ma had failed her — this time, not in an outright lie, but in failing to tell the truth.

'She wouldn't,' said Henry. 'Savitri always hated a fuss made about her own self. But I had an idea. I thought it was a good one. Her children were almost adult now; there could be no harm in it — what of reuniting her with David and Nat? What of bringing her to London for treatment? I knew David would pay for the treatment, even if the National Health wouldn't. Just knowing they were alive would make her want to live, I thought. So — well, to make a long story short, I went to London myself to check, to find out what specialists could and would treat her, before telling anyone else. I didn't want to raise hopes. But I did write to Savitri, telling her about Nat and David—Gopal had given me her address. I wanted to give her that one solace! That's when I met you in London, Nat, and brought you back by the scruff of your neck!'

'That must have been the letter she got just before she died — the one with all the good news!' said Saroj.

Henry nodded. 'She wrote to Gopal then, and to me. So excited! She told me she would come. She didn't want treatment, but she was coming to India, to see David again, and Nat. She begged me not to tell you, David. She wanted to surprise you.'

David could only shake his head.

'A while after that Gopal wrote to say she was dead — no details. He asked for Nat's address in London — I gave it to him. That was all. I haven't heard from him since then.'

'He's been too busy since then.' Nat's voice was bitter.

'You can't blame Gopal, Nat. He meant well. And he really does believe you're his son.'

I wish it too, Saroj thought. *I wish it with all my heart.*

Her mind wearily picked out the memories that corresponded to David's tale, and clicked them together. She felt sick. That was what the letter had been all about, the letter Ma received the day before her death, the letter she had wanted to share with Saroj, the reason she had wanted to rush off to London, and India. Henry had told her the truth, and she wanted to rush back to India, to her real, true life, to her past. She'd wanted Saroj to meet 'some people' — Nat, of course, and David. A wonderful reunion.

Except that Saroj did not fit in. Not at all. Saroj had nothing at all to do with Savitri's story, Savitri's life, Savitri's past, and as she listened she shrank back into the shadows, watched the two men who reached out for each other and drew closer together —

without her, Saroj. Sharing a past. Rewriting history. Wishing away her existence. Nauseated, she watched Nat claim his past.

'What luck, that someone else didn't adopt me before you came!' said Nat. David shook his head. 'We have Mani to thank for that,' he said. 'He'd left that note, saying the child's mother was insane. That was his final trump — he didn't want you to be adopted into a good home. He probably left a similar note with the other baby – or would have done, if it had lived. Finally, I think the notes just got mixed up. Paul's note ended up with you, and Paul died. I did have some doubt, at first. I remember when I went to him afterwards; I showed him the note, and wanted the truth from him: were you Fiona's baby, or Savitri's? He only smirked. "You'll never truly know, will you? Take it or leave it," he said. He already had the money. He didn't care which child had lived or died. And he wanted me to stay in that uncertainty. There was nothing I could do. And in the end it didn't matter.'

'The death certificate he showed Savitri was in Nataraj's name,' said Henry, 'but it would have been, wouldn't it? He had custody of Nataraj, and his birth certificate. It didn't matter which name went with the body. I suppose he wanted to cover his tracks, in case there ever was an inquiry into Nataraj's whereabouts.'

'Evil — pure evil!' said Nat. 'But surely Fiona wasn't insane back then? I thought her illness developed much later?'

David shook his head again. 'No. Getting gang-raped as a young girl, a virgin, was the real trigger for her illness. There had been — incidents. Mani knew of it. Gopal loved her truly, and thought marriage and motherhood would help; he felt guilty, you see. And it *did* help. But losing Paul sent her over the edge. To tell you the truth, I did have my doubts. I took you to her after I brought you from the orphanage. I even told her you were Paul… but she was already too far gone. She only wanted her doll.'

'Poor Fiona!' said Nat. 'I'd like to meet her one day.'

'You will,' said David. 'I only wish you could have met Savitri.'

Silence followed those words. A deep, eloquent silence. And then:

'I'm sorry, Dad. I really am. Things would have been so different! If only she'd waited! Waited till you came back from Changi!'

David shrugged. 'There's no such thing as "if only", Nat. That's the way she would have seen it. *Everything happens for a purpose,* she always said. She would have said it's all God's will.'

David laid a hand fondly on Nat's. They exchanged a look of such deep love and unity that a pang of jealousy gripped Saroj's heart.

'I should have told you about Savitri long ago, Nat. But I pushed her and the memory of her right to the back of my mind and held it there by a giant hand. I feared that even thinking of her, mentioning her name to you, conjuring up the past, would destroy me. I lost myself in my work — it was what she would have wanted, what we would have done together if things had taken a straight, direct path. What I built here, Nat, I built for her, in her memory. Prasad Nagar is a monument to her. It was my way of bringing her to life, but without the pain. She was my inspiration.'

'And mine, too. Even without knowing her.'

'She lives in you, Nat. Her hands are your hands — golden hands. She lives in you. She moves through you.'

Nat held up his hands, palms upward, and looked at them, nodding. In the candlelight he was beautiful, so beautiful and golden it was painful to behold.

Saroj listened to the two of them in a state of shock. They were speaking of her mother, but with every word they spoke they were stealing Ma from her, transforming her into this stranger, *Savitri.* David, Nat and Savitri — that would have been the proper ending for this story, the happy ending. And she, Saroj, would never have been born. If Ma had found out earlier that they were together she would have left Deodat. Saroj could not question that. Left Deodat, and returned to the man and the son she had really wanted, not even considered bearing Deodat's children.

Savitri should never even have made that trip to Georgetown, never have married Deodat, should have waited for her man, for David, and Nat! Should have believed! Kept the faith! That would have been the fairytale come true! Cinderella should have found her prince! *I was a mistake,* Saroj reflected. *I should never have been born. I was a substitute, a surrogate, I and all of us Roy children. We are the anti-climax of Savitri's life!*

The Savitri she knew, her Ma, was a lie, a make-believe, an actress playing a part, trying to forget her real life, the life that should have been. And Nat! He could be happy now. He had gained a mother, but she had lost hers, and a lover, a life.

Chapter 72

Saroj
A Village in Madras State, 1971

*H*ow can he sleep? How can he possibly sleep?
Saroj wanted to wake him up, shake him, slap him, scream at him. *How can you sleep, you bastard, don't you see what this has done to us? How can you lie there and smile in your sleep, happy because you've found your darling mother, when you very well know that your finding a mother is the end of us?*

She looked at Nat and her silent cry seemed to fill all space with anguish. *My brother! He is my brother! My lover is my brother!*

Nat slept on, sprawled next to her on the verandah. The only man she had ever loved, and he was her brother. *We are Savitri's children!* She threw herself down and buried her face in her pillow, smothering racking sobs, biting into the pillow-case. Last night she had wanted to discuss it, to go over all the implications, the horror of it all, to let the dreadful truth wash over them both and to wallow in it through the night, but David had called a halt to all that. It was late, he said, and there was work waiting for him in the morning. It was time to sleep and they had talked enough. Time in the morning to solve their problems.

Solve their problems! As if this problem could ever be solved! But Nat had quickly pulled himself together, tucked the horror of it all in some safe corner of his mind — *Oh, how I hate this equanimity of mind which is the Indian disease!* — made a bed for himself and for Saroj on the verandah mats, given her a sheet to cover herself with. They had lain down next to each other, she in his arms. He had been trembling as he held her but his embrace had been that of a brother. He had dried her tears and bid her sleep.

'I love you, Saroj,' had been his last words. 'No matter what, remember that. I truly love you. We will work this thing out. We'll go through it together.' He had kissed her cheek and then he had slept, like a baby, and left her to brood and cry into her pillow and bite the sheet and toss.

Hours had passed and she could not bear it. Dawn was near and it was a dawn she never wanted to know, because no matter how they twisted and turned the facts — Nat was her brother.

If she waited to say goodbye they would try to persuade her to stay. Out of politeness, they would bid her stay, to hear her side of Savitri's story, to marvel at what had become of Savitri, to mourn her death. This was not Saroj's place. Better to go now, at once, and easier for them all.

She had not unpacked the day before. It was easy to pull on her clothes and brush her hair in the dark, sling her bag across her shoulder, and walk off towards Town. There she woke a rickshaw-wallah sleeping in his rickshaw and got a ride to the bus-station. The first bus left at four. She did not bother to go into Madras. The airport lay on the bus route anyway, so she got off there, had her ticket changed, and waited for the next flight out.

London was deserted. Among its millions, the ones Saroj most loved were absent. Her need for friendship and for comfort, though, were greater than ever before in her life, greater even than in the time following Ma's death. She was a stranger in a strange land, homeless, abandoned. She wanted to go home, to Trixie and Ganesh and the streets she had known as a child.

Two weeks later she took a stand-by flight to Georgetown. Ganesh and Trixie were waiting for her. She fell into their arms and they held her close and wrapped her in their love, even before they had heard her story. Because her grief was written all over her face and poured out of her eyes and her brother and her friend knew and held her close.

Recovery would take an age, but here in the familiar streets of her childhood, in this cosy town where each face seemed to smile and welcome her home, recovery *would* come.

And at home there was someone else. Her father. Now that

she had lost everything she would build on that. Now that she was completely orphaned, Balwant — for she no longer thought of him as uncle — would have to acknowledge her, at least secretly, without Aunt Kamla's knowledge. Maybe she could live with them, rebuild her life from that lovely breeze-swept house, a safe haven. Warm in the glow of a father's love. It was only a consolation prize, for sure — but it was a beginning.

There were questions, of course, that might never find answers. How could Ma, after having loved David, ever turn to another man? But Savitri — Ma — had believed David dead. There had been too much tragedy in her life; a completely new beginning had been vital. In leaving India Ma had shed her past — completely. Cast off the Savitri persona entirely. And: Ma was human. A man like Balwant must have been a ray of light in an otherwise bleak life in Deodat's shadow. These answers satisfied Saroj.

She moved in with Balwant Uncle, resting her hopes on him. But Balwant Uncle was a disappointment: curiously unresponsive to her overtures and hints. Why wouldn't he respond? Acknowledge her as a daughter? Balwant Uncle was as jovial as ever, but Saroj wanted more, so much more, more than he could ever give. How could Balwant Uncle ever stand in for Nat, fill the gap inside her?

She could not bring back the past, nor rewrite it. Living abroad had changed her, and as the weeks passed she felt raggedly out of place. Trixie's and Ganesh's happiness only reminded her of her own loss; and anyway, they would not be staying long. Trixie was a temporary celebrity here — a big fish in a small pond — but she missed the excitement of London, as did Ganesh, who was restless without the city and his job, and harboured plans for his own catering service. Should she, too, return to the uncaring Moloch, London? Start again there? She felt in limbo, neither here not there, and the one place she longed for was forbidden. But worse was to come.

After a month she knew for certain she was pregnant — with her brother's child.

Chapter 73

Saroj
Georgetown, 1971

Saroj sat in Dr Lachmansingh's waiting room, mentally wringing her hands, heart pounding. Trixie, sitting beside her, must have felt her agony for she reached out and clasped Saroj's sweating hand and squeezed it. Saroj glanced at the contented faces and swelling bellies of the Indian women around her. Trixie was the odd woman out here, the only black. Even in their choice of doctor, Guyana's women were racially divided.

It wasn't meant to be this way, Saroj protested, but there was no-one to hear except her own rebellious thoughts, every single one of which cried out with all its might against abortion. The voice of reason rose above them like a stern relentless father, forefinger raised: *you must. There is no other way.*

And behind them all: Nat. Never receding even for a moment, looming large like the backdrop to a battle scene, watching the whole mess with calm, benevolent eyes. For five long weeks Saroj had fought to dispel the thought of him, but he was not a thought, he was there, always, so much a part of her that to tear him from her life would be to destroy herself.

She had tried reason. *He is your brother, she told herself. Of course you love him! You love him as a brother, the way you love Ganesh. That is why you were attracted to him; it was the call of your blood. You recognised him, because Ma is in him as she is in you, and all you did was make the mistake of seeing him as a lover, as a man, instead of as your brother.* But behind it all, Nat smiled on.

She had considered reconciliation. She had left him too abruptly, she told herself. She should not have dashed off like that into the night. She should have given herself the chance to talk it out. Nat and David would have had clever and calming words to say and Nat and she would have grown into a new relationship.

And it was all no good. She loved him, but not as a brother. She knew the difference.

And she was going to have his child — her brother's child — if she did not stop this *thing* growing inside her.

'Miss Roy?' Trixie was shaking her arm and a nurse was calling and she woke from her reverie. The nurse smiled. 'The doctor is waiting, Miss Roy. Oh, and are you coming too?' This to Trixie, who had stood up and was close behind Saroj in the narrow passageway outside the waiting room.

'Yes, she's coming with me,' Saroj said firmly, and clasped Trixie's hand. They exchanged a look of amused complicity and entered the doctor's consulting room, and took their seats behind the desk that filled half the space.

Dr Lachmansingh's pleasure at seeing Saroj was obviously genuine.

'So, you're back! I thought you'd left the country for good — contributing to the brain drain. I hope you've changed your mind and come home to settle! Why anyone should want to live in that cold England I don't understand at all!'

Saroj smiled and agreed with him and the small talk sallied to and fro for several minutes before she took matters in hand and said outright: 'Dr Lachmansingh — I have a big problem.'

Immediately they were all sitting straight in their chairs and looking appropriately serious. Saroj decided not to beat about the bush. She simply blurted it out:

'I'm pregnant and I need an abortion because it's from my brother.'

Dr Lachmansingh's neatly bearded chin dropped in horror. 'From... from *Ganesh?*'

Saroj gave a wry chuckle. 'No, no. Not from Ganesh — I've not sunk *that* deep. It's a long story.'

The roads in La Penitence were pot-holed and the houses grey and dilapidated: one-storey wooden cottages, the paint peeling off, the shutters broken, the gutters before them black and stinking, the grass verges unkempt and strewn with rubbish. They crawled through the area for a quarter of an hour before finding the house. It was tiny, little more than one room on stilts, but an attempt had been made to beautify it for green and red curtains hung at all the open windows. A group of limp, tattered, coloured flags attached to tall bamboo poles near the front palings signified that it was a Hindu home. The yard was a small square of dried mud and weeds, and the wreck of a rusty green Ford Prefect against the back palings had been claimed by a gigantic pumpkin plant pushing thick green tendrils through the gaping windows. The road outside was narrow and Trixie parked as near as she could to the gutter without falling in, so that they all had to exit through the opposite doors.

Saroj looked at the house and at the address on the piece of notepaper in her hand, torn from Dr Lachmansingh's pad.

She climbed the rickety staircase, raised the knocker and let it fall.

'Who dat?'

The voice was close by, almost at her elbow, and she swung around. A woman was looking out of the window not a yard away from her. She seemed aged and tired but the face was so familiar Saroj's heart missed a beat. When the woman saw Saroj she simply raised her eyebrows and said, 'Oh. I comin'.'

Her face disappeared, then the door opened.

'Sarojini,' she said. That was all. They faced each other in silence, neither moving. But Saroj could hear the pounding of her heart. Her hands were slippery with sweat and she wiped them on her hips. Nat and Trixie stood close behind her and they too were silent. The resemblance! Despite her age, despite the fatigue and dullness in the older woman's eyes and the lines around her mouth and the pockmarks on her cheek, Saroj stood face to face with herself.

'Well, don't just stan' dere. Come in. Come in.'

She turned and moved away to let them in, and then Saroj saw her hair, greasy with coconut oil, and endlessly long, down almost to her knees, plaited in a thick rope up to her waist and from that point loose, reddish, wiry, split-ended — but long.

As if hearing Saroj's thoughts, the woman turned around and touched Saroj's own hair.

'I see you cut yuh hair,' she commented. 'You had such lovely hair. Like mine use to be. Mistress Dee she ain't gon' cut you hair, so you hair gon' be like my own. To honour me, she say.'

'I cut it myself,' Saroj told her then. 'I cut it, I cut it just after... I was in hospital,' Saroj almost whispered the last words as it dawned on her that the cutting of her hair symbolised the greatest folly of her life. She had cut her hair to punish the mother who was not, in fact, her mother.

'I saw you in hospital,' the woman said, in a pleasant, conversational tone. 'Come, chile, sit down, sit down. Look, take de Morris chair. Leh me bring some mo' chairs for your friends.'

She stepped back into the tiny room and lifted a chair from the little dining table and brought it to face the big Morris chair by the window in the gallery. She brought another chair which she placed to complete the circle, and Saroj and Trixie sat down. The woman stayed standing.

'I got another chair in de bedroom,' she laughed. 'I gon' get dat jus' now, but you-all don't want some lime juice? Coconut water? Or tea?'

'Lime juice, please!' Saroj whispered, and Trixie nodded.

The woman was speaking again. 'That was de last time I see yuh, in the hospital,' she said. 'When I come to give yuh some blood.'

'I saw you,' Saroj told her. 'I saw you looking down at me. I thought it was a dream, or a hallucination. I thought it was myself. You looked so much like me! Or, I look so much like you!'

'Yes, dear.' She had opened a small fridge and took out a jug of lime juice. She poured three glasses for her visitors, put them on a tray and came out to serve it.

'Dat's what Mistress Dee say. She say you look jus' like me. An' she give me photos, yuh know. She always bring photos. I got a whole album full ah photos. After Mr Roy send me away

I start collecting photos.'

She sighed, and stopped speaking.

'You — you're Parvati, aren't you? My nanny?'

'You remember me?'

'Hardly at all, it's just a vague memory of being close to you, loving you; and then Baba sent you away... I was so angry with Baba. I hated him after that! Such a childish hatred, and yet it was so real.'

'He not really a bad man, yuh know. He buy dis house fuh me. So at least I had that. But he so shame! He shame because of what happen wid me.'

'What did happen, Parvati?'

'You don't know? Then I tell you.'

Savitri gave birth to two children, Indrani and Ganesh, and after that something happened. Savitri could read her husband's face like a book and guilt and shame were written all over it. She wished he would tell her, but that was too much to expect.

But finally he was forced to tell her: about the beautiful young Parvati, poor as a mouse, whose newly widowed mother, a year ago, had come to him begging for help.

'We in't got nuttin', Mr Roy. Nuttin',' wailed the woman, and Deodat rubbed his cheek and regarded her and her daughter. 'Who sent you to me? Why do you come to me of all people?'

'My poor dead husband always talk 'bout you. He is you second cousin twice remove. He say he used to play wid you when you was chirren.'

'What was your husband's name?'

'Ram Verasamy.'

Deodat thought back and remembered. These were distant relatives of his, then; Verasamy had moved to New Amsterdam and lost touch with him. Yes, he had heard of the death, but had not gone to the funeral. And yet, family duty dictated that he help. He brought mother and daughter to Georgetown, installed them in a rented house, found a cleaning job for the mother, made sure they had enough to eat and to clothe themselves — and fell in love with the beautiful daughter. Uncontrollably in love.

His head hanging now, he confessed all to Savitri, and she smiled and laid a hand on his in understanding as he wept.

'It is all right,' she said. 'You are only human; a man. Men are weak in this respect. It's all right.'

'But that's not all,' Deodat said, and could not look her in the eye. 'Parvati is now with child — my child!'

Neither of them spoke for a long time. And then Deodat said with an unsteady voice, 'It is all my fault and I must make it up to her. I cannot allow her to raise a child out of wedlock! She and the child — my child! — would be treated as vermin. And I thought, I was wondering, I always wanted a large family, more children, but...'

'I know,' said Savitri. She knew: between him and her there would be no more children. It had been that way since Ganesh's birth.

'So you want us to adopt the child? Is that it?'

'What a terrible thing to ask a wife! What an insult to you!'

But Savitri only laughed. 'It is no insult. I would do it gladly! But what about the child's mother? You would take her child from her? Do you know what a terrible thing that is?'

'I told you, she cannot raise the child herself. She will have to give it up for adoption anyway. She would be happy to give her child a happy home and a good mother.'

'But no-one must ever know,' Savitri said firmly. 'They must not know that she has had a baby — an unmarried mother. She will never find a husband if they know. We must do this in secret. We must pass the child off as mine. We'll hire her as a nanny, maybe leave the country for a while. I must think. Leave this to me.'

So Savitri went to Trinidad, in good time, taking Indrani and Ganesh with her, and Parvati as nanny. When they returned Savitri had a baby girl, named Sarojini. Savitri, knowing what it was for a woman to lose a child, shared the baby with Parvati, and Parvati was Saroj's beloved nanny, a second mother.

Saroj turned to Trixie. 'Remember the photo, Trix? The one of Gan's second birthday, on the beach? I knew there was something strange about it but I couldn't think what. It was taken in August; I was born that September. Ma should have been eight months pregnant, but she wasn't. She was slim as a reed in that photo.'

When Deodat looked at his little daughter, the child nearest to his heart, he feared for her, for she was a child of sin and guilt. He had to get rid of that bad influence, that woman of sin, that Parvati, who had once had power over his lower senses, but who had subsequently, in the wake of the resulting problems, lost that power. It would be difficult to get rid of Parvati, because Saroj loved her so, and his wife — whom he feared to cross in any way — encouraged her. But then Parvati let the child play with the negroes next door. It was a serious transgression. Absolutely forbidden. It was the chance he was waiting for. He threw her out.

From that day on Deodat watched hawk-like over Saroj, for she carried the seed of immorality within her. What if she inherited that woman's beauty! Those loose morals! He vowed to do his best for this child. Protect her from the perils of straying lust. Keep her hidden from mankind, fostered, preserved and treasured. His heart ached when he saw her, the poor little thing. The finding of a good husband for her, Deodat swore, would be his first and sacred duty.

When Parvati's mother was dying, Savitri came and cared for her, brought medicines and laid hands on her and wiped the sweat from her face. As far as her husband and her family were concerned she was at the temple. It was the beginning of a double life, a life of subterfuge.

Soon after her mother's death Parvati developed a wicked red rash on her hands and arms, painful to the touch. She went to the Georgetown hospital but nothing helped. Then Savitri laid her hands on the rash, rubbed an ointment into it, and in a few days the rash flaked off and the skin healed, and after that she had no trouble. Parvati told all her friends, and the next time Savitri came the sick people lined up on the road to see her.

Savitri began to treat the sick of La Penitence. At first just once a week in the afternoon, when she was supposed to be in the temple. But demand for her grew. She came for an hour in the mornings as well, when the children were at school and Deodat in the office. She brought herbs and tinctures, teas and roots and powders, and she went to people in their homes and laid her hands on them.

Parvati's home became a hospital. The people of La Penitence flocked to Savitri, because Savitri had a smile and she had a special touch. When Savitri laid her hand on them they felt they were well again. They believed, and they were healed.

When Parvati's mother died there wasn't enough money, and of course no-one would marry her, for it was rumoured that she had once been the mistress of a married man, though nobody could exactly name him. And it was rumoured that she had borne a bastard child and given it up for adoption. But Parvati was still beautiful and though no man would have her as a wife several wanted her as a mistress, and she chose another married man who kept her fed and clothed. After him there was another, and another.

But physical beauty is evanescent, and Parvati's faded quickly. Savitri helped with gifts of money and food, but after her death the bad times came; and more men.

'I is a bad woman, a woman of shame,' said Parvati. 'You should not have come. And now you know you should go and forget me. I am glad you came but I will understand. Go now and try to forgive me. Pray for me.'

But Saroj was hardly listening. She was grinning at Trixie, in triumph.

Chapter 74

Saroj
London, 1971

It was a small, messy, poky room, a bedsit near Streatham Common. Dark, for the curtains were drawn, and lit only by a dirty electric bulb hanging naked from the ceiling, giving off a tepid yellow glow. In one corner, an unmade bed, in the other, a wardrobe with a broken door. The smell was a mélange of old stale sweat and sickly-sweet incense. Saroj looked around in distaste; then she looked at Baba, dressed in grubby longjohns and an even grubbier singlet, sitting in an armchair facing the dead fireplace. The two stared at each other in silence.

'Tell me about Parvati,' said Saroj.

Baba looked away.

'You found out — you know! I didn't want…'

'No theatricals, please. Just tell me the story.'

And so Baba began to speak. A broken, humble Baba, stumbling over the words, pausing when he couldn't find the right ones, rambling when his thoughts took him on journeys to the past.

'I was weak… I gave in to lust… She was so young, so pretty. How could I resist? It was wrong, I know… to take advantage. Then… she told me she was in trouble. What could I do… your mother was strong so I turned to her, confessed, asked for forgiveness. And help. She is so wise… now she is gone… this is all I have left of her…'

Baba gestured vaguely towards the fireplace. On the mantelpiece was a shrine, with an urn as centrepiece, surrounded by fresh roses, and a small photo of Ma. Three sticks of incense is gave off white tendrils of pungent smoke, and a thick candle burned with a single unwavering flame. The mantelpiece shrine was the only clean part of the room.

'Every day I lay fresh roses for her,' Said Baba, 'she loved roses!

He removed a grubby handkerchief from his pocket and wiped his face, and his eyes. Saroj walked to the window, drew back the curtains, turned off the overhead bulb.

'Go on,' she said.

'I made full confession. She was so understanding. She knew what to do. She took care of it. They went to Trinidad. She and Parvati went there, for six months. She told people she was going to have a baby, she needed long rest. Then the baby was born. You! Your mother —Parvati I mean — was weak — I was weak — so afraid. Afraid you would be weak too. I know what men are like. Full of lust. And you — so sweet, so innocent. I thought marriage was the best protection for you. I was wrong. I lost you. You always hated me. I deserved it! God has punished me!'

'Ha! So you're getting a bit of sense in your old age. But look at this place! This mess! You stink! When did you last change those—those knickers? And those sheets? Pfui — filthy!'

Saroj pulled the sheets from the unmade bed, rolled them up and threw them in the corner.

'Where do you keep clean sheets?'

Baba waved his hand towards a chest of drawers. Saroj opened all the drawers until she found clean bedclothes. She made the bed and continued to move around tidying up the room while Baba mumbled memories from the past.

Now and then Saroj glanced at the harmless old man slumped in the armchair, and after a while her eyes softened.

'You need a wife!' she said. 'I better arrange a marriage for you!'

A smile played on her lips.

'No, no wife — oh, you are joking. I had the best wife in the world and lost her. Nobody could replace her — a saint! Such a harsh man I was. Too harsh. Too harsh. With you too

— too harsh. Tried to force you…. Now all I have are her ashes. All gone. Ganesh has gone to Guyana with his wife. Ganesh got marred.

'Did you go to Ganesh's wedding? Not me. Not invited. A nice girl, nice girl. Christian girl. What does it matter, Christian, Hindu, Moslem — many paths, one goal. What was I saying. Ashes. One day I want to return to India. My beloved India, and sprinkle her ashes in the Ganges. Nat promised to take me. Did you ever meet Nat? Ganesh's friend. A kind boy. Used to come here and read to me – the Ramayana, the Mahabharata — like a son. He will take me to India. He is there right now. He will come back. Next time he will take me. Such a nice, kind boy.'

Saroj said nothing, and looked at her watch. She walked to the window and opened the curtains. Daylight flooded the room. She tried to open the window, but it was stuck.

'That window is hard to open,' said Baba. 'The paint is sticky. I don't open it much You have to pull hard.'

So Saroj pulled hard and the window unstuck; she threw it open and looked out on to the street. As if on cue, a man walking past looked up. It was Nat. He stopped, looked up at her and smiled.

'Well — hi there!'

Saroj smiled back, and leaned on the windowsill, chin on her hands, relaxed, happy. They gazed at each other in silence.

'I got your cable,' said Nat.

'And I got yours.'

'What's your big wonderful news?'

'What's yours?'

'You first`.'

'No, you.'

Nat smiled, and patted his shirt pocket.

'It's all in here. The letter Ma wrote Gopal. The famous letter.'

Saroj continued to smile, serene, relaxed, patient. She had all the time in the world.

'Baba was just telling me about some nice, kind boy. Why not come in?'

'After you ran off I was pretty devastated,' said Nat. 'The whole story nagged at me and I just had to find out more. So I went to see Gopal. I told him to come out with the truth at last, and he did.'

'What did he say?'

'He loved Savitri. He wanted to make all things right for her at the end. You know, he's a screenwriter with a terrific imagination. It seemed to him a wonderfully dramatic idea for us to marry — his son (as he thought) with Savitri's daughter. A kind of poetic justice, karmatic balance, making everything right again, a story fit for a screenplay. That's what he said. Then he added the words that changed everything — "though she is only adopted."

'My God, Saroj, when he said that I yelled out loud. Literally! I made him repeat, explain. Yes, he said, and he seemed surprised that we didn't know.

'He didn't know all the details, not about Parvati and your dad, but he did know Savitri wasn't your biological mother; she had told him in a letter. And that was enough for me. I came over here like a shot! But you were gone!'

'Ma would have told me — but she died. She wanted to tell me, Nat. That was the letter… She was all excited about it, the day that she died. She wanted to bring me to India, to meet some special people, she said. You and David. She was going to tell me everything. And then she died.'

'Anyway. Read this.'

And he reached into his shirt pocket, took out an envelope folded in two, and handed it to Saroj.

Dear Brother Gopal,

I have just received Henry's letter with the wonderful news. Why did you not tell me? Years ago? But how can I complain! I forgive you! The happiness I now feel at their resurrection more than makes up for even a moment of my years of anguish, believing David and Nataraj to be dead.

I have had a difficult life, Gopal, but I know that now my bad karma is at last exhausted — Henry's letter is the proof. My darlings are alive! And out of the ashes of the past years, brother, so much good has come! Such beautiful children have been granted me — three, to make up for the five I lost. Amrita, Shanti, Anand, Ganesan, and Nataraj. Yet I did not lose five, but only four, for Nataraj has been returned to me! And once again I have four children. I give thanks to God!

Gopal, I am hurrying to London and India as soon as possible, and I shall bring my younger daughter Sarojini with me. You remember, she is the girl we adopted, and we have been having some difficulties finding a suitable husband for her, as she is very modern-minded and headstrong as I myself once was.

I wonder how she will get along with Nataraj? After all, he is half-English and as he is living in London he will certainly have modern ideas, just like Sarojini. She is very intelligent, as well as beautiful. So, I am bringing her along. I am so looking forward to the meeting of these two dear children of mine! (Oh we mothers! Sometimes I think matchmaking is in our blood! Yet I shall keep my opinion to myself, and let nature take its course.)

I am going to telephone Sarojini right away. She might not want to go to India but the moment I mention the word London I just know she'll need no persuasion.

Saroj smiled as she folded the letter. 'Savitri, Mrs Dee, Ma. Whatever her name is, she's still right here. Attending to every single detail. Like she always did.'

Saroj sat up with a jolt. 'Oh my goodness, Nat, I quite forgot…'

She took his hand, placed it on her belly, and pressed it there. 'The most important detail…'

EPILOGUE

A shes to ashes . . .' The vicar's voice droned on. Boring .. .
Gita tugged at the hem of Mummy's *shalwar kameez.*
Mummy's head, lowered in respect for the dead, turned slightly
and she looked down sideways. Gita looked up at her in bright-
eyed eagerness, just dying to speak, words gathered inside like
a little brook about to bubble out of the earth. No funereal
solemnity here. Mummy suppressed a smile and raised a finger
to her lips. 'Ssshhhh!' she mouthed.

Gita's eyes clouded in disappointment and she wrinkled her
nose and shook her black curls. Then she raised one little bare
foot to scratch the back of her calf with her toenails, wrote her
name in the sand with her big toe, poked Granny in the bottom
and giggled and everybody looked at her and frowned. Daddy
secretly waggled a finger at her and that made her giggle again.
After that the vicar finished speaking and everybody walked
slowly round and shovelled spadefuls of sand into Auntie Fiona's
open grave, and flowers, lots and lots of flowers. Even Grandad
Deodat, sitting in his wheelchair, managed a small spadeful.
And so did Khan, his wheelchair-pusher. Then it was over and
they walked away, towards the house.

Gita walked between Mummy and Granny, holding a
hand of each, jumping and swinging. Daddy pushed Grandad
Deodat's wheelchair; Khan didn't want to let him but Daddy
insisted. Grandad Deodat's head lolled to one side — he had
fallen asleep again. He was always sleeping. Mummy was
speaking to Granny, telling Granny to take her, Gita, for a walk
to see the sea. They had been promising to show her the sea for
a long time so when she heard that she danced around Granny
tugging at her hand, crying, 'Yes, yes, yes, let's go to the sea!'

'Ah comin', chile, but ah can't run so fas' like you, yuh know!' said Granny, so Gita tugged all the harder.

'Take your time, Parvati,' said Mummy. 'Take off her clothes and let her bathe. We'll come and join you in a while — I just want to look around here first.'

Granddad David explained to Parvati how to get to the sea. He pointed down the curve of the driveway, through the tangle of bougainvilleas hiding the gate around the bend. 'Turn left into Atkinson Avenue,' he said, 'and walk for a few minutes till you come to the flame-of-the-forest tree. Cross the avenue there — you'll see a little path. Just walk down it and you'll come straight to the sea. You can't miss it!'

Saroj and Nat watched as Gita dragged Parvati away.

'Little imp of mischief !' Saroj said, shaking her head and smiling fondly. 'D'you know, she tried to take the doll out of Fiona's coffin this morning, just before they nailed it up? She said she can take better care of it than Fiona can down in the earth. I had to promise to buy her one of her own!'

'Well, it's about time she had one of her own,' said David. 'Three-year-old girls need dolls, you know!'

'But not Fiona's,' said Saroj firmly. 'Poor Fiona needs her doll.'

'Who knows, maybe right now she's with the real thing. With Paul.'

David and Henry had wandered off and stood now in the rose arbour, talking about the old days. It was all overgrown, of course, and none of the roses were blooming. A thorny tangle of bush.

'It needs Savitri's touch,' said Henry. 'The whole place does.'

'A gardener…' mused David as Saroj and Nat approached.

'This place is paradise gone wild,' Saroj said, looking around her in wonder. 'All it needs is a little loving care and my goodness, what a sanctuary we'd have! And in the middle of Madras! I wouldn't have believed it!'

'That's India,' Nat said. 'Heaven in the midst of hell.'

'Shall I show you the house?' David asked. 'Of course, it'll be black with mildew now but maybe you'll get an idea of what it once was.'

Inside it was cool, damp, musty, dark. David walked from room to room throwing open the shutters, but even then no sunshine entered the rooms for the verandah encircling the house kept out the glare — that was its purpose. The rooms were empty, except for the little servants' area where Fiona had lived out her last years. Forlorn, neglected, violated by time, the house seemed to cringe under their inspection, as if ashamed of its nakedness, of the blue-green mould covering the tiles and creeping up the once immaculate walls.

'It's huge,' said Saroj. 'What a pity no-one lives here, no-one cares, no-one looks after it. What a waste!'

'Now Fiona's gone maybe we could sell it, or else...' David began.

'I've got a much better idea,' Nat broke in. 'We'll clean it up. Get the garden put straight. And Saroj moves in when she starts at university.'

'Live here?' Saroj exclaimed. 'But it's much too big for me alone. I'd be lost!'

'You needn't live in the whole house. We'll begin with the front room and the verandah and the kitchen. And you needn't be here alone. Gita and Parvati can live here too. They'd both prefer to be near you in Madras than up country with me and Dad. And if you live in the city it wouldn't be much fun for Gita, but here...'

'It'd be perfect!' Saroj caught Nat's thought and as it took root her eyes began to shine. 'She'd be just like Savitri, living in paradise — but what about school?'

'Henry can move in too. He can teach her just as well here as in the village, the way he taught the Fairwinds children back then. What about it, Henry? Wouldn't you like to come back to Fairwinds?'

'Would I ever!'

'But... Savitri wasn't alone. She had me to play with,' objected David. 'Gita'd die of loneliness here, paradise or not.

You know what she's like. You know how she needs friends, other children around her!'

'Well, why shouldn't she have them? If Henry's going to teach her he can teach others as well. Bring in some children — from the neighbourhood.'

'A school! That's what we'll do! Open a school for girls! Girls from the poorest families, bright little girls, eager to learn…'

'Oh, yes! I can just imagine it — so many rooms, so many classrooms…' Saroj almost ran out of the door and into the next room, seeing it all in her mind's eye, the little girls at their desks, shining dark eyes turned on the teacher, the chant of eager voices, their cries as they ran out at break, pigtails flying and skirts whirling, little bare feet pattering around the verandah. A playground, she thought. Swings, a seesaw… Fresh milk every day… We'll keep some cows. Someone to cook lunch…   A Tamil teacher, art, music, a gymnasium…

'There's not enough room for everything,' she said. 'We need the whole house for classrooms. We'll build another house, a small one, living quarters for me and Gita and Parvati — over there — come Nat, let me show you, and maybe a boarding house for girls from the country, and —'

She took Nat's hand and dragged him down the verandah steps into the garden, pointing, exclaiming, gesturing.

David and Henry followed slowly.

'I've never seen her like this before,' David marvelled. Saroj had proved, till now, an interested, diligent, yet somehow restrained daughter-in-law, trying hard to find her bearings but never completely connecting. The dedication was all there but something was lacking. A vital spark? Zest, spirit, an elusive factor X? A certain glow, inimitable, ineffable. The thing beneath the surface, beyond technique: inspiration, imagination. Soul. Vision. Love.

As they joined her and Nat he said, 'We were just saying, Saroj, are you quite sure you want to be a gynaecologist? What about teaching as a vocation?'

Saroj threw back her head with a laugh. She put her arm around Nat's waist, leaning into him. 'No, no, I know what I want, and I know where I belong. But it'll take a few years to get there, and by then this —' she spread her arms to embrace all of Fairwinds '— should be on its feet and walking. We'll name it after Savitri. We'll dedicate it to her. The Savitri Iyer School. The SIS.'

David's eyes met Nat's and they both smiled. 'You know what, Saroj?' David said. 'I recognise the symptoms. You've got the Savitri fever. You'll never recover.'

Letter from Sharon

First of all, I want to say a huge thank you for choosing *Of Marriageable Age*, I hope you enjoyed reading Savitri, Nat and Saroj's story just as much as I loved writing it.

If you did enjoy it, I would be forever grateful if you'd **write a review**. I'd love to hear what you think, and it can also help other readers discover one of my books for the first time.

Also, if you'd like to **keep up-to-date with all my latest releases**, just sign up at:

www.bookouture.com/sharonmaas

A story is a wonderful thing to share with others—it connects us in so many ways, makes us all part of the same world, unites us in spirit. If that's how you feel too, I'd love to hear from you—drop me a line on my Facebook or Goodreads page, or through my website contact form below.

Thank you so much for your support – until next time.

Sharon Maas

www.sharonmaas.com

Glossary

Advaita — Non-duality; philosophical doctrine that nothing exists apart from the Spirit, that all forms are constituted of Spirit and physical differences are but illusion. The principal doctrinal division in Hinduism is between the schools of Advaita and Dvaita, duality, whereas Advaita is considered a natural development from Dvaita.

Ahamkara — sense of 'I', ego

Amma — Tamil: mother

Appa — Tamil: father

Arathi — the slow waving of a sacred flame during worship

Asramam — Tamil: ashram, spiritual centre, hermitage

Bhakti — spiritual love, devotion to God

Brahmin — member of the priestly caste in Hinduism

Dhal puri — flat bread filled with split-peas

Dhobi — Washerman, washerwoman

Dravidian — dark-skinned original inhabitant of South India

Dvaita — Duality. Dvaitists worship a Personal God separate from the worshipper — see *Advaita.*

Fakir — religious mendicant

Iddly — rice cake of South India

Jaggary — dumpy brown sugar

Kama — eroticism, sensual desire

Kolam — elaborate chalk or powder pattern before the threshold of a house or temple

Ksatriya — member of the warrior caste in Hinduism

Kum-kum — red powder worn on forehead

Kurta pyjamas — knee-length shirt or tunic worn over cotton drawstring trousers

Lingam — upright stone pillar representing Shiva or the Absolute

Lungi — wide cloth wrapped about the hips, typical men's wear in South India

Mantra — a sacred formula used as an incantation

Mitthai — a crisply fried sweet bread

Mudra — positions of hands and fingers in Indian dance, each with a specific meaning

Patti — Tamil: grandmother

Pradakshina — walking clockwise in a circle around a temple or a shine Puja — ritualistic worship

Rajasic — tendency outwards into activity; desire, aggression, ambition

Rudrakshra beads — rosary of beads dedicated to Shiva, used in the repetition of mantras

Sambar — spicy South Indian dish eaten with rice

Sannyasin — one who in quest of God has renounced home, property, caste and all worldly attachments and desires. Wears an ochre-coloured robe.

Sattvic — tendency inwards towards light; spirituality, purity, bliss

Shalwar kameez — women's wear consisting of knee-length dress over wide trousers

Sharpai — simple bed consisting of wooden framework and strapped surface

Shehnai — musical instrument like an oboe, often played at weddings in North India

Sruti — scriptural text, musical term

Tamasic — tendency into matter; darkness, sloth, ignorance

Tamby — Tamil: "little brother", "little boy"

Tapasvi — person performing religious abstinence, austerities

Thatha — Tamil: grandfather

Tinnai — raised platform or front porch of a South Indian home

Vibhuti — sacred ash